PUFFIN BOOKS

THE DARK IS RISING SEQUENCE

Susan Cooper was born in Buckinghamshire, read English at Oxford and began her career as a reporter and feature-writer for the *Sunday Times*. She then married an American and moved to the United States. Her sequence of fantasy novels for young adults, *The Dark is Rising*, has won numerous international awards including the Newbery Medal, and has been translated into eleven languages. She has written a number of other books for children and adults, a Broadway play, and several films for television and the cinema. She has two children and lives in Fairfield, Connecticut. Susan is married to the Canadian actor Hume Cronyn.

Other books by Susan Cooper

THE BOGGART
THE BOGGART AND THE MONSTER

KING OF SHADOWS

SUSAN COOPER

THE DARK IS RISING SEQUENCE

PUFFIN BOOKS

PUFFIN BOOKS

Published by the Penguin Group
Penguin Books Ltd, 80 Strand, London WC2R 0RL, England
Penguin Putnam Inc., 375 Hudson Street, New York, New York 10014, USA
Penguin Books Australia Ltd, Ringwood, Victoria, Australia
Penguin Books Canada Ltd, 10 Alcorn Avenue, Toronto, Ontario, Canada M4V 3B2
Penguin Books India (P) Ltd, 11 Community Centre, Panchsheel Park, New Delhi – 110 017, India
Penguin Books (NZ) Ltd, Cnr Rosedale and Airborne Roads, Albany, Auckland, New Zealand
Penguin Books (South Africa) (Pty) Ltd, 24 Sturdee Avenue, Rosebank 2196 South Africa

Penguin Books Ltd, Registered Offices: 80 Strand, London WC2R 0RL, England

www.penguin.com

Over Sea, Under Stone first published in Great Britain by Jonathan Cape 1965,
now by the Bodley Head Ltd
Published in Puffin Books 1968
Copyright © Susan Cooper, 1965

The Dark is Rising first published in Great Britain by Chatto and Windus Ltd 1973,
now by The Bodley Head Ltd
Published in Puffin Books 1976
Copyright © Susan Cooper, 1973

Greenwitch first published in Great Britain by Chatto and Windus Ltd 1974,
now by The Bodley Head Ltd
Published in Puffin Books 1977
Copyright © Susan Cooper, 1974

The Grey King first published in Great Britain by Chatto and Windus Ltd 1975,
now by The Bodley Head Ltd
Published in Puffin Books 1977
Copyright © Susan Cooper, 1975

Silver on the Tree first published in Great Britain by Chatto and Windus Ltd 1977,
now by the Bodley Head Ltd
Published in Puffin Books 1979
Copyright © Susan Cooper, 1977

This collection published as *The Dark is Rising Sequence* 1984
19

Scanned and phototypeset by Datasolve information, London

Set in Clowes Dante

Made and printed in England by Clays Ltd, St Ives plc

British Library Cataloguing in Publication Data
A CIP catalogue record for this book is available from
the British Library

ISBN 0-140-31688-4

Contents

Over Sea, Under Stone

For my father and mother,
with love

Chapter One

'Where is he?'

Barney hopped from one foot to the other as he clambered down from the trains peering in vain through the white-faced crowds flooding eagerly to the St Austell ticket barrier. 'Oh, I can't see him. Is he there?'

'Of course he's there,' Simon said, struggling to clutch the long canvas bundle of his father's fishing-rods. 'He said he'd meet us. With a car.'

Behind them, the big diesel locomotive hooted like a giant owl, and the train began to move out.

'Stay where you are a minute,' Father said, from a barricade of suitcases. 'Merry won't vanish. Let people get clear.'

Jane sniffed ecstatically. 'I can smell the sea!'

'We're miles from the sea,' Simon said loftily.

'I don't care. I can smell it.'

'Trewissick's five miles from St Austell, Great-Uncle Merry said.'

'Oh, where *is* he?' Barney still jigged impatiently on the dusty grey platform, glaring at the disappearing backs that masked his view. Then suddenly he stood still, gazing downwards. 'Hey – look.'

They looked. He was staring at a large black suitcase among the forest of shuffling legs.

'What's so marvellous about that?' Jane said.

Then they saw that the suitcase had two brown pricked ears and a long waving brown tail. Its owner picked it up and moved away, and the dog which had been behind it was left standing there alone, looking up and down the platform. He was a long, rangy, lean dog, and where the sunlight shafted down on his coat it gleamed dark red.

Barney whistled, and held out his hand.

'Darling, no,' said his mother plaintively, clutching at the bunch of paint-brushes that sprouted from her pocket like a tuft of celery.

But even before Barney whistled, the dog had begun trotting in their direction, swift and determined, as if he were recognizing old friends. He loped round them in a circle, raising his long red muzzle to each in turn, then stopped beside Jane, and licked her hand.

'Isn't he gorgeous?' Jane crouched beside him, and ruffled the long silky fur of his neck.

'Darling, be careful,' Mother said. 'He'll get left behind. He must belong to someone over there.'

'I wish he belonged to us.'

'So does he,' Barney said. 'Look.'

He scratched the red head, and the dog gave a throaty half-bark of pleasure.

'*No*,' Father said.

The crowds were thinning now, and through the barrier they could see clear blue sky out over the station yard.

'His name's on his collar,' Jane said, still down beside the dog's neck. She fumbled with the silver tab on the heavy strap. 'It says Rufus. And something else . . . Trewissick. Hey, he comes from the village!'

But as she looked up, suddenly the others were not there. She jumped to her feet and ran after them into the sunshine, seeing in an instant what they had seen: the towering familiar figure of Great-Uncle Merry, out in the yard, waiting for them.

They clustered round him, chattering like squirrels round the base of a tree. 'Ah, there you are,' he said casually, looking down at them from beneath his bristling white eyebrows with a slight smile.

'Cornwall's wonderful,' Barney said, bubbling.

'You haven't seen it yet,' said Great-Uncle Merry. 'How are you, Ellen, my dear?' He bent and aimed a brief peck at Mother's cheek. He treated her always as though he had forgotten that she had grown up. Although he was not her real uncle, but only a friend of her father, he had been close to the family for so many years that it never occurred to them to wonder where he had come from in the first place.

Nobody knew very much about Great-Uncle Merry, and nobody ever quite dared to ask. He did not look in the least like his name. He was tall, and straight, with a lot of very thick, wild, white hair. In his grim brown face the nose curved fiercely, like a bent bow, and the eyes were deep-set and dark.

How old he was, nobody knew. 'Old as the hills,' Father said, and they felt, deep down, that this was probably right. There was something about Great-

Uncle Merry that was like the hills, or the sea, or the sky; something ancient, but without age or end.

Always, wherever he was, unusual things seemed to happen. He would often disappear for a long time, and then suddenly come through the Drews' front door as if he had never been away, announcing that he had found a lost valley in South America, a Roman fortress in France, or a burned Viking ship buried on the English coast. The newspapers would publish enthusiastic stories of what he had done. But by the time the reporters came knocking at the door, Great-Uncle Merry would be gone, back to the dusty peace of the university where he taught. They would wake up one morning, go to call him for breakfast, and find that he was not there. And then they would hear no more of him until the next time, perhaps months later, that he appeared at the door. It hardly seemed possible that this summer, in the house he had rented for them in Trewissick, they would be with him in one place for four whole weeks.

The sunlight glinting on his white hair, Great-Uncle Merry scooped up their two biggest suitcases, one under each arm, and strode across the yard to a car.

'What d'you think of that?' he demanded proudly.

Following, they looked. It was a vast, battered estate car, with rusting mudguards and peeling paint, and mud caked on the hubs of the wheels. A wisp of steam curled up from the radiator.

'Smashing!' said Simon.

'Hmmmmmm,' Mother said.

'Well, Merry,' Father said cheerfully, 'I hope you're well insured.'

Great-Uncle Merry snorted. 'Nonsense. Splendid vehicle. I hired her from a farmer. She'll hold us all, anyway. In you get.'

Jane glanced regretfully back at the station entrance as she clambered in after the rest. The red-haired dog was standing on the pavement watching them, long pink tongue dangling over white teeth.

Great-Uncle Merry called: 'Come on, Rufus.'

'Oh!' Barney said in delight, as a flurry of long legs and wet muzzle shot through the door and knocked him sideways. 'Does he belong to you?'

'Heaven forbid,' Great-Uncle Merry said. 'But I suppose he'll belong to you three for the next month. The captain couldn't take him abroad, so Rufus goes with the Grey House.' He folded himself into the driving seat.

'The Grey House?' Simon said. 'Is that what it's called? Why?'

'Wait and see.'

The engine gave a hiccup and a roar, and then they were away. Through the streets and out of the town they thundered in the lurching car, until hedges took the place of houses; thick, wild hedges growing high and green as the road wound uphill, and behind them the grass sweeping up to the sky. And against the sky they saw nothing but lonely trees, stunted and bowed by the wind that blew from the sea, and yellow-grey outcrops of rock.

'There you are,' Great-Uncle Merry shouted, over the noise. He turned his head and waved one arm away from the steering-wheel, so that Father moaned softly and hid his eyes. 'Now you're in Cornwall. The real Cornwall. Logres is before you.'

The clatter was too loud for anyone to call back.

'What's he mean, Logres?' demanded Jane.

Simon shook his head, and the dog licked his ear.

'He means the land of the West,' Barney said unexpectedly, pushing back the forelock of fair hair that always tumbled over his eyes. 'It's the old name for Cornwall. King Arthur's name.'

Simon groaned. 'I might have known.'

Ever since he had learned to read, Barney's greatest heroes had been King Arthur and his knights. In his dreams he fought imaginary battles as a member of the Round Table, rescuing fair ladies and slaying false knights. He had been longing to come to the West Country; it gave him a strange feeling that he would in some way be coming home. He said, resentfully: 'You wait. Great-Uncle Merry knows.'

And then, after what seemed a long time, the hills gave way to the long blue line of the sea, and the village was before them.

Trewissick seemed to be sleeping beneath its grey, slate-tiled roofs, along the narrow winding streets down the hill. Silent behind their lace-curtained windows, the little square houses let the roar of the car bounce back from their white-washed walls. Then Great-Uncle Merry swung the wheel round, and suddenly they were driving along the edge of the harbour, past water rippling and flashing golden in the afternoon sun. Sailing-dinghies bobbed at their moorings along the quay, and a whole row of Cornish fishing-boats that they had seen only in pictures painted by their mother years before: stocky workman-like boats, each with a stubby mast and a small square engine-house in the stern.

Nets hung dark over the harbour walls, and a few fishermen, hefty, brown-faced men in long boots that reached their thighs, glanced up idly as the car passed. Two or three grinned at Great-Uncle Merry, and waved.

'Do they know you?' Simon said curiously.

But Great-Uncle Merry, who could become very deaf when he chose not to answer a question, only roared on along the road that curved up the hill, high over the other side of the harbour, and suddenly stopped. 'Here we are,' he said.

In the abrupt silence, their ears still numb from the thundering engine, they all turned from the sea to look at the other side of the road.

They saw a terrace of houses sloping sideways up the steep hill; and in the middle of them, rising up like a tower, one tall narrow house with three rows of windows and a gabled roof. A sombre house, painted dark-grey, with the door and window-frames shining white. The roof was slate-tiled, a high blue-grey arch facing out across the harbour to the sea.

'The Grey House,' Great-Uncle Merry said.

They could smell a strangeness in the breeze that blew faintly on their faces down the hill; a beckoning smell of salt and seaweed and excitement.

As they unloaded suitcases from the car, with Rufus darting in excited frenzy through everyone's legs, Simon suddenly clutched Jane by the arm. 'Gosh – *look!*'

He was looking out to sea, beyond the harbour mouth. Along his pointed finger, Jane saw the tall graceful triangle of a yacht under full sail, moving lazily towards Trewissick.

'Pretty,' she said, with only mild enthusiasm. She did not share Simon's passion for boats.

'She's a beauty. I wonder whose she is?' Simon stood watching, entranced. The yacht crept nearer, her sails beginning to flap; and then the tall white mainsail crumpled and dropped. They heard the rattle of rigging, very faint across the water, and the throaty cough of an engine.

'Mother says we can go down and look at the harbour before supper,' Barney said, behind them. 'Coming?'

'Course. Will Great-Uncle Merry come?'

'He's going to put the car away.'

They set off down the road leading to the quay, beside a low grey wall with tufts of grass and pink valerian growing between its stones. In a few paces Jane found she had forgotten her handkerchief, and she ran back to retrieve it from the car. Scrabbling on the floor by the back seat, she glanced up and stared for a moment through the wind-screen, surprised.

Great-Uncle Merry, coming back towards the car from the Grey House, had suddenly stopped in his tracks in the middle of the road. He was gazing down at the sea; and she realized that he had caught sight of the yacht. What startled her was the expression on his face. Standing there like a craggy towering statue, he was frowning, fierce and intense, almost as if he were looking and listening with senses other than his eyes and ers. He could never look frightened, she thought, but this was the nearest thing to it that she had ever seen. Cautious, startled, alarmed . . . what was the matter with him? Was there something strange about the yacht?

Then he turned and went quickly back into the house, and Jane emerged thoughtfully from the car to follow the boys down the hill.

*

the side of the mountain of fishy-smelling boxes, which had probably been having more effect on her imagination than the thought of the sea.

'Girls!' said Simon cheerfully.

There was suddenly an ear-splitting crash from the other side of the boxes, a scream, and a noise of metal jingling on concrete. Simon and Barney gazed horrified at one another for a moment, and rushed round to the other side.

Jane was lying on the ground with a bicycle on top of her, its front wheel still spinning round. A tall dark-haired boy lay sprawled across the quay not far away. A box of tins and packets of food had spilled from the bicycle carrier, and milk was trickling in a white puddle from a broken bottle splintered glittering in the sun.

The boy scrambled to his feet, glaring at Jane. He was all in navy-blue, his trousers tucked into Wellington boots; he had a short, thick neck and a strangely flat face, twisted now with ill temper.

'Look where 'ee's goin', can't 'ee?' he snarled, the Cornish accent made ugly by anger. 'Git outa me way.'

He jerked the bicycle upright, taking no heed of Jane; the pedal caught her ankle and she winced with pain.

'It wasn't my fault,' she said, with some spirit. 'You came rushing up without looking where you were going.'

Barney crossed to her in silence and helped her to her feet. The boy sullenly began picking up his spilled tins and slamming them back into the box. Jane picked one up to help. But as she reached it towards the box the boy knocked her hand away, sending the tin spinning across the quay.

'Leave 'n alone,' he growled.

'Look here,' Simon said indignantly, 'there's no need for that.'

'Shut y' mouth,' said the boy shortly, without even looking up.

'Shut your own,' Simon said belligerently.

'Oh Simon, don't,' Jane said unhappily. 'If he wants to be beastly let him.' Her leg was stinging viciously, and blood trickled down from the graze on her knee. Simon looked at her flushed face, hearing the strain in her voice. He bit his lip.

The boy pushed his bicycle to lean against the pile of boxes, scowling at Barney as he jumped nervously out of the way; then rage suddenly snarled out of him again. '— off, the lot of 'ee,' he snapped; they had never heard the word he used, but the tone was unmistakable, and Simon went hot with resentment and clenched his fists to lunge forward. But Jane clutched him back, and the boy moved quickly to the edge of the quay and climbed down over the edge, facing them, the box of groceries in his arms. They heard a thumping, clattering noise, and looking over the edge they saw him lurching about in a rowing-dinghy. He untied its mooring-rope from a ring in the wall and began edging out through the other boats into the open harbour, standing up with one oar thrust down over the stern. Moving hastily and angrily, he clouted the dinghy hard against the side of one of the big fishing-boats, but took no notice. Soon he was out in open water, sculling rapidly, one-handed, and glaring back at them in sneering contempt.

As he did so they heard a clatter of feet moving rapidly over hollow wood from inside the injured fishing-boat. A small, wizened figure popped up suddenly from a hatch in the deck and waved its arms about in fury, shouting over the water towards the boy in a surprisingly deep voice.

The boy deliberately turned his back, still sculling, and the dinghy disappeared outside the harbour entrance, round the jutting wall.

The little man shook his fist, then turned towards the quay, leaping neatly from the deck of one boat to another, until he reached the ladder in the wall and climbed up by the children's feet. He wore the inevitable navy-blue jersey and trousers, with long boots reaching up his legs.

'Clumsy young limb, that Bill 'Oover,' he said crossly. 'Wait'll I catch 'n, that's all, just wait.'

Then he seemed to realize that the children were more than just part of the quay. He grunted, flashing a quick glance at their tense faces, and the blood on Jane's knee. 'Thought I heard voices from below,' he said, more gently. 'You been 'avin' trouble with 'n?' He jerked his head out to sea.

'He knocked my sister over with his bike,' Simon said indignantly. 'It was my fault really, I made her run into him, but he was beastly rude and he bashed Jane's hand away and – and then he went off before I could hit him,' he ended lamely.

The old fisherman smiled at them. 'Ah well, don't 'ee take no count of 'n. He'm a bad lot, that lad, evil-tempered as they come and evil-minded with ut. You keep away from 'n.'

'We shall,' Jane said with feeling, rubbing her leg gingerly.

The fisherman clicked his tongue. 'That's a nasty old cut you got there, midear, you want to go and get 'n washed up. You'm on holiday here, I dessay.'

'We're staying in the Grey House,' Simon said. 'Up there on the hill.'

The fisherman glanced at him quickly, a flicker of interest passing over the impassive brown wrinkled face. 'Are 'ee, then? I wonder maybe' – then he stopped short, strangely, as if he were quickly changing his mind about what he had been going to say. Simon, puzzled, waited for him to go on. But Barney, who had not been listening, turned round from where he had been peering over the edge of the quay.

'Is that your boat out there?'

The fisherman looked at him, half taken aback and half amused, as he would have looked at some small unexpected animal that barked. 'That's right, me 'andsome. The one I just come off.'

'Don't the other fishermen mind you jumping over their boats?'

The old man laughed, a cheerful rusty noise. 'I'd'n no other way to get ashore from there. Nobody minds you comin' across their boat, so long's you don't mark 'er.'

'Are you going out fishing?'

'Not for a while, midear,' said the fisherman amiably, pulling a piece of dirty rag from his pocket and scrubbing at the oilmarks on his hands. 'Go out with sundown, we do, and come back with the dawn.'

Barney beamed. 'I shall get up early and watch you come in.'

'Believe that when I see 'n,' said the fisherman with a twinkle. 'Now look, you run and take your liddle sister home and wash that leg, don't know what scales and muck have got into it off here.' He scuffed at the quay with his glistening boot.

'Yes, come on, Jane,' Simon said. He took one more look out at the quiet line of boats; then put up his hand to peer into the sun. 'I say, that oaf with the bicycle, he's going on board the yacht!'

Jane and Barney looked.

Out beyond the far harbour wall, a dark shape was bobbing against the long white hull of the silent yacht. They could just see the boy climbing up the side, and two figures meeting him on the deck. Then all three disappeared, and the boat lay deserted again.

'Ah,' said the fisherman. 'So that's it. Young Bill were buying stores and petrol and all, yesterday, enough for a navy, but nobody couldn't get it out of him who they was for. Tidy old boat, that'n – cruisin', I suppose. Can't see what he made all the mystery about.'

He began to walk along the quay: a rolling small figure with the folded tops of his boots slapping his legs at every step. Barney trotted beside him, talking earnestly, and rejoined the others at the corner as the old man, waving to them, turned off towards the village.

'His name's Mr Penhallow, and his boat's called the *White Heather*. He says they got a hundred stone of pilchard last night, and they'll get more tomorrow because it's going to rain.'

'One day you'll ask too many questions,' said Jane.

'Rain?' said Simon incredulously, looking up at the blue sky.

'That's what he said.'

'Rubbish. He must be nuts.'

'I bet he's right. Fishermen always know things, specially Cornish fishermen. You ask Great-Uncle Merry.'

But Great-Uncle Merry, when they sat down to their first supper in the Grey House, was not there; only their parents, and the beaming red-cheeked village woman, Mrs Palk, who was to come in every day to help with the cooking and cleaning. Great-Uncle Merry had gone away.

'He must have said *something*,' Jane said.

Father shrugged. 'Not really. He just muttered about having to go and look for something and roared off in the car like a thunderbolt.'

'But we've only just got here,' Simon said, hurt.

'Never mind,' Mother said comfortably. 'You know what he is. He'll be back in his own good time.'

Barney gazed dreamily at the Cornish pasties Mrs Palk had made for their supper. 'He's gone on a quest. He might take years and years. You can search and search, on a quest, and in the end you may never get there at all.'

'Quest my foot,' Simon said irritably. 'He's just gone chasing after some stupid old tomb in a church, or something. Why couldn't he have told us?'

'I expect he'll be back in the morning,' Jane said. She looked out of the window, across the low grey wall edging the road. The light was beginning to die, and as the sun sank behind their headland the sea was turning to a dark grey-green, and slow mist creeping into the harbour. Through the growing haze she saw a dim shape move, down on the water, and above it a brief flash of light; first a red pinprick in the gloom, and then a green, and white points of light above both. And she sat up suddenly as she realized that what she could see was the mysterious white yacht, moving out of Trewissick harbour as silently and strangely as it had come.

Chapter Two

Next day, as they sat eating breakfast, Great-Uncle Merry came back. He loomed in the doorway, tall and hollow-eyed under the thatch of white hair, and beamed at their surprised faces.

'Good morning,' he said cheerfully. 'Any coffee left?' The ornaments seemed to rattle on the mantelpiece as he spoke; Great-Uncle Merry always gave the impression of being far too big for any room he was in.

Father reached out imperturbably to pull up another chair. 'What's it like out this morning, Merry? Doesn't look so good to me.'

Great-Uncle Merry sat down and helped himself to toast, holding the slice in one large palm while he spread butter on it with Father's knife. 'Cloud. Thick, coming in from the sea. We're going to have rain.'

Barney was fidgeting with unbearable curiosity. Suddenly, forgetting the family rule that they should never ask their mysterious great-uncle questions about himself, he burst out: 'Gumerry, where have you *been*?' In the heat of the the moment he used the pet name which he had invented when he was very small. They all used it sometimes still, but not for everyday.

Jane hissed quietly between her teeth, and Simon glared at him across the table. But Great-Uncle Merry seemed not to have heard. 'It may not last,' he went on conversationally to Father, through a mouthful of toast. 'But I think we shall have it for most of the day.'

'Will there be thunder?' Jane said.

Simon added hopefully, 'Shall we have a storm at sea?'

Barney sat silent while their voices eddied round the table. The weather, he said to himself in exasperation, all of them talking about the weather, when Great-Uncle Merry's just come back from his quest.

Then over their voices there came a low rumble of thunder, and the first spattering sounds of rain. As everyone rushed to the window to look out at the heavy grey sky, Barney crossed unnoticed to his great-uncle and slipped his hand into his for a moment.

'Gumerry,' he said softly, 'did you find it, what you were looking for?'

He expected Great-Uncle Merry to look past him with the familiar amiable-obstinate expression that greeted any question. But the big man looked down at him almost absently. The eyebrows were drawn forbiddingly together on the craggy, secret face, and there was the old fierceness in the dark hollows and lines. He said gently, 'No, Barnabas, I didn't find it this time.' Then it was as if a blanket came down again over his face. 'I must go and put the car away,' he called to Father, and went out.

The thunder rolled quietly, far out over the sea, but the rain fell with grey insistence, blurring the windows as it washed down outside. The children wandered aimlessly about the house. Before lunch they tried going for a walk in the rain, but came back damp and depressed.

Half-way through the afternoon Mother put her head round the door. 'I'm going upstairs to work until supper. Now look, you three – you can go where you like in the house but you must promise not to touch anything that's obviously been put away. Everything valuable is all locked up, but I don't want you poking at anyone's private papers or belongings. All right?'

'We promise,' Jane said, and Simon nodded.

In a little while Father muffled himself in a big black oilskin and went off through the rain to see the harbour-master. Jane wandered round the bookshelves, but all the books within reach seemed to have titles like *Round the Horn*, or *Log-Book of the* Virtue, *1886*, and she thought them very dull.

Simon, who had been sitting making darts out of the morning paper, suddenly crumpled them all up irritably. 'I'm fed up with this. What shall we do?'

Barney stared gloomily out of the window. 'It's raining like anything. The water in the harbour's all flat. And on our first proper day. Oh I hate the rain, I hate it, I hate it, I hate the rain . . .' He began to chant morosely.

Simon prowled restlessly around the room, looking at the pictures on the dark wallpaper. 'It's a very dreary house when you're shut up inside. He doesn't seem to think about anything but the sea, does he, the captain?'

'This time last year you were going to be a sailor too.'

'Well, I changed my mind. Oh well, I don't know. Anyway, I should go on a destroyer, not a potty little sailing-ship like that one. What is it?' He peered up at the inscription under an engraving. '*The Golden Hind*.'

'That was Drake's ship. When he sailed to America and discovered potatoes.'

'That was Raleigh.'

'Oh well,' said Barney, who didn't really care.

'What useless things they discovered,' Simon said critically. 'I shouldn't have bothered about vegetables, I should have come back loaded with doubloons and diamonds and pearls.'

'And apes and peacocks,' said Jane, harking vaguely back to a poetry lesson at school.

'And I should have gone exploring into the interior and the rude natives would have turned me into a god and tried to offer me their wives.'

'Why would the natives be rude?' said Barney.

'Not that sort of rude, you idiot, it means – it means – well, it's the sort of things native *are*. It's what all the explorers call them.'

'Let's be explorers,' Jane said. 'We can explore the house. We haven't yet, not properly. It's like a strange land. We can work from the bottom all the way up to the top.'

'And we should have to take provisions with us, so we can have a picnic when we get there,' said Barney, brightening.

'We haven't got any.'

'We can ask Mrs Palk,' said Jane. 'She's making cakes for Mother in the kitchen. Come on.'

Mrs Palk, in the kitchen, laughed all over her red face and said, 'What will 'ee think of next, I wonder?' But she gave them, neatly wrapped, a stack of freshly-baked scones cut in half, thickly buttered and put together again; a packet of squashed-fly biscuits, three apples and a great slab of dark yellow-orange cake, thick and crumbling with fruit.

'And something to drink,' said Simon commandingly, already captain of the expedition. So Mrs Palk good-humouredly added a big bottle of home-made lemonade 'to finish 'n off'.

'There,' she said, 'that'll take 'ee to St Ives and back, I reckon.'

'My rucksack's upstairs,' said Simon, 'I'll get it.'

'Oh really,' said Jane, who was beginning to feel a little foolish. 'We aren't even going outdoors.'

'All explorers have rucksacks,' Simon said severely, making for the door. 'I won't be a minute.'

Barney nibbled at some yellow cake-crumbs from the table. 'This is smashing.'

'Saffron cake,' Mrs Palk said proudly. 'You won't get that in London.'

'Mrs Palk, where's Rufus?'

'Gone out, and a good job too, though I dare say we shall have his great wet feet all over the floor afore long. Professor took'n for a walk. Now stop pickin' at that cake, midear, or you'll spoil that picnic o' yours.'

Simon came back with his rucksack. They filled it, and went out into the little dark passage away from the kitchen, Mrs Palk waving them farewell as solemnly as if they were off to the North Pole.

'Who did she say had taken Rufus for a walk?' said Jane.

'Great-Uncle Merry,' Barney said. 'They all call him the Professor, didn't you know? Mr Penhallow did as well. They talk as if they've known him for years.'

They were on the first-floor landing, long and dark, lit only from one small window. Jane waved her hand at a big wooden chest half hidden in one corner. 'What's that?'

'It's locked,' said Simon, trying the lid. 'One of the things we mustn't touch, I suppose. Actually it's full of native gold and ornaments, we'll collect it on the way back and stow it in the hold.'

'Who's going to carry it?' demanded Barney practically.

'Easy, we've got a string of native porters. All walking behind in a row and calling me Boss.'

'Catch me calling you Boss.'

'Actually you ought to be the cabin-boy, and call me Sir. Aye, aye, Sir!' Simon bellowed suddenly.

'Shut up,' said Jane. 'Mother's working at the other end of the landing, you'll make her do a smudge.'

'What's in here?' said Barney. There was a dark door in the shadows at the far end of the landing. 'I haven't noticed it before.' He turned the handle, and the door opened outwards with a slow creak. 'I say, there's another little corridor down some steps, and a door at the end of it. Come on.'

They went down over the worn carpet, beneath rows of old maps hanging on the walls.

The little corridor, like all the house, had a smell of furniture polish and age and the sea; and yet nothing like these things really but just the smell of strangeness.

'Hey,' said Simon as Barney reached for the door. 'I'm the captain, I go first. There might be cannibals.'

'Cannibals!' said Barney with scorn, but he let Simon open the door.

It was an odd little room, very small and bare, with one round leaded window looking out inland across the grey slate roofs and fields. There was a bed, with a red-and-white gingham coverlet, and a wooden chair, a wardrobe, and a wash-stand with an outsize willow-pattern bowl and ewer. And that was all.

'Well, that's not very interesting,' said Jane, disappointed. She looked about, feeling something was missing. 'Look, there isn't even a carpet, just a bare floor.'

Barney pattered across to the window. 'What's this?' He picked something up from the window-sill, long and dark with the glint of brass. 'It's a sort of tube.'

Simon took it from him and turned it about curiously. 'It's a telescope in a case.' He unscrewed the case so that it came apart in two halves. 'No it's not, what a swizz, it's just the case with nothing inside.'

'Now I know what this room reminds me of,' Jane said suddenly. 'It's like a cabin in a ship. That window looks just like a porthole. I think it must be the captain's bedroom.'

'We ought to take the telescope with us in case we lose our way,' said Simon. Holding it made him feel pleasantly important.

'Don't be silly, it's just an empty case,' Jane said. 'Anyway, it's not ours, put it back.'

Simon scowled at her.

'I mean,' Jane said hastily, 'we're in the jungle, not at sea, so there are landmarks.'

'Oh all right.' Simon put the case down reluctantly.

They emerged from the little dark corridor, its door, as they closed it behind them, vanishing once more into the shadows so that they could hardly see where it had been.

'Not much else here. That one's Great-Uncle Merry's bedroom, there's the bathroom this side of it and Mother's studio room the other.'

'What an odd way this house is built,' Simon said, as they turned into another narrow corridor towards the stairs leading up to the next floor. 'All little bits joined together by funny little passages. As if each bit were meant to be kept secret from the next.'

Barney looked round him in the dim light, tapping at the half-panelled walls. 'It's all very solid. There ought to be secret panels and things, secret entrances into native treasure-caves.'

'Well, we haven't finished yet.' Simon led the way up the stairs to the familiar top landing, where their bedrooms were. 'Isn't it getting dark? I suppose it's the low clouds.'

Barney squatted on the top stair. 'We ought to have torches, burning brands to light the path and keep the wild animals off. Only we couldn't because there are hostile natives all round, and they'd see.'

Simon took over. Somehow imagination worked easily in the friendly silence of the Grey House. 'Actually they're already after us, creeping along our tracks up the hill. We'll be able to hear their feet rustling soon.'

'We ought to hide.'

'Make camp somewhere that they can't get at.'

'In one of the bedrooms, they're all caves.'

'I can hear them *breathing*,' Barney said, gazing down the dark stairs into the shadow. He was half beginning to believe it.

'The obvious caves wouldn't do,' Simon said, remembering he was in command. 'They'd look there first of all.' He crossed the landing and began thoughtfully opening and shutting doors. 'Mother's and Father's room – no good, very ordinary cave. Jane's – just the same. Bathroom, our room, no escape route anywhere. We shall all be turned into sacrifices and eaten.'

'Boiled,' said Barney, sepulchrally. 'In a great big pot.'

'Perhaps there's another door, I mean cave, that we haven't noticed. Like the one downstairs.' Jane peered round the darkest end of the landing, beside her brothers' door. But the passage came to a dead end, the wall running unbroken round all three sides. 'There ought to be one. After all the house goes straight up, doesn't it, and there's a door directly underneath there' – she pointed at the blank wall – 'and a room behind it. So there ought to be a room the same size behind this wall.'

Simon became interested. 'You're quite right. But there isn't any door.'

'Perhaps there's a secret panel,' Barney said hopefully.

'You read too many books. Have you ever seen a real secret panel in a real house? Anyway there isn't any panelling on this wall, just wallpaper.'

'Your room's on the other side,' Jane said. 'Is there a door in there?'

Simon shook his head.

Barney opened the door into their bedroom and went in, kicking his slippers under the bed as he went past. Then he stopped suddenly.

'Hey, come in here.'

'What's the matter?'

'That bit between our beds, where the wall makes a sort of alcove for the wardrobe. What's on the other side?'

'Well, the landing, of course.'

'It can't be. There's too much wall in here. You stand in the doorway and look on both sides – the landing stops before it gets that far.'

'I'll bang on the wall where it does stop, and you listen in here,' said Jane. She went outside, pulling the door shut, and they heard a faint tapping on the wall just over the head of Barney's bed.

'There you are!' Barney said, hopping with excitement. 'The landing only reaches to there, but the wall in here goes on for yards, right over your bed to the window. So there must be a room on the other side.'

Jane came back into the bedroom. 'The wall doesn't look nearly as long out there as it does in here.'

'It isn't. And I think that means,' Simon said slowly, 'that there *must* be a door behind the wardrobe.'

'Well that finishes it, then,' Jane said, disappointed. 'That wardrobe's enormous, we shall never be able to move it.'

'I don't see why not.' Simon looked thoughtfully at the wardrobe. 'We shall have to pull it from down low, so the top doesn't overbalance. If we all pull at one end perhaps it'll swing round.'

'Come on then,' Jane said. 'You and I pull, and Barney hold the top and shout if he feels it overbalancing.'

They both bent and heaved at the nearest leg of the wardrobe. Nothing happened.

'I think the stupid thing's nailed to the floor,' said Jane in disgust.

'No it's not. Come on, once more. One two three – *heave*!'

The great wooden tower squeaked unwillingly a few inches across the floor.

'Go on, go on, it's coming!' Barney could hardly stand still.

Simon and Jane tugged and puffed and blew, their plimsolls slithering on the linoleum; and gradually the wardrobe moved out at an angle from the wall. Barney, peering into the gloom behind, suddenly shrieked.

'There it is! There *is* a door! Ouf –' He staggered backwards, gasped, and sneezed. 'It's all covered in dust and cobwebs, it can't have been opened for years.'

'Well go on, try it,' panted Simon, pink with breathlessness and success.

'I hope it doesn't open towards us,' Jane said, sitting weakly on the floor. 'I can't pull this thing another inch.'

'It doesn't,' Barney said, muffled from behind the wardrobe. They heard the door creak protestingly open. Then he reappeared, with a large dark smudge down one cheek. 'There isn't a room. It's a staircase. More like a ladder really. It goes up to a sort of hatchway and there's light up there.' He looked at Simon with a crooked grin. 'You can go first, Boss.'

One by one they slipped behind the wardrobe and through the little hidden door. Inside, it was at first very dark, and Simon, blinking, saw before him a wide-stepped ladder, steeply slanting, rising towards a dimly-lit square beyond which he could see nothing. The steps were thick with dust, and for a moment he felt nervous of disturbing the stillness.

Then very faintly, he heard above his head the low familiar murmur of the sea outside. At once the comfortable noise made him more cheerful, and he even remembered what they were supposed to be. 'Last one up shut the door,' he called down over his shoulder. 'Keep the natives at bay.' And he began to climb the ladder.

Chapter Three

As Simon's head emerged through the hatch at the top he caught his breath just as Barney had: 'Aah – aah –' and sneezed enormously. Clouds of dust rose, and the ladder shook.

'Hey,' said Barney protestingly from below, drawing his face back from his brother's twitching heels.

Simon opened his watering eyes and blinked. Before him and all round was one vast attic, the length and breadth of the whole house, with two grubby windows in its sloping roof. It was piled higgledy-piggledy with the most fantastic collection of objects he had ever seen.

Boxes, chests and trunks lay everywhere, with mounds of dirty grey canvas and rough-coiled ropes between them; stacks of newspapers and magazines, yellow-brown with age; a brass bedstead and a grandfather clock without a face. As he stared, he saw smaller things: a broken fishing-rod, a straw hat perched on the corner of an oil-painting darkened by age into one great black blur; an empty mousetrap, a ship in a bottle, a glass-fronted case full of chunks of rock, a pair of old thigh-boots flopped over sideways as if they were tired, a cluster of battered pewter mugs.

'Gosh!' said Simon.

Muffled noises of protest came from below, and he hauled himself out through the opening and rolled sideways out of their way on the floor. Barney and Jane came through after him.

'Simon!' said Jane, gazing at him in horror. 'You're filthy!'

'Well, isn't that just like a girl. All this round you, and you only see a bit of dust. It'll brush off.' He patted ineffectually at his piebald shirt. 'But isn't it marvellous? Look!'

Barney, cooing with delight, was picking his way across the littered floor. 'There's an old ship's wheel . . . and a rocking-chair . . . and a saddle. I wonder if the captain ever had a horse?'

Jane had been trying to look insulted, but failed. 'This is something like exploring. We might find anything up here.'

'It's a treasure-cave. This is what the natives were after. Hear them howling with frustrated rage down there.'

'Dancing round in a circle, with the witch-doctor cursing us all.'

'Well, he can curse away,' Barney said cheerfully. 'We've got enough provisions for ages. I'm hungry.'

'Oh not yet, you can't be. It's only four o'clock.'

'Well, that's tea-time. Anyway, when you're on the run you eat little and often, because you daren't ever stop for long. If we were Eskimos we'd be chewing an old shoe-lace. My book says –'

'Never mind your book,' Simon said. He fished inside the rucksack. 'Here, have an apple and keep quiet. I want to look at everything properly, before we have our picnic, and if I can wait so can you.'

'I don't see why,' Barney said, but he bit into his apple cheerfully and wandered across the floor, disappearing between the high brass skeleton of the old bed and an empty cupboard.

For half an hour they poked about in a happy dusty dream, through the junk and broken furniture and ornaments. It was like reading the story of somebody's life, Jane thought, as she gazed at the tiny matchstick masts of the ship sailing motionless for ever in the green glass bottle. All these things had been used once, had been part of every day in the house below. Someone had slept on the bed, anxiously watched the minutes on the clock, pounced joyfully on each magazine as it arrived. But all those people were long dead, or gone away, and now the oddments of their lives were piled up here, forgotten. She found herself feeling rather sad.

'I'm ravenous,' Barney said plaintively.

'I'm thirsty. It's all that dust. Come on, let's unload Mrs Palk's tea.'

'This attic's rather a swizz,' Simon said, squatting on a crackling edge of canvas and undoing the rucksack. 'All the really interesting boxes are locked. Look at that one, for instance.' He nodded towards a black metal chest with two rusting padlocks on its lid. 'I bet it's full of the family jewels.'

'Well,' Jane said regretfully, 'we aren't supposed to touch anything locked, are we?'

'There's a lot not locked,' Simon said, handing her the bottle of lemonade. 'Here. You'll have to swig from the bottle, we forgot to bring any cups. Don't worry, we won't pinch anything. Though I shouldn't think anyone's been up here for years.'

'*Food*,' Barney said.

'The scones are in that bag there. Help yourself. Four each. I've counted.'

Barney reached out an extremely dirty hand.

'Barney!' Jane squeaked. 'Wipe your hand. You'll eat all sorts of germs and get typhoid or – or rabies or something. Here, have my handkerchief.'

'Rabies is mad dogs,' Barney said, looking with interest at the black fingerprints on his scone. 'Anyway, Father says people make too much fuss about germs. Oh all *right*, Jane, stop waving that silly thing at me, I've got a proper handkerchief of my own. I don't know how girls ever blow their noses.'

Scowling, he thrust his free hand into his pocket, and then his expression changed to disgust. 'Ugh,' he said, and brought out a brown, squashed apple core. 'I'd forgotten that. All cold and horrible.' He flung the core away from him into the far corner of the attic. It bounced, slithered, and rolled into the shadows.

Simon grinned. 'Now you'll bring the rats out. All attics have rats. We shall hear greedy little squeakings and see twin green points of fire and there'll be rats all over the floor. First they'll eat the apple core, and then they'll come after us.'

Jane turned pale. 'Oh no. There wouldn't be rats up here, would there?'

'If there were they'd have eaten all the newspaper,' Barney said hopefully. 'Wouldn't they?'

'I expect they don't like ink. All old houses have rats. We've got them at school, you can hear them scuttling about in the roof sometimes. Come to think of it their eyes are red, not green.' Simon's voice began to lose its brightness. He was beginning to feel slightly unhappy about the rats himself now. 'I think maybe you'd better pick that apple core up, you know, just in case.'

Barney gave an exaggerated sigh and got to his feet, swallowing his scone in two gigantic bites. 'Where did it go, then? Over there somewhere. I wonder why they didn't put anything in this corner.'

He crawled about on his hands and knees, aimlessly. 'Come and help, I can't find it.' Then he noticed a triangular gap in the sloping wall of the attic where its planks joined the floor. He peered through, and saw daylight gleaming dimly through the tiles. Just inside the gap the floorboards ended and he could feel wide-spaced beams.

'I think it must have gone through this hole,' he called. 'I'm going to look.'

Jane dived across the floor towards him. 'Oh do be careful, there might be a rat.'

'Couldn't be,' Barney said, half-way through the gap. 'There's light comes through the tiles and I can see, more or less. Can't see any core, though. I wonder if it fell between the floorboards and the underneath part. Ow!'

His rear half jerked suddenly.

'What is it? Oh do come out!' Jane tugged at his shorts.

'I touched something. But it can't be a rat, it didn't move. Where's it gone . . . here it is. Feels like cardboard. Blah – here's that disgusting core next to it as well.'

His voice grew suddenly louder as he backed out of the hole, flushed and blinking. 'Well, there it is,' he said, triumphantly, flourishing the apple core. 'Now the rats'll have to come and get it. I still don't believe there are any.'

'What's that other thing you've got?' Simon looked curiously at a tattered, scroll-like object in Barney's other hand.

'Piece of wallpaper, I think. I bet you've eaten all the scones, you pigs.' Barney bounded back across the floor, making the floorboards rattle. He sat down, pulled out his handkerchief, waved it ostentatiously at Jane, wiped his hands and began to munch another scone. As they ate, he reached over and idly unrolled the scroll he had found, holding one end down on the floor with his toe and pushing the other back with a piece of wood until it lay stretched open before them.

And then, as they saw what it was, they all suddenly forgot their eating and stared.

The paper Barney had unrolled was not paper at all, but a kind of thick brownish parchment, springy as steel, with long raised cracks crossing it where it had been rolled. Inside it, another sheet was stuck down: darker, looking much older, ragged at the edges, and covered with small writing in strange squashed-looking dark brown letters.

Below the writing it dwindled, as if it had been singed by some great heat long ago, into half-detached pieces carefully laid back together and stuck to the outer sheet. But there was enough of it left for them to see at the bottom a rough drawing that looked like the uncertain outline of a map.

For a moment they were all very quiet. Barney said nothing but he could feel a strange excitement bubbling up inside him. He leant forward in silence and carefully stretched the manuscript flat, pushing the piece of wood aside.

'Here,' Simon said, 'I'll get something to weight the edges down.'

They put an old paper-weight, a pewter mug and two carefully dusted chunks of wood on the corners, and sat back on their heels to look.

'It's terribly old,' Jane said. 'Centuries, thousands of years.'

'Like those papers in glass cases in museums, with little curtains to keep the light out.'

'Where did it come from? How did it get up here?'

'Somebody must have hidden it.'

'But it's older than the house. I mean look at it, it must be, some of the writing's nearly faded away.'

'It wasn't hidden,' Barney said, with absolute conviction, though he had no clear idea why. 'Someone just threw it down where I found it.'

Simon whooped suddenly, making them jump. 'This is terrific! Do you realize, we've got a real live treasure map? It could lead us to anything, anywhere, secret passages, real hidden caves – the treasure of Trewissick' – he rolled the words lovingly round his tongue.

'There isn't much map, it's all writing.'

'Well then, that's instructions. Look in ye little room on ye second floor, I expect it says, ye second floorboard on the, I mean ye, left –'

'When this was written there weren't such things as floorboards.'

'Oh come off it, it's not that old.'

'I bet it is,' Barney said, quietly. 'Anyway, you look at this writing. You can't read it, it's all in some funny language.'

'Course you can read it if you look properly,' Simon said impatiently. In his mind he was already half-way through a sliding panel, throwing back the lid of a chest to reveal hoards of untold wealth. He could almost hear the chink of doubloons.

'Let's have a look.' He leaned forward, the floorboards hard and rough under his knees, and peered at the manuscript. There was a long pause. 'Oh,' he said at last, reluctantly.

Barney said nothing, but looked at him very expressively indeed.

'Well all right,' said Simon. 'There's no need to look so cocky. It isn't in English. But that doesn't mean we shan't be able to find out what it says.'

'Why isn't it in English?'

'How on earth should I know?'

'I mean,' Barney said patiently, 'that we're in England, so what other language could it possibly be in?'

'Latin,' Jane said unexpectedly. She had been looking quietly at the manuscript over Simon's shoulder.

'Latin?'

'Yes. All old manuscripts are written in Latin. The monks used to write them down with a goose-feather for a pen, and put flowers and birds and things all squiggling round the capital letters.'

'There isn't anything squiggling here. It looks as if it's been written in rather a hurry. I can't even see any capital letters at all.'

'But why *Latin*?' demanded Barney.

'I don't know, the monks just always used it, that's all, it was one of their things. I suppose it's a religious-sounding kind of language.'

'Well, Simon does Latin.'

'Yes, come on, Simon, translate it,' Jane said maliciously. At school she had not yet begun Latin, but he had been learning it for two years, and was rather superior about the fact.

'I don't think it's Latin at all,' Simon said rebelliously. He peered at the manuscript again. 'This writing's so odd, the letters all look the same. Like a lot of little straight lines all in a row. The light in here isn't very good either.'

'You're just making excuses.'

'No, I'm not. It's jolly difficult.'

'Well, if you can't even recognize Latin when you see it you can't be nearly as good as you make out.'

'Have another look,' said Barney hopefully.

'I think it's in two parts,' Simon said slowly. 'One little paragraph on top, and then a lot more all together after a gap. The second bit I can't make out at all, but the first paragraph does look as if it might be Latin. The first word looks like *cum*, that means with, but I can't see what comes after it. Then later on there's *post multos annos*, that's after many years. But the writing's all so small and squashy I can't – wait a minute, there's some names in the last line. It says *Mar* – no, *Marco Arturoque*.'

'Like Marco Polo,' Jane said doubtfully. 'What a funny name.'

'Not one name, it's two. *Que* means and, only they put it on the end instead of in the middle. And *o* on the end is the ablative of -*us*, so this means by with or from Marcus and Arturus.'

'By with or from? What a – Barney! Whatever's the matter?'

Barney, red in the face and spluttering, had suddenly thumped his fist on the floor, caught his breath trying to say something, and collapsed into a thunderous fit of coughing. They patted him on the back and gave him a drink of lemonade.

'Marcus and Arturus,' he said hoarsely, gulping his breath back. 'Don't you see, it's Mark and Arthur! It's about King Arthur and his knights. Mark was one of them, and he was King of Cornwall. It must be about them.'

'Gosh,' Simon said. 'I think he's right.'

'It *must* be that. I bet old King Mark left some treasure behind somewhere and that's why there's a map.'

'Suppose we find it.'

'We'd be rich.'

'We'd be famous.'

'We shall have to tell Mother and Father,' Jane said.

The two boys stopped thumping each other ecstatically and looked at her. 'Whatever for?'

'Well –' Jane said lamely, taken aback. 'I suppose we ought to, that's all.'

Barney sat back on his heels again, frowning, and riffled his fingers through his hair, which by now looked several shades darker than it had when they came up to the attic.

'I wonder what they'd say?'

'I know what they'd say,' Simon said promptly. 'They'd say it was all our imagination, and anyway they'd tell us to put the manuscript back where we found it because it isn't ours.'

'Well,' said Jane, 'it isn't, is it?'

'It's treasure trove. Finding's keepings.'

'But we found it in someone else's house. It belongs to the captain. You know what Mother said about not touching anything.'

'She said anything that was put away. This wasn't put away, it was just chucked down in a corner.'

'I found it,' Barney said. 'It was all forgotten and dusty. I bet you anything the captain hadn't a clue it was there.'

'Oh honestly, Jane,' Simon said. 'You can't find a treasure map and just say Oh, how nice, and put it back again. And that's what they'd make us do.'

'Oh well,' Jane said doubtfully, 'I suppose you're right. We can always put it back afterwards.'

Barney had turned to the manuscript again. 'Hey,' he said, 'look at this top part, the old manuscript that's stuck down on the parchment. What's it made of? I thought it was parchment like the outside bit, but when you look properly it isn't, and it's not paper either. It's some funny thick stuff, and it's hard, like wood.'

He touched an edge of the strange brown surface gingerly with one finger.

'Be careful,' Jane said nervously. 'It might crumble away into dust before our eyes or something.'

'I suppose you'd still want to go showing everyone even then,' Simon said acidly. '"Look what we've found, does it matter if we touch it?" and show them a little heap of dust in a match-box.'

Jane said nothing.

'Oh well, never mind,' Simon said, relenting. She meant well, after all. 'Hey, it's getting awfully dark up here, d'you think we ought to go down? They'll be looking for us soon, Mother will have stopped painting.'

'It *is* getting late.' Jane looked round the attic and shivered suddenly. The big echoing room was growing dark, and there was a dismal sound now to the rain faintly tapping on the glass.

Back in their bedrooms, the boys' wardrobe pushed in again to hide the small secret door, they washed and changed hurriedly as the curt clang of the ship's bell calling them to supper echoed up the stairs. Simon changed his dusty shirt, rolling the clean one into a crumpled ball before he put it on, and hoping no one would notice it was fresh. There was not very much they could do about Barney's hair, now khaki. 'It's like what Mother says about that rug in the living-room at home,' Jane said in despair, trying to brush out the dust while her brother wriggled in protest. 'It shows every mark.'

'Perhaps we ought to wash it.' Simon peered at Barney critically.

'*No*,' Barney said.

'Oh well, there isn't time really. Anyway, I'm hungry. You'll just have to sit away from the light.'

But when they were all sitting round the supper-table, it soon became clear that no one was going to ask questions about where they had been. The evening began as one of those times when everything seemed determined to go wrong. Mother looked tired and depressed, and did not say very much; signs, they knew, that her day's painting had not been a success. Father, gloomy after the grey day, erupted into wrath when Rufus bounced in dripping from his walk, and banished him to the kitchen with Mrs Palk. And Great-Uncle Merry had come in silent and thoughtful, mysteriously brooding. He sat at one end of the table, alone, staring into the middle distance like a great carved totem-pole.

The children eyed him warily, and took care to pass him the salt before he had to ask. But Great-Uncle Merry scarcely seemed to see them. He ate automatically, picking up his food and guiding it to his mouth without taking the slightest notice of it. Barney wondered for a wistful moment what would happen if he were to slip a cork table-mat on to his great-uncle's plate.

Mrs Palk came in with an enormous apple tart and a dish of mounded yellow cream and clattered the dirty plates into a pile. She went out down the hall, and they heard the rich rolling contralto of 'O God, our help in ages past' echoing into the distance.

Father sighed. 'There are times,' he said irritably, 'when I could dispense with devotions at every meal.'

'The Cornish,' boomed Great-Uncle Merry from the shadows, 'are a devout and evangelical people.'

'I dare say,' said Father. He passed Simon the cream. Simon helped himself to a large spoonful, and a yellow blob dropped from the spoon to the table-cloth.

'Oh *Simon*,' Mother said. 'Do look what you're doing.'

'I couldn't help it. It just fell.'

'That comes of trying to take too much at once,' Father said.

'Well, you like it too.'

'Possibly. But I don't try to transport a quart in a pint pot.'

'What d'you mean?'

'Never mind,' Father said. 'Oh for heaven's sake, Simon, that's just making it worse.' Simon, in an attempt to retrieve the blob of cream with his spoon, had left a large yellow smear on the cloth.

'Sorry.'

'I should think so.'

'Did you go fishing today, Father?' Jane said hopefully from across the table, feeling that it was time to change the subject.

'No,' said Father.

'Don't be stupid,' Simon said ungratefully, still smarting. 'It was raining.'

'Well, Father does go fishing in the rain sometimes.'

'No, he doesn't.'

'Yes, he does.'

'If I may be allowed to explain my own actions,' Father said with heavy sarcasm. 'Occasionally I have been known to go fishing in the rain. Today I did not. Is that comprehensible?'

'Have some apple tart, dear,' said Mother, handing him a plate.

'Hrmm,' Father said, glancing at her sideways, and he lapsed into silence. After a moment he said, hopefully: 'Might be an idea if we all went for a walk after supper. It seems to be clearing up.'

Everyone looked out of the window, and the temperature of the room rose several degrees. Over the sea the clouds had broken, leaving a deepening blue sky, and the opposite headland glowed suddenly a brighter green as the sinking sun shone for the first time that day.

Then they heard the doorbell ring.

'Bother,' Mother said wearily. 'Whoever can that be?' Mrs Palk's footsteps rang briskly past the door, and then back again. She put her head in. ''Tis some people for you, Dr Drew.'

'Stand by to repel boarders,' Father said, and he went out into the hall. In a few moments he was back, talking to someone over his shoulder as he came through the door. '. . . very kind of you indeed, we hadn't really thought what we were going to do tomorrow. They're an independent lot, you know. Well, here we are.' He beamed heartily round with what the family called his public face. 'My wife, Simon, Jane, Barney . . . this is Mr and Miss – er – Withers. From that yacht you admire so much, Simon. We met in the harbour this morning.'

A man and a girl stood behind him in the doorway. Both were dark-haired, with beaming smiles bright in sun-tanned faces. They looked like beings suddenly materialized from another very tidy planet. The man stepped forward, holding out his hand: 'How do you do, Mrs Drew?'

They sat staring blankly at him as he advanced towards Mother; he wore dazzling white flannel trousers, and a blazer, with a dark-blue scarf tucked in the neck of his white shirt, and they had not expected to see anything like him in Trewissick at all. Then they jumped hastily as Mother stood to shake hands, and Simon knocked over his chair. Into the confusion Mrs Palk appeared with a large teapot and a tray of cups and saucers.

'Two extra cups,' she said, smiling blandly, and departed again.

'Do sit down,' the girl said. 'We only popped in for a moment, we didn't want to interrupt.' She bent to help Simon pick up his chair. Her black curls bobbed forward over her forehead. She was a very pretty girl, Jane thought, watching her. Much older than any of them, of course. She wore a bright green shirt and black trousers, and her eyes seemed to twinkle with a kind of hidden private laughter. Jane suddenly felt extremely young.

Mr Withers, showing a lot of very white teeth, was talking to Mother. 'Mrs Drew, do please forgive this intrusion, we had no intention of breaking into your supper.'

'Not at all,' said Mother, looking faintly bemused. 'Won't you have a cup of tea?'

'Thank you, no, no, most kind, but we have a meal waiting on the boat. We simply came to issue an invitation. My sister and I are in Trewissick for some days, with the yacht to ourselves – on our way round the coast, you know – and we wondered whether you and the children would care to spend a day out at sea. We have –'

'Gosh!' Simon nearly upset his chair again. 'How marvellous! You mean go out in that fabulous boat?'

'I do indeed,' said the smiling Mr Withers.

Simon spluttered without words, his face glowing with delight. Mother said hesitantly: 'Well . . .'

'Of course I realize we're descending on you out of the blue,' Mr Withers said soothingly. 'But it would be pleasant to have company for a change. And when we met your husband in the harbour-master's office this morning, and discovered we are neighbours in London –'

'Are you?' said Barney curiously from the table. 'Where?'

'Marylebone High Street, just round the corner from you,' said the girl, dimpling at him. 'Norman sells antiques.' She looked across at Mother. 'I expect you and I use the same shops, Mrs Drew – you know that little *pâtisserie* where you can get those gorgeous rum babas?'

'I try not to,' Mother said, beginning to smile. 'Well really, this is very kind, considering we're strangers. But I'm not sure whether . . . well, the three of them can be rather a handful, you know.'

'Mother!' Simon looked aghast.

Mr Withers puckered his nose boyishly at her. 'But my invitation extends to the whole family, Mrs Drew. We sincerely hope you and your husband will join our little crew as well. Just a trip out and back, you understand – round the bay, as the commercial gentlemen have it. With perhaps a little fishing. I shall enjoy showing off the boat. Tomorrow perhaps? They say it should be a fine day.'

What an old-fashioned way of talking he has, Jane thought idly; perhaps it comes of selling antiques. She looked at Simon and Barney, both all eagerness at the idea of a day on the strange yacht, gazing anxiously at their parents; and then back at Mr Withers's immaculate white flannels and folded scarf. I don't like him, she thought. I wonder why?

'Well, thank you very much indeed,' Mother said finally. 'I don't think I shall come, if you'll forgive me – if the sun comes out I shall go and work up above the harbour. But I know Dick and the children would love to go.'

'Ah yes, Dr Drew was telling us about your painting,' Mr Withers said warmly. 'Well, the loss will be ours – but if the muse calls, dear lady . . . The rest of the family will come, though, I hope?'

'Not half,' said Simon swiftly.

'It sounds smashing,' Barney said. He added, as an afterthought : 'Thank you very much.'

'Well,' said Father cheerfully, 'this is a noble gesture, I must say. We're all very grateful to you. As a matter of fact' – he looked vaguely round the room – 'there should have been one other member of the family here, but he seems to have disappeared. My wife's uncle. He rented the house for us.'

The children automatically followed his gaze round the room. They had forgotten Great-Uncle Merry. Now they realized that there had been no sign of him since the two sudden visitors appeared. The door that led into the breakfast room at the back of the house stood slightly open – but when Barney ran across to look in, there was no one there.

'Professor Lyon, you mean?' the girl said.

'That's right.' Father stared at her for a moment. 'I didn't think I'd mentioned him this morning. D'you know him, then?'

Mr Withers answered for her, quickly and smoothly. 'I believe we have met, once or twice. In another sphere than this. In the course of our work, you know. A charming old gentleman, as I remember, but a little unpredictable.'

'That he certainly is,' Mother said ruefully. 'Always dashing off somewhere. He hasn't even finished his supper this time. But do let me give you some tea, or coffee.'

'Thank you, but I think we should be getting back,' the girl said 'Vayne will have supper waiting.'

Mr Withers pulled down the edges of his immaculate blazer with a precise, feminine gesture. 'You're quite right, Polly, we mustn't be late.' He swung his white smile round the room like a lighthouse. 'Vayne is our skipper – the professional on board. And an excellent chef too. You must sample his cooking tomorrow. Well now, shall we see you all down in the harbour, if the weather is fine? Nine thirty, perhaps? We will have the dinghy waiting at the quay.'

'Splendid.' Father moved with him out into the hall, and everyone straggled after them. On the way Polly Withers paused, and looked up over Simon's head at the old Cornish maps hanging among the oil-paintings on the dark wall. 'Do look, Norman. Aren't they marvellous?' She turned to Mother. 'This really is a wonderful house. Did your uncle rent it from a friend?'

'A Captain Toms. We've never met him – he's abroad. Quite an old man – a retired sailor of some kind. I believe his family have owned the Grey House for years.'

'A fascinating place.' Mr Withers was looking about him with a professional eye. 'He has some beautiful old books, I see.' He reached one hand idly down to the door of a long low bookcase in the hall ; but it would not open.

'I keep everything locked,' Father said. 'You know what it is with a furnished house – one's always nervous of damaging things.'

'An admirable principle,' Mr Withers said formally. But his sister was smiling down at Simon. 'I bet it's a wonderful place to explore, though, isn't it?' she said. 'Have you children been looking for secret tunnels and things yet? I know I should have done, in an old house. Do let us know if you find one.'

Simon said politely, feeling Barney's anxious eyes on his back: 'Oh, I don't think there's anything like that here.'

'Well, till tomorrow, then,' Mr Withers said from the doorstep; and they were gone.

'Isn't that terrific?' Barney said eagerly, when the door closed. 'A whole day out on that yacht! D'you think they'll let us help sail her?'

'Mind you keep out of their way until you're asked,' said Father. 'We don't want any casualties.'

'Well, you could be ship's doctor.'

'I'm on holiday, remember?'

'Why didn't you tell us you'd met them?' demanded Simon.

'I was going to,' Father said meekly. 'I expect I was too busy being irritable.' He grinned. 'You can let Rufus out now if you want to, Barney – but he's *not* going on the boat tomorrow, so don't ask.'

Jane said suddenly: 'I don't think I will either.'

'Well, for goodness' sake!' Simon stared at her. 'Why ever not?'

'I should get seasick.'

'Of course you wouldn't – not under sail. There won't be any smelly old engine running. Oh come on, Jane.'

'No,' said Jane, more firmly. 'I'm not batty about boats like you are. I really don't want to go. They won't mind, will they, Father?'

Simon said in disgust: 'You must be nuts.'

'Leave her alone,' said his father. 'She knows her own mind. No, they'll understand, Jane. No one would want you to be worried about getting ill. See how you feel about going in the morning, though.'

'I do think it would be safer not,' Jane said. But she said nothing about her real reason for not wanting to go. It would have sounded too silly to explain that she felt a strange uneasiness about the tall white yacht, and about the smiling Mr Withers and his pretty sister. The more she thought about it, the sillier it seemed; so that in the end she convinced herself, as well as everybody else, that her reason for avoiding the trip was nothing but fear of seasickness.

But again nobody knew where Great-Uncle Merry had gone.

Chapter Four

A white morning haze lay over the sea, and down in the harbour the boats shifted idly on still water, bright under the sun. Jane peered down from her window. The fishing-boats were deserted, but she could see two small figures clambering from a dinghy beside the quay.

Simon said, behind her: 'I brought this for you to look after, if you really aren't coming.' She turned and saw him holding out a grey woollen sock. It looked peculiarly stiff and cylindrical.

'What on earth's so special about your socks?'

Simon grinned, but lowered his voice. 'It's the manuscript. I couldn't think of anything else to put it in.'

Jane laughed, took the sock and pulled the manuscript out half-way. But even though she handled it gently, the edges cracked and crumbled ominously as they caught in the wool. 'Hey,' she said, alarmed. 'If that's going to happen every time, the whole thing'll fall to bits in a week. It was all right up in the attic, lying there for years without anyone touching it, but if we're going to carry it around –'

Simon looked anxiously at the curled parchment, its battered edges dark with age, and saw cracks that had not been there before. He said, troubled: 'But we'll have to handle it so much if we're going to find out what it means . . . wait a minute, though. That room –'

Leaving Jane baffled, he seized the manuscript and ran downstairs to the small dark door on the first-floor landing which led to the passage they had discovered on the way to the attic. It was still unlocked. He stepped down into the tiny passage, and across to the bare, austere room that they had decided was the captain's bedroom. It was just as it had been the day before, and the telescope was still lying on the window-sill.

Simon picked up the case, and unscrewed it. The thread of each half was bright and untarnished, shining with a faint film of oil; and the copper lining inside, when he held it up to the light, glinted dry and clean. He dropped the rolled manuscript inside. It fitted perfectly, resting snugly between the two halves when he screwed them together again. Simon looked thoughtfully round the room, as if it might tell him something. But there was nothing but the silence and the mysterious lived-in emptiness, and he closed the door again, gently, and ran back upstairs.

'Look,' he said to Jane. 'Might have been made for it.'

'Perhaps it was,' said Jane, taking the case.

'You'd better hide it somewhere,' said Simon. 'What about the top of our wardrobe?'

'I'll think of a good place,' said Jane thoughtfully.

But Simon, half-way back to his own room already, hardly heard her; already his mind was racing ahead to the day on the Witherses' yacht. And by the time he, Barney and Father were gone, in a great scuffle of argument over oilskins and pull-overs and bathing-trunks, Jane was almost beginning to wish she had changed her mind and gone too.

But she said firmly, to Simon's final jeers: 'No. I'd only spoil it all if I got sick.' And instead she stood watching from the window as they ran down to the quay, and the little dinghy bobbed out to the tall, slim white yacht.

Her mother, easel under one arm and a bag of sandwiches and paints in the other hand, looked at her doubtfully. 'Darling, are you sure you aren't going to be lonely?'

'Goodness no,' said Jane stoutly. 'I shall just wander about, it'll be fun. Honestly. I mean you don't get lonely when you're painting, do you?'

Mother laughed. 'All right, independence, you wander. Don't get lost. I shall be up above the harbour on the other side if you want me. Mrs Palk's going to be here all day, she'll get your lunch. Why don't you take Rufus for a walk?'

She went out into the sunshine, her eyes already vague with the shape and colour of her painting. Jane felt a wet nose push at her hand, looked down at Rufus's large hopeful brown eyes, laughed, and ran off with him down into the village, through the small strange streets and the Cornish voices lilting from the doorways of the shops.

But all the morning she felt curiously restless, as if something were jostling to push itself to the front of her mind. As if, she thought, her mind were trying to say something to her that she couldn't quite hear. When she brought Rufus home, to collapse in a panting red heap in the kitchen beside Mrs Palk, she was still thoughtful and subdued.

'Nice walk, lovey?' said Mrs Palk, sitting back on her heels. She had a bucket of soapy water beside her, and her face was red and shiny; she had been scrubbing the grey slate floor.

'Mmm,' Jane said vaguely. She fiddled with the bow on her pony-tail.

'Have 'ee's lunch ready in just a minute,' Mrs Palk said, scrambling to her feet. 'My, just look at that dog, proper wore out. Needs a drink of water, I'll be bound –' She reached for Rufus's dish.

'I'll go up and wash.' Jane wandered out through the hall, the cool dark passage with the sunlight shafting in on one of the old maps that Polly Withers had exclaimed over with delight. Miss Withers . . . why should she and her brother have seemed sinister? They were perfectly ordinary people, there was no real reason to think otherwise. It was kind of them to have asked everyone out for the day on the yacht . . . Odd, though, that remark she had made about exploring, and finding things . . .

Finding things. Half-way up the stairs, Jane remembered with a sudden shock of guilt that she had left the manuscript alone all the morning, shut in its new case in the drawer of her bedside table. Should she have taken it with her? No, don't be silly, she thought; but she scuttled up the stairs and into her room anxiously, and felt a surge of relief as she saw the case lying quietly glinting in the drawer.

She drew out the brown roll of parchment and took it to the window, gingerly straightening it out. The lines of cramped black lettering gave her the same shiver of uneasy excitement that she had felt in the attic, at that moment when suddenly they had all three realized what they were looking at. She peered at it, but the squat chunks of words were no more legible now than they had been then. She could just make out the initials of the words that Simon had said were Mark and Arthur.

How were they ever to find out what it all meant?

She looked down at the bottom of the curling sheet, at the few thin wavering lines that they had thought might be a map. In the dim light of the attic there had been little there to see; but now Jane had the full white glare of midday. She bent closer, suddenly realizing that there were more lines in the map than she had noticed at first; lines so faint that before she had mistaken them for cracks. And among them, fainter still, some words were written.

It was a very rough map, as if it had been hurriedly drawn. It seemed to be coastline, looking rather like a letter W lying on its side, with two inlets and a headland. Or was it two headlands and an inlet? There was no way of telling which side was supposed to be the sea. And although she could just see that there was a word written across one of the projecting arms of land – or sea – it was made totally unreadable by one of the breaks in the ancient crumbling parchment: a crack crossing the word out as neatly as if it had been a thick ink line.

'Bother,' said Jane crossly, aloud. She realized as she said it that she had become determined in the last half-minute to have some discovery of her own about the manuscript to announce to Simon and Barney when they came back from their day on the boat. That was what had been niggling at the back of her mind all the morning.

One other name was written across the map. If it was a name. The letters were small and brown, but more distinct than those on the rest of the manuscript. Jane worked them out one by one and found they made three words. 'Ring Mark Hede.' She stared, disappointed. It meant nothing. 'Ring, mark, heed,' she said experimentally. It wasn't even a place. How could a place have a name like that?

The clang of the ship's bell in the hall came echoing up the stairs, breaking into the stillness of the sea's murmur and the distant gulls, and she heard Mrs Palk calling faintly below. 'Jane! Ja—ne!' Hastily she rolled up the manuscript and dropped it back into the telescope case, screwing the two halves tight together. She opened the drawer of her bedside table, hesitated for a moment, then shut it again. Better not let it out of her sight. She snatched a cardigan from the bed, wrapped it round the case and ran out and down the stairs two at a time.

But she ran too fast. Swinging round a corner of the first-floor landing, she bumped heavily against a long low wooden chest lying in the shadows, and yelped with pain. It *would* have to be the same leg she had hurt down on the quay . . . but as she bent to rub her knee, something drew her attention away. The chest she had knocked against was the one they had noticed the day before, with the lid locked. 'Native gold and ornaments,' Simon had said, and then found he couldn't open it. But now the lid had sprung open a few inches, and was rocking gently up and down. It must have been stuck, not locked; her collision had jerked it loose.

Curiously Jane lifted it fully open. There was not much inside: some old newspapers, a big pair of leather gloves, two or three heavy woollen sweaters and, half hidden, a small black-covered book. A very dull treasure, she thought. But the book might be interesting. She reached down inside and picked it up.

'Ja—ne!' Mrs Palk's voice was nearer, coming up the stairs. Guiltily Jane dropped the lid and bundled the little book inside the folds of her cardigan with the telescope case. Mrs Palk's face puffed into view through the banisters.

'Coming,' Jane said meekly.

'Ah, there, thought 'ee'd gone to bed. Gettin' too fat for they stairs, I am.' Mrs Palk beamed at her. 'Lunch is on the table. I were takin' me pastry out of the oven or I'd not have kept 'ee so long.' She waddled back to the kitchen. A mounded plateful of ham and salad waited for Jane in the dining-room, like a small bright island in the glossy sea of the polished mahogany table. Beside it was a dish of gooseberry tart and a small jug of cream.

Jane sat down and ate everything absently, leafing with one hand through the little book she had found in the chest. It was a guide-book to the village, written by the local vicar. 'A Short Guide to Trewissick' said the title-page, in flowing, curly type. 'Compiled by the Reverend E. J. Hawes-Mellor, M.A. (Oxon.) LL.D. (Lond.), Vicar of the Parish Church of St John, Trewissick.'

Not exciting, thought Jane, her interest dying. She flipped through the narrow pages, full of details of 'rambles' through the countryside around. The words from the manuscript were still swimming before her mind. If only she could have something to tell Simon and Barney about the map . . .

It was then that the guide-book fell open at its centre page under her fingers. Jane glanced down idly, and then paused. The page showed a detailed map of Trewissick village, with every street, straight and winding, patterned behind the harbour that lay snug between its two headlands. The churches, the village hall, were all separately marked; she saw with a quick thrill of pride that the Grey House was marked by name, on the road that led up to the tip of Kemare Head and then faded into nothing. But what caught her attention was the name written neatly across the headland. It read: 'King Mark's Head'.

'King Mark's Head,' said Jane slowly, aloud. She reached down to the bundled cardigan lying beside her chair, drew out the telescope case and unrolled the manuscript on the table. The words stared up at her, cramped and enigmatic: 'Ring Mark Hede'. And as she looked she saw that the first letter of the first word, blurred with age and dirt, might very well be not an 'R' but a 'K'. She gulped with excitement and took a deep breath.

King Mark's Head: the same name on both maps. So that the map on the manuscript from the attic must be a map of Trewissick – of that very part of Trewissick on which the Grey House stood. The strange words must be an old name for Kemare Head.

But when the first delighted shock had washed over her she looked again from one map to the other, and her spirits sank a little. There was something very odd about the wavering outline of the coast drawn on the old manuscript; something more than the inaccuracies you always found in a rough free-hand drawing. The lines of the coast were not the same as those on the guide-book map; the headlands bulged strangely, and the harbour was the wrong shape. Why?

Puzzled, Jane fetched a stub of pencil from the sideboard and did her best to draw a faint copy of the manuscript coastline over the one on the guide-book. There was no doubt about it; the shapes were not the same.

Perhaps the manuscript didn't show Trewissick after all. Perhaps there were two headlands in Cornwall called King Mark's Head. Or perhaps the coast had changed its shape in the hundreds of years since the manuscript had been drawn. How on earth were they to find out?

She put the manuscript reluctantly away, and stared at the two outlines, one in print, one in pencil, that she now had on the page of the book. But still she could find no answer. In exasperation she flipped back the pages of the book, and suddenly caught sight of the title-page again.

'. . . the Reverend E. J. Hawes-Mellor, M.A. . . .'

Jane jumped to her feet. That was it! Why not? The vicar of Trewissick must know all about the district. He was the expert, he had written the guide-book. He would know whether the coast had changed its shape, and what it had been like before. That was the way to find out – the only way. He was the only person who wouldn't ask why she wanted to know; he would think she was just interested in his book. She must go and find him, and ask.

And then think how much she would have to tell Simon and Barney when they came home . . .

That was the final thought which decided Jane, normally the shy member of the family, on the way she would spend her afternoon. She turned quickly as the door opened, and Mrs Palk came rolling in. 'Finished, 'ave 'ee? Enjoy it?'

'Lovely. Thank you very much.' Jane gathered up the guide-book, and the precious woolly bundle of her cardigan. 'Mrs Palk,' she said tentatively, 'do you know the vicar of Trewissick?' Surely, she thought, with all those hymns . . .

'Well, not meself personally, no.' Mrs Palk became very grave and solemn. 'Bein' chapel, I don't have no contact with'n, though I see 'n about, of course. Tur'ble clever man, they do say the vicar is. Was 'ee thinkin' of takin' a look at the church, midear?'

'Yes,' Jane said. After all I probably shall, she added defensively to herself.

''Tis a beautiful old place. Long way though – up the hill at the top of the village. You can just see the tower through the trees going up Fish Street, from the quay.'

'I think I know.'

'Don't get sunstroke, now.' Mrs Palk sailed benevolently out with the dishes, and in a moment Jane heard 'Abide with me' echoing with rich gloomy relish down the hall from the kitchen. She ran upstairs, looked hastily round for a place where she might hide the manuscript case, and finally tucked it among the covers at the foot of her bed, so that it could lie along the edge of the mattress and leave no bump. Then before her nervousness could get the better of her new idea, she went out, clutching her guide-book, into the sleepy afternoon sun.

The church at the top of the hill seemed cut off from the sea. Jane could see nothing from there but trees and the hills, and even the little village houses ended some twenty yards down the road. The square grey church with its low tower, and the big gate-posts opposite it, might have been in any wooded valley a hundred miles from the sea.

In the churchyard a wizened old man in shirt-sleeves and braces was cutting the grass with a pair of shears. Jane stopped near him on the other side of the wall. 'Excuse me,' she said loudly, 'but is that the vicarage over there?'

The old man, wheezing, straightened himself by holding one arm round to push himself in the small of the back. 'A's right,' he said laconically, and then just stood there, staring without expression, watching her all the way across the road and up the drive. Jane heard her feet crunching on the gravel, enormously loud in the silent afternoon. The big square grey house, its windows empty and lifeless, seemed to dare her to disturb it.

It was a very scruffy house, she thought, for a vicarage. The gravel of the drive was clotted with weeds, and in the rambling garden hydrangea bushes grew spindly and neglected, with the grass of the lawns as high as hay. She pressed the bell-push by the side of the peeling door, and heard a bell ring faintly inside the house, echoing a long way off.

After a long time, when she had just begun to decide with relief that no one was there to answer the bell, she heard footsteps inside the house. The door opened, creaking resentfully as if it did not often open at all.

The man standing there was tall and dark, untidy in an old sports jacket, but at the same time forbidding, with the thickest black eyebrows that Jane had ever seen growing almost straight across his brow without a break in the middle. He stared down at her.

'Yes?' His voice was very deep, without a trace of accent.

'Is Mr Hawes-Mellor in, please?'

The tall man frowned. 'Mr who?'

'Mr Hawes-Mellor. The vicar.'

His face cleared a little, though still the intent black-browed stare did not relax. 'Ah, I see. Mr Hawes-Mellor, I'm afraid, is no longer vicar here. He died a number of years ago.'

'Oh,' said Jane, and stepped back off the doorstep, not at all sorry at the chance to go away. 'Oh well, in that case –'

'Perhaps I can be of some help,' he said in the deep mournful voice. 'My name is Hastings, I have replaced Mr Hawes-Mellor here.'

'Oh,' Jane said again; she was beginning to find the lone Mr Hastings and his strange neglected house and garden rather unnerving. 'Oh no, I don't want to be a nuisance, it was only something about a book he wrote, a guide-book to the village.'

A flicker of interest seemed to wake in the vicar's dark face. 'A guide-book to Trewissick? There was some talk that he had written one, but I have never been able to trace a copy. What was it that you wanted to ask? I'm afraid that if you are looking for the book I can be of no help –'

'Oh no,' Jane said, not without pride. 'I've got one.' She held her little guide-book up to show him. 'It was just something inside it, about the village, that I wondered if he'd got wrong.'

The vicar stared down at the book, opened his mouth to say something and then seemed to change his mind. He held the door wider open and moved his mouth into an uneasy mile. 'Well, do come in for a few moments, young lady, and we'll see what we can do. I know a little about Trewissick myself after my years here.'

'Thank you very much,' Jane said nervously. She stepped inside the door, hitching up the ribbon on her pony-tail as she followed him down the passage, and hoping she looked reasonably tidy. Not that she would have been out of place if she had been in rags: she thought, looking around her, that the vicarage was one of the most unloved-looking and shabbiest houses she had ever seen. It was big, and rambling, with more sense of space than the Grey House; but the paint was peeling, the walls grubby and the floors all bare with one or two faded rugs. She began to feel rather sorry for the vicar as he strode stiffly along ahead of her.

He led her into a room which was obviously his study, with a big desk strewn with papers, two battered cane chairs with faded cushions, and shelves of books all round the walls. Tall French windows stood wide open to show the stretch of long grass that Jane had glimpsed from the front drive.

'Now,' he said, sitting down behind his desk and clearing a space impatiently in the litter of papers on its top. 'Sit yourself down and tell me what you were going to ask Mr Hawes-Mellor. You've found a copy of his book, have you?'

He stared again at the book in Jane's hand. It seemed to fascinate him.

'Yes,' Jane said. 'Would you like to have a look at it?' She held the book out to him.

The vicar took it, slowly, closing his long fingers round the narrow cover as if it were something infinitely precious. He did not open it, but put it down on the desk before him and looked at it so hard that he seemed not to be seeing it but thinking about something else. Then he turned his grave, heavy-browed face towards Jane again.

'You are on holiday here?'

'Yes. My name's Jane Drew. I'm staying with my family in the Grey House.'

'Are you indeed? That is not a house I am very familiar with.' Mr Hastings smiled rather grimly. 'Captain Toms has no time for me, I am afraid. A strange, solitary man.'

'We've never met him,' Jane said. 'He's gone abroad.'

'And this book of yours.' His fingers caressed its cover almost unconsciously. 'Is it interesting?'

'Oh tremendously. I love all the stories about Trewissick when there were smugglers and things.' For a moment Jane wondered doubtfully whether to mention the map after all. But her curiosity overcame any doubts. She stood up and crossed to stand beside him, leafing through the book to the page with the map of south Cornwall. 'This was the bit that puzzled me, the shape of the coastline. I wanted to ask if it had ever been different once.'

Standing behind the vicar, she could not see his face, but his shoulders seemed to stiffen as he looked at the map, and the fingers of his hand lying on the desk curled gently underneath into the palm.

'A curious question,' he said.

'I just wondered.'

'I see there is another line pencilled over the coastline of the map here. Is that yours?'

'Yes.'

'From your imagination?' The deep voice was very quiet.

'More or less. Well, that is . . . I saw something like it somewhe.e, in a book or something.' Jane floundered, trying to avoid mentioning their manuscript from the attic without actually telling untruths. 'If you know about Trewissick, Mr Hastings, do you know if the coast has always been the same shape?'

'I should have thought so. A granite coast takes a very long time to change.' He was staring it the pencilled line. 'You say you saw this outline in a book?'

'Oh, a book, or another map, or something,' Jane said vaguely.

'In the Grey House?'

'We don't touch the captain's books,' Jane said automatically, forgetting that the guide-book must be one of them.

'But you have looked around them, no doubt?' The vicar rose to his feet, towering above her, and reached out a long arm to take a book from one of the shelves. He handed it to Jane; it was very old and covered with shiny scuffed leather, and the pages crackled and gave off a smell of musty age when she opened it. It was called *Tales of Lyonesse*, and a lot of the 's's were printed like 'f's.

'Have you seen any book there like that?' His voice was persistent. He stood between Jane and the light and looking up at him, she could see nothing but a faint glint of light reflected from his eyes in the shadowed face. The effect was for a moment exceedingly sinister, and Jane felt creeping over her the small cold uneasiness that was becoming familiar about the holiday: a sense of something mysterious, that everyone else knew about but that was hidden from her brothers and her.

'No, I don't think so.'

'Are you sure? A title like that, perhaps? You might have seen a map in such a book?'

'No, really. We just haven't looked.'

'Might you not have seen a volume on a shelf similar to this?'

'I honestly don't know,' Jane said, shrinking back in her chair at the urgency that had come into his voice. 'Why don't you ask the captain?'

Mr Hastings took the book from her and tucked it back in its place on the shelf. The grave near-frown was back on his face. 'He is not a communicative man,' he said shortly.

Uneasiness was nudging more insistently at Jane's mind, and she began to fidget from one foot to another.

'Well, I must be off home,' she said, using one of Mother's phrases brightly and hoping it sounded polite. 'I'm sorry to have interrupted you.' She glanced rather wildly from the window to the door.

The vicar, standing silent and intent, pulled himself together and moved towards the French windows. 'You can come out this way, it's quicker. The front door is seldom used.'

He held out his hand to Jane. 'I am pleased to have met you, Miss Drew. I am sorry not to have been more helpful, but I must say I think it unlikely that our coast here has ever had any characteristics that are not shown on Mr Hawes-Mellor's map. He was, I understand, a cartographer of some repute. I am glad you came to see me.'

He inclined his head gravely as he shook Jane's hand, with a strange, archaic gesture that reminded her suddenly of Mr Withers when he left the Grey House. But this, she thought, seemed more genuine, as if it were something which Mr Withers had been trying to imitate.

'Good-bye,' she said quickly, and ran off through the long feathery grass towards the drive of the silent shabby house, and the road that led back home.

Chapter Five

When Jane reached the Grey House, Simon and Barney were chattering like monkeys in the living-room to Great-Uncle Merry, who sat quietly listening from the depths of a big armchair. Both boys were glowing with excitement, and even Barney's fair skin had been flushed by the wind and sun to a faint pinkish-brown.

'There you are, darling,' Mother said. 'I was just beginning to worry about you.'

Simon hailed her with a yell from across the room, 'Oh you should have come! It was fabulous, like being right out to sea, and when the wind was behind us we went tremendously fast, far better than a motor boat . . . only we came back in on the engine, because the wind dropped, and that was fun too. Mr Withers came back with us for a drink, but he's gone now. Father went with him, to fetch up some of the mackerel we caught.'

'And what's Jane been doing?' said Great-Uncle Merry quietly from his corner.

'Oh, nothing much,' Jane said. 'Wandering about.'

But when all three children were upstairs (sent early up to bed because, Father said ominously when Simon imitated a lightship siren right behind his chair, they were all 'overtired'), Jane knocked at the door of the boys' room and went in to tell them about her discovery and her visit to the vicar. She did not meet quite the enthusiastic response that she had expected.

'You copied out part of the manuscript?' Simon demanded, his voice rising to a squeak of horror. 'And showed it to him?'

'Yes, I did,' Jane said defensively. 'Well, for goodness' sake, what harm can that possibly do? A little pencilled line in a guide-book can't mean anything to anybody.'

'You jolly well shouldn't have done anything connected with the manuscript unless we all agreed it together.'

'It wasn't connected with the manuscript, not as far as he knew. I just told him I wanted to find something out about the coast.' Jane forgot any uneasiness she had felt about the vicar in building a defence against Simon's indignation. 'I thought you'd be grateful, my finding out the manuscript map shows Kemare Head.'

'She's quite right, you know,' Barney said from his pillow. 'It's terrifically important finding that out. For all we knew up to now it might have been a map of Timbuctoo. And if it turns out from what the vicar says that Trewissick hasn't changed since when our map was drawn, that's going to help us when we find if there are any clues in the manuscript.'

'I dare say,' Simon said grudgingly, clambering into bed and kicking off all the blankets. 'Oh well, yes, it does help. We'll talk about it tomorrow.'

'Then we can start our quest,' Barney said sleepily. 'Night, Jane. See you in the morning.'

'Good night.'

*

But the morning brought more than any of them had bargained for.

Simon woke first, very early. The air was still as warm as it had been the day before. He lay in his pyjamas staring up at the ceiling for a little while, listening to Barney's peaceful breathing from the other bed. Then he grew restless, so he went out and padded downstairs barefoot, feeling hungry. If he found Mrs Palk already in the kitchen he might manage to have two breakfasts.

But Mrs Palk seemed not to have arrived yet, and the house was quite silent. It was not until he reached the flight of stairs leading down into the hall that Simon first noticed something wrong.

Always on his way down to breakfast he stopped to look at the old map of Cornwall that hung on the wall at the turn of the stairs. But when he looked for it this morning, it was not there. Only a rectangular mark on the wallpaper showed where it had hung; and as Simon glanced along the wall of pictures down the stairs he saw there were several more gaps as well.

Puzzled, he went slowly down into the hall. He found several strange naked-looking patches where pictures had been taken down, and the barometer, next to one empty space, was leaning sideways.

Simon went across and straightened it, feeling the bare wooden blocks of the floor cool under his bare feet. Looking down the long hall, he could see nothing else unusual at first. Then he noticed that at the far end, where the sun was streaming in from the kitchen through the open doorway, several of the blocks had been wrenched out and were strewn all over the floor. Simon stared, puzzled.

He started down the hall towards the kitchen, and then on an impulse turned to his right and reached for the handle of the door into the living-room. It squeaked under his touch as it always did, and nervously Simon opened the door and peered round. Then he gasped.

The room looked as though a tornado had blown through it in the night. The pictures hung crooked on the walls, or lay torn from their frames on the floor, and the furniture seemed to Simon's first startled glance to be completely buried in books.

Everywhere there were books, scattered over the floor, open, closed, upside-down; heaped on the tables and chairs, mounded on the sideboard; and a lonely few still lying on the empty shelves. All the locked bookcases around the walls, that they had been forbidden to touch, were empty. The glass doors hung loose from their hinges with splintered wood showing round their locks; and one or two, completely wrenched away, were propped against the wall. The shelves had been swept clear of everything they held, and the drawers below were open, with papers spilling from them loose on to the chaos of books on the floor. There was a faint musty smell, and a thin pall of dust seemed to hang in the air.

For one frozen moment Simon stood staring, aghast. Then he turned on his heel and raced upstairs, shouting for his father.

Everyone was woken out of their early half-sleep by his shouts. Led by Father, they all stumbled out into the passage in pyjamas and nightdresses and followed Simon downstairs, trying dazedly to understand the words tumbling over each other out of his mouth.

'What is it?'

'What's the matter, is the house on fire?'

'Burglars!' Father said incredulously, following down the stairs. 'But you don't get burgled in a village like – good heavens!' He caught sight of the devastation in the living-room through the open door. As Mother, Jane and Barney followed his gaze they fell silent too, but not for long.

Wherever they went on the ground floor of the house they found the same thing. The doors of bookcases had been ripped off, and the books tumbled off the shelves into a chaotic jumble on the floor. Every locked drawer or cupboard had been forced, and the papers from inside scattered wildly about. Even in the breakfast room half a dozen elderly cookery books had been scattered from a shelf.

'I don't understand this,' Father said slowly. 'The place is practically wrecked, but one or two obvious things that are clearly valuable haven't been touched. That statuette on the mantelpiece there, for instance, and that big silver cup on the sideboard in the front room. There doesn't seem any point to it all.'

'Someone was rejoicing in destruction,' Barney said solemnly.

Simon said slowly, 'They must have made an awful noise. Why didn't it wake us up?'

'We're two floors away,' Barney said. 'You can't hear anything up there. I like this, it's mysterious.'

'I don't,' Jane shivered. 'Imagine someone wandering about down here all night while we were asleep upstairs. It gives me the creeps.'

'Perhaps there wasn't anyone,' Barney said.

'Don't be an idiot, of course there was. Or do you think all the books jumped off the shelves?'

'It needn't have been human. It might have been one of those special sort of ghosts that throws things about just for fun. A polter – polt –'

'Poltergeist,' said Father absently. He was opening all the silver cupboards to see if anything had gone.

'There you are. One of those.'

'Well, Mrs Palk says the house is supposed to be haunted,' Jane said. 'Oh dear.'

They all looked at one another round-eyed, and suddenly shivered.

Mother said, appearing suddenly in the doorway and making them all jump: 'Well, it's the first ghost I've ever heard of who wore crêpe-soled shoes. Dick, come and have a look out here.'

Father straightened up and followed her out into the kitchen, with the children close at his heels. Mother pointed, without a word.

Two kitchen windows were open, the big one over the sink and a small one above it; and so was the door. And on the flat white tiles of the table-top beside the sink there was the faint but unmistakable outline of a footprint. A large footprint, with bar markings across the sole; and traces of the same markings on the window-sill above.

'Gosh!'

'There's your ghost,' Father said cheerfully, though he did not look cheerful at all.

Then he turned on them briskly. 'Now come on, all of you, off upstairs and get dressed. You've seen all there is to see. No' – he waved his hands as all three children began to protest vigorously. 'This isn't a game, it's extremely serious. We shall have to call the police, and I don't want anything touched before they arrive. *Off*!'

Father had one voice which stopped all argument, and this was it. Simon, Jane and Barney trailed reluctantly out of the kitchen door and along the hall, and then stopped still at the foot of the stairs, looking up. Great-Uncle Merry was heavily descending the stairs towards them, clad in a pair of brilliant red pyjamas and with his white hair all standing up on end.

He was yawning prodigiously and rubbing his eyes in a puzzled kind of way. 'Won't do,' he was muttering to himself. 'Can't make it out . . . heavy sleep . . . most unusual . . .' Then he caught sight of the children. 'Good morning,' he said with dignity, as if he were fully and impeccably dressed. 'Befuddled though I am this morning, a great clamour has been penetrating up the stairs from down here. Is anything wrong?'

'We've had *burglars* . . . !' Simon began, but Father came striding out after them from the kitchen and clapped his hands. 'Come on, come on, I told you to go and get dressed . . . Oh good, there you are, Merry. The most extraordinary thing has happened –' He glared at the children, and they hastily ran upstairs.

After breakfast the police arrived from St Austell: a solid, red-faced sergeant and a very young constable following him like a mute shadow. Simon was looking forward to eager questions about his discovery of the crime. At the very least, he thought vaguely, he would have to make a statement. He was not quite sure what this meant, but it sounded familiar and important.

But the sergeant only said to him, his warm Cornish accent stroking the words: 'Came down first, did 'ee?'

'Yes, that's right.'

'Touch anythin'?'

'No, not a thing. Well, I did straighten the barometer. It was crooked.' Looking round at the chaos, Simon thought how silly this sounded.

'Ah. Hear anythin'?'

'No.'

'All quite as usual, eh, apart from the mess?'

'Yes, it was really.'

'Ah,' said the sergeant. He grinned at Simon sitting eagerly on the edge of his chair. 'All right, I'll let 'ee off this time.'

'Oh,' said Simon, deflated. 'Is that all?'

'I reckon so,' the sergeant said placidly, tugging his jacket down over his stout middle. 'Now, sir,' he said to Father, 'if we might take a look at this footprint you say you found . . .'

'Yes, of course.' Father led them out of the kitchen. The children, drifting behind, peeped through the door. The sergeant gazed impassively at the footprint for some moments, said to his speechless constable, 'Now take good note o' that, young George,' and moved ponderously out to the disorder of the living-room.

'You say there seems to be nothin' gone, sir?'

'Well, it's difficult to tell, of course, since it's a rented house,' Father said. 'But certainly nothing valuable seems to be missing. The silver's all intact, not that there's much of it anyway. That cup, as you see, wasn't touched. But they seemed to go for the books, and I can't vouch for those. There may well be some missing that we don't know about.'

'"Tis a proper mess, surely.' The sergeant bent down, with some effort, and picked up a book. A small deflated black cobweb lay along the top of its pages. 'Very old, these – valuable, maybe. Quite well off, the captain is, I believe.'

'If I might suggest, sergeant –' Great-Uncle Merry said diffidently, from the edge of the group.

'What is it, Professor?' The sergeant beamed at him all over his rosy countryman's face; even he seemed to know Great-Uncle Merry inexplicably well.

'I had no chance to look very thoroughly, since most of the bookcases were locked. But I should have said that very few of the books in this house were valuable, to a dealer at any rate. None of them was worth more than a few pounds, at the outside.'

'Funny. They seem to have been looking for something . . . hey, look here.' The sergeant shifted aside some of the papers whitening the floor, and they saw a pile of empty picture-frames.

'Those are from the hall,' Simon said at once. 'That bumpy gold frame had a map in it at the top of the stairs.'

'Hmm. No map in ut now. All of 'em been ripped out. Still, I dare say we'll find them somewhere in all this clutter.' The sergeant rocked to and fro on his heels, gazing with an expression of mild regret at the battered bookcases and piles of books. He rubbed one of his shiny silver buttons thoughtfully, and finally turned to Father with an air of decision. 'Sheer hooliganism, I reckon, sir. Can't be no other explanation. Seldom is round these parts, anyway.'

'Ah,' said the young constable regretfully, and immediately turned crimson and looked down at his feet.

The sergeant beamed at him. 'Someone with a grudge against the captain, I dare say, havin' a go at his belongings. Might well be one or two people hereabouts don't like him, he's a funny old bird. Wouldn't 'ee say so, Professor?'

'You might call him that,' Great-Uncle Merry said abstractedly. He was standing looking about him with a puzzled frown.

'Breakin' in idn' difficult in a place the size of Trewissick,' the sergeant said. 'People don't expect it, they leave their windows open . . . did 'ee lock up last night, Dr Drew?'

'Yes, I always do, back and front.' Father scratched his head. 'I could swear there weren't any windows open downstairs, but I must admit I didn't go round trying them all.'

'Well no, you wouldn't expect this sort of thing . . . beats me why anyone should want to take the risk, just to rough the place up and not pinch anything. Now if I could have one more look at that print –' He led the way out of the room.

Simon beckoned Jane and Barney to stay behind. 'Hooligans,' he said thoughtfully. He picked up a book that lay sprawled open face downwards on the carpet, and shut its covers gently.

'It doesn't sound right, somehow,' Jane said. 'It's all so thorough. Every drawer opened, and almost every book taken down.'

'And every map taken out of its frame,' said Barney. 'It's just the maps, have you noticed? None of the pictures.'

'The burglars must have been looking for something.'

'And they went on all through the house because they couldn't find it.'

'perhaps it wasn't down here,' Simon said slowly.

'Well, it couldn't have been upstairs.'

'How d'you know?'

'Don't be silly, there just isn't anything upstairs. Except us.'

'Isn't there?'

'Well —' Jane said, and then suddenly they were all three looking at one another in horror. They turned and dashed out of the room and up the stairs, to the second-floor bedroom where the great square wardrobe stood between Simon's and Barney's beds.

Simon hastily dragged a chair forward and jumped up on it to feel round on top of the wardrobe. His face went blank with alarm. 'It's gone!'

There was a fearful moment of silence. Then Jane sat down with a bump on Barney's bed and began to giggle hysterically.

'Stop it!' Simon said sharply, sounding for a moment as authoritative as his father.

'Sorry . . . it's all right, it hasn't gone,' Jane said weakly. 'It's in my bed.'

'In your *bed*?'

'Yes, I've got it. It's still there. I clean forgot.' Jane babbled, then pulled herself together. 'When I went to see the vicar I didn't want to take it with me, and I had to hide it somewhere in my room. So I shoved it right down under the bedclothes. It was the nearest place. Then last night I forgot it was there, and I must have gone to sleep without feeling it. Come on.'

The front bedroom was full of sunlight, and through the window the sea sparkled as merrily as if nothing could ever disturb the world. Jane hauled back the sheet of her rumpled bed and there, tucked in a corner at the bottom, was the telescope case.

They perched in a row on the edge of the bed, and Jane opened the case on her lap. They stared in silent relief at the familiar hollow cylinder of the old manuscript inside.

'Do you realize,' Simon said gravely, 'this was the safest place it could possibly have been? They could have looked anywhere else, but not in your bed without waking you up.'

'You don't think they came up and looked in our rooms?' Barney turned pale.

'They might have looked anywhere.'

'Oh, but this is silly.' Jane swung her pony-tail as if she were trying to clear her head. 'How on earth could they have known anything about the manuscript at all? We found it in the attic, all hidden away, and it had obviously been there for years and years. And no one can even have been up in the attic for ages — think of all that dust on the stairs.'

'I don't know,' Simon said. 'There's a lot of things I don't understand. I only know I've been feeling funny about the manuscript ever since you said that vicar of yours got all excited about the copy of the map.'

Jane shrugged. 'I don't see how a vicar could be bad. Anyway he didn't know about the manuscript. He asked a few questions, but I think he was just being nosy.'

'Wait a minute,' Barney said slowly. 'I've remembered something. There was someone else asking questions. It was Mr Withers, on the boat yesterday, when I was down in the cabin with him getting lunch. He started saying a lot of peculiar things about the Grey House, and to tell him if we saw anything that looked very old . . . any' – he swallowed – 'any old books or maps or papers . . .'

'Oh no,' Simon said. 'It couldn't have been him.'

'But whoever it was,' said Barney in a small clear voice, 'they were looking for the manuscript – weren't they?'

Sitting there in the silence of the Grey House they all three knew that it was the truth.

'They must want it awfully badly.' Simon looked down at the manuscript. 'It's that map part, that's what it is. Somehow someone knows it's in the house. Oh, I *wish* we knew what it said.'

'Look here,' Jane said, making up her mind, 'we've got to tell Mother and Father about finding it.'

Simon stuck his chin out. 'It wouldn't do any good. Mother would be worried stiff. Anyway, don't you see, we shouldn't have a chance to work it out ourselves then. And suppose it *does* lead to buried treasure?'

'I don't want to find any beastly treasure. Something horrible's bound to happen if we do.'

Barney forgot his fright in outraged ownership. 'We can't tell anyone about it now. We found it. I found it, it's my quest.'

'You're too young to understand,' Jane said pompously. 'We shall have to tell someone about it – Father, or the policeman. Oh do see,' she added plaintively. 'We've got to do something, after last night.'

'Children!' Mother's voice came from the stairs outside, very close. They jumped guiltily to their feet at once, and Simon held the manuscript case behind his back.

'Hallo?'

'Oh there you are.' Mother appeared in the doorway; she looked preoccupied. 'Look, the house is going to be chaotic all this morning – would you like to go off swimming and come home for a late lunch – about one thirty? Then this afternoon Great-Uncle Merry wants to take you all out.'

'Fine,' Simon said, and she vanished again.

'That's it!' Barney thumped the pillow in excitement and relief. 'That's it, of course, why didn't we think of it before? We can tell someone and still have things all right. We can tell Great-Uncle Merry!'

Chapter Six

'Now then,' said Great-Uncle Merry as they strode down the hill to the harbour. 'It's a splendid afternoon for a walk. Which way d'you want to go?'

'Somewhere lonely.'

'Somewhere miles from anywhere.'

'Somewhere where we can talk.'

Great-Uncle Merry looked down at them, from one strained face to the next. His bleak, impassive expression did not change and he simply said, 'Very well,' and lengthened his stride so that they had to trot to keep up. He asked no questions, but walked in silence. They climbed the winding little street on the side of the harbour opposite Kemare Head and the Grey House, and followed the cliff path past the last straggling houses of the village, until the great purple-green sweep of the opposite headland rose before them.

Up the slope they toiled, through heather and prickling gorse, past rough outcroppings of grey rock patched yellow with lichen and weathered by the wind. There had been no breath of a breeze down in the harbour, but here the wind was loud in their ears.

'Gosh,' Barney said, pausing and turning outwards to look down. 'Look!' They turned with him, and saw the harbour far below and the Grey House tiny on the threading road. Already they were higher than their own headland, and still the rock-scarred slope stretched above them to meet the sky.

They turned again and scrambled up the slope, and at last they were at the top of the headland, with the line of the surf laid out like a slow-moving map below them on either side, and beyond it the great blue sweep of the sea. One big slanting boulder of granite stood higher than any they had passed on the way up, and Great-Uncle Merry sat down with his back against it, his legs arched up before him, long and knobbly in their flapping brown corduroys.

The children stood together, looking down. The land before them was unfamiliar, a silent, secret world of mounded peaks and invisible valleys, all its colours merging in a haze of summer heat.

'*Hic incipit regnum Logri* . . .' Great-Uncle Merry said, looking out with them them across it all, as if he were reading out an inscription.

'What does that mean?'

'Here begins the realm of Logres . . . Now come on, the three of you, and sit down.'

They squatted down beside him, in a semi-circle before the big rock. Great-Uncle Merry surveyed them as if he were enthroned. 'Well,' he said gently, 'who tells me what's wrong?'

In the quiet with only the sound of the wind stirring the air Jane and Barney looked at Simon. 'Well, it was the burglar,' he said haltingly. 'We were worried . . .' and then the three of them were all tumbling out the words.

'When Miss Withers came the other night she was asking questions about the Grey House, and whether we'd found anything.'

'And so did Mr Withers on their yacht, he asked me about old books.'

'And whoever it was last night, they only touched the books and all the old maps . . .'

'. . . they were looking for it, they must have been . . .'

'. . . only they didn't know where to look, and they didn't know we already had it.'

'Suppose they know we've got it, they might come after us . . .'

Great-Uncle Merry raised one hand, though he did not move. His chin was up. He looked as if he were waiting for something. 'Gently now,' he said. 'If you have found something in the Grey House, what is it you have found?'

Simon felt inside the rucksack. He held out the roll of parchment to Great-Uncle Merry. 'We found this.'

Great-Uncle Merry took the parchment without a word, and gently unrolled it on his knees. He gazed at it in silence for a long while, and they could see his eyes moving over the words.

The wind on the headland whined softly round them, and although, as they watched, Great-Uncle Merry's expression did not change, they suddenly knew that some enormous emotion was flooding through him. Like an electric current it tingled in the air, exciting and frightening at the same time; though they could not understand what it was. And then he raised his head at last and looked out across the hills of Cornwall rolling far into the distance; and he breathed a great sigh of relief that was like a release from all the worry of the whole world.

'Where did you find it?' he said, and the three children jumped at the quiet, ordinary tone of his voice as if it brought them out of a spell.

'In the attic.'

'There's a great big attic, all full of dust and junk, we found a door behind our wardrobe, and a staircase leading up.'

'I found it,' Barney said. 'I threw my apple core away, and I went to get it back because of the rats, and I found the manuscript by accident in a corner under the floor.'

'What is it, Gumerry?'

'What does it say?'

'It's terribly old, isn't it?'

'Is it important? Is it about buried treasure?'

'In a way,' Great-Uncle Merry said. His eyes seemed dazed, unable to focus anywhere, but there was a twitching at the corners of his mouth. Somehow, without smiling, he looked happier than they had ever seen him look before. Jane thought, watching: it is a sad face usually, and that's why there is such a difference.

He laid the manuscript down on his lap and looked from Jane to Simon to Barney and back again. He seemed to be searching for words.

'You have found something that may be more important than you can possibly realize,' he said at last.

They stared at him. He looked away again over the hills.

'You remember the fairy stories you were told when you were very small – "once upon a time..." Why do you think they always began like that?'

'Because they weren't true,' Simon said promptly.

Jane said, caught up in the unreality of the high remote place, 'Because perhaps they were true once, but nobody could remember when.'

Great-Uncle Merry turned his head and smiled at her. 'That's right. Once upon a time . . . a long time ago . . . things that happened once, perhaps, but have been talked about for so long that nobody really knows. And underneath all the bits that people have added, the magic swords and lamps, they're all about one thing – the good hero fighting the giant, or the witch, or the wicked uncle. Good against bad. Good against evil.'

'Cinderella.'

'Aladdin.'

'Jack the Giant-killer.'

'And all the rest.' He looked down again, his fingers caressing the curving edge of the parchment. 'Do you know what this manuscript is about?'

'King Arthur,' Barney said promptly. 'And King Mark. Simon found the names, in Latin.'

'And what do you know about King Arthur?'

Barney looked round triumphantly at his captive audience and drew breath for a long recital, but somehow found himself stammering instead.

'Well . . . he was King of England, and he had his knights of the Round Table, Lancelot and Galahad and Kay and all of them. And they fought jousts and rescued people from wicked knights. And Arthur beat everyone with his sword Excalibur. It was good against bad, I suppose, like you said about, in the fairy stories. Only he was real.'

Great-Uncle Merry's quiet pleased smile was flickering again. 'And when was Arthur King of England?'

'Well –' Barney waved his hands vaguely. 'A long time ago . . .'

'. . . like in the fairy stories,' Jane finished for him. 'I see. But Gumerry, what are you trying to tell us? Was King Arthur a fairy story too?'

'No!' Barney said indignantly.

'No,' said Great-Uncle Merry. 'He was real. But the same thing has happened, d'you see – he lived such a long time ago that there's no record of him left. And so he's become a story, a legend, as well.'

Simon fidgeted with the strap of his rucksack. 'But I don't see where the manuscript comes in.'

The wind over the headland stirred Great-Uncle Merry's white hair outlined against the sky, and as he glanced down he looked magisterial and severe.

'Patience a little. And listen carefully now, because you may find this difficult to understand.

'First of all, you have heard me talk of Logres. It was the old name for this country, thousands of years ago; in the old days when the struggle between good and evil was more bitter and open than it is now. That struggle goes on all round us all the time, like two armies fighting. And sometimes one of them seems to be winning and sometimes the other, but neither has ever triumphed altogether. Nor ever will,' he added softly to himself, 'for there is something of each in every man.

'Sometimes, over the centuries, this ancient battle comes to a peak. The evil grows very strong and nearly wins. But always at the same time there is some leader in the world, a great man who sometimes seems to be more than a man, who leads the forces of good to win back the ground and the men they seemed to have lost.'

'King Arthur,' Barney said.

'King Arthur was one of these,' Great-Uncle Merry said. 'He fought against the men who wanted Logres, who robbed and murdered and broke all the rules of battle. He was a strong and good man, and the people of those days trusted him absolutely. With that faith behind him, Arthur's power was very great – so great that in the stories that have grown up since, people have talked about his having magical help. But magic is just a word.'

'I suppose he didn't win,' Jane said with sudden conviction, 'or there wouldn't have been any wars since.'

'No, he didn't win,' Great-Uncle Merry said, and even in the clear afternoon sunshine he seemed with every word to become more remote, as ancient as the rock behind him and the old world of which he spoke.

'He wasn't altogether beaten, but he didn't altogether win. So the same struggle between good and evil sides has gone on ever since. But the good has grown very confused, and since the ancient days of Logres it has been trying to regain the strength it was given by Arthur. But it never has. Too much has been forgotten.

'But those men who remembered the old world have been searching for its secret ever since. And there have been others searching as well – the enemies, the wicked men, who have the same greed in their cold hearts as the men whom Arthur fought.'

Great-Uncle Merry looked out into the distance, his head outlined against the sky like the proud carved head of a statue, centuries old and yet always the same. 'I have been searching,' he said. 'For many, many years.'

The children stared at him, awed and a little afraid. For a moment he was a stranger, someone they did not know. Jane had a sudden fantastic feeling that Great-Uncle Merry did not really exist at all, and would vanish away if they breathed or spoke.

He looked down at them again. 'I was beginning to know that this part of Cornwall held what we sought,' he said. 'I did not know that you children would be the ones to find it. Or what danger you would be putting yourselves in.'

'Danger?' Simon said incredulously.

'Very great danger,' said Great-Uncle Merry, looking him full in the face. Simon swallowed. 'This manuscript, Simon, puts you all right in the middle of the battle. Oh, nobody will stick a knife in your back – their methods are more subtle than that. And perhaps more successful.' He looked down at the manuscript again. 'This,' he said more normally, 'is a copy.'

'A copy?' said Barney. 'But it's so old.'

'Oh yes, it's old. About six hundred years old. But it's a copy of something even older than that – written more than nine hundred years ago. The part at the beginning is in Latin.'

'There, I said so,' Jane said in triumph.

Simon stuck out his lower lip. 'Well, I translated bits of it, didn't I? Not much, though,' he confessed to Great-Uncle Merry. 'I couldn't recognize any of the words.'

'I don't suppose you could. This is medieval Latin, not like the Latin you learn at school . . . it's written by a monk who must have lived near here, and I think about six hundred years ago, though there's no date. He says, roughly, that near his monastery an old English manuscript has been found. He says it tells of an old legend from the days of Mark and Arthur, and that he has copied out the story to save its being lost, because the manuscript was falling to bits. He says he copied out a map that was with the manuscript too. Then all the rest, underneath, is the story that he copied out – and you can see the map right at the bottom.'

'If the original manuscript was so old that it was falling to bits six hundred years ago . . .' Barney said, bemused.

Simon broke in impatiently. 'Gumerry, can you understand the copied-out part? That's not Latin, is it?'

'No, it's not,' Great-Uncle Merry said. 'It's one of the Early English dialects, the old language that used to be spoken centuries ago. But it's a very old form of it, full of words from the old Cornish and even some from Brittany. I don't know – I'll read it out as best I can. But I may turn it into rather curious English, and I may have to stop . . .'

He peered at the manuscript again. Then, stumblingly and with many pauses while he held it to the sunlight or fumbled in his mind for a word, he began to read, in his deep, far-away voice. The children sat and listened, with the sun hot on their faces and the wind still whispering in their ears.

'This I write, that when the time comes it shall be found by the proper man. And I leave it in the care of the old land that soon shall be no more.

'Into the land of Cornwall, the kingdom of Mark, there came in the days of my fathers a strange knight fleeing towards the west. Many fled hither in those days, when the old kingdom was broken by the invader and the last battle of Arthur was lost. For only in the western land did men still love God and the old ways.

'And the strange knight who came to the place of my fathers was called Bedwin, and he bore with him the last trust of Logres, the grail, made in the fashion of the Holy Grail, that told upon its sides all the true story of Arthur soon to be misted in men's minds. Each panel told of an evil overcome by Arthur and the company of God, until the end when evil overcame all. And the last panel showed the promise and the proof of Arthur's coming again.

'For behold, said the knight Bedwin to my fathers, evil is upon us now, and so shall it be for time beyond our dreaming. Yet if the grail, that is the last trust of the old world, be not lost, then when the day is ripe the Pendragon shall come again. And at the last all shall be safe, and evil be thrust out never to return.

'And so that the trust be kept, he said, I give it into your charge, and your sons', and your sons' sons', until the day come. For I am wounded near death from the last of the old battles, and I can do no more.

'And very soon he died, and they buried him over the sea and under the stone, and there he lies until the day of our Lord.

'And so the grail passed to my fathers' charge, and they guarded it in the land of Cornwall where men still strove to keep alive the old ways, while in the east the men of evil grew more numerous and the land of Logres grew dark. For Arthur was gone, and Mark was dead, and the new kings were not as the old had been. And with each turn of years the grail came to the charge of the eldest son, and at the last it came to me.

'And since the death of my father I have kept it safe as best I might, in secret and in true faith; but now I grow old, and am childless, and the greatest darkness of all comes upon our land. For the heathen men of evil, who came to the east in years past and slew the Englishmen and took their land, are turning westward now, and we shall not long be safe from them.

'The darkness draws toward Cornwall, and the long ships creep to our shore, and the battle is near which must lead to final defeat and the end of all that we have known. No guardian for the grail is left, since my brother's son whom I loved as my own is turned already to the heathen men, and guides them to the west. And to save my life, and the secret of the grail that only its guardian knows, I must flee even as Bedwin the strange knight fled. But in all the land of Logres no haven remains, so that I must cross the sea to the land where, they say, Cornishmen have fled whenever terror comes.

'But the grail may not leave this land, but must wait the Pendragon, till the day comes.

'So therefore, I trust it to this land, over sea and under stone, and I mark here the signs by which the proper man in the proper place, may know where it lies: the signs that wax and wane but do not die. The secret of its charge I may not write, but carry unspoken to my grave. Yet the man who finds the grail and has other words from me will know, by both, the secret for himself. And for him is the charge, the promise and the proof, and in his day the Pendragon shall come again. And that day shall see a new Logres, with evil cast out; when the old world shall appear no more than a dream.'

Great-Uncle Merry stopped reading; but the children sat as still and speechless as if his voice still rang on. The story seemed to fit so perfectly into the green land rolling below them that it was as if they sat in the middle of the past. They could almost see the strange knight Bedwin riding towards them, over the brow of a slope, and the long ships of the invaders lurking beyond the grey granite headland and its white fringe of surf.

Simon said at last, 'Who is the Pendragon?'

'King Arthur,' Barney said.

Jane said nothing, but sat thinking of the sad Cornishman sailing away over the sea from his threatened land. She looked at Great-Uncle Merry. He was gazing unseeing down at the sea and the headland beyond Trewissick, the taut lines of his face relaxed and wistful. '. . . when the old world,' he repeated softly to himself, 'shall appear no more than a dream . . .'

Simon scrambled to his feet and went to crouch close to him, peering at the manuscript on his knee. 'Then the map must show where the grail is. I say, suppose we find it! What will it mean?'

'It will mean all kinds of things,' Great-Uncle Merry said grimly. 'And not all of them pleasant, perhaps.'

'What will it look like? What is a grail, anyway?'

'A kind of drinking-vessel. A chalice. A cup. But not like an ordinary cup.' Great-Uncle Merry looked at them gravely. 'Now listen to me. This map you have found shows the way to a sign which men have been seeking for centuries. I said that I had been looking for it. But you remember I said that there were others too – the enemy side, if you like. These people are evil, and they can be very, very dangerous indeed.' Great-Uncle Merry spoke with great seriousness, leaning forward, and the children gazed rather nervously back.

'They have been very close to me for a long time now,' he said. 'And here in Trewissick they have been close to you too. One of them is the man Norman Withers. Another is the woman who calls herself his sister. There may be others, but I do not know.'

'Then the burglary.' They stared at him and Jane said, 'Was it them?'

'Undoubtedly,' Great-Uncle Merry said. 'Not in person, perhaps. But they must have been behind it all – the ransacked books, the stolen maps, the attempt to look for a secret hiding-place under the floor. They were very near, you know, nearer than I. When I rented the Grey House it was no more than a shot in the dark. I had narrowed the search down to the Trewissick area, but that was all. And I had no idea what I was looking for. It might have been anything. But they knew. Somehow, in some dark way, they had found out about the manuscript and they came after it last night. Only, they hadn't bargained for your finding it by chance first.' He smiled slightly. 'I should like to see Withers's face today.'

'Everything fits now,' Simon said slowly. 'The way he made friends so quickly with Father, the way he took us out in the boat –' For an unpleasant moment he heard Great-Uncle Merry's voice saying again emphatically, 'They can be very dangerous indeed . . .'

Barney said: 'But Gumerry, did you know that *we* should find whatever it was? Us, I mean, me and Simon and Jane?'

His great-uncle looked at him sharply. 'What makes you say that?'

'Well – I don't know –' Barney fumbled for words. 'You must have looked yourself, before we came, and not found anything. But when we did come, you were never there. You kept on disappearing, almost as if you were leaving the house to us.'

Great-Uncle Merry smiled. 'Yes, Barney,' he said, 'I did have an idea you might find it, because I know you three very well. That was one idea I had before our friends did, so that for all their interest in the Grey House they were still worried about what I was up to. And I led them a high old dance all over south Cornwall while you were at home. I was, you might say, a red herring.'

'But what –' Barney said.

'Oh never mind,' Simon broke in. He had been hovering restlessly at Great-Uncle Merry's elbow. 'It's all obvious now. The thing is, what about the map?'

'You're quite right.' Great-Uncle Merry sat down by the rock again. 'We haven't any time to lose.'

'It's a map of Trewissick,' Simon said eagerly. 'Jane found that out. Only the coast seems to have changed –'

'I was comparing it with the map in a guide-book at the Grey House,' Jane said. It hardly seemed worth mentioning her visit to the vicar. 'The funny thing is that though the outlines of the coast don't look alike, the names are the same. If you look very closely on the manuscript one of the headlands is called King Mark's Head, only it's spelt all wrong. And that's the name the guide-book uses for Kemare Head. So the manuscript must show Trewissick.'

'That's right,' Great-Uncle Merry said, bent over the parchment. 'Simple corruption, dropping consonants –' His head shot up. '*What* did you say?'

Jane looked puzzled. 'Mmm?'

'Did you say it was called King Mark's Head in the guide-book?'

'Yes, that's right. Does it matter?'

'Oh no.' The usual remote expression came back over Great-Uncle Merry's face like a veil. 'Only that particular name hasn't been used for a very long time, and most people have forgotten about it. I should like to have a look at that guide-book of yours.'

'I don't understand this.' Simon was peering over the old map. 'Even if it is Trewissick, where does that get you? It's the most useless treasure map I ever saw, there are all sorts of peculiar marks on it but none of them means anything. Nothing leads to anything else, so how can it show you where the grail is?'

Great-Uncle Merry pointed at the manuscript. 'Remember what the text says – for the proper man, in the proper place, to find . . .'

'Perhaps it's like one of those mazes you see in books sometimes,' Jane said, thinking hard. 'The ones that are simple once you get going but it's awfully hard to find where to start. That could be what he meant by "in the proper place". If you took the map to the right starting-point, then it would tell you where to go from there.'

Simon almost wailed, 'But how do we find out where to start from?'

Barney, standing at Great-Uncle Merry's elbow, had not been listening. He had lapsed into one of his dreaming silences, gazing wide-eyed out over the harbour and occasionally glancing back at the map. 'I know what it reminds me of,' he said musingly.

No one took any notice. Barney went on dreamily to himself, 'It's like one of Mother's drawings, the ones she calls perspective sketches. It looks like a picture, not a map at all really. You've got the bump of this hill coming over the edge of the harbour when you look down, and the headland curving like that' – he traced his finger through the air over the view before him – 'and those stones on top of it make the funny little knobs on the side of the map . . .'

'Golly, he's got it!' Simon shouted, jerking Barney out of his reverie. 'That's what it is, look! It *is* a picture, and not a map, and that's why the shape looked all wrong compared with the guide-book. Look, you can see –' He took the manuscript carefully from Great-Uncle Merry's hands and held it up in front of them, against the long rocky arm of Kemare Head. And as they looked from the headland back to the manuscript, the scrawled brown lines suddenly seemed so obviously a picture of the scene before them that they wondered how they could possibly have thought it was a map.

'Well then,' Jane said, incredulity spreading over her face as she looked from one to the other, '*this* must be the proper place. The beginning of the maze. All this time without knowing it we've been standing on the very same spot as the man who drew the picture. Just think!' She looked at the manuscript in awe.

'Well, come on,' Barney said, glowing with excitement at what he had discovered. 'We know where he started from. How do we find out where he went from here?'

'Look at the picture. There's a sort of blodge marked on this headland.'

'There are blodges all over the place. Half of them are blots and the rest are dirt marks.'

'The marks of age,' Great-Uncle Merry said sepulchrally.

'No, but this one's intentional,' Simon persisted. 'Right here, where – gosh! It must be that rock you're leaning on, Gumerry!'

His great-uncle looked round critically. 'Well, it's possible, I suppose. Yes indeed, it's possible. A natural outcropping, I think, not erected by the hands of men.'

Barney got up and trotted all round the rock, gazing closely at its yellow lichened scars and every small crevice and cleft, but noticing nothing unusual. 'It looks very ordinary,' he said in disappointment, reappearing at the other side.

Jane burst out laughing. 'You look just like Rufus, sniffing along after a rabbit and then finding there's nothing there after all.'

Barney slapped his knee. 'I knew we should have brought Rufus. He'd have been terrifically useful on a hunt, sniffing things out.'

'You can't sniff things out when they've been hidden for centuries, idiot.'

'I don't see why not. You wait, I bet you he'll help.'

'Not a hope.'

'Where is he, anyway?'

'With Mrs Palk. Shut up somewhere, I suppose, poor thing. You know Father said he wouldn't have him in the house any more when he got in a rage the other night.'

'Mrs Palk takes him home every evening.'

'If she hadn't taken him home yesterday evening he might have caught the burglars.'

'Gosh, so he would.' There was a moment's silence as they all digested the thought.

'I don't trust Mrs Palk,' Jane said darkly.

'Well, don't worry about it,' Great-Uncle Merry said easily. 'From what I know of that dog he'd just have licked their hands and told them to go ahead.'

'He doesn't like Mr Withers,' Barney said. 'He came to meet us wagging his tail when we came in off the boat yesterday, but when he saw Mr Withers his tail went right down and he barked. We all laughed about it at the time,' he added thoughtfully.

'Well, we'll bring him out tomorrow. But we shall have to go home soon and we still aren't any nearer the beginning. Gumerry, could this rock really mean anything?' Simon rubbed its grey surface doubtfully.

'Perhaps it's in line with something,' Jane said hopefully. 'Like a compass bearing. Look at the map, I mean the picture.'

'Doesn't help. It could be in line with any one of those blodges.'

'Well then, we ought to find out where all the blodges are and go and see if there's anything near one of them.'

'But that would take months.'

'Oh!' Barney stamped his foot with impatience. 'This is awful. What are we going to do?'

'Leave it,' Great-Uncle Merry said unexpectedly.

'*Leave* it?' They stared at him.

'Leave it until tomorrow. Come to it with fresh minds. We haven't much time, and it's going to be a race in the end, but we're all right at the moment. The other side don't know that we've found anything. They watch me like hawks, but they don't suspect you, and with any luck they won't. You can afford to go away and think about it for tonight.'

'Won't they come back and burgle us again?' Jane said nervously.

'They wouldn't dare. No, that was a long shot – they staked everything on being able to find a clue the first time, and they failed. They'll try something different now.'

'I wish we knew what.'

'Great-Uncle Merry,' Simon said, 'why can't we tell the police it was them? Then they wouldn't be able to come after us at all.'

'Yes,' said Jane, eagerly. 'Why not?'

'We can't possibly,' Barney said with conviction.

'Why not?'

'I don't know.'

They looked at Great-Uncle Merry.

He said non-committally, 'Why didn't you tell the police that you thought you knew what the burglars had been after?'

'Well – they'd have laughed. They'd have thought it was just an old bit of paper.'

'And if we'd gone to them it wouldn't have been a secret any more and we shouldn't have been able to follow up the map.'

'And anyway,' Jane said, with a return of the old guiltiness, 'we hadn't told Mother and Father about finding it in the first place.'

'Well,' Great-Uncle Merry said, 'you would have said to them, we found an old parchment in the attic and we think that's what the burglars were looking for when they turned the house upside-down. And our worthy sergeant, who is satisfied that the culprits were just hooligans, would have smiled indulgently and told you to go away and play.'

'That's right, that's just it. That's why we didn't.'

Great-Uncle Merry smiled. 'Now, I could go to him and say this manuscript is a clue to a kind of ancient cup, called a grail, that is hidden in Trewissick. It tells the real story of King Arthur. The man from the yacht called the *Lady*

Mary wants it, and he burgled the house, and he has me followed night and day to discover if I have found it before him. And what would happen?'

'They'd go and arrest Mr Withers,' Simon said hopefully, but he sounded less convinced than before.

'The sergeant would go to Mr Withers, who would of course have a perfect alibi for the night of the burglary, and he would question him rather apologetically about my odd-sounding story. Mr Withers would impress him as a courteous and gentlemanly antique-dealer on a harmless holiday with his pretty sister.'

'That's what we thought he was,' Barney pointed out.

'The sergeant knows of me,' Great-Uncle Merry went on, 'and knows I do things that sometimes seem' – he chuckled – 'eccentric. He would think things over, and he'd say to himself: Poor old Professor, 'tis all been too much for 'n at last. All that book-learnin', tidn' natural, it do 'ave turned the poor old chap's head.'

'You do it even better than Simon,' Jane said admiringly.

'I see now,' Simon said. 'It would just sound fantastic. And if we told the sergeant about Mr Withers and his sister asking questions about old books, it would just seem perfectly normal to him and not suspicious at all.'

He looked up and grinned. 'Of course, we couldn't possibly tell them. Sorry. I didn't think.'

'Well, you must think now, and seriously,' Great-Uncle Merry said, turning his grave dark eyes on each face in turn. 'I'm going to say something I shan't say again. You may think the same as the sergeant would, that this is all a business of a private rivalry. An old professor and a book-collector, both intent on beating the other to something that doesn't matter much to anyone else anyway.'

'No!'

'Of course not.'

'It's much more than that,' Jane said impulsively. 'I've got a feeling...'

'Well – if you all have a feeling, if you understand just a little of the things I was trying to say earlier on, then that's more than enough. But I am not happy about having the three of you mixed up in this at all, and I should be even less happy if I thought you didn't have any idea of what you were doing.'

'You make it sound fearfully serious,' Simon said curiously.

'So it is... I worry because I can only be on the edge all the time, acting as decoy, making them think they have nobody to bother about except me. So that you are left all on your own, with the responsibility of unravelling this.' He touched the manuscript in Simon's hand. 'Step by difficult step.'

'Smashing,' Barney said happily.

Simon glanced at his brother and sister and drew himself up trying to look as dignified as it is possible to look in shorts and sandals.

'Well, I'm the eldest –'

'Only by eleven months,' said Jane.

'Well I am, anyway, and I'm responsible for you two and I ought to be spokesman, and – and' – he floundered, and then gave up all attempt at dignity in a rush – 'and honestly, Gumerry, we do know what we're doing. In a way it is a kind of quest, like Barney said. And it isn't as if we were altogether on our own.'

'All right,' Great-Uncle Merry said. 'It's a bargain.' And he shook hands solemnly with each of them in turn. Everyone looked at everyone else, wide-eyed and a little breathless, and then they all suddenly felt rather foolish, and burst out laughing. But behind the laughter they were dimly aware of a new kind of comforting closeness, in the face of possible danger.

When they packed up, and were starting down the hill, Great-Uncle Merry said, stopping them in their tracks, 'Take a good look at it first.' He swept his arm out over the harbour, the cliffs and the sea. 'Take the real picture with you too. Learn what it looks like.'

They looked across from the slope once more. The sun was setting down in the westward sky, over Kemare Head and the Grey House, lighting the top of the headland and the strange grey rocks that prickled its skyline. But the harbour was already darkening into shadow. As they looked, the sun seemed gradually to fall, until the unbearable brightness of it was over the outlined fingers of the group of standing stones, and the stones themselves became invisible in the blaze.

Chapter Seven

'Well, I think it's underneath the Grey House.'

'Yes – look how the burglars tried to take up the floor.'

'But they were looking for the map, not the grail.'

'No they weren't. Remember what Great-Uncle Merry said. They didn't know what they were looking for, nor did he. It might have been a clue to it, like the map, or it might have been the thing itself.'

'Well, the clue was there, why shouldn't the thing itself be there as well?'

'But look, idiot,' Simon said, unrolling the map, 'the Grey House isn't marked. There isn't even a blodge. It just wasn't there then. Remember our Cornishman lived nine hundred years ago.'

'Oh.'

They were sitting on the grass half-way up Kemare Head, at the side of one of the rough-trodden tracks which ran zigzagging up its slope. Great-Uncle Merry had left them on their own. 'A day's grace to find the first clue,' he had said, 'while I draw off the hounds. Just one piece of advice – don't start till the afternoon. Spend the morning on the beach or something. Then you'll be sure the hounds are gone.'

Then he had gone out fishing for the day with Father, who was intent on trying a part of the sea off a headland a mile down the coast. And sure enough, as their small boat puttered out of the harbour with Father at the tiller and Great-Uncle Merry towering stiff-backed in the bows, the yacht *Lady Mary*, gleaming white in the sun, had within minutes moved silently out after them, her engine purring faintly over the quiet morning sea. Watching from the house, they had seen her sails gradually unfurl and billow as she came into the bay. She took a wide course out to sea, but one from which Great-Uncle Merry and Father would always be just in sight.

Up on the headland now the afternoon sun prickled their bare legs, and there was a small breeze. 'Oh dear,' Jane said despondently, edging a blade of grass from its sheath and nibbling it. 'This is hopeless. We just don't know where to start. Perhaps we should go back to where we were yesterday.'

'But we know what things look like from there.'

'Well, so what? Which things?'

'Well – the headland, and the sea, and the sun – and those stones up on the top there.' Barney gestured vaguely above their heads, up the slope. 'I think they've got something to do with it. The Cornishman must have been able to see them. Gumerry says they're three thousand years old, so they'd have been almost as ancient-looking nine hundred years ago as they are now.'

'You can certainly see them clear enough from the other side.' Simon sat up, interested.

'But they're such a long way across,' Jane pointed out. 'I mean, the first clue might be that you have to take ten paces to your left, or something. It always is in stories about buried treasure. But to get to the standing stones, up here, from over there, you'd have to take thousands of paces right across the harbour. It doesn't make sense.'

'It doesn't have to be like that,' Simon said. 'It could be the thing like compass bearings again. You know – perhaps we have to get something in line with something else to lead us on to a third thing.'

Barney closed his eyes and screwed up his face, trying to bring back a picture of the scene they had gazed at so hard the evening before. 'D'you remember when the sun set yesterday?' he said slowly. 'The biggest standing stone was right bang in line with the sun, from where we were. I remember because you could only see it if you didn't look straight at it, if you see what I mean.'

Simon looked closely at the manuscript again, excitement beginning to dawn on his face.

'D'you know, I think you've got something there. This round thing drawn here over the standing stones, that we thought was just decoration – perhaps it's supposed to be the sun. I mean, if he knew the map wouldn't be found for years and years and years he'd have to use signs like the sun, that wouldn't be likely to change.'

'Come on then, let's go further up and look.' Jane jumped eagerly to her feet; and then suddenly she froze, stock-still. 'Simon, quick,' she said quietly, in a strained, tight voice. 'Put the map away. Hide it.'

Simon frowned. 'What on earth –'

'Quickly! It's Miss Withers. She's coming up the path, and someone else with her. They'll be right on top of us in a minute.'

Simon hastily rolled up the manuscript and stuffed it into his rucksack. 'Who is it with her?' he hissed.

'I can't see – yes, I can.' Jane turned away quickly as if it hurt her to look, and sat down again. She was very flushed. 'It's that boy. The one who knocked me over. I *knew* he was mixed up in all this somehow.'

They heard voices then, coming nearer up the slope. Miss Withers's clear tones floated up to them. 'I don't care, Bill, we have to check on everything. He may already have –' Then she was on them, silhouetted against the skyline, and she stopped short as she saw the three children all sitting looking expressionlessly up at her. The boy stopped too, glowering.

For a moment Miss Withers stood with her mouth slightly open, taken aback. Then she pulled herself together and flashed a smile at them. 'Well!' she said pleasantly, coming forward. 'What a nice surprise! All the Drew family at once. I hope you boys didn't get too tired after all that sea air we gave you the other day.'

'Not a bit, thank you,' Barney said in his clearest, most public voice.

'It's a marvellous boat,' said Simon, equally distant and polite.

'And what are you all doing up here?' Miss Withers inquired innocently. She was wearing slacks, with a sleeveless white blouse that made her arms look very brown; and her dark hair was tumbled by the breeze. She looked very attractive and healthy.

She glanced at Jane expectantly. Jane gulped. 'We were just looking at the sea. We saw your boat go out this morning.'

'We thought you'd be on board her,' Simon added, without thinking.

A flicker of weariness crossed Polly Withers's face. She said easily, 'Ah, I'm not the best of sailors, as I probably told you.'

Simon looked deliberately down at the sea. It lay as flat and unrippled as a pond. Miss Withers said, following his gaze, 'Ah, it'll blow up later, you mark my words.'

'Oh?' Simon said. His face was expressionless still, but there was the faintest note of insolent disbelief in his tone. For the first time Miss Withers's smile faded slightly.

Before she could say anything, the boy with her spoke. 'Miss Polly be allus right about the sea,' he said gruffly, glaring at Simon. 'She do know more about 'n than all they old men down there put together.' He jerked his head contemptuously down at the harbour.

'Oh – I haven't introduced you,' Miss Withers said brightly. 'Do forgive me. Jane, Simon, Barnabas, this is Bill, our right-hand man. Without him the *Lady Mary* couldn't do a thing.'

The boy flushed darkly and looked down at his grubby plimsolls, after a quick glance up at her. Jane thought, pityingly: he thinks she's wonderful.

'We've met before,' Simon said shortly.

Barney said: 'How is your bicycle?'

'No better for your askin',' the boy snapped.

'Watch your manners, Bill.' Through the sweet smile Miss Withers's voice was cold and tight as a steel wire. 'That's not the way we speak to our friends.'

Bill looked at her in sullen reproach, jerked forward and went on up the path without a word.

'Oh dear.' Miss Withers sighed. 'Now I've hurt his feelings. These village people are so touchy.' She made a charming, conspiratorial little grimace at them. 'I suppose I'd better go after him.' She turned to follow the boy, and then swung round again. The words shot out like a flick of lightning: 'Have you found a map?'

For a moment of roaring silence that seemed like an hour they stared at her. And then Barney, driven by pure naked alarm, took refuge in gabbling nonsense. 'Did you say a map, Miss Withers? Or was it a gap? We did find a gap in the hedge, down there, that was how we got through up to the headland. But we haven't got a map, at least I haven't, I don't know about Simon and Jane . . . don't you know your way up the hill?'

Miss Withers, staring fixedly at them, relaxed into friendliness again. 'Yes, that's right, Barnabas, a map . . . I don't know my way about at all well, as a matter of fact. And I couldn't find a map anywhere in the shops this morning. There's one little footpath I'm looking for, just over the other side, and Bill isn't very much help.'

'I believe Great-Uncle Merry has a map,' Jane said, vaguely. She was watching closely from the corner of her eye; but not a muscle moved in Miss Withers's face. 'You haven't met our great-uncle, have you, Miss Withers? He's gone out fishing with Father today. What a pity. I'm awfully sorry we can't help.'

'I do hope you find your way,' Simon said kindly.

'Well, well, I expect I shall,' Miss Withers said. She flashed her brightest smile at them, and turned away up the path, raising her hand. 'Good-bye, all of you.'

They watched in silence until she disappeared over the line where the slope met the sky. Then Barney flung himself face down on the ground and rolled over and over, letting out a long relieved breath. 'Wheeee-ee-ee-ee! How awful! When she suddenly said . . . !' He buried his face in the grass.

'D'you think she realizes?' Jane said anxiously to Simon. 'Did we give it away?'

'I don't know.' Simon gazed thoughtfully up the quiet green slope. There was no sign there now of Miss Withers, or of anything except one far-away grazing sheep. 'I don't think so. I mean, we must have all looked pretty silly when she asked about a map, I know you did . . .'

'So did you. Like a fish.'

'All right . . . well, we could perfectly well have looked surprised anyway, her saying it out of the blue like that. I don't think she'd be able to tell if we were looking guilty or just startled. I expect,' he added, gaining confidence as he went on, 'she believes we really did think she just wanted an ordinary map to find her way.'

'Perhaps that's all she did want.'

'No fear!' Barney said, emerging from the grass. 'She was testing us out, all right. Otherwise why did she say "found"? Have you *found* a map? Any normal person would have said, I say, have you *got* a map?'

'He's quite right.' Simon stood up, rubbing the dust from his legs. 'Great-Uncle Merry was right too. They aren't taking chances. Miss Withers was surprised to see us, you could tell, but it wasn't five seconds before she was having a go about the map.'

'It was nasty altogether,' Jane said, wriggling her shoulders as if she could shake off the memory. She looked up the slope. 'How can we go on up there now? We shan't be able to tell if she and that horrible little boy are hidden away somewhere, watching everything we do.'

'Well, it's no good letting that stop us,' Simon stuck out his chin. 'If we think about being watched we shall never do anything. So long as we behave normally, as if we were just wandering about, it ought to be all right.' He picked up his rucksack. 'Come on.'

The side of Kemare Head was steeper than the opposite headland had been, and for a long time as they toiled up the zigzag path they saw nothing above them but the line of the slope against the sky, with the sun blazing down into their eyes. The end of the headland, rocky and grey, stretched out far beyond them into the sea, and sweeping towards it the land looked immensely solid, as if it were all rock and the soil above it no more than a skin.

And then they were at the top of the slope, where the grass grew short in a great dry-green sweep, and they could see the standing stones. As they drew nearer, the stones seemed to grow, pointing silently to the sky, like vast tombstones set on end.

'Stones,' Simon said, 'is the biggest understatement I've ever heard. Like calling Nelson's Column a stick.'

He stood considering the giant granite pillars rising above him. There were four of them; one much higher than the rest, with the other three grouped irregularly round it.

'Perhaps the grail's buried under one of those,' Barney said tentatively.

'It can't be, they're too old . . . anyway, I think you're wrong about it being buried.'

'Oh come on, it must be,' Jane said. 'How else could anything stay hidden all that time?'   .

'And remember that bit in the manuscript,' said Barney. 'Over sea and under stone.'

Simon rubbed his ear, still dissatisfied. 'We aren't over the sea here. The sea's miles away. Well all right, not miles, but I bet it's four hundred yards to the end of the headland.'

'Well, we're still above the sea, aren't we?'

'I'm sure that's not what he meant. Over sea, over sea – I wonder – anyway, we're trying to go too fast. Step by step, Gumerry said. We ought to stick to the step we're on.'

Simon looked at the sun, gradually sinking over the coast where cliff after cliff curved into the mist beyond Kemare Head. 'Have a look at the stones. The sun'll be as low as it was yesterday soon.'

'They look so different when you're close.' Jane wandered round the weather-beaten pillars of rock. 'We want to know which one it was that looked in line with the sun from the other side, isn't that it? But how do we find that out from here?'

'It was the biggest one,' Barney said. 'It stood up higher than the rest.'

The sun glowed deep towards the horizon, casting an orange-gold warmth over their faces. 'Look at the shadows,' Simon said suddenly. His shadow on the ground before him moved a long arm, dapple-edged by the grass, as he pointed. 'That's the way we can do it from this side. *Backwards.* If one stone was was directly between us and the sun yesterday, that means that from here its shadow would be pointing directly to where we were standing then. Towards the rock Gumerry was sitting against. Look, you can just see it from here.'

Following his arm, they saw the one chunky rock on the opposite headland; a small far-away bump on its skyline, lit bright by the gold of the setting sun. It was higher than the standing stone on Kemare Head, and further out towards the sea. But it was undoubtedly the spot where they had stood the day before.

Jane gazed at Simon in open and unusual admiration. He flushed slightly, and became very brisk. 'Come on, Barney, quick before the sun goes. Which stone d'you think it was?'

'Well, it was the biggest, so it must have been this one.'

Barney moved a yard or two downhill to the tallest stone. He crossed to its other side, facing the harbour, and crouched down in the shadow, peering at the lone stone across the bay. He frowned, doubtfully. Simon and Jane moved to one side of him, waiting impatiently.

Barney, his frown deepening, suddenly lay down on his stomach in the grass, so that he was lying along the line of the pointing shadow and looking straight ahead. 'Am I lying straight?' he said, rather muffled.

'Yes, yes, dead straight. Is it the right one?'

Barney scrambled to his feet, looking doleful. 'No. That shadow doesn't point exactly at the rock. You can see the rock clearly enough, but you have to shift your eyes slightly to be looking straight at it. And that's cheating.'

'But you *said* it was the tallest stone you saw.'

'I still say it was.'

'I don't see how it could have been,' Jane said, petulant with disappointment.

Simon was thinking hard, holding the rucksack swinging by its strap and banging it absently against his leg. He turned and looked back at the other three stones, standing black now and gold-rimmed against the blaze of the sun. Then he yelped, dropped the rucksack and rushed towards the furthest stone, scrambling down as Barney had done to lie in its shadow. Holding his breath, he dropped his chin to the grass and shut his eyes.

'Move your top half a bit to the left, you're not straight,' Jane said, close beside him, beginning to understand.

Simon shifted a few inches, raising himself on his elbows. 'That right?'
'Okay.'

Simon crossed his fingers and opened his eyes. Straight in front of him over the blades of grass, right in the middle of his line of vision, the bright sunlit rock on the opposite headland was staring him in the face. 'This is the one,' he said in a curiously subdued voice.

Barney rushed across and dropped down beside him. 'Let me, let me –' He elbowed Simon out of the way and squinted across the harbour at the rock. 'You're right,' he said rather reluctantly. 'But it was the biggest stone that I saw, I know it was.'

'That's right,' said Jane.

'What d'you mean, that's right?'

'Look at the way the stones are put up. Look at the way the ground slopes. This is the top of the headland, but it isn't flat, and the big stone is lower down than the others. The one you're next to now is higher up the hill, even though it's not the tallest. So where you saw its outline against the sky yesterday, it *looked* as if it was the tallest.'

'Gosh,' Barney said. 'I never thought of that.'

Simon said loftily, 'I thought you might get there in the end.'

'It was jolly clever of you,' Jane said. 'If you hadn't been so quick we might never have realized. The shadows'll be gone soon.' She pointed down at the grass. The blaze of the sun was sinking over the far horizon behind them, and the shadow creeping up over the ground, swallowing up the long shadows of the stones. But across the harbour the rock on the other headland, higher up and longer exposed to the sun, still shone bright like a beacon.

Barney whooped with delight. 'We've got it! We've got it!' He thwacked one hand against the hard warm rock of the standing stone, and whirled round in a circle. 'We're on the first step, isn't it fabulous?'

'Only the first step, though,' Simon said. But pleasure was bubbling within him as well. They all three felt suddenly enormously energetic.

'But we've started . . .'

'We know where to look for the next clue now.'

'We go from here.' Barney ran his hand over the surface of the standing stone again. 'From this one.'

'But where?' Simon said, determined to be realistic. 'And how?'

'We shall just have to look at the map again. It's bound to tell us. I mean, really the first clue was marked plain as plain, how to get from the other headland over to the stone here, if only we'd known how to understand it.' Barney ran across to where Simon had dropped his rucksack, flipped the straps open and fumbled inside, bringing out the grubby brown roll of the manuscript from its case. 'Look,' he said, sitting down with a bump and spreading it out on the grass before him. 'Here's where the stone's marked . . .'

'Bring it farther up,' Simon said, looking over his shoulder. 'The sun's still on the grass a bit higher up, and you need the brightest light you can get to look at it. Anyway it'll be warmer.'

Barney clambered obligingly up the slope, past the massive grey foot of the last and tallest standing stone, to where the grass was still a brighter green in the last golden light of the sun. Simon and Jane followed him, standing on either side so that their own shadows should not darken the faint indistinct scrawl on the curling parchment. They bent down, intent, staring at the crude quick outline that was the Cornishman's picture, made nine hundred years before, of the standing stones.

Miss Withers's voice said, behind them: 'So you have found a map after all.'

A great wave of horror enveloped Barney, and he froze hunched over the manuscript. Simon and Jane wheeled round in alarm.

Miss Withers stood close behind them, higher up the slope. Her outline was dark and menacing against the sunset sky, and they could not see her face. The boy Bill appeared silently behind her, and stood at her elbow. The sight of them both poised there filled Jane with panic, and she suddenly felt frightened at the silence and emptiness of the headland.

Barney's finger unconsciously curled into his palm, and the edge of the manuscript, released, sprang back into a closed roll. The faint crackle of its movement sounded like a gunshot in the silence. 'Oh, don't put it away,' Miss Withers said clearly. 'I want to have a look.'

She took a step forward, stretching out her hand, and in terror of the flat expressionless voice Jane cried out suddenly.

'*Simon!*'

As the dark figure loomed swiftly towards him from the hill, Simon felt himself wake up. Quicker than his own thought he swung round, dipped swiftly and snatched up the manuscript from Barney's knee. And then he was gone, half slithering, half running down the slanting side of Kemare Head, towards the village.

'Bill! Quickly!' Miss Withers snapped. The big silent figure beside her shot into sudden life, tearing down the hill at Simon's heels. But he was too clumsy for his speed, and in mid-flight on the edge of the slope he stumbled and half fell. He recovered himself almost at once, but not before Simon, running and slipping straight down over the grass and the zigzagging paths, had gained thirty yards' lead.

'He won't catch him,' Jane said, her voice wavering with excitement, feeling a broad smile of relief spreading over her stiff cheeks.

'Run it, Simon!' Barney shrilled down the hill, scrambling to his feet.

Miss Withers came down towards them, and they drew back from the sight of her face, twisted by rage into something frightening and unfamiliar, no longer attractive, no longer even young. She snarled at them: 'You stupid children, tampering with things you don't understand –'

She swung away from them and made off down the slope in the same direction that Simon had taken, in a long quick stride. They watched her angry erect back cross and recross the slope on the zigzag path, until she disappeared over the edge of the headland.

'Come on,' Barney said. 'We've got to find Gumerry. Simon's going to need help.'

The dry grass was like polished wood under Simon's feet, giving no grip as he slipped and slithered down the hillside; now on his feet, now flat on his back and elbows, holding one arm up always to keep the manuscript from damage. Behind him he heard the noise of the boy from the village slipping and stumbling more heavily, his breath rasping in his throat, and an occasional gasping curse as he lost his footing and fell.

Facing outwards across the harbour as he ran down, Simon felt that he could almost jump straight out into the sea. The slope seemed much steeper than when they had climbed up by the path, dropping below him in an endless green curve. His heart was thumping wildly, and he was too intent on getting away to imagine what might happen if the boy caught up with him. But gradually, minute by minute, the panic at the pit of his stomach was disappearing.

Everything depended on him now – to keep the manuscript safe, and get away. He was almost enjoying himself. This was something that he could understand; it was like a race or a fight at school, himself against the boy Bill. And he wanted to win. Panting, he glanced over his shoulder. The boy seemed to be gaining on him a little. Simon flung himself down the rest of the slope, sliding and bumping on his back, alarmingly fast, now and again coming to his feet for a couple of staggering steps.

And then suddenly he was at the bottom of the slope, stumbling and gulping for breath. With a brief glance up at the pursuing Bill, who yelled and glared at him as he saw him looking round, Simon was off and away over the field, running like a hare and feeling confidence surge stronger as he ran. But he could not lose the boy behind him. Stronger, bigger and longer-legged, the village boy pounded after him with grim determination, striding more heavily but never losing ground.

Simon made for a stile in the hedge at the far side of the field and leapt over, gripping the shaky wooden bar at its top with one hand. He came out at the other side into a quiet lane, pitted with deep dry ruts hard as rock, lined with trees, arching overhead in a thick-leaved roof. With the sunlight quite gone now, it was half dark under the branches, and both ends of the lane vanished within a few yards into impenetrable shadow.

Simon looked wildly up and down, clutching the manuscript and feeling the sweat damp in the palms of his hands. Which way would lead him to the Grey House? He could no longer hear the sea.

Making a blind choice, he turned right and ran up the lane. Behind him he heard the clatter of the boy's boots climbing over the stile. The lane seemed never-ending as he ran, dodging light-footed from side to side to avoid the ruts. Round every bend there stretched another, curving on in a gloomy tunnel of branches and banks, with no break anywhere into a gateway or another field.

He could hear the beat of the boy's feet behind him on the hard dry mud of the lane.

The boy shouted nothing now, but pounded along in grim silence. Simon felt a thread of panic creep back into his mind, and he ran more wildly, longing to get out of the cavernous lane and into the open air.

Then facing him round the next bend he saw the sky, bright after the gloom, and within moments he was out again, running on a paved road past quiet walls and trees. Again he turned automatically without time to think where he was going, and the rubber soles of his plimsolls pattered softly along the deserted road.

The long high grey wall along one side, and the hedge of a field on the other, gave no sign to tell him where he was running – more slowly now, he knew, for try as he might he was beginning to tire. He began to long for someone, anyone, to appear walking along the road.

The boy's footsteps rang more loudly behind him now, over the quiet evening twitter of birds hidden in the trees. The sound of the feet so much noisier than his own gave Simon the beginnings of an idea, and when at last the road branched off he put on a desperate burst of speed and ran down the side turning.

The wall ended at two battered gate-posts through which he glimpsed an overgrown drive. Further down the road he caught sight of the rising tower of Trewissick church, and his heart sank as he realized how far he was from home.

The boy Bill had not turned the corner yet; Simon could hear his steps gradually growing louder from the main road. Quickly he slipped inside the deserted gateway of the long drive and wriggled into the bushes which grew in an unruly tangle beside the gate-post. He jumped with pain as thorns and sharp twigs stuck into him from all sides. But he crouched quite still behind the leaves, trying to quieten his gasping breaths, certain that the pounding of his heart must be audible all up and down the road.

The idea worked. He saw Bill, dishevelled and scarlet, pause at the end of the road, peering up and down. He looked puzzled and angry, listening with his head cocked for the sound of feet. Then he turned and walked slowly towards Simon's hiding-place down the side road, glancing back uncertainly over his shoulder.

Simon held his breath, and crouched further back into the bushes.

Unexpectedly he heard a noise from behind him. Turning his head sharply, wincing as a fat purple fuchsia blossom bobbed into his eye, he listened. In a moment he recognized the sound of feet crunching on gravel, coming towards the road down the drive. The gaps of light through the branches darkened for an instant as the figure of a man passed very close to him, walking down the drive and out through the gateway. Simon saw that he was very tall, and had dark hair, but he could not see his face.

The figure wandered idly out into the road. Simon saw now that he was dressed all in black; long thin black legs like a heron, and a black silk jacket with the light glinting silvery over the shoulders. The boy Bill's sullen face brightened as he caught sight of the man, and he ran forward to meet him in the middle of the road. They stood talking, but out of earshot, so that Simon could hear their voices only as an indistinct low blur. Bill was waving his hands and pointing back behind him to the road and then down the drive. Simon saw the tall dark man shake his head, but still he could not see his face.

Then they both turned back towards the drive and began to walk in his direction, Bill still talking eagerly. Simon shrank nervously back into his hiding-place, feeling suddenly more frightened than he had done since the chase began. This was no stranger to Bill. The boy was smiling. This man was someone he had recognized with relief. Someone else on the enemy side . . .

He could see nothing now but the leaves before his face, and did not dare move forward to peer through a gap. But the footsteps ringing on the metalled road outside did not change to the crunch of gravel; they went past, outside the wall, and on up the road. Simon heard the murmur of voices, but could distinguish nothing except one phrase when the village boy raised his voice. '. . . got to get 'n, she said, 'tis surely the right one, and now I've lost . . .'

Lost me, thought Simon with a grin. His terror faded as their footsteps died away, and he began to feel triumphant at having outwitted the bigger boy. He glanced down at the manuscript in his hand and gave it a conspiratorial squeeze. There was silence again now, and he could hear nothing but the song of the birds in the approaching dusk. He wondered how late it was. The chase seemed to have lasted for a week. The muscles of his legs began to nag protestingly at their long cramped stillness. But still he waited, straining his ears for any sound showing that the man and the boy were still near.

At last he decided that they must have gone out of sight down the road. Clutching the manuscript firmly, he parted the bushes before his face with one hand and stepped out into the drive. No one was there. Nothing moved.

Simon tiptoed gingerly across the gravel and peered up and down round the gate-post. He could see no one, and with growing cheerfulness he crossed from the gateway to make his way back to the road from which he had come.

It was not until he was several paces out in the open that he saw the boy Bill and the dark man standing together beside the wall fifty yards away, in clear view.

Simon gasped, and felt his stomach twist with panic. For a moment he stood there, uncertain whether to bolt back to the shelter of the drive before they could see him. But as he hesitated, mesmerized, Bill turned his head, shouted and began to run, and the man with him, realizing, turned to follow. Simon swung round and dashed for the main road. The silence all round seemed suddenly as menacing as the leaf-roofed lane had been; he ached for the safety of crowds, people and cars, so that at least he would lose the awful sensation of being alone, with feet pounding after him in implacable pursuit.

Down the side road, round the corner and along the wall of the churchyard, faster, faster; Simon's heart sank as he ran. His legs were stiff after the cramped pause in the bushes, and his whole body was very tired. He knew that he would not be able to last very much longer.

A car passed him, travelling fast in the opposite direction. Wild thoughts flickered through Simon's mind, as he felt the road beating hard through his thin rubber soles: he could shout and wave at a car, perhaps, or run for refuge into one of the little houses that were fringing the road as he neared the village. But the boy Bill had a man with him now, and the man could tell some story to any stranger Simon approached, and the stranger would probably believe that instead . . .

'Stop!' a deep voice called behind him. Desperately Simon tried to fling himself forward faster. Everything would be over if they caught him. They would have the manuscript, they would have the whole secret. There would be nothing left to do. He would have broken the trust, he would have let Gumerry down . . .

His breath began to come in great painful gasps, and he staggered as he ran. There was a cross-roads ahead. The fast decisive footsteps behind him sounded louder and louder; almost he heard his pursuers breathing in his ears. He heard the boy call, on a note of triumph: 'Quick . . . *now* . . .' The voice was farther away than the footsteps. It must be the man who was behind him, almost at his heels, his feet thudding nearer, nearer . . .

Simon's ears were singing with the fight for breath. The cross-roads loomed ahead, but he could hardly see it. He heard half consciously the noisy roar of a car's engine, very near, but it barely registered in his weary brain. There was a rattle and a squeal of brakes, and half-way across the cross-roads he almost collided with the rusting bonnet of a big car.

Simon slithered to a halt and made to dodge round it, aware only of the danger at his heels. And then, as if the darkening twilit sky were once more suddenly flooded with sunlight, he realized Great-Uncle Merry was leaning from the window of the car.

The car's engine revved up again with a thunderous roar. 'The other side! Get in!' Great-Uncle Merry yelled at Simon through the window.

Sobbing with relief, Simon stumbled round the back of the big estate car and wrenched at the handle of the door on the other side. He collapsed into the creaking seat and pulled the door shut as Great-Uncle Merry let in the clutch and slammed his foot down on the accelerator. The car leapt forward, jerking round the corner, and then they were down the road and away.

Chapter Eight

'But how did you know where to come?' Simon said, as Great-Uncle Merry changed gear noisily at the foot of the hill up to the Grey House.

'I didn't really. I was just driving round the village hoping I should find you. I left as soon as Jane and Barney came tumbling back into the house. Poor mites, they were in a dreadful state – they rushed into the drawing-room and grabbed me bodily. Your parents were rather amused. They seem to think we're playing some great private game.' Great-Uncle Merry smiled grimly.

'Gosh, it was lucky you chose that road to drive along,' Simon said. 'I've never been so glad to see anybody in my life.'

'Well, you must remember I know Trewissick. When the children said they hadn't been able to find you on the path back to the house I knew there was only one way you could have gone. You came out into Pentreath Lane, didn't you?'

'There was a lane,' Simon said. 'All shut in by trees. I didn't really have time to see what it was called.'

Great-Uncle Merry chuckled. 'No, I dare say not. Anyway I gambled on your turning out of that lane on to the main Tregoney road, which in fact you did. Good job you didn't go the other way.'

'Why?' Simon said, remembering the blind choice he had made in the lane, with the boy scrambling over the stile behind him.

'In the other direction that lane is a dead end. It leads up to Pentreath Farm. If you can call it a farm – it's been hopelessly neglected for years. Mrs Palk's no-good brother lives there – young Bill Hoover's father. So does the boy himself when he bothers to go home, which I gather isn't very often. But on the whole it wouldn't have been a very healthy place for you to run to.'

'Golly!' Simon felt cold at the thought.

'Well, never mind. You didn't anyway.' Great-Uncle Merry stopped the car with a final rattle and roar and heaved at the hand-brake. 'Here we are. Safe home. Now you run along in and clean yourself up before your mother sees you. There's some friend of hers come to supper, luckily, so she'll be shut up in the drawing-room. Out you get. I'll put the car away. And Simon –'

Simon, half-way out of the door with the manuscript clutched to his breast, paused and looked back. He could only just see Great-Uncle Merry's face, his ruffled white hair turned to a dark tangle by the shadow, and light from a street lamp up the hill reflecting eerily back to make his eyes two glinting points in the dark.

'It was very well done,' Great-Uncle Merry said quietly.

Simon said nothing, but slammed the door feeling suddenly more grown-up than he ever had before. And when the car had coughed on up the hill he forgot all his weariness and crossed the road holding his back very straight.

Jane and Barney were at the door before he had one foot on the step. They hustled him inside and towards the stairs.

'Did he catch you?'

'You've still got it! Oh well done . . .'

'We thought you'd get all beaten up . . .' This was Barney, wide-eyed and solemn.

'You didn't get hurt, did you? What happened?' Jane ran her eyes critically over Simon like a doctor.

'I'm all right . . .'

There was a sudden bright streak of light in the hall as the drawing-room door opened. Mother called, over a murmur of voices from inside. 'Is that you, children?'

'Yes,' Jane called across the banisters.

'Supper's nearly ready, don't be long. Come straight down when you've washed.'

'All right, Mother.' The door closed again. 'They're all talking like anything in there,' Jane said to Simon. 'Mother and Father met some long-lost friend in the harbour and it turns out she lives in Penzance. I think she paints too. She's staying to supper. She seems quite nice. Did he chase you for *miles*?'

'Hundreds of miles,' Simon said. He yawned. 'Hundreds and hundreds . . . and then Great-Uncle Merry turned up just when I was going to get caught.'

'We sent him out after you,' Barney said eagerly. They went on up the stairs.

'We didn't send him,' Jane said reprovingly. 'He went. Like a rocket, as soon as he heard what had happened.'

'Well, he wouldn't have gone if we hadn't told him, and then Simon wouldn't have got rescued.' Barney was glowing with excitement. He would have given his ears to have been the hero of the chase. 'We didn't know which way you'd gone. We tailed Miss Withers for a bit, but she just went down the headland and sat down on the grass at the bottom *looking out at the sea*.' His voice rose to an incredible squeak. 'So we rushed home, and Great-Uncle Merry was just back from fishing. We were jolly glad to see you getting out of the car,' he added unexpectedly.

'Not half so glad as me,' Simon yawned again, and rubbed his forehead. 'I do feel mucky. It must have been when I hid in those bushes . . . come on, I can tell you while I wash.'

First they were too busy eating to talk, and then towards the end of supper, too busy trying not to fall asleep; so all three children were grateful that Miss Hatherton was there. She was a small, bright, bouncy person, quite old, with cropped grey hair and twinkling eyes. She was a sculptress – a famous one, Great-Uncle Merry told them afterwards – and had taught Mother when she was a student at art school. She also seemed to have a passion for catching sharks, and at the supper-table she alternated between enthusiastic discussions of art with Mother and fishing with Father. The children listened with interest, but were relieved when Mrs Palk brought the coffee in and Mother, who had not missed their yawns, sent them to bed.

'Nothing like Cornish air to send you to sleep,' Miss Hatherton said cheerfully as they pushed back their chairs and said good night. 'If any of these follows in your footsteps,' she added to Mother, 'it'll be that one.' She pointed, disconcertingly, at Barney.

Barney blinked at her.

'What do you want to do when you grow up, young man?' she asked him.

'I'm going to be a fisherman,' Barney said promptly. 'With a big boat, like the *White Heather*.'

Miss Hatherton roared with laughter. 'You tell me that in ten years' time,' she said, 'and I shall be very surprised. Good night. I'll buy your first picture.'

'She's dotty,' Barney said as they went upstairs. 'I don't want to be a painter.'

'Never mind,' Simon said. 'She's nice. Don't go, Jane, come in our room for a minute. I think Gumerry's coming up, he made a sort of face at me as I closed the door.'

They waited, and in a few moments Great-Uncle Merry appeared in the doorway. 'I can't stay more than a minute,' he said. 'I am engaged in the beginnings of what promises to be a long and heated discussion with Miss Hatherton and your mother over the relative merits of Caravaggio and Salvator Rosa.'

'Coo,' said Barney.

'As you say, Barnabas, coo. I rather think I am out of my class with those two. However –'

'Gumerry, we found it,' Jane said eagerly. 'We found the second step, and we've started properly now. It's one of the standing stones on Kemare Head. The boys did it between them really,' she added honestly. 'Come on, Simon, get the manuscript out.'

Simon got up and retrieved the telescope case, grubbier and more battered now than it had been, from the top of the wardrobe. They laid the scroll out on the bed and showed Great-Uncle Merry the rock where it had all begun, and the small rough sketch of the sun, and how they had worked their way to the standing stone.

'But we can't tell which standing stone it is on the map,' Simon said. 'Because they don't look the same here as they actually do on the headland.'

They all bent over the drawing that they still could not help calling a map. Great-Uncle Merry looked at it in silence.

'Gumerry,' Jane said tentatively, an idea that she could not quite grasp beginning to chase about her brain, 'would he have done the whole thing on the same system, do you think?'

'Whatever do you mean?' Simon said, bouncing flat on his back on the bed.

'Well, you remember when we were trying to work out the first bit, and I said that it ought to be the way all treasure maps start – six paces to the east, or something. And you said, no, it might be done by getting one thing in line with another as a sort of pointer.'

'Well?'

'Well, does that mean that you have to get everything in line with something else, at every step? Are all the clues going to be the same kind of clue?'

'You mean, next we shall have to get something else in line with the standing stone?'

Great-Uncle Merry was still gazing down at the map. 'It's possible. What makes you think so?'

'That,' Jane said. She pointed at the map. Everyone peered.

'I can't see anything,' Barney said querulously.

'Look, there. Over the end of Kemare Head.'

'But that's just another of those blodges,' Simon said in disgust. 'How can that mean anything?'

'Doesn't it remind you of anything else?'

'No,' Simon said. He lay back again, and yawned.

Great-Uncle Merry looked from one to the other, and smiled to himself.

'Oh really,' Jane said, exasperated. 'I know you've done jolly well today and I know you're tired, but honestly –'

'*I'm* listening,' Barney said at her elbow. 'What about the blodge?'

'It's not a blodge at all,' Jane said. 'At least I don't think so. It's a bit smudged, but it's a circle, a properly drawn one, and I think it means something. It looks just like the other one, the one over the standing stones that turned out to be the setting sun.'

Simon propped himself up on his elbows and began to take an interest again.

Jane went on, thinking aloud: 'The way the first clue worked, we had to find the stone that was in line with the sun and the rock we started from. And then we had to go to the stone and check that it was the right one by the shadow. Well, perhaps now we have to do the same thing. Find something that's in line with the stone, and then go to it and see if its shadow points back to the stone.'

Great-Uncle Merry said softly, 'The signs that wax and wane but do not die . . .'

Jane turned to him eagerly. 'That's it. That's what he said, isn't it, in the manuscript? There must be all sorts of clues in the writing, as well as in the drawing. Only they're even more buried and we don't know how to get at them.'

'This shadow business,' Simon said doubtfully. 'Couldn't it be simpler than the way you just said? Perhaps all we have to do is find out what the shadow of our standing stone points at.'

'But it points back at the place we started,' Barney said. 'Because he didn't use it as his first clue. His first clue was "Look and see what's between you and the setting sun." The shadow was just our way of proving it.'

'Well, it doesn't have to be a shadow made by the setting sun this time.'

'That's where my blodge comes in,' Jane said.

Barney said sleepily: 'Perhaps it's the rising sun. Only it can't be, it isn't in the right place.'

'No,' Simon said. 'Of course it isn't. It's just a blodge.'

Jane spluttered with impatience and glared at him. 'Oh . . . why does it have to be the sun at all?'

Great-Uncle Merry was still sitting silent and statuesque on the edge of the bed. He said again lovingly to himself: 'The signs that wax and wane but do not die . . .'

Simon gazed at him blankly.

'Don't you see?' Jane almost howled at him. 'It isn't the sun – it's the moon!'

Simon's face began to change like the sky on a windy day, different expressions chasing one another across it. He looked from Jane, to the map, to Great-Uncle Merry. 'Gumerry,' he said accusingly, 'I believe you knew all the time. Is she right?'

Great-Uncle Merry stood up. The bed creaked as he rose, and his height seemed to fill the room; the light, swinging from the ceiling behind his head, cast his face into shadow and brought back once more to all three of them the old sense of mystery. His great dark figure, with a mist of light faintly silver round his head, left them silent and awed.

'This is your quest,' he said. 'You must find the way every time yourselves. I am the guardian, no more. I can take no part and give you no help, beyond guarding you all the way.' He turned slightly so that the light shone on his face and then his voice was ordinary again. 'I imagine you'll need some guarding on this next stage, too. You know what it is now, don't you?'

Simon said slowly: 'We have to find which way the shadow of the standing stone points at night. Under the moon.'

Barney said, matter-of-fact: 'The full moon.'

'The full moon?'

'Jane's blodge – he drew it round, not crescent-shaped, so it must mean the full moon.'

'What's it like now?'

'You are *not* going up on the headland to look at the moon tonight,' Great-Uncle Merry said firmly.

'No, I didn't really mean that. I don't think I could manage it anyway.' Simon stifled another yawn. 'I wondered whether the moon was full or not now. We should have to wait for ages if it were all thin and new.'

'It's full tonight,' Jane said. 'I could see it shining in through my bedroom window. So that means it will be almost as bright tomorrow. Would that do, Gumerry? I mean, could we go and look tomorrow night?'

Before their great-uncle could answer Simon was sitting up again, looking thoughtful. 'There's one thing wrong with all this. If we've got a moon that's only just past full, then we've got all the light we ought to have. But the moon changes, doesn't it? I mean, it rises and sets at different times, and in different places, according to the time of year. Well – we're in August now, but how do we know that the Cornishman wasn't working out his clues in the middle of January or April or something, when the moon wouldn't look the same as it does to us?'

'You're just being awkward,' Barney said.

'No,' said Great-Uncle Merry. 'He's right. But I will say just one thing. I think you will find that this is the right time of the year. Call it luck, call it anything you like. But since you were able to follow the first clue, I think you'll find you're able to follow the rest as well. And yes, Jane, tomorrow night would do very well for looking at the moon and the standing stones. Especially well, for a reason you don't know yet – just after you came up, Miss Hatherton was asking your parents to go and see her studio in Penzance tomorrow, and to stay the night.'

'Ooh! Will they go?'

'Wait and see. Go to bed. And try not to put all your faith in the moon. There may be greater problems still waiting for you than you think.'

Mother stood with her hand on the door of Miss Hatherton's small beetle-like car. 'Now you're sure you'll be all right?' she said doubtfully.

'Oh Mother, of course we shall,' Jane said. 'What could possibly happen to us?'

'Well, I don't know, I'm not altogether happy about leaving you . . . what with that burglary . . .'

'That was ages ago now.'

'So long as you don't set the place on fire,' Father said cheerfully. Miss Hatherton had promised to take him shark-fishing the next day, and he was as excited as a schoolboy.

'Don't let them go to bed too late, Uncle Merry,' Mother said, getting into the car.

'Now don't worry, Ellen,' Great-Uncle Merry said paternally from the doorstep, looking like an Old Testament patriarch with the children clustering round him. 'I shan't have a chance to lead them astray with Mrs Palk living in. We shall all probably die of overeating instead.'

'Are you sure you won't all come too?' Miss Hatherton leant across the steering-wheel, blinking in the morning sun. The car lurched slightly as Father squeezed himself into the back. Simon handed in his fishing-rods after him.

'No, honestly, thank you,' he said.

'It's no good, you can't tear these three away from Trewissick,' Father said. 'I've never seen anything like it. Even trying to get them as far as the next village is like prising a limpet off a rock. I daren't think what's going to happen when the time comes to go home.'

'Well, well, they know their own minds. And I can't tempt you away, Professor Lyon?'

'Oh dear,' Mother said. 'I'm sorry you're stuck with them, Merry.' She made a face at the children.

'Nonsense,' Great-Uncle Merry said. 'This is my element. Disgusting place, Penzance, anyway.' He scowled horribly at Miss Hatherton, who grinned amiably back. 'Trippers, ice-cream and little brass piskies. Commercialized. You can keep it.'

'Well,' Miss Hatherton said with a grin, starting the engine, 'off to the piskies. We'll send you a stick of rock, Professor. Good-bye. Good-bye, children.' The car moved off, a ragged chorus of farewell following it.

'Good-bye!' Mrs Palk shrilled, appearing suddenly behind them on the doorstep and waving a tea-cloth. The little car chugged up the hill and out of sight.

'Well now, idn' that nice, the two of them going off together?' Mrs Palk said sentimentally. 'Quite like old times, I'll be bound, before their troubles began.' She wagged her tea-cloth at the children.

'Do you mean us?' demanded Barney indignantly.

'That I do. Proper 'eadache, you be ... still, you'll do, I dare say.' She vanished, beaming, back to the kitchen.

'Jolly useful, that Miss Hatherton,' Simon said with satisfaction. 'Of course I hope they have a lovely time and all that, but it does leave the coast clear, doesn't it?'

'That moonlight shadow ...' Jane said thoughtfully. 'You know, I've been thinking ...'

'No thinking today,' Great-Uncle Merry said firmly. 'We can't do anything until tonight. I haven't been in the sea since I came down here this year, I think you should all take me down for a bathe.'

'For a *bathe*?' Barney's voice rose in amazement.

'That's right.' Great-Uncle Merry glared down at him through bristling white eyebrows. 'D'you think I'm too old to swim, is that it?'

'Er – no, no, not at all, Gumerry,' Barney said, confused. 'I just never thought of you in the water, that's all.'

'But what about the map?' Jane wailed.

'We've just got going,' Simon said reproachfully.

'Well, and we shan't stop. We'll spend a nice quiet day on the beach in the sunshine.' Great-Uncle Merry grinned at them. 'And who knows, perhaps there'll be a moon tonight.'

And there through the windows of the Grey House the moon hung, in the late August evening, when they were back from their day and washing before Mrs Palk called them down to supper. The sun had flamed down on the beach all day, and they were all tanned – Barney's fair skin was burning an angry red. But now the moon dominated the sky; a sky deepening after the sunset to a strange grey-black, with all but the brightest stars dimmed by the milky luminous sheen that flowed over sky and sea without seeming to come from the moon at all.

Simon said, low and excited: 'It's a perfect night.'

'Mmm,' Jane said. She had been outside to look at the sky, and to study nervously the black outline of Kemare Head rising dark and impenetrable behind the house. Like Simon, she was excited, but the old uneasiness was back as well.

It would be better, she told herself severely, not to think about the dark, or at least to think of it as the same dark in which the long-ago Cornishman worked out the clues that they were following now. But perhaps in this darkness too there still lurked the evil which had been creeping up on him then, from the unfriendly east, threatening the grail as he sought urgently for a hiding-place ... perhaps it was waiting for them, out there ... why was there no light burning on the Witherses' yacht ... ?

'Oh, stop it,' Jane said aloud.

'What?' said Simon in surprise.

'Nothing ... I was talking to myself ... Oh good, there's the bell. Come on.'

Mrs Palk, in the intervals of carrying heaped plates from the kitchen and empty ones back out again, was in a very firm motherly mood. Great-Uncle Merry told her that they were going out night-fishing off the outer harbour, and at once she began laying great plans for filling thermos flasks with hot coffee, and leaving plates of sandwiches ready in the kitchen for their return. But she would not hear of Barney going too.

'You'm not goin' anywhere wi' sunburn like that, midear, twouldn' be sensible, now. You stay here wi' me and have a nice early night, that'd be the best thing by far. If you go out you'll be rubbin' and blisterin' quick as anything, and then you'd find yourself in bed tomorrow when you could be out in the sunshine, and you wouldn't like that, would you?'

'I should be perfectly all right,' Barney said, half-heartedly. Mrs Palk had painted calamine on his sunburned legs, but they were very sore and tender, and although he tried to hide the pain he winced every time he took a step. And he was very sleepy after the day spent running and swimming in the open air.

Great-Uncle Merry said, 'I think it would be best, Barney. If you're awake we'll come and report to you when we get in.'

'That 'ee won't,' Mrs Palk said. She treated Great-Uncle Merry, for all her respect for 'the Professor', with exactly the same indulgent strictness that she did Simon and Barney and Jane. 'He'll have a good long sleep, undisturbed, till mornin', and then he'll wake up fresh as a daisy with all that soreness gone. And he can hear all about everything then.'

'Mrs Palk,' Great-Uncle Merry said meekly, 'you are a good soul and you remind me overwhelmingly of my old nanny, who would never let me go outside the door without taking my goloshes. Well, young Barnabas, I think . . .'

'Oh, all right,' Barney said sadly. 'I suppose so. I'll stay here.'

'That's right,' Mrs Palk beamed. 'I'll go and make 'ee a nice hot drink before bed.' She bustled out of the room.

'You lucky things,' Barney said enviously to Simon and Jane. 'I bet you find all sorts of marvellous clues, just because I can't come. It isn't fair.'

'As a matter of fact you'll have the most important job of all tonight,' Simon said impressively. 'And the most dangerous too. We decided it would be too risky to take the map with us, so you'll be in charge of it here. You might have to guard it with your life – suppose the burglars came back again.'

'Oh don't,' Jane said in alarm.

'That isn't very likely, don't worry,' Great-Uncle Merry said, getting to his feet. 'But it's a responsibility all the same, Barney, so you aren't altogether out of things.'

Barney was not sure whether to feel important or pathetic, but he went obediently to bed. Looking back as they set off into the dark, they saw his face pressed white against one of the upstairs windows, and a dim hand waving them good-bye.

'Gosh, it's cold,' Jane said, shivering slightly, as they went up the road away from the village.

'You'll be all right once we've been walking for a bit,' Great-Uncle Merry said. He had insisted before they went out that they should wear sweaters and scarves under their coats, and they were grateful now.

'Everything seems terribly big,' Simon said suddenly. They all spoke softly by instinct, for there was no sound in the dark night but the soft tread of their own feet. Only, occasionally, they heard a car humming past in the village, and, very faint, the wash of the sea and the creak of boats at their moorings in the harbour below.

Jane looked round at the silver roofs and the patches of black shadow cast by the moon. 'I know what you mean. You can only see one edge of everything, there's always one side in shadow. So you can't see where it ends . . . and the headland looks awfully sinister. I'm glad I'm not on my own.'

This was a confession she would never have made in daylight. But somehow in the dark night it seemed less shameful. Simon said unexpectedly: 'So am I.'

Great-Uncle Merry said nothing. He walked along beside them in silence, very tall, brooding, his face lost in the shadows. With every long stride he seemed to merge into the night, as if he belonged to the mystery and the silence and the small nameless sounds.

Round the corner of the road, away from the harbour, they turned off and climbed over a fence on to the headland. The road curved round inland again, and above them stretched the dark grassy sweep of the slope, up towards the standing stones. In a little while they found the footpath, and began the long to-and-fro climb to the top.

'Listen!' Jane said suddenly, stopping in mid-stride.

There was no sound as they stood there, but only the sigh of the sea.

'You're hearing things,' Simon said nervously.

'No – I'm sure –'

Above their heads, from the top of the headland still out of sight, there came drifting down a faint ghostly call. 'Whoo-oo.'

'Oh,' Jane said in relief. 'Only an owl. Horrible, I couldn't think what it was.'

Great-Uncle Merry still said nothing. They began to climb again. Then all at once they hesitated, as if by some unspoken agreement. A dark curtain seemed to have come down all round them.

'What is it?'

'A cloud's come over the moon. Look. It's only a little one.'

Like a puff of smoke the cloud drifted away from the face of the moon as suddenly as it had come, and the land and sea were silver again.

'You said there wouldn't be any cloud.'

'Well, there isn't much, only a few little ones.'

'The wind has changed,' Great-Uncle Merry said. His voice, out of his long silence, sounded very deep. 'It comes from the south-west, Cornwall's wind. It brings cloud sometimes, and sometimes other things.' He went on up the hillside, and they did not like to ask him what he meant.

As they climbed after him more clouds came up, ragged and silver-edged in the moonlight; scudding swiftly across the sky as if another wind were up there, stronger and more purposeful than the gentle breeze blowing down into their faces over the slope.

And then, looming over the dark brow of the headland, they saw the outline of the standing stones. Magnified by the darkness, they towered mysteriously against the silver-washed sky, and vanished unnervingly into shadow whenever a cloud rushed over the face of the moon. In the daylight the stones had seemed tall, but now they were immense, dominating the headland, and all the dim moonlit valleys that stretched inland from the lights of the village twinkling faintly below. Jane clutched at Simon's arm, suddenly overawed.

'I'm sure they don't want us here,' she said unhappily.

'Who don't?' Simon demanded, bravado making his voice louder than he intended.

'Ssh, don't make such a noise.'

'Oh, grow up,' Simon said roughly. He did not feel happy in the dark emptiness of the night, but he was determined not to think about it. Then he felt a coldness at the pit of his stomach, as his great-uncle's deep voice came back to them in a way that seemed to confirm all that Jane felt.

'They don't mind,' Great-Uncle Merry said softly. 'If anything, we're welcome here.'

Simon shook himself slightly, pretending not to have heard. He looked round at the stones, surrounding them now, rearing up against the sky. 'This was the one.' He crossed to the stone they had found the day before. 'I remember this funny sort of hole in the side.'

Jane joined him, calmed by his matter-of-fact tone. 'Yes, that's it. When we looked across from here we were absolutely in line with the sun, and that rock we started from. Over on that other headland. Funny you can't see it now. I'd have thought the moon would shine on it like the sun did.'

'The moon's in another direction, out over the sea,' Simon said. 'Look at the shadow, come on, that's what we've got to follow.'

'Oh bother,' Jane said, as another cloud crossed the moon and they were left in the dark again. 'The clouds are getting much thicker, I wish they'd go away. There seems to be much more wind up here too.' She clutched her duffle coat round her, and tucked her scarf in more tightly.

'Don't be long,' Great-Uncle Merry said suddenly out of the darkness. He was standing against another of the stones, swallowed up in its outline so that they could not even make out his shape. Jane felt a shiver of alarm return.

'Why? Is anything wrong?'

'No, nothing ... look, here's the moon again.'

The night became silver again; looking up, it was as if they saw the moon sailing through the clouds instead of the other way round; racing smoothly across the sky, passing puffs and wisps of cloud on either side, and yet never moving from its place.

Simon said, in flat, dull disappointment: 'It doesn't point at anything!' He stared at the ground beside the towering stone. Dark on the silvered gloom of the grass lay the shadow cast by the high bright moon; and it pointed like a blunt finger away from Kemare Head, towards the long dark inland horizon of the Cornish moors.

'Perhaps it points to some landmark we haven't noticed,' Jane said doubtfully, gazing in vain over the shadow-masked hills.

'More likely the Cornishman used a landmark that's fallen down, or been destroyed, or just crumbled away. There's always been that risk. And it would mean we could never get any further than this.'

'But he wouldn't have done that, I know he wouldn't.' Jane looked wildly round her into the night, into the wind gusting over the bleak headland; and then suddenly she stood still, and stared. From her place beside the great stone that was their only sure mark, she had turned her head to the moon that raced motionless high over the top of Kemare Head, over the sea; and she saw, as if for the first time, the pathway of light that it laid down.

Straight as an arrow the long white road of the moon's reflection stretched towards them across the surface of the sea, like a path from the past and a path to the future; at its edges it danced and glimmered as the waves rose beneath the wind. And where it ended, at the tip of Kemare Head, a clear dark silhouette stood against the shining sea-carried light.

She said to Simon, huskily: 'Look.'

He turned to see, and she knew that in a moment he was as certain as she that this was what they were supposed to find.

'It's those rocks on the end of the headland,' she said. 'Outlined there. It must be. And we weren't supposed to use the shadow as a pointer this time – we had to stand here by this stone and let the moonlight itself show us the next clue.'

'And that's what it does.' Simon's voice rose as the familiar excitement of the chase came flooding back. 'And if that's what he meant by the signs that wane but do not die, then the grail must be hidden somewhere in that clump of rocks. Buried on the end of Kemare Head. Gosh – Gumerry, we've found it!' He turned back towards the silent dominating circle of the standing stones, and then hesitated: 'Gumerry?' he said uncertainly.

Jane came quickly to stand close to him. Out of the shelter of the rock the wind blew her pony-tail round across her face. She called more loudly, 'Gumerry! Where are you?'

There was no answer but the rise and fall of the sighing wind, loud enough now to drown the distant murmur of the sea. Jane, feeling very small indeed under the ghostly group of great stones, took hold of Simon's sleeve. Her voice quavered in spite of itself. 'Oh Simon – where's he gone?'

Simon called into the growing wind: 'Great-Uncle Merry! Great-Uncle Merry! Where are you?'

But still there was nothing but the darkness, and the high white moon sailing now dark, now light, and the noise of the wind. They heard the husking wail of the owl again, nearer this time, over the headland in the opposite valley; a friendless, inhuman, desolate sound. Jane forgot everything but the loneliness of the dark. She stood speechless with fright, as if she knew a great wave was bearing down on her and she could not move out of its path. If she had not been there Simon would have been as paralysed by fright himself. But he took a deep breath, and clenched his fists.

'He was over here before,' he said, swallowing. 'Come on.' He moved in the direction of the other standing stones, barely visible now in the blackness.

'Oh no –' Jane's voice rose hysterically, and she clutched at his sleeve. 'Don't go near them.'

'Don't be stupid, Jane,' Simon said coolly, sounding much braver than he felt.

Another owl hooted, unexpectedly, on their other side, towards the end of the headland. 'Oh,' Jane said miserably. 'I want to go home.'

'Come on,' Simon said again. 'He must be over here. I expect he can't hear us, this wind's getting up like anything.' He took Jane's hand, and unwillingly she moved with him towards the dark looming shapes of the standing stones. The moon dimmed and disappeared into the depths of a bigger cloud, so that only a dim luminous glow from the stars gave shape to anything at all. They went gingerly through the darkness, feeling that at any moment they might collide with something unseen; panic suppressed only by the desperate hope of finding their great-uncle suddenly at their side. He seemed a very strong and necessary refuge now that he was not there.

They were right among the standing stones now, and they could feel rather than see the black rock pillars rearing up around them. The wind blew gustily, singing through the grass, and again they heard the owl cry below them out of the dark. They moved slowly together, straining their eyes to peer ahead. Then the ragged cloud turned silver again, and the moon came sailing out through the flying wisps at its edge; and in the same moment they became aware of a tall dark shape looming up before them where no stone had been before.

It seemed to swell as the wind blew, so that suddenly they saw that it was no stone, but the tall figure of a man all in black, with a long cloak that swirled in the wind as he turned towering over them. For an instant the moonlight caught his face as he turned, and they saw eyes shadowed under dark jutting brows, and the flash of white teeth in what was not a smile. Jane screamed, terrified, and hid her face in Simon's shoulder.

And then at once the moon was covered again by cloud, and the threat and roar of the darkness seemed to rear up all around them. Without a word they swung round and ran, stumbling, driven by panic, away from the silent standing stones and down the hill, until with an enormous flooding of relief they heard the call of a familiar deep voice. As they looked ahead, gasping, they saw Great-Uncle Merry silhouetted against the lighter background of the sea, standing before them on the path.

They rushed to him, and Jane flung her arms round his waist and clung to him, sobbing with relief. Simon had just enough self-possession left to stand on his own. 'Oh Gumerry,' he said breathlessly, 'we couldn't find you anywhere.'

'We must go down from here quickly,' his great-uncle said low and urgently, holding Jane to him and stroking the back of her quivering head. 'I was looking for you. I knew there was something in those cries that was not like any owl. Come quickly.'

He bent down and picked Jane up in his arms in one swift movement as if she had been a baby, and with Simon close at his heels he strode off down the hill, keeping to the path that they could just see as moonlight flashed through the racing clouds.

Simon said, panting as he trotted along, 'There was a man up there. We saw him, all of a sudden, out of the dark. He was all muffled up in a big coat like a cloak, all in black. It was horrible.'

'I went to find them,' Great-Uncle Merry said. 'He must have got past me. Then there were others. I shouldn't have left you alone.'

Jane, shaken in his arms as he loped down the hill, opened her eyes and looked back over his shoulder at the top of the headland, where the dark fingers of the standing stones still pointed up into the sky. And in the moment before they disappeared over the horizon she saw that there were twice as many shapes as there had been before, with other black figures standing among the stones.

'Gumerry, they're coming after us!'

'They dare not follow while I am here,' Great-Uncle Merry said calmly, and he went down the slope at the same long easy stride.

Jane swallowed. 'I think I'm all right now,' she said in a small voice. 'Could you put me down?'

Hardly pausing, Great-Uncle Merry set her on her feet again, and like Simon she half ran beside him to keep up. They reached the bottom of the slope, and crossed the field to the road, feeling it a reassuring place after the vast bleak emptiness of the headland. The wind no longer whined round their ears down here, and they heard again the friendly soft murmur of the sea.

'That man,' Simon said. 'That man we saw. It was him, Gumerry, the one we'd never seen before. It was the man you rescued me from. The man who chased me, with the boy.'

Jane said in a small frightened voice, looking straight ahead of her at the twinkling village lights as she walked, 'But I recognized him straight away, when the moonlight shone on his face. That's why I was so scared. It was the vicar of Trewissick. And he's the man who saw my outline of the map in the guide-book.'

Chapter Nine

Barney, left behind, flattened his nose against the window of Jane's bedroom. He saw Simon and Jane glance up and wave, but Great-Uncle Merry was marching along without looking to right or left, a tall thin figure vanishing into the dark. Barney smiled to himself. He knew that determined stride very well.

He peered after them until he could see nothing in the darkness but the lights of the village dancing in the black rippled water, among the ghostly boats. From the Witherses' yacht, there was no light at all. He turned away from the window, sighing a little at the frustration of being left out. To comfort himself he took a firmer hold on the telescope case which Simon had solemnly handed over to him when they came up to say good-bye. At once he felt better. He was a knight entrusted with a sacred mission; he had been wounded in battle but had to guard his secret just the same . . . he bent each leg gently in turn, and winced at the burning tightness of the skin over his knees. The enemy were all round, hunting the secret which he held in his charge, but none of them would be able to get near . . .

'Now then, back 'ee come to bed,' Mrs Palk said behind him, unexpectedly. Barney swung round. She was standing massive in the doorway, with the light from the landing streaming round her, watching him. Barney's fingers instinctively curled tighter round the cool metal case, and he came towards her, padding softly on his bare feet. Mrs Palk backed out on to the landing to let him through the door. As he passed close to her she reached out her hand curiously.

'What's that 'ee got there?'

Barney jerked the case out of her reach, and then quickly forced a laugh. 'Oh,' he said as casually as he could, 'it's a telescope of the captain's I borrowed. It's jolly good. You can see all the ships going past out in the bay. I thought I might be able to watch the others go down to the harbour with it, but it's not much good in the dark.'

'Oh ah.' Mrs Palk seemed to lose interest. 'Fancy that, I never seen the captain use any telescope. Still, there be all sorts of strange things in this house, more than I shall ever know about, I'll be bound.'

'Well, good night, Mrs Palk,' Barney said, making for his own room.

'Good night, midear,' Mrs Palk said. 'Just give me a shout if 'ee want anything. I reckon I'll be going to bed myself soon, my days of waitin' up for fishermen are over.' She disappeared downstairs, and the landing light went out.

Barney switched on the lamp at the side of his bed and quietly closed the door. He felt unprotected, and rather excited still, without Great-Uncle Merry in the house. He thought of pushing a chair against the door, but changed his mind when he remembered that Simon would fall over it when he came back. The last thing he wanted was for anyone to think he had been worried at being alone.

He took the manuscript out to have one last look, and to guess what Simon and Jane might find from the shadow of the standing stone. But he could see nothing in the rough picture of the stones and the moon. Suddenly sleepy, he slipped the roll back and turned out the light; snuggled down into the bed-clothes with the case clutched to his chest, and fell asleep.

He never knew exactly what it was that woke him. When, through the confusion of half-dreams and imagined noises, he realized that he was awake, the room was quite dark. There was no sound but the constant murmur of the sea, very faint on this side of the house but always in the air. But from the way all his senses were straining to catch something, he knew that a part of him which had not quite gone to sleep at all was warning him of some danger very near. He lay very still, but he could hear nothing. Then there was a very faint creak behind him, from the direction of the door.

Barney felt his heart begin to thump a little faster. He was used to hearing noises at night; their flat in London was part of a very old house which creaked and muttered all the time at night, as if the walls and floors were breathing.

Although he had never been awake here long enough to find out, he guessed that the Grey House probably did the same. But this noise, somehow, was not as friendly as those . . .

Barney did what he did at home whenever he woke up and heard a noise that sounded more like a burglar than an ordinary creak of the floor. He made the small grumbling, yawning whimper that people give sometimes in their sleep, and turned over in bed as if he were settling himself down without waking up. As he turned, he half opened one eye for a quick look round the room.

At home when he did this there was never anything to see at all, and he fell asleep again feeling rather foolish. But this time it was different. By a faint line of light he could see that the door was standing open, and near it the glow of a small torch was moving across the room. The light of the torch stopped quite still as he moved. Barney snuggled into his new position, lay still and breathed deeply for several minutes with his eyes closed. Gradually he heard the small noises begin again. He lay listening, more perplexed than frightened now. Who was it? What were they doing? It can't be someone who wants to knock me on the head, he said to himself, or they'd have knocked me on the head before this. They don't want to wake me up, and they don't want to make a noise. *They're looking for something . . .*

He groped under the bedclothes, careful not to show any movement or make a noise. The telescope case was still there, and he kept tight hold of it.

Then he heard another sound. The person moving noiselessly about his room in the dark sniffed, very slightly. The noise was almost imperceptible, but Barney recognized it as a sniff he had heard before. He grinned to himself in relief, feeling his muscles relax. Very slowly he edged his hand out from under the bedclothes towards the bed-side table, and switched on the light.

Mrs Palk jumped, dropped her torch with a clatter and clapped her hand to her heart. For some seconds Barney was completely dazzled by the sudden light flooding the room, but he blinked his eyes clear in time to see disappointment and surprise on her face. Quickly she pulled herself together, and gave him a broad reassuring smile.

'There now, and I thought I hadn't waked 'ee up. What a pity. I'm so sorry, midear. Did I frighten 'ee?'

Barney said bluntly: 'Whatever are you doing, Mrs Palk?'

'Came up to see if 'ee was all right and sleepin' properly. And I thought while I was up here I'd pick up your dirty cup to wash up wi' the rest of the things downstairs. Had your Horlicks up here, remember? Bless the boy,' she added fondly, 'he's half asleep still.'

Barney stared at her. He did feel sleepy, but not too sleepy to remember Jane coming into his room when he had first gone up to bed and saying, 'Mrs Palk said would I pick up your cup if you'd finished, or do you want any more?'

'Jane took my cup down.'

Mrs Palk looked vaguely round the room, and gazed wide-eyed at his empty bed-side table. 'So she did then, it quite slipped my mind. What a silly old thing I be. Well, I'll leave 'ee to go back to sleep, my love, I'm so sorry to have waked 'ee.' She bustled with almost comical speed out of the room.

Barney had almost fallen asleep again when he heard low voices outside the door, and Simon came in. He shot up in bed. 'What happened? Did you find anything? Where did you go?'

'Nothing happened much,' Simon said wearily. He peeled off his windcheater and sweater and dropped them on to the floor. 'We found where we've got to go next. Where the next clue leads. It's those rocks at the end of Kemare Head, right over the sea.'

'Did you go and look? Is there anything there?'

'No, we didn't.' Simon was abrupt, trying not to remember the nastiness of the moments when he and Jane had been alone in the dark.

'Why not?'

'The enemy were up there, that's why. All round us in the dark, and one of them was the man who chased me that day with the boy. Only Jane says it was the vicar. I don't know, it's all awfully complicated. Anyway, we ran away and nobody followed us. Funny, they all seem scared of Gumerry.'

'Who were *they*?'

'Dunno.' Simon yawned hugely. 'Look, I'm going down to have some cocoa. We can talk in the morning.'

Barney lay down again, sighing. 'All right. Ooh –' He jerked up again. 'Wait a minute. Shut the door.'

Simon looked at him curiously and pushed the door shut. 'What is it?'

'You mustn't say anything in front of Mrs Palk. Not a word. Tell Jane.'

'We shouldn't. She wouldn't understand anyway.'

'Ho,' Barney said importantly. 'That's what you think. I woke up just now and she was snooping around the room in the dark with a torch. Good job I had the map all safe. She's after it. I bet you she's after it. I think she's *bad*.'

'Hmmm,' Simon said, sceptically, looking at him. Barney's hair was ruffled, and his eyes shadowed with sleep. It was very easy to believe that what he was describing had been no more than a dream.

When they went downstairs in the morning Mrs Palk was bustling energetically about the kitchen beating eggs in a bowl with her elbow flicking up and down like a machine. 'Breakfast?' she said brightly. Barney watched her closely, but he could see nothing but good humour and beaming honesty. And yet, he said insistently to himself, she looked so guilty when I turned on the light . . .

'It's a wonderful day again,' Jane said happily as they sat down. 'The wind's still quite strong, but there isn't a cloud anywhere. It must have blown them all away.'

'Ah well, let's hope ut doesn't blow the marquee away as well,' Mrs Palk said, putting an enormous jug of creamy yellow milk on the table.

'What marquee?'

'What!' Mrs Palk opened her eyes. 'Haven't 'ee seen the posters? Why, 'tis Carnival day today. People come in from all round, even from St Austell. All sorts of things go on . . . there's a swimming gala in the harbour, then the band comes out, and there's dancing all the way up the street from the sea. They play the "Floral Dance". You know the tune, surely.' She began to sing lustily.

'I know it,' Simon said, 'but I thought they only danced it somewhere else.'

'Helston,' said Jane. 'The Helston Furry Dance.'

''Es, so they do,' Mrs Palk said. 'I reckon they copied it from us myself. Everyone knows Trewissick's Floral Dance, it was danced in my grandmother's time. Everyone dressed up gay and fancy in costume, and there's a great crowd in the street all dancin' and laughin'. No one goes out fishing today. There's a great marquee in the field behind the village, and all kinds of stalls and games, and wrestling . . . Then when the sun begins to go down they crown the carnival queen, and they stay round the harbour long after it gets dark, and dance in the moonlight . . . 'tis a long time before anyone wants to go to sleep in Trewissick, carnival day.'

'What fun,' Jane said.

'Hmmm,' said Simon.

'Oh, you mustn't miss it,' Mrs Palk said earnestly. 'I shall be there every minute, 'tis like the old days all over again. Eh, but now here I stand talking and your scrambled eggs will be getting hard on the stove.' She turned and sailed out of the room.

'It does sound fun,' Jane said reproachfully to Simon.

'I dare say. We've got other things to do. Of course if you'd rather go to the carnival than find the grail . . .'

'Sssh!' Barney looked nervously at the door.

'Oh, don't worry about her, she's all right. Great-Uncle Merry's a long time coming down, isn't he?'

'I didn't mean it,' Jane said meekly. 'Actually what I want to do more than anything is get back up on the headland, so we can go and find that rock.'

'We can't go without Gumerry. I wonder if he's awake?'

'I'll go and see.' Barney slipped from his chair.

'Hey, where be off to?' Mrs Palk nearly collided with him, carrying her tray through the door. 'Sit down and eat this now while 'tis hot.'

'I was going to call Great-Uncle Merry.'

'Now you leave him be, poor old gentleman,' Mrs Palk said firmly. 'Gadding about in the middle of the night, tidn' natural at his age, no wonder he's having a good long sleep. Night-fishin', indeed. And not a fish to show for it after all that traipsin' about. You proper wearied him last night, I reckon. You remember we aren't all as young as you three.' She wagged her finger at them. 'Now you get along into the sun after your breakfast, and let him have his sleep out.' She departed again, shutting the door behind her.

'Oh dear,' Jane said, abashed. 'She's right, you know. Great-Uncle Merry is quite old really.'

'Well, he's not doddering,' Simon said defensively. 'He doesn't seem old at all sometimes. He went like a rocket last night – *and* carrying you. It was all I could do to keep up with him.'

'Well, perhaps this is the after-effect.' Jane's conscience was beginning to nag. 'Last night must have been an awful strain on him, what with one thing and another. I don't think we should wake him up. It's only nine o'clock, after all.'

'But we haven't made any plans or anything,' said Barney.

'Perhaps we just ought to wait here till he does wake up,' Simon said despondently.

'Oh no, why should we? He wouldn't mind if we went on to the headland. He can follow us when he's had his sleep.'

'Didn't he say we shouldn't go anywhere without him from now on?' Barney said doubtfully. 'Or anyway, not without telling him?'

'Well, we can leave a message for him with Mrs Palk.'

'No, we can't!'

'Barney thinks Mrs Palk is one of the enemy,' said Simon sceptically.

'Oh, surely not,' Jane said vaguely. 'Well anyway, we don't really have to leave a message. He's bound to guess where we've gone. There's only one place any of us would want to go, and that's to the rocks on Kemare Head.'

'We can say to Mrs Palk that he'll know where we've gone. Just like that. And then she'll tell him and he'll understand.'

'We can say we've taken Rufus for a walk,' said Barney hopefully.

'That's not a bad idea. Where is he?'

'In the kitchen. I'll go and get him.'

'Tell Mrs Palk while you're there. And tell her we'll see her at her beloved carnival. We probably will anyway.'

Barney bolted the last of his scrambled egg and went out to the kitchen, munching a piece of toast.

Simon suddenly had an idea. He got up and crossed to the window, and peered out down the hill. He turned back quickly to Jane. 'We might have known. They're watching us already. That boy's at the bottom of the road, sitting on the wall. Not doing anything – just sitting there, looking up here. They must be waiting for us to come out, because they don't know whether we found a clue last night that will lead us somewhere.'

'Oh gosh.' Jane bit her lip. Their night on the headland had left her more deeply nervous than ever before. It was as if they were fighting not people, but a dark force that used people as its tools. And could do what it liked with them. 'Isn't there a back way out of the house up to the headland?'

'I don't know. How funny, we've never looked.'

'Well, we've been doing other things. I suppose even if there was one, they'd be watching it.'

'Well . . . the only person who'd be likely to know about a back way is that Bill, and he's at the front. There's no harm in looking.'

Barney had come back, with Rufus lolloping joyfully at his side. 'There is a way,' he said. 'You can get through the hedge at the top of the back garden. I found it one morning before you were up. Rufus showed me, actually – he was dashing about and suddenly he disappeared, and then I heard him barking miles away outside, half-way up the headland. You come out into a lane and then you're out on Kemare Head before you know it. It's a good way out because they wouldn't expect us to go through – there's no gate or anything.'

'Gumerry won't know about that way,' Jane said suddenly. 'He'll come out the front way, and they'll follow him, and it'll be just as bad as if they'd followed us in the first place.'

'No fear,' Barney said confidently. 'He'll shake them off somehow. I bet you this is one time they won't have the slightest idea where we are.'

When the children were gone and the house lay silent, Mrs Palk spent two brisk hours working downstairs. She took care not to make a noise. Then she sat down in the kitchen to drink a leisurely cup of tea.

She made the tea very strong, using one of the captain's best cups: very large, and made of thin, almost translucent white china. She sat at the kitchen table sipping from it, a look of great secret satisfaction on her face. After a while she went to a cupboard under the sink, pulled out her big shopping-bag and took from it a brilliant jumble of coloured ribbons, with an elaborate feathery structure not unlike a Red Indian head-dress. She set this on her head, looked at herself in the mirror, and chuckled. Then she carefully put it aside and poured out some more tea in a fresh cup. She put this on a tray and sailed out into the hall and up the stairs, a great smiling mysterious galleon of a woman.

Without knocking, she opened the door of Great-Uncle Merry's room, went in, and set down the tray by the bed. Great-Uncle Merry was buried in the bed-clothes, breathing heavily. Mrs Palk pulled back the curtains to let the light pour into the dim room, bent down and shook him roughly by the shoulder. As he stirred she drew back quickly and stood waiting, beaming down at him with her usual doting motherly smile.

He yawned, groaned and clutched his head sleepily, running his fingers back through the untidy white hair.

'Time to get up, Professor,' said Mrs Palk brightly. 'Nice long rest I let 'ee have, after all that gadding about last night. Done 'ee good, I'll be bound. Not all as young as we used to be, are we now?'

Great-Uncle Merry looked at her and grunted, blinking himself awake.

'Drink 'ee's tea now, and I'll go and get 'ee's breakfast.' Mrs Palk's rich voice flowed on as she turned to twitch the curtains tidy. 'Can have it in peace and blessed quiet for once. They children have been out for hours.'

Suddenly Great-Uncle Merry was very wide awake. He sat up straight-backed, a startling sight in his bright red pyjama jacket. 'What time is it?'

'Why, 'tis gone eleven.' Mrs Palk beamed at him.

'Where have the children gone?'

'Now don't 'ee worry about them. They can look after theirselves well enough for one day.'

'Little idiots – where are they?' His forehead creased.

'Now, now, Professor,' Mrs Palk said chidingly. 'Gone off to save 'ee a journey, they have, as a matter of fact. Thoughtful, well-brought-up little things, they are, for all their mother's a bit higgledy-piggledy, begging your pardon. Gone off to Truro for 'ee.'

'*Truro!*'

Mrs Palk smiled innocently. ''Es, that's right. Young Simon answered the telephone this morning. Nasty machine,' she added confidingly, shuddering slightly. 'Near scared me out of my life, screeching away. Talked to the man on the other end for a long time, he did. And after, he came to me and said, all serious, bless his heart – Mrs Palk, he says, that was a friend of Great-Uncle Merry's on the telephone from the museum at Truro, saying he's got to see us all very urgently about something.'

'Who was it?'

'Wait a minute now, Professor, I'm not finished . . . I reckon we ought to go off at once if our great-uncle's still asleep, young Simon says to me, and catch the bus. Then he can come on after us when he wakes up.'

'Who was it?' Great-Uncle Merry insisted.

'Simon didn't give me no name . . . very important he made it sound. So off they all went, the three of them, and got the bus into St Austell. Don't you worry, Mrs Palk, they said, just you tell our great-uncle for us.'

'You should never have let them go alone,' Great-Uncle Merry said curtly. 'If you'll excuse me, Mrs Palk, I should like to get up.'

'Course,' said Mrs Palk indulgently, still smiling and unruffled, and she sailed out of the room.

Within minutes Great-Uncle Merry was downstairs, fully dressed, frowning to himself and occasionally muttering anxiously. He waved away his breakfast, and went striding out of the Grey House. Mrs Palk, watching from the doorstep, saw his big battered car appear on the road and roar off, leaving a great black smear of smoke hanging in the air as it disappeared out of the village.

She smiled to herself and went back into the Grey House. A few moments later she came out again, the small secret smile still hovering round her mouth; locked the door behind her and went off with her shopping-bag down the hill to the harbour. A few bright red and blue feathers nodded over the top of the bag as it swung at her side.

Chapter Ten

'This isn't nearly as simple as I thought it would be,' Simon said, frowning. He looked about him at the jagged rocks. 'From the standing stones last night it looked as if there was just one lump of rock here, sticking out on its own. But there are so many of them, and they're all so big.'

The wind blowing in from the open sea tossed Jane's pony-tail to and fro on the back of her neck. She looked back inland. 'It's just like being out at sea. As if we were cut off, and looking at the land from the outside.'

The end of Kemare Head was a more desolate place than any they had yet seen, even with the sunlight glittering on the water far below, and the smell of the sea in the wind. They stood in the midst of a bleak patch of rocks, rising bare out of the grass almost at the headland's tip. The ground fell away before them in a steep grassy slope, and from there the sheer edge of the cliff dropped to meet the other rocks, two hundred feet below, where the white waves endlessly grunted and sighed. They could see no sign of life or movement anywhere around.

'It's lonely,' Barney said. 'It feels lonely itself, I mean, somehow. Different from us feeling lonely. I wonder what the next clue is, if there is one.'

'I don't think there is,' Jane said slowly. 'This is so much an end of a place. It doesn't lead anywhere, everything leads towards it . . . Funny how we didn't see anybody at all on the way up. There are usually one or two people wandering about, even on the headlands.'

'There certainly were last night,' Simon said.

'Oh don't, I keep trying not to remember. But there just isn't a living thing up anywhere near here. I think it's odd.'

'Mr Penhallow says the locals keep away from the end of the headland,' Barney said, clambering to perch above their heads on one of the rocks. Rufus tried to climb up beside him, slithered back again and licked his ankle whining. 'They don't like the standing stones much either, but they never come up here at all. He wouldn't talk about it much. He said people thought the rocks were haunted, and unlucky, and he sounded as if he believed it himself. He said they call them the Gravestones.'

'They call the standing stones that?'

'No, these rocks here.'

'Funny, I should have thought it would be the other way round. The others do look rather like gravestones in a kind of way. But these are just rocks, like any other rocks.'

'Well, that's what he said.' Barney shrugged his shoulders and nearly overbalanced. 'Just that people didn't like them.'

'I wonder why.' Jane gazed up at the nearest crag of rock, rising just above her head. Simon, next to her, tapped idly at its surface with the old brass telescope case, the manuscript safely rolled up inside; Barney had ceremonially handed it back that morning. Then suddenly he stopped tapping and stood stock-still.

'Whatever's the matter? Have you found anything?' Jane peered at the rock.

'No . . . yes . . . Oh, it's all right, I'm not looking at anything. Don't you remember, in the manuscript? I can hear Great-Uncle Merry saying it now. Where the Cornishman said he hid the grail. Over sea and under stone.'

'That's right, and the same when they buried the strange knight, what was his name . . .'

'Bedwin,' Barney said. 'Golly, I see what you mean. Over sea and under stone. *Here!*'

'But –' Jane said.

'It must be!' Simon hopped distractedly on one foot. 'Over sea – well, we couldn't be anywhere that was much more obviously over the sea, could we? And under stone. Well, here are the stones.'

'And this must be where they buried Bedwin as well!' Barney hastily slithered down from his rock. 'And that's why they call it the Gravestones, and think it's haunted. They've forgotten all the real story, because it's hundreds and hundreds of years ago. But they remember that bit, or at least they remember people being frightened to come here, and so they don't come either.'

'Perhaps they're right,' Jane said nervously.

'Oh come off it. Well, anyway, even if Bedwin's ghost was floating about somewhere, he wouldn't want to scare us because we're on the same side as he was.'

'Great-Uncle Merry said something like that last night.' Jane screwed up her forehead to remember.

'Oh never mind, don't you realize what this means? We're *there*, we've found it!' Barney spluttered with delight. Rufus, catching his mood, pranced joyfully round them barking into the wind.

Simon looked at him. 'All right then. Where is it?'

'Well,' Barney said, pausing a little. 'Here. Under one of the rocks.'

'Yes, well, just stop rushing about like a madman and think for a minute. What do we have to do, dig them all up? They're part of the headland. It's all rock. Look.' Simon took out his penknife, a hefty steel weapon with two big blades and a marlin-spike, and went down on his knees to dig away the earth at the foot of one of the crags. He tore away tufts of grass, dug a hole, and three inches from the surface came to solid rock. 'There. You see?' He scraped at the rock with his knifeblade, making a depressing grating sound. 'How can there be anything buried there?'

'It doesn't all have to be like that,' Barney said rebelliously.

'Perhaps there's a different bit somewhere,' Jane said hopefully. 'If we all three divide up and search every inch we're bound to find something. We ought to have brought spades with us really. Come on.'

So Barney went to one end of the rocks and Jane, twenty yards away, to the other. Simon, glancing nervously down at the steep edge of the headland, went round to the seaward side and began working his way in from there. They clambered up and down, over the sharp-edged granite, searching the patches of wiry grass between the rocks, tugging at boulders to see if they would move and show a place where something could be buried underneath. But no stone ever shifted an inch, and they found nothing but granite and grass, with no hint of a hiding-place.

Jane was holding something carefully in her hand as they came together again. 'Look,' she said, holding it out. 'Don't you think it's peculiar finding a sea-shell up here? I mean how on earth could it have got up from the beach, specially if no one ever comes up here?'

'It's more like a stone than a shell,' Simon said curiously, taking it from her hand. It was a cockleshell, but its hollow was solid and hard, filled with what looked like rock; and the surface of the shell was not white and roughened like those they found on the beach, but smooth and dark grey.

'A visitor must have dropped it,' Barney said easily. 'Visitors wouldn't be frightened of coming up here, they wouldn't know anything about what the Trewissick people say.'

'I suppose so.' They all thought of visitors, scornfully.

'Oh well.' Jane put the shell in her pocket and looked around helplessly. 'This is awful. We're stuck. What can we do now?'

'There must be something up here, there must.'

'We don't really know . . . perhaps it's just another step on the ladder after all.'

'But there's nothing else marked to follow. Let's have a look at the map again.'

Simon squatted down on the grass and unscrewed the telescope case, and they peered at the manuscript, its words and lines faint brown in the sun.

'I'm certain he meant this to be the end of the quest,' Barney said obstinately. 'Look at the way the end of the headland stands all on its own. There's nothing to lead anywhere else.'

Simon stared pensively at the map. 'Perhaps it just leads back where we started from. He might have been pulling our legs all the while. A sort of insurance policy, to make it difficult for anyone to find the grail.'

'Perhaps he hid it somewhere we shall never find.'

'Perhaps he took it with him after all.'

'Perhaps it doesn't exist.'

They sat round in a gloomy group, ignoring the sunshine and the magnificent sweep of coast and sea. There was a long despondent silence. Barney glanced up idly. 'Where's Rufus got to?'

'Dunno,' Simon said morosely. 'Fallen over the cliff, I expect. Sort of stupid thing that animal would do.'

'Oh no!' Barney scrambled to his feet in concern. 'I hope he's all right. Rufus! Rufus!' He put two fingers in his mouth and let out an ear-splitting whistle. Jane winced.

They saw nothing, and heard nothing but the wind, and then they became aware of a curious noise just above their heads; a kind of snuffling, scrabbling whine.

'He's up there!' Barney clambered round the side of the rocks, and they saw the top of his fair head appear behind a jutting grey hump as he stood up. Then he suddenly vanished. His voice came over the rocks to them on the wind muffled but tense with excitement. 'Hey! Come over here, quick!'

The rocks made a kind of fortress, rising one after the other like rows of battlements. They found him in the middle, crouching beside one of the peaks, watching Rufus. The dog stood quivering and intent, his nose close against the rock, one paw scraping feebly as he whined and sniffed.

'Quick,' Barney said without turning round. 'I don't know what he's trying to do, but I think he's found something. I've never seen him like this before. If it's rats or rabbits he just goes mad and barks and rushes about, but this is different. Look at him.'

Rufus seemed to be standing in a trance, unable to tear himself away from the rock-face.

'Let me look,' Simon said. He stepped carefully past Barney and put one arm round Rufus's neck, fondling him under the chin as he drew him away from the rock. 'There's a tiny gap here.' His voice came back to them. 'I can get my fingers inside – ow! I say, this top rock moves! I felt it shift, I'm sure I did. It nearly caught my hand. It's terrifically big, but I think . . . Jane, can you get round on my other side?'

Jane squeezed herself between the rocks next to him.

'Now get hold there,' Simon directed her. 'That jutting-out bit . . . when I tell you, push as hard as you can away from you, towards the sea. Wait a minute, I've got to get a grip on my side . . . I don't know if this'll work . . . now, *heave!*'

Obediently, but without any idea of what she was supposed to be doing, Jane pushed with all her might at the rock-face, with Simon panting and heaving beside her. For a long strained moment nothing happened. Then just as their lungs seemed about to burst, they felt the rock move beneath their hands. It gave a very slight tremor, and then a grinding, grating lurch. They staggered back, and the great rough round rock rolled away from their hands and down into the nearest hollow. They could feel the crunching thud of its fall shake the rock where they stood.

Where the boulder had been there was a dark, shapeless hole about two feet across.

They stood still, gaping. Rufus pattered forward across the rocks, bent his head to sniff delicately at it and then turned back, his tail waving and his tongue hanging out over his teeth as if he were grinning.

Simon moved forward at last and pulled away a couple of smaller rocks from the edge of the hole. He knelt down by it and peered inside then put his arm in to see how deep it was.

His arm disappeared up to the shoulder, until he was lying flat, and he could feel nothing but rough rock at the sides. He blinked up at Barney and Jane. 'I can't feel any bottom to it,' he said, hushed.

His voice brought back their own, and they found they had been holding their breath.

'Get up, let's have a look.'

'This must be it, mustn't it? It must be where he hid the grail!'

'How deep d'you think it goes?'

'Gosh, this is terrific! Clever old Rufus!'

Rufus waved his tail faster.

'That chunk of rock,' Jane said, looking at it reverently where it lay tumbled on its side. 'It must have been there for nine hundred years. Imagine . . . nine hundred years . . .'

'Well, it wasn't exactly loose, was it?' Simon flexed his strained arm muscles tenderly. 'Though it must have been fairly delicately balanced, or we shouldn't have been able to shift it at all. Anyway, we've got to find how deep this goes before we know if there's anything there.'

He looked thoughtfully at the gaping dark mouth in the rock. Jane sighed to herself and stopped thinking about the centuries.

'Drop a stone down, then you can hear how deep it is. Like thunderstorms. You know, counting the seconds between the lightning and the thunder to see how far away the storm is.'

Simon picked up a loose chunk of rock from the edge of the hole and poised it over the blackness. He let go, and it dropped out of sight. They listened.

After a long time Jane sat back on her heels. 'I couldn't hear anything.'

'Nor could I.'

'Try again.'

Simon dropped another stone into the hole, and again they strained their ears to hear it strike the bottom. Nothing happened.

'There wasn't anything then either.'

'No.'

'It must be *bottomless*!'

'Don't be an idiot, it can't be.'

'Perhaps it comes out in Australia,' Barney said. He looked nervously at the hole.

'It just means the noise was too far away for us to hear,' Simon said. 'But it must be tremendously deep. I wish we'd brought a rope.'

'Look in your pockets,' Jane said. 'They're always full of junk. So are Barney's. At least Mother's always saying so when she has to empty them. You might have some string or something.'

'Junk yourself,' Simon said indignantly, but he turned out his pockets on to the rock.

The results, though interesting, were not very much help. Simon laid out an array of belongings including his knife, a very dirty handkerchief, a little scratched glass-covered compass, two fifty-pence pieces, a stump of candle, two screwed-up bus tickets, four toffees in battered cellophane wrappings and a ballpoint pen.

'Well,' he said, 'we can have a toffee each anyway.' He handed them round solemnly. The toffees were slightly furry at the edges where the cellophane had come loose, but tasted none the worse for that. Simon gave the fourth to Rufus, who made a few grimacing attempts to chew it and then swallowed it whole.

'What a waste,' Barney said. He emptied his own pockets, in a shower of sand; a green glass marble with an orange pip in the middle, a small white pebble, twenty pence, a headless lead sailor, a handkerchief miraculously much cleaner than Simon's, and a thick piece of wire curved round at both ends.

'Whatever do you carry that around for?' demanded Jane.

'Well, you never know,' Barney said vaguely. 'It might come in useful. Come on, let's have a look at yours.'

'Nothing in them,' Jane said, a trifle smugly. She pulled both her pockets inside out.

'Well, you brought your duffle coat,' said Simon. He crossed the rocks, climbed down to the grass of the headland where they had been standing, and brought the jacket back. 'Here we are. One handkerchief. Two hair-grips. Just like a girl. Two pencils. A box of matches. Whatever d'you want those for?'

'Like Barney – they might come in useful. A lot more useful than that old bit of wire anyway.'

Simon felt in the other pocket. 'Money, a button ... what's this?' He brought out a reel of cotton. 'Now that's an idea. Pretty daft thing to carry about, but it might help us find how deep the hole is.'

'I'd forgotten I had that,' Jane said. 'All right, you win, I carry junk round too. But you must admit it's sensible junk.' She took the cotton-reel from him. 'It says there's a hundred yards of cotton on this. Well, no hole could be that deep, surely?'

'I wouldn't be surprised, with this one,' Simon said. 'Tie something to the cotton, and lower it down.'

'Have to be something pretty light,' Barney said. 'Or it'll break.'

Jane unwound a length of cotton and pulled on it. 'Oh I don't know, it's pretty strong. Here, I know, give me that bit of wire.'

Barney looked at her doubtfully, but handed it over. Jane tied one end of the cotton to its curved end. 'There. Now we just lower away and wait till it hits bottom.'

'I know a better way.' Simon took the reel back, and put one of Jane's pencils through the hole in the middle. It was just long enough to protrude at either side. 'See, you hold on to both ends of the pencil and the reel unwinds of its own accord, because of the weight. Like playing a fish.'

'Let me do it.' Jane knelt down beside the hole and dropped the wire into its dark mouth. The cotton-reel spun round as the thread disappeared, and they held their breath. Then suddenly the reel slowed, turned wearily and came to a halt. Just as they were thinking that the wire had reached firm ground, they saw the end of the cotton blowing loose.

'Bother,' Jane said in disappointment. 'It's broken.' She looked down into the blackness in a vain attempt to see where the cotton had gone. Simon took the reel from her and examined it.

'Half the cotton's gone, anyway, and it still hadn't hit anything. That means the hole must be at least fifty yards deep. That's a hundred and fifty feet. Good grief!' He tapped Jane on the shoulder. 'Come on, dopey, you won't see anything down there.'

Jane flapped her hand at him, still bending over the hole. 'Shut up.'

They waited patiently until she straightened herself, red in the face. 'I can hear the sea,' she said, blinking in the sunlight.

'Of course, you can hear the sea. So can I. It's just over the edge of the headland.'

'No, no, I mean you can hear it down there.'

Simon looked at her, tapped his head and sighed.

But Barney lay down close to the hole and put his head inside. 'She's right, you know,' he said eagerly, looking up. 'Come and put your ear down here.'

'Hmmm,' said Simon sceptically, and lay down beside him. Then he heard very faintly, coming up from the depths of the hole, a hollow booming sound. It faded and then rose again, slow and regular. 'Is that the sea?'

'Of course it is,' Jane said. 'That deep gonging sort of noise, don't you recognize it? The sort of noise waves make when they wash into a cave. And think what it means . . . the hole must go all the way down through the cliff to the sea, and there must be an entrance down there. *And that's where the Cornishman hid the grail.*'

'But it can't go all that way.' Simon sat up slowly, rubbing his ear. 'Couldn't this be vibration or something, coming through from the edge of the rocks down below?'

'Well, I ask you, does it sound like it?'

'No,' Simon admitted. 'It doesn't. Only . . . how could anyone have made such a narrow little hole so deep?'

'Goodness knows. But he did, didn't he? Perhaps that little shell I found was thrown up through it somehow.'

'Then if the grail is down there, we have to get at it from the entrance where the sea comes in. There must be a cave. I wonder if we can climb round from the harbour?'

'Listen!' Barney suddenly scrambled to his feet and stood upright, his head cocked. 'I heard something. Like an engine.'

Simon and Jane stood up, and listened to the distant waves and the wind. They could hear sea-gulls crying, the plaintive yelping calls blown gustily towards them from below. And then the noise Barney had heard; the low thrumming of an engine from the direction of the harbour.

It was Simon who caught sight of the long white bow of the yacht moving out round the curve of Kemare Head. He crouched low. 'Get down, quickly!' he said hoarsely. 'It's them! It's the *Lady Mary*!'

Barney and Jane dropped to the ground beside him. 'They can't see us if we keep behind the rocks,' Simon said quietly. 'Don't move, anyone, until they've gone out of sight.'

'I've got a gap here,' Barney whispered. 'I can just see them through the rock . . . Mr Withers is on deck, and his sister with him. Their skipper's not there, he must be in the cockpit . . . they're looking this way, not up here, they seem to be looking at the cliffs . . . Mr Withers has got binoculars . . . now he's put them down, and he's turned to his sister to say something. I can't see the expression on his face, they aren't near enough. I wish they'd come closer in.'

'Oh!' Jane swallowed, husky with agitation. 'Suppose there is a cave down there, where the grail is, and they see it!'

The idea was paralysing, and they lay rigid, three minds wishing the boat away. The noise of the *Lady Mary's* engine grew louder, passing the end of the headland close below them.

'What are they doing?' Simon hissed urgently.

'I can't see, there's a rock in the way now.' Barney wriggled with frustration.

The noise of the engine filled the air. But it did not stop. As they listened, breathless, it grew gradually less, moving away across the sea.

'I can see them again now, there's another gap . . . he's still looking at the coast through the binoculars. I don't think he's seen anything, it looks as if he's still hunting . . . now they've gone round the corner.' Barney rolled over and sat up. 'If they are looking for a cave, how did they know?'

'They *can't* know, they haven't seen the map,' Jane said in anguish. 'They couldn't possibly. I mean even if the vicar is in league with them, and they know about the outline I drew in the guide-book, it hasn't got any sort of clue. I didn't put any of the clue marks in.'

'But if they don't know where to look, why are they looking in the right place?'

'I think,' Simon said reassuringly, 'it's just part of their routine. I mean, they don't know where to look, so they look everywhere. Great-Uncle Merry said something like that the very first day we talked. It's like the way they searched the house – all at random, without any sort of plan. Perhaps they've thought of the idea of a cave, vaguely, and they're scouring the whole coast in case they find one. Not just this part, but all the way up and down. They don't *know* there is one.'

'Well, we do. If it's there, why didn't they see it?'

'Perhaps they did,' Barney said gloomily.

'Oh no, they can't have done. They'd have stopped. At any rate they wouldn't have gone on looking like you said they were. You did say that, didn't you?' Jane looked at him nervously.

'Oh yes – old Withers was still squinting hard through his glasses when they went out of sight.'

'Well then.'

'There's one other thing it might be,' Simon said reluctantly. He paused.

'What?'

'We heard the sea, so the mouth of the cave might be covered. It might be under water. That could be why they didn't see it. There are lots of underwater caves in Cornwall, I remembered reading about them somewhere. It might not have been like that when our Cornishman hid the grail, but perhaps the land's sunk a bit in nine hundred years.'

'Well, that's good,' Barney said. 'They'd never be able to find it then.'

Simon looked at him, and raised his eyebrows, 'Nor should we.'

Barney stared. 'Oh. Oh, surely we could. You can dive pretty well.'

'We wouldn't have a chance. I can dive, but I'm not a fish.'

'I suppose the whole thing would be full of water,' Jane said slowly. 'And the grail would be under the sea, and all eaten away like wrecks of ships.'

'Covered in barnacles,' said Simon.

'It can't be. It mustn't be. He said over the sea, and it must *be* over the sea.'

'We shall just have to find out. Great-Uncle Merry will know.'

They stared at one another in consternation.

'Gumerry! I'd forgotten all about him.'

'Where is he?'

'We've been up here for ages. He must have woken up hours ago.'

'Barney, what exactly did you ask Mrs Palk to tell him?'

'I said would she say we'd gone for a walk with Rufus, he'd know where. She looked at me a bit funny, but she said she'd give him the message. I tried to make it sound like a game,' said Barney, very serious.

'I do hope nothing's happened to him,' said Jane anxiously.

'Don't worry, I expect he's still snoring,' Simon said. He looked at his watch. 'It's half past eleven. Let's get down quickly before the yacht comes back. We might not be so lucky next time – if they come back under sail we shouldn't hear them. I wonder why they didn't last time, there's more than enough wind.' He frowned.

'Oh never mind,' Barney said. 'Let's go and find Gumerry. Round the back again – that boy might still be watching the front.'

'No, we shall have to go the front way. Gumerry might be coming up. I've got a feeling we haven't much time left. We shall just have to risk getting caught. Come on.'

Chapter Eleven

But as soon as they came down within sight of the harbour they saw that there was no question either of passing unseen or of being caught.

The streets round the harbour were thronged with people; fishermen and shopkeepers in their Sunday suits, wives in their best summer dresses, and more gay crowding tourists than the children had ever seen in Trewissick before. All the boats, swaying level with the quays on the high tide, were moored at one side, leaving a clear rectangle of water marked out with strings of bobbing white floats. As they came down the road they heard the faint thud of a starting-pistol, and six brown bodies flung themselves into the water and began thrashing in a white flurry of spray across the marked course. The crowd began to cheer.

'It must be the end of the swimming gala,' Jane said eagerly, caught up in the carnival atmosphere below them. 'Let's go and watch for a minute.'

'For heaven's sake,' Simon said in despair. 'We're on a mission. We've got to find Great-Uncle Merry before we do anything else.'

But there was no answer to the doorbell of the Grey House, as they stood on the doorstep with knots of shirt-sleeved visitors chattering past them up and down the hill. And when Simon had gone round to the back and retrieved the front-door key from its secret place in the toolshed, they went inside to find the house quite deserted.

Great-Uncle Merry's bed was neatly made, but there was no sign, in his bedroom or anywhere else, to tell them where he had gone. Mrs Palk was nowhere to be found. There were three plates of cold mackerel and salad covered up on the kitchen table, left for their lunch. But that was all. The house was spotless, silent and neat – and empty.

'Where can he have gone? And where's Mrs Palk?'

'Well, that's easy enough. She'll be outside watching the swimming with everyone else. You know how she was drooling about carnival day.'

'Let's go and find her. She must know where he is.'

'Tell you what,' Barney said. 'You two go down to the harbour and I'll run up to the top of the hill and see if Gumerry has gone up there after all. I'd be able to see him if he's climbing the headland, it takes quite a time to get to the top.'

Simon thought for a moment. 'All right, that seems sensible enough. But for goodness' sake keep out of sight of the yacht if you see it coming back. And come down to us as quick as you can, we don't want to get separated. We'll be down there on the quay where the start of the swimming is.'

'Righto.' Barney made off, but then turned back. 'I say, what are you going to do with the manuscript? If we don't find Gumerry and we're all on our own, d'you think it's safe to go on carrying it about?'

'A lot safer than I'd feel if we left it anywhere,' Simon said grimly, looking down at the case in his hand. 'I'm going to hang on to it whatever happens.'

'Oh well,' Barney said cheerfully. 'Don't drop it in the harbour, that's all. Cheerio. Shan't be long.'

'I'm glad he's so bright about it all,' Jane said, as the front door slammed. 'I wish I were. It's as if there's someone waiting behind every corner to pounce on us. I only feel safe when I'm in bed.'

'Cheer up,' said Simon. 'You're still suffering from last night. I was scared then too, but I'm not now. Try and forget about it.'

'That's all very well,' said poor Jane miserably, 'but everyone seems to be turning out to be bad now, and it isn't even as if we knew what sort of badness it is. Why do they all want the manuscript so much?'

'Well,' Simon wrinkled his forehead, trying to remember what Great-Uncle Merry had said on the first day, 'it's the grail they want, isn't it? Because it stands for something, somehow. And that's why Gumerry wants to find it as well. It's like two armies fighting in history. You're never quite sure what they're actually fighting about, but only that one wants to beat the other.'

'Great-Uncle Merry's like an army sometimes, all in one person. Those times when he goes all peculiar and distant and you feel he's not quite there.'

'Well, there you are, then. It's the same with the others. They're a kind of bad army. Up on the standing stones last night, even before we knew they were there, you could still feel the badness.'

'I know,' Jane said fervently. 'Oh dear, I should feel much better if we knew where Great-Uncle Merry was.'

'We shall know as soon as we find Mrs Palk. Buck up, Jane.' Simon patted her awkwardly on the shoulder. 'Come on, let's go down to the harbour. Barney'll get there before us at this rate.'

Jane nodded, feeling a little better. 'Oh – Mother and Father will be coming back this afternoon. D'you think we ought to leave a note?'

'No, we'll be back long before them.'

They went out of the Grey House, leaving it to its silence, and walked down the hill to the harbour. Unfamiliar children were running all over the place, ignoring their anxious calling parents; and the sleepy little shop which sold ice-cream down on the quay was festooned with flags and posters and doing a roaring trade.

Simon and Jane threaded their way along the side of the harbour, through the wandering crowds, to the course marked out for the swimming gala. But they felt as if they were paddling against a current; all the crowds were moving towards them, and when they reached the right place they found everything was over. Only a few boys and girls dodging wet through the crowds in swim-suits, and the bobbing lines of floats on the empty water, showed that there had been a swimming gala at all.

One of the swimmers brushed past Simon, and as he glanced up at the wet brown body he recognized the face below the dark water-flattened hair. It was Bill.

The boy's mouth opened and he paused belligerently; but then in an instant, changing his mind, he scowled and disappeared, running barefoot through the crowds towards the front quay.

'Hey, Jane! Jane!' Simon called urgently. She was a few paces ahead of him, and had not noticed Bill.

A deep voice said in Simon's ear, 'Your young friend lost un's race. He'm not in a very good temper. They Hoovers be all the same.'

Simon looked round, and saw the beaming wrinkled brown face of the old fisherman they had met on the day they first encountered the boy Bill.

'Hallo, Mr Penhallow,' he said, reflecting how odd the greeting sounded. 'Was he in the swimming gala, then?'

'Aye, that he were, the race for the championship. Be'aved 'isself badly as usual too, lost by a few yards and turned 'n's back on the winner when the lad went to thank'n for a good race.' He chuckled. 'The winner were my youngest.'

'Your son?' said Jane, who had turned back to Simon's call.

She looked at Mr Penhallow's weather-beaten face; he looked much too old to have a son young enough for a swimming race.

'A's right,' said the fisherman equably. 'Tough little lad. He'm sixteen now, on leave from the Merchant Navy.'

'I say,' said Simon, impressed. 'Could I join the Merchant Navy when I'm sixteen, d'you think?'

'You wait awhile,' said Mr Penhallow, twinkling at him. ''Tis a hard life at sea.'

'Barney says he wants to be a fisherman like you now,' Jane said. 'With a boat like the *White Heather*.'

Mr Penhallow laughed. 'That's an idea won't last long, neither. I'd take 'n out with us one night if he were a bit bigger, then he'd soon change his tune.'

'Are you going out tonight?'

'No. Havin' a rest.'

Jane, suddenly feeling one of her shoes damp, looked down and found she was standing in a pool of water. She moved hurriedly. 'Those swimmers must have splashed about a lot. There's puddles all along the quay.'

'Not just the swimming, my love,' Mr Penhallow said. ''Tis the tide. It came right over there this morning – spring tides be higher than usual this month.'

'Oh yes,' said Simon. 'Look – there are bits of seaweed right at the back of the path. It must have washed right up to the wall. Does it often come as high as that?'

'Not often. Once or twice a year, usually – March and September. 'Tis strange to have such big tides in August. I reckon 'tis because of these strong winds we been havin'.'

'How low will it go down?' Jane said, fascinated.

'Oh, a long way. Th'arbour don't look pretty at any low tide, but it do look worse at the biggest springs. Lot of stinkin' old mud and weed that 'ee don't normally see. You wait till about five o'clock today. Still, I dare say you'll be watching the carnival like everyone else then.'

'I expect so,' Simon said vaguely. He was thinking furiously; it was as if the fisherman's words had touched a spring in his brain. 'Mr Penhallow,' he said, carefully casual, 'I suppose when you get a really low tide like that there's a lot more rocks than usual uncovered outside the harbour?'

'Oh, a good old lot,' the fisherman said. 'They do say 'tis possible to walk all the way round from Trewissick harbour to the Dodman, that's two-three bays beyond Kemare Head. But that be nothing more'n a tale – I dare say the rocks be uncovered, but the tide'd be coming up again before you was half-way there.'

Jane was only half-listening. 'Mr Penhallow, we were looking for Mrs Palk, she's the lady who keeps house for us. Do you know her?'

'Know Molly Palk?' said Mr Penhallow, chuckling. 'I should say I do. Nice lass, she used to be – still is, but she turned a bit miserly when old Jim Palk died. Costing your mum and dad a pretty penny, I'll be bound. Do anything for a few extra pound, would old Moll. Now I come to think of it, course, she'm your young friend Bill's auntie, too.'

'Mrs Palk is?' Jane said amazed. 'That awful boy?'

'Ah,' Mr Penhallow said, placidly. 'The two sides of the family don't have much to do with each other mind. Most of Trewissick forgets they'm even related. Don't suppose Moll likes people to know.'

'I think Great-Uncle Merry told me once,' Simon said. 'I'd clean forgotten. He said Bill was Mrs Palk's no-good brother's son.'

Jane said thoughtfully: 'I wonder whether . . . Oh well, it doesn't matter now. Have you seen her anywhere about?'

'Let me see, now, I did pass the time of day with her. Oh ah, up on the front quay. She were all dressed up for the carnival, some funny affair on her head, helping with the procession, most like, I reckon you'll still find her up by there, unless she've popped in to have her dinner.'

The crowds had thinned round them now, milling about instead on the front quay, with here and there groups of bandsmen in bright blue uniform, clutching large curly silver instruments and wearing ill-fitting blue peaked caps. Simon and Jane peered across the harbour, but they were too far away to be able to distinguish faces.

'Well, I must be off to find my young Walter. Real cock-a-hoop he'll be. Remember me to our liddle fisherman, midears.' Mr Penhallow toddled off along the quay, grinning to himself. Jane, who had been wondering what it was about him that seemed different, realized for the first time that instead of the blue jersey and long thigh-boots he was in a stiff black suit, and shoes that squeaked.

'I don't think he should have talked like that about Mrs Palk,' she said, troubled.

'You don't know, it might be important,' Simon said. 'Anyway, what are we going to do now? We've got to find Mrs Palk to know where Great-Uncle Merry's gone. But Mr Penhallow says he saw her on the other side of the harbour, and we told Barney we'd meet him here.'

'I wonder where Barney is? He's surely had time to get up to the top of the road and back by now. Look, you go and see if Mrs Palk is over there, and I'll wait here till he comes.'

Simon rubbed his ear. 'I don't know, I don't like all this splitting up. We haven't got Great-Uncle Merry, we haven't got Barney for the moment, and if you and I split up, nobody will have anybody else at all. Any one of us could get nobbled and the others not know. I think we ought to keep together.'

'Well, all right,' Jane said. 'We'll wait a bit longer. Let's go back to the corner of the front quay and we can cut him off. That's the only way down here, he'll have to pass it.'

As they walked back they saw the Trewissick band forming up across the harbour, with the crowd bobbing and weaving round them and children darting excitedly to and fro on the edge. One or two strange figures stood out among the white shirts and summer dresses; tall, fantastically coloured, decked with ribbons and leaves, with monstrous false heads set on their shoulders.

'They must be part of the carnival procession.'

'I think it's starting. Listen, what a horrible noise.'

The band had begun a wavering brassy tune that resolved itself gradually into a recognizable march.

'Oh come on, it's not that bad,' Jane said. 'I expect they're more used to fishing than playing trumpets. Anyway, it's very cheerful-sounding. I like it.'

'Hmmf. Let's sit on the wall here at the corner, we can catch Barney when he passes.' Simon crossed into the road and looked up the hill. 'I can't see any sign of him. But there's so many people about it's difficult to see properly.'

'Oh well,' Jane hoisted herself up on to the wall, wincing as the rough slate rubbed the skin behind her knees. 'We'll just wait. Hey listen, the music's getting louder.'

'Music!' said Simon.

'Well, it is . . . Oh look, the procession's started! And they're coming this way!'

'I thought Mrs Palk said they would go straight up the hill.'

'Perhaps they go up from this corner of the harbour instead of the other. Or perhaps they go all round the village first . . . look, they're all dressed up. And they're playing that thing Mrs Palk was singing this morning, the "Floral Dance".'

'We've got a good view, anyway,' Simon hopped up to sit on the wall beside her.

Slowly the crowd drew near them along the front quay, children running and jumping about in front of the red-faced puffing band. Behind them, edged by delighted pushing throngs of visitors, came a dancing file of the fantastic figures they had seen from across the harbour, the monstrous heads lurching and hopping in a slow parody of dance, and others, masked and disguised, weaving in and out of the crowds. Here and there they swooped on the bystanders, taking pretty girls by the hand, pretending to strike squealing old ladies with a ribboned wand, guiding the visitors and villagers to join hands and dance with them in rows across the width of the street. 'Pom . . . pom . . . di-pom-pom-pom . . .' the music boomed in the children's ears where they sat on the wall, and the crowds eddied all round them on the corner, overflowing up the hill as well as down.

Jane, beaming round her in delight at the tops of the giant grinning heads, suddenly stared across the crowd. She pointed, and shouted something in Simon's ear.

Simon could hear nothing but the music, thrumming round him till the wall seemed to shake. 'What?' he shouted back.

Jane ducked her head close to his ear. 'There's Mrs Palk! Look! Just over there, with feathers on her head, behind the man covered in leaves. Quickly, let's catch her!' And before Simon could stop her she had slipped down from the wall and was on the edge of the crowd.

Simon jumped down after her and caught at her arm just as she was about to push her way across the crowd between two dancing, laughing files. 'Not now, Jane!' But he too was swept along for several yards by the dancing crowd before he could draw her back into a clear space. They stood pinned against the far wall of the road, away from the harbour, hemmed in by others standing watching the carnival procession dance by.

And that was why they did not see Barney, who had been threading his way down the hill-road past the Grey House, dodge between people's legs to slip round the corner of the wall, ignoring the procession; and run as fast as he could along the inner quay to the place where they had agreed to meet.

Chapter Twelve

It took Barney a long time to make his way down the hill past the house. There had been no sign of Great-Uncle Merry on the headland. On the road, knots of wandering people were scattered maddeningly about in his path, and three times he had to stand aside as a car came grinding up the steep narrow slope. Barney dodged impatiently to and fro, in and out, with Rufus at his heels.

Half-way down the hill he heard music from the other side of the harbour, and through the heads he caught sight of the dancing procession moving forward along the quay. Slipping his finger inside Rufus's collar, he side-stepped through the thickening crowd and down the hill as fast as he could, darting through every visible gap like a shrimp in a pool.

But when he reached the corner of the harbour the procession was upon him, and he could see nothing at all but an impenetrable wall of legs and backs. He wriggled through behind them, the din of the music thumping in his ears, until he was out of the crowd at last and on the quay. With a sigh of relief he let go of Rufus's collar, and ran with him towards the deserted corner where he had arranged to meet Simon and Jane.

There was nobody there.

Barney looked round wildly. He could see nothing to give him the slightest hint of where the others had gone. Reasoning with himself, he decided they must have caught sight of Mrs Palk. She had been very keen on the idea of the carnival and the dancing; she must be in the procession. And it had been Simon's and Jane's job to go and find her, as it had been his to go and scout on the headland. They must have gone chasing her, knowing that he would guess where they had gone.

Satisfied, Barney went off to find the carnival. He followed the last of the crowd still drifting up the road. Even down in the sheltered harbour the wind was blowing in from the sea, but now and again it dropped for a moment, and Barney heard a tantalizing snatch of music come wafting over the roofs from somewhere in the village. 'Pom . . . pom . . . di-pom-pom-pom . . .' All round him people were wandering aimlessly about, idly talking . . . 'Where've they gone?' . . . 'We can meet them at the ground' . . . 'But they dance through the streets for ages yet' . . . 'Oh, come *on*.'

Disregarding them, Barney set off down a little side turning, with Rufus still loping patiently at his heels. He wandered from one winding lane to another, down narrow passages where the slate roofs almost touched overhead, past neat front doors with their brass knockers gleaming golden in the sun, through cobbled alleys where front doors opened not on to a pavement but straight on to the street. For a small place, Trewissick seemed to be an extraordinary endless maze of winding little roads. Straining his ears all the time, Barney followed the sound of the music through the maze.

He made one or two false turns, losing the sound. Then gradually the band grew louder, and with it he began to hear the hum of voices and the rasping shuffle of feet. He snapped his fingers to Rufus, and broke into a trot, swinging from one quiet deserted little alley into the next. And then suddenly the noise burst on him like a storm, and he was out of the muffling narrow street and among the crowds, out in the sunshine filling a broad road where the procession jogged and danced by. 'Come on, my white-headed boy,' someone called to him, and the people near by turned and laughed.

Barney could not see Simon and Jane amongst the dancers, and there seemed little chance of being able to get to them even if he did. He gazed fascinated round him at the bobbing giant heads, the bodies beneath them fantastic and gay in doublets and red, yellow, blue hose. Everywhere he saw costumed figures: a man dancing stiff as a tree, a solid flapping mass of green leaves, pirates, sailors, a hussar in bright red with a tall cap. Slave-girls, jesters, a man in a long blue silk gown made up as a pantomime dame; a girl all in black, twirling sinuous as a cat, with a cat's bewhiskered head. Little boys in green as Robin Hood, little girls with long fair hair as Alice; highwaymen, morris-men, flower-sellers, gnomes.

It was like nothing he had ever seen before. The dancers whirled in and out of the crowd on the edge of the street where he stood; and then suddenly, before Barney knew what was happening they were dancing round him.

He felt someone catch at his hand, and he was drawn out into the centre of the dancing crowd, among the ribbons and feathers and bright bobbing heads, so that his feet fell into step with the rest.

Breathless, grinning, he glanced up. The black-gloved hand holding one of his own belonged to the figure of the cat, twirling in the skin-close black tights with a long black tail swinging out behind, and whiskers bristling long and straight from the headmask fitting over the cheeks. He saw the eyes glint through the slits, and the teeth flash. For a moment, among the dancing figures all round, he saw close to him one in a great feathered Red Indian head-dress, with a face startlingly like Mrs Palk's. But as he opened his mouth to call, the black cat seized both his hands and wheeled him round and round in a dizzy spiral through the ranks of the crowd. People glanced down at him and smiled as he passed, and Barney, giddy with the music and the speed and the twisting black limbs of the cat before his eyes, flung himself laughing round where it swung him . . .

. . . Until he came up with a sudden halt against the long white robes of a figure dressed as an Arab sheikh, moving with the rest so that the robes were swung wide and billowing by the breeze. And glancing up through a world swaying with his own giddiness, Barney had time only to glimpse a slim figure and a dark-skinned lean face, before the cat swung him by the hands straight into the out-swung muffling folds of the man's white robes.

The robe twisted round him as he staggered, still laughing, in the sudden gloom. And then, so quickly that he had no time even to feel alarmed, the man's arm came round him like an iron band and lifted him from the ground, and the other hand muffled his mouth in the folds of the cloth, and Barney felt himself being carried away.

Before he could struggle, he was swung in a scuffling moment through the roaring music and the crowd. Pushing ineffectually against the man's chest, he felt him run a few steps and heard the noise of the voices and the band suddenly grow fainter. He kicked out blindly and felt his toes hit the man's shins. But he was only wearing sandals, and could do no great harm: the man gave a muffled curse but did not pause, jolting him along for a few more steps until Barney felt himself swung higher into the air and dropped on to a padded seat that protested with the noise of springs.

The robe fell loose from his mouth. He yelled, and went on yelling until a hand came back and pressed hard against his face.

A girl's voice said urgently: 'Quickly! Get him away!'

A voice almost as light as a girl's but masculine, said curtly: 'Get in. You'll have to drive.'

Barney suddenly lay quite still, all his senses alerted. There was something familiar about the second voice. He felt a coldness at the back of his neck. Then the pressure of the hand over his mouth relaxed a little through the cotton folds, and the voice said softly, close to his ear, 'Don't make a noise, Barnabas, and don't move, and nobody will be hurt.'

And suddenly Barney knew the black-masked figure of the cat, and the dark man in sheikh's robes. He felt the seat judder slightly as the noise of a powerful car's engine coughed and then rose in a throbbing howl. Then the note deepened, and he felt a lurch, and knew that he was being driven away.

Rufus jumped nervously back from the shuffling, dancing feet that had enclosed Barney in the crowd. Tentatively he put his nose forward to follow, once, twice, but always a heel came up in the way with an accidental kick, and he had to dodge away.

From a safer distance, he barked, loudly. But the sound was lost at once in the booming music and the clamour of the crowd. Alarmed by the shattering noise and bustle suddenly filling his small world, he put his ears back flat against the side of his head; his tail was down between his legs, and he showed the whites of his eyes.

He retreated further from the noise, waiting hopefully on the corner of the street for Barney to reappear. But there was no sign of him. Rufus moved uneasily.

Then as the band drew directly opposite, blowing and banging only a few yards away, rocking every corner with the rise and fall of music that to a dog's ears was a menacing roaring noise, Rufus could suddenly stand it no longer. He gave up all hope of Barney, and turning his back on the clamour of the carnival, he padded away down the alley with the tip of his tail sweeping the ground and his nose lowered, sniffing his way home.

Simon and Jane rejoined one another at the corner of the harbour, quiet again now in the sunny afternoon.

'Well, I've been back to where we said. He isn't there.'

'I had a good look in the house. He hasn't been there either.'

'D'you think he could have gone off after Mrs Palk?'

'I keep telling you, it couldn't have been Mrs Palk you saw.'

'I don't see why not. If only you hadn't stopped me I could have grabbed her.'

'How could we meet Barney here if you –' Simon began.

'Oh all right, all right. But we haven't met him.'

'Well then, he can't have come down from the headland yet.'

Jane's expression changed. 'Oh dear. Perhaps he's got into trouble up there.'

'No, no, don't worry when we don't need to. More likely he's found Great-Uncle Merry after all and they're both up there still.'

'Well, come on then, let's go and look.'

The car swayed and growled as if it were alive. Barney lay wrapped up like a parcel in the robe which Mr Withers had slipped from his own shoulders as he dropped him in the car. He decided that it must be a sheet; the smell of it under his nose was like clean laundry on the beds at home. But he wasn't at home. He muttered peevishly under his breath, and kicked at the side of the car.

'Now, now,' said Mr Withers. He took hold of Barney's legs and swung him none too gently round into a sitting position, at the same time pulling the sheet clear of his face. 'I think perhaps we might let you emerge now, Barnabas.'

Barney blinked, dazzled by the sudden sunlight. Before he could open his eyes properly to look at the road the car swung squealing through a gap in a high wall, and slowed down, its wheels crunching on gravel, along a tree-lined drive.

'Nearly there,' Mr Withers said placidly.

Barney twisted his head to glare up at him. He could still barely recognize Mr Withers's face through the dark-brown stain that turned him into an Arab; the eyes and teeth glinted unnaturally white, and behind the make-up the man seemed withdrawn and pleased with himself, almost arrogant.

'Where are we? Where are you taking me?'

'Don't you know? Ah no' – the dark head nodded wisely – 'of course, you would not. Well, you will know soon, Barnabas.'

'What do you want?' Barney demanded.

'Want? Nothing, my dear boy. We're just taking you for a little ride, to meet a friend of ours. I think you'll get on very well together.'

Barney saw, through the trees, that they were coming to a house. He looked down at the sheet still twined round him, and wriggled to move his arms free. Mr Withers turned quickly.

'Take this stupid thing off me. I feel silly.'

'Just a little joke of ours,' Mr Withers said. 'Where's your sense of humour, Barnabas? I thought you were enjoying yourself.'

He leaned over and began pulling the sheet free as the car drew up outside the peeling front door of a big, deserted-looking house. 'You'll have to hop out, if you can. I can't loosen it properly in here.' He spoke casually, easily, with no trace of menace in his voice, and as Barney glanced up at him suspiciously the white teeth shone briefly again in a smile.

The girl slipped out of the driving seat, moving like a snake in her black tights, and came round to open the door at Barney's side. She helped him out, and spun him round to pull the sheet away. Barney staggered, his arms and legs so stiff with cramp that he could hardly move.

Polly Withers laughed. Her head was still a fantastic sight in the close-fitting black cat's mask, covering all her face but the eyes and mouth. 'I'm sorry, Barney,' she said companionably. 'We did overdo it a bit, didn't we? You danced jolly well, I thought, I was almost sorry to stop. Still, never mind, now we'll go and have some tea, if it isn't too early for you.'

'I haven't had any lunch,' Barney said irrelevantly, suddenly remembering.

'Well, in that case we must certainly get you something to eat. Good gracious, no lunch? And it's all our fault, I expect. Norman, ring the bell, we must feed the poor boy.'

Mr Withers, making a concerned clicking noise with his tongue, crossed from the car and pressed the bell next to the big door. He was all in white still, but in shirt-sleeves and white flannels without his Arab robe. His bare arms were stained the same dark-brown as his face.

Barney, following him slowly with the girl's hand resting lightly on his shoulder, was puzzled by their friendliness. He began to wonder whether he had been seeing everything in the wrong light. Perhaps this was after all only a joke, part of the fun of carnival day. Perhaps the Witherses were perfectly ordinary people after all ... they had never actually done anything to prove beyond doubt that they were the enemy ... perhaps he and Simon and Jane had got things all wrong ...

Then he heard footsteps echoing faintly within the house, clumping gradually nearer, and the door was opened. At first he did not recognize the figure in tight black jeans and a green shirt. Then he saw that it was the boy Bill Hoover, who had chased Simon for the map. And in a moment he remembered the scene on Kemare Head that day, and the greed on Miss Withers's face when she had looked at the map, and he knew that they had not been wrong after all.

Bill's face lit up out of its down-turned sullenness as he saw Barney, and he grinned across at Miss Withers.

'You got'n, then?' he said.

Mr Withers cut in quickly, stepping forward and almost pushing the boy out of the way. 'Hallo, Bill,' he said smoothly, 'we've brought a young friend of ours on a visit. I don't think anyone will mind. We could all do with something to eat, run and see if you can manage to rustle anything up, will you?'

'Mind?' the boy said, 'I should say not.' He looked at Barney again with the same eager, unpleasant grin, then turned and disappeared down the long corridor, calling something into an open doorway as he passed.

'Come along in, Barney,' the girl said. She propelled him gently through the door and shut it behind her. Barney looked round him in the long empty passage, at the marks of damp on the fading wallpaper; and he felt very small and lonely. He heard a deep voice call from somewhere inside the house: 'Withers? Is that you?'

Mr Withers, who had been standing surveying Barney with a slight smile, jumped and put his hand half-consciously up to his collar. 'Come,' he said curtly. He took Barney by the hand and led him down the corridor, their footsteps echoing on the uncarpeted wooden floor, to the doorway of a room at the far end.

It was a big room, dark after the blazing sunlight outside. Long windows stretched from the floor to ceiling in one wall, with long shabby velvet curtains half pulled across, and the light that shafted in between them fell on a big, square desk in the centre of the room, its top littered with papers and books.

The room seemed empty. Then Barney jumped as he saw a tall man move in the shadow beyond the sunlight.

'Ah,' said the deep voice, 'I see you have brought the youngest of them. The white-haired child. I am most interested to make his acquaintance. How do you do, Barnabas?'

He held out his hand, and Barney, bemused, took it. The voice was not unpleasant, and rather kind.

'How do you do?' he said faintly.

He looked up at the tall man, but in the half-light he had only a vague impression of deep-shadowed eyes under dark, heavy brows, and a clean-shaven face. The smooth edge of a silk jacket brushed his hand.

'I was about to have a cool drink, Barnabas,' the man said, as courteously as if he were talking to someone older than himself. 'Will you join me?' He waved his hand towards the shadows, and Barney saw the glint of silver and a white cloth on a low table beside the desk.

'The boy has had nothing to eat, sir,' Miss Withers said behind Barney, in a peculiarly hushed, reverent voice. 'We thought perhaps Bill could fetch something...' Her voice died away. The man looked at her, and grunted.

'Very well, very well. Polly, for goodness' sake go and change into some normal clothes. You look ridiculous. The necessity for fancy dress is over, you are not at the carnival now.' He spoke sharply, and Barney was astonished at the meekness with which Miss Withers answered him.

'Yes, sir, of course...' She slipped away into the passage, sleek and inhuman in the black cat's skin.

'Come in, my boy, and sit down.' He spoke softly again, and Barney came slowly forward into the room and sat down in an armchair. It creaked with the crackling rustle of wickerwork, and he suddenly felt for an instant that he had been in the room before. He glanced round, his eyes growing accustomed to the dim light, at the dark walls and the shelves of books rising to the ceiling. There was something... but he could not place it. Perhaps it was just that the room reminded him a little of the Grey House.

As if he read his thoughts, the man said: 'I hear you are on holiday in the Grey House, above the harbour.'

Barney said, surprised at his own daring, 'It must be a very interesting house. That seems to be the only thing anyone ever says to us.'

The man leant forward, resting his hand on the edge of the desk. 'Oh?' The deep voice rose a little with eagerness. 'Who else has asked you about it?'

'Oh, no one important,' Barney said hastily. 'After all, it's a nice house. Do you live here, Mr – ?'

'My name is Hastings,' the big man said, and at the sound of the name

Barney again felt the flicker of familiarity, vanishing as soon as it came. 'Yes, I do. This is my house. Do you like it, Barnabas?'

'It's rather like the Grey House, as a matter of fact,' Barney said.

The man turned back towards him again. 'Indeed? Now what makes you say that?'

'Well –' Barney began; but then the door opened again and the boy Bill came in carrying an enormous tray with a big jug of milk and some bottles of lager, glasses, and a plate piled with sandwiches. He crossed the room to where the tall man stood and put the tray down on the desk; nervously, just within reach, as if he were frightened to come too near. 'Mis' Withers said for someth'n to eat, sir,' he said, gruffly, already backing towards the door. The man waved him away without speaking.

The sight of the sandwiches made Barney realize how long it was since breakfast, and he felt more cheerful. He sat back in the creaking chair and glanced round him. It could have been worse, he thought. The mysterious Mr Hastings seemed to mean him no harm, and he was beginning to enjoy the sight of all their enemies cringing in terror before someone else. He took a sandwich from the plate held out to him and bit into it cheerfully. The bread was soft and new, with plenty of butter, and in the middle there was some delicious kind of potted meat. He began to feel better still.

Mr Withers moved silently across to the desk and poured him out a glass of milk, then began opening the bottles of lager. The big man called Hastings sat down in the chair behind the desk and swung gently from side to side, regarding Barney thoughtfully from beneath his heavy brows. He said softly, conversationally, 'Is it buried under the Grey House, Barnabas, or one of the standing stones?'

Half-way through a gulp of milk, Barney suddenly choked. He groped for the desk and put his glass down with a bang, and leaned forward, coughing and spluttering. Mr Withers, soft-footed, crossed to pat him on the back. 'Dear me, Barnabas,' he murmured, 'has something gone down the wrong way?'

Barney, his mind working furiously, went on coughing for rather longer than he needed to. When he looked up he took refuge instinctively in innocence. 'I'm sorry, I caught my breath,' he said. 'Did you say something?'

'I think you heard perfectly well what I said,' Mr Hastings said. He stood up again, towering very tall over Barney in the low chair, and walked over to the window with a glass of lager in his hand. The light fell on his face for the first time, and watching, Barney felt a slight chill of uneasiness at the flat permanent scowl of the brows and the grim lines running down to the mouth. It was a strong, far-away face, something like his great-uncle's, but with a frightening coldness behind it that was not like Great-Uncle Merry at all.

Barney found himself wishing very much that there was somebody to tell Great-Uncle Merry where he had gone.

Mr Hastings held up his glass to the window. The sunlight shone through it clear and golden. 'An ordinary glass of beer,' he said, abstractedly, 'until you hold it against the light. And then it becomes quite transparent, you can see right through it . . .' He swung round on Barney so that he was silhouetted dark and menacing against the window again. '. . . As transparent as every single thing that you children have been doing, these past days. Do you think we have not seen through it all? Do you think we have not been watching?'

'I don't know what you mean,' Barney said.

'You may be a stupid little boy,' Mr Hastings said, 'but not I think as stupid as all that . . . come along. We know that you have found a map, and that with the help of your esteemed great-uncle, Professor Lyon'– his mouth twisted on the words as if he were tasting something unpleasant – 'you have been attempting to trace the place to which it leads. We know that you have come very near the end of that track. And since, my dear Barnabas, we cannot afford to risk your reaching the end of it, we have decided at last to draw in the net and put a stop to your little quest. That is what you are doing here.'

Barney shivered at the menace in the cold deep voice. His mouth felt very dry. He reached forward and picked up the glass of milk again, and took a long drink. 'I'm sorry,' he said blinking wide-eyed at Mr Hastings over the rim of the glass and licking a moustache of milk away from his upper lip. 'I don't know what you mean. Could I have another sandwich, please?'

Behind him he heard Mr Withers's sharp intake of breath, and for a second a very small voice deep inside his brain crowed with triumph. But he watched the tall figure by the window apprehensively. It seemed to grow for a moment and loom still more menacingly over him. And then it moved abruptly, back into the dim shadow of the rest of the room.

'Give him another sandwich,' Mr Hastings said. 'And then you can go, Withers. You know what you have to do. We haven't much time. Come back when I ring.'

Mr Withers, his dark-stained face scarcely visible in the gloom, pushed the plate of sandwiches across to Barney's elbow. He said obsequiously, 'Yes, sir,' and ducking his head in a bow he went out of the room.

Barney took another sandwich, feeling fatalistically that whatever was likely to happen, he might as well eat. 'Why do they all call you sir?' he said curiously.

The tall man came and sat down at the desk again, playing with a pencil between his fingers. 'Who is there that you would call sir?'

'Well, nobody really. Only the masters at school.'

'Perhaps I am one of their masters,' Mr Hastings said.

'But they aren't at school.'

'I think you would not really understand, Barnabas. In fact there are a great many things that you do not understand. I wonder what stories that great-uncle of yours has put into your head. He has told you that we are bad and wicked, no doubt, and that he is a good man?'

Barney blinked at him, and took another bite of his sandwich.

Mr Hastings smiled grimly. 'Ah, but of course you do not know what I am talking about. You haven't the slightest idea.' The heavy irony in the deep voice made Barney wrinkle his nose. 'Well, let us forget that, just for a moment, and pretend, just pretend, that you do know what I mean. You have been led to believe, I think, that my friends and I are everything that is evil. That we want to follow up the clues in the map because we can do bad things with what we find. You have nothing to go on but your great-uncle's word, and perhaps one or two strange things that Polly or Norman Withers may seem to have done.'

The voice dropped until it was silky and very gentle. 'But just think, Barnabas, of the strange things your great-uncle does. Coming out of nowhere and vanishing again . . . he has vanished again today, has he not? Well no, of course, you can't answer me, because we are only pretending that you know what I am talking about. But this is not the first time he has unexpectedly disappeared, I think, and it will not be the last.'

He stared at Barney, dark eyes penetrating and level from beneath the overhanging brow. Barney ate his sandwich a little more slowly, unable to take his own gaze away. 'As for our being evil . . . well, now, Barnabas, do I strike you as being a bad man? Have I done you any harm? There you sit, eating and drinking quite happily, certainly not looking alarmed. Are you frightened of me?'

'You had me kidnapped,' Barney said flatly.

'Oh come now, that was just a little joke of Polly's. I wanted to talk to you, that's all.'

Mr Hastings sat back in his chair and spread his arms wide, with the tips of his fingers just touching the edge of the desk. 'Now look, my boy, I will make a bargain with you. I will tell you what is actually behind everything that has been going on these last days, and you will stop playing this game of not having seen the map.'

He did not wait for Barney to say anything. 'We are indeed hunting the same thing that your great-uncle is hunting, my friends and I. But whatever story he has spun you about us is, quite frankly, a lot of moonshine. Your great-uncle is a scholar, and an outstanding one. Nobody would dispute that, and I probably know it better than you. The trouble is that he himself knows it, and thinks about it much too much.'

'What d'you mean?' said Barney indignantly.

'When a man is famous for being a very great scholar he wants very much to go on being famous. You found this old manuscript, you and your brother and sister, and when you told your great-uncle about it he realized, as you did not, how important it was. When he saw it he was even more certain. Now I, Barnabas, am the curator, that means the director, of one of the most important museums in the world. I have been hunting the manuscript that you found, and especially what it leads to, for a very long time. They are both very important to the people who study such things, and could make a lot of difference to the total knowledge there is in the world. And your great-uncle knew that I was hunting them.

'But when you found the manuscript he saw that he had a chance of achieving the quest himself. The more he thought about this, the more attractive an idea it seemed. He has always been famous as a man who knows a great deal about the part of history these things are connected with. If he were to find them, he would know more than anyone else in the world. People would say, what an amazing man Professor Lyon is, to know so much, there's no one like him anywhere . . .'

'To know *how* much?' Barney said.

'You would not understand the details,' Mr Hastings said shortly. Then his voice dropped again to the same deep persuasive note. 'Don't you see, Barnabas? Your great-uncle is concerned only with his own fame. Do you think for one moment that when you have ended the hunt, any of the credit will go to you children? It will all go to him . . . Whereas I and my museum, and the people I employ, believe that all knowledge should be shared, and that no one man has the right to it alone. And if you were to help us, we should take care that you had whatever credit was due to you. The whole world should know what you had done.'

In spite of himself Barney had forgotten his sandwich and milk. He sat listening, troubled; trying to understand the truth for himself. Yes, Great-Uncle Merry was strange, often, not like other men; but all the same . . .

He said, slow and perplexed, 'Well, I don't know – all this just doesn't sound like Great-Uncle Merry. Surely he couldn't do anything like that?'

'But I assure you –' Mr Hastings jumped to his feet and began walking to and fro between the desk and the door. He seemed unable to keep still any longer. 'Many people one knows well, often most excellent people, can prove capable of the most curious acts. I do realize that you may be surprised, and shocked.

But this is the truth, Barnabas, and it is very much more simple than you have been led to believe.'

Barney said : 'So we ought to give the map to you, and let you find the –' Just in time he caught the word 'grail'. Through the whole conversation there had been no mention of what the map led to. Perhaps they knew less than they said they did. Perhaps that was one of the things they wanted to trap him into telling them.

Mr Hastings paused for a second. 'Yes?' he said.

'Well, and let you find whatever it leads to.'

Barney picked up his glass of milk again and drank reflectively. 'Because then you would put whatever it is in your museum and everyone would be able to know about it.'

Mr Hastings nodded gravely. 'There you have it, Barnabas. All knowledge is sacred, but it should not be secret. I think you understand. This is something you should do – that *we* should do – in the name of scholarship.'

Barney looked down into his milk, swishing it gently round the glass. 'But isn't that what Great-Uncle Merry's doing?'

'No, no!' Mr Hastings swung impatiently on his heel, striding impatient and very tall up and down the room. 'Whatever he does he is doing in the name of Professor Lyon, and that is all. What else would he do anything for?'

Barney never knew afterwards what put the words into his head; he spoke before he thought, almost as if someone else were speaking through him. He heard himself saying clearly, 'In the name of King Arthur, and of the old world before the dark came.'

The tall dark figure stopped abruptly, completely still, with its back still turned. For a moment there was absolute silence in the room. It was as if Barney had pressed a switch that would any moment bring an avalanche thundering down. He sat motionless and almost breathless in his chair. Then very slowly the figure turned. Barney gulped, and felt a prickling at the roots of his hair. Mr Hastings was at the darker end of the room, near the door, and his face was hidden in shadow. But he seemed to loom taller and more threatening than he had ever done before, and when he spoke there was a different throb in the deep voice that paralysed Barney with fright.

'You will find, Barnabas Drew,' it said softly, 'that the dark will always come, and always win.'

Barney said nothing. He felt as if he had forgotten how to speak, and his voice had died for ever with his last words.

Mr Hastings did not take his eyes off him. He reached out beside him and tugged twice at a cord hanging down from the ceiling beside the door. Within seconds the door swung open and Mr Withers slipped noiselessly inside. He had washed the dark-brown stain from his arms and face.

'Is everything ready?' said the deep voice.

'Yes, sir,' Mr Withers hissed obsequiously. 'The car is at the side door. The girl has changed. She will drive again.'

'You will drive with her. I shall follow in the closed car with the boy. Bill has it ready?'

'The engine is running already . . .'

'Where are you taking me?' Barney's voice rose shrill in fright, and he jumped down from his chair. But he could not run out of the room, past the tall figure that still held his gaze.

'You are coming with us to the sea,' said the voice behind the dark intent eyes. 'You will cause no trouble, and you will do whatever I say. And when we are on the sea, Barnabas, you are going to tell us about your map, and show us where it leads.'

Chapter Thirteen

The Grey House was as calm and empty as it had been when they left. 'Barney!' Simon shouted up the stairs. 'Barney?' His voice dwindled away uncertainly.

'He can't be inside,' Jane said. 'The key was still in its hiding-place. Oh Simon, what can have happened to him?' She turned back anxiously to the open front door, and stared down the hill.

Simon came back down the dark, shadowy hall to join her in the pool of sunlight. 'He must have missed us in the harbour.'

'But surely he'd have come back here after that? There isn't a soul about down there now, they've all gone after the band. That awful Bill passed us – you don't think –'

'No,' Simon said hastily. 'Anyway Barney's got Rufus with him. He can't get into much trouble. You wait, he'll be back soon. I expect he's found Gumerry and they're looking for us.'

He was turning back into the house when Jane suddenly shouted joyfully: 'Look! You're right!'

Rufus was loping up the hill towards them, a swift streak of red on the grey road. But they could see no one behind him. Jane called, and he raised his muzzle and trotted more quickly up the steps, between their legs and into the house. Then he stood facing them, his long ribbon of a tongue dangling over his jaws. But his tail was down, and there was none of the bouncing, barking delight with which he usually came home.

'No sign of Barney.' Jane came slowly in from the doorstep. She looked down at Rufus. 'What is it, then? What's happened?'

The dog took no notice of her. He stood there apathetically, his eyes blank. Even when they had given him a drink of water and taken him into the room overlooking the harbour, he still gave no sign that he knew he was home. It was as if he were thinking of something quite different.

'I expect it's the heat,' Simon said. He sounded unconvinced. 'Come on, there's nothing we can do except wait. The yacht's still down in the harbour, anyway.'

'That doesn't mean anything,' Jane said miserably.

'Well, it does mean –' But Simon had no chance to explain. Jane had clutched his arm nervously. He saw that she was staring at Rufus.

They could never explain it afterwards. It was as if Rufus had been lying there listening for something, and had at last caught the thing he was waiting for; though they knew that they had heard no sound at all. He raised his head, his eyes so wide open that the whites were showing, and stood up slowly in a way more like an old man than a dog. His ears were pricked and his muzzle raised high, pointing straight at something they could not see. He began to walk, very slowly and deliberately, towards the door.

Mesmerized, Simon and Jane followed. Rufus went out into the hall until he reached the front door, and stood waiting. He did not turn his head. He simply stood there rigid, looking ahead at the door, as if quite certain that they knew what he wanted them to do.

Simon reached forward, glancing nervously down at the long, straight red back, and opened the door; and they stood on the step watching in complete bewilderment as Rufus stalked with the same ageless confidence straight ahead across the road. When he reached the other side he leapt up with a quick light flurry to stand erect on the wall which kept the road from the sheer sixty-foot drop down to the harbour side. He seemed to be looking out at the sea.

'He's not going to jump?' Jane jerked in alarm, but found that she was whispering.

And then they heard the noise that they never afterwards forgot.

*

Barney knew, dimly, that he had been taken out of the big silent house and driven away in a car; and that now they were walking in a group with the noise of the sea somewhere near. But he was not certain how many of them there were, or where they were taking him. Since the moment in the shadowy room when those blazing dark eyes had glared into his face, he had been conscious of nothing except that he was to do what he was told. He no longer had any thoughts of his own; it was a strange, relaxed feeling, as if he were comfortably half asleep. There could be no argument now. No fighting. He knew only that the tall dark figure walking at his side, wearing a wide-brimmed black hat, was his master.

Master . . . who else had used the word that day?

'Come, Barnabas,' said the deep voice above him. 'We must hurry. The tide is going out, we must reach the yacht.'

Reach the yacht, said Barney dreamily to himself, we're going on the sea . . . that was the sea he could smell, the water lapping beside them at the edge of Trewissick harbour.

Far away, as if it came from a great height, he heard Polly Withers's voice say urgently: 'Anyone could see us from the road up by the house. They'll see us, I know they will –'

'Polly,' said the deep slow voice, 'I am the one who sees. If our old Cornish friend has done her work well, there will be no one there. And if the other two children have been let slip . . . well, are they a match for us?'

Somewhere Mr Withers laughed, soft and sinister.

Barney walked on, like a machine. The air was warm and thick; he could feel the sun fierce on his face. He had heard them talking ever since they left the house, but nothing they said seemed to have meaning for him any more. He was not frightened; he had forgotten Simon and Jane. He was somehow floating outside himself, watching with mild interest while his body walked along, but feeling nothing at all.

And then, like the sudden snapping of a bow, the noise came.

Into the air over their heads, a dog howled: a long weird note so unexpected and anguished that for a moment they all stopped dead. It echoed slow through the harbour, a freezing inhuman wail that had in it all the warning and terror that ever was in the world. Even Mr Hastings stood listening, paralysed.

And the Barney who was outside Barney, floating half detached in the air, felt the noise wake him up with a savage jolt. He looked up, and saw Rufus standing above him, outlined red against the sky, with the sound still throbbing from his throat. And suddenly he knew where he was, and that he must get away.

He swung round on his heel, ducked under the arms that grabbed too late to catch him, and raced along the quay towards the road. The hill was empty, drained of people by the carnival procession, and he was twenty-five yards clear of the confused group on the quay before they could properly begin to give chase. He heard the shouts and pounding feet behind him, and flung himself up the hill towards the Grey House.

Simon and Jane stared in amazement from the steps. Suddenly there had been Rufus's blood-chilling howl; now suddenly Barney, with four threatening figures at his heels. They ran instinctively down the steps towards him, and then swung back in alarm at the worst sound of all. Behind them, the door of the Grey House had slammed; and the key was inside.

Barney staggered up to them, and Rufus came bounding down from the wall. Jane said, panic-stricken: 'Which way?'

Simon turned frantically to the great wooden door in the wall which was the Grey House's side entrance; often it was kept locked. He pressed the latch, his heart thumping. Relief flooded over him in a wave as the door opened, and he pushed it wide. 'Quick!' he yelled.

The four figures pounding grim and intent at Barney's heels were only a few steps behind. Jane and Barney shot inside the door, with Rufus a swift red flurry among their feet. The wall itself seemed to shake as Simon slammed the door shut and hurriedly pushed home the three big iron bolts. They ran up the cold, narrow alley between the side of the Grey House and the house next door, and paused at the far end. Outside, footsteps skidded up to the door. They saw the latch rise as someone on the other side pressed it. It rattled angrily, and there was a thump against the door. Then there was silence.

'Suppose they climb over the wall?' Jane whispered fearfully.

'They couldn't possibly,' Simon whispered back. 'It's too high.'

'Perhaps they'll break the door down!'

'Those bolts are jolly strong. Anyway people would see them and get suspicious . . . Listen. They've gone away.'

They all strained their ears. There was no sound from the door at the other end of the alley. Rufus looked up at them inquiringly and whined, whistling plaintively through his nose.

'What are they doing? They must be up to something . . .'

'Quick!' Simon said decisively. 'We've got to get away from the house before they have time to get round the back. They'll have it surrounded soon.'

In panic they ran into the little back garden, and up through the knee-high grass to the hedge at the top. Rufus bounded round them cheerfully, jumping to lick Barney's face. He seemed to have forgotten the uncanny impulse that had made him utter that one long, lost howl, and now he was behaving as if everything were just a great game.

'I hope that dog's going to keep quiet,' Jane said anxiously.

Simon peered through the gap in the hedge.

'He will,' Barney said. He bent down and cupped one hand gently over Rufus's long red muzzle, murmuring to him under his breath.

Simon straightened. 'It's all clear. Come on.'

One by one they slipped out of the garden into the road that curved round behind the houses from the harbour, along the edge of Kemare Head.

'Oh,' Jane said in sudden anguish, 'if *only* we knew where Gumerry had gone.'

Barney said, horrified, 'Didn't you find him? What about Mrs Palk?'

'No, we didn't find him. We did see Mrs Palk, but we couldn't get to her through the crowd. Didn't you see him? Why were they chasing you? Where did you come from? We thought something awful must have happened when Rufus came back on his own, but we didn't know where to look for you.'

'Wait a minute,' Barney said. The shock of waking from his bewitched daze was turning into an enormous sense of urgency. A dozen things that he had heard in the last hour were dodging about in his mind; and as he began to see their meaning he was feeling more and more alarmed.

'Simon,' he said earnestly, 'we've got to get the grail. *Now*. Even without Great-Uncle Merry. There isn't time to look for him, or wait, or anything. I think they're very nearly on to it. Only not quite, that's why they wanted me.'

'First thing is to get away from here.' Simon looked about him wildly. 'They could come up either way from the harbour. We'll have to get off the road and hide in that field at the back of the headland. The land doesn't slope there, we ought to be able to keep hidden.'

They crossed the road and came out into the fields at the bottom of Kemare Head. The sun blazed high up in the sky still, beating down with a heat that pressed on them like a giant hand. But not even Jane was worrying about the chances of sunstroke now.

As they reached the hedge on the far side of the first field, they heard voices. They scrambled hastily through the hedge, without pausing to look round, and flattened themselves in the long grass on the other side. Barney slid his arm apprehensively over Rufus's back, but the dog lay quiet, with his long pink tongue lolling out.

Nobody saw quite where they came from, but suddenly the figures were standing there on the road. Mr Withers, slight and stooping a little, darting his head about like a weasel; the boy Bill, walking wary and belligerent in his bright shirt; and towering over them both, the tall menacing figure in black, a dark gash across the heat-wavering summer day. Watching, Simon thought suddenly of the desperate day when threatening feet were pounding after him, down a lonely road; and he turned his eyes away from the man.

'The girl's not there,' Barney hissed. 'She must be watching the front, in case we tried to come out that way again.'

Down on the road the little group stood for a moment irresolute. Bill turned and peered across the field, straight towards the hedge. The three children flattened themselves closer to the ground, hardly daring to breathe. But Bill looked away again, apparently satisfied. Withers looked across the field as well, and said something to him. The boy shook his head.

The tall figure in black had been standing a little way apart, motionless. It was difficult to tell which way he was looking. All at once he raised his arm, pointing seaward to the rising bulk of Kemare Head. He seemed to be talking earnestly.

'What are they going to do?' Jane whispered. Cramp was beginning to gnaw agonizingly at her right leg, and she was longing to move.

'If they're going to the end of the headland we're sunk,' Simon said, low and strained.

'How many more of them are there, for goodness' sake? That tall man . . .' Jane stared at him through the erratic leaf-starred gaps in the hedge. She could not see his face, but a cold sense of familiarity was beginning to grow in her mind. Then, as she gazed, he took off his wide black hat for a moment to brush his hand across his forehead, and suddenly she knew the shape of the head with the thick dark hair. The pattern of twigs and grass and sunlight swirled before her eyes, and she clutched at Simon's arm.

'Simon! It's him again! It's –'

'I know that,' Simon said. 'The moment he came round the corner I knew. I thought you did.'

'He's the boss of all of them,' Barney whispered in the same urgent undertone. 'His name's Hastings.'

'That's right,' Jane said faintly. 'Hastings. The vicar.'

Barney wriggled a little in the grass to stare at her. 'He's not the vicar.'

'He is. I saw him at the vicarage. Oh, you remember . . .'

'Is it a big rambling sort of house, all neglected?' Barney said slowly. 'With a long drive, and a room full of books?'

It was Jane's turn to stare. 'I remember saying about the books, but not about the drive. How did you –'

Barney said, with the utmost conviction: 'I don't care what you say, he isn't the vicar. I don't know what he is, but it isn't that. He can't possibly be. There's something perfectly beastly about him. He's like everything Gumerry said about the other side, you can sort of feel it, looking at him. And he says things . . .'

'Keep down!' Simon said abruptly. They all dropped their heads into the grass, and lay silent for a long moment while the sun beat down on their backs and scorched the skin behind their knees, and the cool long grass along the edge of the hedge tickled their cheeks. Rufus stirred and grunted and was quiet again. He had fallen asleep.

In a little while Simon nervously raised his head a few inches from the ground, hearing nothing but the call of one far-away gull high up in the sky. He had seen the three figures turn and move across the field and for a moment he had thought they were caught in a trap. But there was no one now on the road where they had stood, and no one in the silent stretch of the field.

'They've gone!' he whispered exultantly. Barney and Jane raised their heads too, slowly and cautiously.

'Look!' Jane propped herself on one elbow, and pointed out to the coast. There they were, the tall black striding figure and the two smaller ones, one on either side, bobbing out of sight along the side of Kemare Head.

'Oh!' Barney rolled over on his back and groaned with despair. 'We're cut off! How can we get out on the headland now?'

Jane sat up, wincing as she stretched her cramped legs. She said despondently, 'I don't see what there is to get worked up about. We can't do anything. We found where the grail is, but we can't get at it anyway. If there is a bottom entrance, it's under the sea, and the hole we found at the top is too narrow to get through even if we had a rope.'

Barney said, yelping, 'But they'll be able to. I know they will. That man can do anything, he seems to have things planned before he even knows they're going to happen. And if they find the hole in the rocks . . .'

'But they couldn't go down any more than we could,' Jane said reasonably. 'And they couldn't get in from the bottom either, unless they've got diving suits on the yacht. Anyway,' she added without much conviction, 'we aren't really absolutely sure the grail's there at all.'

'But we are, you know we are!' Barney's anxious frustration was mounting unbearably. 'We've got to stop them. Even if we can't do anything ourselves, we've got to *stop* them!'

'Don't be a silly little boy,' Jane said, irritated by disappointment. 'We'll just have to let them go, and keep out of their way till we find Great-Uncle Merry. There isn't a thing we can do.'

'There is one thing,' Simon said. His voice sounded muffled and rather gruff, as it always did when he was trying not to be excited. They looked at him, and

Jane raised an eyebrow sceptically. Simon said nothing. He was sitting hugging his knees, frowning out across the field.

'Well, go on then.'

'The tide.'

'The tide? What d'you mean?'

'The tide's out.'

'Well, what's so marvellous about that? I know it is,' Barney said, wonderingly. 'You could see the mud down in the harbour.'

But Simon was not listening. 'Jane, you remember what Mr Penhallow said down in the harbour. About the tide being low.'

'Oh yes.' Jane began to look less gloomy. 'Yes, that's right. It goes very low today, he said ... spring tide ... right round the rocks...'

'You can walk right round the rocks,' Simon said.

'So what?' demanded Barney.

'If we could walk right round the rocks,' Simon said with careful patience, 'we could walk right round the bottom of Kemare Head.'

Jane interrupted, catching him up, 'And the cave, the under-water entrance – when we heard the noise of the sea coming up the hole this morning, the tide was high. So the waves were still coming over the entrance. But don't you see, Barney, with this special low tide – if it uncovers all the rocks down there, it may uncover the entrance as well, and we should be able to get in.'

Barney's face was a comical mixture of expressions; blankness dissolving into excitement, and then into alarm. 'Gosh! Come on then, let's get down there!' He jumped to his feet, and then wailed. 'But we can't! There's one of them watching the harbour, and the other three out on the headland – how can we get down there without being seen?'

'I've thought of that too.' Simon was pink with importance. 'Just a minute ago. There's the other side. The bay on the other side of the headland, where we bathe from. We can get across the fields to it from here without them seeing us, unless they're actually up by the standing stones looking down in that direction. If they look down we've had it, but it's the only way I can see.'

'They won't be,' Jane said confidently. 'They wouldn't expect us to go down there. They'd be watching the harbour side.'

'Come on, we've got to be quick. Quicker than ever now. The tide was still going out when we were up over the harbour, I think, but it may turn any moment. I wish we knew exactly when.'

Barney, with Rufus roused and leaping round him again, was already several yards across the field. He halted suddenly, looking troubled, and turned slowly back. 'There's still Great-Uncle Merry. He'll never find us now. He'll be worried stiff.'

'He didn't bother much about worrying us stiff when he disappeared this morning,' Simon said shortly.

'Oh, but all the same –'

'Look,' Simon said, 'I'm the oldest, and I'm in charge. It's got to be Gumerry or the grail we look for, Barney, there isn't time for both. And I say we go after the grail.'

'So do I,' Jane said.

'Oh well,' said Barney, and he went on over the field, secretly relieved to be able to accept commands. He felt he had had enough of being the lone hero that day to last him for years – so that his private dreams of acting solitary bold knights in shining armour would never be quite the same again.

They were all three hot and breathless by the time they reached the beach in the next bay from Trewissick, on the other side of Kemare Head. But they saw to their relief that the tide had obviously not yet begun to come back in.

The sea seemed to be miles away, over a vast stretch of silver-white sand unscarred by footprints under the sun, and as they looked eagerly along the side of the headland they could see rocks uncovered at its foot. Before, the waves had always washed up against the cliff, even at the lowest tide.

Their feet sank into the soft dry sand at the top of the beach. Barney flopped down and began to unstrap one sandal. 'Wait a minute, I want to take my shoes off.'

'Oh come on,' Simon said impatiently, 'you'll only have to put them back on again when we get to the rocks.'

'I don't care, I'm taking them off now all the same. Anyway I'm tired.'

Simon groaned, and whacked the telescope case against his knee in exasperation. More than ever now he was determined to carry the manuscript wherever they went, and the case was hot and damp in the palm of his hand.

Jane sat down on the sand beside Barney. 'Come on, Simon, have a rest just for five minutes. It won't hurt, and I'm jolly hot as well.'

Not altogether unwillingly, Simon let his knees give way and collapsed to lie flat on his back. The sun blazed down into his eyes, and he turned over quickly. 'Golly, what a day. I could do with a swim.' He looked longingly out at the sea; but his eyes swivelled at once back to the rocks.

'There's even more uncovered than I thought there would be. Look, it's going to be easy as anything to walk round the cliff. It looks pretty wet in places, where the tide's left some water behind, but we can get through that easily enough.'

'So you'll have to take your shoes off as well,' said Barney triumphantly. He hung his sandals round his neck by their straps and wiggled his toes luxuriously in the sand, looking up at the gulls wheeling and faintly calling high over the beach. Then he stiffened. 'Listen!'

'I heard that too,' Simon said, looking up curiously. 'Funny, it sounded like an owl.'

'It was an owl,' Barney said, peering up at the towering side of the headland. 'It came from up there. I thought you only heard owls at night.'

'You do. And if they come out in the day-time they get mobbed by all the other birds, because they eat their young. We did it at school.'

'Well, the gulls don't seem to be taking any notice,' Barney said. He looked up at the dark specks lazily sailing to and fro over the sky. Then he glanced round the beach. 'Hey, where's Rufus?'

'Oh, he's around somewhere. He was here just a minute ago.'

'No, he isn't.' Barney stood up. 'Rufus! Rufus!' He whistled, on the long lilting note that the dog always answered to. Behind them they heard a bark, and they looked up the beach towards the sloping field to see Rufus on the edge of the grass, facing away from the sea but with his head turned to look back at them.

Barney whistled again, and patted his knee. The dog did not move.

'What's the matter with him?'

'He looks frightened. Has he hurt himself?'

'I hope not.' Barney ran up the beach and took Rufus by the collar, fondling his neck. The dog licked his hand. 'Come on, boy,' Barney said softly. 'Come on, then. There's nothing wrong. Come on, Rufus.' He tugged gently at the collar, moving back towards Simon and Jane. But Rufus would not move. He whined, straining away from the beach; his ears were pricked uneasily, and when Barney pulled more impatiently at his collar he turned his head and gave a low warning growl.

Puzzled, Barney relaxed his grip. As he did so, the dog suddenly jerked as if he had heard something, growled again, and slipped out of his grasp to trot swiftly away over the grass. Barney called, but he went on without a pause, head bent, tail between his legs, loping away in a straight line until he disappeared round the side of the headland.

Barney came slowly back down the beach. 'Did you see that? Something must have frightened him – I bet he's run all the way home.'

'Perhaps it was that owl,' Simon said.

'I suppose it might have been – hey, listen, there it is again!' Barney looked up. 'It *is* up on the headland.'

This time they all heard it; the long husking wail drifting softly down: 'Whooo-oo . . .'

As she listened, Jane felt all her warning instincts mutter deep in her mind.

For a moment she could not understand. She looked up, troubled, at the looming mass of Kemare Head, and the tops of the standing stones outlined against the sky.

'Stupid bird,' Simon said idly, lying down on his back again. 'Thinks it's night-time. Tell it to go back to bed.'

As if something exploded inside her head, Jane remembered. 'Simon, quick! It's not a bird at all. It's not an owl. It's them!'

The others stared at her.

Jane jumped to her feet, the lulling warmth of sun and sand forgotten in a sudden new panic. 'Don't you remember – that night, up on the headland, by the standing stones. We heard some owls hoot, and that was why Gumerry went off to look, because he thought they didn't sound right. And it wasn't owls, it was the enemy. Oh quick, perhaps they've seen us! Perhaps that was a signal from one of them to tell the others we're here!'

Simon was up on his feet before she had finished. 'Come on, Barney. Quick!'

Away from the revealing emptiness of the beach they dashed towards the rocky side of the headland, the sand squeaking against their feet as they ran. Barney's sandals bounced about on his chest, kicking him. Jane lost the hair-ribbon from her pony-tail, and her hair flowed loose, tickling the back of her neck. Simon ran clutching the telescope case grimly like a relay-runner's baton. They made straight for the cliff, and paused under its great grey height to look fearfully back at the grassy slope rising behind the beach. But there was no sign of anyone coming after them, and they heard no owl cry.

'Perhaps they didn't see us after all.'

'I bet they can't really see this beach from anywhere on the top of the headland.'

'Well, we've got to hurry all the same. Come on, or the tide will turn and beat us to it.'

They were still running on sand, along the side of the cliff, towards the end of the headland and the sea. Then they came to the rocks, and they began to climb.

The rocks were perilous to cross. At first they were dry, and fairly smooth, and it was easy to scramble from one grey jagged ridge to the next, skirting the small pools where anemones spread their tentacles like feathered flowers among seaweed leaves, and shrimps darted transparent to and fro. But soon they came to the rocks that were uncovered only at the lowest spring tides. Great masses of seaweed grew there, shining, still wet in the sun; slippery brown weed that squelched and popped under their feet, giving way sometimes without warning to drop them into a pool.

They came to a long stretch of water left trapped in the rocks. Barney, still determinedly barefoot, was trailing some way behind the other two. They waited at the edge of the water as he picked his way gingerly towards them. 'Ow!' he said, as he trod on a winkle.

'Do put your sandals on,' Jane said imploringly. 'It doesn't matter about getting them wet, ours are sopping already. You might step on anything in this pool and cut your feet to bits.'

Barney said, with surprising meekness due to having stubbed three toes, 'All right.' He perched on a jutting rock and unhooked his sandals from round his neck. 'Seems silly to put your shoes on to go paddling, instead of taking them off.'

'You can call it paddling,' Simon said darkly. 'There might be all sorts of ravenous deep-sea fish left in here. Mr Penhallow says the sea's terrifically deep just off the headland.' He gazed into the mass of bulbous brown seaweed floating on the surface of the pool. 'Oh well, here goes.'

They splashed through the weed, keeping close to the cliff and catching nervously at the rock to keep their balance. Simon, first in line, reached out warily with his forward foot, stirring the water so that the seaweed swirled cold and clammy against his skin. The bottom of the pool seemed fairly smooth, and he went more confidently, with the others following behind. Then suddenly his probing foot met no resistance, and before he could throw his weight backwards he had slipped down waist-deep in water. Jane, last in line, squealed involuntarily as she saw him drop. Barney held out a hand to Simon, suddenly a much shorter figure than himself.

'It's all right,' Simon said, more surprised than damaged. After the first shock the water felt pleasantly cold on his sun-baked legs. He moved carefully forward, and after a couple of steps felt rock against his knees under the water of the pool. He hauled himself up, splashing like a stranded fish, and in a few moments was only ankle-deep in water again.

'It's a sort of underwater trough. It goes right up to the cliff. Be careful, Barney. Feel with your toes a bit further out and see if there are any footholds there. There might be some sticking up under the water, like stepping-stones. I went down before I had a chance to feel. If there aren't any you'll just have to come across the way I did. Only slower.'

Barney prodded carefully about with one foot beneath the water and its swaying carpet of seaweed, but even farther away from the cliff he could feel only the edge of the underwater ridge, and beyond it nothing. 'I can't feel anything to tread on at all.'

'You'll have to go down, then. Lower yourself into it.'

'We might as well have gone swimming after all,' Barney said nervously. He crouched with both hands on the bottom until he was sitting in the water with his legs dangling over the hidden crevasse, and let himself slip down.

The water was almost over his shoulders when he felt his feet on firm rock; he had forgotten how much taller Simon was. He waded across and Simon hauled him out into the shallow water. Barney's shorts, wet and dark, clung heavily to his thighs, and he bent to detach odd fronds of seaweed that had twined themselves round his legs. Almost at once he felt the heat of the sun begin to dry his skin, leaving behind only the rasp of salt. Jane followed in the same way, and together they splashed across the last few shallow feet of the pool to where the rocks jutted out dry among the brown mounds of seaweed again.

'I do wish we knew about the tide,' Simon said anxiously to Jane. Barney had gone eagerly slipping and slithering over the rocks ahead of them.

Jane looked towards the sea. It lapped mildly against the edge of the rocks a few yards away, leaving a natural pathway all round the bottom of the cliff.

'It certainly hasn't moved. It might even be going out still. I shouldn't worry yet, we must be nearly there.'

'Well, keep an eye on it. It's that deep bit I'm worried about. When the water does start coming in it'll come into the pool first of all, and it wouldn't have to fill up far for us not to be able to get back the way we came. It'd be over Barney's head in no time.'

Jane blanched, and looked ahead at her younger brother, now scrambling on all fours. 'Oh Simon. D'you think we should have left him behind?'

Simon grinned. 'I'd like to have seen you try. Don't worry, it'll be all right. Just so long as we watch the tide.'

Looking back, Jane suddenly realized how far they had come. They stood now on the rocks at the very tip of the headland. The small distant sounds of the land no longer drifted out from the beach and there was nothing but the gentle sigh of the sea. It was almost as if they were cut off already.

Then Barney yelled in excitement. 'Hey look! Quick! Come here! I've found it!'

He was standing close to the cliff, some yards ahead, almost hidden by a rock. They could see him pointing towards the cliff-face. In an instant they had forgotten the tide, and they jumped and slithered over pools and rocks towards Barney, bladder-wrack popping under their feet like machine-gun fire.

'It's not very big,' he called as they came up. Simon and Jane saw the deep cleft in the rock only when they were very close. It was not the kind of cave they had pictured in their minds. Narrow and triangular, it rose barely high enough for Barney to stand upright inside, and they themselves would certainly have to crouch to go in. Rough boulders lay heaped round the entrance, and water dripped from wet green weed coating the roof. They could not see very far inside.

Jane said doubtfully, 'Are you sure this is it?'

'Of course it is,' Barney said positively. 'There couldn't be more than one.'

'I don't see why not.'

'Neither do I,' Simon said, 'but I think this is the one all right. Look up above – you can just see a sort of green triangle at the top of the cliff where the grass grows over the edge by the rocks. We must be almost directly in line with the place where that hole comes out up there.'

Jane looked, and looked down again quickly, shaken by the unnerving height of the cliff leaning over them out of the sky. 'I suppose so.'

Barney peered into the darkness. 'It isn't a cave at all really, just a hole, like at the top. Pouf' – he sniffed critically – 'it smells all seaweedy and salty. And the sides are all wet and green and dripping. Good job we're wet already.'

'I don't like it,' Jane said suddenly, staring hard at the dark entrance so small in the vast mass of the cliff.

'What d'you mean, you don't like it?'

'It gives me the creeps. We can't go in there.'

'You can't, you mean,' Simon said. 'You'll have to keep watch in case the tide turns. But I can.'

'What about me?' Barney demanded indignantly. 'I found it.'

'D'you *want* to?' said Jane in horror.

'With the grail in there? Who wouldn't? Be much better if I tried,' he said persuasively to Simon, 'I'm the smallest, and it's jolly narrow. You might get stuck, and never get out again.'

'Oh don't,' said Jane.

'If you go in, I'm going in after you,' Simon said.

'Okay,' Barney said cheerfully. He had been so unutterably relieved ever since he found himself free of the clutches of the sinister Mr Hastings that nothing else, in comparison, seemed frightening at all. 'I wish we'd brought a torch, though.' He gazed speculatively into the cave. Within a few feet of the entrance it was black and impenetrable.

'I wish we'd brought a rope,' Jane said unhappily. 'Then if you did get stuck I could pull you out.'

Simon put his hands in his pockets looking up at the sky, and began to whistle nonchalantly. They stared at him.

'Well?'

'What's the matter with you?'

'Good job someone in the family's got brains,' Simon said.

'Who? *You?*'

'I don't know what you'd do without me.'

'Oh come on,' Jane said impatiently, 'you haven't got a rope or a torch, so don't pretend you have.'

'I jolly nearly have.' Simon delved into the pocket of his shorts. 'You know when we went through our pockets up there this morning to see if we had some string, and we only had that cotton of yours – well, I thought we ought to be a bit better equipped just in case. So when we were back at the house I pinched some of Father's fishing-line. He didn't take it all with him.' His hand emerged from his pocket clutching a tight-wound wad of thin brown line. 'That's as tough as any rope.'

'I never thought of that,' Jane said, with new respect.

'I've still got that old bit of candle too. But I bet you haven't still got your matches.'

Jane groaned. 'No, I haven't. They were in my duffle, and I left it at home. Oh bother.'

'I thought you would,' Simon said, and with the smug flourish of a conjuror he produced a box of matches and the candle stump from his shirt pocket. Then his face fell. 'Oh gosh, they've got wet. They must have been splashed when I slipped in that pool. The wick of the candle's soaking, it won't be any good. Still, the matches are all right.'

'They'll do fine,' Barney said encouragingly. 'That's smashing. Come on.'

Simon took the telescope case from where he had tucked it under his arm and handed it to Jane. 'You'd better take charge of the manuscript, Janey. If I dropped it in there we'd never find it again.'

He looked out again at the sea. The rocks where they stood were even more like a causeway here, stretching out almost flat from the base of the cliff into the water. Only one hump of grey rock stood alone near the entrance of the cave.

The water still lapped gently at the edge six or seven yards away, no nearer and no further than it had been when they first left the beach. Simon wondered nervously how much time was left before the tide would turn. 'I reckon we've got about half an hour,' he said slowly. 'After that we shall have to get away quick before the tide catches us. Come here, Barney, and hold still.'

He found the loose end of the roll of fishing-line and tied it securely round Barney's waist. 'If you're going to go first I can hold on to the line behind you.'

'D'you think he ought to?' Jane said.

Barney turned round and glared at her.

'Well, I'm not awfully keen on the idea,' said Simon, 'but he's right about its being narrow, and he may be the only one who can get properly inside. It's all right, I won't lose him. Here –' He handed Jane the roll of line. 'Don't let it go slack.'

'And don't keep it too tight,' said Barney, making for the entrance, 'or you'll cut my middle in half.'

Jane looked at her watch. 'It's nearly five o'clock. When you've been in there ten minutes I'll pull on the line twice to tell you.'

'*Ten minutes*!' said Barney in scorn. 'We may have to go in for miles.'

'You might suffocate,' said poor Jane.

'That's a good idea,' Simon said quickly, glancing at her face. 'You pull twice, and if I pull back twice, it means we're all right but we're staying in there. If I pull three times, it means we're coming out.'

'And if I pull three times it means you've got to come out, because the tide's turned.'

'Fine. And four pulls from either end means a distress signal – not,' Simon added hastily, 'that there's going to be any need for it.'

'All right,' Jane said. 'Oh dear. Don't be long.'

'Well, we shall have to go slowly. But don't get in a flap, nothing's going to go wrong.' Simon patted her on the back, and followed as Barney, straining eagerly at the line round his waist like a dog on a leash, waved one hand briefly and disappeared into the mouth of the cave.

Chapter Fourteen

Barney blinked at the darkness. As his eyes grew accustomed to being out of the sunlight, vague objects took shape in the dark. He realized that the light from the entrance penetrated further inside than they had realized; and for the first few yards at least he could see the faint shine of the slimy green weed covering the walls and roof of the cave, and the glint of water lying along the bottom in a shallow unmoving stream.

He moved warily forward, one hand up touching the roof and the other stretched out to one side. He could feel a slight steady pull on the line round his waist from Simon holding it behind him. Very loud in the enclosed silence of the cave he could hear the splash of their feet through the water, and his brother breathing.

'Go carefully,' Simon said, behind him. He spoke softly, almost in a whisper, but the cave echoed his voice into a husking mutter that filled the space all around them.

'I am.'

'You might bump your head.'

'You might bump yours. Mind this bit here, it comes down lower. Put your hand up on the roof and you'll feel it.'

'I can,' Simon said fervently. His neck was bent uncomfortably downwards; taller than Barney, he had to stoop slightly all the while to avoid hitting his head on the slimy rock above. Occasionally a large cold drop of water dripped down inside his shirt collar.

'Isn't it cold?'

'Freezing.' Barney's shorts were clinging clammily to the tops of his legs, and he felt the air chill through his shirt. He was finding it more and more difficult to make out any shapes around him, and soon he paused uneasily, feeling the darkness close in as if it were pressing on his eyes. Groping upwards, his fingers could no longer feel the roof. Ahead of him it rose out of reach, and he clutched at air.

'Wait a minute, Simon.' His voice came eerily back at him from all sides. 'I think it gets higher here. But I can't see a thing now. Have you got those matches?'

Simon felt his way along the line to where Barney stood. He touched his shoulder, and Barney felt more comforted at the contact than he would have admitted even to himself.

'Don't move. I'm letting go of the line for a minute.' Simon groped in his pocket for the matches and opened the box, feeling the edges carefully to make sure he had it the right way up.

The first two matches grated obstinately on the box as he tried to strike them, and nothing happened. The third flared up but broke as it did so, burning Simon's fingers so that he dropped it with an exclamation before they could blink away the dazzle of the sudden light. There was a small hiss as it dropped into the water around their feet.

'Buck up,' said Barney.

'I'm going as fast as I can ... ah, that's it.'

The fourth match was dry, and rasped into flame, flickering. Simon cupped his hand to shelter it. 'Funny, there must be a draught in here. I can't feel one.'

'The match can. That's good, it means there must be an opening somewhere at the other end. So it is the right cave after all.'

Simon's hand hid the dazzle of the little flame, and Barney peered hastily round in the wavering light. Their shadows danced huge and grotesque on the wall. He looked up, and took a few careful steps forward. 'Hold it up . . . hey, come on, the roof does go up higher here, you'll be able to stand upright.'

Simon stepped cautiously towards him, bent over the match, and straightened his back with a gasp of relief. Then the match burned his fingers, and he dropped it. At once the darkness wrapped them like a blanket again.

'Hang on, I'll light another one.'

'Well, wait a minute, we don't want to waste them. I could see a bit of the way ahead when it went out, so we can go that far before you light the next.'

Barney shut his eyes. Somehow, even though the cave was just as dark when his eyes were open, he found shutting them gave him a sense of being safer. Still touching the slippery wall with his finger-tips, he moved two or three paces forward. Simon followed him with one hand on his shoulder, staring ahead into the darkness but seeing as little as if a thick black curtain were hanging close before his face.

They went on into the cave for what seemed a long time. Every few moments Simon struck a match, and they moved forward while the dim light lasted, and for the few remembered paces after it flickered out. Once they tried to light the candle stump, but it only spluttered obstinately, so Simon put it back in his pocket.

The air was cold, but fresh on their faces. Although there was a smell all round them of salt and seaweed, as if they were under the sea, it was not difficult to breathe. The silence, like the darkness, seemed almost solid, broken only by their own footsteps, and an occasional echoing musical plop as water somewhere dripped from the roof of the cave.

As Simon was standing still, fumbling with the match-box again, Barney felt the line round his waist jerk tight and dig into him; once, twice. 'There's two pulls on the line. It must be Jane. Ten minutes. Gosh, I thought we'd been in here for hours.'

'I'll signal back,' Simon said. He struck a match and saw the line thin and taut in its light. Taking firm hold of it he gave two slow steady pulls on the direction from which they had come.

'Funny to think of Jane on the other end,' Barney said.

'I wonder how much there is left?'

'Gosh – d'you think we shall run out? How much line was there?'

'Quite a lot,' said Simon, more optimistically than he felt. 'We've been going awfully slowly. Ow!' The match burned down to his fingers, and he dropped it hastily.

There was no hiss as it fell. As they moved on, groping, Simon suddenly realized that he had been listening for the noise.

'Stop a tick, Barney.' He scuffed at the ground with one foot and peered down. 'The floor's not wet any more.'

'My shoes still squelch,' Barney said.

'That's the water inside them, idiot, not outside.' Simon's voice boomed hollowly round the cave, and he hastily dropped it to a whisper again, half afraid that the noise might bring the roof down on them.

'The sides aren't slimy here either,' Barney said suddenly. 'It's dry rock. It has been for some time actually, only I hadn't really taken any notice.'

Another match fizzed alight as Simon held it to the one dying in his fingers. He held the flame close to the wall. They saw bare grey granite, veined here and there with a white sparkling rock, and no seaweed. The ground, when Barney stooped to touch it, was covered with a kind of dusty sand.

'We must be going uphill.'

'The sea can't ever have come in this far.'

'But we heard it booming about from up the top, this morning. Does that mean we've come past the opening of the chimney bit?' Barney craned his neck back to look at the roof.

'I don't think so,' Simon said uncertainly. 'The noise would carry a long way. Hey, look ahead quick, this match is going out.'

Barney peered forward at the now-familiar picture that he was never afterwards to forget: of narrow shadow-swung walls tunnelling into the dark, holding them in a cramped, unfriendly grip. And in the second before the darkness came down on them again he thought he saw the curtain of shadow at the end nearer than it had been before.

He moved hesitantly forward, and then some instinct told him to stop. He put out his hand in the silent darkness. It met solid rock a few inches from his face. 'Simon! It's a dead end.'

'What?' Incredulity and disappointment rose in Simon's voice. He struggled with the matches; he could feel the bottom of the box through them now, and realized that there could not be many left.

In the flickering light it was difficult to tell shadow from darkness, but they saw that the cave had not actually come to an end. Instead it changed, just in front of them, to a far narrower passage: tall and thin, with a great boulder wedged between its sides about three feet from the ground. Above their heads, out of reach, the cleft was open to the roof; but there was no way of climbing up to it. The boulder blocked their path.

'We'll never get through that,' Simon said in despair. 'There must have been a fall of rock since the Cornishman went through.'

Barney looked down at the forbidding dark gap that remained at the bottom of the cleft, jagged and sinister through the dancing shadows, and swallowed. He was beginning to wish very much that they were back in the sunlight again.

Then he thought of the grail, and then of Mr Hastings's face. 'I can get through underneath, if I crawl.'

'No,' Simon said at once. 'It's dangerous.'

'But we can't go back now.' Barney gained confidence as he began to argue. 'We've got this far, we may be just a few feet away from it. I'll come out again if it's too narrow. Oh come on, Simon, let me try.'

The match went out.

'We haven't got many left,' Simon said out of the darkness. 'They'll run out soon. We've just got to make that candle light, or we shall be stuck in the dark. Where are you?'

Groping his way along the line towards Barney, he took his hand and put the match-box into it. Then he felt in his own pocket for the stump of candle, rubbing its wick hopefully on his shirt to dry it. 'Now light one of the matches.'

There was a noise behind them in the darkness, like a stone falling; a grating, rattling noise and then silence again.

'What was that?'

They listened nervously, but could hear only the sudden violent thumping of their own hearts. Barney struck a match, his hand shaking. The cave sprang into light again round them, with only the darkness pressing mockingly from the direction of the noise.

'It wasn't anything,' Simon said at last. 'Just a stone we must have brushed loose. Here.' He held the candle stub to the flame. The match burned right down, but still the candle wick only spluttered as it had before. They tried again, holding their breath, and this time the wick caught, and burned with a long smoking yellow flame.

'Hold these,' Barney said with determination. 'I'm going in there.' He gave Simon back the last few loose matches and took the candle. 'Look,' he said, shielding the smoking flame from the draught with his other hand. 'It's not so low really, I can go on my hands and knees.'

Simon peered at the entrance unhappily. 'Well . . . for goodness' sake be careful. And pull at the line if you get stuck, I'll keep hold of it.'

Barney went down on his hands and knees and crawled into the dark opening beneath the wedged rock, holding the dangerously flickering candle in front of him. The draught seemed to be stronger now. The rock brushed his body on all sides, so that he had to keep his head down and his elbows in, and for a moment he almost panicked with the sense of being shut in.

But before the panic could take hold, the shadows looming round the one point of light changed their shape, and he raised his head without hitting the rock. He crawled a little farther, the floor rough and gritty under his knees; and found not only that he could stand upright but that the cave was much wider. The pool of light cast by his carefully guarded flame did not even show the walls on either side.

'Are you all right?' Simon's anxious voice came muffled through the opening behind him.

Barney bent down. 'It's okay, it widens out again here, that must be an entrance . . . I'm going on.'

He felt the line at his waist tighten as Simon jerked an answer and he set off slowly across the cave. The darkness opened before him in the small light from his inch of candle, already burning down and dripping hot wax over his finger-nails. When he glanced back over his shoulder he could no longer see the entrance from which he had come.

'Hallo,' Barney said tentatively into the darkness. His voice whispered back at him in a sinister, eerie way: not booming and reverberating round as it had in the narrow tunnel-like cave they had come through, but muttering far away, high in the air. Barney swung round in a circle, vainly peering into the dark. The space round him must be as big as a house – and yet he was in the depths of Kemare Head.

He paused, irresolute. The candle was burning down, soft between his fingers. The thought of the towering dark man in his strange empty house came back to him suddenly, and with it all the feeling of menace that surrounded their pursuers, the enemy, who so desperately wanted to keep them from finding the grail.

Barney shivered with fright and sudden cold. It was as if they were all round him in the silent darkness, evil and unseen, willing him to go back. His ears sang; even in the great empty space of the cave he felt that something was pressing him down, calling him insistently to turn away. Who are you to intrude here, the voice seemed to whisper; one small boy, prying into something that is so much bigger than you can understand, that has remained undisturbed for so many years? Go away, go back where you are safe, leave such ancient things alone . . .

But then Barney thought of Great-Uncle Merry, whose mysterious quest they were following. He thought of all that he had said, right in the beginning, of the battle that was never won but never totally lost. And although he saw nothing but the shadows, and the blackness all around his small lonely pool of yellow light, he suddenly had a vivid picture of the knight Bedwin who had begun it all when he came fleeing to Cornwall from the east. In full armour he stood in Barney's mind, guarding the last trust of King Arthur. Chased by the same forces that were now pursuing them.

And Barney remembered the story that Bedwin was buried on Kemare Head, perhaps directly above the cave where he stood, and he was not frightened. There was friendliness round him in the dark now as well as fear.

So Barney did not turn back. He went on, sheltering his small dying light, into the dark that gave back in whispering echoes the sound of his own steps. And then, above his head, he became aware of a noise stranger than anything he had ever heard.

It seemed to come from nowhere, out of the air; a husky, unearthly humming, very faint and far-away, yet filling the whole cave. It wavered up and down, high and then low, like the wind that sings in the trees and telegraph-wires. As the thought flickered through Barney's mind, he held the candle up and saw that over his head the roof opened into a kind of chimney, rising up and up and out of sight. He thought for an instant that he saw a point of light shining down, but his own light dazzled his eyes and he could never be sure. And he realized that the noise he could hear was the wind, far above, blowing over the hole in the rocks that they had found that morning. The singing down in the cave was the singing of the wind over Kemare Head.

It was almost by accident, as he was looking up, that he saw the ledge. It jutted out from the rocky side of the chimney at the end of the cave; a bump of rock beneath a hollow, like a kind of natural cupboard, just within his reach. Inside it, he saw the glint of candlelight reflected back from a shape that was not part of the rock.

Hardly daring to breathe, he reached up and found his hand touching the side of something smooth and curved. It rang beneath his finger-nail with the sound of metal. He grasped it and took it down, blinking at the dust which rose from the ledge as he did so. It was a cup, heavy and strangely shaped; swelling out from a thick stem into a tall bell-shape like the goblets he had seen pictured in his books about King Arthur. He wondered how the artists could have known. He could hardly believe that this, at last, must be the grail.

The metal was cold in his hand; dusty and very dirty, but with a dull golden sheen underneath the dirt. There was nothing else on the ledge.

The candle flickered suddenly. The wax felt soft and warm, and Barney guessed with a shock that it would burn for only a few moments more before he would be left alone in the dark. He turned away from the ledge to the direction from which he had come, and realized how lost he would have been without the line tied to his waist. The vast round chamber of the cave stretched out all round him into the dark; only the line, straight and thin, told him the way to go.

He walked towards it; the line dropped to the ground and then drew taut again. Simon must be pulling it in. Barney clutched the grail to him with one hand and held up the candle, now almost burned away, with the other. Excitement bubbled away any of the fears he had felt before. 'Simon!' he called. 'I've found it!'

There was no answer but his own voice, whispering back at him from the empty cave. 'Found it . . . found it . . .' . . . a dozen voices, each his own, from every side.

And the light flickered, and went out.

The line stayed taut as Barney put his hand on it and walked slowly forward. 'Simon?' he said uncertainly. Still there was no answer. For a moment he saw in his mind a terrible picture of Simon overpowered and helpless. And on the other side of the narrow passage in the rock, the tall sneering figure of Mr Hastings, taking in the line as if he were playing a fish on a hook, and waiting . . .

Barney's throat felt suddenly dry. He held the grail tighter to him in the darkness, his heart thumping. Then he heard Simon's voice, low down in the darkness before him and very muffled.

'Barney! . . . Barney?'

Barney put out his hand and felt the rock where the roof dropped suddenly to the narrow part of the cave. 'I'm here . . . Simon, I've found it, I've got the grail!'

But all the muffled urgent voice said was, 'Come on out, quick.'

Barney went down on his hands and knees, wincing again at the pressure of the sharp edges of the rock. Carefully he crawled into the crevice that separated the two parts of the cave, bumping his head in the dark on the low uneven roof. He held the grail upright before him, but it knocked against the side of the rock and rang out, to his surprise, with a long musical note as clear and true as a bell.

He saw a dim glow lighting the farther end of the crack, and then the bright star of a match, and Simon crouching low and pulling in the line with his free hand. The shadows made his eyes look big and dark and alarmed. He stared as Barney emerged, forgetting everything at the sight of the tall cup.

Simon had been growing more and more anxious, and only the feel of Barney still moving at the other end of the line had stopped him from squeezing through the narrow gap himself. He had stood alone in the dark, straining for every sound, longing for light but forcing himself to keep the six remaining matches in his pocket for the journey back. It had seemed a very long time.

He took the cup from Barney's hands. 'I thought it would be a different shape, somehow . . . what's this inside?'

'Where?'

'Look –' Simon felt inside the cup and brought out what looked at first like a short stick, almost as dark with age as the cup itself. It had been wedged between the sides, and Barney had not seen it in his haste.

'It's very heavy. I think it's made of lead.'

'What is it?'

'A kind of tube. Like the telescope case, only a lot smaller. It doesn't seem to unscrew, though. Perhaps it just fits together.' Simon pulled experimentally at the tube, and suddenly one end of it came off like a cap; and wound in a roll inside they saw something very familiar indeed.

'It's another manuscript!'

'So that's what he meant when he said –' Simon broke off. He had taken hold of one end of the rolled parchment in an attempt to pull it out of the tube, and the edge had crumbled away at his touch. With sudden caution he jerked his hand away, and in the same instant remembered why he had called so anxiously for Barney to come out.

'We can't touch it, it's too old. And Barney, we've got to get out as quick as we can. Jane gave three pulls on the line just before you came back. The tide must be coming in. If we don't get out soon we shall be cut off.'

As the boys disappeared into the mouth of the cave Jane had settled herself to lean against the lone standing rock, amongst the wet pillows of seaweed and the grey-green sweep of flat granite causeway round the cliff. She tucked the telescope case carefully under her arm. Even though she had always been with Simon when he was carrying it about, she felt a peculiar unnerving sense of responsibility at the thought of what was inside.

Gradually she paid out the thin fishing-line from the neatly wound wad in her hand. The pressure on it was uneven, as if inside the cave the boys were moving forward and then stopping every few moments. She had to concentrate to keep the line from either pulling too tight or dropping loose on the ground.

It was very hot. The sun beat down over the towering grey cliff, and she felt the heat prickling along her skin. Even the rock she leant on was baked by the sun, and she could feel the warmth of it through her shirt on her back. Behind her, the water swished gently as it washed the edge of the uncovered rocks. There was no other sound anywhere, at the lonely foot of the headland with the sea stretching all around, and without the line moving in her hands Jane could have believed that she was the only person in the world. The land, and the Grey House, seemed very far away.

She wondered idly if their parents had come back from Penzance yet, and what they would think when they found the house completely empty, with nothing to show where anyone had gone.

She thought of the three figures they had seen striding out over Kemare Head, led by the frightening Mr Hastings black and long-legged like some giant insect. Instinctively she looked up at the cliff. But there was no sound, no movement, only the great grey sweep of rock that leant over her in permanent unmoving menace, with the green cap of grass on the headland at the top, two hundred feet above.

And then Great-Uncle Merry followed them into her mind. Where was he? Where had he gone this time? What, so near the end of the quest, could possibly have been important enough to take him away? Never for one moment did Jane think that he could have come to any harm, or have been captured by the enemy. She remembered too clearly the utter confidence with which Great-Uncle Merry had swept her into his arms on the midnight headland: 'They dare not follow if I am here . . .'

'I wish you were here now,' Jane said, aloud, shivering a little in spite of the hot still air. She was not happy with Simon and Barney deep in a darkness where anything might be lurking, where they might get lost and never get out, where the roof might fall in . . .

Great-Uncle Merry would have made sure that nothing like that could happen.

Jane looked at her watch. It was twelve minutes past five, and still the line in her hands was moving slowly and irregularly into the cave. She gave two strong deliberate tugs on the line. After a pause she felt it move twice in reply; but faintly. The line was two-thirds unwound; she wished she had measured it as she let it go. Time dragged by; still the line pulled insistently out of her hand, moving into the dark entrance more slowly now. The sun blazed down immovable out of the empty blue sky, and a small breeze sprang up from nowhere to lift the edges of Jane's long loose hair.

She leant against the rock and let her senses drift, feeling the heat of the sun on her skin, breathing the sea-smell of the wet rocks and seaweed, and listening to the gentle lap-lap of the sea. Then in a kind of sleepy daze, with only her fingers awake, she became aware that the sound of the sea had changed.

She jerked to her feet and swung round. To her horror, the piles of seaweed nearest the sea were swaying up and down in a swell that had not been there before. Waves were washing over what had been the edge of the rocks; nearer her, she thought, than they had been. The tide was on the turn.

Jane felt panic begin to rise within her. The last few loops of the line were loose in her hand now: the boys must be an alarming way inside the cave. She took a firm hold of the line, winding part of the slack round her hand and going right up to the dark mouth of the cave, and jerked it hard one, two, three times.

Nothing happened. She waited, listening to the regular swash of the waves creeping in. Then just as tears of fright were beginning to prickle in her eyes she felt the answering signal; three faint tugs on the line pulling at her hand. Almost at once the strain lessened, and the line began to fall slack. Jane let out a great breath of relief. The line came towards her as she pulled at it; slowly at first and then more easily, faster than she had paid it out. Then at last, Simon and Barney, blinking at the daylight behind hands raised to shield their eyes, came stumbling out of the narrow entrance of the cave.

'Hallo,' Simon said foolishly, sounding dazed. His matches had run out five full minutes before they reached the light, and the last part of the way had been a nightmare journey in the pitch dark, walking blind and trusting to the feel of the line to tell them that the way ahead was clear. He had made Barney let him go first. All the time he felt that every next step might bring him crashing against rock, or face to face in the dark with some nameless Thing, and he would not have been surprised when they emerged to find that all his hair had turned white.

Jane only looked at him with a small wry grin and said as he had, 'Hallo.'

'Look!' Barney said, and held up the grail.

Jane felt her grin widen with delight. 'Then we've beaten them! We've got it! Gosh, I wish Gumerry were here.'

'I think it's made of gold,' Barney rubbed at the metal. Out in the sunlight, the grail seemed far less magical than in the mysterious darkness of the cave; but a bright yellow gleam showed here and there through the dirt on its side. 'There's a sort of pattern scratched all over it, too,' he said. 'But you can't see properly, without cleaning it up.'

'It's terribly ancient.'

'But what does it *mean*? I mean, everyone's trying like mad to get hold of it, because it can tell them something, but when you look at it there doesn't seem to be anything it could possibly tell anyone. Unless that pattern's some sort of message.'

'The manuscript,' Simon said.

'Oh gosh, yes.' Barney took the small, heavy lead tube from the cup, and showed Jane the manuscript inside. 'This was wedged in the grail. It must follow on from where our manuscript leaves off. I bet it's tremendously important. I bet it explains everything. But it breaks up almost as soon as you look at it.' He carefully fitted the cap back on the tube.

'We've got to get it home safely,' Simon said. 'I wonder if there's room . . . wait a minute.' He took the telescope case from under Jane's arm and unscrewed it. Their own familiar manuscript stood up from the lower half, fitting it closely.

Simon took the dark leaden cylinder and dropped it carefully inside the centre of the parchment in the telescope case. 'There. Got a hanky, Jane?'

Jane took her handkerchief from her shirt pocket. 'What for?'

'Like that,' Simon said, fitting the handkerchief in a tight ball inside the top of the parchment roll. 'It'll keep the new one steady. We'll have to run if we're going to get off before the tide catches up with us, and it'll get bounced about a lot.'

Automatically Jane and Barney turned to look again at the sea. And at exactly the same moment each of them gasped, with a noise of pure strangled fright. Simon had bent his head to screw the two halves of the case back together. He looked up quickly. The waves were lifting the seaweed now within six feet of where they stood. But that was not what was wrong. Jane and Barney, arrested in mid-movement, were looking further out to sea.

For a moment, the one jutting rock obscured Simon's view. Then he too saw the tall sweeping lines of the yacht *Lady Mary*, under full sail, come round the end of the headland towards them. And he too saw the tall dark figure standing in the bow with one arm raised, pointing.

'Come on, quick!' He grabbed at Barney and Jane as they stood motionless with shock, and pushed them ahead of him.

They jumped and slithered over the seaweed-cushioned rocks, away from the cave and the pursuing yacht. Barney clutched the grail in one hand as he ran, his arms outstretched to keep his balance, and Simon held the manuscripts in their case grimly to his chest. He glanced back over his shoulder and saw the great white mainsail of the yacht crumpling down on to the deck, and a small dinghy being lowered over the side.

Barney slipped and fell, and nearly brought them both down on top of him. Even as he fell the grail did not leave his grip, but struck the rock once more with the same clear bell-like note as before. It rang out over the sound of their splashing hasty feet.

He struggled up again, biting his lip at the sting of salt eating into a graze on his knee, and they hurried on. They were splashing through water all the while now. The waves had grown, and were washing right over the rocks with every pulse of the rising tide. The water marked the pools and hollows with drifting brown weed, and glossed the bare rock with a swirling coat that would turn, soon, into a current strong enough to dislodge their quick desperate feet.

Barney slipped again, and fell with a splash.

'Let me take it.'

'No!'

He scrambled for a foothold, Jane pulling him up by his free arm, and the frenzied nightmare of a race drove them faster, zigzagging in wild blind leaps over the wave-washed rocks. Simon glanced back again. Two figures in a small dinghy were paddling fast towards them from the yacht. He heard the yacht's engines cough into life.

'Go on, quick!' he gasped. 'We can still do it!' They hastened on, half stumbling, kept on their feet only by their own speed. Still there was no sight of the beach round the headland, but only the sea on one side and the great wall of the cliff rising on the other. And before them, dwindling into the tide, the long path of rocks and weed.

'Stop!' A deep voice rang out across the water behind them. 'Come back! You stupid children, come here!'

'They won't catch us,' Simon panted, catching Barney as he almost fell a third time, and jerking him back to his feet. Jane at his side was sobbing for breath at every step, but running and stumbling with the same desperate haste. Then round the headland in front of them something else came into sight, and dropped their hopes like stones to the bottom of the sea.

It was another dinghy, broad as a tub, breasting the waves like a barge. The boy Bill sat at a chugging outboard motor in the stern, and Mr Withers was leaning eagerly forward in front of him, his long dark hair blowing in the wind. He saw them and shouted with triumph, and they saw an unpleasant grin break on the boy's face as he turned the boat's nose towards the rocks in their path.

They skidded to a halt, appalled.

'Which way?'

'They'll cut us off!'

'But we can't go back. Look! The others are going to land!'

With the edge of the water creeping round their feet they looked distractedly back and forth. Not ten yards ahead, the boat with Mr Withers evilly smiling was heading to cut off their path, and behind them the other dinghy was bobbing almost at the edge of the rocks. They were caught, neatly, in a trap.

'Come over here!' the deep voice called to them again. 'You will not get away. Come here!'

Mr Hastings was standing up in his dinghy, a tall black figure, one arm flung out towards them. With his legs planted apart to keep him balanced, swaying with the boat's rise and fall on the swell, he looked as if he were straddling the sea.

'Barnabas!' The voice dropped lower, to a hypnotic monotone. 'Barnabas, come here.'

Jane clutched at Barney's arm. 'Don't go near him!'

'No fear.' Barney was frightened, but not bewitched into obedience as he had been before. 'Oh Simon, what can we do?'

Simon stared up at the cliff, wondering for a wild moment if they could climb to safety. But the sheer granite face towered implacably up, far, far above their heads. They could never have found footholds there even to climb out of reach, and they would have fallen long before they reached the top.

'Barnabas,' the voice came again, gentle, insidious. 'We know what it is you have in your hand. And you too, Simon. Oh yes, Simon, especially you.'

Simon and Barney each closed a hand instinctively tighter round the manuscripts and the grail.

'They are not yours,' the voice rose, more roughly. 'You have no right to them. They must go back where they belong.'

Mr Hastings was watching them intently, poised in the dinghy waiting for the right moment of the swell to jump across to the rocks. Only the heaving mounds of seaweed, masking the edge, made him hesitate. At the tiller, Polly Withers was struggling to control the boat in the rising waves.

Barney shouted suddenly: 'You can't have them. They're not yours either. Why do you want them anyway? You haven't really got a museum, I don't believe all the things you said.'

Mr Hastings laughed softly. The noise echoed eerie and spine-chilling over the gentle murmur of the sea.

'You'll never win properly,' Simon called defiantly. 'You never do.'

'We shall this time,' a lighter voice said behind them. They swung round again. It was Withers. The outboard motor had cut out, and quietly the other dinghy was edging nearer to them as the boy Bill groped for the rock with an oar.

They drew closer together with their backs against the cliff, pressed as far away as they could; but on either side the boats crept closer towards them. The *Lady Mary* was edging slowly along off the headland. They could hear her engines thrumming faintly, though they could see no one on board.

'If only we had a boat,' Jane said in despair.

'Couldn't we swim for it?'

'Where to?'

'There must be *something* we can do!' Barney's voice rose frantically.

'There is nothing at all you can do.' Withers's light sneering voice came over the rocks to them. He was less than five yards away in the bow of the tossing dinghy. 'Give us the manuscript. Give it to us and we will take you off safely. The tide is rising very fast now. You must give it to us.'

'What if we don't?' Simon called rebelliously.

'Look at the sea, Simon. You can't get back now the way you came. Look at the tide. You're cut off. You can't get away unless you come with us.'

'He's right,' Jane whispered. 'Look!' She pointed. Further along the rocks the sea was already washing the foot of the cliff.

'Where's your boat, Simon?' called the mocking voice.

'We'll have to give in,' Simon said, low and angry.

'Take your time, Simon. We can wait. *We've* got all the time in the world.'

They heard the boy snigger on the other side of the boat.

'They've got us.'

'Oh think – *think* – we can't give it up now.'

'Think of Great-Uncle Merry.'

'It's a pity we ever thought of him in the first place,' Simon said fiercely. 'It's no good, I'm going to say we give in.'

'*No!*' Barney said urgently, and before they realized what was happening he had snatched the manuscript case from Simon and splashed forward over the wet rocks to the edge of the sea. He held up the long glinting case in one hand and the grail in the other, and gazed furiously at Mr Hastings. 'If you don't pick us up and let us take them home I shall throw them in the sea.'

'Barney!' Jane croaked. But Simon held her back, listening.

Mr Hastings did not move. He stood looking across with immense calm arrogance at Barney's small bristling figure, and when he spoke the deep voice was colder than any voice they had ever heard. 'If you do that, Barnabas, I shall leave you and your brother and sister here to drown.'

They had no doubt that he was speaking the truth. But Barney was carried away with a passionate indignation, and he was determined never again to believe anything that Mr Hastings said. If once he did, he knew he would be under the spell again.

'I will, I will! If you don't promise, I will!' He raised the grail higher in his right hand, flexing his muscles to throw it. Simon and Jane gasped.

The whole world seemed to stop and centre round the towering black-clad man and a small boy: one will against another, with Barney saved by his own fury from the full force of the commanding glare driving into his eyes. Then Mr Hastings's face twisted, and he let out a strangled shout. 'Withers!'

And from that moment, for the children, the world cracked into unreality and there seemed no reason in anything that happened.

From either side, Norman Withers and Mr Hastings made a dive for Barney. Simon shouted, 'Barney, *don't!*' and dashed towards him to clasp his outstretched arm. Withers, nearer, made a great leap on to the rocks from his boat, setting it swaying wildly with Bill clinging frantically to the tiller. But as his lunging foot came down where the rock should have been, they saw the viciousness in his face change to alarm, and he flung up his arms and disappeared under the water.

He had jumped down on the masked pool among the rocks: the gap where the retreating sea had left deep water, and which now was filled far deeper by the incoming tide. Jane, cowering back against the cliff, chilled with horror as she realized that they would all three have gone headlong into it if they had run another yard further on.

Withers surfaced again, coughing and spluttering, and Barney hesitated, the grail still held over his head. Mr Hastings had leapt across to the rocks without falling, and was coming at him from the other side with long loping strides, his dark brows a menacing bar across his face and his lips drawn back in a horrible unlaughing grin. Simon dived desperately, and was brushed aside by the sweep of one long arm; but in falling he grabbed at the man's nearest leg and brought him crashing down full length on the wet slippery rocks.

For all his height, Mr Hastings moved like an eel. In a moment he was on his feet again, with one big hand clasped round Simon's arm, and in a swift cruel movement he pulled the arm round behind Simon's back and jerked it upwards so that he cried out with pain. The girl in the boat laughed softly. She had not moved since the beginning. Jane heard, and hated her, but stood transfixed by the look of concentrated evil cruelty on the face above her. It was as if something monstrous blazed behind Mr Hastings's eyes, something not human, that filled her with a horror more vast and dreadful than anything she had felt before.

'Put it down, Barnabas,' Mr Hastings panted. 'Put down the manuscript, or I'll break his arm.' Simon wriggled in his grasp and kicked backwards, but then gasped and went limp as his arm was jerked savagely higher and pain shot through him like water boiling in his blood. But before Barney, his face twisted with concern, could even move, a great yell rang out over the water from the yacht. A rough voice shouted, in anguished warning, '*Master!*'

In the same moment they heard a new noise over the low throb of the yacht's waiting engines: a high-pitched drone that grew louder and nearer. Suddenly round the corner of the headland from Trewissick, they saw a glittering arc of spray shooting up from the bows of a big speed-boat. It was moving tremendously fast, swinging out round the seaward side of the yacht towards the place where they stood. And in a glimpse through the spray, they saw the only figure they knew that could tower as tall as Mr Hastings, and above it the familiar blowing tousle of white hair.

Jane let out a shout high with relief. 'It's Gumerry!'

Mr Hastings snarled and released Simon suddenly, making a desperate lunge forward at Barney where he stood wavering on the edge. Just in time Barney saw him and ducked away backwards under his hand.

Bill, in his dinghy, ripped at the outboard motor and set it roaring; then jumped, slithering on the rocks but landing safe. Chunky and menacing beside the giant height of the man in black, he faced them, crouching slightly. Like dancers in a minuet the two moved forward, groping slowly for the treacherous footholds, and the children shrank back against the cliff.

The speed-boat roared up in a great flurry of spray. Within seconds it was alongside the headland. The engine's note changed to a deeper throb and the boat lurched slowly closer. Looking fearfully over Bill's advancing shoulder Jane could see Great-Uncle Merry standing erect, beside the blue-jerseyed figure of Mr Penhallow crouching over the controls.

Forgetting everything in the overwhelming surge of relief, she dashed forward to the edge of the rocks, taking the boy by surprise so that he grasped at her too late and overbalanced against Mr Hastings. The man snarled at him angrily and made a last reach for Barney as he stood pressed and staring helplessly against the cliff, his arms hanging down now limp.

But Simon, twisting up the last of his strength, snatched the grail and the long cylinder of the telescope case from his brother and slipped out of reach, dodging round him to the edge of the waves.

He shouted urgently, 'Gumerry!' As his great-uncle turned, he raised his arm and flung the grail with all his might towards the speed-boat, watching agonized to see if it could cross the gap. At the controls, Mr Penhallow wrestled to hold the boat steady. The strange bell-like cup wheeled through the air, flashing golden in the sun, and Great-Uncle Merry shot out one arm sideways like a slip fielder and caught it as it curved over towards the water.

'Look out!' Barney yelled. Mr Hastings pivoted towards Simon as he drew back his arm to send the manuscript after the cup, darting sideways to keep out of reach. He threw: but as the case left his hand Mr Withers, rising dripping to his feet in the dinghy, lunged out with an oar in a clumsy attempt to intercept it.

Jane screamed.

The oar struck the case in mid-flight. Withers let out a shout of triumph. But in his throat it changed to terror, as the long unwieldy case spun off the oar with the force of Simon's throw and came apart in the air. The two halves spiralled out away from the boat, scattering fragments of the familiar manuscript that they had studied so often: they saw the small lead case from the cave fall out and splash like a stone into the sea; and almost at the same moment the two halves of the telescope case, with their disintegrating parchment, hit the water and disappeared. The broken pieces of parchment did not float; they were gone at once, as if they had dissolved. Nothing was left but Jane's handkerchief, bobbing forlornly on the waves.

And then their blood stood still and cold within them, as an inhuman sound like the howl of an animal rang out over the sea. It was the second long howl that they had heard that day, but it was not the same as the first. Mr Hastings put back his head like a dog, and gave a great shriek of pain and fear and rage. With two long bounds he leapt from the edge of the rocks, and dived with a mighty splash into the rippled water where the case had gone down.

They stared at the sunlight dancing on the water that had closed over his head, and but for the mutter of the engines and the sea there was no sound. A movement by the yacht caught their gaze, and they saw the girl being pulled aboard, with her dinghy left bobbing below.

Bill stood as immobile as the children, gazing open-mouthed at the sea turning golden now under the late sun. Then Withers shouted at him, lurching towards the outboard motor in the remaining dinghy, and as the boat moved off the boy flung himself aboard.

The children still stood watching. No one moved either aboard the speedboat, as it swayed towards the rocks on the swell. The dinghy moved out, buzzing like an angry wasp, and then beside it they saw a dark head break surface, and heard the rasp of desperate gulping breaths. The dinghy slowed, and the man and boy in it heaved the tall black figure aboard. It held nothing in its hand.

Mr Hastings lay in the bottom of the boat, choking and gasping for breath, but as they watched he raised his head, the dark wet hair flattened over his forehead like a mask, and put out a hand to Withers to pull himself up. With rage and hatred twisting his face, he looked back at Great-Uncle Merry.

Great-Uncle Merry stood in the speed-boat with one hand on the wind-shield and the other holding the grail, the sun behind him blazing in his white hair. He drew himself so tall and erect that he looked for a strange moment like some great creature of the rocks and the sea. And he called across the water, in a strong voice that rang back from the cliffs, some words in a language that the children could not understand, but with a note through it that made them suddenly shiver.

And the dark figure in the other boat seemed to shrink within himself at the sound, so that the menace and power were all at once gone out of him. Suddenly he looked only ridiculous in the skin-wet black clothes, and seemed smaller than he had been before. All three in the boat cowered down, making no move or sound, as the dinghy crossed back to the yacht.

The children stirred. 'Gosh!' Barney whispered. 'What did he say?'

'I don't know.'

'I'm glad I don't know,' Jane said slowly.

They watched as the three figures swung themselves aboard the yacht, and almost at once the engine throbbed higher and the *Lady Mary*'s long white hull slipped away. The broad outboard dinghy trailed forlorn behind, but the other remained, bobbing and drifting empty on the waves.

The yacht headed out across the bay, past Trewissick harbour and down the coast, until she was only a small white shape on the sun-gilded sea. And by the time they had all climbed aboard the speed-boat, and looked again, she was gone.

Epilogue

The sound of clapping echoed through the glossy pillars of the long museum gallery, and Simon, very pink in the face, threaded his way back to Barney and Jane through the crowd of gravely smiling scholars and dons. The crowd began to move about again, and voices rose in a general chatter all round them.

A bright-eyed young man with a notebook materialized at their side. 'That was a very nice speech, Simon, if I may say so. This is Jane and Barnabas, is it?'

Simon blinked at him, and nodded.

'I'm from the Press Association,' said the young man briskly. 'Can I just ask you how large a cheque the curator presented you with?'

Simon looked down at the envelope in his hand, put his finger nervously in the flap and tore it open. He took out the neatly folded cheque, gazed at it for several moments, and without a word passed it across to Jane.

Jane looked at it, and swallowed. 'It says, one hundred pounds.'

'*Gosh*!' said Barney.

'Well, that's nice,' said the young man cheerfully. 'Congratulations. Now then, what will you do with it?'

They looked at him blankly.

'I don't know,' said Simon at last.

'Oh, come now,' the young man persisted. 'You must have some idea. What are the things you've always most wanted to buy?'

The children looked at one another helplessly.

'Young man,' said Great-Uncle Merry's deep voice beside them, 'if you were suddenly presented with a hundred pounds, what would you buy?'

The reporter looked taken aback. 'Well – er – I –'

'Precisely,' said Great-Uncle Merry. 'You don't know. Neither do these children. Good afternoon.'

'Just one more thing,' said the young man, unabashed, writing rapid shorthand squiggles in his notebook. 'What were you actually doing when you found the thing?'

'The grail, you mean,' Barney said.

'Well, yes, that's what you like to call it, isn't it?' said the young man lightly.

Barney glared at him indignantly.

'We just happened to be exploring a cave,' Simon said hastily. 'And we found it on a ledge.'

'Wasn't there talk of someone else having been after it?'

'Moonshine,' said Great-Uncle Merry firmly. 'Now look here, my boy, you go off and talk to the curator, just over there. He knows all about it. These three have had enough excitement for one day.'

The young man opened his mouth to say something else, looked at Great-Uncle Merry, and shut it again. He grinned amiably and disappeared into the crowd, and Great-Uncle Merry steered the children into a quiet corner behind a pillar.

'Well,' he said, 'you'll have your pictures in all the papers tomorrow, you'll be written about in books for years to come by a lot of distinguished scholarly gentlemen, and you've been given a hundred pounds by one of the most famous museums in the world. And I must say you all deserve it.'

'Gumerry,' Simon said thoughtfully. 'I know there'd be no point in telling people the real story behind finding the grail, but wouldn't it be a good thing at least to warn them about Mr Hastings? I mean, he got hold of Mrs Palk and that boy Bill and made them bad, and there's nothing to stop him going round doing it to everyone.'

'He has gone,' Great-Uncle Merry said. Two owl-like men in heavy spectacles, passing, bowed respectfully to him, and he nodded vaguely.

'I know, but he might come back.'

Great-Uncle Merry looked down the long gallery, over the heads, and the old closed look came back into his face. 'When he does come back,' he said, 'it will not be as Mr Hastings.'

'Wasn't his name really Hastings at all?' Simon said curiously.

'I have known him use many different names,' Great-Uncle Merry said, 'at many different times.'

Jane slid one foot unhappily to and fro over the smooth marble floor. 'It seems so awful that a vicar should be so bad.'

'He must have kidded all the bishops and things into thinking he was good,' Simon said. 'Same as he kidded everyone in Trewissick.'

'Not at all,' Great-Uncle Merry said.

Simon stared at him. 'But he must have . . . I mean, they must have heard him preaching sermons on Sundays.'

'No one heard him preach on Sundays. And I doubt if he has ever met a bishop in his life.'

Now they were all staring at him, in such baffled amazement that the sides of his mouth twitched into a half-smile. 'It's quite simple. What they call the power of suggestion. Our Mr Hastings was not the vicar of Trewissick, nor anything to do with him. I know the real vicar slightly, he is a tall man as well, though rather thin and about seventy years old . . . his name is Smith.'

'But Mr Hastings lived in the vicarage,' Barney said.

'It was the vicarage, once. Now it's let out to anyone who wants to rent it . . .

the parish council decided years ago that it was much too big for Mr Smith to live alone in it like a pea in a pod, and they found him a little cottage on the other side of the church.'

'And when I went to find him,' Jane said slowly, trying to remember, 'I didn't ask anyone where he lived, I just said to an old man by the church, is that the vicarage, and all he said was yes . . . he was a rather bad-tempered old man, I think . . . And do you know, Gumerry, I don't think Mr Hastings actually told me he was the vicar, I just took it for granted when he said something about his replacing Mr Hawes-Mellor there. But he must have known I thought he was.'

'Oh yes. He wasn't going to disillusion you until he'd found out what you were up to. He knew perfectly well who you were.'

'Did he really?'

'From the moment he opened his front door.'

'Oh,' said Jane. She thought about it, and felt cold. 'Oh.'

'So from that moment we all went on thinking he was the vicar,' Simon said, 'and if ever we mentioned him to anybody like Mr Penhallow they must have thought we meant the real vicar . . . but Gumerry, didn't you know?'

Great-Uncle Merry chuckled. 'No. That's what I thought as well. For some time – well, right up to the last – I entertained the most terrible suspicions of poor harmless Mr Smith.'

Barney said unexpectedly: 'But if you've been against Mr Hastings before, surely you couldn't mistake anybody else for him?'

'He changes,' Great-Uncle Merry said vaguely, deliberately looking away again. 'There is no knowing what he will look like . . .'

And there was a finality in the ring of his voice that forbade any further question; as they knew there would always be when they tried to ask more about the mysterious enemy of their days in Trewissick. This was one of the things from Great-Uncle Merry's secret world, and even though they had been so much involved, they knew he would keep his secrets as he always had.

Simon looked down at the cheque in his hand. 'We found the grail,' he said. 'And everyone seems frightfully excited about it. But it isn't any use on its own, is it? The Cornishman said, if whoever found it had other words from him, on the second manuscript that we didn't even have a chance to look at, then they'd be able to understand what was written on the grail and know the secret of it all. But we shan't ever know, because the manuscripts are at the bottom of the sea.'

Barney said, gloomily, 'We failed, really.'

Great-Uncle Merry said nothing, and when they looked up at him, hearing only the hum of voices from the crowd, he seemed to be towering over them as tall and still as the pillar at his side.

'Failed?' he said, and he was smiling. 'Oh no. Is that really what you think? You haven't failed. The hunt for the grail was a battle, as important in its way as any battle that's ever been fought. And you won it, the three of you. The powers behind the man calling himself Hastings came very near to winning, and what that victory would have meant, if the secret of the grail had been given into their hands, is more than anyone dare think. But thanks to you the vital secret they needed is safe from them still, for as many centuries perhaps as it was before. Safe – not destroyed, Simon. The first manuscript, your map, will certainly have disintegrated at once in the sea. But that was no more use to anyone once it had led you to the second, and the grail. It might have made my colleagues even more excited' – he glanced round the room, and chuckled – 'but that's no matter. The point is that the second manuscript, down under the sea, is sealed up in its case – which will resist seawater indefinitely if it's made of lead. So the last secret is safe, and hidden. So well hidden at the bottom of Trewissick Bay that they could never even begin the long business of searching for it without our being able to find out, and to stop them. They have lost their chance.'

'And so have we,' Simon said bitterly, seeing again the picture that had never properly left his mind. He thought of the glinting brass telescope case, with both precious manuscripts sealed inside, flying from his desperate hand and then, only yards from Great-Uncle Merry's safe grasp, jerking away from the raised oar to break and plunge its contents for ever into the sea.

'No, we haven't,' said Jane unexpectedly. She was thinking of the same moment, and she was out of the cool marble vastness of the museum, back on Kemare Head in the excitement and the scorching sun. 'We do know where it is. I was standing by the only thing that could mark it – that deep pool in the rocks. I was just on the edge, and the lead case went down right in front of me. So we should know where to look if we ever went back.'

For a moment Great-Uncle Merry looked really alarmed. 'I had no idea of that. Then the others will have noticed the same thing – and they will be able to go straight to the spot, dive for the manuscript, and be away with it before anyone has time even to notice they are there.'

'No, they won't,' Jane said, pink and earnest. 'That's the best thing of all, Gumerry. You see, we only noticed that pool in the first place because we came across it when the tide was at its lowest. By the time we were on our way back to the beach the water had covered it again. Mr Withers fell into it, but he didn't know he had. So if there was ever a tide as low as that again, we should be able to look for the pool and find the second manuscript. But the enemy wouldn't, because they don't know about the pool at all.'

'Can we go back?' Simon said eagerly. 'Can we go back, Gumerry, and have someone dive for it?'

'One day, perhaps,' Great-Uncle Merry said; and then before he could say any more a group of men from the murmuring crowd all round them had turned towards him: 'Ah, Professor Lyon! If you have a moment, might I introduce you to Dr Theodore Reisenstatz –'

'I am a great, great disciple of yours,' an intense little man with a pointed beard said to Great-Uncle Merry as he took his hand. 'Merriman Lyon is a name much honoured in my country . . .'

'Come on,' Simon said in an undertone; and the children slipped away to stand on the edge of the crowd, while the bald heads and grey beards wagged and chattered solemnly. They looked across the shimmering floor to the lone glass case where the grail stood like a golden star.

Barney was gazing into space as if he were coming out of a trance.

'Wake up,' Jane said cheerfully.

Barney said slowly, 'Is that his real name?'

'Whose name?'

'Great-Uncle Merry – is he really called Merriman?'

'Well, of course – that's what Merry is short for.'

'I didn't know,' Barney said. 'I always thought Merry was a nickname. Merriman Lyon . . .'

'Funny name, isn't it?' said Simon lightly. 'Come on, let's go and have another look at the grail. I want to see what it says about us again.'

He moved round the edge of the crowd with Jane; but Barney stayed where he was. 'Merriman Lyon,' he said softly to himself. 'Merry Lyon . . . Merlion . . . *Merlin* . . .'

He looked across the room to where Great-Uncle Merry's white head towered over the rest; slightly bent as he listened to what someone else was saying. The angular brown face seemed more than ever like an old, old carving, deep eyes shadowed and mysterious above the fierce nose.

'No,' Barney said aloud, and he shook himself. 'It's not possible.' But as he followed Simon and Jane he glanced back over his shoulder, wondering. And Great-Uncle Merry, as if he knew, turned his head and looked him full in the face for an instant, across the crowd; smiled very faintly, and looked away again.

All the way up the immense gallery, over its glistening stone floor, row upon row of identical glass cases stretched into the distance, with pots, daggers, coins, strange twisted pieces of bronze and leather and wood all shut quiet inside like butterflies caught on pins. The case which held the grail was taller than the rest; a high glass box in a place of honour in the centre of the great gallery, with nothing inside it but the one shining cup, cleaned now to brilliant gold, poised on a heavy black plinth. A neat silver square beneath was engraved with the words:

Gold chalice of unknown Celtic workmanship, believed sixth century. Found in Trewissick, south Cornwall, and presented by Simon, Jane and Barnabas Drew.

They moved round the case, looking at the grail. Its curved, engraved sides had been meticulously cleaned; and now that the beaten gold was free of the dirt left by centuries in the cave under Kemare Head, every line of the engraving was clear.

They saw that it was divided into five panels, and that four of the five were covered with pictures of men fighting: brandishing swords and spears, crouching behind shields, dressed not in armour but in strange tunics ending above their knees. They wore helmets on their heads; but the helmets, curving down over the backs of their necks, were like no shape the children had ever seen before. Between the figures, interweaving like pictures on a tapestry, words and letters were closely engraved. The last panel, the fifth, was completely covered in words, as close-written as the scrawled black lines had been on the manuscript. But all these words on the golden grail, the children knew, were in a language nobody, from Great-Uncle Merry to the museum experts, had been able to understand.

Behind them, they heard two men from the crowd come up deep in discussion, looking down into the glass case.

'. . . quite unique. Of course the significance of the inscription is difficult to estimate. Clearly runic, I think – strange, in a Roman ambiance . . .'

'But my dear fellow –' The second man's voice was loud and jolly; glancing round, Barney saw that he was red-faced, enormous beside his small bespectacled companion. 'Emphasizing the runic element surely presupposes some Saxon connexion, and the whole essence of this thing is Celtic. Romano-Celtic if you like, but consider the Arthurian evidence –'

'Arthurian?' said the first voice in nasal disbelief. 'I should have to have greater proof for that than Professor Lyon's imaginative surmise. Loomis, I think, would have grave doubts . . . but indeed a remarkable find none the less, remarkable . . .'

They moved away again into the crowd.

'What on earth did all that mean?' said Jane. 'Doesn't he believe it's about King Arthur?' Barney glared resentfully after the little man. Then they heard voices from another group passing the show-case.

'Surely all the theories will have to be revised now; it throws a new light on the entire Arthurian canon.' The voice was as solemn as the rest, but younger;

and then it chuckled. 'Poor old Battersby – all his vapourings about Scandinavian analogues, and now here's the first evidence since Nennius of a Celtic Arthur – a real king –'

'*The Times* asked me for a piece, you know,' said a deeper voice.

'Oh really, did you do that? Bit strong, wasn't it? – "a find to shake the whole field of English scholarship"–'

'Not at all,' said the deeper voice. 'It's undoubtedly genuine, and it undoubtedly gives clues to the identity of Arthur. And as such it can't be overpraised. I'm only sorry about that last panel.'

'Yes, the mysterious inscription. A cipher, I think. It must be. Those strange Old English characters – runic, old Battersby claims, absurd of course – personally I'm sure there was once a key to them. Lost long since, of course, so we shall never know...'

The voices faded like the rest.

'Well, that sounds better,' Simon said.

'They all seem to treat it as a kind of relic,' Jane said sadly. 'I suppose it's what Gumerry said, that the real meaning of it wouldn't have been known unless the enemy had got hold of it, and then it would have been too late.'

'Well, the enemy can come and look at it as much as they like now,' said Simon, 'but it won't mean anything to them without the manuscript. I suppose that was the key to the ciphers in the last panel, that the man was talking about just now.'

Jane sighed. 'And it won't mean anything to us either. So we shan't know the real truth about King Arthur, about the – what did the manuscript call him? – the Pendragon.'

'No. We shan't know exactly who he was, or what happened to him.'

'We shan't know what his secret was, that Gumerry talked about and the enemy wanted.'

'We shan't know about that other odd thing the manuscript said – the day when the Pendragon shall come again.'

Barney, listening to them, looked again at the mysterious words engraved on the gleaming side of the grail. And he raised his head to stare across the room at Great-Uncle Merry's tall figure, with the great white head and fierce, secret face.

'I think we shall know,' he said slowly, 'one day.'

The Dark is Rising

For Jonathan

Contents

PART ONE
The Finding

Midwinter's Eve

'Too many!' James shouted, and slammed the door behind him.

'What?' said Will.

'Too many kids in this family, that's what. Just *too many*.' James stood fuming on the landing like a small angry locomotive, then stumped across to the window-seat and stared out at the garden. Will put aside his book and pulled up his legs to make room. 'I could hear all the yelling,' he said, chin on knees.

'Wasn't anything,' James said. 'Just stupid Barbara again. Bossing. Pick up this, don't touch that. And Mary joining in, twitter twitter twitter. You'd think this house was big enough, but there's always *people*.'

They both looked out of the window. The snow lay thin and apologetic over the world. That wide grey sweep was the lawn, with the straggling trees of the orchard still dark beyond; the white squares were the roofs of the garage, the old barn, the rabbit hutches, the chicken coops. Further back there were only the flat fields of Dawsons' Farm, dimly white-striped. All the broad sky was grey, full of more snow that refused to fall. There was no colour anywhere.

'Four days to Christmas,' Will said. 'I wish it would snow properly.'

'And your birthday tomorrow.'

'Mmm.' He had been going to say that too, but it would have been too much like a reminder. And the gift he most wished for on his birthday was something nobody could give him: it was snow, beautiful, deep, blanketing snow, and it never came. At least this year there was the grey sprinkle, better than nothing.

He said, remembering a duty: 'I haven't fed the rabbits yet. Want to come?'

Booted and muffled, they clumped out through the sprawling kitchen. A full symphony orchestra was swelling out of the radio; their eldest sister Gwen was slicing onions and singing; their mother was bent broad-beamed and red-faced over an oven. 'Rabbits!' she shouted, when she caught sight of them. 'And some more hay from the farm!'

'We're going!' Will shouted back. The radio let out a sudden hideous crackle of static as he passed the table. He jumped. Mrs Stanton shrieked, 'Turn that thing DOWN.'

Outdoors, it was suddenly very quiet. Will dipped out a pail of pellets from the bin in the farm-smelling barn, which was not really a barn at all, but a long, low building with a tiled roof, once a stable. They tramped through the thin snow to the row of heavy wooden hutches, leaving dark foot-marks on the hard frozen ground.

Opening doors to fill the feed-boxes, Will paused, frowning. Normally the rabbits would be huddled sleepily in corners, only the greedy ones coming twitch-nosed forward to eat. Today they seemed restless and uneasy, rustling to and fro, banging against their wooden walls; one or two even leapt back in alarm when he opened their doors. He came to his favourite rabbit, named Chelsea, and reached in as usual to rub him affectionately behind the ears, but the animal scuffled back away from him and cringed into a corner, the pink-rimmed eyes staring up blank and terrified.

'Hey!' Will said, disturbed. 'Hey James, look at that. What's the matter with him? And all of them?'

'They seem all right to me.'

'Well, they don't to me. They're all jumpy. Even Chelsea. Hey, come on, boy –' But it was no good.

'Funny,' James said with mild interest, watching. 'I dare say your hands smell wrong. You must have touched something they don't like. Same as dogs and aniseed, but the other way round.'

'I haven't touched anything. Matter of fact, I'd just washed my hands when I saw you.'

'There you are then,' James said promptly. 'That's the trouble. They've never smelt you clean before. Probably all die of shock.'

'Ha very ha.' Will attacked him, and they scuffled together, grinning, while the empty pail toppled rattling on the hard ground. But when he glanced back as they left, the animals were still moving distractedly, not eating yet, staring after him with those strange frightened wide eyes.

'There might be a fox about again, I suppose,' James said. 'Remind me to tell

Mum.' No fox could get at the rabbits, in their sturdy row, but the chickens were more vulnerable; a family of foxes had broken into one of the henhouses the previous winter and carried off six nicely-fattened birds just before marketing-time. Mrs Stanton, who relied on the chicken-money each year to help pay for eleven Christmas presents, had been so furious she had kept watch afterwards in the cold barn two nights running, but the villains had not come back. Will thought that if he were a fox he would have kept clear too; his mother might be married to a jeweller, but with generations of Buckinghamshire farmers behind her, she was no joke when the old instincts were roused.

Tugging the handcart, a home-made contraption with a bar joining its shafts, he and James made their way down the curve of the overgrown drive and out along the road to Dawsons' Farm. Quickly past the churchyard, its great dark yew trees leaning out over the crumbling wall; more slowly by Rooks' Wood, on the corner of Church Lane. The tall spinney of horse-chestnut trees, raucous with the calling of the rooks and rubbish-roofed with the clutter of their sprawling nests, was one of their familiar places.

'Hark at the rooks! Something's disturbed them.' The harsh irregular chorus was deafening, and when Will looked up at the tree-tops he saw the sky dark with wheeling birds. They flapped and drifted to and fro; there were no flurries of sudden movement, only this clamorous interweaving throng of rooks.

'An owl?'

'They're not chasing anything. Come on, Will, it'll be getting dark soon.'

'That's why it's so odd for the rooks to be in a fuss. They all ought to be roosting by now.' Will turned his head reluctantly down again, but then jumped and clutched his brother's arm, his eye caught by a movement in the darkening lane that led away from the road where they stood. Church Lane: it ran between Rooks' Wood and the churchyard to the tiny local church, and then on to the River Thames.

'Hey!'

'What's up?'

'There's someone over there. Or there was. Looking at us.'

James sighed. 'So what? Just someone out for a walk.'

'No, he wasn't.' Will screwed up his eyes nervously, peering down the little side road. 'It was a weird-looking man all hunched over, and when he saw me looking he ran off behind a tree. *Scuttled*, like a beetle.'

James heaved at the handcart and set off up the road, making Will run to keep up. 'It's just a tramp, then. I dunno, everyone seems to be going batty today – Barb and the rabbits and the rooks and now you, all yak-twitchetty-yakking. Come on, let's get that hay. I want my tea.'

The handcart bumped through the frozen ruts into Dawsons' yard, the great earthen square enclosed by buildings on three sides, and they smelt the familiar farm-smell. The cowshed must have been mucked out that day; Old George, the toothless cattleman, was piling dung across the yard. He raised a hand to them. Nothing missed Old George; he could see a hawk drop from a mile away. Mr Dawson came out of a barn.

'Ah,' he said. 'Hay for Stantons' Farm?' It was his joke with their mother, because of the rabbits and the hens.

James said, 'Yes, please.'

'It's coming,' Mr Dawson said. Old George had disappeared into the barn. 'Keeping well, then? Tell your mum I'll have ten birds off her tomorrow. And four rabbits. Don't look like that, young Will. If it's not their happy Christmas, it's one for the folks as'll have them.' He glanced up at the sky, and Will thought a strange look came over his lined brown face. Up against the lowering grey clouds, two black rooks were flapping slowly over the farm in a wide circle.

'The rooks are making an awful din today,' James said. 'Will saw a tramp up by the wood.'

Mr Dawson looked at Will sharply. 'What was he like?'

'Just a little old man. He dodged away.'

'So the Walker is abroad,' the farmer said softly to himself. 'Ah. He would be.'

'Nasty weather for walking,' James said cheerfully. He nodded at the northern sky over the farmhouse roof; the clouds there seemed to be growing darker, massing in ominous grey mounds with a yellowish tinge. The wind was rising too; it stirred their hair, and they could hear a distant rustling from the tops of the trees.

'More snow coming,' said Mr Dawson.

'It's a horrible day,' said Will suddenly, surprised by his own violence; after all, he had wanted snow. But somehow uneasiness was growing in him. 'It's – creepy, somehow.'

'It will be a bad night,' said Mr Dawson.

'There's Old George with the hay,' said James. 'Come on, Will.'

'You go,' the farmer said. 'I want Will to pick up something for your mother from the house.' But he did not move, as James pushed the handcart off towards the barn; he stood with his hands thrust deep into the pockets of his old tweed jacket, looking at the darkening sky.

'The Walker is abroad,' he said again. 'And this night will be bad, and tomorrow will be beyond imagining.' He looked at Will, and Will looked back in growing alarm into the weathered face, the bright dark eyes creased narrow by decades of peering into sun and rain and wind. He had never noticed before how dark Farmer Dawson's eyes were: strange, in their blue-eyed county.

'You have a birthday coming,' the farmer said.

'Mmm,' said Will.

'I have something for you.' He glanced briefly round the yard, and withdrew one hand from his pocket; in it, Will saw what looked like a kind of ornament, made of black metal, a flat circle quartered by two crossed lines. He took it, fingering it curiously. It was about the size of his palm, and quite heavy; roughly forged out of iron, he guessed, though with no sharp points or edges. The iron was cold to his hand.

'What is it?' he said.

'For the moment,' Mr Dawson said, 'just call it something to keep. To keep with you always, all the time. Put it in your pocket, now. And later on, loop your belt through it and wear it like an extra buckle.'

Will slipped the iron circle into his pocket. 'Thank you very much,' he said, rather shakily. Mr Dawson, usually a comforting man, was not improving the day at all.

The farmer looked at him in the same intent, unnerving way, until Will felt the hair rise on the back of his neck; then he gave a twisted half-smile, with no amusement in it but a kind of anxiety. 'Keep it safe, Will. And the less you happen to talk about it, the better. You will need it after the snow comes.' He became brisk. 'Come on, now, Mrs Dawson has a jar of her mincemeat for your mother.'

They moved off towards the farmhouse. The farmer's wife was not there, but waiting in the doorway was Maggie Barnes, the farm's round-faced, red-cheeked dairymaid, who always reminded Will of an apple. She beamed at them both, holding out a big white crockery jar tied with a red ribbon.

'Thank you, Maggie,' Farmer Dawson said.

'Missus said you'd be wanting it for young Will here,' Maggie said. 'She went down the village to see the vicar for something. How's your big brother, then, Will?'

She always said this, whenever she saw him; she meant Will's next-to-oldest brother Max. It was a Stanton family joke that Maggie Barnes at Dawsons' had a thing about Max.

'Fine, thank you,' Will said politely. 'Grown his hair long. Looks like a girl.'

Maggie shrieked with delight. 'Get away with you!' She giggled and waved her farewell, and just at the last moment Will noticed her gaze slip upward past his head. Out of the corner of his eye as he turned, he thought he saw a flicker of movement by the farmyard gate, as if someone were dodging quickly out of sight. But when he looked, no one was there.

With the big pot of mincemeat wedged between two bales of hay, Will and James pushed the handcart out of the yard. The farmer stood in his doorway behind them; Will could feel his eyes, watching. He glanced up uneasily at the looming, growing clouds, and half-unwillingly slipped a hand into his pocket to finger the strange iron circle. '*After the snow comes.*' The sky looked as if it were about to fall on them. He thought: *what's happening?*

One of the farm dogs came bounding up, tail waving; then it stopped abruptly a few yards away, looking at them.

'Hey, Racer!' Will called.

The dog's tail went down, and it snarled, showing its teeth.

'James!' said Will.

'He won't hurt you. What's the matter?'

They went on, and turned into the road.

'It's not that. Something's wrong, that's all. Something's awful. Racer, Chelsea – the animals are all scared of me.' He was beginning to be really frightened now.

The noise from the rookery was louder, even though the daylight was beginning to die. They could see the dark birds thronging over the treetops, more agitated than before, flapping and turning to and fro. And Will had been right; there was a stranger in the lane, standing beside the churchyard.

He was a shambling, tattered figure, more like a bundle of old clothes than a man, and at the sight of him the boys slowed their pace and drew instinctively closer to the cart and to one another. He turned his shaggy head to look at them.

Then suddenly, in a dreadful blur of unreality, a hoarse, shrieking flurry was rushing dark down out of the sky, and two huge rooks swooped at the man. He staggered back, shouting, his hands thrust up to protect his face, and the birds flapped their great wings in a black vicious whirl and were gone, swooping up past the boys and into the sky.

Will and James stood frozen, staring, pressed against the bales of hay.

The stranger cowered back against the gate.

'Kaaaaaaak ... kaaaaaak ...' came the head-splitting racket from the frenzied flock over the wood, and then three more whirling black shapes were swooping after the first two, diving wildly at the man and then away. This time he screamed in terror and stumbled out into the road, his arms still wrapped in defence round his head, his face down; and he ran. The boys heard the frightened gasps for breath as he dashed headlong past them, and up the road past the gates of Dawsons' Farm and on towards the village. They saw bushy, greasy grey hair below a dirty old cap; a torn brown overcoat tied with string, and some other garment flapping beneath it; old boots, one with a loose sole that made him kick his leg oddly sideways, half-hopping, as he ran. But they did not see his face.

The high whirling above their heads was dwindling into loops of slow flight, and the rooks began to settle one by one into the trees. They were still talking loudly to one another in a long cawing jumble, but the madness and the violence were not in it now. Dazed, moving his head for the first time, Will felt his cheek brush against something, and putting his hand to his shoulder, he found a long black feather there. He pushed it into his jacket pocket, moving slowly, like someone half-awake.

Together they pushed the loaded cart down the road to the house, and the cawing behind them died to an ominous murmur, like the swollen Thames in spring.

James said at last, 'Rooks don't do that sort of thing. They don't attack people. And they don't come down low when there's not much space. They just don't.'

'No,' Will said. He was still moving in a detached half-dream, not fully aware of anything except a curious vague groping in his mind. In the midst of all the din and the flurry, he had suddenly had a strange feeling stronger than any he had ever known: he had been aware that someone was trying to tell him something, something that had missed him because he could not understand the words. Not words exactly; it had been like a kind of silent shout. But he had not been able to pick up the message, because he had not known how.

'Like not having the radio on the right station,' he said aloud.

'What?' said James, but he wasn't really listening. 'What a thing,' he said. 'I s'pose the tramp must have been trying to catch a rook. And they got wild. He'll be snooping around after the hens and the rabbits, I bet you. Funny he didn't have a gun. Better tell Mum to leave the dogs in the barn tonight.' He chattered amiably on as they reached home and unloaded the hay. Gradually Will realized in amazement that all the shock of the wild, savage attack was running out of James's mind like water, and that in a matter of minutes even the very fact of its happening had gone.

Something had neatly wiped the whole incident from James's memory; something that did not want it reported. Something that knew this would stop Will from reporting it too.

'Here, take Mum's mincemeat,' James said. 'Let's go in before we freeze. The wind's really getting up – good job we hurried back.'

'Yes,' said Will. He felt cold, but it was not from the rising wind. His fingers closed round the iron circle in his pocket and held it tightly. This time, the iron felt warm.

The grey world had slipped into the dark by the time they went back to the kitchen. Outside the window, their father's battered little van stood in a yellow cave of light. The kitchen was even noisier and hotter than before. Gwen was setting the table, patiently steering her way round a trio of bent figures where Mr Stanton was peering at some small, nameless piece of machinery with the twins, Robin and Paul; and with Mary's plump form now guarding it, the radio was blasting out pop music at enormous volume. As Will approached, it erupted again into a high-pitched screech, so that everyone broke off with grimaces and howls.

'Turn that thing OFF!' Mrs Stanton yelled desperately from the sink. But though Mary, pouting, shut off the crackle and the buried music, the noise level changed very little. Somehow it never did when more than half the family was at home. Voices and laughter filled the long stone-floored kitchen as they sat round the scrubbed wooden table; the two Welsh collies, Raq and Ci, lay dozing at the far end of the room beside the fire. Will kept away from them; he could not have borne it if their own dogs had snarled at him. He sat quietly at tea – it was called tea if Mrs Stanton managed to produce it before five o'clock, supper if it was later, but it was always the same hearty kind of meal – and kept his plate and his mouth full of sausage to avoid having to talk. Not that anyone was likely to miss your talk in the cheerful babble of the Stanton family, especially when you were its youngest member.

Waving at him from the end of the table, his mother called, 'What shall we have for tea tomorrow, Will?'

He said indistinctly, 'Liver and bacon, please.'

James gave a loud groan.

'Shut up,' said Barbara, superior and sixteen. 'It's his birthday, he can choose.'

'But *liver*,' said James.

'Serves you right,' Robin said. 'On your last birthday, if I remember right, we all had to eat that revolting cauliflower cheese.'

'I made it,' said Gwen, 'and it wasn't revolting.'

'No offence,' said Robin mildly. 'I just can't bear cauliflower. Anyway you take my point.'

'I do. I don't know whether James does.'

Robin, large and deep-voiced, was the more muscular of the twins and not to be trifled with. James said hastily, 'Okay, okay.'

'Double-ones tomorrow, Will,' said Mr Stanton from the head of the table.

'We should have some special kind of ceremony. A tribal rite.' He smiled at his youngest son, his round, rather chubby face crinkling in affection.

Mary sniffed. 'On my eleventh birthday, I was beaten and sent to bed.'

'Good heavens,' said her mother, 'fancy you remembering that. And what a way to describe it. In point of fact you got one hard wallop on the bottom, and well-deserved, too, as far as I can recollect.'

'It was my birthday,' Mary said, tossing her pony-tail. 'And I've never forgotten.'

'Give yourself time,' Robin said cheerfully. 'Three years isn't much.'

'And you were a very young eleven,' Mrs Stanton said, chewing reflectively.

'Huh!' said Mary. 'And I suppose Will isn't?'

For a moment everyone looked at Will. He blinked in alarm at the ring of contemplating faces, and scowled down into his plate so that nothing of him was visible except a thick slanting curtain of brown hair. It was most disturbing to be looked at by so many people all at once, or at any rate by more people than one could look at in return. He felt almost as if he were being attacked. And he was suddenly convinced that it could in some way be dangerous to have so many people thinking about him, all at the same time. As if someone unfriendly might *hear* . . .

'Will,' Gwen said at length, 'is rather an old eleven.'

'Ageless, almost,' Robin said. They both sounded solemn and detached, as if they were discussing some far-off stranger.

'Let up, now,' said Paul unexpectedly. He was the quiet twin, and the family genius, perhaps a real one: he played the flute and thought about little else. 'Anyone coming to tea tomorrow, Will?'

'No. Angus Macdonald's gone to Scotland for Christmas, and Mike's staying with his grannie in Southall. I don't mind.'

There was a sudden commotion at the back door, and a blast of cold air; much stamping, and noises of loud shivering. Max stuck his head into the room from the passage; his long hair was wet and white-starred. 'Sorry I'm late, Mum, had to walk from the Common. Wow, you should see it out there – like a blizzard.' He looked at the blank row of faces, and grinned. 'Don't you know it's snowing?'

Forgetting everything for a moment, Will gave a joyful yell and scrambled with James for the door. 'Real snow? Heavy?'

'I'll say,' said Max, scattering drops of water over them as he unwound his scarf. He was the eldest brother, not counting Stephen, who had been in the Navy for years and seldom came home. 'Here.' He opened the door a crack, and the wind whistled through again; outside, Will saw a glittering white fog of fat snowflakes – no trees or bushes visible, nothing but the whirling snow. A chorus of protest came from the kitchen: 'SHUT THAT DOOR!'

'There's your ceremony, Will,' said his father. 'Right on time.'

Much later, when he went to bed, Will opened the bedroom curtain and pressed his nose against the cold windowpane, and he saw the snow tumbling down even thicker than before. Two or three inches already lay on the sill, and he could almost watch the level rising as the wind drove more against the house. He could hear the wind, too, whining round the roof close above him, and in all the chimneys. Will slept in a slant-roofed attic at the top of the house; he had moved into it only a few months before, when Stephen, whose room it had always been, had gone back to his ship after a leave. Until then Will had always shared a room with James – everyone in the family shared with someone else. 'But my attic ought to be lived in,' his eldest brother had said, knowing how Will loved it.

On a bookcase in one corner of the room now stood a portrait of Lieutenant Stephen Stanton, R.N., looking rather uncomfortable in dress uniform, and beside it a carved wooden box with a dragon on the lid, filled with the letters he sent Will sometimes from unthinkably distant parts of the world. They made a kind of private shrine.

The snow flurried against the window, with a sound like fingers brushing the pane. Again Will heard the wind moaning in the roof, louder than before; it was rising into a real storm. He thought of the tramp, and wondered where he had taken shelter. '*The Walker is abroad . . . this night will be bad . . .*' He picked up his jacket and took the strange iron ornament from it, running his fingers round the circle, up and down the inner cross that quartered it. The surface of the iron was irregular, but though it showed no sign of having been polished it was completely smooth – smooth in a way that reminded him of a certain place in the rough stone floor of the kitchen, where all the roughness had been worn away by generations of feet turning to come round the corner from the door. It was an odd kind of iron: deep, absolute black, with no shine to it but no spot anywhere of discoloration or rust. And once more now it was cold to the touch; so cold this time that Will was startled to find it numbing his fingertips. Hastily he put it down. Then he pulled his belt out of his trousers, slung untidily as usual over the back of a chair, took the circle, and threaded it through like an extra buckle, as Mr Dawson had told him. The wind sang in the window-frame. Will put the belt back in his trousers and dropped them on the chair.

It was then, without warning, that the fear came.

The first wave caught him as he was crossing the room to his bed. It halted him stock-still in the middle of the room, the howl of the wind outside filling his ears. The snow lashed against the window. Will was suddenly deadly cold, yet tingling all over. He was so frightened that he could not move a finger. In a flash of memory he saw again the lowering sky over the spinney, dark with rooks, the big black birds wheeling and circling overhead. Then that was gone, and he saw only the tramp's terrified face and heard his scream as he ran. For a moment, then, there was only a dreadful darkness in his mind, a sense of looking into a great black pit. Then the high howl of the wind died, and he was released.

He stood shaking, looking wildly round the room. Nothing was wrong. Everything was just as usual. The trouble, he told himself, came from thinking. It would be all right if only he could stop thinking and go to sleep. He pulled off his dressing-gown, climbed into bed, and lay there looking up at the skylight in the slanting roof. It was covered grey with snow.

He switched off the small bedside lamp, and the night swallowed the room. There was no hint of light even when his eyes had grown accustomed to the dark. Time to sleep. Go on, go to sleep. But although he turned on his side, pulled the blankets up to his chin, and lay there relaxed, contemplating the cheerful fact that it would be his birthday when he woke up, nothing happened. It was no good. Something was wrong.

Will tossed uneasily. He had never known a feeling like this before. It was growing worse every minute. As if some huge weight were pushing at his mind, threatening, trying to take him over, turn him into something he didn't want to be. That's it, he thought: make me into someone else. But that's stupid. Who'd want to? And make me into what? Something creaked outside the half-open door, and he jumped. Then it creaked again, and he knew what it was: a certain floorboard that often talked to itself at night, with a sound so familiar that usually he never noticed it at all. In spite of himself, he still lay listening. A different kind of creak came from further away, in the other attic, and he twitched again, jerking so that the blanket rubbed against his chin. You're just jumpy, he said to himself; you're remembering this afternoon, but really there isn't much to remember. He tried to think of the tramp as someone unremarkable, just an ordinary man with a dirty overcoat and worn-out boots; but instead all he could see once more was the vicious diving of the rooks. '*The Walker is abroad . . .*' Another strange crackling noise came, this time above his head in the ceiling, and the wind whined suddenly loud, and Will sat bolt upright in bed and reached in panic for the lamp.

The room was at once a cosy cave of yellow light, and he lay back in shame, feeling stupid. Frightened of the dark, he thought: how awful. Just like a baby. Stephen would never have been frightened of the dark, up here. Look, there's the bookcase and the table, the two chairs and the window seat; look, there are the six little square-riggers of the mobile hanging from the ceiling, and their shadows sailing over there on the wall. Everything's ordinary. Go to sleep.

He switched off the light again, and instantly everything was even worse than before. The fear jumped at him for the third time like a great animal that had been waiting to spring. Will lay terrified, shaking, feeling himself shake, and yet unable to move. He felt he must be going mad. Outside, the wind moaned, paused, rose into a sudden howl, and there was a noise, a muffled scraping thump, against the skylight in the ceiling of his room. And then in a dreadful furious moment, horror seized him like a nightmare made real; there came a wrenching crash, with the howling of the wind suddenly much louder and closer, and a great blast of cold; and the Feeling came hurtling against him with such force of dread that it flung him cowering away.

Will shrieked. He only knew it afterwards; he was far too deep in fear to hear the sound of his own voice. For an appalling pitch-black moment he lay scarcely conscious, lost somewhere out of the world, out in black space. And then there were quick footsteps up the stairs outside his door, and a voice calling in concern, and blessed light warming the room and bringing him back into life again.

It was Paul's voice. 'Will? What is it? Are you all right?'

Slowly Will opened his eyes. He found that he was clenched into the shape of a ball, with his knees drawn up tight against his chin. He saw Paul standing over him, blinking anxiously behind his dark-rimmed spectacles. He nodded, without finding his voice. Then Paul turned his head, and Will followed his looking and saw that the skylight in the roof was hanging open, still swaying with the force of its fall; there was a black square of empty night in the roof, and through it the wind was bringing in a bitter midwinter cold. On the carpet below the skylight lay a heap of snow.

Paul peered at the edge of the skylight frame. 'Catch is broken – I suppose the snow was too heavy for it. Must have been pretty old anyway, the metal's all rusted. I'll get some wire and fix it up till tomorrow. Did it wake you? Lord, what a horrible shock. If I woke up like that, you'd find me somewhere under the bed.'

Will looked at him in speechless gratitude, and managed a watery smile. Every word in Paul's soothing, deep voice brought him closer back to reality. He sat up in bed and pulled back the covers.

'Dad must have some wire with that junk in the other attic,' Paul said. 'But let's get this snow out before it melts. Look, there's more coming in. I bet there aren't many houses where you can watch the snow coming down on the carpet.'

He was right: snowflakes were whirling in through the black space in the ceiling, scattering everywhere. Together they gathered what they could into a misshapen snowball on an old magazine, and Will scuttled downstairs to drop it in the bath. Paul wired the skylight back to its catch.

'There now,' he said briskly, and though he did not look at Will, for an instant they understood one another very well. 'Tell you what, Will, it's freezing up here – why don't you go down to our room and sleep in my bed? And I'll wake you when I come up later – or I might even sleep up here if you can survive Robin's snoring. All right?'

'All right,' Will said huskily. 'Thanks.'

He picked up his discarded clothes – with the belt and its new ornament – and bundled them under his arm, then paused at the door as they went out, and looked back. There was nothing to see, now, except a dark damp patch on the carpet where the heap of snow had been. But he felt colder than the cold air had made him, and the sick, empty feeling of fear still lay in his chest. If there had been nothing wrong beyond being frightened of the dark, he would not for the world have gone down to take refuge in Paul's room. But as things were, he knew he could not stay alone in the room where he belonged. For when they were clearing up that heap of fallen snow, he had seen something that Paul had not. It was impossible, in a howling snow-storm, for anything living to have made that soft unmistakable thud against the glass that he had heard just before the skylight fell. But buried in the heap of snow, he had found the fresh black wing-feather of a rook.

He heard the farmer's voice again: *This night will be bad. And tomorrow will be beyond imagining.*

Midwinter Day

He was woken by music. It beckoned him, lilting and insistent; delicate music, played by delicate instruments that he could not identify, with one rippling, bell-like phrase running through it in a gold thread of delight. There was in this music so much of the deepest enchantment of all his dreams and imaginings that he woke smiling in pure happiness at the sound. In the moment of his waking, it began to fade, beckoning as it went, and then as he opened his eyes it was gone. He had only the memory of that one rippling phrase still echoing in his head, and itself fading so fast that he sat up abruptly in bed and reached his arm out to the air, as if he could bring it back.

The room was very still, and there was no music, and yet Will knew that it had not been a dream.

He was in the twins' room still; he could hear Robin's breathing, slow and deep, from the other bed. Cold light glimmered round the edge of the curtains, but no one was stirring anywhere; it was very early. Will pulled on his rumpled clothes from the day before, and slipped out of the room. He crossed the landing to the central window, and looked down.

In the first shining moment he saw the whole strange-familiar world, glistening white; the roof of the outbuildings mounded into square towers of snow, and beyond them all the fields and hedges buried, merged into one great flat expanse, unbroken white to the horizon's brim. Will drew in a long, happy breath, silently rejoicing. Then, very faintly, he heard the music again, the same phrase. He swung round vainly searching for it in the air, as if he might see it somewhere like a flickering light.

'Where are you?'

It had gone again. And when he looked back through the window, he saw that his own world had gone with it. In that flash, everything had changed. The snow was there as it had been a moment before, but not piled now on roofs or stretching flat over lawns and fields. There were no roofs, there were no fields. There were only trees. Will was looking over a great white forest: a forest of massive trees, sturdy as towers and ancient as rock. They were bare of leaves, clad only in the deep snow that lay untouched along every branch, each smallest twig. They were everywhere. They began so close to the house that he was looking out through the topmost branches of the nearest tree, could have reached out and shaken them if he had dared to open the window. All around him the trees stretched to the flat horizon of the valley. The only break in that white world of branches was away over to the south, where the Thames ran; he could see the bend in the river marked like a single stilled wave in this white ocean of forest, and the shape of it looked as though the river were wider than it should have been.

Will gazed and gazed, and when at last he stirred he found that he was clutching the smooth iron circle threaded on to his belt. The iron was warm to his touch.

He went back into the bedroom.

'Robin!' he said loudly. 'Wake up!' But Robin breathed slowly and rhythmically as before, and did not stir.

He ran into the bedroom next-door, the familiar small room that he had once shared with James, and shook James roughly by the shoulder. But when the shaking was done, James lay motionless, deeply asleep.

Will went out on to the landing again and took a long breath, and he shouted with all his might: 'Wake up! Wake up, everyone!'

He did not now expect any response, and none came. There was a total silence, as deep and timeless as the blanketing snow; the house and everyone in it lay in a sleep that would not be broken.

Will went downstairs to pull on his boots, and the old sheepskin jacket that had belonged, before him, to two or three of his brothers in turn. Then he went out of the back door, closing it quietly behind him, and stood looking out through the quick white vapour of his breath.

The strange white world lay stroked by silence. No birds sang. The garden was no longer there, in this forested land. Nor were the outbuildings nor the old crumbling walls. There lay only a narrow clearing round the house now, hummocked with unbroken snowdrifts, before the trees began, with a narrow path leading away. Will set out down the white tunnel of the path, slowly, stepping high to keep the snow out of his boots. As soon as he moved away from the house, he felt very much alone, and he made himself go on without looking back over his shoulder, because he knew that when he looked, he would find that the house was gone.

He accepted everything that came into his mind, without thought or question, as if he were moving through a dream. But a deeper part of him knew that he was not dreaming. He was crystal-clear awake, in a Midwinter Day that had been waiting for him to wake into it since the day he had been born, and, he somehow knew, for centuries before that. *Tomorrow will be beyond imagining* ... Will came out of the white-arched path into the road, paved smooth with snow and edged everywhere by the great trees, and he looked up between the branches and saw a single black rook flap slowly past, high in the early sky.

Turning to the right, he walked up the narrow road that in his own time was called Huntercombe Lane. It was the way that he and James had taken to Dawsons' Farm, the same road that he had trodden almost every day of his life, but it was very different now. Now, it was no more than a track through a forest, great snow-burdened trees enclosing it on both sides. Will moved bright-eyed and watchful through the silence, until, suddenly, he heard a faint noise ahead of him.

He stood still. The sound came again, through the muffling trees: a rhythmical, off-key tapping, like a hammer striking metal. It came in short irregular bursts, as though someone were hammering nails. As he stood listening, the world around him seemed to brighten a little; the woods seemed less dense, the snow glittered, and when he looked upward, the strip of sky over Huntercombe Lane was a clear blue. He realized that the sun had risen at last out of the sullen bank of grey cloud.

He trudged on towards the sound of hammering, and soon came to a clearing. There was no village of Huntercombe any more, only this. All his senses sprang to life at once, under a shower of unexpected sounds, sights, smells. He saw two or three low stone buildings thick-roofed with snow; he saw blue wood-smoke rising, and smelt it too, and smelt at the same time a voluptuous scent of new-baked bread that brought the water springing in his mouth. He saw that the nearest of the three buildings was three-walled, open to the track, with a yellow fire burning bright inside like a captive sun. Great showers of sparks were spraying out from an anvil where a man was hammering. Beside the anvil stood a tall black horse, a beautiful gleaming animal; Will had never seen a horse so splendidly midnight in colour, with no white markings anywhere.

The horse raised its head and looked full at him, pawed the ground, and gave a low whinny. The smith's voice rumbled in protest, and another figure moved out of the shadows behind the horse. Will's breath came faster at the sight of him, and he felt a hollowness in his throat. He did not know why.

The man was tall, and wore a dark cloak that fell straight like a robe; his hair, which grew low over his neck, shone with a curious reddish tinge. He patted the horse's neck, murmuring in its ear; then he seemed to sense the cause of its restlessness, and he turned and saw Will. His arms dropped abruptly. He took a step forward and stood there, waiting.

The brightness went out of the snow and the sky, and the morning darkened a little, as an extra layer of the distant cloudbank swallowed the sun.

Will crossed the road through the snow, his hands thrust deep into his pockets. He did not look at the tall cloaked figure facing him. Instead he stared resolutely at the other man, bent again now over the anvil, and realized that he knew him; it was one of the men from Dawsons' Farm. John Smith, Old George's son.

'Morning, John,' he said.

The broad-shouldered man in the leather apron glanced up. He frowned briefly, then nodded in welcome. 'Eh, Will. You're out early.'

'It's my birthday,' Will said.

'A Midwinter birthday,' said the strange man in the cloak. 'Auspicious, indeed. And you will be eleven years grown.' It was a statement, not a question. Now Will had to look. Bright blue eyes went with the red-brown hair, and the man spoke with a curious accent that was not of the South-East.

'That's right,' Will said.

A woman came out of one of the nearby cottages, carrying a basket of small loaves of bread, and with them the new-baked smell that had so tantalized Will before. He sniffed, his stomach reminding him that he had eaten no breakfast. The red-haired man took a loaf, wrenched it apart, and held out a half towards him.

'Here. You're hungry. Break your birthday fast with me, young Will.' He bit into the remaining half of the loaf, and Will heard the crust crackle invitingly. He reached forward, but as he did so the smith swung a hot horseshoe out of his fire and clapped it briefly on the hoof clenched between his knees. There was a quick smoky smell of burning, killing the scent of the new bread; then the shoe was back in the fire and the smith peering at the hoof. The black horse stood patient and unmoving, but Will stepped back, dropping his arm.

'No, thank you,' he said.

The man shrugged, tearing wolfishly at his bread, and the woman, her face invisible behind the edge of an enveloping shawl, went away again with her basket. John Smith swung the horseshoe out of the fire to sizzle and steam in a bucket of water.

'Get on, get on,' said the rider irritably, raising his head. 'The day grows. How much longer?'

'Your iron will not be hurried,' said the smith, but he was hammering the shoe in place now with quick, sure strokes. 'Done!' he said at last, trimming the hoof with a knife.

The red-haired man led his horse round, tightened the girths, and slid upwards, quick as a jumping cat, into his saddle. Towering there, with the folds of his dark robe flowing over the flanks of the black horse, he looked like a statue carved out of night. But the blue eyes were staring compellingly down at Will. 'Come up, boy. I'll take you where you want to go. Riding is the only way, in snow as thick as this.'

'No, thank you,' Will said. 'I am out to find the Walker.' He heard his own words with amazement. *So that's it*, he thought.

'But now the Rider is abroad,' the man said, and all in one quick movement he twitched his horse's head around, bent in the saddle, and made a sweeping grab at Will's arm. Will jerked sideways, but he would have been seized if the smith, standing at the open wall of the forge, had not leapt forward and dragged him out of reach. For so broad a man, he moved with astonishing speed.

The midnight stallion reared, and the cloaked rider was almost thrown. He shouted in fury, then recovered himself, and sat looking down in a cold contemplation that was more terrible than rage. 'That was a foolish move, my friend smith,' he said softly. 'We shall not forget.' Then he swung the stallion round and rode out in the direction from which Will had come, and the hooves of his great horse made only a muffled whisper in the snow.

John Smith spat, derisively, and began hanging up his tools.

'Thank you,' Will said. 'I hope –' He stopped.

'They can do me no harm,' the smith said. 'I come of the wrong breed for that. And in this time I belong to the road, as my craft belongs to all who use the road. Their power can work no harm on the road through Hunter's Combe. Remember that, for yourself.'

The dream-state flickered, and Will felt his thoughts begin to stir. 'John,' he said. 'I know it's true I must find the Walker, but I don't know why. Will you tell me?'

The smith turned and looked directly at him for the first time, with a kind of compassion in his weathered face. 'Ah no, young Will. Are you so newly awake? That you must learn for yourself. And much more, this your first day.'

'First day?' said Will.

'Eat,' said the smith. 'There is no danger in it now that you will not be breaking bread with the Rider. You see how quickly you saw the peril of that. Just as you knew there would be greater peril in riding with him. Follow your nose through the day, boy, just follow your nose.' He called to the house, 'Martha!'

The woman came out again with her basket. This time she drew back her shawl and smiled at Will, and he saw blue eyes like the Rider's but with a softer light in them. Gratefully, he munched at the warm crusty bread, which had been split now and spread with honey. Then beyond the clearing there was a new sound of muffled footfalls in the road, and he spun fearfully round.

A white mare, without rider or harness, trotted into the clearing towards them: a reverse image of the Rider's midnight-black stallion, tall and splendid and without marking of any kind. Against the dazzle of the snow, glittering now as the sun re-emerged from cloud, there seemed a faint golden glow in its whiteness and in the long mane falling over the arched neck. The horse came to stand beside Will, bent its nose briefly and touched his shoulder as if in greeting, then tossed its great white head, blowing a cloud of misty breath into the cold air. Will reached out and laid a reverent hand on its neck.

'You come in good time,' John Smith said. 'The fire is hot.'

He went back into the forge and pumped once or twice at the bellows-arm, so that the fire roared; then he hooked down a shoe from the shadowed wall beyond and thrust it into the heat. 'Look well,' he said, studying Will's face. 'You've not seen a horse like this ever before. But this will not be the last time.'

'She's beautiful,' Will said, and the mare nuzzled again gently at his neck.

'Mount,' said the smith.

Will laughed. It was so obviously impossible; his head reached scarcely to the horse's shoulder, and even if there had been a stirrup it would have been far out of reach of his foot.

'I am not joking,' said the smith, and indeed he did not look the kind of man who often smiled, let alone made a joke. 'It is your privilege. Take hold of her mane where you can reach it, and you will see.'

To humour him, Will reached up and wound the fingers of both hands in the long coarse hair of the white horse's mane, low on the neck. In the same instant, he felt giddy; his head hummed like a spinning-top, and behind the sound he heard quite plainly, but very far off, the haunting, bell-like phrase of music that he had heard before waking that morning. He cried out. His arms jerked strangely; the world spun; and the music was gone. His mind was still groping desperately to recover it when he realized that he was closer to the snow-thick branches of the trees than he had been before, sitting high on the white mare's broad back. He looked down at the smith and laughed aloud in delight.

'When she is shod,' the smith said, 'she will carry you, if you ask.'

Will sobered suddenly, thinking. Then something drew his gaze up through the arching trees to the sky, and he saw two black rooks flapping lazily past, high up. 'No,' he said. 'I think I am supposed to go alone.' He stroked the mare's neck, swung his legs to one side, and slid the long way down, bracing himself for a jolt. But he found that he landed lightly on his toes in the snow. 'Thank you, John. Thank you very much. Good-bye.'

The smith nodded briefly, then busied himself with the horse, and Will trudged off in some disappointment; he had expected a word of farewell at least. From the edge of the trees, he glanced back. John Smith had one of the mare's hind feet clenched between his knees, and was reaching his gloved hand for his tongs. And what Will saw then made him forget any thought of words or farewells. The smith had done no removing of old horseshoes, or trimming of a shoe-torn foot; this horse had never been shod before. And the shoe that was now being fitted to its foot, like the line of three other shoes he could now see glinting on the far smithy wall, was not a horseshoe at all but another shape, a shape he knew very well. All four of the white mare's shoes were replicas of the cross-quartered circle that he wore on his own belt. Will walked a little way down the road, beneath its narrow roof of blue sky. He put a hand inside his jacket to touch the circle on his belt, and the iron was icycold. He was beginning to know what that meant by now. But there was no sign of the Rider; he could not even see any tracks left by the black horse's feet. And he was not thinking of evil encounters. He could feel only that something was drawing him, more and more strongly, towards the place where in his own time Dawsons' Farm would stand.

He found the narrow side-lane and turned down it. The track went on a long way, winding in gentle turns. There seemed to be a lot of scrub in this part of the forest; the branching tops of small trees and bushes jutted snow-laden from the mounding drifts, like white antlers from white rounded heads. And then round the next bend, Will saw before him a low square hut with rough-daubed clay walls and a roof high with a hat of snow like a thick-iced cake. In the doorway, paused irresolute with one hand on the rickety door, stood the shambling old tramp of the day before. The long grey hair was the same, and so were the clothes and the wizened, crafty face.

Will came close to the old man and said, as Farmer Dawson had said the day before: 'So the Walker is abroad.'

'Only the one,' said the old man. 'Only me. And what's it to you?' He sniffed, squinting sideways at Will, and rubbed his nose on one greasy sleeve.

'I want you to tell me some things,' Will said, more boldly than he felt. 'I want to know why you were hanging around yesterday. Why you were watching. Why the rooks came after you. I want to know,' he said in a sudden honest rush, 'what it means that you are the Walker.'

At the mention of the rooks the old man had flinched closer to the hut, his eyes flickering nervously up at the tree-tops; but now he looked at Will in sharper suspicion than before. 'You can't be the one!' he said.

'I can't be what?'

'You can't be . . . you ought to know all this. Specially about those hellish birds. Trying to trick me, eh? Trying to trick a poor old man. You're out with the Rider, ain't you? You're his boy, ain't you, eh?'

'Of course not,' Will said. 'I don't know what you mean.' He looked at the wretched hut; the lane ended here, but there was scarcely even a proper clearing. The trees stood close all round them, shutting out much of the sun. He said, suddenly desolate, 'Where's the farm?'

'There isn't any farm,' said the old tramp impatiently. 'Not yet. You ought to know . . .' He sniffed again violently, and mumbled to himself; then his eyes narrowed and he came close to Will, peering into his face and giving off a strong repellent smell of ancient sweat and unwashed skin. 'But you might be the one, you might. If you're carrying the first sign that the Old One gave you. Have you got it there, then? Show us. Show the old Walker the sign.'

Trying hard not to back away in disgust, Will fumbled with the buttons of his jacket. He knew what *the sign* must be. But as he pushed the sheepskin aside to show the circle looped on his belt, his hand brushed against the smooth iron and felt it burning, biting with icy cold; at the same moment he saw the old man leap backwards, cringing, staring not at him but behind him, over his shoulder. Will swung round, and saw the cloaked Rider on his midnight horse.

'Well met,' said the Rider softly.

The old man squealed like a frightened rabbit and turned and ran, blundering through the snowdrifts into the trees. Will stood where he was, looking at the Rider, his heart thumping so fiercely that it was hard to breathe.

'It was unwise to leave the road, Will Stanton,' said the man in the cloak, and his eyes blazed like blue stars. The black horse edged forward, forward; Will shrank back against the side of the flimsy hut, staring into the eyes, and then with a great effort he made his slow arm pull aside his jacket so that the iron circle on his belt showed clear. He gripped the belt at its side; the coldness of the sign was so intense that he could feel the force from it, like the radiation of a fierce, burning heat. And the Rider paused, and his eyes flickered.

'So you have one of them already.' He hunched his shoulders strangely, and the horse tossed its head; both seemed to be gaining strength, to be growing taller. 'One will not help you, not alone, not yet,' said the Rider, and he grew and grew, looming against the white world, while his stallion neighed triumphantly, rearing up, its forefeet lashing the air so that Will could only press himself helpless against the wall. Horse and rider towered over him like a dark cloud, blotting out both snow and sun.

And then dimly he heard new sounds, and the rearing black shapes seemed to fall to one side, swept away by a blazing golden light, brilliant with fierce patterns of white-hot circles, suns, stars – Will blinked, and saw suddenly that it was the white mare from the smithy, rearing over him in turn. He grabbed frantically at the waving mane, and just as before he found himself jerked up on to the broad back, bent low over the mare's neck, clutching for his life. The great white horse let out a shrieking cry and leapt for the track through the trees, passing the shapeless black cloud that hung motionless in the clearing like smoke; passing everything in a rising gallop, until they came at last to the road, Huntercombe Lane, the road through Hunter's Combe.

The movement of the great horse changed to a slow-rising, powerful lope, and Will heard the beating of his own heart in his ears as the world flashed by in a white blur. Then all at once greyness came around them, and the sun was blacked out. The wind wrenched into Will's collar and sleeves and boot-tops, ripping at his hair. Great clouds rushed towards them out of the north, closing in, huge grey-black thunderheads; the sky rumbled and growled. One white-misted gap remained, with a faint hint of blue behind it still, but it too was closing, closing. The white horse leapt at it desperately. Over his shoulder Will saw swooping towards them a darker shape even than the giant clouds: the Rider, towering immense, his eyes two dreadful points of blue-white fire.

Lightning flashed, thunder split the sky, and the mare leapt at the crashing clouds as the last gap closed.

And they were safe. The sky was blue before and above them; the sun blazing, warming Will's skin. He saw that they had left his Thames Valley behind. Now they were among the curving slopes of the Chiltern Hills, capped with great trees, beech and oak and ash. And running like threads through the snow along the lines of the hills were the hedges that were the marks of ancient fields – very ancient, as Will had always known; more ancient than anything in his world except the hills themselves, and the trees. Then on one white hill, he saw a different mark. The shape was cut through snow and turf into the chalk beneath the soil; it would have been hard to make out if it had not been familiar. But Will knew it. The mark was a circle, quartered by a cross.

Then his hands were jerked away from their tight clutch on the thick mane, and the white mare gave a long shrill whinnying cry that was loud in his ears and then strangely died away into a far distance. And Will was falling, falling; yet he knew no shock of a fall, but knew only that he was lying face down on cold snow. He stumbled to his feet, shaking himself. The white horse was gone. The sky was clear, and the sunshine warm on the back of his neck. He stood on a snow-mounded hill, with a copse of tall trees capping it far beyond, and two black birds drifting tiny to and fro above the trees.

And before him, standing alone and tall on the white slope, leading to nowhere, were two great carved wooden doors.

The Sign-seeker

Will thrust his cold hands into his pockets, and stood staring up at the carved panels of the two closed doors towering before him. They told him nothing. He could find no meaning in the zigzag symbols repeated over and over, in endless variation, on every panel. The wood of the doors was like no wood he had ever seen; it was cracked and pitted and yet polished by age, so that you could scarcely tell it was wood at all except by a rounding here and there, where someone had not quite been able to avoid leaving the trace of a knot-hole. If it had not been for signs like those, Will would have taken the doors to be stone.

His eyes slid beyond their outline as he looked, and he saw that all around them was a quivering of things, a movement like the shaking of the air over a bonfire or over a paved road baked by a summer sun. Yet there was no difference in heat to explain it here.

There were no handles on the doors. Will stretched his arms forward, with the palm of each hand flat against the wood, and he pushed. As the doors swung open beneath his hands, he thought that he caught a phrase of the fleeting bell-like music again; but then it was gone, into the misty gap between memory and imagining. And he was through the doorway, and without a murmur of sound the two huge doors swung shut behind him, and the light and the day and the world changed so that he forgot utterly what they had been.

He stood now in a great hall. There was no sunlight here. Indeed there were no real windows in the lofty stone walls, but only a series of thin slits. Between these, on both sides, hung a series of tapestries so strange and beautiful that they seemed to glow in the half-light. Will was dazzled by the brilliant animals and flowers and birds, woven or embroidered there in rich colours like sunlit stained glass.

Images leapt at him; he saw a silver unicorn, a field of red roses, a glowing golden sun. Above his head the high vaulted beams of the roof arched up into shadow; other shadows masked the far end of the room. He moved dreamily a few paces forward, his feet making no sound on the sheepskin rugs that covered the stone floor, and he peered ahead. All at once sparks leapt and fire flared in the darkness, lighting up an enormous fireplace in the far wall, and he saw doors and high-backed chairs and a heavy carved table. On either side of the fireplace two figures stood waiting for him: an old lady leaning on a stick, and a tall man.

'Welcome, Will,' the old lady said, in a voice that was soft and gentle, yet rang through the vaulted hall like a treble bell. She put out one thin hand towards him, and the firelight glinted on a huge ring that rose round as a marble above her finger. She was very small, fragile as a bird, and though she was upright and alert, Will, looking at her, had an impression of immense age.

He could not see her face. He paused where he stood, and unconsciously his hand crept to his belt. Then the tall figure on the other side of the fireplace moved, bent, and lighted a long taper at the fire, and coming forward to the table, began putting the taper to a ring of tall candles there. Light from the smoking yellow flame played on his face. Will saw a strong, bony head, with deep-set eyes and an arched nose fierce as a hawk's beak; a sweep of wiry white hair springing back from the high forehead; bristling brows and a jutting chin. And though he did not know why, as he stared at the fierce, secret lines of that face, the world he had inhabited since he was born seemed to whirl and break and come down again in a pattern that was not the same as before.

Straightening, the tall man looked at him, across the circle of lighted candles that stood on the table in a frame like the rim of a flat-resting wheel. He smiled slightly, the grim mouth slanting up at its edges, and a sudden fan of lines wrinkling each side of the deep-set eyes. He blew out the burning taper with a quick breath.

'Come in, Will Stanton,' he said, and the deep voice too seemed to leap in Will's memory. 'Come and learn. And bring that candle with you.'

Puzzled, Will glanced around him. Close to his right hand, he found a black wrought-iron stand as tall as himself, rising to three points; two of the points were tipped by a five-pointed iron star and the third by a candlestick holding a thick white candle. He lifted out the candle, which was heavy enough to need both hands, and crossed the hall to the two figures waiting at the other end. Blinking through the light, he saw as he approached them that the circle of candles on the table was not a complete circle after all; one holder in the ring was empty. He leaned across the table, gripping the hard smooth sides of the candle, lighted it from one of the others, and fitted it carefully into the empty socket. It was identical with the rest. They were very strange candles, uneven in width but cold and hard as white marble; they burned with a long bright flame and no smoke, and smelled faintly resinous, like pine trees.

It was only as he leaned back to stand upright that Will noticed the two crossed arms of iron inside the candlestick ring. Here again, as everywhere, was the sign: the cross within the circle, the quartered sphere. There were other sockets for candles within the frame, he saw now: two along each arm of the cross, and one at the central point where they met. But these were still empty.

The old lady relaxed, and sat down in the high-backed chair beside the hearth. 'Very good,' she said comfortably in that same musical voice. 'Thank you, Will.'

She smiled, her face folding into a cobweb of wrinkles, and Will grinned whole-heartedly back. He had no idea why he was suddenly so happy; it seemed too natural to be questioned. He sat down on a stool which was clearly waiting for him in front of the fire, between the two chairs.

'The doors,' he said, 'the great doors I came through. How do they just stand there on their own?'

'The doors?' the lady said.

Something in her voice made Will look back over his shoulder at the far wall from which he had just come: the wall with the two high doors, and the holder from which he had taken the candle. He stared; there was something wrong. The great wooden doors had vanished. The grey wall stretched blank, its massive square stones quite featureless except for one round golden shield, alone, hanging high up and glinting dully in the light from the fire.

The tall man laughed softly. 'Nothing is what it seems, boy. Expect nothing and fear nothing, here or anywhere. There's your first lesson. And here's your first exercise. We have before us Will Stanton – tell us what has been happening to him, this last day or two.'

Will looked into the urgent flames, warm and welcome on his face in the chill room. It took much effort to wrench his mind back to the moment when he and James had left home for Dawsons' Farm to collect hay – hay! – the previous afternoon. He thought, bemused, about everything that stood between that moment and his present self. After a while he said: 'The sign. The circle with the cross. Yesterday Mr Dawson gave me the sign. Then the Walker came after me, or tried to, and afterwards they – whoever they are – they tried to get me.' He swallowed, cold at the memory of his night's fear. 'To get the sign. They want it, that's what everything is about. That's what today is about too, even though it's so much more complicated because now isn't *now*, it's some other time, I don't know when. With everything like a dream, but real . . . They're still after it. I don't know who they are, except for the Rider and the Walker. I don't know you either, only I know you are against them. You and Mr Dawson and John Wayland Smith.'

He stopped.

'Go on,' said the deep voice.

'Wayland?' Will said, perplexed. 'That's an odd name. That's not part of John's name. What made me say that?'

'Minds hold more than they know,' the tall man said. 'Particularly yours. And what else have you to say?'

'I don't know,' Will said. He looked down and ran a finger along the edge of his stool; it was carved in gentle regular waves, like a peaceful sea. 'Well, yes I do. Two things. One is that there's something funny about the Walker. I don't really think he's one of them, because he was scared stiff of the Rider when he saw him, and ran away.'

'And the other thing?' the big man said.

Somewhere in the shadows of the great room a clock struck, with a deep note like a muffled bell: a single note, a half-hour.

'The Rider,' Will said. 'When the Rider saw the sign, he said: "So you have one of them already." He didn't know I had it. But he had come after me. Chasing me. Why?'

'Yes,' said the old lady. She was looking at him rather sadly. 'He was chasing you. I'm afraid the guess that is in your mind is right, Will. It isn't the sign they want most of all. It's you.'

The big man stood up, and crossed behind Will so that he stood with one hand on the back of the old lady's chair and the other in the pocket of the dark, high-necked jacket he wore. 'Look at me, Will,' he said. Light from the burning ring of candles on the table glinted on his springing white hair, and put his strange, shadowed eyes into even deeper shadows, pools of darkness in the bony face. 'My name is Merriman Lyon,' he said. 'I greet you, Will Stanton. We have been waiting for you for a long time.'

'I know you,' Will said. 'I mean . . . you look . . . I felt . . . don't I know you?'

'In a sense,' Merriman said. 'You and I are, shall we say, similar. We were born with the same gift, and for the same high purpose. And you are in this place at this moment, Will, to begin to understand what that purpose is. But first you must be taught about the gift.'

Everything seemed to be running too far, too fast. 'I don't understand,' Will said, looking at the strong, intent face in alarm. 'I haven't any gift, really I haven't. I mean there's nothing special about me.' He looked from one to the other of them, figures alternately lit and shadowed by the dancing flames of candles and fire, and he began to feel a rising fear, a sense of being trapped. He said, 'It's just the things that have been happening to me, that's all.'

'Think back, and remember some of those things,' the old lady said. 'Today is your birthday. Midwinter Day, your eleventh Midwinter's Day. Think back to yesterday, your tenth Midwinter's Eve, before you first saw the sign. Was there nothing special at all, then? Nothing new?'

Will thought. 'The animals were scared of me,' he said reluctantly. 'And the birds perhaps. But it didn't seem to mean anything at the time.'

'And if you had a radio or a television set switched on in the house,' Merriman said, 'it behaved oddly whenever you went near it.'

Will stared at him. 'The radio did keep making noises. How did you know that? I thought it was sunspots or something.'

Merriman smiled. 'In a way. In a way.' Then he was sombre again. 'Listen now. The gift I speak of, it is a power, that I will show you. It is the power of the Old Ones, who are as old as this land and older even than that. You were born to inherit it, Will, when you came to the end of your tenth year. On the night before your birthday, it was beginning to wake, and now on the day of your birth it is free, flowering, fully grown. But it is still confused and unchannelled because you are not in proper control of it yet. You must be trained to handle it, before it can fall into its true pattern and accomplish the quest for which you are here. Don't look so prickly, boy. Stand up. I'll show you what it can do.'

Will stood up, and the old lady smiled encouragingly at him. He said to her suddenly, 'Who are you?'

'The lady –' Merriman began.

'The lady is very old,' she said in her clear young voice, 'and has in her time had many, many names. Perhaps it would be best for now, Will, if you were to go on thinking of me as – the old lady.'

'Yes, ma'am,' Will said, and at the sound of her voice his happiness came flooding back, the rising alarm dropped away, and he stood up erect and eager, peering into the shadow behind her chair where Merriman had moved a few paces back. He could see the glint of white hair on the tall figure, but no more.

Merriman's deep voice came out of the shadow. 'Stand still. Look at whatever you like, but not hard, concentrate on nothing. Let your mind wander, pretend you are in a boring class at school.'

Will laughed, and stood there relaxed, tilting his head back. He squinted up, idly trying to distinguish between the dark criss-crossing beams in the high roof and the black lines that were their shadows. Merriman said casually, 'I am putting a picture into your mind. Tell me what you see.'

The image formed itself in Will's mind as naturally as if he had decided to paint an imaginary landscape and were making up the look of it before putting it on paper. He said, describing the details as they came to him: 'There's a grassy hillside, over the sea, like a sort of gentle cliff. Lots of blue sky, and the sea a darker blue underneath. A long way down, right down there where the sea meets the land, there's a strip of sand, lovely glowing golden sand. And inland from the grassy headland – you can't really see it from here except out of the corner of your eye – hills, misty hills. They're a sort of soft purple, and their edges dissolve into a blue mist, the way the colours in a painting dissolve into one another if you keep it wet. And' – he came out of his half-trance of seeing and looked hard at Merriman, peering into the shadow with inquisitive interest – 'and it's a sad picture. You miss it, you're homesick for wherever it is. Where is it?'

'Enough,' Merriman said hastily, but he sounded pleased. 'You do well. Now it is your turn. Give me a picture, Will. Just choose some ordinary scene, anything, and think of the way it looks, as if you were standing looking at it.'

Will thought of the first image that came into his head. It was one which he realized now had been worrying away at the back of his thoughts all this while: the picture of the two great doors, isolated on the snowy hillside, with all their intricate carving, and the strange blue at their edges.

Merriman said at once: 'Not the doors. Nothing so close. Somewhere from your life before this winter came.'

For a second Will stared at him disconcerted; then he swallowed hard, closed his eyes and thought of the jeweller's shop his father ran in the little town of Eton.

Merriman said, slowly, 'The door-handle is of the lever kind, like a round bar, to be pushed downward perhaps ten degrees on opening. A small hanging-bell rings as the door moves. You step down a few inches to reach the floor, and the jolt of the drop is startling without being dangerous. There are glass showcases all round the walls, and beneath the glass counter – of course, this must be your father's shop. With some beautiful things inside it. A grandfather clock, very old, in the back corner, with a painted face and a deep, slow tick. A turquoise necklet in the central showcase with a setting of silver serpents: Zuni work, I think, a very long way from home. An emerald pendant like a great green tear. A small enchanting model of a Crusader castle, in gold – perhaps a salt-cellar – that you have loved, I think, since you were a small boy. And that man behind the counter, short and content and gentle, must be your father, Roger Stanton. Interesting to see him clearly at last, free of the mist . . . He has a jeweller's glass in his eye, and he is looking at a ring: an old gold ring with nine tiny stones set in three rows, three diamond chips in the centre and three rubies at either side, and some curious runic lines edging those that I think I must look at more closely one day soon –'

'You even got the ring!' Will said, fascinated. 'That's mother's ring, Dad was looking at it last time I was in the shop. She thought one of the stones was loose, but he said it was an optical illusion . . . However do you do it?'

'Do what?' There was an ominous softness in the deep voice.

'Well – that. Put a picture in my head. And then see the one I had there myself. Telepathy, isn't it called? It's tremendous.' But an uneasiness was beginning in his mind.

'Very well,' Merriman said patiently. 'I will show you in another way. There is a circle of candle flames beside you there on the table, Will Stanton. Now – do you know of any possible way of putting out one of those flames, other than blowing it out or quenching it with water or snuffer or hand?'

'No.'

'No. There is none. But now, I tell you that you, because you are who you are, can do that simply by wishing it. For the gift that you have, this is a very small task indeed. If in your mind you choose one of those flames and think of it without even looking, think of it and tell it to go out, *then that flame will go out*. And is that a possible thing for any normal boy to do?'

'No,' Will said unhappily.

'Do it,' Merriman said. 'Now.'

There was a sudden thick silence in the room, like velvet. Will could feel them both watching him. He thought desperately: I'll get out of it, I'll think of a flame, but it won't be one of those; it'll be something much bigger, something that couldn't be put out except by some tremendous impossible magic even Merriman doesn't know . . . He looked across the room at the light and shadow dancing side by side across the rich tapestries on the stone walls, and he thought hard, in furious concentration, of the image of the blazing log fire in the huge fireplace behind him. He felt the warmth of it on the back of his neck, and thought of the glowing orange heart of the big pile of logs and the leaping yellow tongues of flame. *Go out, fire*, he said to it in his mind, feeling suddenly safe and free from the dangers of power, because of course no fire as big as that could possibly go out without a real reason. *Stop burning, fire. Go out.*

And the fire went out.

All at once the room was chill – and darker. The ring of candle flames on the table burned on, in a small cold pool of their own light only. Will spun round, staring in consternation at the hearth; there was no hint of smoke, or water, or of any way in which the fire could possibly have died. But dead it was, cold and black, without a spark. He moved towards it slowly. Merriman and the old lady said no word, and did not stir. Will bent and touched the blackened logs in the hearth, and they were cold as stone – yet furred with a layer of new ash that fell away under his fingers into a white dust. He stood up, rubbing his hand slowly up and down his trouser-leg, and looked helplessly at Merriman. The man's deep eyes burned like black candle flames, but there was compassion in them, and as Will glanced nervously across at the old lady, he saw a kind of tenderness in her face too. She said gently: 'It's a little cold, Will.'

For a timeless interval that was no more than the flicker of a nerve, Will felt a screaming flash of panic, a memory of the fear he had felt in the dark nightmare of the snowstorm; then it was gone, and in the peace of its vanishing he felt somehow stronger, taller, more relaxed. He knew that in some way he had accepted the power, whatever it was, that he had been resisting, and he knew what he must do. Taking a deep breath, he squared his shoulders and stood straight and firm there in the great hall. He smiled at the old lady; then looked past her, at nothing, and concentrated on the image of the fire. *Come back, fire*, he said in his mind. *Burn again*. And the light was dancing over the tapestried walls once more, and the warmth of the flames was back on his neck, and the fire burned.

'Thank you,' the old lady said.

'Well done,' said Merriman softly, and Will knew that he was not speaking merely of the extinguishing and relighting of a fire.

'It is a burden,' Merriman said. 'Make no mistake about that. Any great gift of power or talent is a burden, and this more than any, and you will often long to be free of it. But there is nothing to be done. If you were born with the gift, then you must serve it, and nothing in this world or out of it may stand in the way of that service, because that is why you were born and that is the Law. And it is just as well, young Will, that you have only a glimmering of an idea of the gift that is in you, for until the first ordeals of learning are over, you will be in great danger. And the less you know of the meaning of your power, the better able it will be to protect you as it has done for the last ten years.'

He gazed at the fire for a moment, frowning. 'I will tell you only this: that you are one of the Old Ones, the first to have been born for five hundred years, and the last. And like all such, you are bound by nature to devote yourself to the long conflict between the Light and the Dark. Your birth, Will, completed a circle that has been growing for four thousand years in every oldest part of this land: the circle of the Old Ones. Now that you have come into your power, your task is to make that circle indestructible. It is your quest to find and to guard the six great Signs of the Light, made over the centuries by the Old Ones, to be joined in power only when the circle is complete. The first Sign hangs on your belt already, but to find the rest will not be easy. You are the Sign-seeker, Will Stanton. That is your destiny, your first quest. If you can accomplish that, you will have brought to life one of the three great forces that the Old Ones must turn soon towards vanquishing the powers of the Dark, which are reaching out now steadily and stealthily over all this world.'

The rhythms of his voice, which had been rising and falling in an increasingly formal pattern, changed subtly into a kind of chanted battle cry; a call, Will thought suddenly, with a chill tightening his skin, to things beyond the great hall and beyond the time of the calling. 'For the Dark, the Dark is rising. The Walker is abroad, the Rider is riding; they have woken, the Dark is rising. And the last of the Circle is come to claim his own, and the circles must now all be joined. The white horse must go to the Hunter, and the river take the valley; there must be fire on the mountain, fire under the stone, fire over the sea. Fire to burn away the Dark, for the Dark, the Dark is rising!'

He stood there tall as a tree in the shadowed room, his deep voice ringing out in an echo, and Will could not take his eyes from him. *The Dark is rising.* That was exactly what he had felt last night. That was what he was beginning to feel again now, a shadowy awareness of evil pricking at his fingertips and the top of his spine, but for the life of him he could not utter a word. Merriman said, in a singsong tone that came strangely from his awesome figure, as if he were a child reciting:

> When the Dark comes rising, six shall turn it back;
> Three from the circle, three from the track;
> Wood, bronze, iron; water, fire, stone;
> Five will return, and one go alone.

Then he swept forward out of the shadow, past the old lady, still and bright-eyed in her high-backed chair; with one hand he raised one of the thick white candles out of the burning ring, and with the other swung Will towards the towering side wall.

'Look well, for each moment, Will,' he said. 'The Old Ones will show something of themselves, and remind the deepest part of you. For one moment, look at each.' And with Will beside him he strode long-legged round the hall, holding the candle aloft again and again beside each of the hanging tapestries on the walls. Each time, as if he had commanded it, one bright image shone for an instant out of each glowing embroidered square, as bright and deep as a sunlit picture seen through a window-frame. And Will saw.

He saw a may tree white with blossom, growing from the thatched roof of a house. He saw four great grey standing stones on a green headland over the sea. He saw the empty-eyed grinning white skull of a horse, with a single stubby broken horn in the bony forehead and red ribbons wreathing the long jaws. He saw lightning striking a huge beech tree and, out of the flash, a great fire burning on a bare hillside against a black sky.

He saw the face of a boy not much older than himself, staring curiously into his own: a dark face beneath light-streaked dark hair, with strange cat-like eyes, the pupils light-bordered but almost yellow within. He saw a broad river in flood and beside it a wizened old man perched on an enormous horse. As Merriman whirled him inexorably from one picture to the next, he saw suddenly with a flash of terror the brightest image of all: a masked man with a human face, the head of a stag, the eyes of an owl, the ears of a wolf, and the body of a horse. The figure leapt, tugging at some lost memory deep within his mind.

'Remember them,' Merriman said. 'They will be a strength.'

Will nodded, then stiffened. All at once he heard noises growing outside the hall, and knew with a dreadful shock of certainty why it was that he had felt such uneasiness a short time before. While the old lady sat motionless in her chair, and he and Merriman stood again beside the hearth, the great hall was filled suddenly with a hideous mixture of moaning and mumbling and strident wailing, like the caged voices of an evil zoo. It was a sound more purely nasty than any he had ever heard.

The hair prickled at the back of Will's neck, and then suddenly there was silence. A log fell, rustling, in the fire. Will heard the blood beating in his veins. And into the silence a new sound came from somewhere outside, beyond the far wall: the heart-broken, beseeching whine of a forsaken dog, calling in panic for help and friendliness. It sounded exactly as Raq and Ci, their own dogs, had sounded when they were puppies crying for comfort in the dark; Will felt himself dissolve into sympathy, and he turned instinctively towards the sound.

'Oh, where is it? Poor thing –'

As he looked at the blank stone of the far wall, he saw a door take shape in it. It was not a door like the huge vanished pair by which he had entered, but far smaller; an odd, pinched little door looking totally out of place. But he knew he could open it to help the imploring dog. The animal whined again in more acute misery than before; louder, more pleading, in a desperate half-howl. Will swung impulsively forward to run to the door; then was frozen in mid-step by Merriman's voice. It was soft, but cold as winter stone.

'Wait. If you saw the shape of the poor sad dog, you would be greatly surprised. And it would be the last thing you would ever see.'

Incredulous, Will stood and waited. The whining died away, in a last long howl. There was silence for a moment. Then all at once he heard his mother's voice from behind the door.

'Will? Wiii – iill . . . Come and help me, Will!' It was unmistakably her voice, but filled with an unfamiliar emotion: there was in it a note of half-controlled panic that horrified him. It came again. 'Will? I need you . . . where are you, Will? Oh, please, Will, come and help me –' And then an unhappy break at the end, like a sob.

Will could not bear it. He lurched forward and ran towards the door. Merriman's voice came after him like a whiplash. 'Stop!'

'But I must go, can't you hear her!' Will shouted angrily. 'They've got my mother: I've got to help –'

'*Don't open that door!*' There was a hint of desperation in the deep voice that told Will, through instinct, that in the last resort Merriman was powerless to stop him.

'That is not your mother, Will,' the old lady said clearly.

'Please, Will!' his mother's voice begged.

'I'm coming!' Will reached out to the door's heavy latch, but in his haste he stumbled, and knocked against the great head-high candlestick so that his arm was jarred against his side. There was a sudden searing pain in his forearm, and he cried out and dropped to the floor, staring at the inside of his wrist where the sign of the quartered circle was burned agonizingly red into his skin. Once more the iron symbol on his belt had caught him with its ferocious bite of cold; it burned this time with a cold like white heat, in a furious flaring warning against the presence of evil – the presence that Will had felt but forgotten. Merriman and the old lady still had not moved. Will stumbled to his feet and listened, while outside the door his mother's voice wept, then grew angry, and threatened; then softened again and coaxed and cajoled; then finally ceased, dying away in a sob that tore at him even though his mind and senses told him it was not real.

And the door faded with it, melting like mist, until the grey stone wall was solid and unbroken as before. Outside, the dreadful inhuman chorus of moaning and wailing began again.

The old lady rose to her feet then and came across the hall, her long green dress rustling gently at every step. She took Will's hurt forearm in both her hands and put her cool right palm over it. Then she released him. The pain in Will's arm was gone, and where the red burn had been he saw now the shiny, hairless skin that grows in when a burn has been long healed. But the shape of the scar was clear, and he knew he would bear it to the end of his life; it was like a brand.

The nightmare sounds beyond the wall rose and fell in uneven waves.

'I'm sorry,' Will said miserably.

'We are besieged, as you see,' Merriman said, coming forward to join them. 'They hope to gain a hold over you while you are not yet grown into your full power. And this is only the beginning of the peril, Will. Through all this midwinter season their power will be waxing very strong, with the Old Magic able to keep it at a distance only on Christmas Eve. And even past Christmas it will grow, not losing its high force until the Twelfth Day, the Twelfth Night – which once was Christmas Day, and once before that, long ago, was the high winter festival of our old year.'

'What will happen?' Will said.

'We must think only of the things that we must do,' the old lady said. 'And the first is to free you from the circle of dark power that is drawn now round this room.'

Merriman said, listening intently, 'Be on your guard. Against anything. They have failed with one emotion; they will try to trap you through another next.'

'But it must not be fear,' she said. 'Remember that, Will. You will be frightened, often, but never fear them. The powers of the Dark can do many things, but they cannot destroy. They cannot kill those of the Light. Not unless they gain a final dominion over the whole earth. And it is the task of the Old Ones – your task and ours – to prevent that. So do not let them put you into fear or despair.'

She went on, saying more, but her voice was drowned like a rock submerged in a high-tide wave, as the horrible chorus that whined and keened outside the walls rose louder, louder, faster and angrier, into a cacophony of screeches and unearthly laughter, shrieks of terror and cackles of mirth, howlings and roars. As Will listened, his skin crept and grew damp.

As if in a dream he heard Merriman's deep voice ring out through the dreadful noise, calling him. He could not have moved if the old lady had not taken his hand, drawing him across the room, back towards the table and the hearth, the only cave of light in the dark hall. Merriman spoke close to his ear, swift and urgent, 'Stand by the circle, the circle of light. Stand with your back to the table, and take our hands. It is a joining they cannot break.'

Will stood there, his arms spread wide, as out of sight beside him each of them took one of his hands. The light of the fire in the hearth died, and he became aware that behind him the flames of the candle-circle on the table had grown tall, gigantic, so high that when he tilted back his head he could see them rising far over him in a white pillar of light. There was no heat from this great tree of flame, and though it glowed with great brilliance it cast no light beyond the table. Will could not see the rest of the hall, not the walls nor the pictures nor any door. He could see nothing but blackness, the vast black emptiness of the awful looming night.

This was the Dark, rising, rising to swallow Will Stanton before he could grow strong enough to do it harm. In the light from the strange candle, Will held fast to the old lady's frail fingers, and Merriman's wood hard fist. The shrieking of the Dark grew to an intolerable peak, a high triumphant whinnying, and Will knew without sight that before him in the darkness the great black stallion was rearing up as it had done outside the hut in the woods, with the Rider there to strike him down if the new-shod hooves did not do their work. And no white mare this time could spring from the sky to his rescue.

He heard Merriman shout, 'The tree of flame, Will! Strike out with the flame! As you spoke to the fire, speak to the flame, and strike!'

In desperate obedience Will filled his whole mind with the picture of the great circle of tall, tall candle-flames behind him, growing like a white tree; and as he did so, he felt the minds of his two supporters doing the same, knew that the three of them together could accomplish more than he ever imagined. He felt a quick pressure in each hand from the hand holding it, and he struck forward in his mind with the column of light, lashing it out as if it were a giant whip. Over his head there came a vast crashing flash of white light, as the tall flames reared forward and down in a bolt of lightning, and a tremendous shriek from the darkness beyond as something – the Rider, the black stallion, both – fell away, out, down, endlessly down.

And in the gap cleft in the darkness there before them, while he still blinked dazzled eyes, stood the two great carved wooden doors through which he had first come into the hall.

In the sudden silence Will heard himself shout triumphantly, and he leapt forward, tugging free of the hands that held his own, to run to the doors. Both Merriman and the old lady cried out in warning, but it was too late. Will had broken the circle, he was standing alone. No sooner did he realize it than he felt giddy, and staggered, clutching his head, a strange ringing sound beginning to thrum in his ears. Forcing his legs to move, he lurched to the doors, leaned against them, and beat feebly on them with his fists. They did not move. The eerie ringing in his head grew. He saw Merriman moving up before him, walking with great effort, leaning far forward as though he were straining against a high wind.

'Foolish,' Merriman gasped. 'Foolish, Will.' He seized the doors and shook them, thrusting forward with the strength of both his arms so that the twisted veins beside his brows stood up from the skin like thick wire; and as he did so, he lifted his head and shouted a long commanding phrase that Will did not understand. But the doors did not move, and Will felt weakness drawing him down, as if he were a snowman melting in the sun.

The thing that brought him back to wakefulness, just as he was beginning to drift into a kind of trance, was something he was never able to describe – or even to remember very well. It was like the ending of pain, like discord changing to harmony; like the lightening of the spirits that you may feel suddenly in the middle of a grey dull day, unaccountable until you realize that the sun has begun to shine. This silent music that entered Will's mind and took hold of his spirit came, he knew instantly, from the old lady. Without speech, she was speaking to him. She was speaking to both of them – and to the Dark. He looked back, dazzled; she seemed taller, bigger, more erect than before, a figure on an altogether larger scale. And there was a golden haze about her figure, a glow that did not come from the candlelight.

Will blinked, but he could not see clearly; it was as if he were separated from her by a veil. He heard Merriman's deep voice, gentler than he had yet heard it, but wrung with some strong sudden unhappiness. 'Madam,' Merriman said wretchedly. 'Take care, take care.'

No voice replied, but Will had a feeling of benison. Then it was gone, and the tall, glowing form that was and yet was not the old lady moved slowly forward in the darkness towards the doors, and for an instant Will heard again the haunting phrase of music that he could never capture in his memory, and the doors slowly opened. Outside there was a grey light and silence, and the air was cold.

Behind him, the light of the candle-ring was gone, and there was only darkness. It was an uneasy, empty darkness, so that he knew the hall was no longer there. And suddenly he realized that the luminous golden figure before him was fading too, vanishing away, like smoke that grows thinner, thinner, until it cannot be seen at all. For an instant there was a flash of rose-coloured brilliance from the huge ring that had been on the old lady's hand, and then that too dimmed, and her bright presence faded into nothing. Will felt a desperate ache of loss, as if his whole world had been swallowed up by the Dark, and he cried out.

A hand touched his shoulder. Merriman was at his side. They were through the doors. Slowly the great wooden carved portals swung back behind them, long enough for Will to see clearly that they were indeed the same strange gates that had opened for him before on the white untrodden slope of a Chiltern hill. Then, at the moment that they closed, the doors too were no longer there. He saw nothing: only the grey light of snow that reflects a grey sky. He was back in the snow-drowned woodland world into which he had walked early that morning.

Anxiously he swung round to Merriman. 'Where is she? What happened?'

'It was too much for her. The strain was too great, even for her. Never before – I have never seen this before.' His voice was thick and bitter; he stared angrily at nothing.

'Have they – taken her?' Will did not know what words to use for the fear.

'No!' Merriman said. The word was so quick with scorn it might have been a laugh. 'The Lady is beyond their power. Beyond any power. You will not ask a question like that when you have learned a little. She has gone away for a time, that is all. It was the opening of the doors, in the face of all that was willing them shut. Though the Dark could not destroy her, it has drained her, left her like a shell. She must recover herself, away alone, and that is bad for us if we should need her. As we shall. As the world always will.' He glanced down at Will without warmth; suddenly he seemed distant, almost threatening, like an enemy; he waved one hand impatiently. 'Close your coat, boy, before you freeze.'

Will fumbled with the buttons of his heavy jacket; Merriman, he saw, was wrapped in a long battered blue cloak, high-collared.

'It was my fault, wasn't it?' he said miserably. 'If I hadn't run forward, when I saw the doors – if I'd kept hold of your hands, and not broken the circle –'

Merriman said curtly: 'Yes.' Then he relented a little. 'But it was their doing, Will, not yours. They seized you, through your impatience and your hope. They love to twist good emotion to accomplish ill.'

Will stood hunched with his hands in his pockets, staring at the ground. Behind his mind a chant went sneering through his head: *you have lost the Lady, you have lost the Lady*. Unhappiness was thick in his throat; he swallowed; he could not speak. A breeze blew through the trees, and sprayed snow-crystals into his face.

'Will,' Merriman said. 'I was angry. Forgive me. Whether you had broken the Three or not, things would have been the same. The doors are our great gateway into Time, and you will know more about the uses of them before long. But this time you could not have opened them, nor I, nor perhaps any of the circle. For the force that was pushing against them was the full midwinter power of the Dark, which none but the Lady can overcome alone – and even she, only at great cost. Take heart; at the proper time, she will return.'

He pulled at the high collar of his cloak, and it became a hood that he drew over his head. With the white hair hidden he was a dark figure suddenly, tall and inscrutable. 'Come,' he said, and led Will through the deep snow, among great beeches and oaks bare of leaves. At length they paused, in a clearing.

'Do you know where you are?' Merriman said.

Will stared round at the smooth snowbanks, the rearing trees. 'Of course I don't,' he said. 'How could I?'

'Yet before the winter is three-quarters done,' Merriman said, 'You will be creeping into this dell to look at the snowdrops that grow everywhere between the trees. And then in the spring you will be back to stare at the daffodils. Every day for a week, to judge from last year.'

Will gaped at him. 'You mean the Manor?' he said. 'The Manor grounds?'

In his own century, Huntercombe Manor was the great house of the village. The house itself could not be seen from the road, but its grounds lay along the side of Huntercombe Lane opposite the Stantons' house, and stretched a long way in each direction, edged alternately by tall wrought-iron railings and ancient brick walls. A Miss Greythorne owned it, as her family had for centuries, but Will did not know her well; he seldom saw her or her Manor, which he remembered vaguely as a mass of tall brick gables and Tudor chimneys. The flowers that Merriman had spoken of were private landmarks in his year. For as long as he could remember, he had slipped through the Manor railings at the end of winter to stand in this one magical clearing and gaze at the gentle winter-banishing snowdrops, and later the golden daffodil-glow of spring. He did not know who had planted the flowers; he had never seen anyone visiting them. He was not even sure whether anyone else knew they were there. The image of them glowed now in his mind.

But rearing questions very soon chased it out. 'Merriman? Do you mean this clearing is here hundreds of years before I first saw it? And the great hall, is it a Manor before the Manor, out of centuries ago? And the forest all round us, that I came through when I saw the smith and the Rider – it stretches everywhere, does it all belong to –'

Merriman looked down at him and laughed, a gay laugh, suddenly without the heaviness that had been over them both.

'Let me show you something else,' he said, and he drew Will further through the trees, away from the clearing, until there was an end to the sequence of trunks and mounds of snow. And before him Will saw not the morning's narrow track that he had been expecting, winding its way through an endless forest of ancient crowding trees – but the familiar twentieth-century line of Huntercombe Lane, and beyond it, a little way up the road, a glimpse of his own house. The Manor railings were before them, somewhat shortened by the deep snow; Merriman stepped stiff-legged over, Will crept through his usual gap, and they were standing on the snow-banked road.

Merriman put back his hood again, and lifted his white-maned head as if to sniff the air of this newer century. 'You see, Will,' he said, 'we of the Circle are planted only loosely within Time. The doors are a way through it, in any direction we may choose. For all times co-exist, and the future can sometimes affect the past, even though the past is a road that leads to the future . . . But men cannot understand this. Nor will you for a while yet. We can travel through the years in other ways too – one of them was used this morning to bring you back through five centuries or so. That is where you were – in the time of the Royal Forests, that stretched over all the southern part of this land from Southampton Water up to the valley of the Thames here.'

He pointed across the road to the flat horizon, and Will remembered how he had seen the Thames twice that morning: once among its familiar fields, once buried instead among trees. He stared at the intensity of remembering on Merriman's face.

'Five hundred years ago,' Merriman said, 'the kings of England chose deliberately to preserve those forests, swallowing up whole villages and hamlets inside them, so that the wild things, the deer and the boars and even the wolves, might breed there for the hunt. But forests are not biddable places, and the kings were without knowing it establishing a haven too for the powers of the Dark, which might otherwise have been driven back then to the mountains and remotenesses of the North . . . So that is where you were until now, Will. In the forest of Anderida, as they used to call it. In the long-gone past. You were there in the beginning of the day, walking through the forest in the snow; there on the empty hillside of the Chilterns; still there when you had first walked through the doors – that was a symbol, your first walking, for your birthday as one of the Old Ones. And there, in that past, is where we left the Lady. I wish that I knew where and when we shall see her again. But come she will, when she can.' He shrugged, as if to shake away the heaviness again. 'And now you can go home, for you are in your own world.'

'And you are in it too,' said Will.

Merriman smiled. 'Back again. With mixed feelings.'

'Where will you go?'

'About and roundabout. I have a place in this present time, just as you do. Go home now, Will. The next stage in the quest depends on the Walker, and he will find you. And when his circle is on your belt beside the first, I shall come.'

'But –' Will suddenly wanted to clutch at him, to beg him not to go away. His home no longer seemed quite the unassailable fortress it had always been.

'You will be all right,' Merriman said gently. 'Take things as they come. Remember that the power protects you. Do nothing rash to draw trouble towards you, and all will be well. And we shall meet soon, I promise you.'

'All right,' Will said uncertainly.

An odd gust of wind eddied round them, in the still morning, and gobbets of snow spattered down from the roadside trees. Merriman drew his cloak around him, its bottom edge swirling a pattern in the snow; he gave Will one sharp look, of warning and encouragement mixed, pulled his hood forward over his face, and strode off down the road without a word. He disappeared round the bend beside Rooks' Wood, on the way to Dawsons' Farm.

Will took a deep breath, and ran home. The lane was silent in the deep snow and the grey morning; no birds moved or chirped; nothing stirred anywhere. The house too was utterly quiet. He shed his outdoor clothes, went up the silent stairs. On the landing he stood looking out at the white roofs and fields. No great forest mantled the earth now. The snow was as deep, but it was smooth over the flat fields of the valley, all the way to the curving Thames.

'All right, all right,' said James sleepily from inside his room.

From behind the next door, Robin gave a kind of formless growl and mumbled, 'In a minute. Coming.'

Gwen and Margaret came stumbling together out of the bedroom they shared, wearing nightdresses, rubbing their eyes. 'There's no need to bellow,' Margaret said reproachfully to Will.

'Bellow?' He stared at her.

'*Wake up everyone!*' she said in a mock shout. 'I mean, it's a holiday, for goodness' sake.'

Will said, 'But I –'

'Never mind,' Gwen said. 'You can forgive him for wanting to wake us up today. After all, he has a good reason.' And she came forward and dropped a quick kiss on the top of his head.

'Happy birthday, Will,' she said.

The Walker on the Old Way

'More snow to come, they say,' said the fat lady with the string bag to the bus conductor.

The bus conductor, who was West Indian, shook his head and gave a great glum sigh. 'Crazy weather,' he said. 'One more winter like this, and I going back to Port of Spain.'

'Cheer up, love,' said the fat lady. 'You won't see no more like this. Sixty-six years I've lived in the Thames Valley, and I never saw it snow like this, not before Christmas. Never.'

'Nineteen forty-seven,' said the man sitting next to her, a thin man with a long pointed nose. 'That was a year for snow. My word it was. Drifts higher than your head, all down Huntercombe Lane and Marsh Lane and right across the Common. You couldn't even cross the Common for two weeks. They had to get snow ploughs. Oh, that was a year for snow.'

'But not before Christmas,' said the fat lady.

'No, it was January.' The man nodded mournfully. 'Not before Christmas, no –'

They might have gone on like this all the way to Maidenhead, and perhaps they did, but Will suddenly noticed that his bus-stop was approaching in the featureless white world outside. He jumped to his feet, clutching at bags and boxes. The conductor punched the bell for him.

'Christmas shopping,' he observed.

'Uh-huh. Three . . . four . . . five . . .' Will squashed the packages against his chest, and hung on to the rail of the lurching bus. 'I've finished it all now,' he said. 'About time.'

'Wish I had,' said the conductor. 'Christmas Eve tomorrow too. Frozen blood, that's my problem – need some warm weather to wake me up.'

The bus stopped, and he steadied Will as he stepped off. 'Merry Christmas, man,' he said. They knew one another from Will's bus rides to and from school.

'Merry Christmas,' Will said. On an impulse he called after him, as the bus moved away. 'You'll have some warm weather on Christmas Day!'

The conductor grinned a broad white grin. 'You gonna fix it?' he called back.

Perhaps I could, Will thought, as he tramped along the main road towards Huntercombe Lane. *Perhaps I could*. The snow was deep even on the pavements; few people had been out to tread it down in the last two days. For Will they had been peaceful days, in spite of the memory of what had gone before. He had spent a cheerful birthday, with a family party so boisterous that he had fallen into bed and asleep with scarcely a thought of the Dark. After that, there had been a day of snowball fights and improvised toboggans with his brothers, in the sloping field behind the house. Grey days, with more snow hanging overhead but inexplicably not falling yet. Silent days; hardly a car came down the lane, except the vans of the milkman and the baker. And the rooks were quiet, only one or two of them drifting slowly to and fro sometimes over their wood.

The animals, Will found, were no longer frightened of him. If anything, they seemed more affectionate than before. Only Raq, the elder of the two collies, who liked to sit with his chin resting on Will's knee, would jerk away from him sometimes for no apparent reason, as if propelled by an electric shock. Then he would prowl the room restlessly for a few moments, before coming back to gaze inquiringly up into Will's face, and make himself comfortable again as before. Will did not know what to make of it. He knew that Merriman would know; but Merriman was out of his reach.

The crossed circle at his belt had remained warm to the touch since he had arrived home two mornings before. He slipped his hand under his coat now as he walked, to check it, and the circle was cold; but he thought that must simply be because he was outdoors, where everything was cold. He had spent most of the afternoon shopping for Christmas presents in Slough, their nearest large town; it was an annual ritual, the day before Christmas Eve being the day when he was certain of having birthday present money from assorted aunts and uncles to spend. This, however, was the first year he had gone alone. He was enjoying it; you could think things out better on your own. The all-important present for Stephen – a book about the Thames – had been bought long before, and posted off to Kingston, Jamaica, where his ship was on what was called the Caribbean Station. Will thought it sounded like a train. He decided he must ask his bus conductor friend what Kingston was like; though since the bus conductor came from Trinidad perhaps he might have stern feelings about other islands.

He felt again the small drooping of the spirits that had come in the last two days, because this year for the first time that he could remember there had been no birthday present from Stephen. And he pushed the disappointment away for the hundredth time, with the argument that the posts had gone wrong, or the ship had suddenly sailed on some urgent mission among the green islands. Stephen always remembered; Stephen would have remembered this time, if something had not got in the way. Stephen couldn't possibly forget.

Ahead of him, the sun was going down, visible for the first time since his birthday morning. It blazed out fat and gold-orange through a gap in the clouds, and all around the snow-silver world glittered with small gold flashes of light. After the grey slushy streets of the town, everything was beautiful again. Will plodded along, passing garden walls, trees, and then the top of a small unpaved track, scarcely a road, known as Tramps' Alley, that wandered off from the main road and eventually curled round to join Huntercombe Lane close to the Stantons' house. The children used it as a short cut sometimes. Will glanced down it now, and saw that nobody had been along the path since the snow began; down there it lay untrodden, smooth and white and inviting, marked only by the picture-writing of birds' footprints. Unexplored territory. Will found it irresistible.

So he turned down into Tramps' Alley, crunching with relish through the clear, slightly crusted snow, so that fragments of it clung in a fringe to the trousers tucked into his boots. He lost sight of the sun almost at once, cut off by the block of woodland that lay between the little track and the few houses edging the top of Huntercombe Lane. As he stomped through the snow, he clutched his parcels to his chest, counting them again: the knife for Robin, the chamois-leather for Paul, to clean his flute; the diary for Mary, the bathsalts for Gwennie; the super-special felt-tipped pens for Max. All his other presents were already bought and wrapped. Christmas was a complicated festival when you were one of nine children.

The walk down the Alley began quite soon to be less fun than he had expected. Will's ankles ached from the strain of kicking a way through the snow. The parcels were awkward to carry. The red-golden glow from the sun died away into a dull greyness. He was hungry, and he was cold.

Trees loomed high on his right: mostly elms, with an occasional beech. At the other side of the track was a stretch of wasteland, transformed by the snow from a messy array of rank weeds and scrub into a moon-landscape of white sweeping slopes and shaded hollows. All around him on the snow-covered track twigs and small branches lay scattered, brought down from the trees by the weight of snow; just ahead, Will saw a huge branch lying right across his path. He glanced apprehensively upward, wondering how many other dead arms of the great elms were waiting for wind or snow-weight to bring them crashing down. A good time for collecting firewood, he thought, and had a sudden tantalizing image of the leaping fire that had blazed in the fireplace of the great hall: the fire that had changed his world, by vanishing at the word of his command and then obediently blazing into life again.

As he stumbled along in the cold snow, a sudden wild cheerful idea sprang up in his mind out of the thought of that fire, and he paused, grinning to himself. *You gonna fix it*? Well, no, friend, I probably can't get you a warm Christmas Day really, but I could warm things up a bit here, now. He looked confidently at the dead branch lying before him, and with easy command now of the gift he knew was in him, he said to it softly, mischievously, 'Burn!'

And there on the snow, the fallen arm of the tree burst into flame. Every inch of it, from the thick rotted base to the smallest twig, blazed with licking yellow fire. There was a hissing sound, and a tall shaft of brilliance rose from the fire like a pillar. No smoke came from the burning, and the flames were steady; twigs that should have blazed and crackled briefly and then fallen into ash burned continuously, as if fed by other fuel within. Standing there alone, Will felt suddenly small and alarmed; this was no ordinary fire, and not to be controlled by ordinary means. It was not behaving at all in the same way as the fire in the hearth had done. He did not know what to do with it. In panic, he focused his mind on it again and told it to go out, but it burned on, steady as before. He knew that he had done something foolish, improper, dangerous perhaps. Looking up through the pillar of quivering light, he saw high in the grey sky four rooks flapping slowly in a circle.

Oh Merriman, he thought unhappily, where are you?

Then he gasped, as someone grabbed him from behind, blocked his kicking feet in a scuffle of snow, and twisted his arms by the wrists behind his back. The parcels scattered in the snow. Will yelled with the pain in his arms. The grip on his wrists slackened at once, as if his attacker were reluctant to do him any real harm; but he was still firmly held.

'Put out the fire!' said a hoarse voice in his ear, urgently.

'I can't!' Will said. 'Honestly. I've tried, but I can't.'

The man cursed and mumbled strangely, and instantly Will knew who it was. His terror fell away, like a released weight. 'Walker,' he said, 'let me go. You don't have to hold me like that.'

The grip tightened again at once. 'Oh no you don't boy. I know your tricks. You're the one all right, I know now, you're an Old One, but I don't trust your kind any more than I trust the Dark. You're new awake, you are, and let me tell you something you don't know – while you're new awake, you can't do nothing to anyone unless you can see him with your eyes. So you aren't going to see me, that I know.'

Will said: 'I don't want to do anything to you. There really are some people who can be trusted, you know.'

'Precious few,' the Walker said bitterly.

'I could shut my eyes, if you'd let me go.'

'Pah!' the old man said.

Will said, 'You carry the second Sign. Give it to me.'

There was a silence. He felt the man's hands fall away from his own arms, but he stood where he was and did not turn round. 'I have the first Sign already, Walker,' he said. 'You know I do. Look, I'm undoing my jacket, and I'll pull it back, and you can see the first circle on my belt.'

He pulled aside his coat, still without moving his head, and was aware of the Walker's hunched form slipping round at his side. The man's breath hissed out through his teeth in a long sigh as he looked, and he turned his head up to Will without caution. In the yellow light from the steadily-burning branch Will saw a face contorted with battling emotions: hope and fear and relief wound tightly together by anguished uncertainty.

When the man spoke, his voice was broken and simple as that of a small sad child.

'It's so heavy,' he said plaintively. 'And I've been carrying it for so long. I don't even remember why. Always frightened, always having to run away. If only I could get rid of it, if only I could rest. Oh, if only it was gone. But I daren't risk giving it to the wrong one, I daren't. The things that would happen to me if I did, they're too terrible, they can't be put into words. The Old Ones can be cruel, cruel . . . I think you're the right one, boy, I've been looking for you a long time, a long time, to give the Sign to you. But how can I be really sure? How can I be sure you aren't a trick of the Dark?'

He's been frightened so long, Will thought, that he's forgotten how to stop. How awful, to be so absolutely lonely. He doesn't know how to trust me; it's so long since he trusted anyone, he's forgotten how . . . 'Look,' he said gently. 'You must know I'm not part of the Dark. Think. You saw the Rider try to strike me down.'

But the old man shook his head miserably, and Will remembered how he had fled shrieking from the clearing the moment the Rider had appeared.

'Well, if that doesn't help,' he said, 'doesn't the fire tell you?'

'The fire almost,' the Walker said. He looked at it hopefully; then his face twisted in recalled alarm. 'But the fire, it'll bring them, boy, you know that. The rooks will already be guiding them. And how do I know whether you lit the fire because you're a new-awake Old One playing games, or as a signal to bring them after me?' He moaned to himself in anguish, and clutched his arms round his shoulders. He was a wretched thing, Will thought pityingly. But somehow he had to be made to understand.

Will looked up. There were more rooks circling lazily overhead now, and he could hear them calling harshly to one another. Was the old man right, were the dark birds messengers of the Dark? 'Walker, for goodness' sake,' he said impatiently. 'You must trust me – if you don't trust someone just once, for long enough to give him the Sign, you'll be carrying it for ever. Is that what you want?'

The old tramp wailed and muttered, staring at him from mad little eyes; he seemed caught in his centuries of suspicion like a fly in a web. But the fly still has wings that can break the web; give him the strength to flap them, just once ... Driven by some unfamiliar part of his mind, without quite knowing what he was doing, Will gripped the iron circle on his belt, and he stood up as straight and tall as he could and pointed at the Walker, and called out, 'The last of the Old Ones has come, Walker, and it is time. The moment for giving the Sign is now, now or never. Think only of that – no other chance will come. Now, Walker. Unless you would carry it for ever, obey the Old Ones now. *Now!*'

It was as if the word released a spring. In an instant, all the fear and suspicion in the twisted old face relaxed into childish obedience. With a smile of almost foolish eagerness the Walker fumbled with a broad leather strap that he wore diagonally across his chest, and he pulled from it a quartered circle identical with the one that Will wore on his belt, but gleaming with the dull brown-gold sheen of bronze. He put it into Will's hands, and gave a high cackling little laugh of astonished glee.

The yellow-flaming branch on the snow before them blazed suddenly brighter, and went out.

The branch lay just as it had when Will first came down the Alley: grey, uncharred, cold, as if no part of it had ever been touched by spark or flame. Clutching the bronze circle, Will stared down at the rough-barked wood, lying there on unmarked snow. Now that its light was gone, the day seemed suddenly much more murky, full of shadows, and he realized with a shock how little of the afternoon was left. It was late. He must go. And then a clear voice said, out of the shadows ahead, 'Hello, Will Stanton.'

The Walker squealed in terror, a thin, ugly sound. Will slipped the bronze circle quickly into his pocket, and stepped stiffly forward. Then he almost sat down on the snow in relief, as he saw that the newcomer was only Maggie Barnes, the dairy-girl from Dawsons' Farm. Nothing sinister about Maggie, Max's apple-cheeked admirer. Her dumpling form was all muffled up in coat and boots and scarf; she was carrying a covered basket, and heading down towards the main road. She beamed at Will, then peered accusingly at the Walker.

'Why,' she said, in her round Buckinghamshire voice, ''tis that old tramp that's been hanging around this past fortnight. Farmer said he wanted to see the back of you, old man. He been bothering you, young Will? I bet he has, now.' She glared at the Walker, who shrank sullenly into his dirty cape-like coat.

'Oh, no,' Will said. 'I was just running down from the bus from Slough, and I – bumped into him. Really bumped. Dropped all my Christmas shopping,' he added hastily, and bent to collect his parcels and packages that still lay scattered on the snow.

The Walker sniffed, hunched himself deeper inside his coat, and made to shuffle off past Maggie up the track. But as he drew level with her, he stopped abruptly, jerking back as if he had struck some invisible barrier. He opened his mouth, but no sound came. Will straightened up slowly, watching, his arms full of bundles. A dreadful sense of misgiving began to creep over him, like the chill of a cold breeze.

Maggie Barnes said amiably: 'Long time since the last bus from Slough, young Will. Fact, I'm just off to catch the next one. You always take half an hour to do that five-minute walk from the bus-stop, Will Stanton?'

'I don't see that it's any business of yours how long I take about anything,' Will said. He was watching the frozen Walker, and some very confused images were turning about in his head.

'Manners, manners,' said Maggie. 'Such a nicely brought-up little boy as you, too' Her eyes were very bright, peering at Will from the scarf-wrapped head.

'Well, good-bye, Maggie,' said Will. 'I've got to get home. Tea's past ready.'

'The trouble with nasty dirty tramps, like this one you just bumped into but who isn't bothering you,' Maggie Barnes said softly, without moving, 'the trouble with them is, they steal things. And this one stole something the other day from the farm, young Will, something belonging to me. An ornament. A big goldeny-brown coloured kind of ornament, circle-shaped, that I wore on a chain round my neck. And I want it back. *Now!*' The last word flicked out viciously, and then she was all soft sweetness again, as if her gentle voice had never changed. 'I want it back, I do. And I do think he might just have slipped it in your pocket when you weren't looking, when you bumped into him. If he saw me coming, that is, as he might well have done in the light of that funny little bonfire I saw burning up here just now. What do you think of all that, young Will Stanton, hey?'

Will swallowed. The hair was prickling upright on the back of his neck as he listened to her. There she stood, looking just the same as ever, the rosy-cheeked, uncomplicated farm girl who ran Dawsons' milking-machine and reared the smallest calves; and yet the mind out of which these words were coming could be nothing but the mind of the Dark. Had they stolen Maggie? Or had Maggie always been one of them? If she had, what else could she do?

He stood facing her, one hand clutching his parcels, one hand sliding cautiously into his pocket. The bronze Sign was cold, cold to his touch. He summoned up all the power of thought that he could find to drive her away, and still she stood there, smiling coldly at him. He conjured her to leave by all the names of power that he could remember Merriman using: by the Lady, by the Circle, by the Signs. But he knew he did not have the right things to say. And Maggie laughed aloud and moved deliberately forward, looking into his face, and Will found that he could not move a muscle.

He was caught, frozen just like the Walker; fixed immobile in a position he could not alter by so much as an inch. He glared furiously at Maggie Barnes, in her smooth red scarf and demure black coat, as she calmly slipped her hand past his into his coat pocket and drew out the bronze Sign. She held it in front of his face, and then rapidly unbuttoned his coat, flicked his belt away from him, and threaded the bronze circle on it to stand next to the iron.

'Hold up your trousers, Will Stanton,' she said mockingly. 'Oh, dear now, you can't, can you . . . But then you don't really wear that belt to keep up your trousers, do you? You wear it to keep this little . . . decoration . . . safe . . .' Will noticed that she held the two Signs as lightly as possible, and winced when she had to touch them with any firmness; the cold that was beating out of them must surely be burning her to the bone.

He watched in utter despair. There was nothing he could do. All his effort and questing was coming to an end before it had even properly begun, and there was nothing he could do. He wanted both to shout with rage and to weep. And then, deep down, something stirred in his mind. Some detail of memory flickered, but he could not catch it. He remembered it only at the moment when fresh-faced Maggie Barnes held up his belt before him with the first and second circle threaded there together, dull iron and gleaming bronze side by side. Staring greedily at the two circles, Maggie broke into a low gurgle of sneering laughter that sounded the more evil for the rosy openness of the face from which it came. And Will remembered.

. . . *when his circle is on your belt beside the first, 'I shall come . . .'*

At that same moment, fire leaped up out of the fallen elm tree branch that Will had briefly lighted before, and flames cracked down from nowhere in a circle of searing white light all around Maggie Barnes, a circle of light higher than her head. She crouched down suddenly on the snow, cringing, her mouth slack with fear. The belt with the two linked Signs dropped out of her limp hand.

And Merriman was there. Tall in the long dark cloak, his face hidden in shadow by the enveloping hood, he was there at the side of the road, just beyond the flaring circle and the cowering girl.

'Take her from this road,' he said in a clear loud voice, and the blazing circle of light moved slowly to one side, forcing the girl Maggie to stumble with it, until it hovered on the rough ground next to the road. Then with an abrupt crackling sound it was gone, and Will saw instead a great barrier of light spring up on either side of the road, edging it on both sides with leaping fire, stretching far into the distance in both directions – a great deal further than the length of the track that Will knew as Tramps' Alley. He stared at it, a little frightened. Out in the dimness he could see Maggie Barnes grovelling wretchedly in the snow, her arms shielding her eyes from the light. But he and Merriman and the Walker stood in a great endless tunnel of cold white flame.

Will bent and picked up his belt, and in a kind of relieved greeting he grasped the two Signs in his hands, iron in his left hand, bronze in his right. Merriman came to his side, raised his right arm so that the cloak swept down from it like the wing of some great bird, and pointed one long finger at the girl. He called out a long strange name, that Will had never heard before and could not keep in his mind, and the girl Maggie wailed aloud.

Merriman said, with scorn death-cold in his voice, 'Go back, and tell them that the Signs are beyond their touching. And if you would remain unharmed, do not try again to work your will while you stand on one of our Ways. For the old roads are wakened, and their power is alive again. And this time, they will have no pity and no remorse.' He called out the strange name again, and the flames edging the road leaped higher, and the girl screamed high and shrill as if she were in great pain. Then she scuffled away across the snowy field like a small hunched animal.

Merriman looked down at Will. 'Remember the two things that saved you,' he said, the light glinting now on his beaked nose and deep-set eyes under the shadowing hood. 'First, I knew her real name. The only way to disarm one of the creatures of the Dark is to call him or her by his real name : names that they keep very secret. Then, as well as the name, there was the road. Do you know the name of this track ?'

'Tramps' Alley,' Will said automatically.

'That is not a real name,' Merriman said with distaste.

'Well, no. Mum won't ever use it, and we're not supposed to. It's ugly, she says. But nobody else I know ever calls it anything else. I'd feel silly if I called it Oldway –' Will stopped suddenly, hearing and tasting the name properly for the first time in his life. He said slowly, 'If I called it by its real name, Oldway Lane.'

'You would feel silly,' said Merriman grimly. 'But the name that would make you feel silly has helped to save your life. Oldway Lane. Yes. And it was not named for some distant Mr Oldway. The name simply tells you what the road is, as the names of roads and places in old lands very often do, if only men would pay them more attention. It was lucky for you that you were standing on one of the Old Ways, trodden by the Old Ones for some three thousand years, when you played your little game with fire, Will Stanton. If you had been anywhere else, in your state of untrained power, you would have made yourself so vulnerable that all the things of the Dark that are in this land would have been drawn towards you. As the witch-girl was drawn by the birds. Look hard at this road now, boy, and do not call it by vulgar names again.'

Will swallowed and stared at the flame-edged Way stretching into the distance like some noble road of the sun, and on a sudden wild impulse he made it a clumsy little bow, bending from the waist as well as his armful of packages would let him. The flames leapt again, and curved inward, almost as if they were bowing in return. Then they went out.

'Well done,' said Merriman, with surprise and a touch of amusement.

Will said, 'I will never, never again do anything with the – the power, unless there is a reason. I promise. By the Lady and the old world. But' – he could not resist it – 'Merriman, it was my fire that brought the Walker to me, wasn't it, and the Walker had the Sign.'

'The Walker was waiting for you, stupid boy,' said Merriman irritably. 'I told you that he would find you, and you did not remember. Remember now. In this our magic, every smallest word has a weight and a meaning. Every word that I say to you – or that any other Old One may say. The Walker? He has been waiting for you to be born, and to stand alone with him and command the Sign from him, for time past your imagining. You did that well, I will say – it was a problem to bring him to the point of giving up the Sign when the time came. Poor soul. He betrayed the Old Ones once, long ago, and this was his doom.' His voice softened a little. 'It has been a hard age for him, the carrying of the second Sign. He has one more part in our work, before he may have rest, if he chooses. But that is not yet.'

They both looked at the motionless figure of the Walker, still standing caught in frozen movement at the side of the road as Maggie Barnes had left him.

'That's an awfully uncomfortable position,' Will said.

'He feels nothing,' said Merriman. 'Not a muscle will even grow stiff. Some small powers the Old Ones and the people of the Dark have in common, and one of them is this catching a man out of Time, for as long as is necessary. Or in the case of the Dark, for as long as they find it amusing.'

He pointed a finger at the immobile, shapeless form, and spoke some soft rapid words that Will did not hear, and the Walker relaxed into life like a figure in a moving film that has been stopped and then started again. Staring wide-eyed, he looked at Merriman and opened his mouth, and made a curious dry, speechless sound.

'Go,' Merriman said. The old man cringed away, clasping his flapping garments around him, and shambled off at a half-run up the narrow path. Watching him as he went, Will blinked, then peered hard, then rubbed his eyes; for the Walker seemed to be fading, growing strangely thinner, so that you could see the trees through his body. Then all at once he was gone, like a star blotted out by a cloud.

Merriman said, 'My doing, not his own. He deserves peace for a while, I think, in another place than this. That is the power of the Old Ways, Will. You would have used the trick to escape from the witch-girl, very easily, if you had known how. You will learn that, and the proper names and much else very soon now.'

Will said curiously, 'What is your proper name?'

The dark eyes glinted at him from inside the hood. 'Merriman Lyon. I told you when we met.'

'But I think that if that had really been your proper name, as an Old One, you would not have told me it,' Will said. 'At any rate, not out loud.'

'You are learning already,' Merriman said cheerfully. 'Come, it grows dark.'

They set off together down the lane. Will trotted beside the striding, cloaked figure, clutching his bags and boxes. They spoke little, but Merriman's hand was always there to catch him if he stumbled at any hollow or drift. As they came out at the far curve of the track into the greater breadth of Huntercombe Lane, Will saw his brother Max walking briskly towards them.

'Look, there's Max!'

'Yes,' Merriman said.

Max called, gaily waving, and then he was close. 'I was just coming to meet you off this bus,' he said. 'Mum was getting in a bit of a tizz because her baby boy was late.'

'Oh, for goodness' sake,' Will said.

'Why were you coming that way?' Max waved in the direction of Tramps' Alley.

'We were just –' Will began, and as he turned his head to include Merriman in the remark he stopped, so abruptly that he bit his tongue.

Merriman was gone. In the snow where he had been standing a moment before, no mark of any kind was left. And as Will looked back the way they had walked across Huntercombe Lane, and down the top curve of the smaller track, he could see only one line of footprints – his own.

He thought he heard a faint silvery music, somewhere in the air, but even as he raised his head to listen, it too was gone.

PART TWO
The Learning

Christmas Eve

Christmas Eve. It was the day when the delight of Christmas really took fire in the Stanton family. Hints and glimmerings and promises of special things, which had flashed in and out of life for weeks before, now suddenly blossomed into a constant glad expectancy. The house was full of wonderful baking smells from the kitchen, in a corner of which Gwen could be found putting the final touches to the icing of the Christmas cake. Her mother had made the cake three weeks before; the Christmas pudding, three months before that. Ageless, familiar Christmas music permeated the house whenever anyone turned on the radio. The television set was never turned on at all; it had become, for this season, an irrelevance. For Will, the day brought itself into natural focus very early. Straight after breakfast – an even more haphazard affair than usual – there was the double ritual of the Yule log and the Christmas tree.

Mr Stanton was finishing the last piece of toast. Will and James stood on either side of him at the breakfast table, fidgeting. Their father held a crust forgotten in one hand as he pored over the sports page of the newspaper. Will too was passionately interested in the fortunes of Chelsea Football Club, but not on Christmas Eve morning.

'Would you like some more toast, Dad?' he said loudly.

'Mmm,' said Mr Stanton. 'Aaah.'

James said, 'Have you had enough tea, Dad?'

Mr Stanton looked up, turned his round, mild-eyed head from one to the other of them, and laughed. He put down the paper, drained his teacup, and crammed the piece of toast into his mouth. 'C'mon, then,' he said indistinctly, taking each of them by an ear. They howled happily, and ran for boots and jackets and scarves.

Down the road with the handcart they went, Will, James, Mr Stanton, and tall Max, bigger than his father, bigger than anyone, with his long dark hair jutting in a comical fringe out of a disreputable old cap. What would Maggie Barnes think of that, Will wondered cheerfully, when she peeped roguishly as usual round the kitchen curtain to catch Max's eye; and then in the same instant he remembered about Maggie Barnes, and he thought in a rush of alarm: *Farmer Dawson is one of the Old Ones, he must be warned about her* – and he was distraught that he had not thought of it before.

They stopped in Dawsons' yard, old George Smith coming out to meet them with his gaping grin. The going had been easier along the road that morning, since a plough had been through; but everywhere the snow still lay unmoving in a constant, grey, windless cold.

'Got you a tree to beat all!' Old George called joyfully. 'Straight as a mast, like Farmer's. Both Royal trees again, I reckon.'

'Royal as they come,' said Mr Dawson, pulling his coat tight round him as he came out. He meant it literally, Will knew; every year, a number of Christmas trees were sold from the Crown plantations round Windsor Castle, and several came back in the Dawson farm lorry to the village.

'Morning, Frank,' said Mr Stanton.

'Morning, Roger,' said Farmer Dawson, and beamed at the boys. 'Hey lads. Round the back with that cart.' His eyes slid impersonally over Will, without so much as a flicker of notice, but Will had deliberately left his jacket swinging open in such a way that it was plain there were now two crossed-circle Signs on his belt, not one.

'Good to see you looking so lively,' said Mr Dawson breezily to them all, as they heaved the handcart round behind the barn; and his hand rested briefly on Will's shoulder with a faint pressure that told him Farmer Dawson had a good idea of what had been happening in the last few days. He thought of Maggie Barnes and searched hastily for words to frame a warning.

'Where's your girl friend, Max?' he said, carefully loud and clear.

'Girl friend?' said Max indignantly. Being deeply involved with a blonde-tressed student at his London art school, from whom enormous blue-enveloped letters arrived in the post every day, he was totally uninterested in all local girls.

'Ho, ho, ho,' said Will, trying hard. '*You* know.'

Fortunately James was fond of this kind of thing, and joined in with enthusiasm. 'Maggie-maggie-maggie,' he chanted gaily. 'Oh, Maggie the dairymaid's sweet on Maxie the great artist, oooh – oooh . . .' Max punched him in the ribs, and he lapsed into snorting giggles.

'Young Maggie's had to leave us,' Mr Dawson said coolly. 'Illness in the family. Needed at home. She packed up and went early this morning. Sorry to disappoint you, Max.'

'I'm not disappointed,' said Max, turning scarlet. 'It's just these stupid little –'

'Ooooh – oooooh,' sang James, dancing about out of arm's length. 'Oooh poor Maxie, lost his Maggie –'

Will said nothing. He was satisfied.

The tall fir tree, its branches tied down with bands of hairy white string, was loaded on to the handcart, and with it the gnarled old root of a beech tree that Farmer Dawson had cut down earlier that year, split in half, and put aside to make Yule logs for himself and the Stantons. It had to be the root of a tree, not a branch, Will knew, though nobody had ever explained why. At home, they would put the log on the fire tonight in the big brick fireplace in the living-room, and it would burn slowly all the evening until they went to bed. Somewhere stored away was a piece of last year's Yule log, saved to be used as kindling for its successor.

'Here,' Old George said, appearing suddenly at Will's side as they all pushed the cart out of the gate. 'You should have some of this.' He thrust forward a great bunch of holly, heavy with berries.

'Very good of you, George,' said Mr Stanton. 'But we do have that big holly tree by the front door, you know. If you know anyone who hasn't –'

'No, no, you take it.' The old man wagged his finger. 'Not half so many berries on that bush o' yours. Partic'lar holly, this is.' He laid it carefully in the cart; then quickly broke off a sprig and slipped it into the top buttonhole of Will's coat. 'And a good protection against the Dark,' the old voice said low in Will's ear, 'if pinned over the window, and over the door.' Then the pink-gummed grin split his creased brown face in a squawk of ancient laughter, and the Old One was Old George again, waving them away. 'Happy Christmas!'

'Happy Christmas, George!'

When they carried the tree ceremonially through the front door, the twins seized it with cross-boards and screwdrivers, to give it a base. At the other end of the room Mary and Barbara sat in a rustling sea of coloured paper, cutting it into strips, red, yellow, blue, green, and gluing them into interlocked circles for paper-chains.

'You should have done those yesterday,' Will said. 'They'll need time to dry.'

'*You* should have done them yesterday,' Mary said resentfully, tossing back her long hair. 'It's supposed to be the youngest's job.'

'I cut up lots of strips the other day,' Will said.

'We used those up hours ago.'

'I did cut them, all the same.'

'Besides,' Barbara said peaceably, 'he was Christmas shopping yesterday. So you'd better shut up, Mary, or he might decide to take your present back.'

Mary muttered, but subsided, and Will half-heartedly stuck a few paper-chains together. But he kept an eye on the doorway, and when he saw his father and James appear with their arms full of old cardboard boxes, he slipped quietly away after them. Nothing could keep him from the decorating of the Christmas tree.

Out of the boxes came all the familiar decorations that would turn the life of the family into a festival for twelve nights and days: the golden-haired figure for the top of the tree; the strings of jewel-coloured lights. Then there were the fragile glass Christmas-tree balls, lovingly preserved for years. Half-spheres whorled like red and gold-green seashells, slender glass spears, spider-webs of silvery glass threads and beads; on the dark limbs of the tree they hung and gently turned, shimmering.

There were other treasures, then. Little gold stars and circles of plaited straw; light, swinging silver-paper bells. Next, a medley of decorations made by assorted Stanton children, ranging from Will's infant pipe-cleaner reindeer to a beautiful filigree cross that Max had fashioned out of copper wire in his first year at art school. Then there were strings of tinsel to be draped across any space, and then the box was empty.

But not quite empty. Rifling his fingers gingerly through the crumpled handfuls of packing-paper, in an old cardboard container nearly as tall as himself, Will found a small flat box not much larger than his hand. It rattled.

'What's this?' he said curiously, trying to open the lid.

'Good heavens,' said Mrs Stanton from her central armchair. 'Let me see that a moment, love. Is it . . . yes it is! Was it in the big box? I thought we'd lost it years ago. Just look at this, Roger. See what your youngest son's found. It's Frank Dawson's box of letters.'

She pressed a catch on the lid of the box, so that it flicked up, and Will saw inside a number of ornate little carvings done in some light wood that he could not name. Mrs Stanton held one up: a curved letter S, with the beautifully detailed head and scaly body of a snake, twirling on an almost invisible thread. Then another: an arched M, with peaks like the twin spires of a faery cathedral. The carvings were so delicate that it was quite impossible to see where they joined the threads from which they hung.

Mr Stanton came down from the step-ladder, and poked one gentle finger into the box. 'Well, well,' he said. 'Clever old Will.'

'I've never seen them before,' said Will.

'Well, you have really,' his mother said. 'But so long ago that you wouldn't remember. They disappeared years and years ago. Fancy them being at the bottom of that old box all the time.'

'But what are they?'

'Christmas-tree ornaments, of course,' Mary said, peering over her mother's shoulder.

'Farmer Dawson made them for us,' Mrs Stanton said. 'They're beautifully carved, as you see. And exactly as old as the family – on our first Christmas Day in this house Frank made an R for Roger' – she fished it out – 'and an A for me.'

Mr Stanton pulled out two letters which both hung together from the same thread. 'Robin and Paul. This pair came a bit later than usual. We hadn't been expecting twins . . . Really, Frank was awfully good. I wonder if he has time for anything like this now?'

Mrs Stanton was still turning the small wooden curlicues in her thin, strong fingers. 'M for Max, and M for Mary . . . Frank was very cross with us for having a repeat, I remember . . . Oh, Roger,' she said, her voice suddenly softening. 'Look at this one.'

Will stood beside his father to look. It was a letter T, carved like an exquisite little tree spreading two branches wide. 'T?' he said. 'But none of us begins with T.'

'That was Tom,' his mother said. 'I don't really know why I've never spoken to you younger ones about Tom. It was just so long ago . . . Tom was your little brother who died. He had something wrong with his lungs, a disease some new babies get, and he only lived for three days after he was born. Frank had the initial already carved for him, because it was our first baby and we had two names chosen; Tom if it was a boy, Tess if it was a girl . . .'

Her voice sounded slightly muffled, and Will suddenly regretted finding the letters. He patted her shoulder awkwardly. 'Never mind, Mum,' he said.

'Oh, gracious,' said Mrs Stanton briskly. 'I'm not sad, love. It was a very long while ago. Tom would have been a grown-up man by now, older than Stephen. And after all' – she gave a comical look round the room, cluttered with people and boxes – 'a brood of nine should be enough for any woman.'

'You can say that again,' said Mr Stanton.

'It comes of having farming forebears, Mum,' said Paul. 'They believed in large families. Lots of free labour.'

'Speaking of free labour,' said his father, 'where have James and Max gone?'

'Fetching the other boxes.'

'Good Lord. Such initiative!'

'Christmas spirit,' said Robin from the step-ladder. 'Good Christian men rejoice, and all that. Why doesn't someone turn some music on?'

Barbara, sitting on the floor beside her mother, took the little carved wooden T from her hand and added it to a row she had made on the carpet of every initial in order. 'Tom, Steve, Max, Gwen, Robin and Paul, me, Mary, James,' she said. 'But where's the W for Will?'

'Will's was there with all the rest. In the box.'

'It wasn't a W actually, if you remember,' said Mr Stanton. 'It was a kind of pattern. I dare say Frank had got tired of doing initials by then.' He grinned at Will.

'But it's not here,' Barbara said. She held the box upside down, then shook it. Then she looked at her youngest brother solemnly. 'Will,' she said, 'you don't exist.'

But Will was feeling a growing uneasiness that seemed to come from some very deep faraway part of his mind. 'You said it was a pattern, not a W,' he said casually. 'What sort of pattern, Dad?'

'A mandala, as I recall,' said Mr Stanton.

'A what?'

His father chuckled. 'Pay no attention, I was only showing off. I don't imagine Frank would have called it that. A mandala is a very ancient kind of symbol dating back to sun-worship and that kind of thing – any pattern made of a circle with lines radiating outward or inward. Your little Christmas ornament was just a simple one – a circle with a star inside, or a cross. A cross, I think it was.'

'I can't think why it isn't there with the rest,' said Mrs Stanton.

But Will could. If there was power in knowing the proper names of the people of the Dark, perhaps the Dark could in its turn work magic over others by using some sign that was a symbol of a name, like a carved initial . . . Perhaps someone had taken his own sign in order to try to get power over him that way. And perhaps, indeed, this was why Farmer Dawson had carved him not an initial, but a symbol that nobody of the Dark could use. They had stolen it anyway, to try . . .

A little while later, Will slipped away from the tree-decorating and went upstairs and pinned a sprig of holly over the door and each of the windows of his room. He tucked a piece into the newly-mended catch of the skylight as well. Then he did the same for the windows of James's room, which he would share for Christmas Eve, and came downstairs and fixed a small bunch neatly over the front and back doors of the house. He would have done the same to all the windows, too, if Gwen hadn't crossed the hall and noticed what he was doing.

'Oh, Will,' she said. 'Not *everywhere*. Put it all along the mantelpiece or somewhere, so it's controllable. I mean, otherwise we shall have holly berries underfoot every time anyone draws the curtains.'

A typical female attitude, Will thought in disgust; but he was not inclined to draw attention to his holly by making any great protest. In any case, he reflected as he tried to arrange the holly artistically over the mantel, up here it would be a protection against the only entry into the house that he had forgotten about. Having left his Father Christmas days behind, he had not thought about the chimney.

The house was glowing now with light and colour and excitement. Christmas Eve was almost accomplished. But last of all there came the carol-singing.

After tea that day, when the Christmas lights had been turned on, and when the last rustling scuttlings of present-wrappings were ending, Mr Stanton stretched back in his battered leather armchair, took out his pipe, and beamed pontifically at them all.

'Well,' he said, 'who's going on the trek this year?'

'Me,' said James.

'Me,' said Will.

'Barbara and I,' said Mary.

'Paul, of course,' said Will. His brother's flute-case was all ready on the kitchen table.

'I don't know whether I shall,' Robin said.

'Yes, you will,' said Paul. 'No good without a baritone.'

'Oh, all right,' said his twin begrudgingly. This brief exchange had been repeated annually now for three years. Being large, mechanically-minded and an excellent footballer, Robin felt it was not quite proper for him to show eagerness for any activity as lady-like as carol-singing. In fact he was genuinely devoted to music, like the rest of them, and had a pleasant dark-brown voice.

'Too busy,' Gwen said. 'Sorry.'

'What she means is,' said Mary from a safe distance, 'that she has to wash her hair in case Johnnie Penn might come round.'

'What do you mean, *might*?' said Max from the armchair next to his father's.

Gwen made a terrible face at him. 'Well,' she demanded, 'and what about you going carolling?'

'Even busier than you,' Max said lazily. 'Sorry.'

'And what *he* means is,' said Mary, now hovering beside the door, 'that he has to sit up in his room and write another enormous long letter to his blonde bird in Southampton.'

Max pulled off one of his slippers to hurl, but she was gone.

'Bird?' said his father. 'Whatever will the word be next?'

'Good grief, Dad!' James looked at him in horror. 'You really do live in the Stone Age. Girls have been birds since the year one. Just about as much brains as birds too, if you ask me.'

'Some real birds have quite a lot of brains,' Will said reflectively. 'Don't you think?' But the episode of the rooks had been so effectively removed from James's mind that he took no notice; the words bounced off.

'Off you all go,' said Mrs Stanton. 'Boots, thick coats, and back by eight-thirty.'

'Eight-thirty?' Robin said. 'If we give Miss Bell three carols, and Miss Greythorne asks us all in for punch?'

'Well, nine-thirty at the very outside,' she said.

It was very dark by the time they left; the sky had not cleared, and no moon nor even a single star glimmered through the black night. The lantern that Robin carried on a pole cast a glittering circle of light on the snow, but each of them had a candle in one coat pocket just the same. When they reached the Manor, old Miss Greythorne would insist on their coming in and standing in her great stone-floored entrance hall with all the lights turned out, each holding up a lighted candle while they sang.

The air was freezing, and their breath clouded out thick and white. Now and then a stray snowflake drifted down from the sky, and Will thought of the fat lady in the bus and her predictions. Barbara and Mary were chattering away as cosily as if they were sitting at home, but behind the chatter the footsteps of all the group rang out cold and hard on the snow-caked road. Will was happy, snug in the thought of Christmas and the pleasure of carol-singing; he walked along in a contented dreamy state, clutching the big collecting box they carried in aid of Huntercombe's small, ancient, famous and rapidly crumbling Saxon church. Then, there ahead of them was Dawsons' Farm with a large bunch of the many-berried holly nailed above the back door, and the carol-singing had begun.

On through the village they sang: 'Nowell' for the rector; 'God Rest Ye Merry Gentlemen' for jolly Mr Hutton, the enormous businessman in the new mock-Tudor house at the end of the village, who always looked as though he were resting very merry indeed; 'Once in Royal David's City' for Mrs Pettigrew, the widowed postmistress, who dyed her hair with tea-leaves and kept a small limp dog which looked like a skein of grey wool. They sang 'Adeste Fideles' in Latin and 'Les Anges dans nos Campagnes' in French for tiny Miss Bell, the retired village schoolmistress, who had taught every one of them how to read and write, add and subtract, talk and think, before they went on to other schools elsewhere. And little Miss Bell said huskily, 'Beautiful, beautiful,' put some coins that they knew she could not afford into the collecting box, gave each of them a hug, and – 'Merry Christmas! Merry Christmas!' – they were off to the next house on the list.

There were four or five more, one of them the home of lugubrious Mrs Horniman, who 'did' for their mother once a week and had been born and bred in the East End of London until a bomb had blown her house to bits thirty years before. She had always given them a silver sixpence each, and so she still did, coolly disregarding changes in the currency. 'Wouldn't be Christmas without sixpences,' Mrs Horniman said. 'I laid a good stock in before we got landed with all them decimals, so I did. So I can go on every Christmas just the way I used to, me ducks, and I reckon my stock'll see me out, until I'm deep in me grave and you're singing to someone else at this here door. Merry Christmas!'

And then it was the Manor, the last stop before home.

> Here we come a-wassailing among the leaves so green,
> Here we come a-wandering, so fair to be seen . . .

They always began with the old Wassail Song for Miss Greythorne, and this year the bit about the green leaves, Will reflected, was even more inappropriate than usual. The carol bounded its way along, and for the last verse Will and James soared up into the high pealing descant that they did not always use for an ending because it took so much breath.

> Good master and good mistress while you're sitting by the fire,
> Pray think of us poor children who are wandering in the mire . . .

Robin tugged the big metal bell-pull, whose deep clanging always filled Will with an obscure alarm, and as they spiralled up in the last verse the great door opened, and there stood Miss Greythorne's butler, in the tail-coat he wore always on Christmas Eve night. He was not a very grand butler; his name was Bates, a tall, lean, morose man who could often be seen helping the one aged gardener in the vegetable garden near the Manor's back gate, or discussing his arthritis with Mrs Pettigrew at the Post Office.

> Love and joy come to you
> And to you your wassail too . . .

The butler smiled and nodded politely at them and held the door wide, and Will all but swallowed his last high note, for it was not Bates; it was Merriman.

The carol ended, and they all relaxed, shuffling in the snow. 'Enchanting,' Merriman said gravely, surveying them impersonally, and Miss Greythorne's high imperious tones came ringing past him. 'Bring them in! Bring them in! Don't keep them waiting on the doorstep!'

She sat there in the long entrance hall, in the same high-backed chair that they saw every Christmas Eve. She had not been able to walk for years after an accident when she was a young woman – her horse had fallen and rolled on her, the village said – but she flatly refused ever to be seen in a wheelchair.

Thin-faced and bright-eyed, her grey hair always swept up on top of her head in a kind of knot, she was a figure of total mystery in Huntercombe.

'How's y'mother?' Miss Greythorne demanded of Paul. 'And y'father?'

'Very well, thank you, Miss Greythorne.'

'Havin' a good Christmas?'

'Splendid, thanks. I hope you are.' Paul, who was sorry for Miss Greythorne, always went to some trouble to be warmly polite; he made sure now that his eyes did not flicker round the high-roofed hall as he spoke. For although the cook-housekeeper and the maid were standing beaming at the back of the hall, and though of course there was the butler who had opened the front door, otherwise in all this great house there was no trace of any visitor, tree, decoration, or any other sign of Christmas festivity, save for one gigantic branch of many-berried holly hanging over the mantel.

'An odd season, this,' Miss Greythorne said, looking at Paul pensively. 'So full of a number of things, as that odious little girl in the poem said.' She turned suddenly to Will. 'And are you having a busy time this year, eh, young man?'

'I certainly am,' said Will frankly, caught off balance.

'A light for your candles,' said Merriman in low respectful tones, coming forward with a box of enormous matches. Hastily they all tugged the candles from their pockets, and he struck a match and moved carefully among them, the light turning his eyebrows into fantastic bristling hedges and the lines from nose to mouth into deep-shadowed ravines. Will looked thoughtfully at his tail-coat, which was cut away at the waist, and which he wore with a kind of jabot at the neck instead of a white tie. He was having some difficulty in thinking of Merriman as a butler.

Someone at the back of the hall turned out the lights, leaving the long room lit only by the group of flickering flames in their hands. There was the soft tap of a foot; then they began with the sweet, soft lullaby carol, 'Lullay lullay, thou little tiny child . . .' ending it with a last wordless verse played only by Paul. The clear, husky sound of the flute fell through the air like bars of light and filled Will with a strange aching longing, a sense of something waiting far off, that he could not understand. Then for contrast they sang 'God Rest Ye Merry, Gentlemen'; then 'The Holly and the Ivy'. And then they were back at 'Good King Wenceslas', always a grand finale for Miss Greythorne, and always making Will sorry for Paul, who had once observed that this carol was so totally unsuited to his kind of music that it must have been written by someone who despised the flute.

But it was fun being the page, trying to make his voice so exactly match James's that the two of them together sounded like one boy.

Sire, he lives a good league hence . . .

. . . and Will thought: we're really doing well this time, I'd swear James wasn't singing at all if . . .

Underneath the mountain . . .

. . . if it weren't for the fact that his mouth's moving . . .

Right against the forest fence . . .

. . . and he glanced through the gloom as he sang, and saw, with a shock as brutal as if someone had thumped him in the stomach, that in fact James's mouth was not moving, nor was any other part of James, nor of Robin or Mary or any of the Stantons. They stood there immobile, all of them, caught out of Time, as the Walker had stood in Oldway Lane when the girl of the Dark enchanted him. And the flames of their candles flickered no longer, but each burned with the same strange, unconsuming pillar of white luminous air that had risen from Will's burning branch that other day. Paul's fingers no longer moved on his flute; he too stood motionless, holding it to his mouth. Yet the music, very much like but even sweeter than the music of a flute, went on, and so did Will, singing in spite of himself, finishing the verse . . .

By Saint Agnes' fou . . . oun . . . tain . . .

. . . And just as he began to wonder, through the strange sweet accompanying music that seemed to come out of the air, quite how the next verse could be done, unless a boy soprano were expected to sound like good King Wenceslas as well as his page, a great beautiful deep voice rolled out through the room with the familiar words, a great deep voice that Will had never heard employed in song before and yet at once recognized.

. . . Bring me flesh and bring me wine
Bring me pine-logs hither;
Thou and I will see him dine
When we bear them thither . . .

Will's head swam a little, the room seemed to grow and then shrink again; but the music went on, and the pillars of light stood still above the candle-flames, and as the next verse began Merriman reached casually out and took his hand, and they walked forward singing together:

> Page and monarch forth they went,
> Forth they went together,
> Through the rude wind's wild lament
> And the bitter weather.

They walked down the long entrance hall, away from the motionless Stantons, past Miss Greythorne in her chair, and the cook-housekeeper, and the maid, all unmoving, alive and yet suspended out of life. Will felt as though he were walking in the air, not touching the ground at all, down the dark hall; no light ahead of them now, but only a glow from behind. Into the dark . . .

> Sire, the night is darker now,
> And the wind blows stronger;
> Fails my heart I know not how,
> I can go no longer . . .

Will heard his voice shake, for the words were right words for what was in his mind.

> Mark my footsteps, good my page;
> Tread thou in them boldly . . .

Merriman sang; and suddenly more was ahead of Will than the dark.

There before him rose the great doors, the great carved doors that he had first seen on a snow-mounded Chiltern hillside, and Merriman raised his left arm and pointed at them with his five fingers spread wide and straight. Slowly the doors opened, and the elusive silvery music of the Old Ones came swelling up briefly to join the accompaniment of the carol, and then was lost again. And he walked forward with Merriman into the light, into a different time and a different Christmas, singing as if he could pour all the music in the world into these present notes – and singing so confidently that the school choirmaster, who was very strict about raised heads and well-moving jaws, would have fallen mute in astonished pride.

The Book of Gramarye

They were in a bright room again, a room unlike anything Will had ever seen. The ceilings were high, painted with pictures of trees and woods and mountains; the walls were panelled in shiny gold wood, lit here and there by strange glowing white globes. And the room was full of music, their own carol taken up by many voices, in a gathering of people dressed like a brilliant scene from a history book. The women, bare-shouldered, wore long full dresses with elaborately looped and ruffled skirts; the men wore suits not unlike Merriman's, with squared-off tail-coats, long straight trousers, white ruffles or black silk cravats at the neck. Indeed now that Will came to look again at Merriman, he realized that the clothes he wore had never really been those of a butler at all, but belonged totally to this other century, whichever it might be.

A lady in a white dress was sweeping forward to meet them, people round her moving respectfully back to make way, and as the carol ended she cried: 'Beautiful! Beautiful! Come in, come in!' The voice was exactly the voice of Miss Greythorne greeting them at the Manor door a little while earlier, and when Will looked up at the face he saw that in a sense this was Miss Greythorne too. There were the same eyes and rather bony face, the same friendly but imperious manner – only this Miss Greythorne was much younger and prettier, like a flower that has unfolded from the bud but not yet been battered by the sun and wind and days.

'Come, Will,' she said, and took his hand, smiling down at him, and he went easily to her; it was so clear that she knew him and that those around her, men and women, young and old, all smiling and gay, knew him too. Most of the bright crowd was leaving the room now, couples and chattering groups, in the direction of a delicious cooking smell that clearly signalled supper somewhere else in the house. But a group of a score or so remained.

'We were waiting for you,' said Miss Greythorne, and drew him towards the back of the room where a fire blazed warm and friendly in an ornate fireplace. She was looking at Merriman too, including him in the words. 'We are all ready, there are no – hindrances.'

'You are sure?' Merriman's voice came quick and deep like a hammer-stroke, and Will glanced up curiously. But the hawk-nosed face was as secret as ever.

'Quite sure,' said the lady. Suddenly she knelt down beside Will, her skirt billowing round her like a great white rose; she was at his eye-level now, and she held both his hands, gazing at him, and spoke softly and urgently. 'It is the third Sign, Will. The Sign of Wood. We call it sometimes the Sign of Learning. This is the time for remaking the Sign. In every century since the beginning, Will, every hundred years, the Sign of Wood must be renewed, for it is the only one of the six that cannot keep its nature unchanged. Every hundred years we have remade it, in the way that we were first taught. And now this will be the last time, because when your own century comes you will take it out for all time, for the joining, and there need be no more renewing then.'

She stood up, and said clearly, 'We are glad to see you, Will Stanton, Sign-seeker. Very, very glad.' And there was a general rumble of voices, low and high, soft and deep, all approving and agreeing; it was like a wall, Will thought, you could lean against it and feel support. Very strongly he could feel the strength of friendship that came out of this small group of unfamiliar, handsomely-dressed people; he wondered whether all of them were Old Ones. Looking up at Merriman beside him, he grinned in delight, and Merriman smiled down at him with a look of more open relaxed pleasure than Will had yet seen on the stern, rather grim face.

'It is almost time,' Miss Greythorne said.

'Some small refreshment for the newcomers first, perhaps,' a man beside them said: a small man, not much taller than Will. He held out a glass. Will took it, glancing up, and found himself staring into a thin, lively face, almost triangular, thickly lined yet not old, with a pair of startlingly bright eyes staring at and somehow into him. It was a disturbing face, with much behind it. But the man had swung away from him, presenting Will only with a neat, green-velvet-covered back, and was handing a glass to Merriman.

'My lord,' he said deferentially as he did so, and bowed.

Merriman looked at him with a comical twist of the mouth, said nothing, but stared mockingly and waited. Before Will had a chance even to begin puzzling over the greeting, the small man blinked and seemed suddenly to collect his wits, like a dreamer abruptly woken. He burst out laughing.

'Ah, no,' he said spluttering. 'Stop it. I have had the habit for long years, after all.' Merriman chuckled affectionately, raised the glass to him, and drank; and since he could make no sense of this odd exchange Will drank too, and was filled with astonishment by an unrecognizable taste that was less a taste than a blaze of light, a burst of music, something fierce and wonderful sweeping over all his senses at once.

'What is it?'

The small man swung round and laughed, his creased face slanting all its lines upwards. 'Metheglyn used to be the nearest name,' he said, taking the empty glass. He blew into it, said unexpectedly, 'An Old One's eyes can see,' and held it out; and staring into the clear base, Will suddenly felt he could see a group of figures in brown robes making whatever it was that he had just drunk. He glanced up to see the man in the green coat watching him closely, with a disturbing expression that was like a mixture of envy and satisfaction. Then the man chuckled and whisked the glass away, and Miss Greythorne was calling for them to come to her; the white globes of light in the room grew dim, and the voices quiet. Somewhere in the house Will thought he could still hear music, but he was not sure.

Miss Greythorne stood by the fire. For a moment she looked down at Will, then up at Merriman. Then she turned away from them and looked at the wall. She stared and stared for a long time. The panelling and the fireplace and the over-mantel were all one, all carved from the same golden wood: very plain, with no curves or flourishes, but only a simple four-petalled rose set in a square here and there. She put up her hand to one of these small rose carvings on the top left-hand corner of the fireplace, and she pressed its centre. There was a click, and below the rose, at the level of her waist, a square dark hole in the panelling appeared. Will did not see any panel slide away; the hole was simply, suddenly, there. And Miss Greythorne put in her hand and drew out an object shaped like a small circle. It was the image of the two that he had himself, and he found that his hand, as once before, had already moved of its own accord and was clasping them protectively. There was total silence in the room. From outside the doors Will could certainly hear music now, but could not make out the nature of it.

The sign-circle was very thin and dark, and one of its inside cross-arms broke as he watched. Miss Greythorne held it out to Merriman, and a little more fell away into dust. Will could see now that it was wood, roughened and worn, but with a grain running through.

'That's a hundred years old?' he said.

'Every hundred years, the renewing,' she said. 'Yes.'

Will said impulsively, into the silent room, 'But wood lasts much longer than that. I've seen some in the British Museum. Bits of old boats they dug up by the Thames. Prehistoric. *Thousands* of years old.'

'*Quercus Britannicus,*' Merriman said, severely and abruptly, sounding like a cross professor. 'Oak. The canoes you refer to were made of oak. And further south, the oaken piles on which the present cathedral of Winchester stands were sunk some nine hundred years ago, and are as tough today as they were then. Oh yes, oak lasts a very long time, Will Stanton, and there will come a day when the root of an oak tree will play a very important part in your young life. But oak is not the wood for the Sign. Our wood is one which the Dark does not love. Rowan, Will, that's our tree. Mountain ash. There are qualities in rowan, as in no other wood on the earth, that we need. But also there are strains on the

Sign that rowan cannot survive as oak might, or as iron and bronze do. So the Sign must be reborn' – he held it up, between one long finger and a deeply back-curved thumb – 'every hundred years.'

Will nodded. He said nothing. He found himself very conscious of the people in the room. It was as if they were all concentrating very hard on one thing, and you could hear the concentration. And they seemed suddenly multiplied, endless, a vast crowd stretching out beyond the house and beyond this century or any other.

He did not fully understand what happened next. Merriman jerked his hand forward suddenly, broke the wooden Sign easily in half and tossed it in the fire, where a great single log like their own Yule log was half-way burned down. The flames leapt. Then Miss Greythorne reached out towards the small man in the green velvet coat, took from him the silver jug from which he had poured drinks, and threw the contents of the jug on the fire. There was a great hissing and smoking, and the fire was dead. And she leaned forward in her long white dress and put her arm into the smoke and the smouldering ashes, and brought out a part-burned piece of the big log. It was like a large irregular disc.

Holding the lump of wood high so that everyone could see, she began to take blackened pieces from it as though she were peeling an orange; her fingers moved quickly, and the burned edges fell away and the skeleton of the wooden piece was left: a clear, smooth circle, containing a cross.

There was no irregularity to it at all, as though it had never before had any other shape than this. And on Miss Greythorne's white hands there was not even a trace of soot or ash.

'Will Stanton,' she said, turning to him, 'here is your third Sign. I may not give it to you in this century. Your quest must all along be fulfilled within your own time. But the wood is the Sign of Learning, and when you have done with your own particular learning you will find it. And I can leave in your mind the movements that the finding will take.' She looked hard at Will, then reached up and slipped the strange wooden circle into the dark hole in the panelling. With her other hand, she pressed the carved rose in the wall above it, and with the same sight-defeating flash as before the hole was suddenly no longer there. The wood-panelled wall was smooth and unbroken as if there had been no change at all.

Will stared. Remember how it was done, remember . . . She had pressed the first carved rose at the top left-hand corner. But now there were three roses in a group at that corner; which one should it be? As he looked more closely, he saw in fearful astonishment that now the whole wall of panelling was covered in squares of carved wood, each containing a single four-petalled rose. Had they grown at this moment, beneath his eyes? Or had they been there all along, invisible because of a trick of the light? He shook his head in alarm and looked round for Merriman. But it was too late. Nobody was close by him. Solemnity had left the air; the lights were bright again, and everybody was cheerfully talking. Merriman was murmuring something to Miss Greythorne, bending almost double to speak close to her ear. Will felt a touch on his arm, and swung round.

It was the small man in the green coat, beckoning to him. Near the doors at the other end of the room, the group of musicians who had accompanied the carol began playing again: a gentle sound of recorders and violins and what he thought was a harpsichord. It was another carol they were playing now, an old one, much older than the century of the room. Will wanted to listen, but the man in green had hold of his arm and was drawing him insistently towards a side door.

Will stood firm, rebellious, and turned towards Merriman. The tall figure jerked upright instantly, swinging round to look for him; but when he saw what was happening Merriman relaxed, merely raising one hand in assent. Will felt the reassurance put into his mind: *go on, it's all right. I'll follow.*

The small man picked up a lamp, glanced casually about him, then quickly swung the side door open just far enough for Will and himself to slip through. 'Don't trust me, do you?' he said in his sharp, jerky voice. 'Good. Don't trust anyone unless you have to, boy. Then you'll survive to do what you're here for.'

'I seem to know about people now, mostly,' Will said. 'I mean, somehow I can tell which ones I can trust. Usually. But you –' he stopped.

'Well?' said the man.

Will said: 'You don't fit.'

The man shouted with laughter, his eyes disappearing in the creases of his face, then stopped abruptly and held up his lamp. In the circle of wavering light, Will saw what seemed to be a small room, wood-panelled, with no furniture except an armchair, a table, a small step-ladder, and a wall-height glass-fronted bookcase in the centre of each wall. He heard a deep measured ticking and saw, peering through the gloom, that a very large grandfather clock stood in the corner. If the room were dedicated only to reading, as it seemed to be, then it held a timepiece that would give a very loud warning against reading for too long.

The small man thrust the lamp into Will's hand. 'I think there's a light over here – ah.' There began an indefinable hissing sound that Will had noticed once or twice in the room next door; then there was the crack of a match lighting and a loud 'Pop!', and a light appeared on the wall, burning at first with a reddish flame and then expanding into one of the great white glowing globes.

'Mantles,' he said. 'Still very new in private houses, and most fashionable. Miss Greythorne is uncommonly fashionable, for this century.'

Will was not listening. 'Who are you?'

'My name is Hawkin,' said the man cheerfully. 'Nothing more. Just Hawkin.'

'Well look here, Hawkin,' Will said. He was trying to work something out, and it was making him most uneasy. 'You seem to know what's happening. Tell me something. Here I am brought into the past, a century that's already happened, that's part of the history books. But what happens if I do something to alter it? I might, I could. Any little thing. I'd be making something in history different, just as if I'd really been there.'

'But you were,' Hawkin said. He touched a spill to the flame in the lamp Will held.

Will said helplessly, '*What?*'

'You were – are – in this century when it happened. If anyone had written a history recording this party here tonight, you and my lord Merriman would be in it, described. Unlikely, though. An Old One hardly ever lets his name be recorded anywhere. Generally you people manage to affect history in ways that no man ever knows . . .'

He touched the burning spill to a three-candle holder on the table beside one of the armchairs; the leather back of the chair shone in the yellow light. Will said, 'But I couldn't – I don't see –'

'Come,' Hawkin said swiftly. 'Of course you do not. It is a mystery. The Old Ones can travel in Time as they choose; you are not bound by the laws of the Universe as we know them.'

'Aren't you one?' Will said. 'I thought you must be.'

Hawkin shook his head, smiling. 'Nay,' he said. 'An ordinary sinful man.' He looked down and smoothed his hand over the green sleeve of his coat. 'But a most privileged one. For like you, I do not belong to this century, Will Stanton. I was brought here only to do a certain thing, and then my Lord Merriman will send me back to my own time.'

'Where,' said Merriman's deep voice to the soft click of the closing door, 'they do not have such stuff as velvet, which is why he is taking such particular pleasure in that pretty coat. Rather a foppish coat, by the present standard, I must tell you, Hawkin.'

The little man looked up with a quick grin, and Merriman put a hand affectionately on his shoulder. 'Hawkin is a child of the thirteenth century, Will,' he said. 'Seven hundred years before you were born. He belongs there. By my art, he has been brought forward out of it for this one day, and then he will go back again. As few ordinary men have ever done.'

Will ran one hand distractedly through his hair; he felt as though he were trying to work out a railway timetable. Hawkin chuckled softly. 'I told you, Old One. It is a mystery.'

'Merriman?' Will said. 'Where do you belong?'

Merriman's dark, beaked face gazed at him without expression, like some long-carved image. 'You will understand soon,' he said. 'We have another purpose here than the Sign of Wood, we three. I belong nowhere and everywhere, Will. I am the first of the Old Ones, and I have been in every age. I existed – exist – in Hawkin's century. There, Hawkin is my liege man. I am his lord, and more than his lord, for he has been with me all his life, reared as if he were a son, since I took him when his parents had died.'

'No son ever had better care,' Hawkin said, rather huskily; he looked at his feet, and tugged the jacket straight, and Will realized that for all the lines on his face Hawkin was not much older than his own brother Stephen.

Merriman said, 'He is my friend who serves me, and I have deep affection for him. And hold him in great trust. So great that I have given him a vital part to play in the quest we must all accomplish in this century – the quest for your learning, Will.'

'Oh,' Will said weakly.

Hawkin grinned at him; then jumped forward and swept him a low bow, deliberately snapping the grave mood. 'I must thank you for being born, Old One,' he said, 'and giving me the chance to scurry like a mouse into another time than my own.'

Merriman relaxed, smiling. 'Did you notice, Will, how he loves to light the gas-lamps? In his day, they use smoky, foul-smelling candles that are not candles at all, but reeds dipped in tallow.'

'Gas-lamps?' Will looked up at the white globe attached to the wall. 'Is that what they are?'

'Of course. No electricity yet.'

'Well,' Will said defensively. 'I don't even know what year this is, after all.'

'Anno Domini eighteen seventy-five,' Merriman said. 'Not a bad year. In London, Mr Disraeli is doing his best to buy the Suez Canal. More than half the British merchant ships that will pass through it are sailing ships. Queen Victoria has been on the British throne for thirty-eight years. In America, the President has the splendid name of Ulysses S. Grant and Nebraska is the newest of the thirty-four states of the Union. And in a remote manor house in Buckinghamshire, distinguished or notorious in the public eye only for its possession of the world's most valuable small collection of books on necromancy, a lady named Mary Greythorne is holding a Christmas Eve party, with carols and music, for her friends.'

Will moved to the nearest bookcase. The books were all bound in leather, mostly brown. There were shiny new volumes with spines glittering in gold leaf; there were fat little books so ancient that their leather was worn down to the roughness of thick cloth. He peered at some of the titles: *Demonolatry, Liber Poenitalis, Discoverie of Witchcraft, Malleus Maleficarum* – and so on through French, German, and other languages of which he could not even recognize the alphabet. Merriman waved a dismissive hand at them, and at the shelves all around.

'Worth a small fortune,' he said, 'but not to us. These are the tales of small people, some dreamers and some madmen. Tales of witchcraft and the appalling things that men once did to the poor simple souls they called witches. Most of whom were ordinary, harmless human beings, one or two of whom truly had dealings with the Dark . . . None of them, of course, had a thing to do with the Old Ones, for nearly every tale that men tell of magic and witches and such is born out of foolishness and ignorance and sickness of mind – or is a way of explaining things they do not understand. The one thing of which they know nothing, most of them, is what we are about. And that is contained, Will, in just one book in this room. The rest are useful now and then as a reminder of what the Dark can accomplish and the black methods it may sometimes use. But there is one book that is the reason why you have come back to this century. It is the book from which you will learn your place as an Old One, and there are no words to describe how precious it is. The book of hidden things, of the real magic. Long ago, when magic was the only written knowledge, our business was called simply Knowing. But there is far too much to know in your day, on all subjects under the sun. So we use a half-forgotten word, as we Old Ones ourselves are half-forgotten. We call it "gramarye".'

He moved across the room towards the clock, beckoning them after him. Will glanced at Hawkin, and saw his thin, confident face tight with apprehension. They followed. Merriman stood in front of the great old clock in the corner, which was a full two feet above even his head, took a key from his pocket, and opened the front panel. Will could see the pendulum in there swaying slowly, hypnotically to . . . and fro, to . . . and fro.

'Hawkin,' Merriman said. The word was very gentle, even loving, but it was a command. The man in green, without a word, knelt down at his left side and stayed there, very still. He said in a beseeching half-whisper: 'My lord –' But Merriman paid no attention. He laid his left hand on Hawkin's shoulder, and stretched his right hand into the clock. Very carefully, he slipped his long fingers back along one side, keeping them as flat as possible to avoid touching the pendulum, and then with a quick flip he pulled out a small black-covered book. Hawkin collapsed into a sitting heap, with a throaty gasp of such terrified relief that Will stared at him in astonishment. But Merriman was drawing him away. He made Will sit down in the room's one chair, and he put the book into his hands. There was no title on the cover.

'This is the oldest book in the world,' he said simply. 'And when you have read it, it will be destroyed. This is the Book of Gramarye, written in the Old Speech. It cannot be understood by any except the Old Ones, and even if a man or creature might understand any spell of power that it contains, he could not use their words of power unless he were an Old One himself. So there has been no great danger in the fact of its existence, these many years. Yet it is not good to keep a thing of this kind past the date of its destiny, for it has always been in danger from the Dark, and the endless ingenuity of the Dark would still find a way of using it if they had it in their hands. In this room now, therefore, the book will accomplish its final purpose, which is to bestow on you, the last of the Old Ones, the gift of gramarye – and after that it will be destroyed. When you have the knowledge, Will Stanton, there will no longer be any need of storing it, for with you the circle is complete.'

Will sat very still, watching the shadows move on the strong, stern face above him; then he gave his head a shake, as if to wake it, and opened the book. He said, 'But it's in English! You said –'

Merriman laughed. 'That is not English, Will. And when we speak to one another, you and I, we do not use English. We use the Old Speech. We were born with it in our tongues. You think you are speaking English now, because your common sense tells you it is the only language you understand, but if your family were to hear you they would hear only gibberish. The same with that book.'

Hawkin was back on his feet, though there was no colour in his face. Breathing unevenly, he leaned against the wall, and Will looked at him in concern.

But Merriman, ignoring him, went on, 'The moment you came into your power on your birthday, you could speak as an Old One. And did, not knowing that you were doing so. That was how the Rider knew you, when you met him on the road – you greeted John Smith in the Old Speech, and he therefore had to answer you in the same, and risk being marked as an Old One himself even though the craft of a smith is outside allegiance. But ordinary men can speak it too – like Hawkin here, and others in this house who are not of the Circle. And the Lords of the Dark can speak it too, though never without a certain betraying accent of their own.'

'I remember,' Will said slowly. 'The Rider did seem to have an accent, an accent I didn't know. Only of course I thought he was speaking English, and that he must just be someone from another part of the country. No wonder he came after me so soon.'

'As simple as that,' Merriman said. He looked at Hawkin for the first time, and laid a hand on his shoulder, but the small man did not stir. 'Listen now, Will. We shall leave you here until you have read the book. It will not be an experience quite like reading an ordinary book. When you have finished, I shall come back. Wherever I may be, I know always when the book is open or when it is closed. Read it now. You are of the Old Ones, and therefore you have only to read it once and it is in you for all Time. After that, we will make an end.'

Will said: 'Is Hawkin all right? He looks ill.'

Merriman looked down at the small drooping figure in green, and pain crossed his face. 'Too much to ask,' he said incomprehensibly, drawing Hawkin upright. 'But the book, Will. Read it. It has been waiting for you for a long time.'

He went out, supporting Hawkin, back to the music and voices of the next room, and Will was left with the Book of Gramarye.

Betrayal

Will was never able afterwards to tell how long he spent with the Book of Gramarye. So much went into him from its pages and changed him that the reading might have taken a year; yet so totally did it absorb his mind that when he came to an end he felt that he had only that moment begun. It was indeed not a book like other books. There were simple enough titles to each page: *Of Flying*; *Of Challenge*; *Of the Words of Power*; *Of Resistance*; *Of Time through the Doors*. But instead of presenting him with a story or instruction, the book would give simply a snatch of verse or a bright image, which somehow had him instantly in the midst of whatever experience was involved.

He might read no more than one line – *I have journeyed as an eagle* – and he was soaring suddenly aloft as if winged, learning through feeling, feeling the way of resting on the wind and tilting round the rising columns of air, of sweeping and soaring, of looking down at patchwork-green hills capped with dark trees, and a winding, glinting river between. And he knew as he flew that the eagle was one of the only five birds who could see the Dark, and instantly he knew the other four, and in turn he was each of them . . .

He read: . . . *you come to the place where is the oldest creature that is in this world, and he that has fared furthest afield; the Eagle of Gwernabwy* . . . and Will was up on a bare crag of rock above the world, resting without fear on a grey-black glittering shelf of granite, and his right side leaned against a soft, gold-feathered leg and a folded wing, and his hand rested beside a cruel steel-hard hooked claw, while in his ear a harsh voice whispered the words that would control wind and storm, sky and air, cloud and rain, and snow and hail – and everything in the sky save the sun and the moon, the planets and the stars.

Then he was flying again, at large in the blue-black sky, with the stars blazing timeless around his head, and the patterns of the stars made themselves known to him, both like and unlike the shapes and powers attributed to them by men long ago. The Herdsman passed, nodding, the bright star Arcturus at his knee; the Bull roared by, bearing the great sun Aldebaran and the small group of the Pleiades singing in small melodic voices, like no voices he had ever heard. Up he flew, and outward, through black space, and saw the dead stars, the blazing stars, the thin scattering of life that peopled the infinite emptiness beyond. And when he was done, he knew every star in the heavens, both by name and as charted astronomical points, and again as something much more than either; and he knew every spell of the sun and moon; he knew the mystery of Uranus and the despair of Mercury, and he had ridden on a comet's tail.

So, down out of the heavens the Book brought him, with one line.

. . . the wrinkled sea beneath him crawls . . .

And down he came plummeting, down towards the creeping wrinkled blue surface that changed, as he grew closer and closer, into a rearing sequence of great buffeting waves. Then he was in the sea, down out of the turmoil, through the green haze, into an astonishing, clear world of beauty and pitilessness and bleak cold survival. Each creature preyed on another, nothing was safe from all. And the Book taught Will here the patterns of survival against malevolence, and the spells of sea and river and stream, lake and beck and fjord, and showed him how water was the one element that could in some measure defy all magic; for moving water would tolerate no magic whether for evil or good, but would wash it away as if it had never been made.

Through deadly sharp corals the Book sent him swimming, among strange waving fronds of green and red and purple, among rainbow-brilliant fish that swam up to him, stared, flicked a fin or tail and were gone. Past the black unkind spines of sea-urchins, past soft waving creatures that seemed neither plant nor fish; and then up on white sand, splashing through gold-flecked shallows – into trees. Dense bare trees like roots ran down into the sea-water all around him in a kind of leafless jungle, and in a flash Will was out of the tangle and blinking again at a page of the Book of Gramarye.

... I am fire-fretted and I flirt with wind ...

He was among trees then, spring trees tender with the new matchless green of young leaves, and a clear sun dappling them; summer trees full of leaf, whispering, massive; dark winter firs that fear no master and let no light brighten their woods. He learned the nature of all trees, the particular magics that are in oak and beech and ash. Then, one verse stood alone on a page of the Book:

> He that sees blowing the wild wood tree,
> And peewits circling their watery glass,
> Dreams about Strangers that yet may be
> Dark to our eyes, Alas!

And into Will's mind, whirling him up on a wind blowing through and around the whole of Time, came the story of the Old Ones. He saw them from the beginning when magic was at large in the world; magic that was the power of rocks and fire and water and living things, so that the first men lived in it and with it, as a fish lives in the water. He saw the Old Ones, through the ages of men who worked with stone, and with bronze, and with iron, with one of the six great Signs born in each age. He saw one race after another come attacking his island country, bringing each time the malevolence of the Dark with them, wave after wave of ships rushing inexorably at the shores. Each wave of men in turn grew peaceful as it grew to know and love the land, so that the Light flourished again. But always the Dark was there, swelling and waning, gaining a new Lord of the Dark whenever a man deliberately chose to be changed into something more dread and powerful than his fellows. Such creatures were not born to their doom, like the Old Ones, but chose it. The Black Rider he saw in all times from the beginning.

He saw a time when the first great testing of the Light came, and the Old Ones spent themselves for three centuries on bringing their land out of the Dark, with the help in the end of their greatest leader, lost in the saving unless one day he might wake and return again.

A hillside rose up out of that time, grassy and sunlit before Will's eyes, with the sign of the circle and cross cut into its green turf, gleaming there huge and white in the Chiltern chalk. Round one arm of the white cross, scraping at it with curious tools like long-bladed axes, he saw a group of figures dressed in green: small men, made smaller still by the width of the great Sign. He saw one of these figures whirl dreamlike out of the group towards him: a man in a green tunic with a short dark-blue cloak, and a hood pulled over his head. The man flung wide his arms, with a short bronze-bladed sword in one hand and a glinting chalice-like cup in the other; spun round, and at once disappeared. Then, caught up by the next page, Will was walking along a path through a thick forest, with some fragrant dark-green herb under his feet; a path that broadened and hardened into stone, a well-worn, undulating stone-like limestone, and led him out of the forest until he was walking along a high, windy ridge under a grey sky, with a dark, mist-filled valley below. And all the while as he walked, though no one walked with him, firmly into his mind in procession came the secret words of power for the Old Ways, and the feelings and signs by which he would know, henceforth, anywhere in the world, where the nearest Old Way ran, either in substance or as the ghost of a road . . .

So it went, until Will found that he was almost at the end of the Book. A verse was written before him.

> I have plundered the fern
> Through all secrets I spie;
> Old Math ap Mathonwy
> Knew no more than I.

Facing the cover, on the very last page, was a drawing of the six circled-cross Signs, all joined into one circle. And that was all.

Will closed the book, slowly, and sat staring at nothing. He felt as though he had lived for a hundred years. To know so much, now, to be able to do so many things; it should have excited him, but he felt weighed down, melancholy, at the thought of all that had been and all that was to come.

Merriman came through the door alone, and stood looking down at him. 'Ah yes,' he said softly. 'As I told you, it is a responsibility, a heaviness. But there it is, Will. We are the Old Ones, born into the Circle, and there is no help for it.' He picked up the book, and touched Will's shoulder. 'Come.'

As he crossed the room to the towering grandfather clock, Will followed, and watched him take the key again from his pocket and unlock the front panel. There still was the pendulum, long and slow, swinging like the beat of a heart. But this time, Merriman took no care to avoid touching it. He reached in with the book in his hand, but he moved with an odd jerkiness, like an actor over-playing the part of a clumsy man; and as he pushed the book in, a corner of it brushed the long arm of the pendulum. Will had just the flash of a moment to see the slight break in the swing. Then he was staggering backwards, his hands flying up to his eyes, and the room was filled with something he could never afterwards describe – a soundless explosion, a blinding flare of dark light, a great roar of energy that could not be seen or heard and yet made him feel for an instant that the whole world had blown up. When he took his hands from his face, blinking, he found that he was pressed against the side of the armchair, ten feet from where he had been before. Merriman was spread-eagled against the wall beside him. And where the grandfather clock had been, the corner of the room was empty. There was no damage, nor any sign of violence or explosion. There was simply nothing.

'That was it, you see,' Merriman said. 'That was one protection of the Book of Gramarye, since our time began. If the thing protecting it should be so much as touched, it and the book and the man touching it would become – nothing. Only the Old Ones were immune from destruction, and as you see' – he rubbed his arm ruefully – 'even we, in the event, can be bruised. The protection has taken many forms, of course – the clock was simply for this century. So now we have destroyed the Book, by the same means that through all these ages we used to preserve it. That is the only proper manner for using magic, as you have now learned.'

Will said shakily, 'Where's Hawkin?'

'He was not needed this time,' Merriman said.

'Is he all right? He looked –'

'Quite all right.' There was a strange tight note in Merriman's voice, like sadness, but none of his new art could tell Will the emotion that put it there.

They went back to the gathering in the next room, where the carol that had begun as they left was only now coming to an end, and where nobody behaved as though they had been away for more than a moment or two, or for any real time at all. But then, Will thought, we are not in real time; at least, we are in past time, and even that we seem to be able to stretch as we wish, to make it go fast, or slow . . .

The crowd had grown, and more people were still drifting back from the supper-room. Will realized now that most of these were ordinary folk, and that only the small group who had remained in the room earlier were Old Ones. Of course, he thought: only they would be able to witness the renewing of the Sign.

There were others, and he was turning to study them when suddenly astonishment and horror caught him up out of all reflection. His eye had caught a face in the very back of the room, a girl, not looking at him but busy in conversation with someone unseen. As he watched, she tossed her head with a bright self-conscious laugh. Then she was bent listening again, and then she was gone, as other guests blocked the group from view. But it had been long enough for Will to see that the laughing girl was Maggie Barnes, Maggie of Dawsons' Farm a century hence. She was not even a fore-shadowing, as this Victorian Miss Greythorne was a kind of early echo of the Miss Greythorne that he knew. This was the Maggie he had last seen in his own time.

He swung round in consternation, but as soon as he met Merriman's eyes he saw that he already knew. There was no surprise in the hawk-nosed face, but only the beginnings of a kind of pain. 'Yes,' he said wearily. 'The witch-girl is here. And I think you should stay beside me, Will Stanton, for this next while, and watch with me, for I do not greatly care to watch alone.'

Wondering, Will stood with him in the corner, unobserved. The girl Maggie was still concealed in the crowd somewhere. They waited; then saw Hawkin, in his dapper green coat, thread his way through the crowd to Miss Greythorne and stand deferentially beside her, in the way of a man accustomed to making himself available for help. Merriman stiffened slightly, and Will glanced up; the lines of pain had deepened on the strong face, as if Merriman were anticipating some great hurt about to come. He looked across again at Hawkin and saw his gay smile flash at something Miss Greythorne had said; showing no sign now of whatever had afflicted him in the library, the small man had a brightness, like a precious stone, that would bring delight to any gloom. Will could see why he was dear to Merriman. But at the same time he had all at once a dreadful, rushing conviction of hovering disaster.

He said huskily, 'Merriman! What is it?'

Merriman looked out over the heads at the lively pointed face. He said, without expression, 'It is peril, Will, that is to come to us through my doing. Great peril, through all this quest. I have made the worst mistake that an Old One may make, and the mistake is about to come down on my head fullfold. To put more trust in a mortal man than he has the strength to take – it is something that all of us learned never to do, centuries ago. Long before the Book of Gramarye came into my charge. Yet in foolishness I made that mistake. And now there is nothing that we can do to put it right, but only watch and wait for the result.'

'It's Hawkin, isn't it? Something to do with the reason why you brought him here?'

'The spell of protection for the Book,' Merriman said painfully, 'was in two parts, Will. You saw the first, the protection against men – it was the pendulum, which would destroy them if they were to touch it, but would not destroy me or any Old One. But I wove another part into that spell that was a protection against the Dark. It set down that I could take the Book out past the pendulum *only if I were touching Hawkin with my other hand.* Whenever the Book was taken out for the last Old One, in whatever century, Hawkin would have to be brought out of his own time in order to be there.'

Will said: 'Wouldn't it have been safer to make an Old One part of the spell, not an ordinary man?'

'Ah no, the whole purpose was to have a man involved. This is a cold battle we are in, Will, and in it we must sometimes do cold things. This spell was woven around me, as keeper of the Book. The Dark cannot destroy me, for I am an Old One, but it could perhaps by magic have tricked me into taking out the Book. In case that happened, there had to be some way in which the other Old Ones could stop me before it was too late. They too could not destroy me, to stop me from doing the work of the Dark. But a man can be destroyed. If it had come to the worst, and the Dark had forced me by magic to take out the Book for them, then before I could begin, the Light would have killed Hawkin. That would have kept the Book safe forever, for in that case, I could not have worked the spell of release by touching him while taking out the Book. And so I should not have been able to reach the Book. Nor would the Dark, nor anyone else.'

'So he risked his life,' Will said slowly, watching Hawkin's sprightly walk as he crossed the floor to the musicians.

'Yes,' Merriman said. 'In our service he was safe from the Dark, but his life was in hazard all the same. He agreed because he was my liege man, and proud of it. I wish that I had made sure that he really knew the risk he ran. A double risk, for he might also have been destroyed today, by me, if I had accidentally touched the pendulum. You saw what happened when at the last I did that. You and I, as Old Ones, were merely shaken; but if Hawkin had been there, under my touch, he would have been killed in a flash, unbodied like the Book itself.'

'He must not only be very brave, he must really love you as if he were your son,' said Will, 'to do things like this for you and the Light.'

'But still he is only a man,' said Merriman, and his voice was rough and the pain back deep in his face. 'And he loves as a man, requiring proof of love in return. My mistake was in ignoring the risk that this might be so. And as a result, in this room in the next few minutes, Hawkin will betray me and betray the Light and mould the whole course of your quest, young Will. The shock just now of actually risking his life, for me and the Book of Gramarye, was too much for his loyalty. Perhaps you saw his face, in the moment when I held his shoulder and took the Book from its perilous place. It was only in that moment that Hawkin fully understood that I was prepared to let him die. And now that he has understood it, he will never forgive me for not loving him as much – in his terms – as he has loved me, his lord. And he will turn on us.' Merriman pointed across the room. 'See where it begins.'

Music struck up brightly, and the guests began forming into couples to dance. One man whom Will had recognized as an Old One moved to Miss Greythorne, bowed, and offered his arm; all around them, couples joined into figures-of-eight for some dance he did not know. He saw Hawkin standing irresolute, moving his head a little to the beat of the music; and then he saw a girl in a red dress appear at his side. It was the witch-girl, Maggie Barnes.

She said something to Hawkin, laughing, and dropped him a small curtsey. Hawkin smiled politely, doubtfully, and shook his head. The girl's smile deepened, she shook her hair coquettishly and spoke to him again, her eyes fast on his.

'Oh,' Will said. 'If only we could hear!'

Merriman regarded him sombrely for a moment, his face absent and brooding.

'Oh,' Will said, feeling foolish. 'Of course.' It would take him some time, clearly, to grow accustomed to using his own gifts. He looked again at Hawkin and the girl, and wished to hear them, and could hear.

'Truly, Madam,' Hawkin said, 'I have no wish to seem churlish, but I do not dance.'

Maggie took his hand. 'Because you are out of your century? They dance here with their legs, just as you do beyond five hundred years. Come.'

Hawkin stared at her aghast as she led him into a set of couples. 'Who are you?' he whispered. 'Are you an Old One?'

'Not for all the world,' said Maggie Barnes in the Old Speech, and Hawkin turned quite white and stood still. She laughed softly and said in English, 'No more of that. Dance, or people will notice. It's easy enough. Watch the next man, as the music begins.'

Hawkin, pale and distressed, stumbled his way through the first part of the dance; gradually he picked up the steps. Merriman said in Will's ear, 'He was told that not one soul here would know of him, and that on pain of death he must not use the Old Speech to any but you.'

Then the speaking below began again.

'You look well, Hawkin, for a man escaped from death.'

'How do you know these things, girl? Who are you?'

'They would have let you die, Hawkin. How could you be so stupid?'

'My master loves me,' said Hawkin, but there was weakness in it.

'He used you, Hawkin. You are nothing to him. You should follow better masters, who would care for your life. And lengthen it through the centuries, not confine it to your own.'

'Like the life of an Old One?' Hawkin said, eagerness waking in his voice for the first time. Will remembered the tinge of envy when Hawkin had spoken to him of the Old Ones; now there was a hint of greed as well.

'The Dark and the Rider are kinder masters than the Light,' Maggie Barnes said softly in his ear, as the first part of the dance ended. Hawkin stood still again and stared at her, until she glanced round and said clearly: 'I need a cool drink, I believe.' And Hawkin jumped and led her away, so that now, with his attention caught and a chance to talk to him privately, the girl of the Dark would have a willing hearer. Will felt suddenly sickened by the approaching treachery, and listened no more. He found Merriman, beside him, still gazing black into space.

'So it will go,' Merriman said. 'He will have a sweet picture of the Dark to attract him, as men so often do, and beside it he will set all the demands of the Light, which are heavy and always will be. All the while he will be nursing his resentment of the way I might have had him give up his life without reward. You can be sure the Dark makes no sign of demanding any such thing – yet Indeed, its lords never risk demanding death, but only offer a black life . . . Hawkin,' he said softly, bleakly, 'liege man, how can you do what you are going to do?'

Will felt fear suddenly, and Merriman sensed it. 'No more of this,' he said. 'It is clear already how it goes. Hawkin now will be a leak in the roof, a tunnel into the cellar. And just as the Dark could not touch him when he was my liege man, now that he is liege to the Dark, he cannot be destroyed by the Light. He will be the Dark's ear in our midst, in this house that has been our stronghold.' His voice was cold, accepting the inevitable; the pain was gone. 'Though the witch-girl managed to make her way in, she could have accomplished no scrap of magic without being destroyed by the Light. But now whenever Hawkin calls them, the Dark can attack us here as elsewhere. And the danger will grow with the years.'

He stood up, fingering his white ruffled cravat; there was a terrible sternness in his fierce-curved profile, and the look that for a moment flared out from the lowering brows made Will's blood run thick and slow. It was a judge's face, implacable, condemning.

'And the doom that Hawkin has brought upon himself, by this act,' Merriman said, without expression, 'is a dread matter, which will make him many times wish that he might die.'

Will stood dazed, caught in pity and alarm. He did not ask what would happen to small, bright-eyed Hawkin, who had laughed at him and helped him and been for so short a while his friend; he did not want to know. Out on the floor, the music of the second part of the dance jingled to a close, and the dancers made one another laughing courtesies. Will stood motionless and unhappy. Merriman's frozen look softened, and he reached out and turned him gently to face the centre of the room.

Will saw there only a gap in the crowd, with beyond it the group of musicians. As he stood there, they struck up once more 'Good King Wenceslas', the carol they had been playing when first he entered the room, through the Doors. Merrily the whole gathering joined in singing, and then the next verse came and Merriman's deep voice was ringing out across the room, and Will realized, blinking, that the verse to come was his.

He drew breath, and raised his head.

> Sire he lives a good league hence,
> Underneath the mountain . . .

And there was no moment of farewell, no moment in which he saw the nineteenth century vanish away, but suddenly with no awareness of change, as he sang he knew that Time had somehow blinked, and another young voice was singing with him, the two of them so nearly simultaneous that anyone who could not see the lips moving would have sworn that it was one boy's voice alone . . .

> Right against the forest fence,
> By St Agnes' fou-ou-ntain . . .

. . . and he knew that he was standing with James and Mary and the rest, and he and James were singing together, and that the music with their voices was Paul's lone flute. He stood there in the dark entrance-hall, with his hands raised before his chest holding the lighted candle, and he saw that the candle had not burned down one millimetre further than when he had last looked at it.

They finished the carol.

Miss Greythorne said, 'Very good, very good indeed. Nothing like Good King Wenceslas, it's always been my favourite.'

Will peered past his candle-flame to look at her motionless form in the big carved chair; her voice was older, harder, more toughened by the years, and so was her face, but otherwise she was just like – her grandmother, must that younger Miss Greythorne have been? Or her great-grandmother?

Miss Greythorne said, 'Huntercombe carol-singers have been singing "Good King Wenceslas" in this house for longer than you or even I can remember, you know. Well now, Paul and Robin and the rest of you, how about a little Christmas punch?' The question was traditional, and so was the answer.

'Well,' said Robin gravely, 'thank you, Miss Greythorne. Perhaps just a little.'

'Even young Will too, this year,' said Paul. 'He's eleven now, Miss Greythorne, did you know?'

The housekeeper was coming forward with a tray of glittering glasses and a great bowl of red-brown punch, and nearly every eye in the room was on Merriman, stepping up to fill the glasses. But Will's gaze was held by the strong, suddenly younger eyes of the figure in the high-backed chair. 'Yes,' said Miss Greythorne softly, almost absent-mindedly, 'I did remember. Will Stanton has had a birthday.' She turned to Merriman, who was already moving towards them, and took from him the two glasses in his hands. 'A happy birthday to you, Will Stanton, seventh son of a seventh son,' said Miss Greythorne. 'And success in your every quest.'

'Thank you, ma'am,' said Will, wondering. And they held up their glasses solemnly to one another, and drank, just as the Stanton children did for the Christmas toast on the one day of the year when they were all allowed wine at dinner.

Merriman was moving round, and now everyone had a glass of punch and was sipping contentedly. The Manor's Christmas punch was always delicious, though no one had ever quite worked out what went into it. As the senior members of the family, the twins strolled dutifully across to chat with Miss Greythorne; Barbara, with Mary in tow, made a beeline for Miss Hampton the housekeeper and Annie the maid, both reluctant members of a village drama group she was trying to force into life. Merriman said to James, 'You and your little brother sing very well.'

James beamed. Though plumper, he was no taller than Will, and it was not often that a stranger gratified him by recognizing him as a superior older brother. 'We sing in the school choir,' he said. 'And solos at arts festivals. Even one in London last year. The music master's very keen on arts festivals.'

'I'm not,' said Will. 'All those mothers, glaring.'

'Well, you were top of your class in London,' James said, 'so of course they all hated you, beating their little darlings. I was only fifth in mine,' he said in matter-of-fact tones to Merriman. 'Will has a lot better voice than me.'

'Oh come off it,' said Will.

'Yes, you have.' James was a fair-minded boy; he genuinely preferred reality to daydreams. 'Till we both break, at any rate. Neither of us might be any good then.'

Merriman said absent-mindedly, 'In point of fact you will become a most accomplished tenor. Almost professional standard. Your brother's voice will be baritone – pleasant, but nothing special.'

'I suppose that might be possible,' said James, polite but disbelieving. 'Of course, there's no way at all for anyone to tell, yet.'

Will said belligerently, 'But he –' and caught Merriman's dark eye and stopped. 'Mmmm, aaah,' he said, and James looked at him with astonishment.

Miss Greythorne called across the room to Merriman, 'Paul would like to see the old recorders and flutes. Take him in, would you?'

Merriman inclined his head in a small bow. He said casually to Will and James, 'Care to come too?'

'No, thank you,' said James promptly. His eyes were on the far door, through which the housekeeper was advancing with another tray. 'I smell Miss Hampton's mince pies.'

Will said, understanding, 'I'd quite like to see.'

He moved with Merriman towards Miss Greythorne's chair, where Paul and Robin stood stiff and rather awkward, one at each side, like guardsmen. 'Off with you,' said Miss Greythorne briskly. 'Are you going too, Will? Of course, you're another musical one, I was forgetting. Quite a good little collection of instruments and stuff in there. Surprised you haven't seen them before.'

Lulled by the words, Will said thoughtlessly, 'In the library?'

Miss Greythorne's sharp eyes glittered at him. 'The library?' she said. 'You must be mixing us up with someone else, Will. There's no library here. Once there was a small one, with some most valuable books, I believe, but it burned down, almost a century ago. This part of the house was struck by lightning. Did a lot of damage, they say.'

'Oh, dear,' said Will in some confusion.

'Well, this is no talk for Christmas,' Miss Greythorne said, and waved them off. Glancing back at her, as she turned to Robin with a bright social smile, Will found himself wondering whether the two Miss Greythornes were not one after all.

Merriman led him, with Paul, to a side door, and they walked through a strange musty-smelling little passage into a high bright room that Will did not at once recognize. It was only when he caught sight of the fireplace that he realized where he was. There was the wide hearth, and the broad mantel with its square panels and carved Tudor rose-emblems. But round the rest of the room the panelling was gone; the walls were instead painted flat white, and brightened here and there by some large improbable-looking seascapes done in lurid blues and greens. In the place where Will had once gone into the little library, there was no longer any door.

Merriman was unlocking a tall, glass-fronted cabinet that stood against a side wall.

'Miss Greythorne's father was a very musical gentleman,' he said in his butler voice. 'And artistic too. He painted all those pictures on the walls over there. In the West Indies, I believe. These, though' – he lifted out a small beautiful instrument like a recorder, black inlaid with silver – 'he didn't actually play, they say. He just liked to look at them.'

Paul was absorbed at once, peering at, into, through the old flutes and recorders as Merriman handed them out of the cupboard. They were both most solemn in their handling; they would put each one carefully back before taking the next out. Will turned to study the panels round the fireplace; then jumped suddenly as he heard Merriman silently calling to him. At the same time he could hear Merriman's voice aloud speaking to Paul; it was an eerie combination.

'Quickly, now!' said the voice in his mind. 'You know where to look. Quick, while you have the chance. It is time to take the Sign!'

'But –' said Will's mind.

'Go on!' Merriman silently roared.

Will glanced back quickly over his shoulder. The door through which they had come was still half open, but his ears would surely warn him of anyone coming up the passage between this room and the next. He moved soft-footed to the fireplace, reached up, and put his hand on the panelling. Shutting his eyes for an instant, he appealed to all his new gifts, and the old world from which they came. Which square panel had it been? Which carved rose? He was confused by the loss of the panelled wall all around; the mantel seemed smaller than before. Was the sign lost, bricked up somewhere behind that flat white wall? He pressed every rose that he could see, round the top left-hand corner of the fireplace, but none moved even a fraction of an inch. Then at the last moment he noticed, at the very point of the corner, a rose part-buried in plaster, jutting out of the wall that clearly had been repaired as well as altered in the last hundred years – ten minutes, he thought wildly – since he had last seen it.

Hastily Will reached up high and pressed his thumb as hard as he could against the centre of the carved flower, as if it were a bell-push. And as he heard the soft click, he was staring into a black square hole in the wall, exactly on the level of his eyes. He reached in and touched the circle of the Sign of Wood, and as he sighed in relief, his finger closing round the smooth wood, he heard Paul begin to play one of the old flutes.

It was very tentative playing: a slow arpeggio first, then a hesitant run; and then, very softly and gently, Paul began playing the melody 'Greensleeves'. And Will stood transfixed, not only by the lovely lilt of the old tune but by the sound of the instrument itself. For though the melody was different, this was his music, his enchantment, the same eerie, faraway tone that he heard always, and then always lost, at those moments in his life that mattered most. What was the nature of this flute that his brother was playing? Was it part of the Old

Ones, belonging to their magic, or simply something very like, made by men? He drew his hand back from the gap in the wall, which closed instantly before he could press the rose again, and he was sliding the Sign of Wood into his pocket as he turned, lost in listening.

And then he froze.

Paul stood playing, across the room, beside the cabinet. Merriman had his back turned and his hands on the glass doors. But now the room held two other figures as well. In the doorway through which they had come stood Maggie Barnes, staring not at Will but at Paul, with a look of dreadful malevolence. And close beside Will, very close, in the spot where the door to the old library had once been, towered the Black Rider. He was within arm's length of Will, though he did not move, but stood transfixed, as if the music had arrested him in mid-stride. His eyes were closed, his lips silently moving; his hands were stretched out pointing ominously towards Paul, as the sweet, unearthly music went on.

Will did one thing well, from the instinct of his new learning. Instantly he flung up a wall of resistance round Merriman and Paul and himself, so that the two of the Dark swayed backward from the force of it. But at the same time he shrieked, 'Merriman!' And as the music broke off, and both Paul and Merriman swung round in swift horror, he knew what he had done wrong. He had not called as the Old Ones should call one another, through the mind. He had made the very bad mistake of shouting aloud.

The Rider and Maggie Barnes vanished, instantly. Paul was striding across the room in concern. 'What on earth's up, Will? Did you hurt yourself?'

Merriman said swiftly, smoothly, from behind him, 'He stumbled, I think,' and Will had the wit to crease his face with pain, bend slowly over as if in anguish, and clutch hard at one arm.

There was the sound of running feet, and Robin burst into the room from the passage, with Barbara close behind. 'What's the matter? We heard the most awful yell –'

He looked at Will and slowed to a halt, puzzled. 'You all right, Will?'

'Uh,' said Will. 'I – uh – I just banged my funny-bone. Sorry. It hurt.'

'Sounded as if someone was murdering you,' Barbara said reproachfully.

Shamelessly Will took refuge in rudeness, his fingers curling in his pocket to make sure the third Sign was safe. 'Well, I'm sorry to disappoint you,' he said petulantly, 'but really I'm all right. I just banged myself and yelled, that's all. Sorry if you were frightened. I don't see what all the fuss is about.'

Robin glared at him. 'Catch me running anywhere to rescue you, next time,' he said witheringly.

'Talk about the boy crying Wolf,' Barbara said.

'I think,' Merriman said gently, closing the cupboard and turning the key, 'that we should all go and give Miss Greythorne one more carol.' And quite forgetting that he was no more than the butler, they all filed dutifully out of the room in his wake. Will called after him, in proper silence this time: 'But I must speak to you! The Rider was here! And the girl!'

Merriman said into his mind, 'I know. Later. They have ways of hearing this kind of talk, remember.' And he moved on, leaving Will twitching with exasperation and alarm.

In the doorway, Paul paused, took Will firmly by the shoulder and turned him to look in his face. 'Are you really all right?'

'Honest. Sorry about the noise. That flute sounded super.'

'Fantastic thing.' Paul let him go, turning to gaze longingly at the cupboard. 'Really. I've never heard anything like it. And of course never played one. You've no idea, Will, I can't *describe* – it's tremendously old, and yet the condition it's in, it might be almost new. And the tone of it –' There was an ache in his voice and his face that something in Will responded to with a deep, ancient sympathy. An Old One, he suddenly knew, was doomed always to feel this same formless, nameless longing for something out of reach, as an endless part of life.

'I'd give anything,' Paul said, 'to have a flute like that one day.'

'Almost anything,' Will said gently. Paul stared at him in astonishment, and the Old One in Will suddenly realized belatedly that this was not perhaps the response of a small boy; so he grinned, stuck out his tongue impishly at Paul, and skipped through the passage, back to the normal relationships of the normal world.

They sang 'The First Nowell' as their last carol; they made their farewells; they were out again in the snow and the crisp air, with Merriman's impassive polite smile disappearing behind the Manor doors. Will stood on the broad stone steps and gazed up at the stars. The clouds had cleared at last, and now the stars blazed like pinpricks of white fire in the black hollow of the night sky, in all the strange patterns that had been a complicated mystery to him all his life, but were endlessly significant now. 'See how bright the Pleiades are tonight,' he said softly, and Mary stared at him in amazement and said, 'The *what*?'

So Will brought his attention down out of the fiery black heavens, and in their own small, yellow, torchlit world the Stanton carollers trooped home. He walked among them speechless, as if in a dream. They thought him tired, but he was floating in wonder. He had three of the Signs of Power now. He had, too, the knowledge to use the Gift of Gramarye: a long lifetime of discovery and wisdom, given to him in a moment of suspended time. He was not the same Will Stanton that he had been a very few days before. Now and forever, he knew, he inhabited a different time-scale from that of everyone he had ever known or loved . . . But he managed to turn his thoughts away from all these things, even from the two invading, threatening figures of the Dark. For this was Christmas, which had always been a time of magic, to him and to all the world. This was a brightness, a shining festival, and while its enchantment was on the world the charmed circle of his family and home would be protected against any invasion from outside.

Indoors, the tree glowed and glittered, and the music of Christmas was in the air, and spicy smells came from the kitchen, and in the broad hearth of the living-room the great twisted Yule root flickered and flamed as it gently burned down. Will lay on his back on the hearth-rug staring into the smoke wreathing up the chimney, and was suddenly very sleepy indeed. James and Mary too were trying not to yawn, and even Robin looked heavy-lidded.

'Too much punch,' said James, as his tall brother stretched gaping in an armchair.

'Get lost,' said Robin amiably.

'Who'd like a mince pie?' said Mrs Stanton, coming in with a vast tray of cocoa mugs.

'James has had six already,' said Mary in prim disapproval. 'At the Manor.'

'Now it's eight,' said James, a mince pie in each hand. 'Yah.'

'You'll get fat,' Robin said.

'Better than being fat already,' James said, through a mouthful, and stared pointedly at Mary, whose plump form had recently become her most gloomy preoccupation. Mary's mouth drooped, then tightened, and she advanced on him, making a snarling sound.

'Ho-ho-ho,' said Will sepulchrally from the floor. 'Good little children never fight at Christmas.' And since Mary was irresistibly close to him, he grabbed her by the ankle. She collapsed on top of him, howling cheerfully.

'Mind the fire,' said Mrs Stanton, from years of habit.

'Ow,' said Will, as his sister thumped him in the stomach, and he rolled away out of reach. Mary stopped, and sat gazing at him curiously. 'Why on earth have you got so many buckles on your belt?' she demanded.

Will tugged his sweater hastily down over his belt, but it was too late; everyone had seen. Mary reached forward and yanked the sweater up again. 'What funny things. What are they?'

'Just decoration,' Will said gruffly. 'I made them in metalwork at school.'

'I never saw you,' said James.

'You never looked, then.'

Mary prodded a finger forward at the first circle on Will's belt and rolled back with a howl. 'It burned me!' she shrieked.

'Very probably,' said her mother. 'Will and his belt have both been lying next to the fire. And you'll both be on top of it if you go on rolling about like that. Come on, now. Christmas Eve drink, Christmas Eve mince pie – Christmas Eve bed.'

Will scrambled gratefully to his feet. 'I'll get my presents while the cocoa cools off.'

'So will I.' Mary followed him. On the stairs she said, 'Those buckle things are pretty. Will you make me one for a brooch next term?'

'I might,' Will said, and he grinned to himself. Mary's curiosity was never much to worry about; it always led to the same place.

They pounded up to their respective bedrooms, and came down laden with packages to be added to the growing pile beneath the tree. Will had been trying hard not to look at this magical heap ever since they came in from carol-singing, but it was sorely difficult, especially since he could see one gigantic box labelled with a name that clearly began with a W. Who else began with W, after all ... ? He forced himself to ignore it, and resolutely piled his own armful in a space at the side of the tree.

'You're watching, James!' Mary shrilled, behind him.

'I am not,' said James. Then he said, because it was Christmas Eve, 'Well, yes, I expect I was. Sorry.' And Mary was so taken aback that she deposited all her parcels in silence, unable to think of anything to say.

On Christmas night, Will always slept with James. Both twin beds were still in James's room from the time before Will had moved up to Stephen's attic. The only difference now was that James kept Will's old bed piled with op art cushions, and referred to it as 'my chaise longue'. There was something about Christmas Eve, they both felt, that demanded company; one needed somebody to whisper to, during the warm beautiful dream-taut moments between hanging the empty stocking at the end of the bed, and dropping into the cosy oblivion that would flower into the marvel of Christmas morning.

While James was splashing in the bathroom, Will slipped off his belt, buckled it again round the three Signs, and put them under his pillow. It seemed prudent, even though he still knew without question that no one and nothing would trouble him or his home during this night. Tonight, perhaps for the last time, he was an ordinary boy again.

Strands of music and the soft rumble of voices drifted up from below. In solemn ritual, Will and James looped their Christmas stockings over their bedposts: precious, unbeautiful brown stockings of a thick, soft stuff, worn by their mother in some unimaginably distant time and misshapen now by years of service as Christmas holdalls. When filled, they would become top-heavy, and could no longer hang; they would be discovered instead lying magnificent across the foot of the beds.

'Bet I know what Mum and Dad are giving you,' James said softly. 'Bet it's a –'

'Don't you dare,' Will hissed, and his brother giggled and dived under the blankets.

'G'night, Will.'

''Night. Happy Christmas.'

'Happy Christmas.'

And it was the same as it always was, as he lay curled up happily in his snug wrappings, promising himself that he would stay awake, until, until . . .

. . . until he woke, in the dim morning room with a glimmer of light creeping round the dark square of the curtained window, and saw and heard nothing for an enchanted expectant space, because all his senses were concentrated on the weighty feel, over and around his blanketed feet, of strange bumps and corners and shapes that had not been there when he fell asleep. And it was Christmas Day.

Christmas Day

When he knelt beside the Christmas tree and pulled off the gay paper wrapping from the giant box labelled 'Will', the first thing he discovered was that it was not a box at all, but a wooden crate. A Christmas choir warbled distant and joyful from the radio in the kitchen; it was the after-Christmas-stocking, before-breakfast gathering of the family, when each member opened just one of his 'tree presents'. The rest of the bright pile would lie there until after dinner, happily tantalizing.

Will, being the youngest, had the first turn. He had made a beeline for the box, partly because it was so impressively large and partly because he suspected it came from Stephen. He found that someone had taken the nails out of the wooden lid, so that he could open it easily.

'Robin pulled out the nails, and Bar and I put the paper on,' said Mary at his shoulder, all agog. 'But we didn't look inside. Come on, Will, come on.'

He took off the lid. 'It's full of dead leaves! Or reeds or something.'

'Palm leaves,' said his father, looking. 'For packing, I suppose. Mind your fingers, they can have sharp edges.'

Will tugged out handfuls of the rustling fronds, until the first hard shape of something began to show. It was a thin strange curving shape, brown, smooth, like a branch; it seemed to be made of a hard kind of papier-mâché. It was an antler, like and yet not like the antler of a deer. Will paused suddenly. A strong and totally unexpected feeling had leapt out at him when he touched the antler. It was not a feeling he had ever had in the presence of the family before; it was the mixture of excitement, security and delight that came over him whenever he was with one of the Old Ones.

He saw an envelope poking out of the packing beside the antler and opened it. That paper bore the neat letterhead of Stephen's ship.

Dear Will:

Happy birthday. Happy Christmas. I always swore never to combine the two, didn't I? And here I am doing it. Let me tell you why. I don't know whether you'll understand, specially after you see what the present is. But perhaps you will. You've always been a bit different from everybody else. I don't mean daft! Just different.

It was like this. I was in the oldest part of Kingston one day during carnival. Carnival in these islands is a very special time – great fun, with echoes going back a long, long way. Anyway I got mixed up in a procession, all laughing people and jingling steel bands and dancers in wild costumes, and I met an old man.

He was a very impressive old man, his skin very black and his hair very white, and he sort of appeared out of nowhere and took me by the arm and pulled me out of the dancing. I'd never seen him in my life before, anywhere, I'm sure of it. But he looked at me and he said, 'You are Stephen Stanton, of Her Majesty's Navy. I have something for you. Not for you yourself, but for your youngest brother, the seventh son. You will send it to him as a present, for his birthday this year and his Christmas, combined in one. It will be a gift from you his brother, and he will know what to do with it in due course, although you will not.'

It was all so unexpected it really knocked me off balance. All I could say was, 'But who are you? How do you know me?' And the old man just looked at me again with very dark, deep eyes that seemed to be looking through me into the day after tomorrow, and he said, 'I would know you anywhere. You are Will Stanton's brother. There is a look that we Old Ones have. Our families have something of it too.'

And that was about it, Will. He didn't say another word. That last bit makes no sense, I know, but that was what he said. Then he just moved into the carnival procession and out again, and when he came out he was carrying – wearing, actually – the thing you will find in this box.

So here I am sending it to you. Just as I was told. It seems mad, and I can think of lots of things you'd have liked better. But there it is. There was something extraordinary about that old man, and I just somehow had to do what he told me.

Hope you like your crazy present, mate. I'll be thinking of you, both days.

Love,
Stephen.

Slowly Will folded the letter and put it back in its envelope. 'A look that we Old Ones have . . .' So the circle stretched all the way round the world. But of course it did, there would be no point in it otherwise. He was glad to have Stephen part of the pattern; it was right, somehow.

'Oh, come *on*, Will!' Mary was hopping with curiosity, her dressing-gown flapping. 'Open it, open it!'

Will suddenly realized that his tradition-minded family had been standing, patiently immobile, waiting for five minutes while he read his letter. Using the lid of the crate as a tray, he hastily began hauling out more and more palm-leaf packing until finally the object inside was clear. He pulled it out, staggering as he took the weight, and everybody gasped.

It was a giant carnival head, brilliant and grotesque. The colours were bright and crude, the features boldly made and easily recognizable, all done in the same smooth, light substance like papier-mâché or a kind of grainless wood. And it was not the head of a man. Will had never seen anything like it before. The head from which the branching antlers sprang was shaped like the head of a stag, but the ears beside the horns were those of a dog or a wolf. And the face beneath the horns was a human face – but with the round feather-edged eyes of a bird. There was a strong, straight human nose, a firm human mouth, set in a slight smile. There was not much else that was purely human about the thing at all. The chin was bearded, but the beard so shaped that it might as easily have been the chin of a goat or deer as of a man. The face could have been frightening; when everyone had gasped, the sound Mary made and hastily muffled had been more like a small scream. But Will felt that its effect would depend on who was looking at it. The appearance was nothing. It was neither ugly nor beautiful, frightening nor funny. It was a thing made to call out deep responses from the mind. It was very much a thing of the Old Ones.

'My word!' his father said.

'That's a funny sort of present,' said James.

His mother said nothing.

Mary said nothing, but edged away a little.

'Reminds me of someone I know,' Robin said, grinning.

Paul said nothing.

Gwen said nothing.

Max said softly, 'Look at those eyes!'

Barbara said, 'But what's it for?'

Will ran his fingers over the strange great face. It took him only a moment to find what he was looking for; it was almost invisible unless you were expecting it, engraved on the forehead, between the horns. The imprint of a circle, quartered by a cross.

He said, 'It's a West Indian carnival head. It's old. It's special. Stephen found it in Jamaica.'

James was beside him now, peering up inside the head. 'There's a kind of wire framework that rests on your shoulders. And a slit where the mouth's just a bit open, I suppose you look out through that. Come on, Will, put it on.'

He heaved up the head from behind to slip it over Will's shoulders. But Will drew away, as some other part of his mind spoke silently to him. 'Not now,' he said. 'Somebody else open their present.'

And Mary forgot the head and her reaction to it, in the happy instant of finding that it was her turn for Christmas. She dived at the pile of presents by the tree, and the cheerful discoveries began again.

One present each; they had almost done, and it was almost time for breakfast, when the knocking came at the front door. Mrs Stanton had been about to reach for her own ritual parcel; her arm dropped to her side, and she looked up blankly.

'Who on earth can that be?'

They all stared at one another, and then at the door, as if it might speak. This was all wrong, like a phrase of music changing in mid-melody. Nobody ever came to the house at this hour on Christmas Day, it was not in the pattern.

'I wonder . . .' said Mr Stanton, with a faint surmise waking in his voice; and he pushed his feet more firmly into his slippers and got up to open the front door.

They heard the door open. His back filled the space and stopped them from seeing the visitor, but his voice rose in obvious pleasure. 'My dear chap, how very good of you . . . come in, do come in . . .' And as he turned back towards the living-room he was holding a small package in one hand that had not been there before, clearly a product of the tall figure that now loomed in the doorway, following him in. Mr Stanton was beaming and glowing, busy with introductions, 'Alice, love, this is Mr Mitothin . . . so kind, all this way on Christmas morning just to deliver . . . shouldn't have taken the . . . Mitothin, my son Max, my daughter Gwen . . . James, Barbara . . .'

Will listened without attention to the grown-up politenesses; it was only at the voice of the stranger that he glanced up. There was something familiar in the deep, slightly nasal voice with a trace of accent, carefully repeating the names: 'How do you do, Mrs Stanton . . . Compliments of the season to you, Max, Gwen . . .' And Will saw the outline of the face, and the longish red-brown hair, and he froze.

It was the Rider. This Mr Mitothin, his father's friend from goodness-knows-where, was the Black Rider from somewhere outside Time.

Will seized the nearest thing to his hand, a sweep of bright cloth that was Stephen's present from Jamaica to his sister Barbara, and pulled it quickly over the carnival head to mask it from view. As he turned again, the Rider raised his head to look further back into the room, and saw him. He stared at Will in open triumphant challenge, a small smile on his lips. Mr Stanton beckoned, flapping a hand, 'Will, come here a minute – my youngest son, Mr –'

Will was instantly a furious Old One, so furious that he did not pause to think what he should do. He could feel every inch of himself, as if he had grown in his rage to three times his own height. He stretched out his right hand with its fingers spread stiff towards his family, and saw them instantly caught into a stop in time, frozen out of all movement. Like waxworks they stood stiff and motionless round the room.

'How dare you come in here!' he shouted at the Rider. The two of them stood facing one another across the room, the only living and moving objects there: no human moved, the hands of the clock on the mantelpiece did not move, and though the flames of the fire flickered, they did not consume the logs that they burned.

'How dare you! At Christmas, on Christmas morning! Get out!' It was the first time in his life he had ever felt such rage, and it was not pleasant, but he was outraged that the Dark should have dared to interrupt this his most precious family ritual.

The Rider said softly, 'Contain yourself.' In the Old Speech, his accent was suddenly much more marked. He smiled at Will without a flicker of change in his cold blue eyes. 'I can cross your threshold, my friend, and pass your berried holly, because I have been invited. Your father, in good faith, asked me to enter the door. And he is the master of this house, and there is nothing you can do about that.'

'Yes, there is,' Will said. Staring at the Rider's confident smile, he focused all his powers in an effort to see into his mind, find what he intended to do there. But he came up sharp against a black wall of hostility, unbreakable. Will felt this should not be possible, and he was shaken. He groped angrily in his memory for the words of destruction with which in the last resort – but only the very last resort – an Old One might break the power of the Dark. And the Black Rider laughed.

'Oh no, Will Stanton,' he said easily. 'That won't do. You cannot use weapons of that kind here, not unless you wish to blast your whole family out beyond Time.' He glanced pointedly at Mary, who stood unmoving next to him, her mouth half-open, caught out of life in the middle of saying something to her father.

'That would be a pity,' the Rider said. Then he looked back at Will, and the smile dropped from his face as if he had spat it away, and his eyes narrowed. 'You young fool, do you think that for all your Gift of Gramarye you can control *me*? Keep your place. You are not one of the masters yet. You may do things as best you can contrive, but the high powers are not for your mastering yet. *And nor am I.*'

'You are afraid of my masters,' Will said suddenly, not knowing quite what he meant, but knowing it was true.

The Rider's pale face flushed. He said softly, 'The Dark is rising, Old One, and this time we do not propose that anything shall hinder its way. This is the time for our rising, and these next twelve months shall see us established at last. Tell your masters that. Tell them that nothing shall stop us. Tell them, all the Things of Power that they hope to possess we shall take from them, the grail and the harp and the Signs. We shall break your Circle before it can ever be joined. *And none shall stop the Dark from rising!*'

The last words keened out in a high shriek of triumph, and Will shivered. The Rider stared at him, his pale eyes glittering; then scornfully he spread out his hands towards the Stantons, and at once they started into life again and the bustle of Christmas was back, and there was nothing Will could do.

'– that box for?' Mary said.

'– Mitothin, this is our Will.' Mr Stanton put his hand on Will's shoulder. Will said coldly, 'How do you do?'

'The compliments of the season to you, Will,' the Rider said.

'I wish you the same as you wish me,' Will said.

'Very logical,' said the Rider.

'Very pompous, if you ask me,' Mary said, tossing her head. 'He's like that sometimes. Daddy, *who* is that box for, that he brought?'

'Mr Mitothin, not "he",' said her father automatically.

'For your mother, a surprise,' the Rider said. 'Something that wasn't finished last night in time for your father to bring it home.'

'From you?'

'From Daddy, I think,' said Mrs Stanton, smiling at her husband. She turned to the Rider. 'Will you have breakfast with us, Mr Mitothin?'

'He can't,' said Will.

'Will!'

'He sees I'm in a hurry,' the Rider said smoothly. 'No, I thank you, Mrs Stanton, but I am on the way to spend the day with friends, and I must be off.'

Mary said, 'Where are you going?'

'North of here ... what long hair you have, Mary. Very pretty.'

'Thank you,' said Mary smugly, shaking her long, loose hair back from her shoulders. The Rider reached out and removed a stray hair delicately from her sleeve. 'Allow me,' he said politely.

'She's always showing it off,' James said calmly. Mary stuck out her tongue.

The Rider looked down the room again. 'That's a magnificent tree. A local one?'

'It's a Royal tree,' James said, 'From the Great Park.'

'Come and see!' Mary grabbed the Rider's hand and tugged him across. Will bit his lip, and deliberately blanked out all thought of the carnival head from his mind by concentrating very hard on what he was likely to have for breakfast. The Rider, he was fairly sure, could see into the top level of his mind but not perhaps the ones buried deeper than that.

But there was no danger. Though the great empty box and its pile of exotic packing stood right beside him, the Rider, surrounded by Stantons, simply peered obediently and admiringly at the ornaments on the tree. He seemed particularly taken with the tiny carved initials from Farmer Dawson's box. 'Beautiful,' he said, absently twirling Mary's left-twined M – which, Will noticed vaguely, was hanging upside-down.

Then he turned back to their parents. 'I really must go, and you must have your breakfasts. Will looks rather hungry, I think.' There was a flash of malice as they looked at one another, and Will knew that he had been right about the limits of the Dark's seeing.

'I'm really immensely grateful to you, Mitothin,' Mr Stanton said.

'No trouble at all, you were right on my way. Compliments of the season to you all –' With a flurry of farewells he was gone, striding down the path. Will rather regretted that his mother shut the door before they had a chance to hear a car's engine start up. He did not think the Rider had come by car.

'Well, my love,' said Mr Stanton, giving his wife a kiss and handing her the box. 'There's your first tree-present. Happy Christmas!'

'Oh!' said their mother, when she had opened it. 'Oh, Roger!'

Will squeezed past his burbling sisters to have a look. Nestled on white velvet, in a box marked with the name of his father's shop, was his mother's old-fashioned ring: the ring he had watched Mr Stanton checking for loose stones some weeks before, the ring that Merriman had seen in the picture he took out of Will's mind. But encircling it was something else: a bracelet made as an enlargement of the ring, exactly matching it. A gold band, set with three diamonds in the centre, and three rubies on either side, and engraved with an odd pattern of circles and lines and curves round them all. Will stared at it, wondering why the Rider should have wanted to have it in his hands. For surely that must have been behind the visit this morning; no Lord of the Dark needed to enter any house merely to see what was inside.

'Did you make it, Dad?' said Max. 'Lovely bit of work.'

'Thank you,' said his father.

'Who was that man who brought it?' Gwen said curiously. 'Does he work with you? Such a funny name.'

'Oh, he's a dealer,' Mr Stanton said. 'In diamonds, mostly. Strange chap, but very pleasant. I've known him for a couple of years, I suppose. We get quite a lot of stones from his people – including these.' He poked one finger gently at the bracelet. 'I had to leave early yesterday while young Jeffrey was still tightening one setting – and Mitothin happened to be in the shop and offered to drop it off to save me coming back. As he said, he was coming past here this morning anyway. Still, it was good of him, he needn't have offered.'

'Very nice,' said his wife. 'But you're nicer. I think it's beautiful.'

'I'm hungry,' said James. 'When are we going to eat?'

It was only after the bacon and eggs, toast and tea, marmalade and honey were all gone, and the debris of the first present-opening cleared away, that Will realized his letter from Stephen was nowhere to be found. He searched the living-room, investigated everyone's belongings, crawled underneath the tree and around the waiting pile of still-unopened presents, but it was not there. It might, of course, have been inadvertently thrown away, in mistake for wrapping-paper; such things sometimes happened in their crowded Christmas Day.

But Will thought he knew what had happened to his letter. And he wondered whether, after all, it had been the chance of investigating his mother's ring that had brought the Black Rider to the house – or a quest for something else.

Before long they noticed that snow was falling again. Gently but inexorably the flakes came fluttering down, without once faltering. The footprints of Mr Mitothin, out on the path from door to drive, were soon covered over as if they had never been there. The dogs, Raq and Ci. who had asked to go out before the snow began, came humbly scratching at the back door again.

'I'm all for a white Christmas now and then,' said Max, staring morosely out, 'but this is ridiculous.'

'Extraordinary,' said his father, looking out over his shoulder. 'I've never known it like this at Christmas, in my lifetime. If much more comes down today, there'll be real transport problems all over the South of England.'

'That's what I was thinking,' said Max. 'I'm supposed to be going to Southampton the day after tomorrow to stay with Deb.'

'Oh, woe, woe,' said James, clutching his chest.

Max looked at him.

'Happy Christmas, Max,' James said.

Paul came clomping into the living-room in boots, buttoning his overcoat. 'Snow or no snow, I'm off ringing. They ol' bells up in thiccy tower don' wait for no one. Any of you heathen mob coming to church this morning?'

'The nightingales will be along,' Max said, looking at Will and James, who between them constituted about one-third of the church choir. 'That should do you, don't you think?'

'If you were to perform your seasonal good deed,' said Gwen, passing, 'with some useful task like peeling the potatoes, then perhaps Mum could go. She does like to, when she can.'

The small muffled group which set out eventually into the thickening snow consisted of Paul, James, Will, Mrs Stanton and Mary, who was, James said unkindly but with truth, probably more interested in avoiding housework than in making her devotions. They plodded up the road, the snowflakes coming down harder now and beginning to sting their cheeks. Paul had gone ahead to join the other ringers, and soon the tumbling notes of the six sweet old bells that hung in the small square tower began chiming through the grey whirling world around them, brightening it back into Christmas. Will's spirits rose a little at the sound, but not much; the heavy persistence of the new snow troubled him. He could not shake off the creeping suspicion that it was being sent as a forerunner of something else, by the Dark. He thrust his hands deep into the pockets of his sheepskin jacket, and the fingertips of one hand found themselves curling round a rook's feather, forgotten since the dreadful night of Midwinter's Eve, before his birthday.

In the snowy road, four or five cars stood outside the church; there were more, usually, on Christmas morning, but few villagers outside walking range had chosen to brave this swirling white fog. Will watched the fat white flakes lie determined and unmelting on his jacket sleeve; it was very cold. Even inside the little church, the snowflakes obstinately remained, and took a long time to melt. He went with James and the handful of other choristers to struggle into surplices in the narrow vestry corridor, and then, as the bells merged into the beginning of the service, to make their procession down the aisle and up into the little gallery at the back of the small square nave. You could see everyone from there, and it was clear that the church of St James the Less was not Christmas-crammed this year, but half full.

The order of Morning Prayer, *as were in this Church of England, by the Authority of Parliament, in the Second Year of the Reign of King Edward the Sixth,* made its noble way through the Christmas pattern led by the Rector's unashamedly theatrical bass-baritone.

'O ye Frost and Cold, bless ye the Lord, praise Him, and magnify Him for ever,' said Will, reflecting that Mr Beaumont had shown a certain wry humour in choosing the canticle.

'O ye Ice and Snow, bless ye the Lord, praise Him, and magnify Him for ever.'

Suddenly he found himself shivering, but not from the words, nor from any sense of cold. His head swam; he clutched for a moment at the edge of the gallery. The music seemed to become for a brief flash hideously discordant, jarring at his ears. Then it faded into itself again and was as before, leaving Will shaken and chilled.

'O ye Light and Darkness,' sang James, staring at him – '*are you all right*? *Sit down* – and magnify Him forever.'

But Will shook his head impatiently, and for the rest of the service he sturdily stood, sang, sat, or knelt, and convinced himself that there had been nothing at all wrong except a vague feeling of faintness, brought on by what his elders liked to call 'over-excitement'. And then the strange sense of wrongness, of discordance, came again.

It was only once more, at the very end of the service. Mr Beaumont was booming out the prayer of St Chrysostom: '. . . who dost promise, that when two or three are gathered together in thy name thou wilt grant their requests . . .' Noise broke suddenly into Will's mind, a shrieking and dreadful howling in place of the familiar cadences. He had heard it before. It was the sound of the besieging Dark, which he had heard outside the Manor Hall where he had sat with Merriman and the Lady, in some century unknown. But in a church? said Will the Anglican choirboy, incredulous: surely you can't feel it inside a church? Ah, said Will the Old One unhappily, any church of any religion is vulnerable to their attack, for places like this are where men give thought to matters of the Light and the Dark. He hunched his head down between his shoulders as the noise beat at him – and then it vanished again, and the Rector's voice was ringing out alone, as before.

Will glanced quickly around him, but it was clear nobody else had noticed anything wrong. Through the folds of his white surplice he gripped the three Signs on his belt, but there was neither warmth nor cold under his fingers. To the warning power of the Signs, he guessed, a church was a kind of no man's land; since no harm could actually enter its walls, no warning against harm should be necessary. Yet if the harm were hovering just outside . . .

The service was over now, everyone roaring out 'O Come, All Ye Faithful' in happy Christmas fervour, as the choir made their way down from the gallery and up to the altar. Then Mr Beaumont's blessing went rolling out over the heads of the congregation: '. . . the love of God, and the fellowship of the Holy Ghost . . .' But the words could not bring Will peace, for he knew that something was wrong, something looming out of the Dark, something waiting, out there, and that when it came to the point he must meet it alone, unstrengthened.

He watched everyone file beaming out of the church, smiling and nodding to each other as they gripped their umbrellas and turned up their collars against the swirling snow. He saw jolly Mr Hutton, the retired director, twirling his car keys, enveloping tiny Miss Bell, their old teacher, in the warm offer of a ride home; and behind him jolly Mrs Hutton, a galleon in full furry sail, doing the same with limp Mrs Pettigrew, the postmistress. Assorted village children scampered out of the door, escaping their best-hatted mothers, rushing to snowballs and Christmas turkey. Lugubrious Mrs Horniman stumped out next to Mrs Stanton and Mary, busily foretelling doom. Will saw Mary, trying not to giggle, fall back to join Mrs Dawson and her married daughter, with the five-year-old grandson prancing gaily in gleaming new cowboy boots.

The choir, coated and muffled, began to leave too, with cries of 'Happy Christmas!' and 'See you on Sunday, Vicar!' to Mr Beaumont, who would be giving only this service here today and the rest in his other parishes. The rector, talking music with Paul, smiled and waved vaguely. The church began to empty, as Will waited for his brother. He could feel his neck prickling, as though with the electricity that hangs strongly oppressive in the air before a giant storm. He could feel it everywhere, the air inside the church was charged with it. The rector, still chatting, reached out an absentminded hand and turned off the lights inside the church, leaving it in a cold grey murk, brighter only beside the door where the whiteness of the snow reflected in. And Will, seeing some figures move towards the door out of the shadows, realized that the church was not empty after all. Down there by the little twelfth-century font, he saw Farmer Dawson, Old George, and Old George's son John, the smith, with his silent wife. The Old Ones of the Circle were waiting for him, to support him against whatever lurked outside. Will felt weak for a moment as relief washed over him in a great warm wave.

'All ready, Will?' said the rector genially, pulling on his overcoat. He went on, still preoccupied, to Paul, 'Of course, I do agree the double concerto is one of the best. I only wish he'd record the unaccompanied Bach suites. Heard him do them in a church in Edinburgh once, at the Festival – marvellous –'

Paul, sharper-eyed, said, 'Is anything wrong, Will?'

'No,' Will said. 'That is – no.' He was trying desperately to think of some way of getting the two of them outside the church before he came near the door himself. Before – before whatever might happen did happen. By the church door he could see the Old Ones move slowly into a tight group, supporting one another. He could feel the force now very strong, very close, all around, the air was thick with it, outside the church was destruction and chaos, the heart of the Dark, and he could think of nothing that he could do to turn it aside. Then as the rector and Paul turned to walk through the nave, he saw both of them pause in the same instant, and their heads go up like the heads of wild deer on the alert. It was too late now; the voice of the Dark was so loud that even humans could sense its power.

Paul staggered, as if someone had pushed him in the chest, and grabbed a pew for support. '*What is that?*' he said huskily. 'Rector? What on earth is it?'

Mr Beaumont had turned very white. There was a glistening of sweat on his forehead, though the church was very cold again now. 'Nothing on earth, I think, perhaps,' he said. 'God forgive me.' And he stumbled a few paces nearer the church door, like a man struggling through waves in the sea, and leaning forward slightly made a sweeping sign of the Cross. He stammered out, 'Defend us thy humble servants in all assaults of our enemies; that we, surely trusting in thy defence, may not fear the power of any adversaries ...'

Farmer Dawson said very quietly but clearly from the group beside the door, 'No, Rector.'

The rector seemed not to hear him. His eyes were wide, staring out at the snow; he stood transfixed, he shook like a man with fever, the sweat came running down his cheeks. He managed to half-raise one arm and point behind him: '... vestry ...' he gasped out. '... book, on table ... exorcize ...'

'Poor brave fellow,' said John Smith in the Old Speech. 'This battle is not for his fighting. He is bound to think so, of course, being in his church.'

'Be easy, Reverend,' said his wife in English; her voice was soft and gentle, strongly of the country. The rector stared at her like a frightened animal, but by now all his powers of speech and movement had been taken away.

Frank Dawson said: 'Come here, Will.'

Pushing against the Dark, Will came forward slowly; he touched Paul on the shoulder as he passed, looking into puzzled eyes in a face as twisted and helpless as the rector's, and said softly: 'Don't worry. It'll be all right soon.'

Each of the Old Ones touched him gently as he came into the group, as if joining him to them, and Farmer Dawson took him by the shoulder. He said,

'We must do something to protect those two, Will, or their minds will bend. They cannot stand the pressure, the Dark will send them mad. You have the power, and the rest of us do not.'

It was Will's first intimation that he could do anything another Old One could not, but there was no time for wonder; with the Gift of Gramarye, he closed off the minds of his brother and the rector behind a barrier that no power of any kind could break through. It was a perilous undertaking, since he the maker was the only one who could remove the barrier, and if anything were to happen to him the two protected ones would be left like vegetables, incapable of any communication, forever. But the risk had to be taken; there was nothing else to be done. Their eyes closed gently as if they had gone quietly to sleep; they stood very still. After a moment their eyes opened again, but were tranquil and empty, unaware.

'All right,' said Farmer Dawson. 'Now.'

The Old Ones stood in the doorway of the church, their arms linked together. None spoke a word to another. Wild noise and turbulence rose outside; the light darkened, the wind howled and whined, the snow whirled in and whipped their faces with white chips of ice. And suddenly the rooks were in the snow, hundreds of them, black flurries of malevolence, cawing and croaking, diving down at the porch in shrieking attack and then swooping up, away. They could not come close enough to claw and tear; it was as if an invisible wall made them fall back within inches of their targets. But that would be only for as long as the Old Ones' strength could hold. In a wild storm of black and white the Dark attacked, beating at their minds as at their bodies, and above all driving hard at the Sign-seeker, Will. And Will knew that if he had been on his own his mind, for all its gifts of protection, would have collapsed. It was the strength of the Circle of the Old Ones that held him fast now.

But for the second time in his life, even the Circle could do no more than hold the power of the Dark at bay. Even together, the Old Ones could not drive it back. And there was no Lady now to bring aid of a greater kind. Will realized once more, helplessly, that to be an Old One was to be very old before the proper time, for the fear he began to feel now was worse than the blind terror he had known in his attic bed, worse than the fear the Dark had put into him in the great hall. This time, his fear was adult, made of experience and imagination and care for others, and it was the worst of all. In the moment that he knew this, he knew too that he, Will, was the only means by which his own fear could be overcome, and thus the Circle fortified and the Dark driven away. Who are you? he asked himself – and answered: you are the Sign-seeker. You have three of the Signs, half the circle of Things of Power. *Use them.*

The sweat was standing on his own forehead now as it had done on the rector's – though now the rector and Paul stood in smiling peace, oblivious, outside everything that was going on. Will could see the strain on the faces of the others, Farmer Dawson most of all. Slowly he moved his hands inwards, bringing the hands each held closer to one another; John Smith's left hand nearer to Farmer Dawson's right. And when they were close enough, he joined his neighbours' hands, shutting himself out. For a panicking moment he clutched them again, as if he were tightening a knot. Then he let go, and stood alone.

Unprotected now by the Circle, though sheltered behind it, he swayed under the impact of the raging ill-will outside the church. Then moving very deliberately, he unclasped his belt with its three precious burdens and draped it over his arm; took from his pocket the rook's feather, and wove it into the centre Sign: the bronze quartered circle. Then he took the belt in both his hands, holding it up before him, and moved slowly round until he stood alone in the church porch, facing the howling, rook-screaming, icy dark beyond. He had never felt so lonely before. He did nothing, he thought nothing. He stood there, and let the Signs work for themselves.

And suddenly, there was silence.

The flapping birds were gone. No wind howled. The dreadful, mad humming that had filled the air and the mind was vanished altogether. Every nerve and muscle in Will's body went limp as the tension disappeared. Outside, the snow still quietly fell, but the flakes were smaller now. The Old Ones looked at one another and laughed.

'The full circle will do the real job,' said Old George, 'but half a circle can do a lot, eh, young Will?'

Will looked down at the Signs in his hand, and shook his head in wonder.

Farmer Dawson said softly, 'In all my days since the grail disappeared, that's the first time I've seen anything but the mind of one of the great ones drive back the Dark. *Things*, this time. They did it alone, for all our willing. We have Things of Power again. It has been a long, long time.'

Will was still looking at the Signs, staring, as if they held his eyes for some purpose. 'Wait,' he said abstractedly. 'Don't move. Stay still for a moment.'

They paused, startled. The smith said, 'Is there trouble?'

'Look at the Signs,' Will said. 'Something's happening to them. They're – they're glowing.'

He turned slowly, still holding the belt with the three Signs as before, until his body was blocking the grey light from the door and his hands were in the gloom of the church; and the Signs grew brighter and brighter, each of them glowing with a strange, inward light.

The Old Ones stared.

'Is it the power of driving back the Dark?' said John Smith's wife in her soft lilt. 'Is it something in them that was sleeping, and begins to wake now?'

Will was trying vainly to sense what the Signs were telling him. 'I think it's a message, it means something. But I can't get through . . .'

The light poured out of the three Signs, filling their half of the dark little church with brilliance; it was a light like sunlight, warm and strong. Nervously, Will reached out a finger to touch the nearest circle, the Sign of Iron, but it was neither hot nor cold.

Farmer Dawson said suddenly, 'Look up there!'

His arm was out, pointing up the nave, towards the altar. In the instant they turned, they saw what he had seen: another light, blazing from the wall, just as beside them the light blazed from the Signs. It shone out like the beam from a great torch.

And Will understood. He said happily, 'So that's why.'

He walked up towards the second patch of brilliance, carrying the belt and the Signs so that the shadows on the pews and on the beams of the roof moved with him as he went. As the two lights grew closer and closer together each seemed to grow brighter still. With Frank Dawson's tall, heavy form looming behind him, Will paused in the middle of the shaft of brilliance reaching out from the wall. It looked as if a slit window were letting light through from some unimaginably bright room beyond. He saw that the light was coming from something very small, as long as one of his fingers, lying on its side.

He said with certainty to Mr Dawson: 'I must take it quickly, you know, while the light still shines from it. If the light is not shining, it can't be found at all.' And putting the belt with the Sign of Iron and the Sign of Bronze and the Sign of Wood into Frank Dawson's hands, he went forward to the light-cleft wall and reached in to the small source of the enchanted beam.

The glowing thing came out of the wall easily from a break in the stucco where the Chiltern flints of the wall showed through. It lay on his palm: a circle, quartered by a cross. It had not been cut into that shape. Even through the light in it, Will could see the smooth roundness of the sides that told him this was a natural flint, grown in the Chiltern chalk fifteen million years ago.

'The Sign of Stone,' Farmer Dawson said. His voice was gentle and reverent, his dark eyes unreadable. 'We have the fourth Sign, Will.'

Together they walked back to join the others, carrying the bright Things of Power. The three Old Ones watched, in silence. Paul and the Rector now sat tranquil in a pew as if sleeping. Will stood with his fellows and took the belt, and threaded on the Sign of Stone to stand there next to the other three. He had to squint through half-closed eyes to keep the brightness from blinding him.

Then when the fourth Sign was in position next to the rest, all the light in them died. They were dark and quiet as they had been before, and the Sign of Stone showed itself as a smooth and beautiful thing with the grey-white surface of an undamaged flint.

The black rook's feather was still woven into the Sign of Bronze. Will took it out. He did not need it now.

When the light went out of the Signs, Paul and the rector stirred. They opened their eyes, startled to find themselves sitting in a pew when a moment ago – it seemed to them – they had been standing. Paul jumped up instinctively, his head turning, questing. 'It's gone!' he said. He looked at Will, and a peculiar expression of puzzlement and wonder and awe came over his face. His eyes travelled down to the belt in Will's hands. 'What happened?' he said.

The rector stood up, his smooth, plump face creased in an effort to make sense of the incomprehensible. 'Certainly it has gone,' he said, looking slowly round the church. 'Whatever – influence it was. The Lord be praised.' He too looked at the Signs on Will's belt, and he glanced up again, smiling suddenly, an almost childish smile of relief and delight. 'That did the work, didn't it? The cross. Not of the church, but a Christian cross, nonetheless.'

'Very old, them crosses are, rector,' said Old George unexpectedly, firm and clear. 'Made a long time before Christianity. Long before Christ.'

The rector beamed at him. 'But not before God,' he said simply.

The Old Ones looked at him. There was no answer that would not have offended him, so no one tried to give one. Except, after a moment, Will.

'There's not really any before and after, is there?' he said. 'Everything that matters is outside Time. And comes from there and can go there.'

Mr Beaumont turned to him in surprise, 'You mean infinity, of course, my boy.'

'Not altogether,' said the Old One that was Will. 'I mean the part of all of us, and of all the things we think and believe, that has nothing to do with yesterday or today or tomorrow because it belongs at a different kind of level. Yesterday is still there, on that level. Tomorrow is there too. You can visit either of them. And all Gods are there, and all the things they have ever stood for. And,' he added sadly, 'the opposite, too.'

'Will,' said the rector, staring at him, 'I am not sure whether you should be exorcized or ordained. You and I must have some long talks, very soon.'

'Yes, we must,' Will said equably. He buckled on his belt, heavy with its precious burden. He was thinking hard and quickly as he did so, and the chief image before his mind was not Mr Beaumont's disturbed theological assumptions, but Paul's face. He had seen his brother looking at him with a kind of fearful remoteness that bit into him with the pain of a whiplash. It was more than he could stand. His two worlds must not meet so closely. He raised his head, gathering all his powers, spread straight the fingers of both hands and pointed one hand at each of them.

'You will forget,' he said softly in the Old Speech. 'Forget. Forget.'

'– in a church in Edinburgh once, marvellous,' the rector said to Paul, reaching to do up the top button of his overcoat. 'The Sarabande in the fifth suite literally had me in tears. He's the greatest cellist in the world, without a doubt.'

'Oh yes,' said Paul. 'Oh yes, he is.' He hunched his shoulders inside his own coat. 'Has Mum gone ahead, Will? Hey, Mr Dawson, hallo, happy Christmas!' And he beamed and nodded at the rest, as they all turned towards the church porch and the scattered flakes of drifting snow.

'Happy Christmas, Paul, Mr Beaumont,' said Farmer Dawson gravely. 'A nice service, sir, very nice.'

'Ah, seasonal warmth, Frank,' said the rector. 'A wonderful season too. Nothing can interfere with our Christmas services, not even all this snow.'

Laughing and chatting, they went out into the white world, where the snow lay mounded over the invisible tombstones and the white fields stretched down to the freezing Thames. There was no sound anywhere, no disturbance, only the occasional murmur of a car passing on the distant Bath Road. The rector turned aside to find his motor-bike. The rest of them went on, in a cheerful straggle, to take their respective paths home.

Two black rooks were perched on the lych-gate as Will and Paul drew close; they rose into the air slowly, half-hopping, dark incongruous shapes against the white snow. One of them passed close to Will's feet and dropped something there, giving a deprecatory croak as he passed. Will picked it up; it was a glossy horse-chestnut from the rooks' wood, as fresh as if it had ripened only yesterday. He and James always collected such nuts from the wood in early autumn for their school games of conkers, but he had never seen one as large and round as this.

'There, now,' said Paul, amused. 'You have a friend. Bringing you an extra Christmas present.'

'A peace offering, perhaps,' said Frank Dawson behind them, with no trace of expression in his deep Buckinghamshire voice. 'And then again, perhaps not. Happy Christmas, lads. Enjoy your dinner.' And the Old Ones were gone, up the road.

Will picked up the conker. 'Well I never,' he said.

They closed the church gate, knocking a shower of snow from its flat iron bars. Round the corner came the coughing roars of a motor-cycle as the rector tried to kick his steed into life. Then, a few feet ahead of them on the trampled snow, the rook flew down again. It walked backwards and forwards irresolutely and looked at Will.

'Caark,' it said, very gently, for a rook. 'Caaark, caark, caark.' Then it walked a few paces forward to the churchyard fence, jumped down again into the churchyard, and walked back a few paces as before. The invitation could hardly have been more obvious. 'Caark,' said the rook again, louder.

The ears of an Old One know that birds do not speak with the precision of words; instead they communicate emotion. There are many kinds and degrees of emotion, and there are many kinds of expression even in the language of a bird. But although Will could tell that the rook was obviously asking him to come and look at something, he could not tell whether or not the bird was being used by the Dark.

He paused, thinking of what the rooks had done; then he fingered the shiny brown chestnut in his hand. 'All right, bird,' he said. 'One quick look.'

He went back through the gate, and the rook, croaking like an old swinging door, walked clumsily ahead of him up the church path and round the corner. Paul watched, grinning. Then he saw Will suddenly stiffen as he reached the corner; vanish for a moment, and then reappear.

'Paul! Come quick! There's a man in the snow!'

Paul called the rector, who had just begun pushing his cycle up the road to start it there, and together they came running. Will was bending over a hunched figure, lying in the angle between the church wall and the tower; there was no movement, and the snow had already covered the man's clothes half an inch thick with its cold, feathery flakes. Mr Beaumont moved Will gently aside and knelt, turning the man's head and feeling for a pulse.

'He's alive, thank God, but very cold. The pulse isn't very good. He must have been here long enough for most men to die of exposure – look at the snow! Let's get him inside.'

'In the church?'

'Well, of course.'

'Let's take him to our house,' Paul said impulsively. 'It's only just round the corner, after all. It's warm, and a lot better, at any rate until an ambulance or something can come.'

'A wonderful idea,' said Mr Beaumont warmly. 'Your good mother is a Samaritan, I know. Just until Dr Armstrong can be called . . . we certainly can't leave the poor fellow here. I don't think there's a broken bone. Heart trouble, probably.' He tucked his heavy cycle gloves under the man's head to keep it from the snow, and Will saw the face for the first time.

He said in alarm, 'It's the Walker!'

They turned to him. 'Who?'

'An old tramp who hangs around . . . Paul, we can't take him home. Can't we get him to Dr Armstrong's surgery?'

'In this?' Paul waved a hand at the darkening sky; the snow was whirling round them, thicker again, and the wind was higher.

'But we can't take him with us! Not the Walker! He'll bring back the –' He stopped suddenly, half-way through a yelp. 'Oh,' he said helplessly. 'Of course, you can't remember, can you?'

'Don't worry, Will, your mother won't mind – a poor man *in extremis* –' Mr Beaumont was bustling now. He and Paul carried the Walker to the gate, like a muffled heap of ancient clothes. He managed finally to start the motor-cycle, and they propped the inert shape on it somehow; then half riding, half pushing, the strange little group made its way to the Stantons' house.

Will glanced behind him once or twice, but the rook was nowhere to be seen.

'Well, well,' said Max fastidiously, as he came down into the dining-room. 'Now I've *really* met a dirty old man.'

'He smelled,' Barbara said.

'You're telling me. Dad and I gave him a bath. My Lord, you should have seen him. Well, no, you shouldn't. Put you off your Christmas dinner. Anyway, he's as clean as a new-born babe now. Dad even washed his hair and his beard. And Mum's burning his horrible old clothes, when she's made sure there's nothing valuable in them.'

'Not much danger of that, I should think,' said Gwen, on her way in from the kitchen. 'Here, move your arm, this dish is hot.'

'We should lock up all the silver,' said James.

'What silver?' said Mary witheringly.

'Well, Mum's jewellery then. And the Christmas presents. Tramps always steal things.'

'This one won't be stealing much for a time,' said Mr Stanton, coming to his place at the head of the table with a bottle of wine and a corkscrew. 'He's ill. And fast asleep now, snoring like a camel.'

'Have you ever heard a camel snore?' said Mary.

'Yes,' said her father. 'And ridden one. So there. When's the doctor coming, Max? Pity to interrupt his dinner, poor man.'

'We didn't,' said Max. 'He's out delivering a baby, and they don't know when he'll be back. The woman was expecting twins.'

'Oh, Lord.'

'Well, the old boy must be all right if he's asleep. Just needs rest, I expect.

Though I must say he seemed a bit delirious, all that weird talk coming out.' Gwen and Barbara brought in more dishes of vegetables. In the kitchen their mother was making impressive clattering noises with the oven. 'What weird talk?' said Will.

'Goodness knows,' said Robin. 'It was when we first took him up. Sounded like a language unknown to human ear. Maybe he comes from Mars.'

'I only wish he did,' Will said. 'Then we could send him back.'

But a shout of approval had greeted his mother, beaming over the glossy brown turkey, and nobody heard him.

They turned on the radio in the kitchen while they were doing the washing-up.

'Heavy snow is falling again over the South and West of England,' said the impersonal voice. 'The blizzard which has been raging for twelve hours in the North Sea is still immobilizing all shipping on the South-east coasts. The London docks closed down this morning, due to power failures and transport difficulties caused by heavy snow and temperatures approaching zero. Snowdrifts blocking roads have isolated villages in many remote areas, and British Rail is fighting numerous electrical failures and minor derailments caused by the snow. A spokesman said this morning that the public is advised not to travel by rail except in cases of emergency.'

There was a sound of rustling paper. The voice went on: 'The freak storms which have intermittently raged over the South of England for the last few days are not expected to diminish until after the Christmas holiday, the Meteorological Office said this morning. Fuel shortages have worsened in the South-east, and householders have been asked not to use any form of electrical heating between the hours of nine a.m. and midday, or three and six p.m.'

'Poor old Max,' Gwen said. 'No trains. Perhaps he can hitch-hike.'

'Listen, listen!'

'A spokesman for the Automobile Association said today that road travel was at present extremely inadvisable on all roads except major motorways. He added that motorists stranded in heavy snowstorms should if possible remain with their vehicles until the snow stops. Unless a driver is quite certain of his location and knows he can reach help within ten minutes, the spokesman said, he should on no account leave his car.'

The voice went on, among exclamations and whistles, but Will turned away; he had heard enough. These storms could not be broken by the Old Ones without the power of the full circle of Signs – and by sending the storms, the Dark hoped to stop him from completing the circle. He was trapped; the Dark was spreading its shadow not only over his quest but over the ordinary world too. From the moment the Rider had invaded his cosy Christmas that morning, Will had watched the dangers grow; but he had not anticipated this wider threat. For days now, he had been too much caught up in his own perils to notice those of the outside world. But so many people were threatened now by the snow and cold: the very young, the very old, the weak, the ill ... The Walker won't have a doctor tonight, that's certain, he thought. It's a good job he isn't dying ...

The Walker. Why was he here? There had to be some meaning behind it. Perhaps he had simply been hovering for his own reasons, and been blasted by the attack of the Dark on the church. But if so, why had the rook, an agent of the Dark, brought Will to save him from freezing to death? Who was the Walker, anyway? Why could all the powers of Gramarye tell him nothing about the old man at all?

There were carols on the radio again. Will thought bitterly: Happy Christmas, world.

His father, passing, slapped him on the back. 'Cheer up, Will. It's bound to stop tonight, you'll be tobogganing tomorrow. Come on, time to open the rest of the presents. If we keep Mary waiting any longer she'll explode.'

Will went to join his cheerful, noisy family. Back in the cosy, brilliant cave of the long room with the fire and the glowing tree, it was untouched Christmas for a while, just as it had always been. And his mother and father and Max had joined to give him a new bicycle, with racing handlebars and eleven gear-speeds.

Will was never quite sure whether what happened that night was a dream.

In the darkest part of the night, the small chill hours that are the first of the next day, he woke, and Merriman was there. He stood towering beside the bed in a faint light that seemed to come from within his own form; his face was shadowed, inscrutable.

'Wake up, Will. Wake up. There is a ceremony we must attend.'

In an instant Will was standing; he found that he was fully dressed, with the Signs on their belt round his waist. He went with Merriman to the window. It was mounded to half its height with snow, and still the flakes were quietly falling. He said, suddenly desolate, 'Isn't there anything we can do to stop it? They're freezing half the country, Merriman, people will be dying.'

Merriman shook his white-maned head slowly, heavily. 'The Dark has its strongest power of all rising between now and the Twelfth Day. This is their preparing. Theirs is a cold strength, the winter feeds it. They mean to break the Circle forever, before it is too late for them. We shall all face a hard test soon.

But not all things go according to their will. Much magic still flows untapped, along the Old Ones' Ways. And we may find more hope in a moment. Come.'

The window ahead of them flew open, outwards, scattering all the snow. A faint luminous path like a broad ribbon lay ahead, stretching into the snow-flecked air; looking down, Will could see through it, see the snow-mounded outlines of roofs and fences and trees below. Yet the path was substantial too. In one stride Merriman had reached it through the window and was sweeping away at great speed with an eerie gliding movement, vanishing into the night. Will leapt after him, and the strange path swept him too off through the night, with no feeling either of speed or cold. The night around him was black and thick; nothing was to be seen except the glimmer of the Old Ones' airy way. And then all at once they were in some bubble of Time, hovering, tilted on the wind as Will had learned from his eagle of the Book of Gramarye.

'Watch,' Merriman said, and his cloak swirled round Will as if in protection.

Will saw in the dark sky, or in his own mind, a group of great trees, leafless, towering over a leafless hedge, wintry but without snow. He heard a strange, thin music, a high piping accompanied by the small constant thump of a drum, playing over and over again a single melancholy tune. And out of the deep dark and into the ghostly grove of trees a procession came.

It was a procession of boys, in clothes of some time long past, tunics and rough leggings; they had hair to their shoulders and bag-like caps of a shape he had never seen before. They were older than he: about fifteen, he guessed. They had the half-solemn expressions of players in a game of charades, mingling earnest purpose with a bubbling sense of fun. At the front came boys with sticks and bundles of birch twigs; at the back were the players of pipe and drum. Between these, six boys carried a kind of platform made of reeds and branches woven together, with a bunch of holly at each corner. It was like a stretcher, Will thought, except that they were holding it at shoulder height. He thought at first that it was no more than that, and empty; then he saw that it supported something. Something very small. On a cushion of ivy leaves in the centre of the woven bier lay the body of a minute bird: a dusty-brown bird, neat-billed. It was a wren.

Merriman's voice said softly over his head, out of the darkness: 'It is the Hunting of the Wren, performed every year since men can remember, at the solstice. But this is a particular year, and we may see more, if all is well. Hope in your heart, Will, that we may see more.'

And as the boys and their sad music moved on through the sky-trees and yet did not seem to pass, Will saw with a catch in his breath that instead of the little bird, there was growing the dim shape of a different form on the bier. Merriman's hand clutched at his shoulder like a steel clamp, though the big man made no sound. Lying on the bed of ivy between the four holly tufts now was no longer a tiny bird, but a small, fine-boned woman, very old, delicate as a bird, robed in blue. The hands were folded on the chest, and on one finger glimmered a ring with a huge rose-coloured stone. In the same instant Will saw the face, and knew that it was the Lady.

He cried out in pain, 'But you said she wasn't dead!'

'No more she is,' Merriman said.

The boys walked to their music, the bier with the silent form lying there came close, and then moved away, vanishing with the procession into the night, and the piping sad tune and the drumbeats dwindled after it. But on the very edge of disappearance, the three boys who had been playing paused, put down their instruments, and turned to stand gazing without expression at Will.

One of them said: 'Will Stanton, beware the snow!'

The second said: 'The Lady will return, but the Dark is rising.'

The third, in a quick sing-song tone, chanted something that Will recognized as soon as it began:

> 'When the Dark comes rising, six shall turn it back;
> Three from the circle, three from the track.
> Wood, bronze, iron; water, fire, stone;
> Five will return, and one go alone.'

But the boy did not end there, as Merriman had done. He went on:

> 'Iron for the birthday, bronze carried long;
> Wood from the burning, stone out of song;
> Fire in the candle-ring, water from the thaw;
> Six signs the circle, and the grail gone before.'

Then a great wind came up out of nowhere, and in a flurry of snowflakes and darkness the boys were gone, whirled away, and Will too felt himself whirling backwards, back through Time, back along the shining way of the Old Ones. The snow lashed at his face. The night was in his eyes, stinging. Out of the darkness he heard Merriman calling to him, urgently, but with a new hope and resonance in his deep voice: 'Danger rises with the snow, Will – be wary of the snow. Follow the Signs, beware the snow ...'

And Will was back in his room, back in his bed, falling into sleep with the one ominous word ringing in his head like the chiming of the deepest church bell over the mounting snow. 'Beware ... beware ...'

PART THREE
The Testing

The Coming of the Cold

The next day the snow still fell, all day. And the next day too.

'I do wish it would stop,' said Mary unhappily, gazing at the blind white windows. 'It's horrible the way it just goes on and on – I hate it.'

'Don't be stupid,' said James. 'It's just a very long storm. No need to get hysterical.'

'This is different. It's creepy.'

'Rubbish. It's just a lot of snow.'

'Nobody's ever seen so much snow before. Look how high it is – you couldn't get out of the back door if we hadn't been clearing it since it started to fall. We're going to be buried, that's what. It's pushing at us – it's even broken a window in the kitchen, did you know that?'

Will said sharply, 'What?'

'The little window at the back, near the stove. Gwennie came down this morning and the kitchen was cold as ice, with snow and bits of glass all over that corner. The snow had pushed the window in, the weight of it.'

James sighed loudly. 'Weight isn't pushing. The snow gets blown into a drift at that side of the house, that's all.'

'I don't care what you say, it's horrible. As if the snow was trying to get in.' She sounded close to tears.

'Let's go and see if the Wa – the old tramp's woken up yet,' Will said. It was time to stop Mary before she came too near the truth. How many other people in the country were being made as frightened as this by the snow? He thought fiercely of the Dark, and longed to know what to do.

The Walker had slept through the previous day, hardly stirring except for occasional meaningless mutterings, and once or twice a small hoarse shout. Will and Mary went up to his room now carrying a tray, with cereal and toast and milk and marmalade. 'Good morning!' Will said loudly and brightly as they went in. 'Would you like some breakfast?'

The Walker opened a slit of an eye and peered at them through his shaggy grey hair, longer and wilder than ever now that it was clean. Will held out the tray towards him.

'Faugh!' the Walker croaked. It was a noise like spitting.

Mary said, '*Well!*'

'D'you want something else instead, then?' said Will. 'Or are you just not hungry?'

'Honey,' the Walker said.

'Honey?'

'Honey and bread. Honey and bread. Honey and –'

'All right,' Will said. They took the tray away.

'He doesn't even say please,' Mary said. 'He's a nasty old man. I'm not going near him any more.'

'Suit yourself,' Will said. Left alone, he found the tail-end of a jar of honey in the back of the larder, rather crystalline round the edges, and spread it lavishly on three hunks of bread. He took this with a glass of milk up to the Walker, who sat up greedily in bed and wolfed the lot. When eating, he was not a pretty sight.

'Good,' he said. He tried to wipe some honey off his beard and licked the back of his hand, peeping at Will. 'Still snowing? Still coming down, is it?'

'What were you doing out in the snow?'

'Nothing,' the Walker said sullenly. 'Don't remember.' His eyes narrowed craftily, and he gestured at his forehead and said in a plaintive whine, 'Hit my head.'

'D'you remember where we found you?'

'No.'

'Do you remember who I am?'

Very promptly he shook his head. 'No.'

Will said softly again, this time in the Old Speech, 'Do you remember who I am?'

The Walker's shaggy face was expressionless. Will began to think that perhaps he really had lost his memory. He leaned over the bed to pick up the tray with its empty plate and glass, and suddenly the Walker let out a shrill scream and flinched away from him, cowering down at the far side of the bed. 'No!' he screeched. 'No! Get away! Take them away!'

Eyes wide and terrified, he was staring at Will in loathing. For a moment Will was baffled; then he realized that his sweater had lifted as he reached out his arm, and the Walker had seen the four Signs on his belt.

'Take them away!' the old man howled. 'They burn! Get them out!'

So much for lost memory, Will thought. He heard concerned feet running up the stairs, and went out of the room. Why should the Walker be terrified by the Great Signs, when he had carried one of them himself for so long?

*

His parents were grave. The news on the radio grew worse and worse as the cold gripped the country and one restriction followed another. In all records of temperature Britain had never been so cold; rivers that had never frozen before stood as solid ice, and every port on the entire coast was iced in. People could do little more than wait for the snow to stop; but still the snow fell.

They led a restless, enclosed life – 'like cavemen in winter', said Mr Stanton – and went to bed early to save fires and fuel. New Year's Day came and went and was scarcely noticed. The Walker lay in bed fidgeting and muttering and refused to eat anything but bread and milk, which by now was tinned milk, watered down. Mrs Stanton said kindly that he was regaining his strength, poor man. Will kept away. He was growing increasingly desperate as the cold tightened and the snow floated down and down; he felt that if he did not get out of the house soon he would find the Dark had boxed him up forever. His mother gave him an escape, in the end. She ran out of flour, sugar, and tinned milk.

'I know nobody's supposed to leave the house except in dire emergency,' she said anxiously, 'but really this counts as one. We do need things to eat.'

It took the boys two hours to shovel a way through the snow in their own garden to the road, where a kind of roofless tunnel, the width of one snowplough, had been kept clear. Mr Stanton had announced that only he and Robin would go to the village, but throughout the two hours Will, panting and digging, begged to be allowed to go too, and by the end his father's resistance was so much lowered that he agreed.

They wore scarves over their ears, heavy gloves, and three sweaters each under their coats. They took a torch. It was mid-morning, but the snow was coming down as relentlessly as ever, and nobody knew when they might get home. From the steep-sided cutting in the one road of the village, tiny uneven paths had been trodden and shovelled to the few shops and most of the central houses; they could see from the footprints that someone had brought horses out from Dawsons' Farm to help carve a way to the cottages of people like Miss Bell and Mrs Horniman, who could never have managed it for themselves. In the village store, Mrs Pettigrew's tiny dog was curled up in a twitching grey heap in one corner, looking limper and unhappier than ever; Mrs Pettigrew's fat son Fred, who helped run the store, had sprained his wrist by falling in the snow and had one arm in a sling, and Mrs Pettigrew was in a state. She twittered and dithered with nervousness, she dropped things, she hunted in quite the wrong places for sugar and flour and found neither of them, and in the end she sat down suddenly in a chair, like a puppet dropped from its strings, and burst into tears.

'Oh,' she sobbed, 'I'm so sorry, Mr Stanton, it's this terrible snow. I'm so frightened, I don't know . . . I have these dreams that we're cut off, and nobody knows where we are . . .'

'We already are cut off,' said her son lugubriously. 'Not a car's been through the village for a week. And no supplies, and everyone running out – there's no butter, and not even any tinned milk. And the flour won't last long; there's only five bags after this one.'

'And nobody with any fuel,' Mrs Pettigrew sniffed. 'And the little Randall baby sick with a fever and poor Mrs Randall without a piece of coal, and goodness knows how many more –'

The shop-bell twanged as the door opened, and in the automatic village habit, everyone turned to see who had come in. A very tall man in a voluminous black overcoat, almost a cloak, was taking off his broad-brimmed hat to show a mop of white hair; deep-shadowed eyes looked down at them over a fierce hooked nose.

'Good afternoon,' Merriman said.

'Hallo,' said Will, beaming, his world suddenly bright.

'Afternoon,' said Mrs Pettigrew, and blew her nose hard. She said, muffled by the handkerchief, 'Mr Stanton, do you know Mr Lyon? He's at the Manor.'

'How d'you do?' said Will's father.

'Butler to Miss Greythorne,' Merriman said, inclining his head respectfully. 'Until Mr Bates comes back from holiday. That is to say, when the snow stops. At present, of course, I can't get out, and Bates can't get in.'

'It'll never stop,' Mrs Pettigrew wailed, and she burst into tears again.

'Oh, *Mum*,' said fat Fred in disgust.

'I have some news for you, Mrs Pettigrew,' said Merriman in loud soothing tones. 'We have heard an announcement over the local radio – our telephone being dead, of course, like yours. There's to be a fuel and food drop in the Manor grounds, as the place most easily visible from the air in this snow. And Miss Greythorne is asking if everyone in the village would not like to move into the Manor, for the emergency. It will be crowded, of course, but warm. And comforting, perhaps. And Dr Armstrong will be there – he is already on his way, I believe.'

'That's ambitious,' Mr Stanton said reflectively. 'Almost feudal, you might say.'

Merriman's eyes narrowed slightly. 'But with no such intention.'

'Oh, no, I do see that.'

Mrs Pettigrew's tears ceased. 'What a lovely idea, Mr Lyon! Oh dear, it would be such a relief to be with other people, especially at night.'

'I'm other people,' said Fred.

'Yes, dear, but –'

Fred said stolidly, 'I'll go and get some blankets. And pack some stuff from the shop.'

'That would be wise,' Merriman said. 'The radio says the storm will grow very much worse this evening. So the sooner everyone can gather, the better.'

'Would you like some help with telling people?' Robin began pulling up his collar again.

'Excellent. That would be excellent.'

'We'll all help,' said Mr Stanton.

Will had turned to look out of the window at the mention of the storm, but the snow floating down out of the solid grey sky seemed much as before. The windows were so misted that it was difficult to see out of them at all, but he caught a glimpse now of something moving outside. There was someone out there on the snow-road carved through Huntercombe Lane. He saw clearly only for a second, as the figure passed the end of the Pettigrews' path, but a second was all he needed to recognize the man sitting erect on the great black horse.

'The Rider has passed!' he said quickly and clearly in the Old Speech.

Merriman's head jerked round; then he collected himself and ostentatiously swept his hat on to his head. 'I shall be very grateful to have assistance.'

'*What* did you say, Will?' Robin, distracted, was staring at his brother.

'Oh, nothing.' Will went to the door, making a great fuss over buttoning his coat. 'Just thought I saw someone.'

'But you said something in some funny language.'

'Of course I didn't. I just said "Who's that out there?" Only it wasn't anyone anyway.'

Robin was still staring at him. 'You sounded just like that old tramp, when he was babbling when we first put him to bed . . .' But he was not given to wasting time on surmise; he shook his practical head and dropped the subject. 'Oh well.'

Merriman managed to walk closely behind Will, as they were leaving the Pettigrews' to scatter and warn the rest of the villagers. He said softly in the Old Speech, 'Get the Walker to the Manor if you can. Quickly. Or he will stop you from getting out yourself. But you may have a little trouble with your father's pride.'

By the time the Stantons reached home, after their struggling tour of the village, Will had almost forgotten what Merriman had said about his father. He was too busy working out how they could get the Walker to the Manor without actually having to carry him. He remembered only when he heard Mr

Stanton talking in the kitchen, as they pulled off their coats and delivered their supplies.

'. . . good of the old girl, having everyone in there. Of course they've got the space, and the fires, and those old walls are so thick they keep the cold out better than anyone's. Much the best thing for the people from the cottages – poor Miss Bell wouldn't have lasted long . . . Still, of course, we're all right here. Self-contained. No point in adding to the manorial load.'

'Oh, Dad,' Will said impulsively, 'don't you think we ought to go too?'

'I don't think so,' said his father, with the lazy assurance that Will should have known was harder to break than any fervour.

'But Mr Lyon said it would be much more dangerous later on, because of the storm getting worse.'

'I think I can make my own judgement of the weather, Will, without help from Miss Greythorne's butler,' said Mr Stanton amiably.

'Oh, wow,' said Max with cheerful rudeness. 'You rotten old snob, hark at you.'

'Come on, that's not what I meant.' His father threw a wet scarf at him. 'Inverted snobbery, more like. I simply don't see any good reason for our trooping off to partake of the bounty of the Lady of the Manor. We're perfectly all right here.'

'Quite right,' Mrs Stanton said briskly. 'Now out of the kitchen, all of you. I want to make some bread.'

The only hope, Will decided, was the Walker himself.

He slipped away and went upstairs to the tiny spare room where the Walker lay in bed. 'I want to talk to you.'

The old man turned his head on the pillow. 'All right,' he said. He seemed muted and unhappy. Suddenly Will felt sorry for him.

'Are you better?' he said. 'I mean, are you actually ill now, or do you just feel weak?'

'I am not ill,' the Walker said listlessly. 'No more than usual.'

'Can you walk?'

'You want to throw me out in the snow, is that it?'

'Of course not,' Will said. 'Mum would never let you go off in this weather, and nor would I, not that I've got much say in it. I'm the very youngest in this family, you know that.'

'You are an Old One,' the Walker said, looking at him with dislike.

'Well, that's different.'

'It's not different at all. Just means there's no point talking about yourself to me as if you were just a little kid in a family. I know better.'

Will said, 'You were guardian of one of the Great Signs – I don't see why you should seem to hate us.'

'I did what I was made to do,' the old man said. 'You took me . . . you picked me out . . .' His brows creased, as though he were trying to remember something from a long time ago; then he grew vague again. 'I was made to.'

'Well, look, I don't want to make you do anything, but there's one thing we all have to do. The snow's getting so bad that everyone in the village is going to live at the Manor, like a kind of hostel, because it'll be safer and warmer.' He felt as he talked that the Walker might know what he was going to say already, but it was impossible to get inside the old man's mind; whenever he tried, he found himself floundering, as if he had broken into the stuffing of a cushion.

'The doctor will be there too,' he said. 'So if you were to let everyone feel you needed to be somewhere with a doctor, we could all go to the Manor.'

'You mean you aren't going otherwise?' The Walker squinted suspiciously at him.

'My father won't let us. But we have to, it's safer –'

'I won't go either,' the Walker said. He turned his head away. 'Go away. Leave me be.'

Will said softly, warningly, in the Old Speech, 'The Dark will come for you.'

There was a pause. Then very slowly the Walker turned his shaggy grey head back again, and Will flinched in horror as he saw the face. For just a moment, its history was naked upon it. There were bottomless depths of pain and terror in the eyes, the lines of black experience were carved clear and terrible; this man had known somewhere such a fearful dread and anguish that nothing could really ever touch him again. His eyes were wide for the first time, stretched open, with his knowledge of horror looking out.

The Walker said emptily, '*The Dark has already come for me.*'

Will took a deep breath. 'But now the circle of the Light comes,' he said. He pulled off the belt with the Signs and held it before the Walker. The old man flinched away, screwing up his face, whimpering like a frightened animal; Will felt sickened, but there was no help for it. He brought the Signs closer and closer to the twisted old face, until, like a piece of breaking wire, the Walker's self-control snapped. He shrieked and began to babble and thrash about, screaming for help. Will ran outside and called for his father, and half the family came running.

'I think he's having some sort of fit. Awful. Shouldn't we get him to Dr Armstrong at the Manor, Dad?'

Mr Stanton said doubtfully, 'We could get the doctor to come here, perhaps.'

'But he might very well be better off there,' said Mrs Stanton, staring at the Walker in concern. 'The old man, I mean. With the doctor able to watch him –

and more comfort and food. Really, this is alarming, Roger. I don't know what to do for him here.'

Will's father gave in. They left the Walker still tossing and raving, with Max near by in case of accidents, and went to turn the big family toboggan into a mobile stretcher. Only one thing nagged in Will's mind. It had to be his imagining, but in the moment when the Walker had cracked at the sight of the Great Signs, and become a mad old man once more, he had thought he saw a flash of triumph in the flickering eyes.

The sky hung grey and heavy, waiting to snow, as they left for the Manor with the Walker. Mr Stanton took the twins with him, and Will. His wife watched them go with unfamiliar nervousness. 'I hope it really is over. D'you really think Will should go?'

'Comes in handy to have someone light sometimes, in this snow,' said his father, over Will's splutter, 'He'll be all right.'

'You aren't going to stay there, are you?'

'Of course not. The only point of the exercise is to deliver the old man to the doctor. Come on, Alice, this isn't like you. There's no danger, you know.'

'I suppose not,' Mrs Stanton said.

They set off, heaving the toboggan, with the Walker strapped to it so trussed in blankets that he was invisible, a thick human sausage. Will left last; Gwen handed him the torches and a flask. 'I must say I'm not sorry to see your discovery go,' she said. 'He frightens me. More like an animal than an old man.'

It seemed a long while before they reached the Manor gates. The drive had been cleared, and trodden down by many feet, and two bright pressure-lamps hung by the great door, lighting the front of the house. Snow was falling again, and the wind beginning to blow chill round their faces. Before Robin's outstretched hand reached the doorbell, Merriman was opening the door. He looked first for Will, though no one else noticed the urgent flicker of his eyes. 'Welcome,' he said.

'Evening,' Roger Stanton said. 'Shan't stay. We're fine at the house. But there's an old chap here who's ill, and he needs a doctor. All things considered, it seemed better to bring him here, rather than have Dr Armstrong going to and fro. So we hopped out before the storm broke.'

'It is rising already,' Merriman said, gazing out. Then he stooped and helped the twins carry the Walker's motionless swaddled form into the house. At the threshold the bundle of blankets jerked convulsively, and the Walker could be heard muffled through his covers shouting, 'No! No! No!'

'The doctor, please,' said Merriman to a woman standing near by, and she scurried away. The great empty hall where they had sung their carols was filled with people now, warm and bustling, unrecognizable.

Dr Armstrong appeared, nodding briskly all round; he was a small bustling man with a monkish fringe of grey hair circling his bald head. The Stantons, like all Huntercombe, knew him well; he had cured every ailment in the family for more years than Will had been alive. He peered at the Walker, now twisting and moaning in protest. 'What's this, eh?'

'Shock, perhaps?' said Merriman.

'He really behaves very oddly,' Mr Stanton said. 'He was found unconscious in the snow some days ago, and we thought he was recovering, but now –'

The big front door slammed itself shut in the rising wind, and the Walker screamed. 'Hum,' said the doctor, and beckoned two large young helpers to carry him off to some inner room. 'Leave him to me,' he said cheerfully. 'So far, we've got one broken leg and two sprained ankles. He'll provide variety.'

He trotted off after his patient. Will's father turned to peer out of a darkening window. 'My wife will start worrying,' he said. 'We must go.'

Merriman said gently, 'If you go now, I think you will leave but not arrive. Probably in a little while –'

'The Dark is rising, you see,' Will said.

His father looked at him with a half-smile. 'You're very poetic all of a sudden. All right, we'll wait just a bit. I could do with a breather, to tell the truth. Better say hallo to Miss Greythorne in the meantime. Where is she, Lyon?'

Merriman, the deferential butler, led the way into the crowd. It was the oddest gathering Will had ever seen. Suddenly half the village was living in close intimacy, a tiny colony of beds and suitcases and blankets. People hailed them from small nests scattered all round the huge room: a bed or a mattress tucked into a corner or fenced in by a chair or two. Miss Bell waved gaily from a sofa. It was like an untidy hotel with everyone camping in the foyer. Miss Greythorne was sitting stiff and upright in her wheelchair beside the fire, reading *The Phoenix and the Carpet* to a speechless group of village children. Like everyone else in the room, she looked uncommonly bright and cheerful.

'Funny,' Will said, as they picked their way through. 'Things are absolutely awful, and yet people look much happier than usual. Look at them all. Bubbling.'

'They are English,' Merriman said.

'Quite right,' said Will's father. 'Splendid in adversity, tedious when safe. Never content, in fact. We're an odd lot. You're not English, are you?' he said suddenly to Merriman, and Will was astonished to hear a slightly hostile note in his voice.

'A mongrel,' Merriman said blandly. 'It's a long story.' His deep-set eyes glittered down at Mr Stanton, and then Miss Greythorne caught sight of them all.

'Ah, there you are! Evenin', Mr Stanton, boys, how are you? What d'you think of this, eh? Isn't it a lark?' As she put down the book, the circle of children parted to admit the newcomers, and the twins and their father were absorbed into talk.

Merriman said softly to Will, in the Old Speech, 'Look into the fire, for the length of time that it takes you to trace the shape of each of the Great Signs with your right hand. Look into the fire. Make it your friend. Do not move your eyes for all that time.'

Wondering, Will moved forward as if to warm himself, and did as he was told. Staring at the leaping flames of the enormous log fire in the hearth, he ran his fingers gently over the Sign of Iron, the Sign of Bronze, the Sign of Wood, the Sign of Stone. He spoke to the fire, not as he had done long ago, when challenged to put it out, but as an Old One, out of Gramarye. He spoke to it of the red fire in the king's hall, of the blue fire dancing over the marshes, of the yellow fire lighted on the beacon hills for Beltane and Hallowe'en; of wild-fire and need-fire and the cold fire of the sea; of the sun and of the stars. The flames leaped. His fingers reached the end of their journey round the last Sign. He looked up. He looked, and he saw . . .

. . . he saw, not the genial muddle of collected villagers in a tall, panelled modern room, lit by electric standard lamps, but the great candle-shadowed stone hall, with its tapestry hangings and high vaulted roof, that he had seen once before, a world ago. He looked up from the log fire that was the same fire, but blazing now in a different hearth, and he saw as before, out of the past, the two heavy carved chairs, one on either side of the fireplace. In the chair on the right sat Merriman, cloaked, and in the chair on the left sat a figure whom he had last seen, not a day before, lying on a bier as if dead. He bent quickly and knelt at the old lady's feet. 'Madam,' he said.

She touched his hair gently. 'Will.'

'I am sorry for breaking the circle, that first time,' he said. 'Are you – well – now?'

'Everything is well,' she said in her soft clear voice. 'And will be, if we can win the last battle for the Signs.'

'What must I do?'

'Break the power of the cold. Stop the snow and cold and frost. Release this country from the hold of the Dark. All with the next of the circle, the Sign of Fire.'

Will looked at her helplessly. 'But I haven't got it. I don't know how.'

'One sign of fire you have with you already. The other waits. In its winning, you will break the cold. But before that, our own circle of flame must be completed, that is an echo of the Sign, and to do that you must take power away from the Dark.' She pointed to the great wrought-iron ring of candle-sockets on the table, the circle quartered by a cross. As she raised her arm, the light glinted on the rose ring on her hand. The outer ring of candles was complete, twelve white columns burning exactly as they had when Will was last in the hall. But the cross-arms still stood empty-socketed; nine holes gaped.

Will stared at them unhappily. This part of his quest left him in despair. Nine great enchanted candles, to come out of nowhere. Power to be seized from the Dark. A Sign that he had already, without knowing it. Another that he must find without knowing where or how.

'Have courage,' the old lady said. Her voice was faint and tired; when Will looked at her, he saw that she herself seemed faint in outline, as if she were no more than a shadow. He reached out his hand in concern, but she drew back her arm. 'Not yet . . . There is another kind of work to be done yet, too . . . You see how the candles burn, Will.' Her voice dwindled, then rallied. 'They will show you.'

Will looked at the brilliant candle flames; the tall ring of light held his eyes. As he looked, he felt a strange jolting sensation, as if the whole world had shuddered. He looked up, and he saw . . .

. . . and he saw, when he raised his eyes, that he was back in the manor of Miss Greythorne's time, Will Stanton's time, with the panelled walls and the murmur of many voices, and one voice speaking in his ear. It was Dr Armstrong.

'. . . asking for you,' he was saying. Mr Stanton was standing beside him. The doctor paused and looked oddly at Will. 'Are you all right, young man?'

'Yes – yes, I'm fine. Sorry. What was it you said?'

'I was saying that your old tramp friend is asking for you. "The seventh son", he lyrically puts it, though how he knew that I can't say.'

'I am though, aren't I?' Will said. 'I didn't know till the other day about the little brother who died. Tom.'

Dr Armstrong's eyes went a long way away for a moment. 'Tom,' he said. 'The first baby. I remember. That's a while ago.' His gaze came back. 'Yes, you are. So's your father, for that matter.'

Will's head jerked round, and he saw his father grin.

'You were a seventh son, Dad?'

'Certainly,' Roger Stanton said, his round pink face reminiscent. 'Half the family was killed in the last war, but there were twelve of us once. You knew that, didn't you? Proper tribe, it was. Your mother loved it, being an only child herself. I dare say that's why she had all you lot. Appalling, in this over-populated age. Yes, you're the seventh son of a seventh son — we used to joke about it when you were a baby. But not later on, in case you got ideas about having second sight, or whatever it is they say.'

'Ha, ha,' said Will with some effort. 'Did you find out what's wrong with the old tramp, Dr Armstrong?'

'To tell you the truth he has me rather confused,' the doctor said. 'He should have a sedative in his disturbed state, but he's got the lowest pulse rate and blood pressure I've ever come across in my life, so I don't know ... There's nothing physically wrong with him, so far as I can tell. Probably he's just feeble-minded, like so many of these old wanderers – not that you see many of them nowadays. They've nearly disappeared. Anyway, he keeps shouting to see you, Will, so if you can put up with it I'll take you in for a moment. He's harmless enough.'

The Walker was making a lot of noise. He stopped when he saw Will, and his eyes narrowed. His mood had clearly changed; he was confident again, the lined, triangular face bright. He looked over Will's shoulder at Mr Stanton and the doctor. 'Go away,' he said.

'Hum,' said Dr Armstrong, but he drew Will's father with him nearer the door, within sight but out of earshot. In the small cloakroom that was serving as sick-bay, one other casualty – the broken leg – lay in bed, but he appeared to be asleep.

'You can't keep me here,' the Walker hissed. 'The Rider will come for me.'

'You were scared stiff of the Rider once,' Will said. 'I saw you. Have you forgotten that too?'

'I forget nothing,' the Walker said scornfully. 'That fear is gone. It went when the Sign left me. Let me go, let me get out to my people.' A curious stiff formality seemed to be coming into his speech.

'Your people didn't mind leaving you to die in the snow,' Will said. 'Anyway I'm not keeping you here. I just had you brought to the doctor. You can hardly expect him to let you go out in the middle of a storm.'

'Then the Rider will come,' the old man said. His eyes glittered, and he raised his voice so that he was shrieking to everyone in the room. 'The Rider will come! The Rider will come!'

Will left him, as his father and the doctor came rapidly towards the bed.

'What on earth was all that about?' said Mr Stanton.

The Walker, with the doctor bending over him, had fallen back and lapsed into angry mumbling again.

'Goodness knows,' said Will. 'He was just talking nonsense. I think Dr Armstrong's right, he's a bit cracked.' He looked all round the room, but saw no sign of Merriman.

'What's happened to Mr Lyon?'

'He's somewhere,' his father said vaguely. 'Find the twins, would you, Will? I'll go and see if the storm's dropped enough to let us out yet.'

Will stood in the bustling hall, as people came and went with blankets and pillows, cups of tea, sandwiches from the kitchen, empty plates going back again. He felt odd, detached, as though he were suspended in the middle of this preoccupied world and yet not part of it. He looked at the great hearth. Even the roar of the flames could not drown out the howling wind outside, and the lash of icy snow against the window-panes.

The flames leapt, holding Will's eyes. From somewhere outside Time, Merriman said into his mind: '*Take care. It is true. The Rider will come for him. That is why I had you bring him here, to a place strengthened by Time. The Rider would have come to your own house otherwise, and all that comes with the Rider too . . .*'

'Will!' Miss Greythorne's imperious contralto came ringing. 'Come over here!' And Will looked back into the present, and went to her. He saw Robin beside her chair, and Paul approaching with a long flat box of a familiar shape in his hands.

'We thought we'd have a kind of concert until the wind drops,' said Miss Greythorne briskly. 'Everyone doin' a little bit. Everyone who fancies the idea, that is. A cailey, or whatever the Scots call 'em.'

Will looked at the happy gleam in his brother's eye. 'And Paul's going to play that old flute of yours that he likes so much.'

'In due course,' Paul said. 'And you're going to sing.'

'All right.' Will looked at Robin.

'I,' said Robin, 'am going to lead the applause. There'll be a lot of that – we appear to be a madly talented village. Miss Bell will recite a poem, three boys from the Dorney end have a folk group – two of them even brought their guitars. Old Mr Dewhurst will do a monologue, just try and stop him. Somebody's little daughter wants to dance. There's no end to it.'

'I thought, Will,' said Miss Greythorne, 'that perhaps you would begin. If you were just to start singing, you know, anything you like, then gradually people would stop to listen until there'd be a complete hush – much better than me ringin' a bell or something and saying, "We will all now have a concert", don't you agree?'

'I suppose so, yes,' said Will, though nothing could have been further from his mind at that moment than the idea of making peaceful music. He thought briefly, and into his mind came a melancholy little song that the school music master had transposed for his voice just the term before, as an experiment. Feeling rather a show-off, Will opened his mouth where he stood, and began to sing.

> 'White in the moon the long road lies,
> The moon stands blank above;
> White in the moon the long road lies
> That leads me from my love.
>
> Still hangs the edge without a gust,
> Still, still the shadows stay:
> My feet upon the moonlit dust
> Pursue the ceaseless way.'

The talking around him fell away into silence. He saw faces turned in his direction, and nearly dropped a note as he recognized some that he had hoped to see, but had not found before. There they were, keeping quietly in the background; Farmer Dawson, Old George, John Smith and his wife, the Old Ones ready again to make their circle if need be. Near by was the rest of the Dawson family, Will's father standing with them.

> 'The world is round, so travellers tell,
> And straight though reach the track,
> Trudge on, trudge on, 'twill all be well,
> The way will guide one back.'

From the corner of one eye he saw, with a shock, the figure of the Walker; with a blanket wrapped round him like a cloak, the old man was standing in the doorway of the little sickroom, listening. For an instant Will saw his face, and was astonished. All guile and terror were gone from that lined triangle; there was only sadness on it, and hopeless longing. There was even a glint of tears in the eyes. It was the face of a man shown something immensely precious that he had lost.

For a second, Will felt that with his music he could draw the Walker into the Light. He gazed at him as he sang, making the plaintive notes an appeal, and the Walker stood limp and unhappy, looking back.

> 'But ere the circle homeward hies
> Far, far must it remove;
> White in the moon the long road lies
> That leads me from my love.'

The room had stilled dramatically as he sang, and the boy's clear soprano that always seemed to belong to a stranger soared high and remote through the air. Now there was a small silence, the only part of performing that really meant anything to him, and afterwards quite a lot of clapping. Will heard it from a long way away. Miss Greythorne called to them all, 'We thought, to pass the time, that anyone who feels inclined might do a little entertainin'. To drown out the storm. Who'd like to join in?'

There was a cheerful buzz of voices, and Paul began to play the old Manor flute, very soft and low. Its gentle sweetness filled the room, and Will stood more confidently as he listened and thought of the Light. But in the next moment the music could no longer bring him strength. He could not hear it at all. His hair prickled, his bones ached; he knew that something, somebody was coming near, wishing ill to the Manor and all inside it, and most of all himself.

The wind rose. It whipped screeching at the window. There was a tremendous thump of a knock at the door. Across the room, the Walker jumped up, his face twisted again, tight with waiting. Paul played, unhearing. The crashing knock came again. None of them could hear, Will realized suddenly; though the wind was near to deafening him, it was not for their ears, nor would they know what was happening now. The crash came a third time, and he knew that he was bound to answer. He walked along through unheeding people to the door, took hold of the big iron circle that was the handle, muttered some words under his breath in the Old Speech, and flung open the door.

Snow spat in at him, sleet slashed his face, winds whistled through the hall. Out in the darkness, the great black horse reared up high over Will's head, hooves flailing, eyes rolling white, the foam flying from bared teeth. And above it gleamed the blue eyes of the Rider and the flaring red of his hair. In spite of himself Will cried out, and threw up one arm instinctively in self-defence.

And the black stallion screamed and fell back with the Rider into the Dark; and the door swung shut, and there was all at once nothing in Will's ears except the sweet lilt of the old flute as Paul played on. People sat and sprawled tranquilly about just as they had before. Slowly Will brought down his arm, still crooked defensively up over his head, and as he did so he noticed something that he had totally forgotten. On the underside of the forearm, which had been facing the Black Rider when he threw up his arm, was the burned-in scar of the Sign of Iron. In that other great hall, the first time, he had burned himself on the Sign when the Dark was making its first attempt on him. The Lady had healed the burn. Will had forgotten it was there. '*One sign of fire you have with you already . . .*'

So that was what she had meant.

One sign of fire had kept the Dark at bay; driven it out of its strongest attack, perhaps. Will leaned limply against the wall, and tried to breathe more slowly. But as he looked across the tranquil crowd listening to their music, he saw again a figure that sent all his confidence crashing into nothing, and the quick instinct of Gramarye told him that he had been tricked. He had thought he was out-facing a challenge, and so he was. But in doing it, he had opened the door between the Dark and the Walker, and thus in some way so strengthened the Walker that the old man had gained a power he had been waiting for.

For the Walker was standing tall now, his eyes bright, his head flung up, and his back straight. He held one arm high, and called out in a strong clear voice: 'Come wolf, come hound, come cat, come rat, come Held, come Holda, I call you in! Come Ura, come Tann, come Coll, come Quert, come Morra, come Master, I bring you in!'

The summons went on, a long list of names, all familiar to Will from the Book of Gramarye. In Miss Greythorne's hall, no one could see or hear; all went on as before, and through the ending of Paul's music, and the loud determined beginning of old Mr Dewhurst's monologue, no eyes that glanced in Will's direction seemed to see him. He wondered whether his father, still standing talking to the Dawsons, would shortly notice that his youngest son was not to be seen.

But very soon as the ringing summons from the Walker went on and on, he ceased to wonder, for under his senses the hall began subtly to change; the old hall of the Lady came back into his consciousness and absorbed more and more of the appearance of the present. Friends and family faded; only the Walker remained clear as before, standing now at the far end of the great hall away from the fire. And while Will still stared at the group in which his father stood, even while it faded he saw take place the doubling by which the Old Ones were able to move themselves in and out of Time. He saw one form of Frank Dawson step easily out of the first, leaving his other self to fade as part of the present; the second form grew clearer and clearer as it came towards him, and after it in the same way came Old George, Young John, and the blue-eyed woman, and Will knew this had been the manner of his own arrival too.

Soon the four were grouped round him in the centre of the Lady's hall, each facing outward, four corners of a square. And as the Walker called his long summons of the Dark, the hall itself began again to change. Strange lights and flames flickered along the walls, obscuring the windows and hangings. Here and there at the sound of a particular name, blue fire would dart up into the air, hiss, and die down again. On each of the three walls facing the hearth, three great sinister flames shot up which did not afterwards die down, but remained dancing and curving in ominous brilliance, filling the hall with cold light.

Before the hearth, in the big carved chair he had occupied from the beginning, Merriman sat motionless. There was a terrible restrained strength in his sitting; Will looked at the broad shoulders with foreboding, as he would have looked at a gigantic spring that might at any moment snap loose.

The Walker chanted louder: 'Come Uath, come Truith, come Eriu, come Loth! Come Heurgo, come Celmis, I bring you in . . .'

Merriman stood up, a great black white-plumed pillar. His cloak was wrapped round him. Only his carved-stone face was clear, with the light blazing in his mass of white hair. The Walker looked at him and faltered. Thick round the hall, the fires and flames of the Dark hissed and danced, all white and blue and black, with no gold or red or warm yellow in any. The nine tallest flames stood up like menacing trees.

But the Walker seemed to have lost his voice again. He looked once more at Merriman and shrank back a little. And through the mixture of longing and fear in the bright eyes, suddenly Will knew him.

'Hawkin,' Merriman said softly, 'there is still time to come home.'

The Hawk in the Dark

The Walker said in a whisper, 'No.'

'Hawkin,' Merriman said again, gently, 'every man has a last choice after the first, a chance of forgiveness. It is not too late. Turn. Come to the Light.'

The voice was scarcely audible, a mere husking breath. 'No.'

The flames hung still and stately round the great hall. No one moved.

'Hawkin,' Merriman said, and there was no command in the tone but only warmth and entreaty. 'Hawkin, liege man, turn away from the Dark. Try to remember. There was love and trust between us, once.'

The Walker stared at him like a doomed man, and now in the pointed, lined face Will could see clearly the traces of the small, bright man Hawkin, who had been brought forward out of his time for the retrieving of the Book of Gramarye, and had through the shock of facing death betrayed the Old Ones to the Dark. He remembered the pain that had been in Merriman's eyes as they watched that betrayal begin, and the terrible certainty with which he had contemplated Hawkin's doom.

The Walker still stared at Merriman, but his eyes did not see. They looked back through time, as the old man rediscovered all that he had forgotten, or pushed out of his mind. He said slowly, with mounting reproach, 'You made me risk my life for a book. For a book. Then because I looked at kinder masters, you sent me back to my own time, but not as I had been before. You gave me then the doom of bearing the Sign.' His voice grew stronger with pain and resentment as he remembered. 'The Sign of Bronze, through the centuries. You changed me from a man into a creature always running, always searching, always hunted. You stopped me from growing decently old in my own time, as all men after their lives grow old and tired and sink to sleep in death. You took away my right to death. You set me in my own century with the Sign, long, long ago, and you made me carry it through six hundred years until this age.'

His eyes flickered towards Will, and flashed with hatred. 'Until the last of the Old Ones should be born, to take the Sign from me. You, boy, it is all through you. This turning in time, that took away my good life as a man, it was all on your account. Before you were born, and after. For your damned gift of Gramarye, I lost everything I had ever loved.'

'I tell you,' Merriman cried out, 'you may come home, Hawkin! Now! It is the last chance, and you may turn to the Light and be as you were.' His proud, towering figure leaned forward, beseeching, and Will felt pain for him, knowing that he felt it was his own misjudgement that had brought his servant Hawkin into betrayal and the life of the wretched Walker, a whining shell committed to the Dark.

Merriman said huskily: 'I pray you, my son.'

'No,' the Walker said. 'I found better masters than you.' The nine flames of the Dark round the walls sprang cold and high and burned with a blue light, quivering. He clutched closer at the dark blanket wrapped round him, and stared wildly about the hall. Shrilly defiant, he shouted, 'Masters of the Dark, I bring you in!'

And the nine flames moved in closer from the walls to the centre of the room, approaching Will and the four outward-facing Old Ones. Will was blinded by their blue-white brilliance; he could no longer see the Walker. Somewhere beyond the great lights, the shrill voice shrieked on, high and mad with bitterness. 'You risked my life for the Book! You made me carry the Sign! You let the Dark hound me through the centuries, but never let me die! Now it is your turn!'

'Your turn! Your turn!' echoed the scream round the walls. The nine tall flames moved slowly closer, and the Old Ones stood in the centre of the floor and watched them approach. Beside the hearth Merriman turned slowly towards the centre of the room. Will saw that his face was impassive again, the deep eyes dark and empty and the lines drawn firm, and he knew that no one would see any strong self-revealing emotion on that face for a very long time. The Walker's chance to turn back to the mind and heart of Hawkin had come and been rejected, and now it was gone forever.

Merriman raised both his arms, and the cloak fell from them like wings. His deep voice whipped into the crackling silence: 'Stop!'

The nine flames paused, and hung.

'In the name of the Circle of Signs,' Merriman said, clear and firm, 'I command you to leave this house.'

The cold light of the Dark that was all around the hall behind the great standing flames flickered and crackled like laughter. And out of the blackness beyond, the voice of the Black Rider came.

'Your circle is not complete and has not that force,' he called mockingly. 'And your liege man has called us into this house, as he did before, and can again. *Our* liege man, my lord. The hawk is in the Dark . . . You can drive us from here no longer. Not with flame, nor force, nor conjoined power. We shall break your sign of Fire before it can be released, and your Circle will never be joined. It will break in the cold, my lord, in the Dark and the cold . . .'

Will shivered. It was growing cold indeed in the hall, very cold. The air was like a current of chill water, coming at them from all sides. The fire in the great hearth gave out no warmth now, no warmth that was not sucked in by the cold blue flames of the Dark all around. The nine flames quivered again, and as he looked at them, he could have sworn that they were not flames but gigantic icicles, blue-white as before but solid, menacing, great pillars ready to topple inward and crush them all with weight and cold.

'. . . cold . . .' said the Black Rider softly from the shadows, '. . . cold . . .'

Will looked at Merriman in alarm. He knew that each of them, every Old One in the room, had been thrusting against the Dark with every power he possessed since the Rider's voice began, and he knew that none of it had had any effect.

Merriman said softly, 'Hawkin lets them in, as he did in his first betrayal, and we cannot prevent that. He had my trust once, and it gives him still that power even though the trust is gone. Our only hope is what it was in the beginning: that Hawkin is no more than a man . . . When the spells of the deep cold are made, there is little that can be done against them.'

He stood frowning as the ring of blue-white fire flickered and danced; even he looked cold, with a dark pinched look round the bones of his face. 'They bring in the deep cold,' he said, half to himself. 'The cold of the void, of black space . . .'

And the cold grew more and more intense, cutting through the body to the mind. Yet the flames of the Dark seemed at the same time to grow dim, and Will realized that his own century was again fading in around them, and that they were back in Miss Greythorne's manor.

And the cold was there too.

Everything was changing now; the murmur of voices had dropped from a cheerful buzz to an anxious mutter, and the tall room was only dimly lit, by candles set in candlesticks and cups and plates, wherever there was space. All the bright electric lamps were dark, and the long metal radiators that warmed most of the room gave off no heat.

Merriman swooped bafflingly up near him with the speed of one returned from a brisk errand; his cloak was subtly different, changed to the sweeping overcoat he had worn earlier that day. He said to Miss Greythorne, 'There's not much we can do down there, ma'am. The furnace is out, of course. All the electric power lines are quite dead. So is the telephone. I have had all the house blankets and quilts brought out, and Miss Hampton is making quantities of soup and hot drinks.'

Miss Greythorne nodded in brisk approval. 'Good thing we kept the old gas stoves. They wanted me to change, y'know, Lyon, when we had the central heating done. I wouldn't, though. Electricity, bah – always knew the old house didn't approve.'

'I am having as much wood as possible brought in to keep the fire up,' Merriman said, but in the same instant, as if in mockery, a great hissing and steaming came from the broad fireplace, and those nearest it jerked away, choking and spluttering. Through the sudden inblown cloud of smoke Will could see Frank Dawson and Old George working to clear something out of the fire.

But the fire had gone out.

'Snow down the chimney!' Farmer Dawson called, coughing. 'We'll need buckets, Merry, quickly. There's a right mess here.'

'I'll go,' Will shouted, and bolted for the kitchen, glad of the chance to move. But before he could get to the door through the huddled groups of chilled, frightened people, a figure rose up before him to block his way, and two hands caught his arms in a grip so tight that he gasped in sudden pain. Bright eyes bored into his, glittering with wild triumph, and the Walker's high, thin voice was screeching in his ear.

'Old One, Old One, last of the Old Ones, you know what's going to happen to you? The cold is coming in, and the Dark will freeze you. Cold and stiff and all of you helpless. No one to protect the little Signs on your belt.'

'Let go!' Will twisted angrily, but the old man's hold on his wrist was the clasp of madness.

'And you know who will take the little Signs, Old One? I shall. The poor Walker, I shall wear them. They are promised to me in reward for my services – no lords of the Light ever offered me such reward. Or any other . . . I shall be the Sign-seeker, I shall, and all that would have been yours at the last shall come to me . . .'

He grabbed for Will's belt, his face twisted with triumph, spittle ringing his mouth like foam, and Will yelled for help. In an instant John Smith was at his side with Dr Armstrong close behind, and the big smith had pinned the Walker's clutching hands behind his back. The old man cursed and shrieked, his eyes burning with hatred at Will, and both men had to struggle to hold him back. At length they had him trapped and harmless, and Dr Armstrong drew back with an exasperated sigh.

'This chap must be the only warm object in the country,' he said. 'Of all times to run berserk – pulse or no pulse I'm going to put him to sleep for a while. He's a danger to the community and to himself.'

Will thought rubbing his sore wrist: if you only knew quite what sort of danger he is . . . Then suddenly he began to see what Merriman had meant. *Our only hope is what it was in the beginning: that Hawkin is no more than a man . . .*

'Keep him there, John, while I get my bag.' The doctor disappeared. John Smith, one big fist grasping the Walker's shoulder and the other both his wrists, winked encouragingly at Will and jerked his head to the kitchen; Will suddenly remembered his original errand, and ran. When he came tearing back with two empty buckets swinging from each hand, there was a fresh commotion at the fireplace; a new hissing had begun, smoke spewed out, and Frank Dawson came staggering backwards.

'Hopeless!' he said furiously. 'Hopeless! You get the hearth clear for a moment and more snow comes pouring down. And the cold –' He looked despairingly about him. 'Look at them, Will.'

The room was misery and chaos: small babies wailing, parents huddling their bodies round their children to keep them warm enough to breathe. Will rubbed his chill hands together, and tried to feel his feet and his face through the numbness of cold. The room was becoming colder and colder, and from the freezing world outside there was no sound even of the wind. The sense of being within two levels of Time at once still hovered in his mind, though all that he could feel now of the ancient manor was the awareness, ominous and persistent, of the nine great ice-candles glimmering round three sides of the room. They had been ghost-like, scarcely visible, when first he found himself brought back by the new cold to his own time, but as the cold grew more intense, so they were growing clearer. Will stared at them. He knew that somehow they embodied the power of the Dark at its Midwinter peak; yet he knew too that they were part of an independent magic harnessed by the Dark, which like so much else in their long battle could be taken away by the Light if only the right thing were done at the right time. How? *How?*

Dr Armstrong was coming back towards the sickroom with his black bag. Perhaps there might after all be one way, just one, of stopping the Dark before the cold could reach the point of destruction. One man, unwitting, giving help to another: this might be the one small event to turn aside all the supernatural force of the Dark . . . Will waited, suddenly taut with excitement. The doctor moved towards the Walker, who still cursed incoherently in John the Smith's grip, and he had slipped a needle deftly in and out of his arm before the old man knew what he was doing. 'There,' he said soothingly. 'That'll help you. Have a sleep.'

Instinctively Will moved forward in case there was need of help, and saw as he did so that Merriman and Farmer Dawson and Old George were drifting closer too. Doctor and patient were closed in by a ring of Old Ones, all round, protecting against interference.

The Walker caught sight of Will and snarled like a dog, showing broken, yellowing teeth. 'Freeze, you'll freeze,' he spat out at him, 'and the Signs will be mine, whatever . . . you try . . . whatever . . .' But he faltered and blinked, his voice dropping as the drug began to spread its drowsiness over him, and even as suspicion began to show in his eyes, the eyelids drooped. Each of the Old Ones took a step or two forward, tightening the circle. The old man blinked again, showing the whites of his eyes in a horrid flash, and then he was unconscious.

And with the mind of the Walker closed, the Dark's way into the house was closed too.

Instantly there was a difference in the room, a slackening of tension. The cold was less fierce, the unhappiness and alarm all round them like a fog began to lessen. Dr Armstrong straightened up, a questing, puzzled expression in his eyes; the eyes grew wider as he saw the circle of intent faces ringing him round. He began indignantly, 'What do – ?'

But the rest of the words were lost to Will, for all at once Merriman was calling them out of the crowd, urgently, silently, in the speech of the mind that men could not hear. '*The candles! The candles of the winter! Take them, before they fade!*'

The four Old Ones scattered hastily into the hall, where the strange blue-white cylinders still hung ghostly round the three walls, burning with their dead cold flames. Going swiftly to the candles, they grasped them, one in each hand; Will, smaller, leapt hastily on a chair to seize the last. It was cold and smooth and heavy to his touch, like ice that did not melt. In the moment that he touched it he was giddy; his head whirled . . .

. . . and he was back in the great hall of that earlier time with the other four, and beside the hearth the Lady was sitting in her high-backed chair again, with the smith's blue-eyed wife sitting at her feet.

It was clear what was to be done. Bearing the candles of the Dark, they advanced towards the great iron mandala-ring of holders on the massive table, and one by one fitted the candles into the nine sockets that still stood empty in the central cross-piece. Each candle changed subtly as it was put in place; its flame rose thinner and higher, taking on a golden-white tinge instead of the cold, threatening blue. Will, with his one candle, came last. He reached through to fit it into the last holder in the very centre of the pattern, and as he did so the flames of all the candles shot upwards in a triumphant circle of fire.

The old lady said, in her frail voice, 'There is the power seized from the Dark, Will Stanton. By cold magic they called up the candles of winter for destruction. But now that we have seized them for better purposes, the candles become stronger, able to bring you the Sign of Fire. See.'

They drew back, watching, and the last central candle that Will had put in place began to grow. When its flame stood high above the rest it took on colour, becoming yellow, orange, vermilion-red; as it still grew, it changed and became a strange flower on a strange stem. A curved, many-petalled blossom blazed there, each petal a different shade of the colours of flame; slowly and gracefully each petal opened and fell, floating away, melting into the air. And in the end, at the tip of the long curved stem of the flame-red plant, a glowing round seedpod was left, waving gently for a moment and then in a quick, silent burst breaking open, its five sides unfolding all at once like stiffer petals. Inside was a golden-red circle of a shape they all knew.

The Lady said: 'Take it, Will.'

Will took two wondering paces towards the table, and the great slender stalk bent over towards him; as he put out his hand, the golden circle fell into it. Instantly a surge of invisible power struck him, an echo of what he had felt at the destruction of the Book of Gramarye – and as he staggered and balanced himself again, he saw that the table was empty. In a flash of time, everything that was on it had vanished: the strange flower and the nine great blazing candles and the Sign-shaped iron holder that had contained them all. Gone. All gone: all except the Sign of Fire.

It was in his palm, warm to the touch, one of the most beautiful things he had ever seen. Gold of several different colours had been beaten together with great craftsmanship to make its crossed-circle shape, and on all sides it was set with tiny gems, rubies and emeralds and sapphires and diamonds, in strange runic patterns that looked oddly familiar to Will. It glittered and gleamed in his hand like all kinds of fire that ever were. Looking closer, he saw some words written very small around the outer edge:

LIHT MEC HEHT GEWYRCAN

Merriman said softly: 'The Light ordered that I should be made.'

They had all but one of the Signs now. Jubilantly Will flung up his arm into the air, holding the Sign high for the others to see; and from every light in the hall the circle of worked gold caught brilliance, flickering as if it were made of flame.

From somewhere outside the hall, there came a great crashing roar with a long wail of anger through it. The sound rumbled and growled and came crashing out again . . .

. . . and as it beat in his ears, suddenly Will was back again in Miss Greythorne's hall, with all around him the familiar village faces turned wondering to the roof, and to the grumbling roar beyond.

'Thunder?' someone said, puzzled.

Blue light flickered in all the windows, and the thunder slammed so earsplittingly close that everyone flinched. Again the light came, again the thudding roar, and somewhere a child began to weep, thin and high. But as all the crowded room waited for the next crash, there was nothing. No flash came, no thunder, not so much as a distant murmur. Instead, after a short breathless silence filled only by the hissing of the ashes in the hearth, there came a soft pattering sound outside, growing gently, gradually louder into an unmistakable slurred staccato against windows and doors and roof.

The same anonymous voice cried out joyfully, 'Rain!'

Voices broke out all round in excitement, grim faces beamed; figures rushed to peer out of the dark windows, beckoning to others in delight. An old man Will never recalled seeing in his life before turned to him with a toothless grin. 'Rain'll melt thic snow!' he piped. 'Melt 'n in no time at all!'

Robin appeared out of the crowd. 'Ah, there you are. Am I going loopy, or does this perishing room suddenly feel warm?'

'It's warmer,' said Will, pulling down his sweater. Beneath it, the Sign of Fire was now looped on his belt secure with the rest.

'Funny. It was so hideously cold for a while. I suppose they've got the central heating going again . . .'

'Let's see the rain!' A pair of boys dashed past them to the main door. But while they still fumbled with the handle, a series of quick, loud knocks came from outside; and there on the step, when the door opened, his hair flattened to his head by the soft, pouring rain, stood Max.

He was out of breath; they could see him urgently gulp air to make the words. 'Miss Greythorne there? My father?'

Will felt a hand on his shoulder and saw Merriman beside him, and knew from the concern in his eyes that in some way this was the next attack of the Dark. Max caught sight of him and came forward, rain running down his face; he shook himself like a dog.

'Get Dad, Will,' he said. 'And the doctor if he can be spared. Mum's had an accident, she fell downstairs. She's still unconscious, and we think she's got a broken leg.'

Mr Stanton had already heard; he dashed for the doctor's room. Will stared unhappily at Max. He called silently to Merriman, frightened, 'Did they do that? Did they? The Lady said –'

'It's possible,' said the answering voice in his mind. 'They cannot harm you, true, and they cannot destroy men. But they can encourage men's own instincts to do them harm. Or bring an unexpected clap of thunder, when someone is standing at the top of a flight of stairs . . .'

Will heard no more than that. He was out of the door with his father and brothers and Dr Armstrong, following Max home.

The King of Fire and Water

James still looked pale and distressed, even when the doctor was safely arrived and examining Mrs Stanton in the living-room. He drew aside his nearest brothers, who happened to be Paul and Will, and moved them out of earshot of the rest. He said unhappily, 'Mary's disappeared.'

'Disappeared?'

'Honestly. I told her not to go. I didn't think she would, I thought she'd be too scared.' Worry had sent stoical James close to tears.

'Go where?' said Paul sharply.

'Out to the Manor. It was after Max went to get you. Gwennie and Bar were in the living-room with Mum. Mary and I were in the kitchen making some tea, and she got all upset and said Max had been gone far too long and we ought to go and check whether anything had happened to him. I told her not to be so daft, of course we shouldn't go, but just then Gwen called me to go and make up the fire in there, and when I came back, Mary was gone. And so were her coat and boots.' He sniffed. 'I couldn't see any sign of where she'd gone, outside – the rain had started, and there weren't any footprints. I was just going to go out after her without saying anything, because the girls had enough to worry about, but then you came, and I thought she'd be with you. Only she wasn't. Oh, dear,' said James woefully. 'She is a silly ass.'

'Never mind,' Paul said. 'She can't have gone far. Just go and wait for a good moment to explain to Dad, and tell him I've gone out to pick her up. I'll take Will, we're both still dressed for it.'

'Good,' said Will, who had hastily been trying to think of arguments for his going.

When they were out in the rain again, the snow already beginning to squelch grey-white underfoot, Paul said, 'Don't you think it's time you told me what all this is about?'

'What?' said Will, astounded.

'What are you mixed up in?' Paul said, his pale blue eyes peering severely through the heavy spectacles.

'Nothing.'

'Look. If Mary's going off might have something to do with it, you've absolutely got to explain.'

'Oh dear,' Will said. He looked at Paul's threatening determination, and wondered how you explained to an elder brother that an eleven-year-old was no longer quite an eleven-year-old, but a creature subtly different from the human race, fighting for its survival . . .

You didn't, of course.

He said, 'It's these, I think.' Glancing cautiously about him, he tugged his jacket and sweater clear of his belt and showed Paul the Signs. 'They're antiques. Just buckle things that Mr Dawson gave me for my birthday, but they must be really valuable because two or three weird people keep on turning up trying to get hold of them. One man chased me in Huntercombe Lane once . . . and that old tramp was mixed up with them somehow. That was why I didn't want to bring him home, that day we found him in the snow.'

He thought how very improbable it all sounded.

'Mmm,' Paul said. 'And that fellow at the Manor, the new butler? Lyon, isn't it? Is he mixed up with these clowns?'

'Oh, no,' Will said hastily. 'He's a friend of mine.'

Paul looked at him for a moment, expressionless. Will thought of his patient understanding that night in the attic, at the beginning, and of the way he played the old flute and knew that if there were any one of his brothers that he could confide in, it would be Paul. But that was out of the question.

Paul said, 'Obviously you haven't told me the half of it, but that'll have to do. I take it you think these antique-chasers might have nobbled Mary as some sort of hostage?'

They had reached the end of the driveway. The rain beat down on them, hard yet not vicious; it ran down the snow-banks, poured from the trees, turned the road into the beginning of a rapidly moving stream. They looked up and down in vain. Will said, 'They must have. I mean, she'd have gone straight towards the Manor, so why didn't we see her on our way home?'

'We'll go that way anyway, to check.' Paul tilted his head suddenly and glared at the sky. 'This rain! It's ridiculous! Just suddenly, out of all that snow – and it's so much warmer too. Makes no sense.' He splashed off up the running stream that was Huntercombe Lane and glanced at Will with a baffled half-grin. 'But then a lot of things aren't making much sense to me at the moment.'

'Ah,' Will said. 'Um. No.' He splashed away noisily to cover his remorse, and peered through the sheets of rain for some sign of his sister. The noise round them was astonishing now: an ocean noise of spattering foam and washing shingle and breaking waves, as the wind brought the rain sluicing rhythmically through the trees. A most ancient noise, as if they stood on the edge of some great ocean before men or their ancestors were ever born. Up the road they went, peering and doggedly calling, anxious now; everything they saw became strange all over again, as the rain carved the snow into new lanes and hillocks. But when they came to one corner, Will knew suddenly very well where they were.

He saw Paul duck defensively behind one raised arm; heard the harsh, raucous croaking abruptly loud and then gone; saw, even through the flying rain, the flurry of black feathers as the gaggle of rooks swooped low past their heads.

Paul straightened slowly, staring. 'What on earth – ?'

'Get over the other side of the road,' Will said, pushing him firmly sideways. 'The rooks go sort of crazy sometimes. I've seen it before.'

Another shrieking swoop of birds came at Paul from behind, driving him forward, while the first dived again to force Will against the snowbank along the edge of the drift-buried wood. Again they came, and again. Will wondered, dodging, whether his brother had realized that they were being herded like sheep, driven where the rooks wanted them to go. But even as he wondered, he knew that he was too late. The grey sheet of rain had separated them entirely; he had no idea where Paul had gone.

He yelled in panic, 'Paul? Paul!'

But as the Old One in him took control, calming the fear he cut off the shout. This was not a matter for ordinary human beings, even of his own family; he should be glad to be alone. He knew now that Mary must be caught, somewhere, held by the Dark. Only he had any chance of getting her back. He stood in the driving rain, staring about him. The light was dying rapidly. Will unbuckled his belt and strapped it round his right wrist; then he said a word in the Old Speech and held up his arm, and from the Signs a steady pathway of light beamed out as from a torch. It shone on ruffled brown water, where the road was becoming a river, deeper and flowing fast.

He remembered that Merriman had said, long before, that the most dangerous peak of the Dark's power would come at Twelfth Night. Was that time now come? He had lost his place in the days, they ran into one another in his mind. Water washed at the edge of his boot as he stood wondering; he jumped hastily backwards to the snowbank edging the wood, and a brown wave in the road-river took a large bite out of the snow-wall on which he had been standing. In the light from the Signs, Will saw that now other chunks of dirty snow and ice bobbed in the water; as it flowed past, it was gradually undercutting the hard-packed banks left on either side by the snowplough, and carrying away broken pieces like miniature icebergs.

Other things were there in the water too. He saw a bucket bob past him, and a tufted object that looked like a sack of hay. The water must be rising high enough to carry things away from people's gardens – perhaps his own among them. How could it rise so fast? As if in answer, the rain hammered at his back, and more snow broke beneath his foot, and he remembered that the ground underneath him must still be frozen bone-hard by the great cold that had paralysed the land before the rain came. Nowhere would this rain be able to soak into the soil. The thawing of the land would take far longer than the melting of the snow – and in the meantime the snow-water had nowhere to go, no alternative but to run over the surface of the frozen countryside looking for a river to join. The floods will be dreadful, Will thought: worse than they've ever been before. Worse even than the cold . . .

But a voice broke in on him, a shout through the rushing water and roaring rain. He stumbled up over the slush-edged mounds of snow to peer through the murk. The shout came again. 'Will! Over here!'

'Paul?' Will called hopefully, but he knew it was not Paul's voice.

'Here! Over here!'

The shout came from the river-road itself, out in the dark. Will held up the Signs; their light beamed out over the churning water and showed him what he took at first for clouds of steam. Then he saw that the curling steam was the puffing of breath: great deep breaths, from a gigantic horse standing four-square in the water, small wild waves foaming past its knees. Will saw the broad head, the long chestnut mane plastered wet to the neck, and he knew that this was either Castor or Pollux, one of the two great shire horses from Dawsons' Farm.

The light from the Signs flicked higher; he saw Old George, muffled in black oilskins, perched high on the back of the massive horse.

'Over here, Will. Through the water, before it rises too fast. We have work to do. Come on!'

He had never heard Old George sound demanding before; this was the Old One, not the amiable old farm-hand. Leaning against the horse's neck, the old man urged it closer through the water. 'Come up, Polly, come by, Sir Pollux.' And big Pollux snorted puffs of steam through his broad nostrils and took a few solid paces forward so that Will was able to stumble out into the river-road and grasp at his tree-like leg. The water came almost to his thighs, but he was so wet from the rain already that it made little difference. There was no saddle on the great horse, only a sodden blanket; but with astonishing strength Old George leaned down and heaved at his hand, and with much struggling he was up. The light from the Signs strapped to his wrist did not waver through all the turning and twisting, but remained directed firmly forwards at the way they should go.

Will slipped and slithered on the broad back, too wide for his straddling. George tugged him to sit in front, astride the great curving neck. 'Polly's shoulders have taken greater weight than you,' he shouted in Will's ear. Then they were swaying forward as the stolid cart-horse lurched off again, splashing through the growing stream, away from the rooks' wood, away from the Stantons' house.

'Where are we going?' Will yelled, staring fearfully out at the darkness; he could see nothing anywhere, only the swirling water in the light of the Signs.

'We go to raise the Hunt,' the cracked old voice said close to his ear.

'The Hunt? What Hunt? George, I must find Mary, they've got Mary, somewhere. And I lost sight of Paul.'

'We go to raise the Hunt,' the voice at his back said steadily. 'I have seen Paul, he is safe on his way home by now. Mary you will find in due course. It is time for the Hunter, Will, the white horse must come to the Hunter, and you must take her there. This is the ordering of things, you have forgotten. The river is coming to the valley, and the white horse must come to the Hunter. And then we shall see what we shall see. We have work to do, Will.'

And the rain beat down on them harder, and somewhere distant thunder rumbled in the early night, as the huge shire horse Pollux splashed patiently on through the rising brown river that had once been Huntercombe Lane.

It was impossible to tell where they were. A wind was rising, and Will could hear the sounds of swaying trees above the steady churning of Pollux's feet. Scarcely a light showed in the village; he supposed that the electric power must still be cut off, either by accident or by agent of the Dark. In any case, most of the people of this part of the village were still at the Manor. 'Where's Merriman?' he called through the loud rain.

'At the Manor,' George shouted in his ear. 'With Farmer. Beset.'

'You mean they're trapped?' Will's voice turned shrill with alarm.

Old George said, hissing close, hard to hear, 'They hold attention, so we may work. And floods make them busy too. Look down, boy.'

In the churning water the light from the Signs showed a scatter of unlikely objects bobbing past: a wicker basket, several disintegrating cardboard boxes, a bright red candle, some tangled strands of ribbon. Suddenly Will recognized one piece of ribbon, a lurid purple and yellow check, as a wrapping he had seen Mary carefully pull off a parcel and roll up on Christmas Day. She was a great hoarder, like a squirrel; this had gone into her hoard.

'Those things are from our house, George!'

'Floods there too,' the old man said. 'Land's low. No danger though, be easy. Just water. And mud.'

Will knew he was right, but again he longed to see for himself. Rushing about, they would all be; moving furniture and rugs, clearing books and everything movable. These first floating objects must have escaped before anyone noticed the water was actually carrying things off . . .

Pollux stumbled for the first time, and Will clutched at the wet chestnut mane; for a moment he had almost slipped and been carried off himself. George made soothing noises, and the big horse sighed and snuffled through his nose. Will could see a few dim lights now that must come from the bigger houses on high ground at the end of the village; that meant they must be nearing the Common. If it was still the Common, and not a lake.

Something was changing. He blinked. The water seemed further away, harder to see. Then he realized that the light from the Signs linked on his wrist was growing dim, fading away to nothing; in a moment they were in darkness. As soon as all the light had died, Old George said softly: 'Whoa, Polly,' and the great shire horse splashed to a halt and stood there with the water rippling past his legs.

George said, 'This is where I have to leave you, Will.'

'Oh,' Will said, forlorn.

'There is the one instruction,' Old George said. 'That you are to take the white horse to the Hunter. That will happen, if you fall into no trouble. And there are two bits of advice to keep you from trouble, just from me to you. The first is that you will find enough light to see by if you stand for a count of a hundred after I am gone. The second is to remember what you know already, that moving water is free of magic.' He patted Will comfortingly on the shoulder. 'Put the Signs round your waist again now,' he said, 'and get down.'

It was a wet business getting down, worse than getting up; Pollux was so high from the ground that Will splashed into the water like a falling brick. Yet he felt no cold; though the rain beat at him still, it was gentle, and in some curious way it seemed to keep him from being chilled.

Old George said again, 'I go to gather the Hunt,' and with no other word of farewell he set Pollux splashing off again towards the Common, and was gone.

Will clambered up the snowbank beside the river-road, found space to stand without toppling, and began counting up to one hundred. Before he had reached seventy, he began to see what Old George had meant. Gradually, the dark world was taking on a glimmer of light from within itself. The rushing water, the pitted snow, the gaunt trees; he could see them all, in a grey dead light like dawn. And while he looked round, puzzling, something floating past him on the quick stream brought him such astonishment that he almost fell into the water again.

He saw the antlers first, turning lazily from side to side, as if the great head were nodding to itself. Then the colours showed, the bright blues and yellows and reds, just as he had first seen them on Christmas morning. He could not see the details of the strange face, the bird-like eyes, the pricked ears of the wolf. But it was his carnival head without a doubt, the inexplicable present that the old Jamaican had given Stephen to give to him, his most precious possession in the world.

Will let out a noise like a sob, and leapt forward desperately to seize it before the water carried it out of reach; but he slipped as he jumped, and by the time he had recovered his balance the bright grotesque head was bobbing out of sight. Will began to run along the bank; it was a thing of the Old Ones, and from Stephen, and he had lost it; he must at all costs get it back. But memory caught him in mid-stride, and he paused. 'The second thing,' Old George had said, 'is to remember that moving water is free of magic.' The head was in moving water, only too clearly. So long as it remained there, no one could harm it or use it for the wrong ends.

Reluctantly, Will put it out of his mind. The great open Common stretched before him, lit by a strange glimmer of its own. Nothing moved. Even the cattle that normally grazed there year round, looming up out of nowhere on misty days like solid ghosts, were away under cover now on the farms, driven off by the snow. Will moved on, carefully. Then the noise of the water that had been in his ears for so long began to change, growing louder, and before him the torrent filling Huntercombe Lane turned aside, joining a tiny local stream that had swollen now into a foaming river rushing over the Common and away. The road that had been the river-road wound on, unhindered, solid and gleaming; Old George, Will sensed, had gone that way. He would have liked to take the road too, but he felt that he was to stay with the river; through the extra sense of the Old Ones, he knew that it would show him how to take the white horse to the Hunter.

But who was the Hunter, and where was the white horse?

Will went gingerly forward, along the lumpy snowbank edging the new-swollen stream. Willows lined it, squat and pollarded. Then suddenly, out of the dark line of trees on the far side of the stream a white shape leapt. There was a glimmer of silver, in the darkness that was not quite dark, and in a spray of wet snow the great white mare of the Light was standing before Will, her breath clouding round the streaks of rain. She was tall as a tree, her mane blown wild by the wind.

Will touched her, gently. 'Will you carry me?' he said, in the Old Speech. 'As you did before?'

The wind spurted as he spoke, and bright lightning flashed jagged round the edge of the sky, closer than it had been. The white horse shuddered, her head jerking up. But she relaxed again almost at once, and Will too felt instinctively that this brewing thunderstorm was not a storm of the Dark. It was expected. It was part of what was to come. The Light was rising, before the Dark could rise.

He made sure the Signs were secure on his belt, and then as once before he reached up to wind his fingers in the long coarse hair of the white mane. Instantly his head spun in giddiness, and clear but far-off he heard his same music, bell-like and haunting, the same heart-catching phrase – till with a great jolt the world turned, the music vanished, and he was up on the back of the white mare, high among the willow trees.

Lightning was flickering all round the growling sky now. Muscles bunched in the tremendous back beneath Will, and he gripped the long mane as the horse leapt out across the Common, out over the hillocks and ravines of snow, its hooves grazing the surface to leave a wake of icy spray. Through the rush of the wind he thought, as he clung close to the mare's arched neck, that he could hear a strange, high yelping in the wind, like the sound of migrating geese flying high. The sound seemed to curve around them, and then to go on ahead, dying out of range.

The white horse leapt high; Will clung tighter as they rose over hedges, roads, walls, all emerging from the melting snow. Then a new noise louder than the wind or the thunder was in his ears, and he saw glinting ruffled black glass ahead of them and knew that they had come to the Thames.

The river was far wider than he had ever seen it here. For more than a week it had been shut tight and narrow by icy walls of overhanging snow; now it had broken loose, foaming and roaring, with great chunks of snow and ice tossing like icebergs. This was not a river, it was a fury of water. It hissed and howled, it was not reasonable. As he looked, Will was frightened as he had never been by the Thames; it was as wild as a thing of the Dark could be, out of his knowledge or control. Yet he knew it was not of the Dark, but beyond either Light or Dark, one of the ancient things from the beginning of Time. The ancient things: fire, water, stone . . . wood . . . and then, after the beginning of men, bronze, and iron . . . The river was loose, and would go according to its own will. '*The river will come to the valley* . . .' Merriman had said.

The white mare paused irresolute on the edge of the wild cold water, then surged forward and leapt. It was only as they rose over the churning river that Will saw the island, an island where none had been before in this swollen torrent, divided by strange glinting channels. He thought, as the white horse jolted him to earth again among bare dark trees: it's a hill really, a piece of high ground cut off by the water. And suddenly he knew very clearly that he would meet great danger here. This was his place of testing, this island that was not an island. Once more he looked up into the sky and silently, desperately called for Merriman; but Merriman did not come, and no word or sign from him came into Will's mind.

The storm was not breaking yet, and the wind had dropped a little; the noise of the river was louder than all else. The white mare bent her long neck and Will scrambled awkwardly down.

Through the mounded snow, sometimes ice-hard and sometimes soft enough to drop him thigh-deep, he set out to explore his strange island. He had thought it a circle, but it was shaped like an egg, its highest point at the end where the white mare stood. Trees grew round the foot; above them was an open, snowy slope; above that a cap of rough scrub dominated by a single gnarled, ancient beech tree. Out of the snow at the foot of this great tree, most perplexingly, four streams ran down over the hill-island, dividing it into four quarters. The white horse stood motionless. Thunder rumbled out of the flickering sky. Will climbed to the old beech tree, and stood watching the nearest spring foam out from beneath a huge snow-mounded root. And the singing began.

It was wordless; it came in the wind; it was a thin, high, cold whine with no definable tune or pattern. It came from a long way off, and it was not pleasant to hear. But it held him transfixed, turning his thoughts away from their proper direction, turning them away from everything except contemplation of whatever happened to be closest at hand. Will felt he was growing roots, like the tree above him. As he listened to the singing, he saw a twig on a low branch of the beech close to his head that seemed for no reason so totally enthralling that he could do nothing but gaze at it, as if it contained the whole world. He stared for so long, his eyes moving very gradually along the tiny twig and back again, that he felt as if several months had passed, while the high, strange singing went on and on in the sky from its distant beginnings. And then suddenly it stopped, and he was left standing dazed with his nose almost touching a very ordinary beech twig.

He knew then that the Dark had its own way of putting even an Old One outside Time for a space, if they needed a space for their own magic. For before him, next to the trunk of the great beech, stood Hawkin.

He was more recognizably Hawkin now, though still the Walker in age. Will felt that he was looking at two men in one. Hawkin was dressed still in his green velvet coat; it seemed still fresh, with the touch of white lace at the neck. But the figure within the coat was no longer neat and lithe, it was smaller, bent and shrunk by age. And the face was lined and battered beneath long, wisping grey hair; the centuries that had beaten at Hawkin had left only his sharp bright eyes unchanged. Those eyes looked at Will now with cold hostility, across the mounded snow.

'Your sister is here,' Hawkin said.

Will could not stop himself from glancing quickly round the island. But it was empty as before. He said coldly: 'She is not here. You're not going to catch me with a silly trick like that.'

The eyes narrowed. 'You are arrogant,' Hawkin hissed. 'You do not see all that is to be known in the world, Old One with the gift, and nor do your masters. Your sister Mary is here, in this place, though she is not to be seen by you. This is a meeting for the only bargain that my lord the Rider will make. Your sister for the Signs. You scarcely have much choice. You people are good at risking the lives of others' – the bitter old mouth curved up in a sneer – 'but I do not think Will Stanton would enjoy watching his sister die.'

Will said, 'I can't see her. I still don't believe she's here.'

Staring at him, Hawkin said to the empty air, 'Master?' And at once the high, wordless singing began again, catching Will back into the slow contemplation that was warm and relaxing as the summer sun, but at the same time horrible in its soft clutch of the mind. It changed him, while he was listening; made him forget the tension of fighting for the Light; submerged him, this time, in watching the way the shadows and hollows made patterns on a patch of snow near his feet. He stood there loose and relaxed, gazing at a point of white ice here, a hollow of darkness there, and the singing whined in his ears like the wind through chinks in a crumbling house.

And then again it stopped, and there was nothing, and Will saw with a shock like sudden cold that he was staring not at a pattern of mere shadows on snow, but at the lines and curves of his sister Mary's face. There she lay on the snow, in the clothes she had worn when he last saw her; alive and unharmed, but gazing blankly up at him without any sign that she recognized him or knew where she was. Indeed, Will thought unhappily, he did not know where she was either, for although he was being shown the appearance of her, it was most unlikely that she was really there lying on the snow. He moved to touch her, and as he expected she vanished completely away, and only the shadows lay on the snow as before.

'You see,' said Hawkin, unmoving beside the beech tree. 'There are some things that the Dark can do, many things, over which you and your masters have no control at all.'

'That's pretty obvious,' Will said. 'Otherwise there wouldn't be such a thing as the Dark, would there? We could just tell it to go away.'

Hawkin smiled, unruffled. He said softly, 'But it will never go away. Once it comes, it breaks all resistance into nothing. And the Dark will always come, my young friend, and always win. As you see, we have your sister. Now you will give me the Signs.'

'Give them to you?' Will said with scorn. 'To a worm who crawled to the other side? Never!'

He saw the fists clench briefly at the cuffs of the green velvet jacket. But this was an old, old Hawkin, not to be drawn; he had himself under control now that he was no longer the wandering Walker but part of the Dark. There was only a small catch of fury in the voice. 'You would do well to deal with the messenger of the Dark, boy. If you will not, you may call up more than you will wish to see.'

The sky flickered and rumbled, bringing a brief, bright light to the dark roaring water all round, the great tree peaking the tiny island, the bowed green-jacketed figure beside its trunk. Will said, 'You are a creature of the Dark. You chose betrayal. You are nothing. I will not deal with you.'

Hawkin's face twisted as he stared venomously at him; then he looked towards the dark empty Common and called: 'Master!' Then again, an angry shriek this time: 'Master!'

Will stood, tranquil, waiting. On the edge of the island he saw the white mare of the Light, almost invisible against the snow, raise her head and sniff the air, snorting softly. She looked once towards Will as if in communication; then wheeled round in the direction from which they had come, and galloped away.

Within seconds, something came. There was no sound, still, but the rushing river and the grumbling, looming storm. The thing that came was utterly silent. It was huge, a column of black mist like a tornado, whirling at enormous speed upright between the land and the sky. At either end it seemed broad and solid, but the centre wavered, grew slender and then thicker again; it wove to and fro as it came, in a kind of macabre dance. It was a hole in the world, this whirling black spectre; a piece of the eternal emptiness of the Dark made visible. As it came closer and closer to the island, bending and weaving, Will could not help backing away; every part of him shouted silently in alarm.

The black pillar swayed before him, covering the whole island. Its whirling, silent mist did not change, but parted, and standing within it was the Black Rider. He stood with the mist wreathing round his hands and head, and smiled at Will: a cold, mirthless smile, with the heavy bars of eyebrows furrowed and ominous above. He was all in black again, but the clothes were unexpectedly modern; he wore a heavy black donkey-jacket and rough, dark denim trousers.

Without a flicker in the chill smile he moved aside a little, and out of the snaking black mist of the column came his horse, the great black beast with fiery eyes, and on its back sat Mary.

'Hallo, Will,' Mary said cheerfully.

Will looked at her. 'Hallo.'

'I suppose you were looking for me,' Mary said. 'I hope nobody got worried. I only went for a little ride, just for a minute or two. I mean, when I went looking for Max, and then I met Mr Mitothin and found Dad had sent him to look for me, well, obviously it was all right. I had a lovely ride. It's a super horse ... and such a lovely day now ...'

The thunder rumbled, behind the massing grey-black cloud. Will shifted unhappily. The Rider, watching him, said loudly, 'Here's some sugar for the horse, Mary. I think he deserves it, don't you?' And he held out his hand, empty.

'Oh, thank you,' Mary said eagerly. She leaned forward over the horse's neck and took the imaginary sugar from the Rider's hand. Then she reached down beside the stallion's mouth, and the animal licked briefly at her palm. Mary beamed. 'There,' she said. 'Is that good?'

The Black Rider still gazed at Will, his smile widening a little. He opened his palm in mockery of Mary, and lying in it Will saw a small white box, made of an icy translucent glass, with lines of runic symbols engraved on the lid.

'Here I have her, Old One,' said the Rider, his nasal, accented voice softly triumphant. 'Caught by the marks of the Old Spell of Lir, that was written long ago on a certain ring and then lost. You should have looked more closely at your mother's ring, you and that simple craftsman your father, and Lyon your careless master. Careless . . . Under that spell I have your sister bound by totem magic, and yourself bound too, powerless to rescue her. See!'

He flicked the little box open, and Will saw lying in it a round, delicately-carved piece of wood, wound about with a fragile gold thread. With dismay he remembered the only ornament that had been missing from the Christmas collection carved by Farmer Dawson for the Stanton family, and the golden hair that Mr Mitothin, his father's visitor, had with casual courtesy flicked away from Mary's sleeve.

'A birth-sign and a hair of the head are excellent totems,' the Rider said. 'In the old days when we were all less sophisticated, you could, of course, work the magic even through the ground a man's foot had trod.'

'Or where his shadow had passed,' Will said.

'But the Dark casts no shadow,' the Rider said softly.

'And an Old One has no birth-sign,' said Will.

He saw uncertainty flicker over the intent white face. The Rider shut the white box and slipped it into his pocket. 'Nonsense,' he said curtly.

Will looked at him thoughtfully. He said, 'The masters of the Light do nothing without reason, Rider. Even though the reason may not be known for years and years. Eleven years ago Farmer Dawson of the Light carved a certain sign for me at my birth – and if he had made the sign with the letter of my name, as the tradition was, then perhaps you could have used it to trap me into your power. But he made it in the sign of the Light, a circle cut by a cross. And as you know well, the Dark can use nothing of that shape for its own purpose. It is forbidden.'

He looked up at the Rider. He said, 'I think you are trying to bluff me again, Mr Mitothin. Mr Mitothin, Black Rider of the black horse.'

The Rider scowled. 'Yet still you are powerless,' he said. 'For I have your sister. And you cannot save her except by giving me the Signs.' Malignance glittered again in his eyes. 'Your great and noble Book may have told you that I cannot harm those who are of the same blood as an Old One – but look at her. She will do anything that I suggest she should do. Even jump into this swollen

Thames. There are parts of the craft that you people neglect, you know. It is so simple to persuade folk into situations where they bring accidents upon themselves. Like your mother, for instance, so clumsy.'

He smiled again at Will. Will stared back, hating him; then he looked at Mary's happy sleeping-waking face and ached that she should be in such a place. He thought: and all because she's my sister. All because of me.

But a silent voice said into his mind: 'Not because of you. Because of the Light. Because of all that must always happen, to keep the Dark from rising.' And with a surge of joy Will knew that he was no longer alone; that because the Rider was abroad, Merriman was near by again too, free to give help if need be.

The Rider put out his hand. 'This is the time for your bargain, Will Stanton. Give me the Signs.'

Will took the deepest breath of his life, and let it out slowly. He said, 'No.'

Astonishment was an emotion that the Black Rider had forgotten long ago. The piercing blue eyes stared at Will in total disbelief. 'But you know what I shall do?'

'Yes,' Will said. 'I know. But I will not give you the Signs.'

For a long moment the Rider looked at him, out of the vast black pillar of swirling mist in which he stood; in his face incredulity and rage were mingled with a kind of evil respect. Then he swung round to the black horse and to Mary and called aloud some words in a language that Will guessed, from the chill they put into his bones, must be the spell-speech of the Dark, seldom used aloud. The great horse tossed his head, white teeth flashing, and bounded forward, with happy witless Mary clutching his mane and gurgling with laughter. He came to the overhanging snowbank that bordered the river, and paused.

Will clenched the Signs on his belt, agonized by the risk he was taking, and with all his might summoned the power of the Light to come to his aid.

The black horse gave a shrill, shrieking whinny and leapt high into the air over the Thames. Half-way through his leap he twisted strangely, bucking in the air, and Mary screamed in terror, grabbing wildly at his neck. But her balance was gone, and she fell. Will thought he would faint as she turned through the air, his risk bursting into disaster; but instead of splashing into the river, she fell into the soft wet snow at its brink. The Black Rider cursed savagely, lunging forward. He never reached her. Before he was in mid-stride, a great arrow of lightning came from the storm amassed now almost overhead, and a gigantic crack of thunder, and out of the flash and the roar a blazing white streak rushed over the island towards Mary, catching her up so that in an instant she was gone, seized away, safe. Will hardly managed to get a glimpse of Merriman's lean form, cloaked and hooded, on the white mare of the Light, with Mary's blonde hair flying where he held her. Then the storm broke, and the whole world whirled flaming round his head.

The earth rocked. He saw for an instant Windsor Castle outlined black against a white sky. Lightning seared his eyes, thunder beat at his head. Then through the singing in his dazed ears he heard a strange creaking and crackling close by. He swung round. Behind him, the great beech tree was cleft down the middle, blazing with great flames, and he realized with amazement that the eager current of the island's four streams was growing less and less, dwindling down to nothing. He looked up fearfully for the black column of the Dark, but it was nowhere to be seen in the raging storm, and the strangeness of all else that was happening drove the thought of it out of Will's head.

For it was not only the tree that had been split and broken. The island itself was changing, breaking open, sinking towards the river. Will stared speechless, standing now on an edge of snow-mounded land left by the vanished streams, while around him snow and land slid and crumpled into the roaring Thames. Above him, he saw the strangest thing of all. Something was emerging out of the island, as the land and snow fell away. There came first, from what had been the taller end of the island, the roughly shaped head of a stag, antlers held high. It was golden, glinting even in that dim light. More came into sight; Will could see the whole stag now, a beautiful golden image, prancing. Then came a curious curved pedestal on which it stood, as if to leap away; then behind this a long, long horizontal shape, as long as the island, rising again at the other end to another high, gold-glinting point, tipped this time by a kind of scroll. And suddenly Will realized that he was looking at a ship. The pedestal was its high curving prow, and the stag its figurehead.

Astounded, he moved towards it, and imperceptibly the river moved after him, until there was nothing left of the island but the long-ship on a last circle of land, with a last rearing snowdrift all around it. Will stood staring. He had never seen such a ship. The long timbers of which it was built overlapped one another like the boards of a fence, heavy and broad; they looked like oak. He could see no mast. Instead there were places for row upon row of oarsmen, up and down the whole length of the vessel. In the centre was a kind of deckhouse that made the ship look almost like a Noah's Ark. It was not a closed structure; its sides seemed to have been cut away, leaving the corner beams and roof like a canopy. And inside, beneath the canopy, a king lay.

Will drew back a little at the sight of him. The mailed figure lay very still, with sword and shield at his side, and treasure piled round him in glittering mounds. He wore no crown. Instead a great engraved helmet covered the head and most of the face, crested by a heavy silver image of a long-snouted animal that Will thought must be a wild boar. But even without a crown this was clearly the body of a king. No lesser man could have merited the silver dishes and jewelled purses, the great shield of bronze and iron, the ornate scabbard, the gold-rimmed drinking-horns, and the heaps of ornaments. On an impulse Will knelt down in the snow and bowed his head in respect. As he looked up again, rising, he saw over the gunwale of the ship something he had not noticed before.

The king was holding something in his hands, where they lay tranquilly folded on his breast. It was another ornament, small and glittering. And as Will saw it more closely, he stood still as stone, gripping the high, oaken edge of the ship. The ornament in the quiet hands of the long-ship king was shaped as a circle, quartered by a cross. It was wrought of iridescent glass, engraved with serpents and eels and fishes, waves and clouds and things of the sea. It called silently to Will. It was without any question the Sign of Water: the last of the Six Great Signs.

Will scrambled over the side of the great ship and approached the king. He had to take care where his feet moved, or he would have crushed fine work of engraved leather and woven robes, and jewellery of enamels and cloisonné and filigree gold. He stood looking down for a moment at the white face half-hidden by the ornate helmet, and then he reached reverently across to take the Sign. But first he had to touch the hand of the dead king, and it was colder than any stone. Will flinched and drew back, hesitating.

Merriman's voice said softly, from close by, 'Do not fear him.'

Will swallowed. 'But – he's dead.'

'He has lain here in his burial-ground for fifteen hundred years, waiting. On any other night of the year he would not be here at all, he would be dust. Yes, Will, this appearance of him is dead. The rest of him has gone out beyond Time, long since.'

'But it's wrong to take tribute away from the dead.'

'It is the Sign. If it had not been the Sign, and destined for you the Sign-seeker, he would not be here to give it to you. Take it.'

So Will leaned across the bier and took the Sign of Water from the loose grip of the dead cold hands, and from somewhere far off a murmur of his music whispered in his ears and then was gone. He turned to the side of the ship. There beside it was Merriman, sitting on the white mare; he was cloaked in dark blue, with his wild white hair uncovered; the hollows of his bony face were dark with strain, but delight gleamed in his eyes.

'It was well done, Will,' he said.

Will was gazing at the Sign in his hands. The sheen over it was the iridescence of all mother-of-pearl, all rainbows; the light danced on it as it danced on water, 'It's beautiful,' he said. Rather reluctantly he loosened the end of the belt and slipped the Sign of Water on, to lie next to the glimmering Sign of Fire.

'It is one of the oldest,' Merriman said. 'And the most powerful. Now that you have it, they lose their power over Mary forever – that spell is dead. Come, we must go.'

Concern sharpened his voice; he had seen Will grasp hastily at a beam as the long ship, suddenly, unexpectedly lurched to one side. It rose upright, swayed a little, then tipped in the opposite direction. Will saw, scrambling for the side, that the Thames had risen still further while he was not watching. Water lapped round the great ship, and had it almost afloat. Not for long now would the dead king rest on the land that had once been an island.

The mare wheeled towards him, snuffling a greeting, and in the same enchanted, music-haunted moment as before Will was up on the white horse of the Light, sitting in front of Merriman. The ship tilted and swung, fully afloat now and the white horse wheeled out of its way to stand near by, watching, the river-water foaming round its sturdy legs.

Creaking and rattling, the long ship gave itself to the rush of the swollen Thames. It was too large a vessel to be overwhelmed; its weight kept it steady even on that swirling water, once it had found a balance. So the mysterious dead king lay in dignity still, among his weapons and gleaming tribute, and Will had a last glimpse of the mask-like white face as the great ship moved away downstream.

He said over his shoulder, 'Who was he?'

There was grave respect on Merriman's face as he watched the long-ship go. 'An English king, of the Dark Ages. I think we will not use his name. The Dark Ages were rightly named, a shadowy time for the world, when the Black Riders rode unhindered over all our land. Only the Old Ones and a few noble brave men like this one kept the Light alive.'

'And he was buried in a ship, like the Vikings.' Will was watching the light glimmer on the golden stag of the prow.

'He was part Viking himself,' Merriman said. 'There were three great ship-burials near this Thames of yours, in days past. One was dug up in the last century near Taplow, and destroyed in the process. One was this ship of the Light, not destined ever to be found by men. And one was the greatest ship, of the greatest king of all, and this they have not found and perhaps never will. It lies in peace.' He stopped abruptly, and at a movement of his hand the white horse turned, ready to leap away from the river to the south.

But Will was still straining to watch the long-ship, and something of his tension seemed to infect both horse and master. They paused. In that moment, an extraordinary streak of blue light came hurtling out of the east, not from the thundering sky but from somewhere across the Common. It struck the ship. A great silent rush of flame burst there, over the broad river and its craggy white banks, and from prow to stern the king's ship was outlined by leaping fire. Will gave a choking wordless cry, and the white horse stirred uneasily, pawing at the snow.

Behind Will, Merriman's strong deep voice said, 'They vent their spite, because they know they are too late. Very easy it is, now and again, to predict what the Dark will do.'

Will said, 'But the king, and all his beautiful things –'

'If the Rider paused for thought, Will, he would have known that his outburst of malice has done no more than create a right and proper ending for this great ship. When this king's father died, he was laid in a ship in the same way, with all his most splendid possessions round him, but the ship was not buried. That was not the way. The king's men set fire to it and sent it off burning alone over the sea, a tremendous sailing pyre. And that, look, is what our King of the Last Sign is doing now: sailing in fire and water to his long rest, down the greatest river of England, towards the sea.'

'And good rest to him,' Will said softly, turning his eyes at last from the leaping flames. But for a long time afterwards, wherever they went, they could see the glow from the blazing long-ship whitening a part of the storm-dark sky.

The Hunt Rides

'Come,' Merriman said, 'we must lose no more time!' And the white mare wheeled them round away from the river and rose into the air, skimming the foaming water, crossing the Thames to the side that is the end of Buckinghamshire, the beginning of Berkshire. She leapt with desperate speed, yet still Merriman urged her on. Will knew why. He had glimpsed, through the flowing folds of Merriman's blue cloak, the great black tornado-column of the Dark gathered again even larger than before, bridging earth and sky, whirling silently in the glow of the burning ship. It was following them, and it was moving very fast.

A wind came up out of the east and lashed at them; the cloak blew forward round Will, enfolding him, as if he and Merriman were shut in a great blue tent.

'This is the peak of it all,' Merriman shouted into his ear, shouting his loudest, but still scarcely to be heard over the rising howl of the wind. 'You have the Six Signs, but they are not yet joined. If the Dark can take you now, they take all that they need to rise to power. Now they will try hardest of all.'

On they galloped, past houses and shops and unwitting people fighting the floods; past roofs and chimneys, over hedges, across fields, through trees, never far from the ground. The great black column pursued them, rushing on the wind, and in it and through it rode the Black Rider on his fire-jawed black horse, spurring after them, with the Lords of the Dark riding at his shoulder like a spinning dark cloud themselves.

The white mare rose again, and Will looked down. Trees were everywhere below them now; great single spreading oaks and beeches in open fields, and then tight-growing woods split by long straight avenues. Surely they were galloping down one such avenue now, past brooding snow-weighed fir trees, and out again into open land . . . Lightning flashed at his left side, leaping in the depths of a huge cloud, and in its light he saw the dark mass of Windsor Castle looming high and close. He thought: if that's the castle, we must be in the Great Park.

He began to feel, too, that they were no longer alone. Twice already he had heard again that strange, high yelping in the sky, but now there was more. Beings of his own kind were about here, somewhere, in the tree-thronged Park. And he felt, too, that the grey-massed sky was no longer empty of life, but peopled with creatures neither of the Dark nor of the Light, moving to and fro, clustering and separating, holding great power . . . The white mare was down in the snow again now, the hooves pounding over drift and slush and icy paths, more deliberately than before. All at once Will realized that she was not responding to Merriman, as he had thought, but following some profound impulse of her own.

Lightning flickered again round them, and the sky roared. Merriman said beside his ear: 'Do you know Herne's Oak?'

'Yes, of course,' Will said at once. He had known the local legend all his life. 'Is that where we are? The big oak tree in the Great Park where –'

He swallowed. How could he not have thought of it? Why had Gramarye taught him everything but this? He went on, slowly, '– where Herne the

Hunter is supposed to ride on the eve of Twelfth Night?' Then he looked round fearfully at Merriman. 'Herne?'

'*I go to gather the Hunt,*' Old George had said.

Merriman said, 'Of course. Tonight the Hunt rides. And because you have played your part well, tonight for the first time in more than a thousand years the Hunt will have a quarry.'

The white mare slowed, sniffing the air. Winds were breaking the sky apart; a half-moon sailed high through the clouds, then vanished again. Lightning danced in six places at once, the clouds roared and growled. The black pillar of the Dark came hurtling towards them, then paused, spinning and undulating, hovering between land and sky. Merriman said, 'An Old Way rings the Great Park, the way through Hunter's Combe. They will take a little while to find their path past that.'

Will was straining to see ahead through the murk. In the intermittent light he could make out the shape of a solitary oak tree, spreading great arms from its short tremendous trunk. Unlike most other trees in sight, it bore not the smallest remnant of snow; and a shadow stood beside its trunk, the size of a man.

The white mare saw the shadow at the same time. She blew hard through her nose, and pawed the ground.

Will said to himself, very softly, '*The white horse must go to the Hunter . . .*' Merriman touched him on the shoulder, and with swift enchanted ease they slid down to the ground. The mare bent her head to them, and Will laid his hand on the tough-smooth white neck. 'Go, my friend,' Merriman said, and the horse swung about and trotted eagerly towards the huge, solitary oak tree and the mysterious shadow motionless beneath. The creature who owned that shadow was of immense power; Will flinched before the sense of it. The moon went behind the clouds again; for a while there was no lightning; in the gloom they could see nothing move beneath the tree. One sound came through the darkness: a whinny of greeting from the white mare.

As if in counterpoint, a deeper, snuffling whinny came out of the trees beside them; as Will swung round, the moon sailed clear of cloud again, and he saw the huge silhouette of Pollux, the shire horse from Dawsons' Farm, with Old George high on his back.

'Your sister is at home, boy,' Old George said. 'She got lost, you know, and fell asleep in an old barn, and had such a curious dream that she is already forgetting . . .'

Will nodded gratefully and smiled; but he was gazing at a curious rounded shape, muffled by wrapping, that George held before him. 'What's that?' His neck was tingling even from being close to it, whatever it was.

Old George did not answer; he leant down to Merriman. 'Is all well?'

'All goes well,' Merriman said. He shivered, and drew his long cloak round him. 'Give it to the boy.'

He looked hard at Will out of his inscrutable deepset eyes, and Will, wondering, went towards the cart-horse and stood at George's knee, looking up. With a quick mirthless grin that seemed to mask great strain, the old man lowered the shadowed burden towards him. It was half as large as Will himself, though not heavy; it was wrapped in sacking. As he laid hands on it, Will knew instantly what it was. It can't be, he thought incredulously; what would be the point?

Thunder rumbled again, all around.

Merriman's voice said, deep in the shadows behind him, 'But of course it is. The water brought it, in safety. Then the Old Ones took it from the water at the proper time.'

'And now,' Old George said, from his place high on patient Pollux, 'you must take it to the hunter, young Old One.'

Will swallowed nervously. An Old One had nothing in the world to fear, nothing. Yet there had been something so strange and awesome about that shadowy figure beneath the giant oak, something that made one feel unnecessary, insignificant, small . . .

He straightened. Unnecessary was the wrong word, at any rate; he had a task to perform. Raising his burden like a standard, he pulled away its covering, and the bright, eerie carnival head that was half-man, half-beast emerged as smooth and gay as if it had just arrived from its distant island. The antlers stood up proudly; he saw that they were exactly the shape of those on the golden stag, the figurehead to the dead king's ship. Holding the mask before him, he walked firmly towards the deep shadow of the broad-spreading oak. At its edge, he paused. He could see a glimmer of white from the mare, moving gently in recognition; he could see that the mare had a rider. But that was all.

The figure on the horse bent down towards him. He did not see the face, but only felt the mask lifted from his hands – and his hands fell back as if they had been relieved of a great weight, even though the head had from the beginning seemed so light. He backed away. The moon came sailing suddenly out from behind a cloud, and for a moment his eyes dazzled as he looked full into its cold white light; then it was gone again, and the white horse was moving out of the shadow, with the figure on its back changed in outline against the dim-lit sky. The rider had a head now that was bigger than the head of a man and horned with the antlers of a stag. And the white mare, bearing this monstrous stag-man, was moving inexorably towards Will.

He stood, waiting, until the great horse came close; its nose gently touched his shoulder, once, for the last time. The figure of the Hunter towered over him. The moonlight now glimmered clear on his head, and Will found himself gazing up into strange tawny eyes, yellow-gold, unfathomable, like the eyes of some huge bird. He gazed into the Hunter's eyes, and he heard in the sky that strange high yelping begin again; with the difficulty of escaping an enchantment, he dragged his gaze aside to look properly at the head, the great horned mask that he had given the Hunter to put on.

But the head was real.

The golden eyes blinked, feather-fringed and round, with the deliberate blink of an owl's strong eyelids; the man's face in which they were set was turned full on Will, and the firm-carved mouth above the soft beard parted in a quick smile. That mouth troubled Will; it was not the mouth of an Old One. It could smile in friendship, but there were other lines round it as well. Where Merriman's face was marked with lines of sadness and anger, the Hunter's told instead of cruelty, and a pitiless impulse to revenge. Indeed he was half-beast. The dark branches of Herne's antlers curved up over Will, the moonlight glinting on their velvety sheen, and the Hunter laughed softly. He looked down at Will out of his yellow eyes, in the face that was no longer a mask but living, and he spoke in a voice like a tenor bell. 'The Signs, Old One,' he said. 'Show me the Signs.'

Without taking his eyes from the towering figure, Will fumbled with his buckle and held the six quartered circles high in the moonlight. The Hunter looked at them and bent his head. When he raised it again, slowly, the soft voice was half-singing, half-chanting words that Will had heard before.

> 'When the Dark comes rising, six shall turn it back;
> Three from the circle, three from the track;
> Wood, bronze, iron; water, fire, stone;
> Five will return, and one go alone.
>
> Iron for the birthday, bronze carried long;
> Wood from the burning, stone out of song;
> Fire in the candle-ring, water from the thaw;
> Six Signs the circle, and the grail gone before.'

But he too did not end where Will expected him to; he went on.

> 'Fire on the mountain shall find the harp of gold
> Played to wake the Sleepers, oldest of the old;
> Power from the green witch, lost beneath the sea;
> All shall find the light at last, silver on the tree.'

The yellow eyes looked at Will again, but they did not see him now; they had grown cold, abstracted, a chill fire mounting in them that brought the cruel lines back to the face. But Will saw the cruelty now as the fierce inevitability of nature. It was not from malice that the Light and the servants of the Light would ever hound the Dark, but from the nature of things.

Herne the Hunter wheeled round on the great white horse, away from Will and the single oak tree, until his fearsome silhouette was in the open, under the moon and the still-lowering stormclouds. He raised his head, and he made to the sky a call that was like the halloo blown by a huntsman on the horn to call up hounds. The hunting horn of his voice seemed to grow and grow, and to fill the sky and come from a thousand throats at once.

And Will saw that this it did, for from every point of the Park, behind every shadow or tree and out of every cloud, leaping round the ground and through the air, came an endless pack of hounds, sounding, belling as hunting dogs do when they are starting after a scent. They were huge white animals, ghostly in the half-light, loping and jostling and bounding together; they paid not the least attention to the Old Ones or to anything but Herne on his white horse. Their ears were red, their eyes were red; they were ugly creatures. Will drew back involuntarily as they passed, and one great silvery dog broke stride to glance at him with as casual a curiosity as if he had been a fallen branch. The red eyes in the white head were like flames, and the red ears stood taut upright with a dreadful eagerness, so that Will tried not to imagine what it would be like to be hunted by such dogs.

Round Herne and the white mare they bayed and belled, a heaving sea of red-flecked foam; then all at once the antlered man stiffened, his great horns pointing as a hunting dog points, and he called the hounds together with the rapid urgent collecting-call, the *menée*, that sends a pack after blood. A bedlam of yelping urgency rose from the milling white dogs, filling the sky, and at the same moment the full strength of the thunderstorm erupted. Clouds split roaring into bright, jagged lightning as Herne and the white horse leapt exultantly up into the arena of the sky, with the red-eyed hounds pouring up into the stormy air after them in a great white flood.

But then a sudden terrible silence like suffocation came, blotting out all sound of the storm. In the moment of its last desperate chance, breaking across the barrier that had been holding it at bay, the Dark came for Will. Shutting out the sky and the earth, the deadly spinning pillar came at him, dreadful in its furious whirling energy and utter quiet. There was no time for fear. Will stood alone. And the towering black column rushed to engulf him with all the monstrous forces of the Dark arrayed in its writhing mist, and at its centre the great foam-mouthed black stallion reared up with the Black Rider, his eyes two brilliant points of blue fire. Will called vainly on every spell of defence at his command, yet knew that his hands were powerless to move to the Signs for help. He stood where he was, despairing, and closed his eyes.

But into the dead, world-muffling silence enwrapping him, one small sound came. It was the same strange high whickering far up in the sky, like the passing of many migrant geese on an autumn night, that he had heard three times that day. Nearer, louder it grew, opening his eyes. And he saw then a scene like nothing he had ever seen before, nor ever saw again. Half the sky was thick and dreadful with the silent raging of the Dark and its whirling tornado power; but now riding down towards it, out of the west with the speed of dropping stones, came Herne and the Wild Hunt. At the peak of their power now, in full cry, they came roaring out of the great dark thundercloud, through streaking lightning and grey-purple clouds, riding on the storm. The yellow-eyed antlered man rode laughing dreadfully, crying out the *avaunt* that rallies hounds on the full chase, and his brilliant, white-gold horse flung forward with mane and tail flying.

And around them and endlessly behind them like a broad white river poured the Yell Hounds, the Yelpers, the Hounds of Doom, their red eyes burning with a thousand warning flames. The sky was white with them; they filled the western horizon; and still they came, unending. At the sound of their bell-like, thousand-tongued yelping, the magnificence of the Dark flinched and swayed and seemed to tremble. Will caught sight of the Black Rider once more, high in the dark mist; his face was twisted in fury and dread and frozen malevolence, and behind these the awareness of defeat. He spun his horse so fiercely round that the lithe black stallion tottered and almost fell. As he jerked at the rein, the Rider seemed to cast something impatiently from his saddle, a small dark object that fell limp and loose to the ground, and lay there like a discarded cloak.

Then the storm and the rushing Wild Hunt were upon the Rider. He rode up into his whirling black refuge. The fantastic tornado-pillar of the Dark curved and twisted, lashed like a snake in agony, until finally there was a great shriek in the heavens, and it began rushing at furious speed northward. Over the Park and the Common and Hunter's Combe it fled, and after it went Herne and the Hunt in full cry, a long white crest on the surge of the storm.

The yelping of the hounds died with distance, fading last of all the sounds of the chase, and above Herne's Oak the silver half-moon was left floating in a sky flecked with small ragged remnants of cloud.

Will drew a long breath, and looked round. Merriman stood exactly as he had last seen him, tall and straight, hooded, a dark featureless statue. Old George had drawn Pollux back into the trees, for no normal animal could have faced the Hunt so close and survived.

Will said, 'Is it over?'

'More or less,' Merriman said, faceless under the hood.

'The Dark – is –' He dared not bring out the words.

'The Dark is vanquished, at last, in this encounter. Nothing may outface the Wild Hunt. And Herne and his hounds hunt their quarry as far as they may, to the very ends of the earth. So at the ends of the earth the Lords of the Dark must skulk now, awaiting their next time of chance. But for the next time, we are this much stronger, by the completed Circle and the Six Signs and the Gift of Gramarye. We are made stronger by your completed quest, Will Stanton, and closer to gaining the last victory, at the very end.' He pushed back his broad hood, the wild white hair glinting in the moonlight, and for a moment the shadowed eyes looked into Will's with a communication of pride that made Will's face warm with pleasure. Then Merriman looked out across the dappled, snow-mounded grassland of the Great Park.

'There is left only the joining of the Signs,' he said. 'But before that, one – small – thing.'

A curious jerkiness caught at his voice. Will followed, puzzled, as he strode forward close to Herne's Oak. Then he saw on the snow, at the edge of the tree's shadow, the crumpled cloak that the Black Rider had let fall as he turned to flee. Merriman stooped, then knelt down beside it in the snow. Still wondering, Will peered closer, and saw with a shock that the dark heap was not a cloak, but a man. The figure lay face upward, twisted at a terrible angle. It was the Walker; it was Hawkin.

Merriman said, his voice deep and expressionless. 'Those who ride high with the Lord of the Dark must expect to fall. And men do not fall easily from such heights. I think his back is broken.'

It occurred to Will, looking at the small still face, that this time he had forgotten that Hawkin was no more than an ordinary man. Not ordinary perhaps – that was not the word for a man who had been used by both Light and Dark, and sent many ways through Time, to become at the last the Walker battered by wandering through six hundred years. But a man nonetheless, and mortal. The white face flickered, and the eyes opened. Pain came into them, and the shadow of a different, remembered pain.

'He threw me down,' Hawkin said.

Merriman looked at him, but said nothing.

'Yes,' Hawkin whispered bitterly. 'You knew it would happen.' He gasped with pain as he tried to move his head; then panic came into his eyes. 'Only my head . . . I feel my head, because of the pain. But my arms, my legs, they are . . . not there . . .'

There was a dreadful, desolate hopelessness in the lined face now. Hawkin looked full at Merriman. 'I am lost,' he said. 'I know it. Will you make me live on, with the worst suffering of all now come? The last right of a man is to die. You prevented it all this time; you made me live on through the centuries when often I longed for death. And all for a betrayal that I fell into because I had not the wit of an Old One . . .' The grief and longing in his voice were intolerable; Will turned his head away.

But Merriman said, 'You were Hawkin, my foster-son and liege man, who betrayed your lord and the Light. So you became the Walker, to walk the earth for as long as the Light required it. And so you lived on, indeed. But we have not kept you since then, my friend. Once the Walker's task was done, you were free, and you could have had rest forever. Instead you chose to listen to the promises of the Dark and to betray the Light a second time . . . I gave you the freedom to choose, Hawkin, and I did not take it away. I may not. It is still yours. No power of the Dark or of the Light can make a man more than a man, once any supernatural role he may have had to play comes to an end. But no power of the Dark or the Light may take away his rights as a man, either. If the Black Rider told you so, he lied.'

The twisted face gazed up at him in agonized near-belief. 'I may have rest? There can be an end, and rest, if I choose?'

'All your choices have been your own,' said Merriman sadly.

Hawkin nodded his head; a spasm of pain flashed across his face and was gone. But the eyes that looked up at them then were the bright, lively eyes of the beginning, of the small, neat man in the green velvet coat. They turned to Will. Hawkin said softly, 'Use the gift well, Old One.'

Then he looked back at Merriman, a long unfathomable private look, and he said almost inaudibly: 'Master . . .'

Then the light went out behind the bright eyes, and there was no longer anyone there.

The Joining of the Signs

In the low-roofed smithy Will stood with his back to the entrance, staring into the fire. Orange and red and fierce yellow-white it burned, as John Smith pushed at the long bellows-arm; the warmth made Will feel comfortable for the first time that day. There was no great harm in an Old One being fish-wet in an icy river, but he was glad to feel warm in his bones again. And the fire lit his spirits, as it lit the whole room.

Yet it did not properly light the room, for nothing that Will could see appeared solid. There was a quivering in the air. Only the fire seemed real; the rest might have been a mirage.

He saw Merriman watching him with a half-smile.

'It's that half-world feeling again,' Will said, baffled. 'The same as that day in the Manor when we were in two kinds of Time at once.'

'It is. Just the same. And so we are.'

'But we're in the time of the smithy,' Will said. 'We went through the Doors.'

So they had; he and Merriman, Old George, and the huge horse Pollux. Out on the wet, dark Common, when the Wild Hunt had driven the Dark away over the sky, they had gone through the Doors into the time six centuries earlier from which Hawkin had once come, and into which Will had walked on the still, snowy morning of his birthday. They had brought Hawkin back to his century for the last time, borne on Pollux's broad back; when they were all come through the Doors, Old George had taken the horse away, bearing Hawkin's body in the direction of the church. And Will knew that in his own time, somewhere in the village churchyard, covered either by more recent burials or by a stone crumbling into illegibility now, there would be the grave of a man named Hawkin, who had died some time in the thirteenth century and lain there in peace ever since.

Merriman drew him to the front of the smithy, where it faced the narrow hard-earth track through Hunter's Combe, the Old Way. 'Listen,' he said.

Will looked at the bumpy track, the dense trees on the other side, the cold grey strip of almost-morning sky. 'I can hear the river!' he said, puzzled.

'Ah,' Merriman said.

'But the river's miles away, the other side of the Common.'

Merriman cocked his head to the rushing, rippling sound of water. It had the sound of a river that is full but not in flood, a river running after much rain. 'What we are hearing,' he said, 'is not the Thames, but the sound of the twentieth century. You see, Will, the Signs must be joined by John Wayland Smith in this smithy, in this time – for not long after this the smithy was destroyed. Yet the Signs were not brought together until your quest, which has been within your own time. So the joining must be done in a bubble of Time between the two, from which the eyes and ears of an Old One may perceive both. That's not a real river we hear. It is the water running in your time down Huntercombe Lane, from the melting of the snow.'

Will thought of the snow and of his family beset by floods, and suddenly he was a small boy wanting very much to be at home. Merriman's dark eyes looked at him compassionately. 'Not long,' he said.

A hammering sound came from behind them; they turned. John Smith had finished pumping the bellows at his red-white fire; he was working at the anvil instead, while the long tongs waited ready before the fire's glow. He was not using his usual heavy hammer, but another that looked ridiculously small in his broad fist; a delicate tool more like those Will saw his father use for jewellery. But then, the object on which he was working was far more delicate than horseshoes; a golden chain, broad-linked, from which the Six Signs would hang. The links lay in a row beside John's hand.

He looked up, his face flushed red by the fire. 'I am almost ready.'

'Very well, then.' Merriman left them and stalked out to the road. He stood there alone, tall and imposing in the long blue cloak, the hood pushed back so that his thick white hair glinted like snow. But there was no snow here, and even through the sound of the water that Will could still hear rushing, no water either . . .

Then the change began. Merriman seemed not to have moved. He stood there with his back to them, his hands loose at his sides, very still, without the least movement. But all around him, the world was beginning to move. The air shivered and quaked, the outlines of trees and earth and sky trembled, blurred, and all things visible seemed to swim and intermingle. Will stood looking at this wavering world, feeling a little giddy, and gradually he began to hear over the sound of the unseen, rushing river-road the murmur of many voices. Like a place seen through a shimmering haze of heat, the trembling world began to resolve itself into outlines of visible things, and he saw that a great indistinct throng of people filled the road and the spaces between all the trees and all the open yard before the smithy. They seemed not quite real, not quite firm; they had a ghostly quality as if they might disappear when touched. They smiled at Merriman, greeting him where he stood, his face turned away still from Will. Thronging round him, they gazed eagerly ahead at the smithy like an audience about to watch a play, but as yet none of them seemed to see Will and the smith.

There was an endless variety of faces – gay, sombre, old, young, paper-white, jet-black, and every shade and gradation of pink and brown between, vaguely recognizable, or totally strange. Will thought he recognized faces from the party at Miss Greythorne's manor, the party in a nineteenth-century Christmas that had led Hawkin to disaster and himself to the Book of Gramarye – and then he knew. All these people, this endless throng that Merriman had somehow summoned, were the Old Ones. From every land, from every part of the world, here they were, to witness the joining of the Signs. Will was all at once terrified, longing to sink into the ground and escape the gaze of this his great new enchanted world.

He thought: these are my people. This is my family, in the same way as my real family. The Old Ones. Every one of us is linked, for the greatest purpose in the world. Then he saw a stir in the crowd, running like a ripple along the road, and some began to shift and move as if to make way. And he heard the music: the piping, thrumming sound, almost comical in its simplicity, of the fifes and drums he had heard in his dream that might not have been a dream. He stood stiffly with his hands clenched, waiting, and Merriman swung round and strode to stand beside him, as out of the crowd towards them came the little procession just as it had been before.

Through the thronging figures, and curiously seeming more solid than any, came the little procession of boys: the same boys in their rough, unfamiliar tunics and leggings, shoulder-length hair, and strange bunched caps. Again those at the front carried sticks and bundles of birch twigs, while those at the back played their single repeated melancholy tune, on pipes and drums. Again between these two groups came six boys carrying on their shoulders a bier woven of branches and reeds with a bunch of holly at each corner.

Merriman said, very softly, 'First on St Stephen's Day, the day after Christmas. Then on Twelfth Night. Twice in the year, if it is a particular year, comes the Hunting of the Wren.'

But now Will could see the bier plainly, and even at the beginning, this time, there was no wren. Instead, that other delicate form lay there, the old lady, robed in blue, with a great rose-coloured ring on one hand. And the boys marched up to the smithy and very gently laid the bier down on the ground. Merriman bent over it, holding out his hand, and the Lady opened her eyes and smiled. He helped her to her feet. Moving forward towards Will, she took both his hands in hers. 'Well done, Will Stanton,' she said, and through all the crowd of Old Ones thronging the track, a murmur of approval went up like the wind singing in the trees.

The Lady turned to face the smithy, where John stood waiting. She said, 'On oak and on iron, let the Signs be joined.'

'Come, Will,' said John Smith. Together they moved to the anvil. Will laid down the belt that had borne the Signs through all their seeking. 'On oak and on iron?' he whispered.

'Iron for the anvil,' said the smith softly. 'Oak for its foot. This big wooden base of the anvil is always oak – the root of an oak, strongest part of the tree. Have I not heard someone telling you the nature of the wood a while ago?' His blue eyes twinkled at Will, and then he turned to his work. One by one he took the Signs and joined them with rings of gold. In the centre he set the Signs of Fire and Water; on one side of them the Signs of Iron and Bronze, and on the other, the Signs of Wood and Stone. At each end he fastened a length of the sturdy gold chain. He worked swiftly and delicately, while Will gazed. Outside, the great crowd of Old Ones was still as growing grass. Behind the tapping of the smith's hammer and the occasional hiss of the bellows, there was no sound anywhere but the running water of the invisible river-road, centuries away in the future and yet close at hand.

'It is done,' said John at last.

Ceremonially he handed Will the glittering chain of linked Signs, and Will gasped at the beauty of them. Holding the Signs now, he felt from them suddenly a strange fierce sensation like an electric shock: a strong, arrogant reassurance of power. Will was puzzled: danger was past, the Dark was fled, what purpose had this? He walked to the Lady, still wondering, put the Signs into her hands, and knelt down before her.

She said, 'But it's for the future, Will, don't you see? That is what the Signs are for. They are the second of the four Things of Power, that have slept these many centuries, and they are a great part of our strength. Each of the Things of Power was made at a different point in Time by a different craftsman of the Light, to await the day when it would be needed. There is a golden chalice, called a grail; there is the Circle of Signs; there is a sword of crystal, and a harp of gold. The grail, like the Signs, is safely found. The other two we must yet achieve, other quests for other times. But once we have added those to these, then when the Dark comes rising for its final and most dreadful attempt on the world, we shall have hope and assurance that we can overcome.'

She raised her head, looking out over the unnumbered ghostly crowd of the Old Ones. '*When the Dark comes rising,*' she said, expressionless, and the many voices answered her in a soft, ominous rumble '*six shall drive it back.*'

Then she looked down again at Will, the lines around her ageless eyes creasing in affection. 'Sign-seeker,' she said, 'by your birth and your birthday you came into your own, and the circle of the Old Ones was complete, for now and forever. And by your good use of the Gift of Gramarye, you achieved a great quest and proved yourself stronger than the testing. Until we meet again, as meet we shall, we remember you with pride.'

The far-stretching crowd murmured again, a different, warm response, and with her thin small hands, the great rose ring glimmering, the Lady bent down and set the chain of the linked Signs around Will's neck. Then she kissed him lightly on the forehead, the gentle brushing-by of a bird's wing. 'Farewell, Will Stanton,' she said.

The murmur of the voices rose, and the world spun round Will in a flurry of trees and flame, and rising over it all was the bell-like haunting phrase of his music, louder and more joyful now than ever before. It chimed and rang in his head, filling him with such delight that he closed his eyes and floated in its beauty; it was, he knew for a crack of a second, the spirit and essence of the Light, this music. But then it began gradually to fade, to grow distant and beckoning and a little melancholy, as it always had been before, fading into nothing, fading, fading, with the sound of running water rising to take its place. Will cried out in sorrow, and opened his eyes.

And he was kneeling on the cold beaten snow in the grey dead light of early morning, in a place he did not recognize beside Huntercombe Lane. Bare trees rose out of pitted, wet snow on the other side of the road. Though the Lane itself was once more a clear paved road, water ran furiously in each of its gutters with a sound like a stream, or even a river . . . The road was empty; no one was anywhere to be seen among the trees. Will could have wept with the sense of loss; all that warm crowd of friends, the brightness and light and celebration, and the Lady: all gone, all fled, leaving him alone.

He put his hand to his neck. The Signs were still there.

Behind him, Merriman's deep voice said, 'Time to go home, Will.'

'Oh,' Will said unhappily, without turning round. 'I'm glad you're still there.'

'You sound most glad,' Merriman said dryly. 'Restrain your ecstasy, I pray you.'

Sitting back on his heels, Will looked at him over his shoulder. Merriman gazed down at him with immense solemnity, his dark eyes owlish, and suddenly the emotions that were drawn into a tight, unbearable knot inside Will cracked and broke, and he dissolved into laughter. Merriman's mouth twitched slightly. He put out his hand, and Will scrambled to his feet, still spluttering.

'It was just –' Will said, and stopped, not quite sure yet whether he was laughing or crying.

'It was – an alteration,' Merriman said gently. 'Can you walk now?'

'Of course I can walk,' said Will indignantly. He stared about him. Where the smithy had been, there was a battered brick building like a garage, and around it he could see traces of cold-frames and vegetable beds through the melting snow. He looked quickly up and saw the outline of a familiar house. 'It's the Manor!' he said.

'The back entrance,' Merriman said. 'Near the village. Used mainly by tradesmen – and butlers.' He smiled at Will.

'This really is where the old smithy used to be?'

'In the plans of the old house it is called Smith's Gate,' Merriman said. 'Buckinghamshire historians writing about Huntercombe are very fond of speculating on the reason. They're always wrong.'

Will stared through the trees at the Manor's tall Tudor chimneys and gabled roofs. 'Is Miss Greythorne there?'

'Yes, she is, now. But didn't you see her in the crowd?'

'The crowd?' Will became aware that his mouth was foolishly gaping, and shut it. Conflicting images chased one another through his head. 'You mean she is one of the Old Ones?'

Merriman raised an eyebrow. 'Come now, Will, your senses told you that long ago.'

'Well . . . yes, they did. But I never knew quite which Miss Greythorne it was who belonged to us, the one from today or from the Christmas party. Well. Well, yes, I suppose I knew that too.' He looked up tentatively at Merriman. 'They're the same, aren't they?'

'That's better,' Merriman said. 'And Miss Greythorne gave me, while you and Wayland Smith were intent on your work, two gifts for Twelfth Night. One is for your brother Paul, and one is for you.' He showed Will two shapeless, small packages wrapped in what looked like silk; then drew them again under his cloak. 'Paul's is a normal present, I think. More or less. Yours is something to be used only in the future, at some point when your judgement tells you you may need it.'

'Twelfth Night,' Will said. 'Is that tonight?' He looked up at the grey early-morning sky. 'Merriman, how have you stopped my family wondering where I've been? Is my mother truly all right?'

'Of course she is,' Merriman said. 'And you have spent the night at the Manor, asleep . . . Come now, these are small things. I know all the questions. You will have all the answers, when you are once at home, and in any case really you know them already.' He turned his head down towards Will, and the deep dark eyes stared compelling as a basilisk. 'Come, Old One,' he said softly, 'remember yourself. You are no longer a small boy.'

'No,' said Will. 'I know.'

Merriman said, 'But sometimes, you feel how very much more agreeable life would be if you were.'

'Sometimes,' Will said. He grinned. 'But not always.'

They turned and strode over the little edge-stream of the road to walk together towards the Stantons' house along Huntercombe Lane.

The day grew brighter, and light began to infuse the edge of the sky before them, where the sun would soon come up. A thin mist hung over the snow on both sides of the road, wreathing round the bare trees and the little streams. It was a morning full of promise, with a hazy, cloudless sky tinged faintly with blue, the kind of sky that Huntercombe had not seen for many days. They walked as old friends walk, without often speaking, sharing the kind of silence that is not so much silence as a kind of still communication. Their footsteps rang out on the bare wet road, making the only sound anywhere in the village except the song of a blackbird and, somewhere further off, the sound of someone shovelling. Trees loomed black and leafless over the road on one side, and Will saw that they were at the corner that passed Rooks' Wood. He stared upwards. Not a sound came out of the trees, or the untidy great nests high up there in the misted branches.

'The rooks are very quiet,' he said.

Merriman said, 'They are not there.'

'Not there? Why not? Where are they?'

Merriman smiled, a small grim smile. 'When the Yell Hounds are hunting across the sky, no animal or bird may stay within sight of them and not be driven wild by terror. All through this kingdom, along the path of Herne and the Hunt, masters will not be able to find any creature that was loose last night. It was better known in older days. Countrymen everywhere used to lock up their animals on Twelfth Night Eve, in case the Hunt should ride.'

'But what happens? Are they killed?' Will found that in spite of all the rooks had done for the Dark, he did not want to think of them all destroyed.

'Oh, no,' Merriman said. 'Scattered. Driven willy-nilly across the sky for as long as the nearest hound chooses to drive them. The Hounds of Doom are not of a species that kills living creatures or eats flesh . . . The rooks will come back eventually. One by one, bedraggled, weary, sorry for themselves. Wiser birds who had no dealings with the Dark would have hidden themselves away last night, beneath branches or house-eaves, out of sight. Those who did are still here, unharmed. But it will take a while for our friends the rooks to recover themselves. I think you will have no trouble with them again, Will, though I would never quite trust one if I were you.'

'Look,' Will said, pointing ahead. 'There are two to trust.' Pride came thick into his voice, as down the road towards them came rushing and bounding the two Stanton dogs, Raq and Ci. They leapt at him, barking and whining with delight, licking his hands in a greeting as gigantic as if he had been gone for a month. Will stooped to speak to them and was enveloped in waving tails and warm panting heads and large wet feet. 'Get off, you idiots,' he said happily.

Merriman said, very softly: 'Gently, now.' Instantly the dogs calmed and were still, only their tails enthusiastically waving; both turned to Merriman and looked up at him for a moment, and then they were trotting amiably in silence at Will's side. Then the Stanton driveway was ahead, and the noise of shovels grew loud, and round the corner they found Paul and Mr Stanton, wrapped against the cold, clearing wet snow and leaves and twigs away from a drain.

'Well, well,' said Mr Stanton, and stood leaning on his shovel.

'Hallo, Dad,' said Will cheerfully, and ran and hugged him.

Merriman said: 'Good morning.'

'Old George said you'd be about early,' said Mr Stanton, 'but I didn't think he meant quite this early. However did you manage to wake him up?'

'I woke myself up,' Will said. 'Yah. I turned over a new leaf for the New Year. What are you doing?'

'Turning over old leaves,' Paul said.

'Ho, ho, ho.'

'We are, though. The thaw came so suddenly that the ground was still frozen, and nothing would drain away. And now that the drains are beginning to thaw as well, the flood's got everything jammed up with washed-away rubbish. Like this.' He lifted a dripping bundle.

Will said, 'I'll get another spade, and help.'

'Wouldn't you like some breakfast first?' Paul said. 'Mary's getting us some, believe it or not. There's a lot of leaf-turning going on here, while the year's still new.'

Will suddenly realized that it was a long time since he had last eaten, and felt a gigantic hunger. 'Mmmm,' he said.

'Come on in and have some breakfast or a cup of tea or something,' said Mr Stanton to Merriman. 'It's a chilly walk from the Manor this time of the morning. I really am extremely grateful to you for delivering him, not to mention looking after him last night.'

Merriman shook his head, smiling, and pulled up the collar of what Will saw had now again subtly changed from a cloak to a heavy twentieth-century overcoat. 'Thank you. But I'll be getting back.'

'Will!' a voice shrilled, and Mary came flying up the drive. Will went to meet her, and she skidded into him and punched him in the stomach. 'Was it fun at the Manor? Did you sleep in a four-poster?'

'Not exactly,' Will said. 'Are you all right?'

'Well, of course. I had a super ride on Old George's horse, it was one of Mr Dawson's huge ones, the show horses. He picked me up in the Lane, quite soon after I'd gone out. Seems ages ago, not last night.' She looked at Will rather sheepishly. 'I suppose I shouldn't have gone out after Max like that, but everything was happening so quickly, and I was worried about Mum not having help –'

'Is she really all right?'

'She'll be fine, the doctor says. It was a sprain, not a broken leg. She did knock herself out, though, so she has to rest for a week or two. But she's as cheerful as can be, you'll see.'

Will looked up the drive. Paul, Merriman, and his father were talking and laughing together. He thought perhaps his father had decided that Lyon the butler was a good chap after all, not merely a manorial prop.

Mary said, 'Sorry about you getting lost in the wood. It was all my fault. You and Paul must have been very close behind me actually. Good job Old George ended up knowing where everyone was. Poor Paul, worrying about both of us being lost, instead of just me.' She giggled, then tried to look penitent, without great effort.

'Will!' Paul swung away from the group, excited, running towards them. 'Just look! Miss Greythorne calls it a permanent loan, bless her – look!' His face was flushed with pleasure. He held out the bundle Merriman had been carrying, now open, and Will saw lying on it the old flute from the Manor.

Feeling his face break into a long, slow smile, he looked up at Merriman. The dark eyes looked down at him gravely, and Merriman held out the second package. 'This, the Lady of the Manor sent for you.'

Will opened it. Inside lay a small hunting horn, gleaming, thin with age. His gaze flicked more briefly to Merriman, and down again.

Mary hopped about, giggling. 'Go on, Will, blow it. You could make a noise all the way to Windsor. Go on!'

'Later,' Will said. 'I have to learn how. Will you thank her for me very much?' he said to Merriman.

Merriman inclined his head. 'Now I must go,' he said.

Roger Stanton said, 'I can't tell you how grateful we've been for all your help. With everything, through this mad weather – and the children – you really have been most tremendously –' he lost his words, but thrust out his arm and pumped Merriman's hand up and down with such warmth that Will thought he would never stop.

The craggy, fierce-carved face softened; Merriman looked pleased and a little surprised. He smiled and nodded, but said nothing. Paul shook hands with him, and Mary. Then Will's hand was in the strong grasp, and there was a quick pressure and a brief intent look from the deep, dark eyes. Merriman said, 'Au revoir, Will.'

He raised his hand to them all and strode off down the Lane. Will drifted after him. Mary said, skipping at his side, 'Did you hear the wild geese last night?'

'Geese?' Will said gruffly. He was not really listening. 'Geese? In all that storm?'

'What storm?' said Mary, and went on before he could blink. 'Wild geese, there must have been thousands of them. Migrating, I suppose. We didn't see them – there was just this gorgeous noise, first of all a lot of cackling from those daft rooks in the wood, and then a long, long sort of yelping noise across the sky, very high up. It was thrilling.'

'Yes,' said Will. 'Yes, it must have been.'

'I don't think you're more than half awake,' Mary said in disgust, and she went hopping ahead to the end of the drive-way. Then she stopped suddenly and stood very still. 'My goodness! Will! Look!'

She was peering at something behind a tree, hidden by the remnants of a snowbank. Will came to look, and saw, lying among the wet undergrowth, the great carnival head with the eyes of an owl, the face of a man, the antlers of a deer. He stared and stared without a word in his throat. The head was crisp and bright and dry, as it had always been and always would be. It looked like the outline of Herne the Hunter that he had seen against the sky, and yet not like.

Still he stared, and said nothing.

'Well, I never,' said Mary brightly. 'Aren't you lucky it got stuck there? Mum *will* be pleased. She was awake by then, it was when the floods came up all of a sudden. You weren't there of course; the water came in all over the ground floor and quite a lot of things got washed out of the living-room before we realized. That head was one of them – Mum was all upset because she knew you'd be. Well, look at that, fancy that –'

She peered closer at the head, still prattling gaily, but Will was no longer listening. The head lay very close to the garden wall, which was still buried in snow but beginning to break through the drifts at either side. And on the drift at the outer edge, covering the verge of the road and overhanging the running stream in the gutter, there were a number of marks. They were hoofprints, made by a horse stopping and pivoting and leaping away over the snow. But none of them was in the shape of a horseshoe. They were circles quartered by a cross: the prints of the shoes that John Wayland Smith, once at the beginning, had put on the white mare of the Light.

Will looked at the prints, and at the carnival head, and swallowed hard. He walked a few paces to the end of the driveway and looked down Huntercombe Lane; he could see Merriman's back still, as the tall, dark-clad figure strode away. And then his hair prickled and his pulses stood still, for from behind him came a sound sweeter than seemed possible in the raw air of the cold grey morning. It was the soft, beautiful yearning tone of the old flute from the Manor; Paul, irresistibly drawn, must have put the instrument together to try it out. He was playing 'Greensleeves' once more. The eerie, enchanted lilt floated out through the morning on the still air; Will saw Merriman raise his wild white head as he heard it, though he did not break his stride.

As he looked down the road still, with the music singing in his ears, Will saw that out beyond Merriman the trees and the mist and the stretch of the road were shaking, shivering, in a way that he knew well. And then gradually, out there, he saw the great Doors take shape. There they stood, as he had seen them on the open hillside and in the Manor: the tall carved doors that led out of Time, standing alone and upright in the Old Way that was known now as Huntercombe Lane. Very slowly, they began to open. Somewhere behind Will the music of 'Greensleeves' broke off, with a laugh and some muffled words from Paul; but there was no break in the music that was in Will's head, for now it had changed into that haunting, bell-like phrase that came always with the opening of the Doors or any great change that might alter the lives of the Old Ones. Will clenched his fists as he listened, yearning towards the sweet beckoning sound that was the space between waking and dreaming, yesterday and tomorrow, memory and imagining. It floated lovingly in his mind, then gradually grew distant, fading, as out on the Old Way Merriman's tall figure, swirled round again now by a blue cloak, passed through the open Doors. Behind him, the towering slabs of heavy carved oak swung slowly together, together, until silently they shut. Then as the last echo of the enchanted music died, they disappeared.

And in a great blaze of yellow-white light, the sun rose over Hunter's Combe and the valley of the Thames.

Greenwitch

For Kate

When the Dark comes rising, six shall turn it back;
Three from the circle, three from the track;
Wood, bronze, iron; water, fire, stone;
Five will return, and one go alone.

Iron for the birthday, bronze carried long;
Wood from the burning, stone out of song;
Fire in the candle-ring, water from the thaw;
Six Signs the circle, and the grail gone before.

Fire on the mountain shall find the harp of gold;
Played to wake the Sleepers, oldest of the old;
Power from the green witch, lost beneath the sea;
All shall find the light at last, silver on the tree.

Chapter One

Only one newspaper carried the story in detail, under the headline: TREASURES STOLEN FROM MUSEUM.

Several Celtic works of art were stolen from the British Museum yesterday, one of them worth more than £50,000. Police say that the theft appears to be the result of an intricate and so far baffling plan. No burglar alarms were set off, the showcases involved were undamaged, and no signs have been found of breaking-in.

The missing objects include a gold chalice, three jewelled brooches and a bronze buckle. The chalice, known as the Trewissick Grail, had been acquired by the Museum only last summer, after its dramatic discovery in a Cornish cave by three children. It had been valued at £50,000, but a Museum spokesman said last night that its true value was 'incalculable', due to the unique inscriptions on its sides which scholars have so far been unable to decipher.

The spokesman added that the Museum appealed to the thieves not to damage the chalice in any way, and would be offering a substantial reward for its return. 'The grail is an extraordinary piece of historical evidence, unprecedented in the whole field of Celtic studies,' he said, 'and its importance to scholars far exceeds its intrinsic value.'

Lord Clare, who is a trustee of the British Museum, said last night that the chalice –

'Oh do come out of that paper, Barney,' Simon said irritably. 'You've read it fifty times, and anyway it's no help.'

'You never know,' said his younger brother, folding the newspaper and cramming it into his pocket. 'Might be a hidden clue.'

'Nothing's hidden,' said Jane sadly. 'It's all too obvious.'

They stood in a dejected row on the shiny floor of the museum gallery, before a central showcase taller than the rows of identical glass cases all round. It was empty, save for a black wooden plinth on which, clearly, something had once been displayed. A neat silver square on the wood was engraved with the words: *Gold chalice of unknown Celtic workmanship, believed sixth century. Found in Trewissick, South Cornwall, and presented by Simon, Jane and Barnabas Drew.*

'All that trouble we had, getting there first,' Simon said. 'And now they've simply come and lifted it. Mind you, I always thought they might.'

Barney said, 'The worst part is not being able to tell anyone who did it.'
'We could try,' Jane said.

Simon looked at her with his head on one side. 'Please sir, we can tell you who took the grail, in broad daylight without breaking any locks. It was the powers of the Dark.'

'Pop off, sonny,' Barney said. 'And take your fairy stories with you.'

'I suppose you're right,' Jane said. She tugged distractedly at her pony-tail. 'But if it was the same ones, somebody might at least have seen them. That horrible Mr Hastings –'

'Not a chance. Hastings changes, Great-Uncle Merry said. Don't you remember? He wouldn't have the same name, or the same face. He can be different people, at different times.'

'I wonder if Great-Uncle Merry knows,' Barney said. 'About this.' He stared at the glass case, and the small, lonely black plinth inside.

Two elderly ladies in hats came up beside him. One wore a yellow flowerpot, the other a pyramid of pink flowers. 'That's where they pinched it from, the attendant said,' one told the other. 'Fancy! The other cases were over here.'

'Tut-tut-tut-tut,' said the other lady with relish, and they moved on. Absently Barney watched them go, their footsteps clopping through the high gallery. They paused at a showcase over which a long-legged figure was bending. Barney stiffened. He peered at the figure.

'We've got to do something,' Simon said. 'Just got to.'

Jane said, 'But where do we start?'

The tall figure straightened to let the be-hatted ladies approach the glass case. He bent his head courteously, and a mass of wild white hair caught the light.

Simon said, 'I don't see how Great-Uncle Merry could know – I mean he isn't even in Britain, is he? Taking that year off from Oxford. Sab – whatsit.'

'Sabbatical,' Jane said. 'In Athens. And not even a card at Christmas.'

Barney was holding his breath. Across the gallery, as the crime-loving ladies moved on, the tall white-haired man turned towards a window; his beak-nosed, hollow-eyed profile was unmistakable. Barney let out a howl. 'Gumerry!'

Simon and Jane trailed blinking in his wake as he skidded across the floor. 'Great-Uncle Merry!'

'Good morning,' said the tall man amiably.

'But Mum said you were in Greece!'

'I came back.'

'Did you know someone was going to steal the grail?' Jane said.

Her great-uncle arched one white-bristling eyebrow at her, but said nothing.

Barney said simply, 'What are we going to do?'

'Get it back,' said Great-Uncle Merry.

'I suppose it was them?' Simon said diffidently. 'The other side? The Dark?'

'Of course.'

'Why did they take the other stuff, the brooches and things?'

'To make it look right,' said Jane.

Great-Uncle Merry nodded. 'It was effective enough. They took the most valuable pieces. The police will think they were simply after the gold.' He looked down at the empty showcase; then his gaze flicked up, and each of the three felt impelled to stare motionless into the deep-set dark eyes, with the light behind them like a cold fire that never went out.

'But I know that they wanted only the grail,' Great-Uncle Merry said, 'to help them on the way to something else. I know what they intend to do, and I know that they must at all costs be stopped. And I am very much afraid that you three, as the finders, will be needed once more to give help – far sooner than I had expected.'

'Shall we?' said Jane slowly.

'Super,' said Simon.

Barney said, 'Why should they have taken the grail *now*? Does it mean they've found the lost manuscript, the one that explains the cipher written on the sides of the grail?'

'No,' said Great-Uncle Merry. 'Not yet.'

'Then why –'

'I can't explain, Barney.' He thrust his hands into his pockets and hunched his bony shoulders. 'This matter involves Trewissick, and it does involve that manuscript. But it is part of something very much larger as well, something which I may not explain. I can only ask you to trust me, as you trusted me once before, in another part of the long battle between the Light and the Dark. And to help, if you are sure you feel able to give help, without perhaps ever being able fully to understand what you are about.'

Barney said calmly, pushing his tow-coloured forelock out of his eyes: 'That's all right.'

'Of course we want to help,' Simon said eagerly.

Jane said nothing. Her great-uncle put one finger under her chin, tilted her head up and looked at her. 'Jane,' he said gently. 'There is absolutely no reason to involve any of you in this if you are not happy about it.'

Jane looked up at the strongly-marked face, thinking how much it looked like one of the fierce statues they had passed on their way through the museum. 'You know I'm not scared,' she said. 'Well, I mean I am a bit, but excited-scared. It's just that if there's going to be any danger to Barney, I feel – I mean, he's going to scream at me, but he is younger than we are and we oughtn't –'

Barney was scarlet. 'Jane!'

'It's no good yelling,' she said with spirit. 'If anything happened to you, we'd be responsible, Simon and me.'

'The Dark will not touch any of you,' Great-Uncle Merry said quietly. 'There will be protection. Don't worry. I promise you that. Nothing that may happen to Barney will harm him.'

They smiled at one another.

'*I am not a baby!*' Barney stamped one foot in fury.

'Stop it,' said Simon. 'Nobody said you were.'

Great-Uncle Merry said, 'When are the Easter holidays, Barney?'

There was a short pause.

'The fifteenth, I think,' Barney said grumpily.

'That's right,' Jane said. 'Simon's start a bit before that, but we all overlap by about a week.'

'It's a long way off,' Great-Uncle Merry said.

'Too late?' They looked at him anxiously.

'No, I don't think so . . . Is there anything to prevent the three of you from spending that week with me in Trewissick?'

'No!'

'Nothing!'

'Not really. I was going to a sort of ecology conference, but I can get out of that . . .' Simon's voice trailed away, as he thought of the little Cornish village where they had found the grail. Whatever adventure might now follow had begun there, deep inside a cave in the cliffs, over sea and under stone. And at the heart of things now, as he had been then, would always be Great-Uncle Merry, Professor Merriman Lyon, the most mysterious figure in their lives, who in some incomprehensible way was involved with the long struggle for control of the world between the Light and the Dark.

'I'll speak to your parents,' his great-uncle said.

'Why Trewissick again?' Jane said. 'Will the thieves take the grail there?'

'I think they may.'

'Just one week,' Barney said, staring pensively at the empty showcase before them. 'That's not much for a quest. Will it really be enough?'

'It is not very long,' said Great-Uncle Merry. 'But it will have to do.'

Will eased a stem of grass out of its sheath and sat down on a rock near the front gate, despondently nibbling. The April sunshine glimmered on the new-green leaves of the lime trees; a thrush somewhere shouted its happy self-echoing song. Lilac and wallflowers scented the morning. Will sighed. They were all very well, these joys of a Buckinghamshire spring, but he would have appreciated them more with someone there to share the Easter holidays. Half his large family still lived at home, but his nearest brother James was away at a Scout camp for the week, and the next in line, Mary, had disappeared to some Welsh relations to recuperate from mumps. The rest were busy with boring older preoccupations. That was the trouble with being the youngest of nine; everyone else seemed to have grown up too fast.

There was one respect in which he, Will Stanton, was far older than any of them, or than any human creature. But only he knew of the great adventure which had shown him, on his eleventh birthday, that he had been born the last of the Old Ones, guardians of the Light, bound by immutable laws to defend the world against the rising Dark. Only he knew – and because he was also an ordinary boy, he was not thinking of it now.

Raq, one of the family dogs, pushed a damp nose into his hand. Will fondled the floppy ears. 'A whole week,' he said to the dog. 'What shall we do? Go fishing?'

The ears twitched, the nose left his hand; stiff and alert, Raq turned towards the road. In a moment or two a taxi drew up outside the gate: not the familiar battered car that served as village taxi, but a shiny professional vehicle from the town three miles away. The man who emerged was small, balding and rather rumpled, wearing a raincoat and carrying a large shapeless holdall. He dismissed the taxi, and stood looking at Will.

Puzzled, Will scrambled up and came to the gate. 'Good morning,' he said.

The man stood solemn for a moment, then grinned. 'You're Will,' he said. He had a smooth round face with round eyes, like a clever fish.

'That's right,' Will said.

'The youngest Stanton. The seventh son. That's one up on me – I was only the sixth.'

His voice was soft and rather husky, with an odd mid-Atlantic accent; the vowels were American, but the intonation was English. Will smiled in polite incomprehension.

'Your father was the seventh in that family,' the man in the raincoat said. He grinned again, his round eyes crinkling at the corners, and held out his hand. 'Hi. I'm your Uncle Bill.'

'Well I'm blowed!' said Will. He shook the hand. Uncle Bill. His namesake. His father's favourite brother, who had gone off to America years and years ago and set up some sort of successful business – pottery, wasn't it? Will did not remember ever having seen him before; he was sent a Christmas present each year by this unknown Uncle Bill, who was also his godfather, and he wrote a chatty letter of thanks annually as a result, but the letters had never had a reply.

'You've grown some,' said Uncle Bill as they walked to the house. 'Last time we met, you were a little scrawny bawling thing in a crib.'

'You sound like an American,' Will said.

'No wonder,' said Uncle Bill. 'I've been one for the last ten years.'

'You never answered my Christmas letters.'

'Did that bother you?'

'No, not really.'

They both laughed, and Will decided that this uncle was all right. Then they were in the house, and his father was coming downstairs; pausing, with an incredulous blankness in his face.

'*Billy!*'

'Roger!'

'My God,' said Will's father, 'what's happened to your hair?'

Reunions with long-lost relatives take time, especially in large families. They were at it for hours. Will quite forgot that he had been gloomy over the absence of companions. By lunchtime he had learned that his Uncle Bill and Aunt Fran were in Britain to visit the Staffordshire potteries and the china-clay district of Cornwall, where they had business of some complex Anglo-American kind. He had heard all about their two grown-up children, who seemed to be contemporaries of his eldest brother Stephen, and he had been told rather more than he really wanted to know about the state of Ohio and the china-making trade. Uncle Bill was clearly prosperous, but this seemed to be only his second trip to Britain since he had emigrated more than twenty years before. Will liked his twinkling round eyes and laconic husky voice. He was just feeling that the prospects for his week's holiday had greatly improved when he found that Uncle Bill was staying only one night, on his way from a business trip to London, and travelling on to Cornwall the next day to join his wife. His spirits drooped again.

'Friend of mine's picking me up, and we're driving down. But I tell you what, Frannie and I'll come and spend a few days on our way back to the States. If you'll have us, that is.'

'I should hope so,' said Will's mother. 'After ten years and about three letters, my lad, you don't get away with one mouldy twenty-four hours.'

'He sent me presents,' Will said. 'Every Christmas.'

Uncle Bill grinned at him. 'Alice,' he said suddenly to Mrs Stanton, 'since Will's out of school this week, and not too busy, why don't you let me take him to Cornwall for the holiday? I could put him on a train back at the end of the week. We've rented a place with far more space than we need. And this friend of mine has a couple of nephews coming down, about Will's age, I believe.'

Will made a strangled whooping sound, and looked anxiously at his parents. Frowning gravely, they began a predictable duet.

'Well, that's really very good of –'

'If you're sure he won't be –'

'He'd certainly love to –'

'If Frannie wouldn't –'

Uncle Bill winked at Will. Will went upstairs and began to pack his knapsack. He put in five pairs of socks, five changes of underwear, six shirts, a pullover and a sweater, two pairs of shorts, and a torch. Then he remembered that his uncle was not leaving until the next day, but there seemed no point in unpacking. He went downstairs, the knapsack bouncing on his back like an overblown football.

His mother said, 'Well, Will, if you'd really like to – Oh.'

'Good-bye, Will,' said his father.

Uncle Bill chuckled. 'Excuse me,' he said. 'If I might borrow your phone –'

'I'll show you.' Will led him out into the hall. 'It's not too much, is it?' he said, looking doubtfully at the bulging knapsack.

'That's fine.' His uncle was dialling. 'Hallo? Hallo, Merry. Everything okay? Good. Just one thing. I'm bringing my youngest nephew with me for a week. He doesn't have much luggage' – he grinned at Will – 'but I just thought I'd make sure you weren't driving some cute little two-seater . . . Ha-ha. No, not really in character . . . okay, great, see you tomorrow.' He rang off.

'All right, buddy,' he said to Will. 'We leave at nine in the morning. That suit you, Alice?' Mrs Stanton was crossing the hall with the tea-tray.

'Splendid,' she said.

Since the beginning of the telephone call, Will had been standing very still. 'Merry?' he said slowly. 'That's an unusual name.'

'It is, isn't it?' said his uncle. 'Unusual guy, too. Teaches at Oxford. Brilliant brain, but I guess you'd call him kind of odd – very shy, hates meeting people. He's very reliable, though,' he added hastily to Mrs Stanton. 'And a great driver.'

'Whatever's the matter, Will?' said his mother. 'You look as though you'd seen a ghost. Is anything wrong?'

'Nothing,' said Will. 'Oh no. Nothing at all.'

Simon, Jane and Barney struggled out of St Austell station beneath a clutter of suitcases, paper bags, raincoats and paperbacks. The crowd from the London train was dwindling about them, swallowed by cars, buses, taxis.

'He did say he'd meet us here, didn't he?'

''Course he did.'

'I can't see him.'

'He's a bit late, that's all.'

'Great-Uncle Merry is never late.'

'We ought to find out where the Trewissick bus goes from, just in case.'

'No, there he is, I see him. I told you he was never late.' Barney jumped up and down, waving. Then he paused. 'But he's not on his own. There's a man with him.' A faint note of outrage crept into his voice. 'And a *boy*.'

A car hooted peremptorily once, twice, three times outside the Stantons' House.

'Here we go,' said Uncle Bill, seizing his holdall and Will's knapsack.

Will hastily kissed his parents good-bye, staggering under the enormous bag of sandwiches, thermos flasks and cold drinks that his mother dumped into his arms.

'Behave yourself,' she said.

'I don't suppose Merry will get out of the car,' said Bill to her as they trooped down the drive. 'Very shy character, pay no attention. But he's a good friend. You'll like him, Will.'

Will said, 'I'm sure I shall.'

At the end of the drive, an enormous elderly Daimler stood waiting.

'Well well,' said Will's father respectfully.

'And I was worrying about space!' said Bill. 'I might have known he'd drive something like this. Well, good-bye, people. Here, Will, you can get in front.'

In a flurry of farewells they climbed into the dignified car; a large muffler-wrapped figure sat hunched at the wheel, topped by a terrible hairy brown cap.

'Merry,' said Uncle Bill as they moved off, 'this is my nephew and godson. Will Stanton. Merriman Lyon.'

The driver tossed aside his dreadful cap, and a mop of white hair sprang into shaggy freedom. Shadowed dark eyes glanced sideways at Will out of an arrogant, hawk-nosed profile.

'*Greetings, Old One,*' said a familiar voice into Will's mind.

'*It's marvellous to see you,*' Will said silently, happily.

'Good morning, Will Stanton,' Merriman said.

'How do you do, sir,' said Will.

There was considerable conversation on the drive from Buckinghamshire to

Cornwall, particularly after the picnic lunch, when Will's uncle fell asleep and slumbered peacefully all the rest of the way.

Will said at last: 'And Simon and Jane and Barney have no idea at all that the Dark timed its theft of the grail to match the making of the Greenwitch?'

'They have never heard of the Greenwitch,' Merriman said. 'You will have the privilege of telling them. Casually, of course.'

'Hmm,' Will said. He was thinking of something else. 'I'd feel a lot happier if only we knew what shape the Dark will take.'

'An old problem. With no solution.' Merriman glanced sideways at him, with one bristly white eyebrow raised. 'We have only to wait and see. And I think we shall not wait for long . . .'

Fairly late in the afternoon, the Daimler hummed its noble way into the forecourt of the railway station at St Austell, in Cornwall. Standing in a small pool of luggage Will saw a boy a little older than himself, wearing a school blazer and an air of self-conscious authority; a girl about the same height, with long hair tied in a pony-tail, and a worried expression; and a small boy with a mass of blond, almost white hair, sitting placidly on a suitcase watching their approach.

'*If they are to know nothing about me,*' he said to Merriman in the Old Ones' speech of the mind, '*they will dislike me extremely, I think.*'

'*That may very well be true,*' said Merriman. '*But not one of us has any feelings that are of the least consequence, compared to the urgency of this quest.*'

Will sighed. '*Watch for the Greenwitch,*' he said.

Chapter Two

'I thought we'd put you in here, Jane,' Merriman said, opening a bedroom door and carefully stooping to go through. 'Very small, but the view's good.'

'Oh!' said Jane in delight. The room was painted white, with gay yellow curtains, and a yellow quilt on the bed. The ceiling sloped down so that the wall on one side was only half the height of the wall on the other, and there was space only for a bed, a dressing-table and a chair. But the little room seemed full of sunshine, even though the sky outside the curtains was grey. Jane stood looking out, while her great-uncle went on to show the boys their room, and she thought that the picture she could see from the window was the best thing of all.

She was high up on the side of the harbour, overlooking the boats and jetties, the wharf piled with boxes and lobster-pots, and the little canning factory. All the life of the busy harbour was thrumming there below her, and out to the left, beyond the harbour wall and the dark arm of land called Kemare Head, lay the sea. It was a grey sea now, speckled with white. Jane's gaze moved in again from the flat ocean horizon, and she looked straight across to the sloping road on the opposite side of the harbour, and saw the tall narrow house in which they had stayed the summer before. The Grey House. Everything had begun there.

Simon tapped on the door and put his head round. 'Hey, that's a super view you've got. Ours hasn't any, but it's a nice room, all long and skinny.'

'Like a coffin,' said Barney in a hollow voice, behind the door.

Jane giggled. 'Come on in, look at the Grey House over there. I wonder if we'll meet Captain Thing, the one Gumerry rented it from?'

'Toms,' Barney said. 'Captain Toms. And I want to see Rufus, I hope he remembers me. Dogs do have good memories, don't they?'

'Try walking through Captain Toms' door and you'll find out,' said Simon. 'If Rufus bites you, dogs don't have good memories.'

'Very funny.'

'What's that?' Jane said suddenly. 'Hush!'

They stood in a silence broken only by the sounds of cars and seagulls, overlaid by the murmur of the sea. Then they heard a faint tapping sound.

'It's on the other side of that wall! What is it?'

'Sounds like a sort of pattern. I think it's Morse. Who knows Morse?'

'I don't,' Jane said. 'You should have been a Boy Scout.'

'We were supposed to learn it last year at school,' Barney said hesitantly. 'But I don't . . . wait a minute. That's a D . . . don't know that one . . . E . . . er . . . W . . . and S, that's easy. There it goes again. What on earth –?'

'Drews,' Simon said suddenly. 'Someone's tapping "Drews". Calling us.'

'It's that boy,' said Jane. 'The house is two cottages joined together, so he must have the exact same room as this one, on the other side of the wall.'

'Stanton,' said Barney.

'That's right. Will Stanton. Tap back to him, Barney.'

'No,' Barney said.

Jane stared at him. His long yellow-white hair had fallen sideways, masking his face, but she could see the lower lip jutting mulishly in a way she knew well.

'Whyever not?'

'He's stopped now,' Barney said evasively.

'But there's no harm in being friendly.'

'Well. No. Well. Oh, I don't know . . . he's a nuisance. I don't see why Great-Uncle Merry let him come. How can we find out how to get the grail back with some strange kid hanging round?'

'Great-Uncle Merry probably couldn't get rid of him,' Jane said. She tugged her hair loose and took a comb from her pocket. 'I mean, it's his friend Mr Stanton who's renting the cottages, and Will's Mr Stanton's nephew. So that's that, isn't it?'

'We can get rid of him easily enough,' Simon said confidently. 'Or keep him away. He'll soon find out he's not wanted, he looks fairly quick on the uptake.'

'Well, we can at least be polite,' said Jane. 'Starting now – it's suppertime in a few minutes.'

'Of course,' Simon said blandly. 'Of course.'

'It's a marvellous place,' Will said, glowing. 'I can see right over the harbour from my room. Who do the cottages belong to?'

'A fisherman called Penhallow,' said his uncle. 'Friend of Merry's. They must have been in the family for a while, judging by that.' He waved at a large yellowed photograph over the fireplace, ornately framed, showing a solemn-looking Victorian gentleman in stiff collar and dark suit. 'Mr Penhallow's granddaddy, I'm told. But the cottages are modernized, of course. They can be let either separately or together – we took both when Merry decided to invite the Drew kids. We'll all eat in here together.'

He waved at the cheerful room, a pattern of bookcases and armchairs and lamps, very new and very old, with a large solid table and eight dignified high-backed chairs.

'Have you known Mr Lyon a long time?' Will said curiously.

'Year or two,' Bill Stanton said, stretching in his armchair, ice clinking in a glass in his hand. 'Met him in Jamaica, didn't we, Fran? We were on holiday – I never did find out whether Merry was vacationing or working.'

'Working,' said his wife, busy setting the table. She was calm and fair, a tall, slow-moving person: not at all what Will had expected from an American. 'On some government survey. He's a professor at Oxford University,' she said reverently to Will. 'A very very clever man. And such a sweetie – he came all the way to Ohio to spend a few days with us last fall, when he was over giving a lecture at Yale.'

'Ah,' said Will thoughtfully. He was prevented from asking more questions by a sudden noise from the wall beside him. A large wooden door swung open, narrowly missing his back, revealing Merriman in the act of closing another identical door beyond it.

'This is where the two cottages connect,' Merriman said, looking down at Will's surprise with a faint grin. 'They lock both doors if the two are let separately.'

'Supper won't be long,' said Fran Stanton in her soft drawl. As she spoke, a small stout lady with a grey knot of hair came into the room behind her, bearing a tray rattling with cups and plates.

'Evenin', Perfessor,' she said, beaming at Merriman. Will liked her face instantly; all its lines seemed carved by smiling.

'Evening, Mrs Penhallow.'

'Will,' said his uncle, 'this is Mrs Penhallow. She and her husband own these cottages. My nephew Will.'

She smiled at him, setting down the tray. 'Welcome to Trewissick, m'dear. We'll make sure you do have a wonderful holiday, with those other three scallywags.'

'Thank you,' Will said.

The dividing door burst open, and the three Drews came piling in.

'Mrs Penhallow! How are you?'

'Have you seen Rufus about?'

'Will Mr Penhallow take us fishing this time?'

'Is that awful Mrs Palk still here? Or her nephew?'

'How's the *White Heather*?'

'Slowly, slowly,' she said, laughing.

'Well,' Barney said. 'How's Mr Penhallow?'

'He'm fine. Out on the boat now, o' course. Now you just bide a moment while I get your supper.' She bustled out.

'I can see you three know your way about the place,' said Bill Stanton, his round face solemn.

'Oh yes,' said Barney complacently. 'Everyone knows us here.'

'We shall have a lot of friends to see,' said Simon rather too loudly, with a quick sideways glance at Will.

'Yes, they've been here before. They stayed for two weeks last summer,' said Merriman. Barney looked at him crossly. His great-uncle's craggy, deep-lined face was impassive.

'Three weeks,' said Simon.

'Was it? I beg your pardon.'

'It's lovely to be back,' Jane said diplomatically. 'Thank you very much for letting us come, Mr Stanton, Mrs Stanton.'

'You're very welcome.' Will's uncle waved a hand in the air. 'Things have worked out fine – you three and Will can all have a great time together, and leave us square old characters to ourselves.'

There was a very small silence. Then Jane said brightly, without looking at her brothers, 'Yes, we can.'

Will said to Simon, 'Why is it called Trewissick?'

'Er,' said Simon, taken aback, 'I really don't know. Do you know what it means, Gumerry?'

'Look it up,' said his great-uncle coolly. 'Research sharpens the memory.'

Will said diffidently, 'It's the place where they have the Greenwitch ceremony, isn't it?'

The Drews stared at him. 'Greenwitch? What's that?'

'Quite right,' Merriman said. He looked down at them, a twitch beginning at one side of his mouth.

'It was in some book I read about Cornwall,' Will said.

'Ah,' Bill Stanton said. 'Will is quite an anthropologist, his father was telling me. Watch out. He's very big on ceremonies and such.'

Will seemed to look rather uncomfortable. 'It's just a sort of spring thing,' he said. 'They make a leaf image and chuck it into the sea. Sometimes they call it the Greenwitch and sometimes King Mark's Bride. Old custom.'

'Oh yes. Like the carnival,' Barney said dismissively. 'In the summer.'

'Well no, not quite.' Will rubbed his ear, sounding apologetic. 'I mean, that Lammas carnival, it's more a sort of tourist affair, isn't it?'

'Huh!' said Simon.

'He's right, you know,' Barney said. 'There were far more visitors than locals dancing about the streets last summer. Including me.' He looked at Will rather thoughtfully.

'Here we be!' cried Mrs Penhallow, materializing in the room with a tray of food almost as big as herself.

'Mrs Penhallow must know all about the Greenwitch,' said Fran Stanton in her soft American voice. 'Don't you, Mrs Penhallow?' It was a well-meaning remark intended to keep the peace, in a situation which seemed to her a little prickly. But it had the reverse effect. The small round Cornishwoman set down her tray abruptly on the table, and the smile dropped from her face.

'I don't hold with talk of witches,' she said, politely but finally, and went out again.

'Oh my,' said Aunt Fran in dismay.

Her husband chuckled. 'Yankee, go home,' he said.

'What is this Greenwitch affair really, Gumerry?' Simon said next morning.

'Will told you.'

'All he knew was what he got out of some book.'

'He's going to be a nuisance, I'm afraid,' Barney said with distaste.

Merriman looked down at him sharply. 'Never dismiss anyone's value until you know him.'

Barney said, 'I only meant –'

'Shut up, Barney,' said Jane.

'The making of the Greenwitch,' said Merriman, 'is an old spring rite still celebrated here, for greeting summer and charming a good harvest of crops and fish. In a day or two, as it happens. If you will all tread a little more gently, Jane might be able to watch it.'

'Jane?' said Barney. 'Only Jane?'

'The making of the Greenwitch is very much a private village affair,' Merriman said. Jane thought his voice seemed strained, but his face was so near the roof of the narrow landing as to be lost in shadow. 'No visitors are normally allowed near. And of the locals, only women are allowed to be present.'

'Good grief!' said Simon in disgust.

Jane said, 'Surely we ought to be doing something about the grail, Gumerry? I mean after all that's why we're here. And we haven't got long.'

'Patience,' Merriman said. 'In Trewissick, as you may recall, you never had to go looking for things to happen. They tended to happen to you.'

'In that case,' Barney said, 'I'm going out for a bit.' He held the flat book in his hand unobtrusively against his side, but his great-uncle looked down from a height like a lighthouse.

'Sketching?' he said.

'Uh-huh,' said Barney reluctantly. The Drews' mother was an artist. Barney had always expressed horror at the idea of possessing the same talent, but in the last twelve months he had been disconcerted to find it creeping up on him.

'Try drawing this terrace from the other side,' Merriman said. 'With the boats as well.'

'All right. Why?'

'Oh, I don't know,' said his great-uncle vaguely. 'It might come in handy. A present for someone. Perhaps even for me.'

Crossing the quay, Barney passed a man sitting at an easel. It was a common enough sight in Trewissick, which like many of the more picturesque villages in Cornwall was much frequented by amateur painters. This particular artist had a very great deal of uncombed dark hair, and a square, hefty frame. Barney paused, and peeped over his shoulder. He blinked. On the easel was a wild abstract in crude bright colours, bearing no visible relation at all to the scene in the harbour before them; it was unexpected, compared to the neat, anaemic little water-colours that nineteen out of twenty Trewissick harbour-painters produced. The man was painting away like one demented. He said, without pausing or turning round, 'Go away.'

Barney lingered for a moment. There was real power in the painting, of a peculiar kind that made him oddly uneasy.

'Go away,' the man said more loudly.

'I'm going,' Barney said, moving one step backwards. 'Why green, up in that top corner, though? Why not blue? Or a *better* kind of green?' He was distressed by a lurid zig-zag of a particularly nasty shade, a yellowy, mustard-like green which drew the eye away from the rest of the picture. The man began to make a low rumbling noise like a growling dog, and the broad shoulders stiffened. Barney fled. He said to himself rebelliously, 'But that colour was *all wrong.*'

On the far side of the harbour he perched himself on a low wall, with the steep sliced rock of the headland at his back. The ill-tempered painter was invisible from there, hidden behind one of the inevitable piles of fish-boxes on the quay. Barney sharpened a new pencil with his penknife and began to doodle. A sketch of a single fishing-boat went badly, but a rough outline of the whole harbour began to turn out well, and Barney switched from pencil to an old-fashioned soft-nibbed fountain pen of which he was particularly fond. He worked fast then, pleased with the drawing, absorbed in its detail, sensing the awareness – still new, this spring – that something of himself was going out through his fingers. It was a kind of magic. Coming up for air, he paused, and held the drawing out at arm's length.

And without a sound, a large dark-sleeved hand came from one side and seized the sketch pad. Before Barney could turn his head, he heard a noise of ripping paper. Then the pad was flung back at his feet, tumbling over itself on the ground. Footsteps ran. Barney leapt up with an indignant shout, and saw a man running away up the quayside, the page from the sketch pad flapping white against his dark clothes. It was the long-haired, bad-tempered painter he had seen on the quay.

'Hey!' Barney yelled, furious. 'Come back!'

Without a glance behind, the man swung round the end of the harbour wall. He was a long way ahead, and the harbour path sloped uphill. Barney came tearing up just in time to hear a car engine snarl into life and roar away. He whirled round the corner into the road, and ran smack into someone walking up the hill.

'Uh!' grunted the stranger, as the breath was thumped out of him. Then his voice came back. 'Barney!'

It was Will Stanton.

'A man,' gasped Barney, staring round at him. 'Man in dark sweater.'

'A man came running up from the harbour just ahead of you,' Will said, frowning. 'He jumped into a car and drove off that way.' He pointed down into the village.

'That was him,' Barney said. He peered resentfully at the empty road.

Will looked too, fiddling with his jacket zip. He said with astonishing force, 'Stupid of me, *stupid*, I knew there was something – just not properly awake, thinking of –' He shook his head as if tossing something away from it. 'What did he do?'

'He's loopy. Mad.' Barney could still scarcely speak for indignation. 'I was sitting down there sketching, and he just came up from nowhere, ripped the drawing out of my book and belted off with it. What would any normal person do that for?'

'Did you know him?'

'No. Well, that is, I'd seen him, but only today. He was sitting down on the quay, painting, at an easel.'

Will smiled broadly. A silly smile, Barney thought. 'Sounds as though he thought your picture was better than his.'

'Oh, come off it,' Barney said impatiently.

'Well, what was his picture like?'

'Weird. Very peculiar.'

'There you are, then.'

'There I am not. It was weird, but it was good too, in a nasty sort of way.'

'Goodness me,' Will said, looking vacant. Barney glared at his round face with its thick brown fringe of hair, and felt more irritated than ever. He began trying to think of an excuse to get away.

'He had a dog in the car,' Will said absent-mindedly.

'A dog?'

'Barking like anything. Didn't you hear it? And jumping about. It nearly jumped out when he got in. Hope it didn't chew up your drawing.'

'I expect it did,' Barney said coldly.

'Lovely dog,' Will said, in the same vague, dreamy tone. 'One of those long-legged Irish setters, a super reddish colour. No decent man would shut a dog like that up in a car.'

Barney stood stock-still, looking at him. There was only one dog like that in Trewissick. He realized suddenly that directly across the road he could see a tall familiar grey house. At the same moment a gate at the side of the house swung open, and a man came out: a stout, elderly man with a short grey beard, leaning on a stick. Standing in the road, he put his fingers in his mouth and gave a sharp two-note whistle. Then he called, 'Rufus? Rufus!'

Impulsively Barney ran towards him. 'Captain Toms? You are Captain Toms, aren't you? Please, look, I know Rufus, I helped look after him last summer, and I think someone's stolen him. A man went off with him in a car, a dark man with long hair, an awful man.' He paused. 'Of course, if it was someone you know –'

The man with the beard looked carefully at Barney. 'No,' he said slowly, deliberately. 'I don't know a gentleman of that description. But you do seem to know Rufus. And by that hair of yours I fancy you'd be maybe Merriman's youngest nephew. One of my tenants, last year, eh? The children with the sharp eyes.'

'That's right.' Barney beamed. 'I'm Barnabas. Barney.' But something puzzled him about Captain Toms' manner: it was almost as if he were carrying on some other conversation at the same time. The old man was not even looking at him; he seemed to be gazing blankly at the surface of the water, seeing nothing, lost in his own mind.

Barney suddenly remembered Will. He turned – and saw to his astonishment that Will too was standing near him staring vacantly at nothing, expressionless, as if listening. What was the matter with everybody? 'This is Will Stanton,' he said loudly to Captain Toms.

The bearded face did not change expression. 'Yes,' said Captain Toms gently. Then he shook his head, and seemed to wake up. 'A dark man, you said?'

'He was a painter. Very bad-tempered. I don't know who he was or anything. But Will saw him going off with a dog who sounded just like Rufus – and just outside your door –'

'I will make inquiries,' Captain Toms said reassuringly. 'But come in, come in, both of you. You shall show your friend the Grey House, Barnabas. I must find my key . . . I was busy in the garden . . .' He felt in his pockets, patting at his jacket ineffectually with the arm not leaning on the stick. Then they were at the front door.

'The door's open!' Will said sharply. His voice was crisp, very different from his inane babbling of a few moments before, and Barney blinked.

Captain Toms pushed the half-open door with his stick, and stumped inside. 'That's how the fellow got Rufus out. Opened the front door while I was round the back . . . I still can't find that key.' He began fumbling in his pockets again.

Following him in, Barney felt something rustle at his feet; he bent, and picked up a sheet of white paper. 'You didn't pick up your –' He stopped abruptly. The note was very short, and in large letters. He could not help taking it in at a glance. He held it out to the captain, but it was Will, this strange brisk Will, who took the paper, and stood staring at it with the old man, the two heads close, young and old, brown and grey.

The note was made of large black capital letters cut from a newspaper and stuck very neatly together on the sheet. It said. 'IF YOU WANT YOUR DOG BACK ALIVE, KEEP AWAY FROM THE GREENWITCH.'

Chapter Three

Under the sunset sky the sea was glass-smooth. Long slow rollers from the Atlantic, rippling like muscles beneath the skin, made the only sign of the great invisible strength of the ocean in all the tranquil evening. Quietly the fishing-boats moved out, a broad fishtail wake spreading behind each one; their engines chugged softly through the still air. Jane stood at the end of Kemare Head, on the crest of a granite outfall that tumbled its rocks two hundred feet to the sea, and she watched them go. Toy boats, they seemed from there: the scatter of a fishing fleet that every week, every month, every year for endless years had been going out after the pilchard or the mackerel before dusk, and staying at the chase until dawn. Every year there were fewer of them, but still every year they went.

The sun dropped at the horizon, a fat glowing ball spreading yellow light over all the smooth sea, and the last boat crept out of Trewissick harbour, its engine thumping like a muffled heart-beat in Jane's ears. As the last spreading lines of the boat's wake washed against the harbour wall, in a final swift rush the great sun dropped below the horizon, and the light of the April evening began very slowly to die. A small wind sprang up. Jane shivered, and pulled her jacket around her; there was suddenly a coldness in the darkening air.

As if in answer to the beginning breeze, a light starred up suddenly across Trewissick Bay, on the headland opposite Kemare Head. At the same time there was a sudden warmth behind Jane's back. She swung round, and saw dark figures against tall flames, where a light had been set to the towering pile of driftwood and branches that had lain waiting to become a bonfire for this one night. Mrs Penhallow had told her that the two beacons would burn until the fishing-boats came back, flames leaping all through the night until the dawn.

Mrs Penhallow: now there was a mystery. Jane thought again of the moment that afternoon when she had been alone in the living-room, flipping through a magazine, waiting for Simon. She had heard a nervous clearing of the throat, and there in the kitchen doorway Mrs Penhallow was standing, round and rosy and unusually fidgetty.

'Ef you fancy comin' to the makin' tonight, m'dear, you'm welcome,' she said abruptly.

Jane blinked at her. 'The making?'

'The makin' of the Greenwitch.' The lilt of Mrs Penhallow's Cornish accent seemed more marked than usual. 'It do take all the night, 'tes a long business, and no outsiders allowed near, generally. But if you feel you'd like ... you being the only female close to the Perfessor, and all ...' She waved a hand as if to catch words. 'The women did agree it's all right, and I'd be happy to take 'ee.'

'Thank you very much,' said Jane, puzzled but pleased. 'Er ... can Mrs Stanton come too?'

'No,' Mrs Penhallow said sharply. She added more gently, as Jane's eyebrows went up, 'She'm a furriner, you see. Tisn't fitting.'

Up on the headland, gazing at the fire, Jane remembered the flat finality of the words. She had accepted the pronouncement and, without even trying to explain the situation to Fran Stanton, had come out after supper to the headland with Mrs Penhallow.

Yet still she had been given no idea of what was to happen. Nobody had told her what the thing called the Greenwitch would be like, or how it would be made, or what would happen to it. She knew only that the business would occupy the whole night, and end when the fishermen came home. Jane shivered again. Night was falling, and she was not over-fond of the nights of Cornwall; they held too much of the unknown.

Black shadows ran over the rocks around her, dancing and disappearing as the flames leapt. Instinctively seeking company, Jane moved forward into the circle of bright light around the bonfire; yet this too was unnerving, for now the other figures moved to and fro at the edge of the darkness, out of sight, and she felt suddenly vulnerable. She hesitated, frightened by the tension in the air.

'Come, m'dear,' said Mrs Penhallow's soft voice, beside her. 'Come by here.' There was a hint of urgency in her tone. Hastily she took Jane by the arm and led her aside. 'Time for the makin',' she said. 'You want to keep out of the way, if you can.'

Then she was gone again, leaving Jane alone near a group of women busying themselves with something not yet visible. Jane found a rock and sat down, warmed by the fire; she watched. Scores of women were there, of all ages: the younger ones in jeans and sweaters, the rest in sturdy dark skirts, long as overcoats, and high heavy boots. Jane could see a big pile of stones, each the size of a man's head, and a far higher pile of green branches – hawthorn, she thought – too leafy to be intended for the fire. But she did not understand the purpose of either of these.

Then one tall woman moved out before the rest, and held one arm high in the air. She called out something Jane could not understand, and at once the women set to working, in a curiously ordered way in small groups. Some would take up a branch, strip it of leaves and twigs, and test it for flexibility; others then would take the branch, and in some swift practised way weave it together with others into what began very slowly to emerge as a kind of frame.

After a while the frame began to show signs of becoming a great cylinder. The cleaning and bending and tying went on for a long time. Jane shifted restlessly. The leaves on some of the branches seemed to be of a different shape from the hawthorn. She was not close enough to see what they might be, and she did not intend to move. She felt she would only be safe here, half-invisible on her rock, unnoticed, watching from a little way off.

At her side suddenly she found the tall woman who had seemed the others' leader. Bright eyes looked down at her out of a thin face, framed by a scarf tied under the chin. 'Jane Drew, it is,' the woman said, with a Cornish accent that sounded oddly hard. 'One of those who found the grail.'

Jane jumped. The thought of the grail was never fully out of her mind, but she had not linked it with this strange ceremony here. The woman, however, did not mention it again.

'Watch for the Greenwitch,' she said conversationally. It was like a greeting.

The sky was almost black now, with only a faint rim of the glow of daylight. The lights of the two bonfires burned brightly on the headlands. Jane said hastily, clutching at this companionship against the lonely dark, 'What are they doing with those branches?'

'Hazel for the framework,' the woman said. 'Rowan for the head. Then the body is of hawthorn boughs, and hawthorn blossoms. With the stones within, for the sinking. And those who are crossed, or barren, or who would make any wish, must touch the Greenwitch then before she be put to cliff.'

'Oh,' Jane said.

'Watch for the Greenwitch,' said the woman pleasantly again, and moved away. Over her shoulder she said, 'You may make a wish too, if you like. I will call you, at the right time.'

Jane was left wondering and nervous. The women were busier now, working steadily, singing in a strange kind of wordless humming; the cylinder shape grew more distinct, closer-woven, and they carried the stones and put them inside. The head began to take shape: a huge head, long, squarish, without features. When the framework was done, they began weaving into it green branches starred with white blossoms. Jane could smell the heavy sweetness of the hawthorn. Somehow it reminded her of the sea.

Hours went by. Sometimes Jane dozed, curled beside her rock; whenever she woke, the framework seemed to look exactly as it had before. The work of weaving seemed endless. Mrs Penhallow came twice with hot tea from a flask. She said anxiously, 'Now if you do feel you've had enough, m'dear, you just say. Easy to take you along home.'

'No,' Jane said, staring at the great leafy image with its court of steady workers. She did not like the Greenwitch; it frightened her. There was something menacing in its broad squat shape. Yet it was hypnotic too; she could scarcely take her eyes off it. *It.* She had always thought of witches as being female, but she could feel no *she* quality in the Greenwitch. It was unclassifiable, like a rock or a tree.

The bonfire still burned, fed carefully with wood, its warmth was very welcome in the chill night. Jane moved away to stretch her stiff legs, and saw inland a faint greyness beginning to lighten the sky. Morning would be coming soon. A misty morning: fine drops of moisture were flicking at her face already. Against the lightening sky she could see Trewissick's standing stones, five of them, ancient skyward-pointing fingers halfway along Kemare Head. She thought: that's what Greenwitch is like. It reminds me of the standing stones.

When she turned back again towards the sea, the Greenwitch was finished. The women had drawn away from the great figure; they sat by the fire, eating sandwiches, and laughing, and drinking tea. As Jane looked at the huge image that they had made, out of leaves and branches, she could not understand their lightness. For she knew suddenly, out there in the cold dawn, that this silent image somehow held within it more power than she had ever sensed before in any creature or thing. Thunder and storms and earthquakes were there, and all the force of the earth and sea. It was outside Time, boundless, ageless, beyond any line drawn between good and evil. Jane stared at it, horrified, and from its sightless head the Greenwitch stared back. It would not move, or seem to come alive, she knew that. Her horror came not from fear, but from the awareness she suddenly felt from the image of an appalling, endless loneliness. Great power was held only in great isolation. Looking at the Greenwitch, she felt a terrible awe, and a kind of pity as well.

But the awe, from her amazement at so inconceivable a force, was stronger than anything else.

'You feel it, then.' The leader of the women was beside her again; the hard, flat words were not a question. 'A few women do. Or girls. Very few. None of those there, not one.' She gestured contemptuously at the cheerful group beyond. 'But one who has held the grail in her hands may feel many things . . . Come. Make your wish.'

'Oh no.' Jane shrank back instinctively.

In the same moment a cluster of four young women broke away from the crowd and ran to the broad, shadowy leaf-image. They were shaking with giggles, calling to one another; one, larger and noisier than the rest, rushed up and clasped the hawthorn sides that stretched far above her head.

'Send us all rich husbands, Greenwitch, pray thi' !' she shouted.

'Or else send her young Jim Tregoney!' bellowed another. Shrieking with laughter, they all ran back to the group.

'See there!' said the woman. 'No harm comes to the foolish, which is most of them. And therefore none to those with understanding. Will you come?'

She walked over to the big silent figure, laid a hand on it, and said something that Jane could not hear.

Nervously Jane followed. As she came close to the Greenwitch she felt again the unimaginable force it seemed to represent, but again the great loneliness too. Melancholy seemed to hover about it like a mist. She put out her hand to grasp a hawthorn bough, and paused. 'Oh dear,' she said impulsively, 'I wish you could be happy.'

She thought, as she said it: how babyish, when you could have wished for anything, even getting the grail back . . . even if it's all a lot of rubbish, you could at least have tried . . . But the hard-eyed Cornishwoman was looking at her with an odd surprised kind of approval.

'A perilous wish!' she said. 'For where one may be made happy by harmless things, another may find happiness only in hurting. But good may come of it.'

Jane could think of nothing to say. She felt suddenly extremely silly.

Then she thought she heard a muffled throbbing sound out at sea; she swung round. The woman too was looking outward, at a grey streak of horizon where none had been before. Out on the dark sea, lights were flickering, white and red and green. The first fishermen were coming home.

Afterwards, Jane remembered little of that long waiting time. The air was cold. Slowly, slowly, the fishing-boats came closer, over the stone-grey sea glimmering in the cold dawn. And then, when at last they neared the wharf, the village seemed to splutter into life. Lights and voices woke on the jetties; engines coughed; the air was filled with shouting and laughing and a great bustle of unloading; and over all of it the gulls wheeled and screamed, early-woken for thievery, eddying in a great white cloud round the boats to dive for discarded fish. Afterwards, Jane found herself remembering the gulls most of all.

Up from the harbour, when the unloading was done, and lorries gone to market and boxes gone into the little canning factory – up from the harbour came a procession of the fishermen. There were others too, factory men and mechanics and shopkeepers and farmers, all the men of Trewissick, but the dark-jerseyed fishermen, shadow-eyed, bristle-chinned, weary, smelling of fish, led the long crowd. They came along the headland, calling cheerfully to the women; no meeting could have been less romantic, Jane thought, up there in the sleepless cold under the dead grey light of the dawn, and yet there was a great light-heartedness among them all. The bonfire still burned, a last stock of wood newly blazing; the men gathered round it, rubbing their hands, in a tumult of deep voices that sounded harsh in Jane's ears after the lighter chattering of the women all night.

High and low in the sky the gulls drifted, uncertain, hopeful. Amongst all the bustle stood the Greenwitch, vast and silent, a little diminished by light and noise but still brooding, ominous. Despite all the raucous exchanges tossed between the men and women there was a curious respectfulness towards the strange leafy image; a clear reluctance to make any fun of the Greenwitch. Jane found that for some reason this left her feeling relieved.

She caught sight of Merriman's tall figure at the edge of the crowd of Cornishmen, but made no attempt to reach him. This was a time simply to wait and see what might happen next. The men seemed to be gathering in one group, the women moving away. All at once Mrs Penhallow was at Jane's side again.

'Come, let me show 'ee where to go, m'dear. Now, as the sun comes up, the men do put the Greenwitch to cliff.' She smiled at Jane, half earnest, half offering a self-conscious apology. 'For luck, you see, and for good fishing and a good harvest. So they say . . . But we must keep our distance, to give them a clear run.' She beckoned, and Jane followed her away from the Greenwitch to the side of the headland. She had only half an idea what this was all about.

The men began to crowd round the Greenwitch. Some touched it ostentatiously, laughing, calling aloud a wish. For the first time, in the growing daylight, Jane noticed that the square, leaf-woven figure had been built on a kind of platform, like a huge tray made of boards, and that this platform had a heavy wheel at each corner, carefully wedged with big stones. Calling and whooping, the men pulled the stones from the wheels, and Jane saw the figure sway as the platform moved free. Greenwitch was perhaps half again as high as a man, but very broad for its height, with its huge square head almost as wide as its body. It did not look like a copy of a human being. It looked, Jane thought, like a single representative of a fearful unknown species, from another planet, or from some unthinkably distant part of our own past.

'Heave, boys!' a voice called. The men had attached ropes to all four sides of the platform; they milled round, holding, steadying, gently pulling the swaying image towards the end of the headland. Greenwitch lumbered forward. Jane could smell the heavy scent of the hawthorn. The blossoms seemed brighter, the green boughs of Greenwitch's sides almost luminous; she realized that inland, over the moors beyond Trewissick, the sun was coming up. Yellow light blazed out over them; a cheer rose from the crowd, and the platform with the green figure moved almost to the clutter of rocks at the edge of the cliff.

Suddenly a shout, high-pitched as a scream, rang out over the crowd; Jane jumped, and turned to see a scuffle of jostling bodies at the edge of the crowd. A man seemed to be trying to break through; she glimpsed a dark-haired head, the face twisted with fury, and then the group closed again.

'Another of they newspaper photographers, I shouldn't wonder,' Mrs Penhallow said with a hint of smugness in her pleasant voice. ''Tisn't allowed to take pictures of the Greenwitch, but there's always one or two do try. The younger lads usually take care o' them.'

Jane thought the younger lads were probably taking good care of this year's intruder, judging by the speed with which his threshing form was being hustled away. She looked again for Merriman, but he seemed to have disappeared. And a change in the voice of the crowd drew her eyes back to the end of Kemare Head.

A voice called again, this time with familiar words of childhood. 'One to be ready . . . two to be steady . . . three to be *off*!' Only the ropes at the rear and sides of the trolley were held now, Jane saw, by perhaps a dozen men each. At the last word of command the crowd buzzed and murmured, the lines of men ran forwards and sideways, Greenwitch lurching faster and faster before them; and then in one swift complex movement the trolley was jerked outwards over the edge of the cliff, and brought up short from falling by its ropes.

And the great green tree-woven figure of the Greenwitch, with no rope to hold it back, was flung out into the air and down over the end of Kemare Head. For a split second it was there, visible, falling, in the blue and the green among the wheeling screaming white gulls, and then it was gone, plunging down, driven by the weight of the stones inside its body. There was a silence as if all Cornwall held its breath, and then they heard the splash.

Cheers and shouts rose from the headland. People rushed to the edge of the cliff, where the rope-holders were slowly dragging the wheeled trolley back up over the rock. After a swift glance over the edge, they surrounded the heaving string of men, cheering them back along Kemare Head. When the crowd near the rocks had thinned away Jane clambered to the edge, and peered cautiously down.

Down there, the sea washed its great slow swells against the foot of the cliff as if nothing had happened. Only a few scattered twigs of hawthorn floated on the water, rising and falling with the swells, drifting to and fro.

Suddenly giddy, Jane drew back from the rocks to the edge of the cheerful Trewissick crowd. There was no smell of hawthorn now, only a mixture of wood-smoke and fish. The bonfire had burned out, and people were beginning to drift away, back to the village.

Jane saw Will Stanton before he saw her. Beside her, a group of fishermen moved away and there was Will, outlined against the grey morning sky, straight brown hair flopping down to his eyebrows, chin jutting in a way that for a split second reminded her oddly of Merriman. The boy from Buckinghamshire was gazing out to sea, unmoving, lost in some fierce private contemplation. Then he turned his head and looked straight at her.

The fierceness became a polite relaxed smile with such speed that Jane felt it was unnatural. She thought: we've been so chilly to him, he can't really be as pleased to see me as all that.

Will came towards her. 'Hallo,' he said. 'Were you here all night? Was it exciting?'

'It went on a long time,' Jane said. 'The exciting part was sort of spread out. And the Greenwitch –' She stopped.

'What was the making of it like?'

'Oh. Beautiful. Creepy. I don't know.' She knew she could never describe it, in the sensible light of day. 'Have you been with Simon and Barney?'

'No,' Will said. His gaze slid past her. 'They were – busy – somewhere. With your great-uncle, I expect.'

'I expect they were dodging you,' Jane said, astounded at her own honesty. 'They can't help it, you know. I don't think it'll last long, once they've got used to you. There's something else bothering them, you see, nothing connected with you . . .'

'Don't worry about it,' Will said. For an instant Jane was looking at a quick reassuring grin; then his eyes flicked away again. She had an embarrassing feeling that she was wasting her breath; that the Drews' rudeness had not troubled Will Stanton in the least. Hastily she took refuge in prattle.

'It was nice when the fishermen and everyone came up from the harbour. And seagulls everywhere . . . and I saw Gumerry too, but he seems to have gone again now. Did you see him?'

Will shook his head, pushing his hands deep into the pockets of his battered leather jacket. 'We're lucky he got us the chance to come up here. They're supposed to go to a lot of trouble keeping visitors out, normally.'

Jane said, remembering: 'There was one newspaper photographer who tried to get up close to the Greenwitch when they were taking it to the edge of the cliff. A lot of boys dragged him off. He was yelling like anything.'

'A dark man? With long hair?'

'Well yes, as a matter of fact. At least I think so.' She stared at him.

'Ah,' Will said. His amiable round face was vacant again. 'Was that before you saw Merriman, or afterwards?'

'After,' Jane said, puzzled.

'Ah,' Will said again.

'Hey, Jane!' Barney came skidding up, out of breath, oversize boots flapping, with Simon close behind him. 'Guess what we did, we saw Mr Penhallow and he let us go on board the *White Heather*, and we helped them unload –'

'Poof!' Jane backed away. 'You certainly did!' Wrinkling her nose at their scale-spattered sweaters, she turned back to Will.

But Will was not there. Gazing round, she could see no sign of him anywhere.

'Where's he gone?' she said.

Simon said, 'Where's who gone?'

'Will Stanton was here. But he's vanished. Didn't you see him?'

'We must have frightened him away.'

'We really ought to be nicer to him, you know,' Barney said.

'Well, well, well,' Simon said indulgently. 'We'll keep him happy. Take him for a climb, or something. Come on, Jane, tell us about the Greenwitch.'

But Jane was not listening. 'That was odd,' she said slowly. 'I don't mean Will going off, I mean something he said. He's only known Gumerry for three days, and he's a polite sort of boy. But when he was talking about him just now, without thinking, the way things slip out naturally because you aren't watching – he didn't call Gumerry " your great-uncle" or "Professor Lyon", the way he usually does. He called him "Merriman". Just as if they were both the same age.'

Chapter Four

It was the sky that began the oddness of the rest of that day. As the Drews walked back along Kemare Head to the harbour the sun rose higher ahead of them, but gave no warmth, for as it rose a fine hazy mist began to grow too. In a little while the mist covered all the sky, so that the sun hung there familiar and yet strange, like a furry orange.

'Heat haze,' said Simon when Jane pointed this out to him. 'It's going to be a nice day.'

'I don't know,' said Jane doubtfully. 'It looks funny to me, more like a kind of danger signal . . .'

By the time they had finished their large breakfast at the cottage, served by a sleepy Mrs Penhallow, the haze was thicker.

'It'll burn off,' Simon said. 'When the sun gets higher.'

'I wish Great-Uncle Merry would come home,' said Jane.

'Stop worrying. Will Stanton isn't back yet either, they could be talking to Mr Penhallow, or someone. What's the matter with you this morning?'

'Needs a nap,' Barney said. 'Poor child. Had no sleep.'

'Poor child, indeed,' said Jane, and was overtaken by a huge yawn.

'See?' said Barney.

'Perhaps you're right,' Jane said meekly, and she went to her room, setting the alarm clock to waken her in an hour's time.

When the shrilling bell buzzed through her head, it woke her into total confusion. Though the curtains were open, the room was almost dark. For a moment Jane thought it was night, and she waking early, until into her mind swam the image of the Greenwitch falling, falling down to the early-morning sea, and in alarm she jumped out of bed. The sky outside was solid with heavy dark clouds; she had never seen anything quite like it. The light was so dim that it was as if the sun had never risen that day.

Simon and Barney were alone downstairs, gazing anxiously out at the sky. Mr and Mrs Stanton, Jane knew, had left Trewissick early that morning for a two-day tour of china-clay pits; Mrs Penhallow, the boys reported, had retreated to bed. And Merriman and Will had still not appeared at all.

'But what could Gumerry be doing? Something must have happened!'

'I don't know quite what we can do, except wait.' Simon was subdued now too. 'I mean, we could go out to look for him, but where would we start?'

'The Grey House,' Barney said suddenly.

'Good idea. Come on, Jane.'

*

'He seems to be taking the appearance of a painter,' Will said to Merriman as they made their way back along Kemare Head, behind the last straggle of cheerful villagers. 'A swarthy kind of man, of middle height, with long dark hair and apparently a real but rather nasty talent. A nice touch, that.'

'The nastiness may be unintentional,' Merriman said grimly. 'Even the great lords of the Dark cannot keep their true nature from colouring their dissimulations.'

'You think he is one of the great lords?'

'No. No, almost certainly not. But go over the rest of it.'

'He has already made a contact with the children. With Barney. And he has a totem – he stole a drawing that Barney had done, of the harbour.'

Merriman hissed between his teeth. 'I had a purpose for that drawing. Our friend is further ahead of us than I gave him credit for. Never under-estimate the Dark, Will. I have been on the verge of it this time.'

'He has also,' said Will, 'stolen Captain Toms' dog Rufus. He left a note warning that the dog would die if the captain went near the Greenwitch – taking care Barney would see the note too. A very neat piece of blackmail. If Captain Toms had gone up to Kemare Head after that, Barney would have thought him a murderer . . . Of course the Dark knew he would be keeping only one of the Old Ones away from the making, but it could have helped him a lot . . . Rufus really is a marvellous animal, though, isn't he?' For a moment Will's voice was that not of an ageless Old One but of an enthusiastic small boy.

The concern in Merriman's bleak, craggy face relaxed into a small smile. 'Rufus played a part of his own in the winning of the grail last summer. He has more talent for communicating with ordinary human beings than most four-legged creatures.'

At the end of the grassy headland, most of the villagers turned downhill to the quayside and the main village road. Merriman led Will straight ahead, to the higher road overlooking the harbour. Pausing to let a few other weary Greenwitch-makers pass, they crossed to the narrow grey-painted house that stood tallest of any in the terraced row. Merriman opened the front door, and they went in.

A long hallway stretched before them, hazy in the early-morning light. From an open door on their right Captain Toms said: 'In here.'

It was a broad room of bookshelves, armchairs, pictures of sailing-ships; he sat in a leather armchair with his right leg outstretched. Its foot, wearing a carpet slipper over a bandage, was propped on a leather-padded footstool. 'Gout,' said Captain Toms apologetically to Will. 'Kicks up now and again, you know. Sign of a misspent youth, they say. It immobilizes me just as effectively as any gentleman of the Dark could do – if our friend had had any foresight, he needn't have bothered to grab poor Rufus.'

'That is a gift he lacks, I think.' Merriman spreadeagled himself on a long sofa, with a small sigh of relief. 'I am not quite sure why, since he is clearly of some rank. Something he dares not exercise, perhaps? Anyway the theft of the grail, the attention paid to linking up with the children, and especially Barney – they all add up in the same direction.'

Captain Toms ran a finger reflectively over his close grey beard. 'You think he plans to have the boy look into the grail, to find him the future . . . the old scrying? . . . Well, it's possible.'

Will said: 'But is that what he wants *first*?'

'Whether it is or not, Barney will need careful watching.'

'I shall haunt him,' Will said. 'He'll hate it.' He prowled restlessly round the room, staring at pictures without seeing them. 'But where is the Dark? Where is he? Not far away, I think.'

'I have had that feeling too,' Captain Toms said quietly from his armchair. 'He is quite close by. Just after sunrise this morning I felt him go past the house, quite quickly, and there has been a faint sense of his nearness ever since.'

'That was when he tried to get to the Greenwitch, before the throwing,' Merriman said. 'Lucky for us he failed, or the creature might have responded. The fishermen hustled him off this way – they were most indignant, and rather rough . . . I followed into the village, until they released him. Then he put a shadow round himself, and I lost the way. But yes, he is near. One senses the ill-will.'

Will stopped his prowling abruptly, stiffening like a pointing dog. Hastily Merriman swung his long legs off the sofa and stood up. 'What is it?'

'Do you feel anything? Hear anything?'

'I did, I think. You're right.' Captain Toms hobbled to the door, leaning heavily on his stick. 'Come outside, quick.'

The sound of barking rose even while they crossed the hall, and as they stood together on the steps of the Grey House it grew louder, nearer, the straining hysterical noise of a dog demanding freedom. Overhead the sky was leaden grey, and the daylight had become grim and murky. Along the road from the village, further down the hill where the harbour and the jetties began, a red flurry of speed came hurtling towards them, with the dark figure of a man running after it.

Will said sharply, on a high note of alarm: 'But look – the children!'

On the quayside along the edge of the harbour road they saw Simon, Jane and Barney breaking into a run, excited, not yet seeing Rufus but responding eagerly to the sound of his bark. 'Rufus!' Barney was shouting gleefully. 'Rufus!'

The Old Ones stood poised, waiting.

As Rufus rushed joyfully round the corner towards the children, they saw the dark man raise his hand. In mid-air the dog froze, motionless, and dropped like a log of wood right in the children's path. Simon, thrown off balance too late to veer aside, tripped helplessly over him and fell hard to the ground. He lay still. Jane and Barney skidded to a halt, aghast. The dark-haired man neared them, paused, raised a hand pointing at Barney –

Only Simon saw. Lying on the ground, facing the hill, drifting back out of the moment of black unconsciousness that had swallowed him when he hit the ground, he blinked his dazed eyes open. And he saw, or thought he saw, three shining figures in a great blaze of white light. They towered and grew, their brilliance blinding Simon's eyes; they seemed to be swelling towards him, and he closed his eyes against the pain of the light. His head was full of whirling noise still, he was not properly out of unconsciousness. Afterwards he was able to tell himself that it was all imagination: confusion after a blow. But the overwhelming sense of awe that had swept over him never afterwards quite left his memory.

And Jane and Barney, caught out of movement, staring horrified at the dark-haired man almost upon them now, saw only the dreadful change on his face as suddenly he reeled back, spun away from them, beneath the impact of some unseen force. Snarling with malignant fury, he seemed to be fighting a tremendous battle with – nothing. His body was rigid; the fighting was all in his eyes and the cold line of his mouth. There was a long horrible moment of waiting, as the dark figure froze, fiercely twisted under the grey light of the dark sky. Then something in him seemed to snap, and he flung round without another glance at them; rushed away and was gone.

Rufus moved, whining; Simon stirred and sat up. He got to his hands and knees over the dog, and patted his head groggily. Rufus licked his hand, struggling to his four wobbly feet like a newborn calf.

'I feel like that too,' said Simon. Carefully, he stood up.

Jane prodded him with a nervous finger. 'Are you all right?'

'Not a scratch.'

'What happened?'

'I don't know. There was such a bright light . . .' His voice trailed away, as he tried to remember.

'That was from banging your head,' said Barney. 'The man, you didn't see him, he was right on top of us and then – I don't know, something stopped him. It was weird.'

'As if he had some kind of fit,' said Jane. 'He sort of writhed about, with this awful look on his face, and then he just dashed off.'

'He was the painter. The one who took my drawing.'

'Was he really? Of course, he stole Rufus too, that was why –'

But Barney was not listening. He stood gazing up at the high-sloping road beside the harbour. 'Look,' he said in a strange flat voice.

They looked with him, and striding down towards them from the direction of the Grey House came Merriman. His jacket flapped open, his hands were in his pockets, his wild white hair lifted in the breeze that was beginning to stir all around. He said when he reached them. 'You're going to get wet if you stand about waiting for the rain.'

Jane glanced up distractedly at the darkening sky. 'Didn't you see what happened, just this minute?'

'Some of it,' Merriman said. 'Are you hurt at all, Simon?'

'I'm fine.'

Barney was still gazing at him with a bemused look on his face. 'It was you, wasn't it?' he said softly. 'You stopped him, somehow. He's from the Dark.'

'Come now, Barney,' Merriman said briskly. 'That's a large assumption. Let us not conjecture where your unpleasant friend came from – just enjoy the fact that he is gone, and Rufus safe and sound back again.'

The red dog licked his hand, feathery tail waving furiously. Merriman rubbed his soft ears. 'Go home,' he said. Without a glance round, Rufus made off up the hill beside the harbour, and they watched in silence as he disappeared into the side entrance of the Grey House.

Barney said, 'That's all very well, but I thought you brought us here to help?'

'Barney!' said Jane.

'You are already helping,' Merriman said gently. 'I told you, be patient.'

Simon said, 'We came out to look for you. We thought something might have happened.'

'I was just in the Grey House, chatting with Captain Toms.'

'Will Stanton hasn't come home since the Greenwitch thing, either.'

'Just sight-seeing, I dare say. I expect we shall find him at home when we go back.' Merriman glanced up again at the lowering grey clouds. A long low rumbling came from the sky over the sea. 'Come along,' he said. 'Home. Before the storm breaks.'

Jane said absently, as they trotted obediently to keep up with his long loping strides, 'The poor Greenwitch, all alone there in the sea. I hope the waves don't smash it all to bits.'

They scrambled up the last narrow steps to the cottage; as they reached the door, white light ripped open the sky, and a huge thumping crash echoed and re-echoed around the bay.

Merriman said, through the noise, 'I don't think they will.'

Jane stood again on Kemare Head, but now she was alone, and the storm at its height. It seemed neither night nor day. The sky was grey all around, heavy, hanging; sharp lightning split it, thunder rumbled and thudded, echoing back from the inland moors. Gulls whirled and screamed in the wind. Below, the sea boiled, waves raging, tearing at the rocks. Jane felt herself lean on the wind, lean out over the cliff – and then leap high in the air, out, down, falling through the wind with the gulls swooping round her as she fell.

There was sick horror in the falling, but a kind of wild delight too. The great waves swirled to meet her, and with no shock nor splash nor sense of another element she was still falling, falling slowly, floating down through the green underwater where none of the wild frenzy from the storm above could reach. There was no movement but a slow swaying of weed, from the deepest touch of the great ocean swells. And before her, she saw the Greenwitch.

The great leafy image rested upright against a group of craggy rocks; they gave it shelter. The Greenwitch stood undamaged, just as Jane had seen it before, the square unhuman head set on the gigantic broad body. Its leaves and hawthorn blossoms were spread like weed in the gentle tug of the water, rippling to and fro. Small fish darted round the head. The whole structure swayed now and then, rhythmically, when the long reach of the stormswell pulled at it.

Then as Jane watched, the swaying grew more pronounced, as though the storm were reaching deeper into the sea. She could feel the pull of the waves herself; she moved like a fish, both obeying and resisting them. Greenwitch began to turn and sway, faster, further, drawn so far in each direction that it seemed the whole figure must topple and be carried away. Jane felt a dark chill in the water, a sense of great threatening power, and to her horror the movement of the Greenwitch changed. Limbs stirred of themselves, the leafy head rippled and stirred as if it were a face. Then the coldness suddenly was gone, the sea was muted blue and green again with the weed and the fish swaying in the swell – but now the Greenwitch, she knew, was alive. It was neither good nor evil, it was simply alive, aware of her as she had all along been aware of it.

The huge leafy head turned towards her, and without a voice the Greenwitch spoke, spoke into her mind.

'I have a secret,' the Greenwitch said.

Jane felt the loneliness that she had felt in the thing up on the headland, in the beginning: the sorrow and emptiness. But through it she felt the Greenwitch clutching at something for comfort, like a child with a toy – though this child was hundreds of years old, and through all its endlessly renewed life had never had such comfort before.

'I have a secret. I have a secret.'

'You are lucky,' Jane said.

The living tower of branches bent towards her, nearer. 'I have a secret, it is mine. Mine, mine. But I will show you. If you promise not to tell, not to tell.'

'I promise,' Jane said.

The Greenwitch lurched sideways, all its twigs and leafy armlets rippling together in the water, and as it moved away from the shallow niche in the rocks against which it had been leaning, Jane saw something there in the shadows. It was a small bright shining thing, lying within the cleft in the rock, on the white sand; it was like a small glowing stick. It looked like nothing of importance, except that it glowed with this strange light.

As to a small child showing its toy, she said to the Greenwitch: 'It's lovely.'

'My secret,' said the Greenwitch. 'I guard it. No-one shall touch it. I guard it well, for always.'

Without warning, the darkness and the chill came again over the water, infusing the whole undersea world. The Greenwitch changed utterly, in an instant. It became hostile, angry, threatening. It loomed over Jane.

'You'll tell! You'll tell!'

The leafy head split horribly into a parody of a face, snarling, furious; the branching form seemed to spread, opening, grasping out to envelop her as the Greenwitch lurched inexorably forward. Jane backed away in terror, cowering down. The water was very hot suddenly, fierce, oppressive, full of roaring noise.

'I won't tell! I promise! I promise! *I promise* . . .'

Cold air was on her face. 'Jane! Wake up! Come on, Jane, wake up now, it's all over, it's not real . . . Jane, wake up . . .' Merriman's deep voice was soft but insistent, his hands strong and reassuring on her shoulders. Jane sat bolt upright in the little bedroom, looked at his face, leant her damp forehead on his arm and burst into tears.

'Tell me about it,' said Merriman soothingly.

'I can't! I promised!' The tears came faster.

'Now look here,' Merriman said when she was calmer. 'You had a bad nightmare, and it's all over. I heard a very muffled sort of shout in here and when I came in you were right down among the bedclothes, must have been as hot as blazes. No wonder you dreamed. Now tell me about it.'

'Oh dear,' said Jane miserably. She told him.

'Mmm,' said Merriman, when she had finished. His bleak, bony face was in shadow; she could read nothing from it.

'It was awful,' Jane said. 'The last bit.'

'I'm sure it was. Last night's doings were too rich a diet for your imagination, I'm afraid.'

Jane managed a small weak grin. 'We had apple pie and cheese for supper tonight. That might have helped too.'

Merriman chuckled and stood up, looming against the low ceiling. 'All right now?'

'All right. Thank you.' As he went out she said, 'Gumerry?'

'What is it?'

'I really do feel sorry for the Greenwitch, still.'

'I hope you may retain that emotion,' said Merriman obscurely. 'Sleep well now.'

Jane lay tranquil, listening to the rain against the window, and the last rumbles of the dying storm. Just before she drowsed away she thought, in a sudden flash of remembering, that she recognized the small bright object that in her dream had been the Greenwitch's secret. But before she could catch at the memory, she was asleep.

Chapter Five

Simon burrowed deeper into the small cosy cave between pillow and bedclothes. 'Mmmmmff, Nya. Go away.'

'Oh come on, Simon.' Barney tugged persistently at the sheet. 'Get up. It's a super morning, come and see. Everything's all shiny from the rain last night, we could go down to the harbour before breakfast. Just for a walk. No-one else is awake. Come on.'

Growling, Simon opened one eye and blinked at the window. In the clear blue sky a seagull turned and lazily drifted, arching down on unmoving wings. 'Oh well,' he said. 'All right.'

In the harbour, nothing moved. Boats hung motionless at their moorings, their mast-images unrippled in the still water. There was a sea-smell of creosote from nets draped for mending over the harbour wall. Nothing broke the silence but the clatter of a distant milk-van somewhere high up in the village. The boys pattered down rainpatched steps and through narrow alleys.

As they stood looking down at the nearest boats a village mongrel trotted up, sniffed amiably at their heels, and went on his way.

'Rufus might be out too,' Barney said. 'Let's go and see.'

'All right.' Simon ambled after him, content, relaxed in the stillness and the sunshine and the gentle swish of the sea.

'There he is!' The rangy red dog came bounding towards them across the quayside. He pranced about them, tail waving, white teeth grinning as the long pink tongue lolled out.

'Idiot dog,' said Simon affectionately as the tongue curled wetly round his hand.

Barney squatted down and gazed solemnly into Rufus's brown eyes. 'I do wish he could talk. What would you tell us, boy, eh? About the painter from the Dark, and where he took you? Where was it, Rufus? Where did he hide you, eh?'

The setter stood still for a moment, looking at Barney; then he cocked his narrow head on one side and gave a curious noise that was half-bark, half-whine, like a kind of question. He swung round, lolloped a few paces along the quay, then stopped and looked back at them. Barney stood up slowly. Rufus trotted away a few more steps, then again turned and looked back, waiting for them.

'What on earth?' said Simon, watching.

'He wants to show us!' Barney hopped nervously up and down. 'Come on, Simon, quick! He'll show us where the painter hides, I bet you, and we shall be able to tell Gumerry!'

Rufus whined, questioning.

'I don't know,' Simon said. 'We ought to get home. Nobody knows where we are.'

'Oh come on, quick, before he changes his mind,' Barney grabbed his arm and tugged him after the lean red dog, already trotting away now confidently across the quay.

Rufus led them straight across the harbour and round into the road that ran inland from the Grey House and the sea; the road was familiar at first, leading back through the narrowest part of the village, past quiet cottages sleeping behind lace-curtained windows, and once or twice a modest house grandly labelled PRIVATE HOTEL. Then they were behind Trewissick, in the hedge-rimmed farmland that curved around the white cones and green ponds of the clay-burrow country, until, far inland, it met the moors.

Simon said, 'We can't go much farther, Barney. We shall have to turn back.'

'Just a little bit more.'

On they went, along silent roads bright with the springtime green of newly full trees. Simon looked around him, with the flickerings of unease in his mind. Nothing was wrong: the sun warmed them; dandelions brightly starred the grass; what could be wrong? Suddenly Rufus turned off the road into a narrow, leafy lane; a signpost at the corner read PENTREATH FARM. On either side, the trees reached their branches up and over to arch in a leafy roof; even in full daylight the lane was shadowed, cool, with only a faint dappling of sunshine filtering through the leaves. All at once Simon was filled with an immense foreboding. He stood stone-still.

Barney looked over his shoulder. 'What's wrong?'

'I don't know, exactly.'

'Did you hear something?'

'No. I just . . . it's as if I've been here before . . .' Simon shivered. 'It's the funniest feeling,' he said. Barney looked at him nervously. 'P'raps we really should go back?'

Simon did not answer; he was staring ahead, frowning. Rufus, who had disappeared round a corner in the lane for a moment, was bounding back again in a great unexplained hurry.

'Into the trees, quick!' Simon grabbed Barney's arm, and with the dog close behind them they slipped into the thicket of trees and brush that edged each side of the road. In there, picking their way carefully from tree to tree to avoid rustling footfalls, they inched forward until they could see the part of the lane that lay ahead, round the corner. They did not speak or whisper; they scarcely breathed and at their feet Rufus crouched still as a dead dog.

There ahead, the trees were no longer thick, the land no longer a leafy tunnel. Instead they saw a wide field scattered with large single trees and clumps of scrub. Across it, the lane was no more than a grassy track, two wheel-worn ruts, winding away to where the trees grew thick again. It did not look as though many people used the path to Pentreath Farm. And there was no sign of any farmhouse. Instead, clear ahead of them in the sunlit field, they saw a caravan.

It stood tall and glittering and handsome: a real old-fashioned gipsy caravan, of a kind they had never seen before except in pictures. Above the high wood-spoked wheels rose white wooden sides, sloping gently outwards, up to the curved wooden roof with its cone-hatted chimney. At each corner between roof and walls, brightly-painted scrollwork filled the eaves. In the side walls, square windows were set, neatly curtained; leaning down from the front of the van were shafts for the horse that stood grazing quietly near-by. At the rear, a sturdy six-rung ladder led up to a door painted with ornate decorations to match the scrollwork: a split door, of the kind used in stables, with the top half hanging open and the lower half latched shut.

As they crouched behind the trees, breathlessly staring, a figure appeared in the doorway, opened this lower door and began descending the steps of the caravan. Barney tightened his grip on Simon's arm. There was no mistaking the long wild dark hair, the snarling brow; the painter was even dressed exactly as he had been both times before, like a fisherman, in navy-blue jersey and trousers. He swallowed nervously at the impact of the man's nearness; it was as if there were a cloud of malevolence all around him. Barney was suddenly very glad that they were deep in the trees out of all possible sight. He stood very still indeed, praying that Rufus would not make a sound.

But although indeed there was no sound anywhere in the clearing except the clear morning song of birds in the trees, the dark man paused suddenly at the bottom of the caravan steps. He lifted his head and turned it all round, like a deer questing; Barney saw that his eyes were shut. Then the man turned full in their direction, the cold eyes opened beneath the lowering brows, and he said clearly, 'Barnabas Drew. Simon Drew. Come out.'

No thought of running away came into their minds, or anything but unquestioning obedience. Barney walked automatically forward out of the trees, and felt Simon moving with him in the same unhesitating way. Even Rufus trotted docile at their side.

They stood together in the sunlit field beside the caravan, facing the dark man in his dark clothes, and although the sun was warm on their skin it seemed to them that the day had become chill. The man looked at them, unsmiling, expressionless. 'What do you want?' he said.

Somewhere in Barney's mind, as a spark flickers and finds tinder and blazes up into a flame, a small light of resentment flared suddenly into a crossness that burned away fear. He said boldly, 'Well, for one thing I'd like my drawing back.'

Beside him he half-saw Simon shake his head a little, like one pushing away sleep, and knew that he too was clear of the spell. He said more loudly, 'You stole my drawing, down in the harbour, goodness knows why. And I liked it, and I want it back.'

The dark eyes contemplated him coolly; it was impossible to read any emotion behind them. 'Quite a promising little scribble, for your age.'

'Well, you certainly don't need it,' Barney said; for a moment he spoke with admiration, thinking of the real power in the man's painting.

'No,' said the man, with an odd, grim half-smile. 'Not now.' He moved back up the steps and through the double door; over his shoulder he said, 'Very well, then. Come on.'

Rufus, who had stood stock-still from the beginning, began a low rumbling growl deep in his throat. Simon put a hand down to quiet him, and said, 'That wouldn't be very sensible, Barney.'

But Barney said lightly, 'Oh no, I think it would be all right,' and he moved towards the caravan steps. Simon had no choice but to follow him. 'Stay, Rufus,' he said. The setter folded his long legs and lay down at the foot of the steps, but still the long low growl went on eerie and unbroken; they could hear it soft in the background like a reminder of warning.

The dark man had his back to them. 'Look well at the Romany vardo,' he said, without turning. 'There are few of them to be seen any more.'

'Romany?' said Simon, 'Are you a gipsy?'

'Half Romany chal,' the man said, 'and half gorgio.' He turned and stood with arms folded, surveying them. 'I am part gipsy, yes. That's the best you'll find these days, on the road at any rate. Even the vardo is only part gipsy.'

He nodded at the roof of the caravan, and they saw, looking up, that it was edged all about with the same brightly-painted scrollwork that decorated the outside, and that tools of some small kind hung all over one wall, with an old fiddle and an oddly-striped woollen rug. But the furniture was shiny-cheap and modern, and the chimney was not a real chimney, but only a vent for carrying away hot air from above the neat electric stove.

Then they saw suddenly that the ceiling was painted. From end to end, above the bright conventional curlicues of the scrollwork, a huge churning abstract painting was spread above their heads. There was no recognizable form to its shapes and colours, yet it was a disturbing, alarming sight, full of strange whorls and shadows and shot through with lurid colours that jarred on the senses. Barney felt again the power and the nastiness that had leapt at him from the canvas he had seen the man painting in the harbour; up on this ceiling too he saw the particular unnerving shade of green he had found so unpleasant out there. He said suddenly to Simon, 'Let's go home.'

'Not yet,' said the dark man. He spoke softly, without moving, and Barney felt a chill awareness of the Dark reaching out to control him — until without warning a faint hissing sound that had been vaguely puzzling him erupted into the boiling of a kettle, and a shrill whistle filled the room and made a sense of evil suddenly ridiculous.

But Simon had felt it too. He looked at the dark man and thought: *you keep steering us away from being frightened, delaying it. Why do you want us to stay?*

The dark-haired man busied himself with the prosaic matter of spooning instant coffee into a mug and pouring on water from the kettle. 'Either of you drink coffee?' he said over his shoulder.

Simon said quickly, 'No thank you.'

Barney said, 'I wouldn't mind a drink of water.' Seeing Simon's scowl, he added plaintively, 'Well, I did get awfully thirsty walking. Not just a drink of water from the tap?'

'In that cupboard by your right foot,' the painter said, 'you will find some cans of orangeade.' He moved to the small table at the end of the caravan, stirring his coffee. 'Sealed,' he added with a deliberate ironic stare at Simon. 'Fizzy. Harmless. Straight from the factory.'

'Thanks,' Barney said promptly, bending to the cupboard door.

The man said, 'You might bring out a cardboard box you'll find in there, too.'

'All right.' After some bumping and rattling, Barney came up with an unremarkable brown box; set it on the table and produced two drinks from the crook of his elbow. Without comment Simon took one, and popped open the top, to a reassuring hiss; but a stubborn caution still made him reluctant to drink, and he made only a pretence of swigging at the can. Barney drank thirstily, with appreciative gurgling noises.

'That's better. Thanks. Now may I have my picture back?'

'Open the box,' the man said, the long hair falling about his face as he drank from his mug.

'Is it in there?'

'Open the box,' the man said again, with a faint edge of strain in his voice. Simon thought: *he's as tense as a strung wire. Why?*

Setting down his drink on the table, Barney opened the top of the brown cardboard box. He took out a sheet of paper, and held it up critically. 'Yes, that's my drawing.'

He glanced back into the box, and then all at once a brightness was in his eyes, a fierce brilliance flashing into his brain, and he was staring in disbelief, crying out in a voice that broke into huskiness.

'Simon! It's the grail!'

In the same instant the world about them changed; with a crash the doors of the little caravan swung shut, and blinds fell over the windows, cutting out all light of day. There was an instant of black darkness, but almost at once Barney found himself blinking in a dim light. Wildly he looked round for its source, and then he realized with a sick shock that the glow, still dim, disturbing, came not from any lamp but from the painted ceiling. Up on the roof, the eerie green whorls that had so troubled him were shining with a cold bleak light. They had shapes, he saw now; angular shapes arranged in groups, like a kind of unknown writing. In the cold green light he looked down, fearful, disbelieving, and saw the same wonderful familiar object that he had seen before gleaming inside the cardboard box. Gently he lifted it out, forgetting everything around him, and set it on the table.

Simon breathed, beside him, 'It is!'

Before them on the table the Cornish grail glowed: the little golden goblet that they had first seen, after so hard a search, deep in a cave beneath the cliffs of Kemare Head, and that they had saved from the people and the power of the Dark, for a while. They did not understand what it was, or what it could do; they knew only that to Merriman and the Light it was one of the great Things of Power, something of infinite value, and that one day it would come into its own when the strange runic signs and words engraved over its sides could be understood. Barney gazed as he had gazed a thousand times before at the pictures and patterns and incomprehensible signs on the golden sides of the grail. If only, if only . . . but the ancient lead-encased manuscript that they had found with the grail, in that deep lost cave, lay now at the bottom of the sea, flung by Barney himself from the end of Kemare Head in the last desperate effort to save grail and manuscript from the pursuing Dark. Though the grail had been saved, the manuscript had come to the sea, and only in that manuscript was the secret by which the vital message written on the grail could be understood . . .

The dim light in the caravan could not dull the glow that came from the grail; yellow it blazed like a fire before them, warm, glittering. Simon said softly, 'It's all right. Not a scratch on it.'

A cold voice from the shadows said, 'It is in good hands.'

Abruptly they were out of their absorption with the grail and back in the ominous half-light of the painter of the Dark. The man's black-bead eyes glittered at them from behind the table; he was a surreal pattern of black and white, black eyes, white face, black hair. And there was a deeper strength and confidence in the voice now, a note of triumph.

'I allow you a sight of the grail,' he said, 'to make a bargain with you.'

'You make a bargain with us?' Simon said, his voice coming out higher and louder than he had intended. 'All you do is steal things. Barney's drawing, Captain Toms' dog. And the grail – it must have been you who stole it from the Museum, or your friends –'

'I have no friends,' said the man unexpectedly, swiftly; it seemed a bitter reaction that he could not help, and for a moment there was a faltering of his cold gaze as he knew it. In the next instant he was composed again, looking down at them both in total self-possession.

'Stealing can be a means to an end, my young friend. My end is very simple, and there is no harm in it. All I require is five minutes of your time. Of your small brother's time, that is, and of a certain ... talent ... that he has.'

'I'm not leaving him alone, not for a minute,' Simon said,

'I did not suggest you should.'

'What, then?'

Barney said nothing, but watched, cautiously. For once he felt no resentment that Simon should be taking over. Deep inside his mind something was beginning to fear this strange taut white-faced man more and more, perhaps because he had so clearly blazing a talent. It would have been much easier to face an uncomplicated monster.

The painter looked at Barney. He said, 'It is very simple, Barnabas Drew. I shall take the cup that you choose to call the grail, and I shall pour into it some water, and a little oil. Then I shall ask you to sit calmly, and look into the cup, and tell me what you see.'

Barney stared at him in amazement. Like a sea-mist a strange idea wreathed into his mind: was the man not evil at all, but simply off his head, a little mad? That could, he suddenly realized, explain everything the strange painter had done; after all, even great artists sometimes did odd things, acted strangely; think of nutty Van Gogh ...

He said carefully. 'Look at the water, and the oil, and tell you what I see? Oil does make nice patterns on water, and colours ... well, that sounds harmless enough. Doesn't it, Simon?'

'I suppose so,' Simon said. He was staring hard at the dark man, at the wild eyes and the pale intent face, and the same hypnotic suggestion was creeping into his own mind. He too was thinking it more and more likely that their supposed adversary might not have anything to do with the Dark at all, whatever Great-Uncle Merry may have thought, but be simply an eccentric, a harmless nut. In which case, it would be safest to humour him,

'Yes,' he said firmly. 'Why not?'

Simon thought: when this daftness is all over, we can grab the grail and run. Give him the slip somehow, call Rufus in, get the grail back to Gumerry ... He looked hard at Barney, trying to communicate; nudged him surreptitiously and flicked his eyes at the grail. Barney nodded. He knew what his brother was trying to tell him; the same thought was only too vivid in his own mind.

The dark man ran some water from the tap into a glass and poured it into the grail. Then he took a small brown bottle from a shelf near the table and added a drop or two of some kind of oil. He looked greedily at Barney. The tension in him sang like a plucked wire.

'Now,' he said. 'Sit down, here, and look hard. Look hard, look long. And tell me what you see.'

Barney sat in the chair before the table, and slowly took the glowing golden chalice in both his hands. Though the inscribed gold of the outside was as bright as it had ever been, the inside surface was a dull black. Barney stared down at the liquid in the bowl. In the cold green light from above his head, incomprehensibly shining out from the patterns of the painted ceiling, he watched the thin, thin layer of oil on the surface of the water swirl and coil into itself, curving, breaking and joining again, forming islands that drifted out and then vanished, merging into the rest. And he saw . . . he saw . . .

Darkness took hold of his brain like sudden sleep, and he knew nothing more.

Chapter Six

Jane was almost in tears. 'But they couldn't just disappear! Something awful must have happened!'

'Nonsense,' Merriman said. 'They'll be rushing in any moment now, demanding their breakfasts.'

'But breakfast was more than an hour ago.'

Jane stared distractedly out over the harbour, busy and bustling in the sunshine. They stood on the little paved path outside the cottages, above the winding web of stairs and alleys that led down to the harbourside.

Will said, 'I'm sure they're all right, Jane. They must have woken up early and wandered out for a walk, and gone farther than they intended. Don't worry.'

'I suppose you're right. I'm sure you are. It's just that I keep having this awful picture in my mind of them going out to Kemare Head, the way we used to, last year, and one of them getting stuck on the cliff, or something . . . Oh dear, I know I'm being stupid. I'm sorry, Gumerry.' Jane shook back her long hair impatiently. 'It all comes of seeing the Greenwitch falling, I suppose. I'll shut up.'

'I tell you what,' said Will. 'Why don't we go out to Kemare Head just to check? You'd feel a lot happier.'

Brightening, she gazed from one to the other of them. 'Could we really?'

'Of course we could,' Merriman said. 'Mrs Penhallow will give the truants their breakfast if they arrive in the meantime. You two start off – I'll have a word with her, and catch you up.'

Jane beamed. 'Oh, that's much better. Waiting's awful. Thank you, Will.'

'Don't mention it,' said Will cheerfully. 'Lovely morning for a walk.'

Into Merriman's mind he said unhappily, '*The Dark has them, I think. You feel it?*'

'*But without harm,*' came the answer cool into his thoughts. '*And perhaps to our gain.*'

Barney stood at the door of the caravan, blinking in the sunlight. 'Well,' he said, 'aren't we going to get them?'

'What?' Simon said.

'The drinks, of course.'

'What drinks?'

'What's the matter with you? The drinks he just offered us. He said, there are cans in the little cupboard, you can help yourselves. And something about a cardboard box.' Turning to go in, he glanced at his brother in amusement. He stopped abruptly.

'Simon, what *is* the matter?'

Simon's face was white and strained, the lines of it drawn downwards in a strange adult expression of concern and distress. He stared at Barney for a moment, and then he seemed to make a great effort and wrench himself on to the same level of conversation. 'You get them,' he said. 'The drinks. You get them. Bring them out here. It's nice in the sunshine.'

There was a sound behind them inside the caravan, and Barney saw Simon jump as if he had been stabbed; then again he saw the same straining for control. Simon leaned back against the wall of the caravan, his face up to the sun. 'Go on,' he said.

Puzzled, Barney went into the caravan, its interior bright with the sunshine streaming in through the windows. The dark painter was sipping a cup of coffee, leaning on the table.

'This one?' Barney waved a foot at the little cupboard under the sink.

'That's right,' the man said.

Down on his knees, Barney took out two cans of orangeade then peered round the dark little cupboard. 'You said a cardboard box, but I can't see one.'

'Not important,' said the painter.

'There's something, though –' Barney reached in, and took out a piece of paper. After one glance he sat back on his heels and looked up at the man without expression. 'It's my drawing. That you took.'

'Well,' said the man. 'That's what you came for, isn't it?' His dark eyes glinted coldly at Barney beneath the scowling brows. 'Take it, and drink your drink, and go.'

Barney said, 'I'd still like to know why you ran off with it.'

'You irritated me,' the man said shortly. He put down his coffee cup and motioned Barney towards the door. 'No brat criticizes my work. Don't start again.' His voice rose ominously as Barney opened his mouth. 'Just go now.'

Simon said from the doorway, 'What's the matter?'

'Nothing,' said Barney. Rolling up the drawing, he picked up the two cans and went to the door.

'I'm not really thirsty,' Simon said,

'Well, I am.' Barney drank deep.

The painter stood watching them, scowling, barring their way back into the caravan. Outside in the sunshine his big horse moved one placid step forward, rhythmically ripping at the grass.

Simon said, 'May we go now?'

The man's eyes narrowed; he said swiftly, 'I have no hold over you. Why ask me?'

Simon shrugged. 'Just now Barney said, let's go home, and you said, not yet. That's all.'

A kind of relief seemed to flicker over the other's dark face. 'Your brother has his precious drawing, so go, go. Up to the left of the farm' – he waved a hand at the grassy lane disappearing on round the corner – 'you'll find a short cut back to the village. The path's a little overgrown, but it will take you to Kemare Head.'

'Thank you,' Simon said.

'Good-bye,' said Barney.

They went on across the field, without looking back. It was like coming out of a dark mist.

'D'you think it's a trap?' Barney whispered. 'Someone might be lying in wait for us at the farm.'

'Too complicated,' Simon said. 'He doesn't need traps.'

'All right.' Trotting alongside, Barney peered at him curiously. 'Simon, you really do look awful. Are you sure you're all right?'

'Do shut up about it,' Simon said, fierce and low. 'I'm fine. Just get a move on.'

'Look!' said Barney in a moment as they rounded the corner. 'It's empty!'

A low grey stone farmhouse faced them, obviously deserted: nothing moved anywhere, old pieces of machinery lay rusting in the yard, and several windows gaped black and jagged-edged. The thatched roof of an out-house was sagging ominously; brambles waved wild green arms where the woods were stealing in towards the house.

'No wonder he's living in a caravan. D'you think he's really half gipsy?'

'I doubt it,' Simon said. 'Just a handy explanation for looking different. And for the caravan. I don't know why but Gumerry will. There's the path.' He headed for a break in the tangled growth near the old house, and they pushed their way along a narrow, bramble-crossed track.

'I'm ravenous,' Barney said. 'Hope Mrs Penhallow's got eggs and bacon.'

Simon glanced round, his face still drawn. 'I've got to talk to Gumerry. We both have. I can't explain yet, but it's terribly urgent.'

Barney stared. 'Well, won't he be at home?'

'Might be. But they'll have had breakfast ages ago, they'll be out looking for us.'

'Where?'

'I don't know. We could try the Grey House, to begin with.'

'Okay,' Barney said cheerfully. 'This path must come out pretty near there. And we can –' He stopped dead, staring at Simon. 'Rufus! We didn't bring him back! Simon, how awful, I clean forgot about him! Where did he go?'

'He ran away. That's one of the things I have to explain about.' Wearily Simon went on up the path. 'It's all part of the same thing. And we've just got to find Great-Uncle Merry as soon as we possibly can, or something's going to go horribly wrong.'

'There's no sign of them up here.' Will came clambering back across the rocks at the tip of Kemare Head.

'No,' Merriman said. He stood still, the sea wind blowing his white hair back like a flag.

'They might have climbed down into the next bay, to the rocks at the bottom,' Jane said. 'Let's go and see.'

'All right.'

'Wait,' Merriman said. As they turned in surprise he raised an arm and pointed inland, back along the headland towards the silent grey group of standing stones that overlooked Trewissick Bay. For a moment Jane noticed nothing. Then she saw a patch of brownish red moving towards them very fast, a patch that resolved itself in a few moments into the form of a desperately-running dog.

'Rufus?'

The red setter skidded to a halt in front of them, panting, trying to bark in odd little gasping coughing sounds.

'He's always rushing up from nowhere trying to tell people things,' said Jane helplessly, crouching to rub his head. 'If only he could talk. Want to come with us, Rufus? Want to come and help find Barney and Simon?'

But it was very soon clear that Rufus wanted nothing but to persuade them to go back along the headland the way they had come. He jumped and whined and barked, and so they followed him. As they came closer to the standing stones, the great grey monoliths of granite in their lonely group up on the windy grass, they saw coming towards them from the village Simon, Barney and Captain Toms. They were moving slowly, the old man still hobbling on a stick; Jane could sense the suppressed impatience in the boys' deliberate pace.

Merriman stood beside the standing stones as they came up to him. He looked only at Simon, and he said, 'Well?'

'So he poured a little drop of some sort of oil into the grail,' Simon said, 'so that it floated on top of the water, and Barney had to sit down and stare at it.'

'Sit down?' Barney said. 'Where?'

'At the table. In the caravan. It was all dark, except for this funny kind of green light coming from the ceiling.'

'I don't remember any green light. And for goodness' sake, Simon, I'd remember if I'd seen the grail for even a second – and I know I didn't.'

'*Barney,*' Simon said; his voice shook with strain, and he leant against the nearest standing stone. 'Will you shut up? You were in a spell of some sort, you don't remember anything.'

'Yes I do, I remember everything we did there, but there was hardly anything. I mean we were only there a minute or two, for me to get my drawing. And I never sat down inside –'

'Barnabas,' Merriman said. The voice was very soft, but there was a cold fierceness in it that made Barney sit still as stone; he said in a whisper, 'I'm sorry.'

Simon was paying him no attention. His eyes were glazed, inturned, as if he were seeing something that was not there. 'Barney looked into the grail for a while, and then the van seemed to go very cold and it was horrible all of a sudden. He started to talk, but' – he swallowed – 'it . . . it wasn't his voice that came out, it was different, and the way he talked was different too, the kind of words . . . He said a lot of things I didn't understand, about someone called Anubis, and making ready for the great gods. Then he said, "*They are here,*" though he didn't say who he meant. And the painter, the man from the Dark, he began asking questions, and Barney would answer them, but in this funny deep voice that just wasn't like his, but like someone else.'

Simon shifted restlessly; they all sat round him among the great stones, listening, intent, silent. The wind sang softly in the grass, and round the towering columns. 'He said, "*Who has it?*" And Barney said. "*The Greenwitch has it.*" He said, "*Where?*" and Barney said, "*In the green depths, in the realm of Tethys, out of reach.*" The painter said, "*Not out of my reach.*" Barney didn't say anything for a bit, and then he went into his own voice, you could tell he was describing something he could see. He sounded very excited, he said, "*There's this weird great creature, all green, and darkness all round it except in one place where there's a terrible bright light, too bright to look at ... and it doesn't like you, or me, or anybody, it won't let anyone come near ...*" The painter was all wound up, so twitchy he could hardly sit still, he said, "*What spell will command it?*" And all of a sudden it wasn't Barney any more, his face went empty again and that other horrible deep voice came out, and it said, "*The spell of Mana and the spell of Reck and the spell of Lir, and yet none of these if Tethys has a mind against you. For the Greenwitch will be the creature of Tethys very soon now, with all the force of all life that came out of the sea.*"'

'Ah,' Captain Toms said.

Will said sharply, 'The spell of Mana and the spell of Reck and the spell of Lir. Are you sure that's what he said?'

Weary and resentful, Simon raised his head and looked at him with dislike. 'Of course I'm sure. If you heard a voice like that coming out of your brother's mouth, you'd remember every word it said for the rest of your life.' Will nodded his head and made a kind of hissing noise and looked very pleased. He 'Get on, get on.'

'The painter came very close to Barney then, whispering,' Simon said. 'I could scarcely hear him. He said, "*Tell me if I am observed.*" I thought Barney was going to pass out. He stared into the grail, and his face got twisted and you could see the whites of his eyes, but then he was all right again and the voice out of him said, "*You are safe if you keep from using the Cold Spells.*" And the man nodded his head and made a kind of hissing noise and looked very pleased, He leant back in his chair and I think he had asked all he wanted to, and he was going to stop. But all of a sudden Barney sat up very straight, and that horrible voice said, very loudly like shouting, "*Unless you find the secret of the Thing of Power in this high part of spring, the grail must go back to the Light. You must make haste, before the Greenwitch departs to the great deeps, you must make haste.*" Then it stopped, and Barney sort of slumped down in his chair, and' – Simon's voice wavered, and he sniffed hard, fiercely raising his head – 'and I grabbed him to make sure he was all right, and the painter was furious and yelled at me. I suppose he thought I'd broken the spell or whatever. So I got cross too, and yelled back that he wouldn't get very far when we told you all about this. And he just sat back then, with a nasty sort of smile, and said that he only had to snap his fingers and we would forget everything that had happened for as far back as he chose.'

'And Barney did,' Jane said shakily. 'But you didn't.'

Simon said, 'We heard Rufus barking outside the door then, so Barney and I both moved to get him, and the dark man jumped up and snapped his fingers once, click, right by our faces. I saw Barney's eyes go sort of vague, and he moved forwards very slowly and opened the door as if he were sleep-walking. So I copied whatever he did, because obviously I had to take terrific care the painter didn't suspect I could remember what had happened. Rufus had gone. Run away. Barney blinked a bit, and shook his head, and almost at once he was talking as if we had just got there a moment or two before. Like going back in time. So I tried to do the same.'

'You didn't do too well,' Barney said. 'You looked awful, I thought you were going to be sick.'

'What happened to the grail?' Jane said.

'I suppose he's still got it.'

'I wouldn't know,' said Barney. 'I don't remember seeing it. I do remember him giving me back my drawing, though. Look.' He waved it at Merriman, who took it and twirled it absently in his fingers as he watched Simon.

'Simon,' Jane said. 'Why did the forgetting work on Barney and not on you?'

'It was the drinks,' Simon said. 'This really sounds stupid, but it must have been. We drank some orangeade, and there must have been a kind of potion in it.'

'Clumsy,' Merriman said. 'Old-fashioned. Interesting.' He looked at Will, and Will looked at him, and their eyes became opaque.

'But the orange was sealed in cans,' Barney said incredulously. 'That's the only reason we drank it, because he couldn't have put anything in it. And anyway, you didn't even open yours.'

'The spell of Mana,' Will Stanton said, very low, to Merriman. 'And the spell of Reck.'

'And the spell of Lir.'

'No, Barney,' Simon said. 'You actually went and got those drinks twice, only the first time was one of the things you've forgotten. And though I didn't have any the second time, I did pretend to drink some the first time. So he thought it worked on us both.'

Will said to Merriman, 'There is no more time. We must go now, at once.'

Simon, Jane and Barney stared at him. There was crisp, unboyish decision in his voice. Merriman nodded, his hawk's face grim and taut; he said unfathomably to Captain Toms, 'Take care of them.' Then he turned his cold grim face to Simon and said, 'You are sure that at the last, the voice that came from Barney said, "Before the Greenwitch departs to the great deeps"?'

'Yes,' said Simon nervously.

'Then it is still here,' Will said, and to the children's bewilderment he and Merriman turned and ran, ran towards the end of the headland, and the sea beyond.

With swift ease of animals they ran, the long lean man and the sturdy boy, an urgent loping running that took away their age and all sense of familiarity in their appearance; faster, faster, faster. And at the rocks ending the headland they did not pause, but went on. Will leapt up light-footed to the crest of Kemare Head and cast himself outwards into the air, into empty sky, arms spread wide, lying on the wind like a bird; and after him went Merriman, his white hair flying like a heron's crest. For an instant the two dark spread-eagled figures seemed to hang in the sky, then with a slowness as if time held its breath they curved downwards, and were gone.

Jane screamed.

Simon said, choking with horror, 'They'll be killed! They'll be killed!'

Captain Toms turned to them, his rosy face stern. He did not lean on his stick; he seemed taller than before. He pointed one arm straight at them with the five fingers spread wide, 'Forget,' he said. 'Forget.'

They stood poised for a moment, caught out of awareness, and compassionately he watched the terror drain out of their faces to leave them empty, expressionless.

He said gently, 'The mission for all of us is to keep the man of the Dark from the Greenwitch. Will and your great-uncle have gone among the fishermen, one way – we four have another way to watch, from your cottage and the Grey House. Know this, now. Have no fear.'

Slowly he lowered his arm, and like puppets the children came back to life.

'We'd better get going, then,' Simon said. 'Come on, Jane.'

'I go with you, Captain, right?' Barney said.

'I'll give you some breakfast,' Captain Toms said, twinkling at him, leaning on his cane. 'It's past time.'

Chapter Seven

Like diving birds they flashed into the water, leaving no ripple in the great Atlantic swells. Down through the green waves, the dim green light; though they breathed as fishes breathe, yet they flickered through the water like bars of light, with a speed no fish could ever attain.

Miles away and fathoms deep they sped, on and on, towards the distant deeps. The sea was full of noises, hissing, groaning, clicking, with great fusillades of thumps like cannon-fire as schools of big startled fish sped out of their way. The water grew warmer; jade-green, translucent. Glancing down, Will saw far below him the last signs of an old wreck. Only stumps remained of the masts and the raised decks, all eaten away by shipworms. From the mounded sand sifting over the hull an ancient cannon jutted, lumpy with coral, and two white skulls grinned up at Will. Killed by pirates, perhaps, he thought: destroyed, like too many men, neither by the Dark nor the Light but by their own kind . . .

Porpoises played above their heads; great grey sharks cruised and turned, glancing curiously down as the two Old Ones flashed by. Down and down they went, to the twilight zone, that dim-lit layer of the ocean where only a little of the day can reach; where all the fish – long slender fish with great mouths, strange flattened fish with telescopic eyes – glowed with a cold light of their own. Then they were down in the deep sea, that covers more of the surface of the earth than any land or grass or tree, mountain or desert; in the cold dark where no normal man may see or survive. This was a region of fear and treachery, where every fish ate every other fish, where life was made only of fierce attack and the terror of desperate flight. Will saw huge toad-like fish with bright-tipped fishing-lines curving up from their backs, to hang cruelly alluring over wide mouths bristling with teeth. He saw a dreadful creature that seemed all mouth, a vast mouth like a funnel with a lid, and a puny body dwindling into a long whiplash tail. Beside it, the body of another began to swell horribly, as a big fish, struggling, disappeared inside the trap-like mouth. Will shuddered.

'No light,' he said to Merriman, as they flashed onwards. 'No joy in anything. Nothing but fear.'

'This is not the world of men,' Merriman said. 'It is Tethys' world.'

Even in the darkest sea they knew they were observed and escorted all the way, by subjects of Tethys invisible even to an Old One's eye. News came to the Lady of the Sea long, long before anyone might approach. She had her own ways. Older than the land, older than the Old Ones, older than all men, she ruled her kingdom of waves as she had since the world began: alone, absolute.

They came to a great crack in the bed of the sea, an abyss deeper than all the ocean deeps. A fine red mud covered the ocean floor. Though they had left all vestige of daylight long behind, miles above their heads, yet there was light of another kind in the black water, by which they could see as the creatures of the deep water saw. Eyes watched them from the darkness, from cracks and crevices. They were reaching the place for which they were bound.

As Will and Merriman slowed their rushing course, there in the lost places of the ocean, they could sense all these watchers around them, but slowly, vaguely, as if in a dream. And when at last the sea brought them to Tethys, they could not see her at all. She was a presence merely, she was the sea itself, and they spoke to her reverently, in the Old Speech.

'Welcome,' said Tethys to them out of the darkness of the deeps of her sea. 'Welcome to you, Old Ones of the earth. I have seen none of your kind for some little time now, for some fifteen centuries or so.'

'And then it was I,' Merriman said, smiling.

'And then indeed it was you, hawk,' said she. 'And one other, greater, with you, but this is not he, I think.'

'I am new on the earth, madam, but I bring you my deep respect,' said Will.

'Ah . . .' Tethys said. 'Aaaaah . . .' And her sigh was the sighing of the sea.

'Hawk,' she said then. 'Why have you come again, this hard voyaging?'

'To beg a favour, lady,' Merriman said.

'Of course,' she said. 'It is always so.'

'And to bring a gift,' he said.

'Ah?' There was a slight stirring in the shadows of the deep, like a gentle swell on the sea.

Will turned his head to Merriman in surprise; he had not known of any gift-bringing, though he realized now how proper it must be. Merriman drew from his sleeve a rolled piece of paper, a glimmering cylinder in the gloom; he unrolled it, and Will saw that it was Barney's drawing of Trewissick. He peered closer, curious, and saw a pen-and-ink sketch, rough but lively; the background of harbour and houses was no more than lightly outlined, and Barney had given all his attention to a detailed drawing in the foreground of a single fishing-boat and a patch of rippled sea. He had even drawn in the name on the boat's stern: she was called the *White Lady*.

Merriman held the drawing at arm's length, and released it into the sea; instantly it vanished into the shadow. There was a pause, then a soft laugh from Tethys. She sounded pleased.

'So the fishermen do not forget,' she said. 'Even after so long, some do not forget.'

'The power of the sea will never change,' Will said softly. 'Even men recognize that. And these are islanders.'

'And these are islanders.' Tethys played with the words. 'And they are my people, if any are.'

'They do as they have always done,' Merriman said. 'They go out to the sea for fish at the going down of the sun, and with the dawn they return again. And once every year, when spring is full and summer lies ahead, they make for you, for the White Lady, a green figure of branches and leaves, and cast it down as a gift.'

'The Greenwitch,' Tethys said. 'It has been born again already, this is the season. It will be here soon.' A coldness came into the voice that filtered from the shadows. 'What is this favour you ask, hawk? The Greenwitch is mine.'

'The Greenwitch has always been yours, and always will. But because its understanding is not as great as your own, it has made the mistake of taking into its possession something that belongs to the Light.'

'That has nothing to do with me,' Tethys said.

A faint light seemed to glimmer from the blue-black shadow in which she was hidden, and all around them lights began to glow and flash from the fish and sea creatures waiting there, watching. Will saw the dangling bait-stars over great gaping mouths; strings of round lights like port-holes running the length of strange slender fish. In the far distance he saw an odd cluster of lights of different colours, that seemed to belong to some bigger creature hidden in the shadow. He shivered, fearful of this alien element in which by enchantment they briefly breathed and swam.

'The Wild Magic has neither allies nor enemies,' Merriman said coldly. 'This you know. If you may not help us, yet it is not right for you to hinder us either, for in so doing you give aid to the Dark. And if the Greenwitch keeps that which it has found, the Dark will be very much strengthened.'

'A poor argument,' Tethys said. 'You mean simply that the Light will then fail to gain an advantage. But I am not permitted to help either Light or Dark to gain any advantage ... You speak deviously, my friend.'

'The White Lady sees everything,' Merriman said, with a soft sad humility in his tone that startled Will, until he realized that it was no more than a delicate reminder of their gift.

'Ha.' There was a flicker of amusement in the voice of the shadow. 'We will have a bargain, Old Ones,' Tethys said. 'You may in my name try to persuade the Greenwitch to give up this ... something ... that is of such value to you.

Before the creature comes to the depths, this is a matter between it and you. I shall not interfere, and the Dark may not interfere either, in my realm.'

'Thank you, madam!' Will said, in quick delight.

But the voice went on, without pause, 'This shall be only until the Greenwitch turns, to come to the deep sea. As it always comes, each year, to its proper home, to me ... and after that time, Old Ones, anything that is in its possession is lost to you. You may not follow. None may follow. You may not return here, then, even by the spell which brings you here today. Should the Greenwitch choose to bring your secret down to the deeps, then in the deeps for ever it shall remain.'

Merriman made as if to speak again, but the voice from the darkness was cold. 'That is all. Go now.'

'Madam –' Merriman said.

'Go!' Rage filled the voice of Tethys suddenly. There was a great flashing and roaring in the depths, all round them; strong currents rose, tugging at their limbs; fish and eels darted wildly round them in all directions, and out of the distant shadow a great shape came. It was the dark thing that carried within it the bright lights that Will had seen; nearer and nearer they came, looming larger and larger, white and purple and green, glaring out of a swelling black mass as high as a house. And Will saw with chill horror that the thing was a giant squid, one of the great monsters of the deep, huge and terrible. Each of its waving suckered tentacles was many times longer than his own height; he knew that it could move as fast as lightning, and that the tearing bite of its dreadful beak-like mouth could have annihilated either of them in a single instant. Fearful, he groped for a spell to destroy it.

'No!' said Merriman instantly into his mind. 'Nothing will harm us here, whatever the danger may seem. The Lady of the Sea is, I think, merely ... encouraging ... us to leave.' He swept a low, exaggerated bow to the shadows of the deep. 'Our thanks, and our homage, lady,' he called in a strong clear voice, and then with Will beside him he swept up and away, past the looming black shape of the huge squid, away to the great open green ocean, the way that they had come.

'We must go to the Greenwitch,' he said to Will. 'There is no time to lose.'

'If there are the two of us,' Will cried to him as they swept along, 'and we work on the Greenwitch the spell of Mana and the spell of Reck and the spell of Lir, will it give up the manuscript to us?'

'That must come afterwards,' called Merriman. 'But those spells will command it to listen, and hear, for only they harness the magic with which the Greenwitch was made.'

They flashed through the sea like bars of light, out of the deep cold, up to the tropic warmth, back to the cold waters of Cornwall. But when they came to the place, beneath the waves beating their long swells against Kemare Head, the Greenwitch was not there. No sign remained. It had gone.

Chapter Eight

When Simon and Jane arrived back at the cottage, they found Fran Stanton setting out plates on the dining-room table. 'Hi,' she said. 'Want some lunch? Mrs Penhallow had to leave, but she made some great-looking Cornish pasties.'

'I can smell them,' Simon said hungrily.

'Lovely,' said Jane. 'Did you have a good time, where you went?'

'We didn't go far,' Mrs Stanton said. 'St Austell, round there. Clay-pits and factories and that sort of thing.' She wrinkled her friendly face. 'Still, after all that's what Bill came over for. And there's a real magic about those big white clay pyramids, and the pools so quiet at the bottom of them. Such green water . . . Are you having fun? What's everyone doing?'

'Will and Great-Uncle Merry went for a walk. Barney's over at the Grey House with Captain Toms. We're supposed to go there too this afternoon, the captain wants us all to stay for supper,' Jane said, boldly improvising. 'That is if you don't mind.'

'Perfect,' Fran Stanton said. 'Bill and I shan't be eating here anyway – I left him seeing some guy near St Austell, and I have to go back tonight to pick him up. This afternoon I came back just to be lazy. Let's eat – and you can tell me all about that Greenwitch deal I wasn't allowed to watch, Jane.'

So Jane, with some difficulty, gave a description of the making of the Greenwitch as of a gay all-night party, an outing for the local girls, while Simon wolfed down Cornish pasties and tried not to catch her eye. Mrs Stanton listened happily, shaking her blonde head in admiration.

'It's just wonderful the way these old customs are kept up,' she said. 'And I think it's great they wouldn't let a foreigner watch. So many of our Indians back home, they let the white man in to watch their native dances, and before you know it the whole thing's just a tourist trap.'

'I'm glad you weren't offended,' Jane said. 'We were afraid –'

'Oh no no no,' said Mrs Stanton. 'Why, I've already got enough material to give a great paper on this trip to my travel group back home. We have this club, you see, it meets once a month and at each meeting someone gives a little talk, with slides, on somewhere she's been. This is the first time,' she added a trifle wistfully, 'I shall have had anywhere unusual to talk about – except Jamaica, and everyone else has been there too.'

Afterwards Jane said to Simon, as they scrambled down towards the harbour, 'She's rather sweet really. I'm glad she'll have us to talk about to her club.'

'The natives and their quaint old customs,' Simon said.

'Come on, you aren't even a native. You're one of they furriners from London.'

'But I'm not so much *outside* it all as she is. Not her fault. She just comes from such a long way away, she isn't plugged in. Like all those people who go to the museum and look at the grail and say, oh, how wonderful, without the least idea of what it really is.'

'You mean people who used to look at it, when it was there.'

'Oh lord. Yes.'

'Well anyway,' said Jane, 'we'd be the same as Mrs Stanton if we were in her country.'

'Of course we would, that's not the point . . .'

They bickered amiably as they crossed the quay and started up the hill towards the Grey House. Pausing to get her breath, Jane looked back the way they had come. All at once she clutched the wall beside her, and stood there, staring.

'Simon!'

'What is it?'

'Look!'

Down in the harbour, in the very centre of the quay, was the painter, the man of the Dark. He sat on a folding stool before an easel, with a knapsack open on the ground beside him, and he was painting. There was no urgency in his movements; he sat there tranquil and unhurried, dabbing at the canvas. Two visitors paused behind him to watch; he paid them no attention, but went serenely on with his work.

'Just *sitting* there!' Simon said, astounded.

'It's a trick. It must be. Perhaps he has an accomplice, someone off doing things for him while he attracts our attention.'

Simon said slowly, 'There was no sign of anyone else having been in the caravan. And the farm looked as if it had been empty for years.'

'Let's go and tell the captain.'

But there was no need to tell him. At the Grey House, they found Barney perched in a small high room overlooking the harbour, studying the painter through Captain Toms' largest telescope. The old man himself, having let them in, remained below. 'This foot of mine,' he said ruefully, 'isn't too grand at climbing up and down stairs.'

'But I bet you he could see as much with his eyes shut, if he wanted to, as I can through this thing,' Barney said, squinting down the telescope with one eye closed and his face screwed up. 'He's special. You know? Just like Gumerry. They're the same kind.'

'But what kind is that, I wonder?' Jane said thoughtfully.

'Who knows?' Barney stood up, stretching. 'A weird kind. A super kind. The kind that belongs to the Light.'

'Whatever that is.'

'Yes. Whatever that is.'

'Hey Jane, look at this!' Simon was bending to the eyepiece of the telescope. 'It's fantastic, like being right on top of him. You can practically count his eyelashes.'

'I've been staring at that face so long I could draw it from memory,' Barney said.

Simon was glued to the lens, entranced. 'It's as good as being able to hear anything he says. You might even be able to lip-read. You can see every single little change of expression.'

'That's right,' Barney said. He looked casually out of the window; breathed on the pane; drew a little face in the misted patch of glass, and then rubbed it out again. 'The view of his face is terrific. The only trouble is, there's no view of his painting at all.'

Jane had taken her turn at the telescope now. She gazed nervously at the face caught out of the distance by the powerful lens: a dark-browed face, grim with concentration, framed by the long unruly hair. 'Well yes, from this angle of course you're just looking at the back of the easel, looking down at his face over the top of the canvas. But that's not important, is it?'

'It is if you're an artist, like Barney,' Simon said. He clasped his head, striking an extravagant artistic pose.

'Ha ha,' said Barney, with heavy patience. 'It's not just that. I thought the picture might be important.'

'Why?'

'I don't know. Captain Toms did ask me what he was painting.'

'What did he say when you said you couldn't see?'

'He didn't say anything.'

'Well then.'

'Your painter doesn't change his expression one bit, does he?' Jane was still peering. 'Just sits there glaring at the canvas. Funny.'

'Not very funny,' Simon said. 'He's a glaring sort of man.'

'No, I mean it's funny he doesn't look anywhere else. If you watch Mother when she's painting a landscape, you can see her eyes going up and down all the time. Flickering. From whatever it is she's painting, down to the picture and then back again. But he's not doing that at all.'

'Let me have another look.' Barney edged her aside and stared eagerly into the lens, grabbing his blond forelock out of the way. 'You know, you're right. Why didn't I notice that?' He thumped his knee with his fist.

'I still don't see what there is to get excited about,' Simon said mildly.

'Well, perhaps it's nothing. But let's go and tell Captain Toms anyway.'

They clattered down three flights of stairs, and into the book-lined living-room at the front of the house. Rufus stood up and waved his tail at them. Captain Toms was standing beside one of the bookcases, gazing at a small book open in his hands. He looked up as they rushed to him, and closed the book.

'What news, citizens?' he said.

Barney said, 'He's still sitting there painting. But Jane just noticed something, he's not painting from life. I mean he just looks at the canvas, without even glancing at anything else at all.'

'So he might just as well be painting in his caravan as painting here,' said Simon, his mind now in gear. 'So, he can't really be here to paint, he must be here for some other reason.'

'That may be quite right,' Captain Toms said. He parted the books on the nearest shelf, carefully, and slipped his volume back. 'And then again it may not be quite right.'

'What do you mean?' Jane said.

'The painting and the other reason may be one and the same thing. The only trouble is,' Captain Toms stared up at his books as if willing them to speak, 'I can't for the life of me work out what that thing is all about.'

Hour after hour they watched, in turn. At length, after an early supper that might equally have been called a late tea, Jane and Simon sat again in the book-clothed living-room with Captain Toms. He puffed contentedly at a friendly-smelling pipe, grey hair wisping out round his bald head like the tonsure of some genial old monk.

'It'll be dark soon,' Jane said, looking out at the orange-red sunset sky. 'He'll have to stop painting then.'

'Yes, but he's still at it,' Simon said, 'or Barney would have come down from the eyrie.' He prowled round the room, peering at the pictures that hung between bookcases. 'I remember these ships from last year. The *Golden Hind* . . . the *Mary and Ellen* . . . the *Lottery* – that's a funny name for a ship.'

'So it is,' said Captain Toms. 'But suitable. A lottery is a gamble, of sorts – and she was owned by gamblers, of sorts. She was a famous smugglers' ship.'

'Smugglers!' Simon's eyes gleamed.

'A regular trade it was in Cornwall, two hundred years ago. Smuggling . . . they didn't even call it that, they called it fair-trading. Fast little boats they had, beautiful sailors. Many a fair-trader's boat was built right here in Trewissick.' The old man gazed absently down at his pipe, turning it in his fingers, his eyes distant. 'But the tale of the *Lottery* is a black tale, about an ancestor of mine I sometimes wish I could forget. Though it's better to remember . . . Out of Polperro, the *Lottery* was, a beauty before the wind. Her crew had years of fair-trading, never caught, until one day east of here a Revenue cutter came up with her, both ships fired on one another, and a Revenue man was killed. Well now, killing was a different thing from smuggling. So all the crew of the *Lottery* became hunted men. Tisn't hard to escape capture in Cornwall, and for a while they were all safe. And they might have been for longer, but one of the crew, Roger Toms, gave himself up to the Revenue and turned King's Evidence, telling them it was a shipmate of his called Tom Potter that fired the dire shot.'

'And Roger Toms was your ancestor,' Jane said.

'He was, poor misguided fellow. The folk of Polperro took him and set him on a boat bound for the Channel Isles, so he shouldn't be able to give evidence against Tom Potter in court. But the Revenue brought him back again, and Tom Potter was arrested, and tried at the Old Bailey in London, and hanged.'

'And wasn't Potter guilty?' Simon said.

'No-one knows, to this day. Polperro folk claimed he was innocent – some even said Roger Toms fired the shot himself. But they may just have been protecting one of their own, for Tom Potter was born in Polperro, but Roger Toms was a Trewissick man.'

Simon said severely, 'He shouldn't have sneaked on his shipmate, even if Potter did do it. That's like murder.'

'So it was,' Captain Toms said gently. 'So it was. And Roger Toms never dared set foot in Cornwall again, from that day until the day he died. But no-one ever knew his real motives. Some Trewissick folk say that Potter was guilty, and that Toms gave him up for the sake of all the wives and children, thinking it sure that unless the one guilty man were accused, sooner or later all the crew of the *Lottery* would be taken and hanged. But most think black thoughts of him. He is the town's shame, not forgotten even yet.' He looked out of the window at the darkening sky, and the blue eyes in the round cherubic face were suddenly hard. 'The very best and the very worst have come out of Cornwall. And come into her, too.'

Jane and Simon stared at him, puzzled. Before they could say anything, Barney came into the room.

'Your turn, Simon. Captain, d'you think I could go and get some more of that super cake?'

'Hungry work, watching,' said Captain Toms solemnly, 'Of course you may.'

'Thank you.' Barney paused for a moment at the door, glancing round the room. 'Watch this,' he said, and he reached for a switch and turned on the lights.

'Goodness!' said Jane, blinking in the sudden brightness. 'It's got really dark. We hadn't noticed, we were talking.'

'And he's still sitting out there,' Barney said.

'Still? In the dark? How can he paint in the dark?'

'Well, he is. He may not be painting what's in front of him, but he's still putting paint on that canvas, cool as a cucumber. The moon's up, it's only a half-moon but it gives enough of a glimmer that you can still see him through the glass. I tell you, he must be stark raving nuts.'

Simon said, 'You don't remember the caravan. He's not nuts. He's from the Dark.'

He went out of the room and up the stairs. Shrugging, Barney headed for the kitchen to fetch his cake.

Jane said, 'Captain Toms, when will Gumerry be back?'

'When he has found out what he went to find out. Don't worry. They will come straight to us.' Captain Toms heaved himself to his feet, reachin for his stick. 'I think I might perhaps take a look through that telescope too, now, if you'll excuse me for a moment, Jane.'

'Can you manage?'

'Oh yes, thank you. I just take my time.' He hobbled out, and Jane went to kneel on the window-seat, staring out at the harbour. A wind was rising, out there; she could hear it beginning to whine softly in the window-frames. She thought: he'll get cold out there soon, the painter from the Dark. Why does he stay there? *What's he doing?*

The wind grew. The moon went out. The sky was dark, and Jane could no longer see the pattern of clouds that had been dimly visible before. All at once she realized that she could hear the sea. Normally the soft swish of the waves against the harbour wall made a constant low music that was part of life; being always there, it was scarcely heard. But now the sound of each wave was distinct; she could hear each smack and splash. The sea, like the wind, was rising.

Simon and Captain Toms came back into the room. Jane saw their reflections ghostly in the window, and turned.

'Can't see him any more,' Simon said. 'There's no light. But I don't think he's gone.'

Jane looked at Captain Toms. 'What should we do?'

The old sailor's face was troubled, creased with thinking; he tilted his head, listening to the wind. 'I shall wait a little to see what the weather does, for more reasons than you might think. After that – after that, we shall see.'

Barney appeared in the doorway, munching a large piece of bright yellow cake.

'Good gracious,' said Jane brightly, to stop herself listening to the sea, 'you must have eaten the whole plateful by now.'

'Mmmmf,' Barney said. He swallowed. 'Do you know, he's still there?'

'What?' They stared at him.

'I haven't been stuffing myself in the kitchen. I popped round the back and crossed the road in front here, to look down from the harbour wall – thought he might see the light if I opened the front door. And he's still there! Right where he was. He really must be cracked, you know, Simon. Dark or not. I mean he's sitting there in the darkness at his easel, still painting. Still painting, in the pitch dark! He's got some sort of light, it's only by the glow that you can see he's there. But all the same, really –'

Captain Toms sat down abruptly in an armchair. He said, half to himself, 'I don't like it. It makes no sense. I try to see, and there is only shadow . . .'

'The wind's making a lot more noise now,' Jane said. She shivered.

'Out there, you can hear the waves really crashing against the headland,' Barney said cheerfully. He crammed the last of his cake into his mouth.

Simon said, 'Is there going to be a storm, captain?'

The old man gave no answer. He sat hunched in his chair, staring into the empty fireplace. Rufus, who had been lying peaceably on the hearth-rug, got up and licked his hand, whining. A sudden gust of wind whistled in the chimney, and rattled the front door. Jane jumped.

'Oh dear,' she said. 'I hope Gumerry's all right. I wish we'd arranged for some great big signal to bring him back if we wnted him. Like Indians and smoke signals.'

'Just a fire, you'd need, now it's dark,' Barney said. 'A beacon fire.'

'In these parts,' Captain Toms said abstractedly, 'beacon fires date back as far as the men who have always lighted them. A warning, from the beginning of time . . .' He leaned forwards, his hands clasped together over the top of his carved walking-stick, and he gazed unseeingly in front of him as if he were looking back into endless centuries, oblivious of the room and the children in it. When he spoke again, the voice seemed younger, clearer, stronger, so that they paused in astonishment where they stood.

'And when last the Dark came rising in this land,' Captain Toms said, 'it came from the sea, and the men of Cornwall lit beacon fires everywhere to warn of its coming. From Estols to Trecobben to Carn Brea the warning fires sprang, from St Agnes to Belovely and St Bellarmine's Tor, and on out to Cadbarrow and Rough Tor and Brown Willy. And the last was at Vellan Druchar, and there the Light gave battle to the Dark. The forces of the Dark were driven back to the sea, and might have escaped that way, to attack again. But the Lady brought home a west wind, that threw all their hope of escape dry upon the shore, and so the forces of the Dark were vanquished, for that time. Yet the first of the Old Ones gave prophecy, that once more from that same sea and shore the Dark should one day come rising.'

He stopped abruptly, and they were left staring at him.

Simon said huskily, at last, 'Is . . . is the Dark rising now?'

'I don't know,' Captain Toms said simply, in his normal voice. 'I think not, Simon. It is all but impossible for them to rise yet. But in that case, something else is happening that I do not understand at all.' He stood up, leaning on the arm of the chair. 'I think perhaps it is time that I went out there, to see what I can see.'

'We'll come with you,' said Simon at once.

'Are you sure?'

'To tell the truth,' Jane said, 'whatever happens out there, I think we'd rather come with you than stay on our own.'

'Too true,' Barney said.

Captain Toms smiled. 'Get your jackets, then. Rufus, you stay here. Stay.'

Leaving the red dog resentful on the hearth-rug, they went out of the Grey House and crept down the hill, slowly, at the captain's painful pace. At the bottom, where the downhill road joined the quay, the old man drew them gently into the shadow of a warehouse at the back of the harbour. Standing huddled there, whipped by the wind blowing in from the sea, they could see the painter from the Dark not twenty yards from them, at the edge of the sea; the light around him made him clear.

As Jane looked at him for the first time, she gasped, and heard the same instinctive strangled sound from the others. For the painter had no torch to make the pool of brightness that surrounded him. The light came from his painting.

Green and blue and yellow it glowed there in the darkness, in great writhing seething patterns like a nest of snakes. Seeing it now for the first time Jane felt an instant dreadful revulsion from the picture, its shape and colour and mood, yet she could not take her eyes from it. The man was still painting, even now. With the wind grabbing at his clothes, and tilting his easel towards him so that he had to hold it still with one hand, he was yet daubing away frenziedly with a brush full of these strange horrible colours, and to Jane's bemused eye it seemed that all the colours came from the brush itself without the least pause for taking up new paint.

'It's horrible!' Barney said violently. He spoke with great force, unthinking, but the wind whipped the words out of his mouth as soon as they were uttered. The painter, standing to windward, would not have heard him even if he yelled at the top of his lungs.

'Now I see!' Captain Toms suddenly thumped his stick on the ground, staring at the picture. 'That's it! Now I understand! He has painted his spells! Mana and Reck and Lir . . . the power is all in the picture! I had forgotten it could be done. Now I see, now I see . . . but too late. Too late . . .'

Jane said fearfully into the wind, 'Too late?'

And the wind rose howling in their ears, lashing at their faces, flinging salt spray into their eyes. There was no rain, nor any lightning or thunder; they heard only the wind and the crashing of the sea. They staggered backwards against the wall, pinned to it by the gale; out on the quay the painter hunched his broad shoulders forwards, leaning into the wind to hold himself upright. He flung away his brush; paints and papers rushed away from him and were gone on the wind; all that he held was the strange glimmering canvas. He raised it above his head, and shouted some words in a tongue the children did not understand.

And suddenly they heard a sound like nothing they had ever heard from the sea before: a great sucking, hissing noise, echoing from side to side of the little harbour. The wind died away. There was all at once a strong, very strong smell of the sea: a smell not of decay but of foam, and waves, and fish and seaweed and tar and wet sand and shells.

For a second the moon sailed out from behind a broken cloud, and they saw a great sideways impossible wave roll back to each side of the harbour. And up out of the water came a towering dark shape, twice as high as a man, looming over the painter, bringing with it even more overpoweringly the tremendous smell of the sea.

The painter flung up his arms holding the canvas, thrusting it at the great black shape, and cried out in a voice that cracked with strain, 'Stay! Stay, I charge you!'

Captain Toms spoke softly, wonderingly, half to himself. 'Watch for the Greenwitch,' he said.

Chapter Nine

They huddled in the dark warehouse doorway, watching. No wind blew now, and the sudden stillness was unnerving, broken only by the rumbling waves. The murmur of passing motor-cars came now and then from the main road higher in the village, but the children did not heed them. Nothing in the world seemed to exist but this thing that loomed before them, rising higher each moment out of the swaying sea.

The thing could not be clearly seen. It had no features, no outline, no recognizable shape. They perceived it only as a great mass of black absolute darkness, blotting out all light or star-glimmer, rearing up over the weird glowing patch that marked the man of the Dark. It was, Jane thought suddenly, far larger than the image of leaves and branches that she had seen cast down into the sea from the point of Kemare Head. And yet, she thought again, the Greenwitch had seemed huge in the dark of that night, rearing up, waiting, shadowed by the flickering beacon fire . . .

The painter said in a loud clear voice, 'Greenwitch!'

Simon felt Barney shiver convulsively, and he moved closer to him. A hand briefly, gratefully, clutched his arm.

'Greenwitch! Greenwitch!'

A great voice came out of the towering massive darkness. It seemed to fill all the night; a voice like the sea, full of shifting music. It said, 'Why do you call me out?'

The painter lowered his dreadful canvas. The light in it was beginning gradually to fade. 'I have need of you.'

'I am the Greenwitch,' the voice said wearily. 'I am made for the sea, I am of the sea. I can do nothing for you.'

'I have a small favour to ask,' the painter said: sweetly, ingratiatingly, but with a strain in his voice as if it would crack into a thousand glittering fragments.

The voice said, 'You are of the Dark. I feel it. I am not permitted to have any dealings with either the Dark or the Light. It is the Law.'

The painter said quickly, 'But you have taken something that the Law does not permit you to take. You know it. You have a part of one of the ancient Things of Power, that you should not have, that no creature of the Wild Magic should have. Greenwitch, you must give it to me.'

The sea-voice of the blackness cried out as if in pain, 'No! It is mine! It is my secret! My secret!' And Jane flinched, for suddenly it was the voice of her dream: plaintive, crying, a child's complaint.

The painter said fiercely, 'It is not yours.'

'It is my secret!' cried the Greenwitch, and the mass of black darkness seemed to rise and swell. 'I guard it, none shall touch it. It is mine, for always!'

At once the painter dropped his tone into gentleness, a soft wheedling. 'Greenwitch, Greenwitch, child of Tethys, child of Poseidon, child of Neptune – what need have you of a secret, in the deeps?'

'As much need as you,' the Greenwitch said.

'Your home is in the deeps.' The painter was still gentle, persuasive. 'There is no need for such secrets there. That is no place for such a thing, woven of different spells that you know nothing of.'

The huge voice of the darkness said obstinately, almost pettishly, 'It is mine, I found it.'

The painter's voice, shaking, began to rise. 'Fool! Wild fool! How dare you play with things of the High Magic!'

The light was fading faster out of his painting now; the children could see nothing around it but the blackness of the Greenwitch against the faint grey glimmer of sky and sea. There were only these two voices, ringing through the empty harbour.

'You are a made creature only, you will do as I say!' Arrogance sharpened the man's tone, gave it an edge of command. 'Give the thing to me, at once, before the Dark shall blast you out of this world!'

The children felt Captain Toms gently but urgently drawing them all back against the wall, into a corner almost cut off from the spot where the two figures confronted one another on the quay. Nervously they moved as they were told.

From the blackness that was the Greenwitch came a hair-raising sound: a long low lamenting, like a moan, rising and falling in a mumbling whine. Then it stopped, and the creature began muttering to itself, broken words that they could not make out. Then there was silence for a moment and all at once it said very clearly, 'You have not the full power of the Dark.'

'Now! I command you!' The painter's voice was shrill.

'You have not the full power of the Dark,' the Greenwitch said again, with a growing, wondering confidence. 'When the Dark comes rising, it is not as one man, but as a terrible great blackness filling the sky and the earth. I see it, my mother shows me. But you are alone. You were sent by the Dark with one small mission only, and you gamble now to make yourself a great Lord, one of the masters. By completing one of the Things of Power for yourself, you think to become great. But you are not great yet, *and you may not command me!*'

Softly, Captain Toms said, 'Tethys has seen what we could not see.'

'I have all the power required!' said the painter loudly. 'Now, Greenwitch, now! Do as the Dark demands!'

The Greenwitch began to make a new sound, a low rumbling so ominous that the children shrank back against the wall. It was somewhere between the growl of a dog and the purring of a cat, and it said, *Beware, beware* . . .

The painter cried out furiously, 'By the spell of Mana and the spell of Reck and the spell of Lir!' and they saw by the last faint glow that he swung up his canvas and its luminous painted magic over his head again, facing the blackness of the Greenwitch. But he could do nothing. The rumbling from the Greenwitch rose into a roar, the air was tight with rebellion and fear, and Jane heard in her mind over and over again the cry *Leave me alone! Leave me alone! Leave me alone!* and never knew whether it had been cried aloud or not.

They were conscious of nothing but a great seething. Resentful fury roared in their ears, throbbing with the slow thunder of waves against rock. And suddenly the whole world was luminous with green light, as for one terrible moment the Greenwitch in all its wild power loomed out of the sky, every live detail clear with a brilliance they never afterwards mentioned even to one another. With a shriek the painter flung himself backwards, and fell to the ground. And the Greenwitch, crying rage from a great mouth, spread terrible arms wide as if to engulf the whole village – and disappeared. It did not go down into the sea. It did not vanish like a burst balloon. It faded, like smoke, dissipating into nothing. And they felt no sense of release from fear, but a greater tension as if there were a storm in the air.

Barney whispered, 'Has it gone?'

'No,' Captain Toms said gravely. 'It is all through the village. It is with us and around us. It is angry and it is everywhere, and there is great danger. I must take you home at once. Merry had good reasons for choosing those cottages – they are as safe as the Grey House, in the protection of the Light.'

Barney was looking at the still figure on the quay. He said fearfully, 'Is he dead?'

'That is not possible,' Captain Toms said quietly. He looked down at the painter. The man lay on his back, breathing evenly, his long hair spread like a black pool around his head. His eyes were closed, but there was no sign of injury. He looked as though he were asleep.

From the road leading into the harbour they heard the engine of a car, growing closer, rounding the corner. Simon stepped out to wave it down, but there was no need. As the car's lights swung on to the group on the quay it slowed abruptly, brakes screaming, and pulled to a halt. From behind the blazing headlamps an American voice called, 'Hey! What goes on?'

'It's the Stantons!' The children rushed to the car doors, and two puzzled figures climbed out. Captain Toms turned quickly; his voice was clear and commanding.

'Evening – you've picked a good time to appear. We've just found this fellow lying here, on our way to the cottage – looks as if a car's knocked him down. Hit and run, I reckon.'

Bill Stanton knelt beside the prostrate painter and felt for his heart; raised one eyelid; gently felt along his arms and legs. 'He's alive . . . no blood anywhere . . . no obvious breaks . . . maybe it's a heart attack, not a car. What should we do? Is there an ambulance here?'

Captain Toms shook his head. 'No ambulance in Trewissick, we're not too good for emergencies. And only one policeman with a motor-bike . . . You know, Mr Stanton, the best thing we could do is get him in your car, and you drive him to the hospital in St Austell. Poor fellow might be dead by the time we get P.C. Tregear out.'

'He's right,' said Fran Stanton, her soft voice concerned. 'Let's do that, Bill.'

'Fine by me.' Mr Stanton looked round the quayside, his eyes searching, quickly efficient. 'We'll have to be very careful lifting him . . . I wonder . . . ah!' He prodded Simon, nearest him. 'See that pile of planks over there? Two of you kids bring one, quick.'

In a struggling group they slid the painter on to the narrow plank; then, with slow lifting and tilting, manoeuvred it to leave him lying on the back seat of the car.

'Do up the seat belts round him, Frannie,' said Mr Stanton, climbing back into the driver's seat. 'He should be okay . . . Will you call the policeman, captain, and have him follow us? Shouldn't like anyone to think it was us knocked the guy down.'

'Yes, of course.'

Fran Stanton paused with the car door open. 'Where's Will?'

Her husband took his hand off the ignition key. 'That's right, it's late. He and Merry can't still be out walking. Where is he, kids?'

They stared at him, speechless.

The brightness died out of Bill Stanton's amiable round face; in its place came suspicion and concern. 'Hey now, what is all this? What's going on here? Where's Will?'

Captain Toms cleared his throat. 'He –' he began.

'Nothing to worry about, Uncle Bill,' said Will, behind them. 'Here I am.'

Chapter Ten

'Very good,' said Merriman, watching, as the Stantons' car hummed round the corner from the harbour and away into the main village street. 'They should just have time to get clear.'

'You make it sound as though somebody was going to drop a bomb,' Simon said.

Jane said nervously, 'Gumerry? What's going to happen?'

'Nothing, to you. Come along,' Merriman swung round and began striding fast and long-legged across the quay towards the cottages; the children scurried after.

'See you later, Merry!' Captain Toms called.

They stopped, turning in consternation; he was beginning to limp back to the Grey House. 'Captain? Aren't you coming with us?'

'Captain Toms!'

'Come along,' Merriman said without feeling, and pushed them before him. They shot him quick glances of irritation and reproach. Only Will marched along without sign of emotion.

'I'm so glad you're back.' Jane slipped round to her great-uncle's side. 'Please, what's going to happen? Really?'

Merriman glanced down at her from his deep-shadowed eyes, without slackening his pace. 'The Greenwitch is abroad. All the power of the Wild Magic, which is without discipline or pattern, is let loose tonight in this place. The power of the Light, since we have so arranged it, will give protection to the cottages and to the Grey House. But elsewhere . . . Trewissick is under possession, this night. It will not be an easy place.' His deep voice was tense and grave, filling them with alarm; they trotted nervously at his side and up the winding zig-zag alleys and stairs to the cottage door. Then they fell into the lighted room like mice diving below-ground from a hunting owl.

Simon swallowed, regaining his breath, feeling slightly ashamed of his haste. He said belligerently to Will, 'Where were you?'

'Talking to people,' Will said.

'Well, what did you find out? You were gone long enough.'

'Nothing much,' Will said mildly. 'Nothing but what hasn't already happened.'

'Wasn't much point in your going then, was there?'

Will laughed. 'Not really.'

Simon stared at him for a moment and then turned irritably away. Will glanced at Jane, and winked. She gave him a quick rueful grin, but studied him afterwards, behind his back. *Simon wanted to quarrel, and you wouldn't,* she thought. *You're like a grown-up, sometimes. Who are you, Will Stanton?*

She said, 'Gumerry, what should we do? Would you like Simon and me to keep watch, upstairs?'

'I should like you all to go to bed,' Merriman said. 'It's late.'

'Bed!' The outrage in Barney's voice was louder even than the others'. 'But everything's just getting really exciting!'

'Exciting is one word for it.' Merriman's bony face was grim. 'Later you might have another. Do as you are told, please.' There was a flicking edge to the words that did not inspire argument.

'Good night,' Jane said meekly. 'Good night, Will.'

'See you in the morning, everyone,' Will said casually, and he disappeared into the Stanton half of the house.

Jane shivered.

'What's the matter?' Simon said.

'Someone walked over my grave . . . I don't know, perhaps I've caught a chill.'

'I'll make you all a hot drink and bring it up,' Merriman said.

Upstairs, Simon paused in the little corridor linking the bedrooms, clutching his head in a kind of despairing fierceness. 'This is ludicrous! Crazy! One minute we're in the middle of some awful great . . . watching that, that *thing* . . . and then Gumerry turns up, and before you know it he's tucking us up with cups of cocoa.'

Barney gave a huge yawn. 'Well yes . . . but I'm . . . tired . . .'

Jane shivered again. 'I am too, I think. I don't know. I feel funny. As if – Can you hear a sort of buzzing noise, very faint, a long way off?'

'No,' Simon said.

'I'm sleepy,' Barney said. 'G'night.'

'I'm coming too,' said Simon. He looked at Jane. 'Are you going to be all right, on your own?'

'Well, if anything happens,' Jane said, 'I'm going to come running in to hide under your bed so fast you won't even see me.'

Simon managed a small grin. 'You do that. There's one thing certain, absolutely no-one is going to get any sleep tonight.'

But when Merriman came tapping gently at Jane's bedroom door in a little while, there were three steaming mugs still on his tray. 'I might have saved myself the effort,' he said. 'Simon and Barney are fast asleep already.'

Jane was sitting in pyjamas and dressing-gown beside the window, looking out. She said, without turning round, 'Have you magicked them?'

Merriman said softly, 'No.' Something in his voice made her turn, then. He was standing in the doorway, his eyes glittering out of black pools of shadow beneath the jutting white-wire eyebrows. He stood so tall in the low little room that his bushy white hair touched the ceiling. 'Jane,' he said. 'Nothing has been done to any of you, or will be. I promised you that in the beginning. And no harm can come to you here. Remember that. You know me well enough, I do not put you into mortal danger, now or ever.'

'I know. Of course I do,' she said.

'Then sleep sound,' Merriman said. He stretched out a long arm, and she reached out and touched his fingertips; it was like a bargain. 'Here, have some cocoa. No potions in it, I promise. Just sugar.'

Jane said automatically, 'I've cleaned my teeth.'

Merriman chuckled. 'Then clean them again.' He put down the mug and went out, closing the door.

Jane took her cocoa and sat beside the window again, warming her fingers on the hot smooth sides of the mug; the room was cold. She looked out of the window, but the reflection of the bedside lamp was in her way. Impulsively she reached out and switched it off, then sat waiting until her eyes grew accustomed to the dim-lit dark.

When at last she could see again, she did not believe what she saw.

From the cottage, high up there on the hillside above the sea, she had a clear view of all the harbour and much of the village. Here and there were pools of yellow light from the lamp-posts: two on the quayside, three across the harbour, up on the road past the Grey House; others, more distant, at points within the village. But the pools of light were small. All else was darkness. And in the darkness, wherever she looked, Jane could see things moving. At first she could tell herself that she was imagining it, for whenever she saw movement from the corner of an eye and shifted her gaze to stare, it was gone. She could never see it clearly, in direct view. But this did not last for long.

It was changed by a single figure of a man. He came up out of the water at the edge of the harbour, climbing a flight of stairs with a strange gliding motion.

He was dripping wet; his clothes clung to him, his long hair was plastered flat and dark round his face, and as he walked a trail of water dripped all round him and was left like a path. He walked slowly up towards the main street of Trewissick, looking neither to left nor right. When he came to the corner of the little canning factory, whose new extension jutted from the old brick buildings set higgledy-piggledy along the quay, the man in the wet clothes did not slow his pace, nor turn aside. He simply walked through the wall as if it had not been there, emerging in a second or two on the other side. Then he disappeared into the darkness of the main street.

Jane stared into the blackness. She said softly, desperately, 'It's not true. It's not true.'

The night was very still, Jane clutched her mug like a talisman of reality; then suddenly jumped so hard that she spilt half the cocoa on the window-sill. She had caught a movement right below her, at the cottage door. Hardly daring to look, she willed her eyes to move downwards, and saw two figures leaving the door. Merriman was unmistakable; though he was hooded and muffled in a long cloak, light from a street-lamp showed Jane the high brow and fierce beak-like nose. But it was a moment before she realized that the second figure, cloaked and hooded in the same way, was Will Stanton. She knew him only by a trick of his walk, which until then she would not have thought she could recognize.

They walked out unhurried into the middle of the quay. Jane felt a frenzied urge to throw open the window and shriek a warning, to bring them back from unknown perils, but she had known her strange great-uncle too long for that. He had never been like other men; he had always had unpredictable powers, seemed somehow larger than anyone they had ever known. He might even be causing these things.

'He is of the Light,' said Jane aloud to herself, gravely, hearing the true impossible seriousness of the words for the first time.

Then she said thoughtfully, amending it a little, 'They are of the Light.' She looked at the smaller hooded figure, discovering in her mind a curious reluctance to believe that there was anything supernatural about Will. His cheerful round face, with the blue-grey eyes and straight mouse-brown hair, had seemed a subtly comforting image from the beginning of this adventure. There would be nothing very comforting about Will if he were like Merriman Lyon.

And then she forgot Merriman, Will and everything around her, for she caught sight of the lights.

They were the lights of a ship, out at sea: bright lights like stars, moving a little as with the waves. They swayed and bobbed out there in the darkness, but they were far too close in. Though they were clearly the lights of a ship of some size, they were close to the rocks of Kemare Head; dreadfully, dangerously close. She heard voices, crying faintly; one of them seemed to call: 'Jack Harry's lights!' And forcing her gaze away from the sea she saw that the harbour was suddenly filled with people: fishermen, women, boys, running and waving and pointing out at the sea. They crowded past and around the still figures of Merriman and Will as if neither of them was there.

Then there seemed to Jane to be a strange blurring of the scene, a moment's vagueness; when her eyes cleared, everything was as it had been the moment before, and though she thought that the crowd of villagers seemed somehow different, in clothes and appearance, she could not be certain. Before she could think further, horror seemed to take hold of the crowd. An eerie flickering light grew over the harbour. And suddenly boats set about with great flaming torches were pouring in past the harbour wall, strange broad boats full of oarsmen, some bareheaded with flowing red hair, some wearing stubby helmets crested with a golden boar and jutting down into a fierce iron nose-guard over the face. The boats reached shallow water; the oarsmen leapt from their oars, seized swords and blazing torches and tumbled out, crowding, splashing, rushing ashore with blood-curdling yells that Jane could hear with dreadful clarity even through the closed window. The villagers scattered, screaming, fleeing in all directions; some few fought the invaders off with sticks and knives. But the red-headed men were intent on one thing only; they hewed and hacked with their swords, slicing at any they could catch with more fearsome brutality than Jane had ever believed possible in human beings. Blood ran bright over the quayside, and streamed down into the sea, clouding out dark and murky in the waves.

Jane stumbled to her feet, feeling sick, and turned away.

When she forced herself back to the window, shivering, the screams and yells had died almost to nothing. The last fugitives and howling invaders were racing out along the furthest roads, and an ominous red glow was rising all over the village, all over the sky. Trewissick was burning. Flames licked round the houses on the hill across the harbour, and glared bright red in the windows; in a great whoosh of fire the warehouse at the far side of the harbour burst into flames. Brick and stone seemed incomprehensibly to burn as fiercely as if they were wood. Fumbling desperately with the catch, Jane flung open the window, and met a great crackling and roaring from the fire and the great billowing clouds of bright-lit smoke. The reflection of the flames danced on the water of the harbour. In her agitation it did not occur to Jane to notice that she did not smell burning, and felt no heat.

Down on the quayside, as if they saw nothing that had happened from the beginning, Will and Merriman stood cloaked and still.

'Gumerry!' Jane shrieked. She could think of nothing but that the fire might reach the cottages. 'Gumerry!' Then the noise outside in the sky was suddenly gone, altogether gone, and she heard her own voice, and found that what she had felt as a high tremendous scream was no more than a whisper. And as she sat watching, disbelieving, the flames died and disappeared, and the red glow in the sky faded away. There was no more blood, nor any trace of it, and everything in the harbour of Trewissick was as if the red-headed, ravening men from the sea had never come.

Somewhere, a dog howled into the night.

Cold, frightened, Jane clutched her dressing-gown tighter around her. She longed to fetch Simon, yet she could not take her eyes from the window. Still unmoving, the dark cloaked figures of Will and Merriman stood over the edge of the sea. They made no sign of having noticed anything that had happened.

There was a glimmering, glittering sheen on the water of the harbour, and Jane saw that over her head the moon had floated free of clouds. A different light brightened the world, cold but gentler: all was black and white and grey. And into it, out of the air, came a voice. It was not a man's voice, but thin and unearthly, chanting one sentence three times on one high heart-catching note.

> The hour is come, but not the man.
> The hour is come, but not the man.
> The hour is come, but not the man.

Jane peered all round the harbour, but could see no-one: only the two unmoving figures below.

Again the dog howled somewhere unseen. Again she felt a strange buzzing, humming sound in the air, and then she began to hear other voices crying far off in the village.

'The *Lottery*! The *Lottery*!' she thought they cried. Then a man's voice, clearer, 'The *Lottery* is taken!'

'Roger Toms! Roger Toms!'

'Hide them!'

'Bring them to the caves!'

'The Revenuers are coming!'

A woman sobbed: 'Roger Toms, Roger Toms . . .'

The harbour filled with people, milling about, anxiously staring out to sea, scurrying to and fro. This time Jane thought she could see faces in the crowd that were like the faces of Trewissick that she knew: Penhallows, Palks, Hoovers, Tregarrens, Thomases, all anxious, all perplexed, casting fearful glances both to land and sea. They seemed to have no real contact with one another; they were like sleep-walkers, sleep-runners, folk desperately turning about in a bad dream. And a great shriek went up from the whole crowd as the last spectre came rushing at them from the sea.

It was not horrible, yet it was more heart-stopping than any. It was a ship: a black ship, single-masted, square-rigged, with a dinghy behind. Silent and unnerving it came gliding into the harbour from the sea, scarcely touching the water, skimming the surface of the waves. It carried no crew. Not a single form moved anywhere on its black decks. And when it reached the land, it did not stop, but went on, sailing silently over harbour and rooftops and hill, away out of Trewissick, to the moors. And as if the phantom ship had swept away with it all sign of life, the crowd vanished too.

Jane found she was clutching the edge of the window-sill so hard that her fingers hurt. She thought miserably: *this is why he wanted us to sleep. Safe and empty with a blanket over our minds, that's where he wanted us. And instead I am in the middle of more nightmares than I ever imagined could come in one night, and the worst nightmare of all is that I am awake* . . .

Nervously she peeped round the curtain again. Merriman and Will strode to the centre of the quay. A third figure, cloaked and hooded, joined them from the other side of the harbour. Standing very tall, facing the village and the hills, Merriman raised both arms in the air. And although nothing could be seen, it was as though a great wave of rage came roaring at them, rearing over them, out of the dark haunted village of Trewissick.

Jane could stand no more of it. With an unhappy little moan she dived across the room and into her bed. Tight over her head she pulled the covers, and lay there stuffy and shivering. She was not afraid for her own safety; Merriman had promised her that the cottage was protected, and she believed him. Nor was she afraid for those figures down in the harbour; if they had survived so strange a succession of monstrosities, they could survive anything. In any case nothing could harm Merriman. It was another fear that possessed Jane: a dreadful horror of the unknown, of whatever force was sweeping through land and sea, out there. She wanted only to cower into her own corner animal-like, away from it, safe.

So this she did, and found, oddly, that because the fear was so large and formless, it proved more ready to go away.

Gradually Jane stopped shivering; grew warm. Her taut limbs relaxed; she began to breathe slowly and deeply. And then she slept.

Down in the harbour with Will and Captain Toms at either side, shadowy hooded figures, Merriman raised both arms higher in a gesture that was half-appeal, half-command, and he called into the darkness over Trewissick in his deep resonant voice the words of the spell of Mana and the spell of Reck and the spell of Lir.

From all around, rage beat at them like waves, a great gale of unseen force.

'No!' cried the great voice of the Greenwitch, thick with fury. 'No! Leave me alone!'

'Come forth, Greenwitch!' Merriman called. 'The spells command it.'

'One coming is all they may command,' the voice roared. 'And out of the sea I came, they commanded me and I came. No more, no more!'

'Come forth, Greenwitch!' Will's clear voice sang out through the darkness like a beam of light. 'The White Lady bids you hear us. Tethys gave us leave to call you, before you should go to the deep.'

Fury enveloped them like a tidal wave. At their backs, the sea growled and murmured; the land quivered beneath their feet.

But then, though they could not see it, the presence was all around them, seething, resentful.

Merriman said: 'The secret is not yours, Greenwitch. You know you should not keep it.'

'I found it. It was in the sea.'

'It would not have been there, but for a battle between the Light and the Dark. It fell, it was lost.'

'It was in the sea, in my mother's realm.'

'Come, my friend,' Captain Toms said gently, in his rounded Cornish voice. 'You know that it is not of the sea, but is a part of a Thing of Power.'

The Greenwitch said, 'I have no friend. It matters nothing to me what happens between the Light and the Dark.'

'Ah,' Merriman said. 'You will find out that it may matter, if this Thing of Power shall belong fully to the Dark. Half of it they have already, half they seek to have from you. If they gain it, and have the power of the whole, things will go hard with the world of men.'

The voice around them mumbled, 'Men have nothing to do with –'

'Men have nothing to do with me?' Will's voice cut light and clear through the night. 'Do you believe that, Greenwitch? Men have everything to do with you. Without them, you would not exist. They make you, each year. Each year, they throw you to the sea. Without men, the Greenwitch would never have been born.'

'They do not make *me*.' The great voice was bitter. 'They serve themselves only, their own needs only. Though they make me in the form of a creature, yet they are making no more than an offering, as once in older days it might have been a slaughtered cock, or sheep, or man. I am an offering, Old Ones, no more. If they thought I had life they would kill me as they killed the cocks and the sheep and the men, to make a sacrifice. Instead they make me as an image, out of branches and leaves. It is a game, a substitute. I am given real life only by the White Lady, life enough to take me down to the deeps. And this once too I have had a different life wake in me, because I was drawn out to the earth, out of the sea, by . . .' the voice grew reflective; a note of cunning crept in . . . 'by the Dark.'

'Put that out of your mind,' Merriman said at once. 'None is more self-serving than the Dark. Tethys has told you that.'

'Self-serving!' The bitterness was back in an instant, and far deeper. 'You are all self-servers, Light, Dark, men. There is no place for the Wild Magic except its own . . . no care . . . no care . . .'

In spite of themselves the three Old Ones swayed backwards as the force of fury rose again abruptly, and the rage of the Greenwitch throbbed all around them like a great heart fiercely beating.

Staggering, Merriman caught himself upright, sweeping his long cloak around him, the hood falling back to leave his wild white hair glistening in the lamplight. 'Has no-one showed care for you, Greenwitch? No-one?'

'No-one!' The huge voice rang through the village, around the hills, over the moors behind; like distant thunder it rumbled and re-echoed. 'No creature! None! Not . . . one . . .' The fierceness died, the thunder grew less. For a long moment they were listening only to the wash of the uneasy sea against the cliffs, out where the swells broke. Then the Greenwitch said in a whisper, 'None except one. None except the child.'

'The child?' Will said involuntarily. A thin note of raw incredulity tipped his voice; for a moment he thought the Greenwitch meant himself.

Merriman said softly, ignoring him, 'The child who wished you well.'

'She was up at the headland at the making,' the Greenwitch said. 'And they told her of the old saying, that whoever touches the Greenwitch before it be put to cliff, and makes a wish, shall have that wish. So then she could have made any wish she chose.' The voice grew warm, for the first time. 'She could have wished for anything, Old Ones, even for the first lost part of your Thing of Power to come back to you. Yet when she touched me she looked at me as if I were human, and she said, "I wish you could be happy."'

The soft thunder died away; the harbour was silent, bursting with the memory that filled it.

'*I wish you could be happy,*' the Greenwitch said softly.

'So she –' Will began; but stopped, as Merriman's hand touched his arm. The air around them was growing bright, light, mild; Trewissick, for this one night, would catch every mood of the Greenwitch like a burning-glass. The echoing voice murmured softly to itself, and it seemed to Will that with every moment the earth and sea in that place grew gentler.

Into the dim-lit spring night a cold voice said, 'The girl too is self-serving, just as the rest of them.'

There was a silence. Then out of the shadows at the back of the quay stepped the painter, the man of the Dark. He stood in a pool of yellow lamplight, facing them, a chunky black silhouette.

'Self-serving,' he said to the air. 'Self-serving.' Then turning to Merriman he said, 'I have the mastery of it, not you. The spells that called it from the ocean were mine. The creature is mine to command, Old One, not yours.'

Will felt a low rumbling around them, and saw the lights faintly quiver.

Merriman said, 'This is not now a matter for command, but for gentleness. The spells that brought it out of the sea can accomplish no more now.'

The painter laughed scornfully. He swung round in a half-circle, arms outstretched. 'Greenwitch!' he shouted. 'I have come back for the secret. I give you one last chance, before the wrath of the Dark will descend!'

The rumbling sound rose into a huge snarl, like a roll of thunder, then died down again.

'Be careful,' said Captain Toms softly. 'Be very careful.'

But the command in the voice of the man of the Dark now was like ice; it was the cold absolute arrogance that through centuries past had brought men down to terror and grovelling obedience. 'Greenwitch!' the man called into the night. 'Give your secret to the Dark! Obey! The Dark is come again, and for the last time, Greenwitch! The hour is come!'

Will clenched his fists so that the nails cut into his palms; even an Old One could feel the force of such a command bite into the mind. He watched without a breath, wondering; he did not know how such a challenge would touch the Wild Magic, a force neither of the Light nor of the Dark nor of men.

The air around them sang with the ferocity of the Dark messenger's will, spinning their wits into uncertainty – and then gradually, subtly, a change began. The force that was in the air faltered, and changed imperceptibly back to the spell-web that had possessed this small part of the earth since the Greenwitch had struck the painter down. The Wild Magic was resisting all challenge, invincible as the Boar Trwyth. Will took a great breath; he began to guess what was to come.

Standing alone on the quay, the painter whirled round, staggering, groping into the air, as if in search for something he could not see. Out of the darkness, high above the village, a weird clear voice called, as it had called before:

> The hour is come, but not the man.
> The hour is come, but not the man.
> The hour is come, but not the man.

And into the silence after the ringing words a whispering began, a gradual murmuring of many voices, calling, whispering: *Roger Toms! Roger Toms!* And shadows came flocking into the harbour, from all sides, all the shades and spirits and hauntings of that one haunted night: the past folk of Trewissick from all the centuries that the little sea-town had ever seen, focused into one black point of time. *Roger Toms! Roger Toms!* they called, softly at first, growing gradually louder, louder. It was a calling and an accusing and a judgement, and it whispered relentlessly round the harbour and over the sea.

Silently, unobtrusively, the three Old Ones drew their hoods over their heads and moved together to one side of the harbour, in the shade of the wall, to stand there unseen.

Out in the centre of the quay, alone, the dark painter turned in a slow circle, incredulously seeing and hearing the past come falling upon him, making him into its long shame. With immense effort he raised his arms, pushing feebly at the air.

But there was no pushing away the unreasoning rage that the Wild Magic had brought out of the village, to make a scapegoat of its attacker. '*Roger Toms! Roger Toms!*' the voices called angrily, stronger, more demanding.

The painter shrieked into the night, 'I am not he! You mistake me!'

'Roger Toms!' came a great triumphant shout.

'No! No!'

They were all around him, crying and calling, pointing, just as the villagers of the present had crowded and called and pushed about the Greenwitch, as it was taken newly made to tumble headlong from the cliff.

And from out of the night, over the roofs of Trewissick from the dark inland moors, came sailing again the phantom ship of Cornwall, single-masted, square-rigged, with a dinghy behind, that had sailed up out of the midnight sea in the haunting. Silently it skimmed over houses and roads and quayside, and this time it was not empty, but had a figure at the helm. The drowned man, dripping and intent, whom Jane had seen glide up out of the sea, stood high on the deck at the wheel, steering his black dead vessel, looking neither to left nor right. And with a glad shriek all the great crowd of shades rushed on to the ship, dragging with them the struggling painter.

'*Roger Toms! Roger Toms!*'

'No!'

The phantom sails filled again with a wind that no man alive could feel, and the ship sailed away, out to sea, out into the night, and on Trewissick quay the Old Ones were left alone.

Jane slept deeply at first, but halfway through the night dreams began to edge into her sleep. She saw the painter, painting; she saw again all the fearful things that she had seen from her window that night. She dreamed of Roger Toms and the fair-traders, with the ship called the *Lottery* fleeing from the Revenue men and the shots ringing out between the two; and in her dream the *Lottery* became the black phantom ship that had sailed unthinkably up out of the sea and away across the land.

She thought, as she tossed in her sleep, that she heard voices calling *Roger Toms! Roger Toms!* And then as they faded, gradually into her dream came the Greenwitch. She could not see it, as she had seen it in a dream once before; this time it was obscure, merely a voice, lost in the shadows. It was unhappy. *Poor thing*, Jane thought, *it's always unhappy*.

She said, 'Greenwitch, what are all these horrible things?'.

'It is the Wild Magic,' the Greenwitch said miserably into her dreaming mind. 'This is how it besets the minds of men, calling up all the terrors they have ever had, or their forefathers have ever had. All the old hauntings of Cornwall, which men there have always feared, that is what these have been.'

'But why tonight?' Jane said.

The Greenwitch sighed, a great gusty sigh like the sea. 'Because I was angry. I am never angry, but the man of the Dark made me so. And the rage of those who are part of the Wild Magic is not a good thing to bring out. The village bore it, the village has been possessed . . .'

'Is it over now?'

'It is over now.' The Greenwitch sighed again. 'The Wild Magic has carried away the man of the Dark. The messenger of the Dark. He was a creature alone, trying to cheat his masters. So they did not protect him, and so the Wild Magic has taken him to outer Time, from which he may never properly come back . . .'

Jane cried, 'But he has the grail! What about the grail?'

'I know nothing of a grail,' the Greenwitch said indifferently. 'What is a grail?'

'It doesn't matter,' Jane said, with effort. 'Did he take your secret, in the end? Did you give it him?'

'It is mine,' the Greenwitch said quickly. 'I found it. And now no-one will let me keep it.'

'Did you give it to the Dark?'

'No.'

'Thank goodness,' Jane said. 'It really is terribly important, Greenwitch. To the Light, to everyone. Really. To the people who made you, to my brothers and me, to all of us.'

The Greenwitch said, 'To you?' Its great melancholy voice echoed round her like waves booming in a cave. 'My secret is important to you?'

'Of course it is,' said Jane.

'Then here,' said the huge voice. 'Take it.'

Jane never knew afterwards what she had been at that moment doing in her dream: standing or sitting or lying, indoors or out, in day or night, under sea or over stone. She remembered only the great wave of astonished delight 'Greenwitch! You will give me your secret?'

'Here,' said the voice again, and there in Jane's hand was the small misshapen lead case, that had fallen into the sea at the end of the adventure that had achieved the grail – and that held inside it the only manuscript able to unravel for them the secret of the grail. 'Take it,' the Greenwitch said. 'You made a wish that was for me, not for yourself. No-one has ever done that. I give you my secret, in return.'

'Thank you,' said Jane, in a whisper. All around her was darkness; it was as though nothing existed in the whole world but herself, standing in emptiness, and the great disembodied voice of this strange wild thing, a creature of the sea made of branches and leaves from the earth. 'Thank you, Greenwitch. I shall find you a better secret, instead.' A quick image came flashing into her mind. 'I shall put it in the same place where you found this one.'

'Too late,' said the great sad voice. 'Too late . . .' It boomed and re-echoed, fading gradually away. 'I go to my mother now, to the great deeps.' Away into the darkness the echoes died, a last whisper lingering. 'Too late . . . too late . . .'

'Greenwitch!' Jane cried in distress. 'Come back! Come back!' She ran blindly into the darkness, reaching out helplessly. 'Come back!'

And in the same moment, the dream dissolved, and she woke.

She woke into the small white room bright with sunshine, gay as the cheerful yellow curtains at the windows, and the yellow quilt pulled up to her chin on the bed. The curtains shifted gently in a small breeze from the window she had left part-open the night before.

And clenched in Jane's hand was a small misshapen lead case, patched with green stains, like a rock that has been a long time under the sea.

Chapter Twelve

Tousle-headed from sleep, rumpled pyjamas flapping, the children rushed unceremoniously into Merriman's bedroom.

'Where is he?'

'Try downstairs. Come on!'

Merriman and Will, looking as though they had been up and dressed for hours, were calmly eating their breakfast in the long low living-room. As Simon, Jane and Barney tumbled into the room Merriman lowered a large rustling stretch of newspaper, and peered at them over a pair of gold-rimmed half-spectacles perched startlingly on his high-arched nose.

He said, looking at the battered leaden cylinder that Jane mutely held out to him, 'Ah.'

Will put down his toast, grinning all over his round face. 'Well done, Jane,' he said.

Jane said, 'But I didn't do anything. It just – it just appeared.'

'You made a wish,' said Will.

She stared at him.

'Aren't we going to open it?' Barney said impatiently. 'Come on, Gumerry.'

'Well,' Merriman said. He took the small lead case from Jane's hand and set it on the table, dark eyes glittering in his deep-lined face. 'Well now.'

Jane was still staring, her gaze flickering between Will and her great-uncle. 'You knew I had it. You knew.'

'We hoped,' Merriman said gently.

Simon put a finger on the case as if he were saying a prayer. 'It's been in the sea so long. Look at it, there's weed and stuff all over it . . . won't the water have got in? That would be my fault, from last summer. I opened it just once, to see what was inside, and then closed it again. Imagine if the manuscript's all ruined in there, if I didn't close it tightly enough . . .'

'Stop it,' said Jane.

Merriman took up the case in his long wiry fingers, and gently he tugged and turned the green-splashed grey metal until suddenly one end of it came away in his hand like a cap. Inside, a small roll of heavy parchment projected from the longer part of the case like a pointing finger.

'It's all right!' Simon said hoarsely. Hastily he cleared his throat and put his shoulders back, though it was hard to recover dignity in pyjamas.

Barney hugged himself, jiggling with impatience. 'What does it say? What does it say?'

Very slowly, and with immense care, Merriman drew the rolled manuscript from the little leaden case. He said, as he unrolled it gently on the table, flat under one large hand, 'We shall be able to do this twice, at the most, unless it is to crumble into dust. So this is the first time.'

His long fingers held the cracking brown parchment open on the white cloth. It was covered with two blocks of heavy black marks. The children stared, dismay chasing horror over their faces.

'But it doesn't say anything! That's not even a language!'

'It's gibberish!'

Jane said slowly, more cautious, 'What is the writing, Gumerry? *Is* there any kind of alphabet like that?'

She looked without hope at the series of black marks: upright strokes, slanting strokes, single and in groups, like the random doodling of a tidy madman.

'Yes,' Merriman said. 'There is.' He lifted his hand so that the manuscript rolled itself again, and Will, who had been looking over his shoulder, went quietly back to his chair. 'There is an ancient alphabet called Ogham, not intended for our kind of writing – this is something like that. But still it is a half-writing, a cipher. Remember, it cannot mean anything until we have the grail – it was written to go with the inscription on the grail, to show its meaning plain. The one will give light to the other.'

Barney wailed, 'But we haven't got the grail!'

'The Dark,' Simon said bitterly. 'The painter.' Then he stiffened, his face full of wild hope. 'But we can get it, we can go and take it from his caravan. They took him to –'

'Morning! Morning!' Mrs Penhallow came bustling in with a tray. 'I heard your voices, m'dears, so here's your breakfasts.'

'Super!' said Barney at once.

Very gently, Merriman let his newspaper droop over the manuscript and its case.

'Well,' Jane said, pulling helplessly at her rumpled dressing-gown. 'We aren't exactly dressed, but thank you.'

'My goodness, who minds about that, on holiday? Now you just help yourselves and relax, and I'll use the time to do your rooms.' Leaving the tray, she bounced out into the kitchen; then reappeared with broom and dusters. When she was safely creaking away up the stairs behind the cottages' connecting door, Simon let out a long breath and burst out again, taut and excited.

'They took him to hospital, so we can go to the caravan, he won't be there! He –'

Will hissed sharply between his teeth, holding up a hand in warning. A stumbling and mumbling came at the other door into the room, and through it appeared Bill Stanton, yawning, blinking, tying the belt of an improbable dressing-gown striped like a deck-chair. He looked at the Drews, covering the last of his yawns. 'Well,' he said. 'I'm glad someone at least looks the same way I do.' Simon sat down hard in his chair and began fiercely slicing bread.

Barney said, 'Did you get on all right last night, Mr Stanton?'

Will's uncle groaned, 'Don't talk about it. What an evening! That crazy guy we were taking to hospital ran away.'

'Ran away?' The room was suddenly very quiet.

Mr Stanton sat down and reached greedily for the teapot. 'I hope he's all right,' he said. 'But he sure gave us enough trouble. He was as quiet as anything there in the back seat, I'd have sworn he was still out like a light. Never made a sound. Then when we were about halfway to St Austell, very bleak part of the road, something ran out in front of the car, and I hit it.' He took a long drink of tea, and sighed gratefully. 'So I stopped, and hopped out to take a look. I mean, you don't want to leave an animal in pain, do you? And while I was out there in the dark, this fellow in the back seat jumped up and opened the door on the other side, and was off out over the fields before Frannie knew what was happening.'

'But he was hurt,' Jane said. 'Could he run?'

'Ran like a hare,' Mr Stanton said, pushing back the hair wisping over his bald head. 'We could hear him crashing about, through hedges I suppose. We looked for him for quite a while, but we didn't have a light and it's none too friendly out there in bad weather in the dark. So in the end we drove on to St Austell and told the police what had happened. Fran thought we should, after getting Captain Toms to tell the Trewissick cop. Though it turned out in the end he didn't, eh, Merry?'

'We tried,' Merriman said blandly. 'P.C. Tregear was out of the village.'

'Well, the St Austell constabulary thought we were nuts,' said Mr Stanton, 'and they were probably right. In the end we came back here. Very late.' He drank some more tea, and sighed again. 'English-born though I am,' he said plaintively, 'I do wish our good Mrs Penhallow would make coffee for breakfast now and again.'

'What was the animal you hit?' Barney said.

'We never found a sign of it. I suppose it was a cat. It looked bigger – might have been a badger perhaps. By the time we were through' – he chuckled – 'we'd decided it was just a good old Cornish ghost.'

'Oh,' Jane said faintly.

'Well, enough of that,' Mr Stanton said. 'We all did our Good Samaritan bit, and I presume the guy's all right somewhere. Hey, this is your last day, kids, isn't it? Looks like it's going to be a nice one. Frannie was wondering if we could all take a picnic on to that big beach the other side of Kemare Head.'

'That sounds delightful,' Merriman said swiftly, before they could react. 'A little later this morning, hmmm? There's one thing I want to show them all first.'

'That's fine. It's going to take me a while to recover from last night. I don't think Fran's even awake yet.'

'What do you want to show us, Gumerry?' said Jane, more from politeness than enthusiasm.

'Oh,' Merriman said. 'Just an old farm.'

They bounced through the village in Merriman's big car: Jane and Captain Toms in front, the boys behind, with a happy, fidgeting Rufus. All the windows were open; with no wind, and the sun rising high already, it promised to be an uncommonly hot spring day.

Simon said, 'But he'll be there waiting for us! He's bound to be, that's why he ran away! Gumerry, how can we possibly just drive up in a car?'

A note of frantic worry was rising in his voice; Will looked at him with sympathy, but said nothing.

Merriman said at last, without turning his head, 'The man of the Dark will not trouble us again, Simon.'

Barney said, 'Why not?'

Simon said, 'How do you know?'

'He tried once more, once too often, to challenge the rights of the Greenwitch,' Merriman said, swinging the car round a corner. 'And the Wild Magic, to which the Greenwitch belongs, carried him away.' He fell silent, in the kind of silence that they knew meant an end of questioning.

'Last night,' said Simon.

'Yes,' Merriman said. Jane, glancing sideways at his eagle-bleak profile, wondered for a cold moment what exactly had happened to the painter of the

Dark, and then, remembering what she had seen, was glad that she did not know.

And before they realized they had gone so far, the big car was turning off the road on to a narrow side-lane, roofed by low-branching trees, past a notice that read: PENTREATH FARM.

Simon said nervously, 'Shouldn't we walk?'

Wilfully misunderstanding, Merriman waved one hand airily. 'Oh no, don't worry, this old bus has stood a lot worse bumps than this in her time.'

Simon tried to swallow his uneasiness. He stared out of the window at the green banks of grass and the thick-swelling trees; at the lacy branches brushing the windows. Unconsciously he clenched his hands together as they approached the last turn in the lane before they would see the painter's caravan, and at the last swing of the car tightened his grip and fought the impulse to close his eyes.

And squinting unhappily out at the green bush-scattered field, he saw that the caravan was not there.

'Stop a moment,' he said, in a high unfamiliar voice. Merriman stopped the car without question, and Simon tumbled out, with Barney close behind him. Together they hurried to the spot where, they both knew very well, the glittering gipsy caravan had stood; where the horse had moved lazily cropping the grass; where the man of the Dark had used Barney's mind for his own ends. There was no sign that anything or anyone had been there for months. Not a blade of grass was bent, not a branch flattened. Rufus, who had jumped out of the car after them, moved restlessly over the ground with his nose down, casting about in circles, finding no scent. Then he paused; lifted his head, shook it from side to side in a strange undog-like manner, like someone with a ringing in his ears, and made off at a swift trot round the next corner in the road.

'Rufus!' Simon shouted. 'Rufus!'

'Let him be,' said Captain Toms clearly from the car. 'Come back here, and we shall follow him.'

On down the lane the big car purred, and then they were round the last corner and facing the farm.

The low grey building seemed even more decrepit than Simon had remembered. He looked with more attention now at the beams of wood nailed cross-shaped over the front door; at the new growth of creeper reaching over windows unhindered; at other windows, here and there, black and broken like missing teeth. Long grass rose lush and new round rusting pieces of farm equipment left in the yard: a skeletal old plough, a harrow, the remnants of a tractor with its great tyres gone. In the pen of a deserted pig-sty, nettles grew tall and rank. Somewhere behind the farmhouse, Rufus barked shrilly, and a flurry of pigeons flapped into the air. There was a wet smell of growing things.

Captain Toms said softly, 'The wild is taking Pentreath Farm, very fast.'

Merriman stood in the middle of the farmyard, looking about him, perplexed. The lines in his face seemed deeper-carved than before. Captain Toms leaned against the car, gazing at the farm, one hand absently tracing patterns in the damp earth with his stick.

Will peered in through one of the front windows of the farm, straining to see through the murk. 'I suppose we should go inside,' he said, without much conviction.

'I don't think so,' Simon said. He stood at Will's shoulder, and for once there was no tension between them, but only the studying of a common problem. 'Somehow I'm sure the painter never went in there. It looked absolutely untouched last time. He seemed just to be living in the caravan on his own. He was a separate sort of man.'

'Separate indeed,' Merriman's deep voice came to them across the yard. 'A strange creature of the Dark, that they sent out as a thief only, to take the grail and hide it. It was a good moment to choose, for we were off our guard, thinking them too preoccupied with licking their wounds after a great defeat ... But the creature of the Dark was willing to betray his masters, having greater ideas. He knew the tale of the lost manuscript, and he thought that if he could secretly get that for himself as well, and thus complete one of the Things of Power, he could by a sort of blackmail make himself one of the great lords of the Dark.'

Jane said, 'But didn't they know what he was doing?'

'They were not expecting him to over-reach his commission,' Merriman said. 'They knew, better perhaps than he did himself, how hopeless a fate lay waiting any lone figure who might venture on such a quest. We think they were not watching him, but simply waiting for his return.'

'The Dark is indeed preoccupied, for a time,' Captain Toms said. 'They have damage to repair, from certain happenings midwinter last. They will make little showing of themselves, until the time of their next great rising.'

Simon said slowly, 'Perhaps that's what the painter meant when he said to Barney, *Am I observed?* Do you remember? I thought he was talking about you, but he must have meant his own masters.'

'Where is Barney?' Will said, looking round.

'Barney? Hey, Barney!'

An unintelligible shout came from somewhere beyond the far side of the farmhouse.

'Oh dear,' said Jane. 'Now what's he up to?'

They ran in the direction of the shout, Merriman following more slowly with Captain Toms. A great rambling tangle of weeds and nettles and brambles rose at the side of the old house, and all around the outbuildings beyond.

'Ow!' Barney howled from somewhere inside the thicket. 'I'm stung!'

'What on earth are you doing?'

'Looking for Rufus.'

They heard a muffled barking; it seemed to come from the further of the two outbuildings, an old stone barn with a perilous half-fallen roof.

'Ow!' Barney yelped again. 'Mind the nettles, they're fierce . . . Rufus just goes on barking and doesn't come out, I think he must be stuck. He went this way . . .'

Captain Toms limped forward. 'Rufus!' he called, very loud and stern. 'Here! Come here!'

There was more muffled excited barking from the ramshackle barn, ending in a snuffling whine.

Captain Toms sighed, and pulled his grey beard. 'Foolish beast,' he said. 'Stand clear a minute. Look out, Barney.' Sweeping his heavy walking-stick from side to side as if it were a scythe, he moved gradually forwards, thrashing a path through the nettles and undergrowth to the crumbling stone sides of the barn. Rufus' barking, inside, became more frenzied still.

'Shut up, dog,' called Barney, at the captain's elbow now. 'We're coming!' He wriggled round to a rotting wooden door, hanging sideways from one hinge, and peered in through the V-shaped gap between door and wall. 'He must have got in here and knocked something over that blocked gap . . . I can get in here, if I . . .'

'Do be careful,' Jane said.

''Course,' said Barney. He squeezed in round the tilted door, pushing aside something that fell with a crumbling clatter, and disappeared. There was a burst of joyful barking inside the barn, and then Rufus came leaping out through the gap, tongue lolling, tail waving. He pranced up to Captain Toms. He was very dirty; small damp pieces of rotten wood speckled his red coat, and cobwebs clung stickily round his nose.

Captain Toms patted him absent-mindedly. He was looking at the barn, with a faint puzzled frown on his face. Then he glanced questioningly at Merriman; following his gaze, Jane saw the same look in her great-uncle's eyes. What was the matter with them? Before she could ask, Barney's head poked out of the gap in the barn door. His hair was dishevelled and one cheek was smeared grey, but Jane's attention was caught only by the unsmiling blankness of his face. He looked as though he had had a very bad shock.

'Come out of there, Barney,' Merriman said. 'That roof's not safe.'

Barney said, 'I'm just coming. But please, Gumerry, could Simon come in here just for a minute first? It's important.'

Merriman glanced from Captain Toms to Will and back to Barney. His stern-lined face was tense. 'All right. For a moment.'

Simon slipped past them to wriggle his way through the gap. Behind him Will said diffidently, 'Would you mind if I came too?'

Jane winced, waiting for the inevitable snub; but Simon only said briefly, 'Fine. Come on.'

The two boys wriggled in after Barney. Simon flinched as a splintered edge scraped his arm; the gap was narrower than it looked. Scrambling to his feet, he stood coughing as Will came in after him. The dust was thick on the floor, and it was hard at first to see clearly in the half-light from dirty, overgrown windows.

Blinking, Simon saw Barney beckoning him.

'Over here. Look.'

He followed Barney to one end of the barn, clear of the piled timber and logs that filled much of the floor. And then he stopped.

Before him, ghostly in the shadows of corner and roof, stood a gipsy caravan, of exactly the same shape and pattern as the one in which they had met the painter of the Dark. There were the tall outward-sloping sides, the insets of carved wood beneath the eaves of the overhanging wooden roof. There, at the far end, were the shafts for the horse, and at this end the divided door – in two halves, swinging, like a stable door – reached by a wooden stairway-ladder of six steps. And the top step was the step on which, at the end, they had stood . . .

But of course it could not be the same. This caravan was not shiny-neat, or newly painted. This caravan had dusty worn sides in which only odd patches of ancient paint remained, flaking away. This caravan had one broken shaft, and the top half of its split door hung from half a hinge. It was old and beaten, unused, unloved; the glass in its windows was long broken. It could not have been moved from its place for the many years since the roof of the old barn had begun to sag, for at the further end of the barn the roof-beams lay rotted with all their remaining weight resting on top of the caravan.

It was a relic, an antique. Simon stared. It was as if he were meeting the great-great-grandfather of a boy he knew well, and finding that the old man had exactly the same face as the boy, but immensely, impossibly aged.

He opened his mouth and looked at Barney, but could think of nothing to say.

Barney said flatly, 'It must have been here for years and years and years. Since long before we were born.'

Will said, 'How well do you remember the inside of the painter's caravan?'

Simon and Barney both jumped at the sound of his voice; they had forgotten he was there. Now they turned; Will stood near the door of the barn, half-hidden in shadow, only his amiable blank face blinking at them in clear light.

Barney said, 'Fairly well.'

'And you, Simon?' Will said. Without leaving time for an answer, he went on, 'Barney doesn't remember seeing the grail at all. But you remember everything, from the moment when he first took out the box it was in.'

'Yes,' Simon said. With a vague, detached interest, he realized that for the first time he was listening to Will as though he were older, without resentment or argument.

Will said nothing more. He crossed from behind them to the steps at the end of the old caravan, pushing aside with his toe the dust and debris that lay cluttered everywhere. He went up the steps. He took hold of the top loose-hanging half of the caravan door, and it came away in his hands, as the rust-eaten hinge crumbled into dust. Then he tugged sharply at the bottom half of the door, and it swung reluctantly towards him with the slow creak of an old farm gate.

'Barney,' he said. 'Do you mind going inside?'

''Course not,' Barney said boldly, but his steps towards the caravan door were reluctant and slow.

Simon said nothing to help him. He was looking at Will, whose voice, as once before, had a crispness and certainty that raised inexplicable echoes in his head.

'Simon,' Will said. 'What did the painter say, word for word, when he first directed Barney to the place where he found the grail?'

Half-closing his eyes, concentrating fiercely, Simon pushed his mind backwards and looked to see what was in it. 'We were both about halfway inside,' he said. Like a sleep-walker he went forwards up the rickety old steps, his hand on Barney's shoulder gently propelling him, and with Will following, the two of them walked into the little room that made the inside of the van.

'And the man said, because Barney had said he was thirsty, "*In that cupboard by your right foot you will find some cans of orangeade. And . . . and you might bring out a cardboard box you'll find in there too.*" So Barney did that.'

Barney turned his head and looked nervously at Will, and the Will who was somehow not quite Will beamed encouragingly, as if he were after all no more than the amiable foolish-looking boy they had met at the beginning of this small strange holiday. So Barney looked down at his right foot, and saw beside it a low cupboard with no handle and the clutter of years mounded against its door; and he crouched on his knees and cleared away the rubbish and scrabbled with his fingernails to find enough leverage to open the small door. When at last it swung open, he felt inside and brought out a battered, damp, evil-smelling cardboard box.

He set it on the floor. All three of them stared at it in silence. Faintly from outside the barn they heard Jane's light voice cry anxiously, 'Are you all right? Hey, do come on out!'

Will said softly, 'Open it.'

Slowly, reluctantly, Barney took hold of the top of the box. The ancient rotting cardboard came away in his hand, and a brightness was in their eyes, a golden radiance that seemed to fill the decrepit, crumbling remnants of what had once a long time ago been a caravan. And there shining beneath their eyes was the grail.

Chapter Thirteen

In the farmyard, in front of the house, a great round piece of granite was set into the ground: an old mill-wheel, worn and grass-fringed. On its bright-flecked grey surface they set the grail, and gathered round as Merriman took from his pocket the battered little cylinder that held the manuscript. He slid out the small roll of parchment, its edges cracked and flaking, and unrolled it to lie on the uneven stone.

'And this is the second time for looking,' he said.

The children picked up stones from the grass and laid them gently on the edges to hold the parchment flat. Then instinctively they drew to one side, to let Merriman and Captain Toms study the grail and manuscript together.

Barney, next to Merriman, suddenly realized that Will was standing quiet and unmoving behind him. He ducked quickly aside. 'Here,' he said. 'Come on.'

The golden grail glittered in the sunlight; the engraving on its sides was clear and clean, but the smooth beaten gold of the inside surface, as Simon had said, was blackened and dark. Will looked now at the close, delicate engraving for the first time in his life, seeing the panels filled with vivid scenes of men running, fighting, crouching behind shields: tunic-clad, strangely-helmeted men brandishing swords and shields. The pictures woke deep memories in him of things he had forgotten he had ever known. He looked closer, at the words and letters interwoven between the figures, and at the last panel on the grail, completely filled with words in this same cipher-language that no living scholar had been able to understand. And like the other two Old Ones, he began methodically to look from the marks on the old manuscript to the marks on the grail, and gradually the interweaving became clear.

Will found himself breathing faster, as the meaning of the inscription began to take shape in his mind.

Staring at the manuscript, Merriman said slowly, painfully, as if he were spelling out a hard lesson:

> On the day of the dead, when the year too dies,
> Must the youngest open the oldest hills
> Through the door of the birds, where the breeze breaks.
> There fire shall fly from the raven boy,
> And the silver eyes that see the wind,
> And the Light shall have the harp of gold.

He stopped, his face tight with concentration. 'Not easy,' he said to himself. 'The pattern is hard to keep.'

Captain Toms leaned on his heavy stick, peering at another panel of the grail. He said softly, his accent cradling the words:

> By the pleasant lake the Sleepers lie,
> On Cadfan's Way where the kestrels call;
> Though grim from the Grey King shadows fall,
> Yet singing the golden harp shall guide
> To break their sleep and bid them ride.

Will knelt down beside the granite slab and turned the grail again. Slowly he read aloud:

> When light from the lost land shall return,
> Six Sleepers shall ride, six Signs shall burn,
> And where the midsummer tree grows tall
> By Pendragon's sword the Dark shall fall.

Merriman stood upright. 'And the last line of all will be the spell,' he said, looking hard at Will; the deep-set dark eyes bored into his mind. 'Remember. *Y maent yr mynyddoedd yn canu, ac y mae'r arglwyddes yn dod.* The mountains are singing, and the Lady comes. Remember.'

He leaned down to the rock, moved aside the stone weights and took up the small curling manuscript in one big hand. As if the Drews did not exist at all, he looked down at Will and Captain Toms.

'You have it all?' he said.

'Yes,' said Will.

'Safe remembered,' Captain Toms said.

In one sharp movement Merriman clenched his fist, and the little roll of stiff, broken-edged parchment crumbled instantly into tiny fragments, small as gravel, light as dust. He opened his long fingers and swung his arm wide, and in a dusty shower the pieces flew away in every direction, into oblivion.

The children cried out sharply.

'Gumerry!' Jane stared at him, appalled. 'You've ruined the whole thing!'

'No,' Merriman said.

'But you can't understand what the grail says, without it. No-one can.' Simon's face was creased with perplexity. 'It'll be just as much of a mystery as it was before!'

'Not to us,' Captain Toms said. He eased himself down to sit on the granite slab, and took up the grail, turning it in his fingers so that the sunlight glinted on the engraved sides. 'We know, now, what is in the hidden message of the grail. It will shape the next twelve months of our lives, and help us to save men from great terror, very soon, for all time. And now that we have it in our minds, we shall never forget.'

'I've forgotten it already,' Barney said plaintively. 'Everything except a bit about a golden harp, and a grey king. How can you have a grey king?'

'Of course you have forgotten it,' Captain Toms said. 'That was the intention.' He smiled at Barney. 'And we do not even need an enchantment to help you forget, as our friend from the Dark did. We can rely on the mortality of your memory.'

'And you don't have to worry about whether anyone else will remember,' Simon said, slowly understanding, 'because no-one else will ever hear or see.'

Jane said sadly, 'It seems a pity that the poor Greenwitch's secret should just be thrown away.'

'It has served its purpose,' Merriman said. His deep voice rose a little, gained a hint of ceremony. 'Its high purpose, for which it was made so very long ago. It has set us the next great step along the road to keep the Dark from rising, and there is nothing more important than that quest.'

'That last bit you said, from the grail and the manuscript,' Barney said. 'What language was it in?'

'Welsh,' Merriman said.

'Is the last part of the quest in Wales?'

'Yes.'

'Are we going to be part of it?'

Merriman said, 'Wait and see.'

*

They lay in variously abandoned attitudes in the sunshine on the beach, recovering from an enormous picnic lunch. Simon and Barney were lazily tossing a ball to and fro, without bothering to stand up. Bill Stanton was eyeing them, and the near-by cricket bat, with nostalgic optimism.

'Just wait,' he said to his sun-bathing wife, 'we'll show you just exactly how it's played, in a little while.'

'Great,' said Fran Stanton sleepily.

Jane, lying on her back blinking up at the blue sky, propped herself up on her elbows and looked out to sea. The sand was hot against her skin; it was a beautiful, sunny, breezeless Cornish day, of a rare and special kind.

'I'm just going for a little walk,' she said to nobody in particular, and over the dry sand she went, across the long golden beach, towards the rocks that glistened with low-tide seaweed at the foot of Kemare Head. The headland reared up above her, grassy slope changing to jagged grey cliff; at the very tip, the cliffs towered in a sheer wall against the sky. Jane's head was full of memories. She began to walk over the rocks, wincing a little as her bare feet, not yet toughened by summer, pressed against rough rock. Out here, last year, she and Barney and Simon had reached the peak of their adventure, the achieving of the grail that had lain for hundreds of years in a cave, the entrance covered totally by water at all but the lowest tides. Out here, they had fled from the pursuing Dark, with the grail and the little lead case they had found inside it. And out here, she thought as she reached the furthest point of the rocks, with the waves breaking white at her feet, just here, in the flurry of saving the grail, the little lead case had plummeted into the waves and down to the bottom of the sea.

And the Greenwitch had found it there, and made it a precious secret.

Jane looked at the deep green water beyond the breaking waves. 'Good-bye, Greenwitch,' she said softly.

She unclasped a small silver bracelet that she wore on her wrist, weighed it experimentally in her hand, and drew back her arm to throw it into the sea.

A voice said gently behind her, 'Don't do that.'

Jane gasped, and nearly lost her balance; swinging round, she saw Will Stanton.

'Oh!' she said. 'You made me jump.'

'Sorry,' Will said. He balanced his way forwards to stand beside her; his bare feet looked very white against the dark seaweed patching the rocks.

Jane looked at his pleasant round face, and then at the bracelet in her hand. 'I know it sounds stupid,' she said reluctantly, 'but I wanted to give the Greenwitch another secret to keep. Instead of the one we took. In my dream' – she paused, embarrassed, but went gamely on – 'in my dream, I said, *I will give you another secret,* and the Greenwitch said in that big sad booming voice, "*Too late, too late,*" and just disappeared . . .'

She was silent, gazing at the sea.

'I only said don't,' Will said, 'because I don't think your bracelet would really do. It's silver, isn't it, and the seawater would turn it all black and dirty-looking.'

'Oh,' Jane said, forlorn.

Will shifted his footing on the wet rock, and felt in his pocket. He said, glancing briefly at Jane and then away, 'I knew you'd want to give the Greenwitch something. I wondered if this would do.'

Jane looked. Lying on Will's outstretched palm was the same small green-patched lead case that had held the manuscript, the Greenwitch's first secret. Will took it and pulled off the cap, shaking out a small object into her hand.

Jane saw a strip of yellow metal, gleaming, with some words engraved on it very small.

'It looks like gold,' she said.

'It is,' said Will. 'Low carat, but gold. Last for ever, even down there.'

Jane read out: '*Power from the green witch, lost beneath the sea.*'

'That's just a line from a poem,' Will said.

'Is it really? It's perfect.' She ran her finger along the bright gold. 'Where did you get it?'

'I made it.'

'You made it?' Jane turned and stared at him with such astonishment that Will laughed. 'My father's a jeweller. He's teaching me to engrave things. I go and help in his shop sometimes after school.'

'But you must have done this before you came down here, before you ever knew we were going to meet the Greenwitch,' Jane said slowly. 'How did you know what to make, what to write?'

'Just a lucky chance, I suppose,' Will said, and there was a polite finality in his tone that reminded Jane instantly of Merriman: it was the voice that forbade any questioning.

'Oh,' she said.

Will put the small golden strip into the case and fitted the cap on tightly. Then he handed it to her.

'Here's your secret, Greenwitch,' Jane said, and she flung it into the sea. The little case vanished into the waves, their foam curling round the weed-fringed rocks. In the sunlight the water glittered like shattered glass.

'Thank you, Will Stanton,' Jane said. She paused, looking at him. 'You aren't quite like the rest of us, are you?'

'Not quite,' said Will.

Jane said, 'I hope we shall see you again, some day.'
Will said, 'I'm pretty sure you will.'

Mr and Mrs Penhallow stood waving from the steps of the cottage, as they left: Merriman to put the four children on the London train, the Stantons on a visit to Truro for the day.

'Good-bye!'

'Good journey to you! Good-bye!'

The cars disappeared across the quay; overhead, seagulls wheeled and cried.

'Perfessor did find what he came for, this time, I do believe,' Mr Penhallow said, sucking pensively at his pipe.

'That liddle gold cup from last year, that was stole in London? Aye. But there was more, I fancy.' Mrs Penhallow gazed at the point where Merriman's car had rounded the corner, with speculation in her eyes.

'More of what?'

''Twas no accident he came down here at Greenwitch time. He've never done that before. This was Cap'n Toms' first Greenwitch makin' at home for a good many years, too . . . I don't know, Walter, I don't know. But something strange have been going on.'

'You'm dreaming,' Mr Penhallow said indulgently.

'That I'm not. But that young Jane was, one night. That same night everyone was dreaming, the night the whole village was hilla-ridden . . . Such talk there was next morning, of things best forgotten . . . And that morning, I was right near the bedrooms, going about my business, when young Jane woke up. And she let out such a hoot, and was out of her room like a wild thing running to her brothers.'

'So she'd been dreaming, sure,' Mr Penhallow said. 'A bad 'un, by the sound of it. What of that?'

''Twasn't her dreaming that stays with me,' Mrs Penhallow looked out at the quiet harbour, and the drifting gulls. ''Twas her room. Clean as a pin it was the night before, she'm a neat little maid. But everywhere in that room, that morning, there was a great mess of little twigs and leaves, hawthorn leaves, and rowan. And everywhere a great smell of the sea.'

The Grey King

for J. B. and Jacquetta

Although all the characters in this books are fictitious, the places are real. I have
however taken certain liberties with the geography of the Dysynni Valley and
Tal y Llyn, and there are no real farms where I have made Clwyd, Prichard's
and Ty-Bont stand.

The Brenin Llwyd I did not invent.

I am grateful to the Rev. Kenneth Francis, Mr J. L. Jones and Mrs Eira Crook for
kindly checking my Welsh.

Contents

On the day of the dead, when the year too dies,
Must the youngest open the oldest hills
Through the door of the birds, where the breeze breaks.
There fire shall fly from the raven boy,
And the silver eyes that see the wind,
And the Light shall have the harp of gold.

By the pleasant lake the Sleepers lie,
On Cadfan's Way where the kestrels call;
Though grim from the Grey King shadows fall,
Yet singing the golden harp shall guide
To break their sleep and bid them ride.

When light from the lost land shall return,
Six Sleepers shall ride, six Signs shall burn,
And where the midsummer tree grows tall
By Pendragon's sword the Dark shall fall.

Y maent yr mynyddoedd yn canu,
ac y mae'r arglwyddes yn dod.

Prologue

'Are you awake, Will? Will? Wake up, it's time for your medicine, love . . .'

The face swung like a pendulum, to and fro; rose high up in a pink blur; dropped again; divided into six pink blurs, all of them spinning madly like wheels. He closed his eyes. He could feel sweat cold on his forehead, panic cold in his mind. *I've lost it. I've forgotten!* Even in darkness the world spun round. There was a great buzzing in his head like rushing water, until for a moment the voice broke through it again.

'Will! Just for a moment, wake up . . .'

It was his mother's voice. He knew, but could not focus. The darkness whirled and roared. *I've lost something. It's gone. What was it? It was terribly important, I must remember it, I must!* He began to struggle, reaching for consciousness, and a long way off heard himself groan.

'Here we go.' Another voice. The doctor. A firm arm, propping his shoulders; cold metal at his lips, a liquid tipped deftly down his throat. Automatically he swallowed. The world wildly spun. Panic came flooding again. A few faint words flashed through his mind and away like a snatch of music; his memory clutched, grasping – '*On the day of the dead –*'

Mrs Stanton stared down anxiously at the white face, the dark-smudged closed eyes, the damp hair. 'What did he say?'

Suddenly Will sat upright, eyes wide and staring. '*On the day of the dead –*' He looked at her, pleading, without recognition. 'That's all I can remember! It's gone! There was something I had to remember, a thing I had to do, it mattered more than anything and I've lost it! I've forgott – en –' His face crumpled and he dropped back helplessly, tears running down his cheeks. His mother leaned over him, her arms round him, murmuring soothingly as if he were a baby. In a few moments he began to relax, and to breathe more easily. She looked up in distress.

'Is he delirious?'

The doctor shook his head, his round face compassionate. 'No, he's past that. Physically, the worst is over. This is more like a bad dream, an hallucination –

though he may indeed have lost something from his memory. The mind can be very much bound up with the health of the body, even in children . . . Don't worry. He'll sleep now. And every day will be better from now on.'

Mrs Stanton sighed, stroking her youngest son's damp forehead. 'I'm very grateful. You've come so often – there aren't many doctors who –'

'Poof, poof,' said little Dr Armstrong briskly, taking Will's wrist between finger and thumb. 'We're all old friends. He was a very, very sick boy for a while. Going to be limp for a long time, too – even youngsters don't bounce back from this kind of thing very fast. I'll be back, Alice. But anyway, bed for at least another week, and no school for a month after that. Can you send him away somewhere? What about that cousin of yours in Wales, who took Mary at Easter?'

'Yes, he could go there. I'm sure he could. It's nice in October, too, and the sea air . . . I'll write to them.'

Will moved his head on the pillow, muttering, but did not wake.

PART ONE

The Golden Harp

The Oldest Hills

He remembered Mary had said, 'They all speak Welsh, most of the time. Even Aunt Jen.'

'Oh, dear,' said Will.

'Don't worry,' his sister said. 'Sooner or later they switch to English, if they see you're there. Just remember to be patient. And they'll be extra kind because of your having been ill. At least they were to me, after my mumps.'

So now Will stood patiently alone on the windy grey platform of the small station of Tywyn, in a thin drizzle of October rain, waiting while two men in the navy-blue railway uniform argued earnestly in Welsh. One of them was small and wizened, gnome-like; the other had a soft, squashy look, like a man made of dough.

The gnome caught sight of Will. '*Beth sy'n bod*?' he said.

'Er – excuse me,' Will said. 'My uncle said he'd meet me off the train, in the station yard, but there's no one outside. Could you tell me if there's anywhere else he might have meant?'

The gnome shook his head.

'Who's your uncle, then?' inquired the soft-faced man.

'Mr Evans, from Bryn-Crug. Clwyd Farm,' Will said.

The gnome chuckled gently. 'David Evans will be a bit late, boy *bach*. You have a nice dreamer for an uncle. David Evans will be late when the Last Trump sounds. You just wait a while. On holiday, is it?' Bright dark eyes peered inquisitively into his face.

'Sort of. I've had hepatitis. The doctor said I had to come away to convalesce.'

'Ah!' The man nodded his head sagely. 'You look a bit peaky, yes. Come to the right place, though. The air on this coast is very relaxing, they say, very relaxing. Even at this time of year.'

A clattering roar came suddenly from beyond the ticket office, and through the barrier Will saw a mud-streaked Land-Rover drive into the yard. But the figure that came bounding out of it was not that of the small neat farmer he vaguely remembered; it was a wiry, gangling young man, jerkily thrusting out his hand.

'Will, is it? Hallo. Da sent me to meet you. I'm Rhys.'

'How do you do.' Will knew he had two grown-up Welsh cousins, old as his oldest brothers, but he had never set eyes on either of them.

Rhys scooped up his suitcase as if it had been a matchbox. 'This all you have? Let's be off, then.' He nodded to the railwaymen. '*Sut 'dach chi?*'

'*Iawn diolch,*' said the gnome. 'Caradog Prichard was asking for you or your father, round about, this morning. Something about dogs.'

'A pity you haven't seen me at all, today,' Rhys said.

The gnome grinned. He took Will's ticket. 'Get yourself healthy now, young man.'

'Thank you,' Will said.

Perched up in the front of the Land-Rover, he peered out at the little grey town as the windscreen wipers tried in vain, twitch-creak, twitch-creak, to banish the fine misty rain from the glass. Deserted shops lined the little street, and a few bent figures in raincoats scurried by; he saw a church, a small hotel, more neat houses. Then the road was widening and they were out between trim hedges, with open fields beyond, and green hills rising against the sky: a grey sky, featureless with mist. Rhys seemed shy; he drove with no attempt at talking – though the engine made so much noise that conversation would have been hard in any case. Past gaggles of silent cottages they drove, the boards that announced VACANCY or BED AND BREAKFAST swinging forlornly now that most of the holiday visitors were gone.

Rhys turned the car inland, towards the mountains, and almost at once Will had a strange new feeling of enclosure, almost of menace. The little road was narrow here, like a tunnel, with its high grass banks and looming hedges like green walls on either side. Whenever they passed the gap where a hedge opened to a field through a gate, he could see the green-brown bulk of hillsides rearing up at the grey sky. And ahead, as bends in the road showed open sky briefly through the trees, a higher fold of grey hills loomed in the distance, disappearing into ragged cloud. Will felt that he was in a part of Britain like none he had ever known before: a secret, enclosed place, with powers hidden in its shrouded centuries at which he could not begin to guess. He shivered.

In the same moment, as Rhys swung round a tight corner towards a narrow bridge, the Land-Rover gave a strange jerking leap and lurched down to one side, towards the hedge. Braking hard, Rhys hauled at the wheel and managed to stop at an angle that seemed to indicate one wheel was in the ditch.

'Damn!' he said with force, opening the door.

Will scrambled after him. 'What happened?'

'There is what happened.' Rhys pointed a long finger at the nearside front wheel, its tyre pressed hopelessly flat against a rock jutting from the hedge. 'Just look at that. Ripped it right open, and so thick those tyres are, you would never think –' His light, rather husky voice was high with astonishment.

'Was the rock lying in the road?'

Rhys shook his curly head. 'Goes under the hedge. Huge, it is, that's just one end . . . I used to sit on that rock when I was half your size . . .' Wonder had banished his shyness. 'What made the car jump, then? That's the funny thing, seemed to jump, she did, right on to it, sideways. It wasn't the tyre blowing, that feels quite different . . .' He straightened, brushing away the rain that spangled his eyebrows. 'Well, well. A wheel change, now.'

Will said hopefully, 'Can I help?'

Rhys looked down at him: at the shadowed eyes and the pale face beneath the thick, straight brown hair. He grinned suddenly, directly at Will for the first time since they had met; it made his face look quite different, untroubled and young. 'Here you come down after being so ill, to be put together again, and I am to have you out in the rain changing an old wheel? Mam would have fifty fits. Back in the warm with you, go on.' He moved round to the rear door of the square little car, and began pulling out tools.

Will clambered obediently up into the front of the Land-Rover again; it seemed a warm, cosy little box, after the chill wind blowing the drizzle into his face out on the road. There was no sound, there among the open fields under the looming hills, but the soft whine of the wind in telephone wires, and an occasional deep *baaa* from a distant sheep. And the rattle of a spanner; Rhys was undoing the bolts that secured the spare wheel to the back door.

Will leaned his head back against the seat, closing his eyes. His illness had kept him in bed for a long time, in a long blur of ache and distress and fleeting anxious faces, and although he had been back on his feet for more than a week, he still grew tired very easily. It was frightening sometimes to catch himself breathless and exhausted, after something as ordinary as climbing a flight of stairs.

He sat relaxed, letting the soft sounds of the wind and the calling sheep drift through his mind. Then another sound came. Opening his eyes, he saw in the side mirror another car slowing to a stop behind them.

A man climbed out, thickset, chunky, wearing a flat cap, and a raincoat flapping over rubber boots; he was grinning. For no good reason, Will instantly disliked the grin. Rhys opened the back of the Land-Rover again, to reach for the jack, and Will heard the newcomer greet him in Welsh; the words were unintelligible, but they had an unmistakable jeering tone. All this short conversation, indeed, lay as open in meaning as if Will had understood every word.

The man was clearly mocking Rhys for having to change a wheel in the rain. Rhys answered, curtly but without crossness. The man looked deliberately into the car, walking forward to peer in at the window; he stared at Will, unsmiling, with strange small light-lashed eyes, and asked Rhys something. When Rhys answered, one of the words was 'Will.' The man in the raincoat said something else, with a sneer in it this time directed at both of them, and then without warning he broke into an astonishing tirade of rapid, bitter speech, the words pouring out flurried and guttural like a churning river in flood. Rhys appeared to pay no attention at all. At last the man paused, angry. He swung round and marched back to his car; then he drove slowly on past them, still staring at Will as he went by. A black-and-white dog was looking out over the man's shoulder, and Will saw that the car was in fact a van, grey and windowless at the back.

He slipped across into the driver's seat and pulled open the window; the Land-Rover lurched gently up into the air beneath him as Rhys heaved on the jack.

'Who was that?' Will said.

'Fellow called Caradog Prichard, from up the valley.' Rhys spat enigmatically on his hands, and heaved again. 'A farmer.'

'He could have stayed and helped you.'

'Ha!' Rhys said. 'Caradog Prichard is not well known for helping.'

'What did he say?'

'He let me know how amusing it was to see me stuck. And some things about a disagreement we have. Of no importance. And asked who you were.' Rhys spun his spanner, loosening the wheel-bolts, and glanced up with a shy conspiratorial grin. 'A good job our mothers were not listening, I was not polite. I said you were my cousin and none of his bloody business.'

'Was he cross?'

Rhys paused reflectively. 'He said – *We shall see about that.*'

Will looked up the valley road where the van had disappeared. 'That's a funny thing to say.'

'Oh,' Rhys said, 'that is Caradog. His hobby is to make people feel uncomfortable. Nobody likes him, except his dogs, and he doesn't even like them.' He tugged at the injured wheel. 'Sit still up there now. We shan't be long.'

By the time he climbed back into the driving seat, rubbing his hands on an oily rag, the fine drizzle had turned to real rain; the dark hair was curling wet over his head. 'Well,' Rhys said. 'This is nice old weather to greet you, I must say. But it won't last. We shall have a good bit of sun yet, off and on, before the winter bites down on us.'

Will gazed out at the mountains, dark and distant, swinging into view as they drove along the road crossing the valley. Grey-white cloud hung ragged round the highest hills, their tops invisible behind the mist. He said, 'The cloud's all tattered round the tops of the mountains. Perhaps it's breaking up.'

Rhys looked out casually. 'The breath of the Grey King? No, I'm sorry to tell you, Will, that's supposed to be a bad sign.'

Will sat very still, a great rushing sound in his ears; he gripped the edge of his seat until the metal bit at his fingers. 'What did you call it?'

'The cloud? Oh, when it hangs ragged like that we call it the breath of the *Brenin Llwyd.* The Grey King. He is supposed to live up there on the high land. It's just one of the old stories.' Rhys glanced sideways at him and then braked suddenly; the Land-Rover slowed almost to a halt. 'Will! Are you all right? White as a ghost, you look. Are you feeling bad?'

'No. No. It was just –' Will was staring out at the grey mass of the hills. 'It was just . . . the Grey King, *the Grey King* . . . it's part of something I used to know, something I was supposed to remember, for always . . . I thought I'd lost it. Perhaps – perhaps it's going to come back . . .'

Rhys crashed the car back into gear. 'Oh,' he called cheerfully through the noise, 'we'll get you better, you just wait. Anything can happen in these old hills.'

Cadfan's Way

'You see?' said Aunt Jen. 'I told you it would clear up.'

Will swallowed his last mouthful of bacon. 'You wouldn't think it was the same country. Marvellous.'

Morning sunshine streamed like banners through the windows of the long farmhouse kitchen. It glinted on the blue slate slabs of the floor, on the willow-pattern china set out on the enormous black dresser; on the shelf of beaming Toby jugs above the stove. A rainbow danced over the low ceiling, cast up in a sun-spell from the handle of the glass milk-jug.

'Warm, too,' said Aunt Jen. 'We are going to have an Indian summer for you, Will. And fatten you up a bit too, my dear. Have some more bread.'

'It's lovely. I haven't eaten so much for months.' Will watched small Aunt Jen with affection as she bustled about the kitchen. Strictly speaking, she was not his aunt at all, but a cousin of his mother's; the two had grown up as close friends, and still exchanged quantities of letters. But Aunt Jen had left Buckinghamshire long before; it was one of the more romantic legends in the family, the tale of how she had come to Wales for a holiday, fallen shatteringly in love with a young Welsh farmer, and never gone home again. She even sounded Welsh herself now – and looked it, with her small, cosily plump form and bright dark eyes.

'Where's Uncle David?' he said.

'Out in the yard somewhere. This is a busy time of the year with the sheep, the hill farms send their yearlings down for the winter . . . he has to drive to Tywyn soon, he wondered if you would like to go too. Go to the beach, you could, in this sunshine.'

'Super.'

'No swimming, mind,' said Aunt Jen hastily.

Will laughed. 'I know, I'm fragile. I'll be careful . . . I'd love to go. I can send Mum a card, saying I got here in one piece.' A clatter and a shadow came in the doorway; it was Rhys, dishevelled, pulling off a sweater. 'Morning, Will. Have you left us some breakfast?'

'You're late,' Will said cheekily.

'Late, is it?' Rhys glared at him in mock fury. 'Just hear him – and us out since six with only an old cup of tea inside. Tomorrow morning, John, we will pull this young monkey out of bed and take him with us.'

Behind him a deep voice chuckled. Will's attention was caught by a face he had not seen before.

'Will, this is John Rowlands. The best man with sheep in Wales.'

'And with the harp, too,' Aunt Jen said.

It was a lean face, with cheekbones carved high in it, and many lines everywhere, creased upward now round the eyes by smiling. Dark eyes, brown as coffee; thinning dark hair, streaked with grey at the sides; the well-shaped, modelled mouth of the Celt. For a moment Will stared, fascinated; there was a curious indefinable strength in this John Rowlands, even though he was not at all a big man.

'*Croeso*, Will,' said John Rowlands. 'Welcome to Clwyd. I heard about you from your sister, last spring.'

'Good heavens,' said Will in unthinking astonishment, and everyone laughed.

'Nothing bad,' Rowlands said, smiling. 'How is Mary?'

'She's fine,' Will said. 'She said she had a marvellous time here, last Easter. I was away too, then. In Cornwall.'

He fell silent for a moment, his face suddenly abstracted and blank; John Rowlands looked at him swiftly, then sat down at the table where Rhys was already poised over bacon and eggs. Will's uncle came in, carrying a batch of papers.

'*Cwpanaid o de, cariad?*' said Aunt Jen, when she saw him.

'*Diolch yn fawr,*' said David Evans, taking the cup of tea she held out to him. 'And then I must be off to Tywyn. You want to come, Will?'

'Yes, please.'

'We may be a couple of hours.' The sound of his words was very precise always; he was a small, neatly-made man, sharp-featured, but with an unexpectedly vague, reflective look sometimes in his dark eyes. 'I have to go to the bank, and to see Llew Thomas, and there will be the new tyre for the Land-Rover. The car that jumped up in the air and got itself a puncture.'

Rhys, with his mouth full, made a strangled noise of protest. 'Now, Da,' he said, swallowing. 'I know how it sounded, but really I am not mad, there was *nothing* that could have made her swerve over to the side like that and hit the rock. Unless the steering rod is going.'

'There is nothing wrong with the steering of that car,' David Evans said.

'Well, then!' Rhys was all elbows and indignation. 'I tell you she just lurched over for no reason at all. Ask Will.'

'It's true,' Will said. 'The car did just sort of jump sideways and hit that rock. I don't see what could have made it jump, unless it had run over a loose stone in the road – but that would have had to be a pretty big stone. And there was no sign of one anywhere.'

'Great allies, you two, already, I can see,' said his uncle. He drained his teacup, gazing at them over the top; Will was not sure whether or not he was laughing at them. 'Well, well, I will have the steering checked anyway. John, Rhys, now that extra fencing for the *fridd* –'

They slid into Welsh, unthinking. It did not bother Will. He was occupied in trying to scorn away a small voice at the back of his mind, an irrational small voice with an irrational suggestion. '*If they want to know what made the car jump,*' this part of his mind was whispering at him, '*why don't they ask Caradog Prichard?*'

David Evans dropped Will at a small newsagent's shop, where he could buy postcards, and chugged off to leave the Land-Rover at a garage. Will bought a card showing a sinister dark lake surrounded by very Welsh-looking mountains, wrote on it 'I GOT HERE! Everyone sends their love,' and sent it off to his mother from the Post Office, a solemn and unmistakable red brick building on a corner of Tywyn High Street. Then he looked about him, wondering where to go next.

Choosing at random, hoping to see the sea, he turned right up the narrow curving High Street. Before long he found that there would be no sea this way: nor anything but shops, houses, a cinema with an imposing Victorian front grandly labelled ASSEMBLY ROOMS, and the slate-roofed lychgate of a church.

Will liked investigating churches; before his illness had overtaken him, he and two friends from school had been cycling all round the Thames Valley to make brass rubbings. He turned into the little churchyard, to see if there might be any brasses here.

The church porch was low-roofed, deep as a cave; inside, the church was shadowy and cool, with sturdy white painted walls and massive white pillars. Nobody was there. Will found no brasses for rubbing, but only monuments to unpronounceable benefactors, like Gruffydd ap Adda of Ynysymaengwyn Hall. At the rear of the church, on his way out, he noticed a strange long grey stone set up on end, incised with marks too ancient for him to decipher. He stared at it for a long moment; it seemed like an omen of some kind, though of what significance he had not the least idea. And then, in the porch on his way out, he glanced idly up at the notice-board with its scattering of parish news, and he saw the name: *Church of St Cadfan.*

The whirling came again in his ears like the wind; staggering, he collapsed on to the low bench in the porch. His mind spun, he was back suddenly in the roaring confusion of his illness, when he had known that something, something most precious, had slipped or been taken away from his memory. Words flickered through his consciousness, without order or meaning, and then a phrase surfaced like a leaping fish: '*On Cadfan's Way where the kestrels call. . . .*' His mind seized it greedily, reaching for more. But there was no more. The roaring died away; Will opened his eyes, breathing more steadily, the giddiness draining gradually out of him. He said softly, aloud, 'On Cadfan's Way where the kestrels call . . . On Cadfan's Way . . .' Outside in the sunshine the grey slate tombstones and green grass glimmered, with jewel-glints of light here and there from droplets of rain still clinging to the longest stems from the day before. Will thought, '*On the day of the dead . . . the Grey King . . .* there must have been some sort of warning about the Grey King . . . and what is Cadfan's Way?'

'Oh,' he said aloud in sudden fury, 'if only I could *remember!*'

He jumped up and went back to the newsagent's shop. 'Please,' he said, 'is there a guide to the church, or to the town?'

'Nothing on Tywyn,' said the red-cheeked girl of the shop, in her sibilant Welsh lilt. 'Too late in the season, you are . . . but Mr Owen has a leaflet for sale in the church, I think. And there is this, if you like. Full of lovely walks.' She showed him a *Guide to North Wales,* for thirty-five pence.

'Well,' said Will, counting out his money rather reluctantly. 'I can always take it home afterwards, I suppose.'

'It would make a very nice present,' said the girl earnestly. 'Got some beautiful pictures, it has. And just look at the cover!'

'Thank you,' said Will.

When he peered at the little book, outside, it told him that the Saxons had settled in Tywyn in A.D. 516, round the church built by St Cadfan of Brittany and his holy well, and that the inscribed stone in the church was said to be the oldest piece of written Welsh in existence, and could be translated: 'The body of Cyngen is on the side between where the marks will be. In the retreat beneath the mound is extended Cadfan, said that it should enclose the praise of the earth. May he rest without blemish.' But it said not a word about Cadfan's Way. Nor, when he checked, did the leaflet in the church.

Will thought: it is not Cadfan I want, it is his Way. A way is a road. A way where the kestrels call must be a road over a moor, or a mountain.

It pushed even the seashore out of his mind, when later he walked absentmindedly for a while among the breakwaters of the windy beach. When he met his uncle for the ride back to the farm, he found no help there either.

'Cadfan's Way?' said David Evans. 'You pronounce it Cadvan, by the way; one *f* is always a *v* sound in Welsh . . . Cadfan's Way . . . No. It does sound a bit familiar, you know. But I couldn't tell you, Will. John Rowlands is the one to ask about things like that. He has a mind like an encyclopedia, does John, full of old things.'

John Rowlands was out somewhere on the farm, busy, so for the time being Will had to content himself with a much-folded map. He went out with it that afternoon, alone in the sunlit valley, to walk the boundaries of the farm; his uncle had roughly pencilled them in for him. Clwyd was a lowland farm, stretching across most of the valley of the Dysynni River; some of its land was marshy, near the river, and some stretched up the soaring scree-patched side of the mountain, green and grey and bracken-brown. But most was lush green valley land, fertile and friendly, part of it left new-ploughed since the harvest of this year's crops, and all the rest serving as pasture for square, sturdy Welsh Black cattle. On the mountain land, only sheep grazed. Some of the lower slopes had been ploughed, though even they looked so steep to Will that he wondered how a tractor ploughing them could have kept from rolling over. Above those, nothing grew but bracken, groups of wind-warped scrubby trees, and grass; the mountain reared up to the sky, and the deep aimless call of a sheep came now and then floating down into the still, warm afternoon.

It was by another sound that he found John Rowlands, unexpectedly. As he was walking through one of the Clwyd fields towards the river, with a high wild hedge on one side of him and the dark ploughed soil on the other, he heard a dull, muffled thudding, somewhere ahead. Then suddenly at a curve in the field he saw the figure, moving steadily and rhythmically as if in a slow, deliberate dance. He stopped and watched, fascinated. Rowlands, his shirt half-open and a red kerchief tied round his neck, was making a transformation. He moved gradually along the hedge, first chopping carefully here and there with a murderous tool like a cross between an axe and a pirate's cutlass, then setting this down and hauling and interweaving whatever remained of the long, rank growth. Before him, the hedge grew wild and high, great arms groping out uncontrolled in all directions as the hazel and hawthorn did their best to grow into full-fledged trees. Behind him, as he moved along his relentless swaying way, he left instead a neat fence: scores of beheaded branches bristling waist-high like spears, with every fifth branch bent mercilessly down at right angles and woven in along the rest as if it were part of a hurdle.

Will watched, silent, until Rowlands became aware of him and straightened up, breathing heavily. He pulled the red kerchief loose, wiped his forehead with it and re-tied it loosely round his neck. In his creased brown face, the lines beside the dark eyes turned upwards just a little as he looked at Will.

'I know,' he said, the velvet voice solemn. 'You are thinking, here is this wonderful healthy hedge full of leaves and hawthorn berries, reaching up to the heavens, and here is this man hacking it down like a butcher jointing a sheep, taming it into a horrid little naked fence, all bones and no grace.'

Will grinned. 'Well,' he said. 'Something like that, yes.'

'Ah,' said John Rowlands. He squatted down on his haunches, resting his axe head down on the ground between his knees and leaning on it. '*Duw*, it's a good job you came along. I cannot go so fast as I used to. Well, let me tell you now, if we were to leave this lovely wild hedge the way it is now, and has been for too long, it would take over half the field before this time next year. And even though I am cutting off its head and half its body, all these sad bent-over shoots that you see will be sending up so many new arms next spring that you will hardly notice any difference in it at all.'

'Now that you come to mention it,' said Will, 'yes, of course, the hedging is just the same at home, in Bucks. It's just that I never actually watched anyone doing it before.'

'Had my eye on this hedge for a year,' John Rowlands said. 'It was missed last winter. Like life it is, Will – sometimes you must seem to hurt something in order to do good for it. But not often a very big hurt, thank goodness.' He got to his feet again. 'You look more healthy already, *bachgen*. The Welsh sun is good for you.'

Will looked down at the map in his hand. 'Mr Rowlands,' he said, 'can you tell me anything about Cadfan's Way?'

The Welshman had been running one tough brown finger along the edge of his mattock; there was a second's pause in the movement, and then the finger moved on. He said quietly, 'Now what put that into your head, I wonder?'

'I don't really know. I suppose I must have read it somewhere. Is there a Cadfan's Way?'

'Oh, yes, indeed,' John Rowlands said. '*Llwybr Cadfan*. No secret about that, though most people these days have forgotten it. I think they have a Cadfan Road in one of the new Tywyn housing estates instead . . . St Cadfan was a kind of missionary, from France, in the days when Brittany and Cornwall and Wales all had close ties. Fourteen hundred years ago he had his church in Tywyn, and a holy well – and he is supposed to have founded the monastery on *Enlli*, that is in English Bardsey, as well. You know Bardsey Island, where the bird-watchers go, out there off the tip of North Wales? People used to visit Tywyn and go on to Bardsey – and so, they say, there is an old pilgrims' road that goes over the mountain from Machynlleth to Tywyn, past Abergynolwyn. And along the side of this valley, no doubt. Or perhaps higher up. Most of the old ways go along high places, they were safer there. But nobody knows where to find Cadfan's Way now.'

'I see,' said Will. It was more than enough; he knew that now he would be able to find the Way, given time. But increasingly he felt that there was very little time left; that it was urgent for his quest, so oddly lost by his memory, to be accomplished very soon. *On the day of the dead*. . . . And what was the quest, and where, and why? If only he could remember . . .

John Rowlands turned towards the hedge again. 'Well –'

'I'll see you later,' Will said. 'Thank you. I'm trying to walk all round the edge of the farm.'

'Take it gently. That is a long walk for a convalescent, the whole of it.' Rowlands straightened suddenly, pointing a finger at him in warning. 'And if you go up the valley and get to the Craig yr Aderyn end – that way – make sure you check the boundaries on your map, and do not go off your uncle's land. That is Caradog Prichard's farm beyond, and he is not kind with trespassers.'

Will thought of the malicious, light-lashed eyes in the sneering face he had seen from the Land-Rover with Rhys. 'Oh,' he said. 'Caradog Prichard. All right. Thanks. *Diolch yn fawr*. Is that right?'

John Rowlands's face broke into creases of laughter. 'Not bad,' he said. 'But perhaps you should stick to just *diolch*.'

The gentle thud of his axe dwindled behind Will and was lost in the insect-hum of the sunny afternoon, with the scattered calls of birds and sheep. The way that Will was going led sideways across the valley, with the grey-green sweep of the mountain rising always before him; it blocked out more and more of the sky as he walked on. Soon he was beginning to climb, and then the bracken began to come in over the grass in a rustling knee-high carpet, with clumps here and there of spiky green gorse, its yellow flowers still bright among the fierce prickling stalks. No hedge climbed the mountain, but a slate-topped drystone wall, curving with every contour, broken now and then by a stile-step low enough for men but too high for sheep.

Will found himself losing breath far more quickly than he would normally have done. As soon as he next came to a humped rock the right size for sitting, he folded thankfully into a panting heap. While he waited for his breath to come properly back, he looked at the map again. The Clwyd farmland seemed to end about halfway up the mountain – but there was, of course, nothing to guarantee that he would come across the old Cadfan's Way before he reached the boundary. He found himself hoping a little nervously that the rest of the mountain above was not Caradog Prichard's land.

Stuffing the map back into his pocket, he went on, higher, through the crackling brown fronds of the bracken. He was climbing diagonally now, as the slope grew steeper. Birds whirred away from him; somewhere high above, a skylark was pouring out its rippling, throbbing song. Then all at once, Will began to have an unaccountable feeling that he was being followed.

Abruptly he stopped, swinging round. Nothing moved. The bracken-brown slope lay still beneath the sunshine, with outcrops of white rock glimmering here and there. A car hummed past on the road below, invisible through trees; he was high above the farm now, looking out over the silver thread of the river to the mountains rising green and grey and brown behind, and at last fading blue into the distance. Further up the valley the mountainside on which he stood was clothed dark green with plantations of spruce trees, and beyond those he could see a great grey-black crag rising, a lone peak, lower than the mountains around it yet dominating all the surrounding land. A few large black birds circled its top; as he watched, they merged together into a shape of a long V, as geese do, and flew unhurriedly away over the mountain in the direction of the sea.

Then from somewhere close, he heard one short sharp bark from a dog.

Will jumped. No dog was likely to be on the mountain alone. Yet there was no sign of another human being anywhere. If someone was near by, why was he hiding himself?

He turned to go on up the slope, and only then did he see the dog. He stood stone-still. It was poised directly above him, alert, waiting; a white dog, white all over with only one small black patch on its back, like a saddle. Except for the curious pattern of colouring, it looked like a traditional Welsh sheep dog, muscular and sharp-muzzled, with feathered legs and tail: a smaller version of the collie. Will held out his hand. 'Here, boy,' he said. But the dog bared its teeth, and gave a low, threatening growl deep in its throat.

Will took a few tentative steps up the slope, diagonally, in the direction he had been going before. Crouching on its stomach, the dog moved with him, teeth glittering, tongue lolling. The attitude was odd and yet familiar, and suddenly Will realized that he had seen it the evening before in the two dogs on his uncle's farm that had been helping Rhys bring in the cows to be milked. It was the movement of control – the watchful crouch from which a working sheepdog would spring, to bring to order the animals it was driving in a particular direction.

But where was this dog trying to drive him?

Clearly, there was only one way to find out. Taking a deep breath, Will turned to face the dog and began deliberately clambering straight up the slope. The dog stopped, and the long, low growl began again in its throat; it crouched, back curved as if all four feet were planted like trees in the ground. The snarl of the white teeth said, very plainly: *Not this way.* But Will, clenching his fists, kept climbing. He shifted direction very slightly so that he would pass close to the dog without touching it. But then unexpectedly, with one short bark, the dog darted towards him, crouching low, and involuntarily Will jumped – and lost his balance. He fell sideways on the steep hillside. Desperately reaching his arms wide to stop himself from rolling headlong down, he slithered and bumped upside-down for a few wild yards, terror loud as a shout in his head, until his fall was checked by something jerking fiercely at his sleeve. He came up against a rock, with a numbing thud.

He opened his eyes. The line where mountain met sky was spinning before him. Very close was the dog, its teeth clamped on the sleeve of his jacket, tugging him back, all warm breath and black nose and staring eyes. And at the sight of the eyes, Will's world spun round and over again so fast that he thought he must still be falling. The roaring was in his ears again, and all things normal became suddenly chaos. For this dog's eyes were like no eyes he had ever seen; where they should have been brown, they were silver-white: eyes the colour of blindness, set in the head of an animal that could see. And as the silver eyes gazed into his, and the dog's breath panted out hot on his face, in a whirling instant Will remembered everything that his illness had taken away from him. He remembered the verses that had been put into his head as guide for the bleak, lone quest he was destined now to follow; remembered who he was and what he was – and recognized the design that under the mask of coincidence had brought him here to Wales.

At the same time another kind of innocence fell away, and he was aware too of immense danger, like a great shadow across the world, waiting for him all through this unfamiliar land of green valleys and dark-misted mountain peaks. He was like a battle leader suddenly given news: suddenly made aware, as he had not been a moment before, that just beyond the horizon a great and dreadful army lay in wait, preparing itself to rise like a huge wave and drown all those who stood in its way.

Trembling with wonder, Will reached across his other arm and fondled the dog's ears. It let go of his sleeve and stood there gazing at him, tongue lolling pink from a pink-rimmed mouth.

'Good dog,' Will said. 'Good dog.' Then a dark figure blotted out the sun, and he rolled abruptly over to sit up and see who stood outlined there against the sky.

A clear Welsh voice said: 'Are you hurt?'

It was a boy. He was dressed neatly in what looked like a school uniform: grey trousers, white shirt, red socks and tie. He had a schoolbag slung over one shoulder, and he seemed to be about the same age as Will. But there was a quality of strangeness about him, as there had been about the dog, that tightened Will's throat and caught him motionless in a wondering stare; for this boy was drained of all colour, like a shell bleached by the summer sun. His hair was white, and his eyebrows. His skin was pale. The effect was so startling that for a wild moment Will found himself wondering whether the hair was deliberately bleached – done on purpose, to create astonishment and alarm. But the idea vanished as swiftly as it had come. The mixture of arrogance and hostility facing him showed plainly that this was not that kind of boy at all.

'I'm all right.' Will stood up, shaking, pulling bits of bracken out of his hair and off his clothes. He said, 'You might teach your dog the difference between people and sheep.'

'Oh,' said the boy indifferently, 'he knew what he was about. He would have done you no harm.' He said something to the dog in Welsh, and it trotted back up the hill and sat down beside him, watching them both.

'Well' – Will began, and then he stopped. He had looked into the boy's face and found there another pair of eyes to shake him off balance. It was not, this time, the unearthliness he had seen in the dog; it was a sudden shock of feeling that he had seen them somewhere before. The boy's eyes were a strange, tawny golden colour like the eyes of a cat or a bird, rimmed with eyelashes so pale as to be almost invisible, they had a cold, unfathomable glitter.

'*The raven boy*,' he said instantly. 'That's who you are, that's what it calls you, the old verse. I have it all now, I can remember. But ravens are black. Why does it call you that?'

'My name is Bran,' the boy said, unsmiling, looking unwinking down at him. 'Bran Davies. I live down on your uncle's farm.'

Will was taken aback for a moment, in spite of his new confidence. 'On the farm?'

'With my father. In a cottage. My father works for David Evans.' He blinked in the sunshine, pulled a pair of sunglasses from his pocket, and put them on; the tawny eyes disappeared into shadow. He said, in exactly the same conversational tone, 'Bran is really the Welsh word for crow. But people called Bran in the old stories are linked up with the raven, too. A lot of ravens in these hills, there are. So I suppose you could say "the raven boy" if you wanted. Poetic licence, like.'

He swung the satchel off his shoulder and sat down beside Will on a rock, fiddling with the leather strap.

Will said, 'How did you know who I was? That David Evans is my uncle?'

'I could just as well ask how you knew me,' Bran said. 'How did you know, to name me the raven boy?'

He ran one finger idly up and down the strap. Then he smiled suddenly, a smile that illuminated his pale face like quick flaring fire, and he pulled off the dark glasses again.

'I will tell you the answer to both questions, Will Stanton,' he said. 'It is because you are not properly human, but one of the Old Ones of the Light put here to hold back the terrible power of the Dark. You are the last of that circle to be born on earth. And I have been waiting for you.'

The Raven Boy

'You see,' Will said, 'it's the first quest, without help, for me – and the last, because this now is the raising of the last defence the Light can build, to be ready. There is a great battle ahead, Bran – not yet, but not far off. For the Dark is rising, to make its great attempt to take the world for itself until the end of time. When that happens, we must fight and we must win. But we can only win if we have the right weapons. That is what we have been doing, and are still, in such quests as this – gathering the weapons forged for us long, long ago. Six enchanted Signs of the Light, a golden grail, a wonderful harp, a crystal sword . . . They are all achieved now but the harp and the sword, and I do not know what will be the manner of the sword's finding. But the quest for the harp is mine . . .'

He picked a sprig of gorse, and sat staring at it. 'Out of a long time ago, there were three verses made,' he said, 'to tell me what to do. They aren't written down any more, though once they were. They are only in my mind. Or at least they used to be – forever, I thought. But then not long ago I was very ill, and when I came out of it, the verses had gone. I'd forgotten them. I don't know if the Dark had a hand in it. That's possible, while I was . . . not myself. They couldn't have taken the words for themselves, but they could have managed to hinder my catching them again. I thought I'd go mad, trying to remember. I didn't know what to do. A few bits came back, but not much . . . not much. Until I saw your dog.'

'Cafall,' Bran said. The dog raised its head.

'Cafall. Those eyes of his, those silver eyes . . . it was as if they broke a spell. He had put me on the Old Way, Cadfan's Way, as well – just here. And I remembered. All the verses. Everything.'

'He is a special dog,' Bran said. 'He is not . . . ordinary. What are your verses?'

Will looked at him, opened his mouth, shut it again, and looked out at the mountains in confusion. The white-haired boy laughed. He said, 'I know. For all you can tell, I might be from the Dark in spite of Cafall. Isn't that it?'

Will shook his head. 'If you were from the Dark, I should know very well. There's a sense, that tells us . . . the trouble is, that same particular sense that says you aren't from the Dark doesn't say anything else about you either. Not a thing. Nothing bad, nothing good. I don't understand.'

'Ah,' Bran said mockingly. 'I have never understood that myself. But I can tell you, I am like Cafall – I am not quite ordinary either.' He glanced at Will, the pale-lashed eyes darting, secretive. Then he said, reciting deliberately, sounding very sing-song Welsh:

> 'On the day of the dead, when the year too dies,
> Must the youngest open the oldest hills
> Through the door of the birds, where the breeze breaks.'

Will sat stone-still, horrified, gazing at him. The land broke in waves. The sky was falling. He said huskily, 'The beginning of it. But you can't know that. It's not possible. There are only three people in the world who –'

He stopped.

The white-haired boy said, 'I was up here with Cafall, a week ago, up here where you never meet anybody, and we met an old man. A strange old man he was, with a lot of white hair and a big beaky nose.'

Will said slowly, 'Ah.'

'He was not English,' said Bran, 'and he was not Welsh either, though he spoke good Welsh, and good English too, for that matter . . . He must have been a *dewin*, a wizard, he knew a lot about me . . .' He pulled a frond of bracken, frowning, and began to pick it to pieces. 'A lot about me . . . Then he told me about the Dark and the Light. I have never heard anything that I believed so very much, right away, without question. And he told me about you. He told me that it was my task to help you on your quest, but that' – a mocking note slid again into the clear voice, perceptible just for an instant – 'but that because you would not trust me, I must learn those three lines, for a sign. And so he taught me them.'

Will lifted his head to look up the valley, at the blue-grey hills hazy in the sunshine and he shivered; the sense of a looming shadow was on him again, like a dark cloud hovering. Then he said, shrugging it aside, speaking without strain of suspicion now, 'There are three verses. But the first two are the ones that matter, for now. The lines my master Merriman taught you come at the beginning.

> 'On the day of the dead, when the year too dies,
> Must the youngest open the oldest hills
> Through the door of the birds, where the breeze breaks.
> There fire shall fly from the raven boy,
> And the silver eyes that see the wind,
> And the Light shall have the harp of gold.
>
> 'By the pleasant lake the Sleepers lie,
> On Cadfan's Way where the kestrels call;
> Though grim from the Grey King shadows fall,
> Yet singing the golden harp shall guide
> To break their sleep and bid them ride.'

He reached out and rubbed Cafall's ears. 'The silver eyes,' he said. There was a silence, with only the distant skylark still trilling faintly in the air. Bran had listened without moving, his pale face intent. At length he said, 'Who is Merriman?'

'The old man you met, of course. If you mean, what is he, that's harder. Merriman is my master. He is the first of the Old Ones, and the strongest, and the wisest ... He will have no part in this quest now, I think. Not in the seeking. There are too many things for all of us to do, in too many places.'

'Cadfan's Way, it said in the verse. I remember he told me one other thing, he said Cafall would get you on to the Way, so that the two things together, the place and Cafall himself, would be important – then he said, *and also the Way for later*. Later – so not yet, I suppose.' Bran sighed. 'What does it all mean?' For all his strangeness, it was the plaintive question of a very normal boy.

'I was thinking,' Will said, 'that the day of the dead might be All Hallows' Eve. Don't you think? Hallowe'en, when people used to believe all the ghosts walked.'

'I know some who still believe they do,' Bran said. 'Things like that last a long time, up here. There is one old lady I know puts out food for the spirits, at Hallowe'en. She says they eat it too, though if you ask me it is more likely the cats, she has four of them ... Hallowe'en will be this next Saturday, you know.'

'Yes,' Will said. 'I do know. Very close.'

'Some people say that if you go and sit in the church porch till midnight on

Hallowe'en, you hear a voice calling out the names of everyone who will die in the next year,' Bran grinned. 'I have never tried it.'

But Will was not smiling as he listened. He said thoughtfully, 'You just said, *in the next year*. And the verse says, "On the day of the dead *when the year too dies*." But that doesn't make sense. Hallowe'en isn't the end of the year.'

'Maybe once upon a time it used to be,' Bran said. 'The end and the beginning both, once, instead of December. In Welsh, Hallowe'en is called *Calan Gaeaf*, and that means the first day of winter. Pretty warm for winter, of course. Mind you, nobody is going to get me to spend the night in St Cadfan's churchyard, however warm.'

'I was there this morning, at St Cadfan's,' Will said. 'That was what put the name back into my head, somehow, to come and look for the Way. But now I have the verse, I must begin at the beginning.'

'The hardest part,' Bran said. He tugged off his school tie, rolled it up and stuffed it into his trouser pocket. 'It says, *the youngest must open the oldest hills, through the door of the birds*. Right? And you are the youngest of the Old Ones, and these are the oldest hills in Britain for sure, these and the Scottish hills. But the door of the birds, that's hard ... The birds have their holes and nests everywhere, the mountains are full of birds. Crows, kestrels, ravens, buzzards, plovers, wrens, wheatears, pipits, curlews – lovely it is, listening to the curlews down on the marshes in spring. And look, there is a peregrine.' He pointed upwards, to a dark speck in the clear blue sky drifting lazily round in a great sweeping curve, far above their heads.

'How can you tell?'

'A kestrel would be smaller, so would a merlin. It isn't a crow. It could be a buzzard. But I think it's a peregrine – you get to know them, they are so scarce now that you look more carefully ... and I have a reason of my own too, because peregrines like to bother ravens, and as you pointed out, I am the raven boy.'

Will studied him: the eyes were hidden again behind the sunglasses, and the pale face, almost as pale as the hair, was expressionless. It must always be difficult to read this boy Bran; to know properly what he was thinking or feeling. Yet here he was, part of the pattern: found by Merriman, Will's master, and now by Will – and described in a prophetic verse that had been made more than a thousand years ago ...

He said, experimentally, 'Bran.'

'What?'

'Nothing. I was just practising. It's a funny name, I never heard it before.'

'The only way it is funny is in that English voice of yours. It is not bran like a breakfast cereal, it is longer-sounding, *braaan, braaan*.'

'*Braaaaaaan*,' said Will.

'Better.' He squinted at Will over the top of the sunglasses. 'Is that a map sticking out of your pocket? Let's have it here a minute.'

Will handed it over. Squatting on the hillside, Bran spread it on the rustling bracken. 'Now,' he said. 'Read out the names that I point to.'

Will peered obediently at the moving finger. He saw: Tal y Llyn, Mynydd Ceiswyn, Cemmaes, Llanwrin, Machynlleth, Afon Dyfi, Llangelynin. He read aloud, laboriously, 'Tallylin, Minid Seeswin, Semeyes, Lan-rin Machine-leth, Affron Diffy, Lang-elly-nin.'

Bran moaned softly. 'I was afraid of that.'

'Well,' said Will defensively, 'that's exactly what they look like. Oh, wait a minute, I remember Uncle David said you pronounce *f* like *v*. So that makes this one "Avon Divvy." '

'Duvvy,' said Bran. 'Written in English, Dovey. The Afon Dyfi is the River Dovey, and that place over there is called Aberdyfi, which means the mouth of the Dovey, Aberdovey. The Welsh *y* is mostly like the English *u* in "run" or "hunt." '

'Mostly?' said Will suspiciously.

'Well, sometimes it isn't. But you'd better stick to that for now. Look here –' He fumbled inside his leather satchel and brought out a school notebook and pencil. He wrote: Mynydd Ceiswyn. 'Now that,' he said, 'is pronounced *Munuth Kice-ooin. Kice* like *rice*. Go on, say it.'

Will said it, peering incredulously at the spelling.

'Three things there,' said Bran, writing. He appeared to be enjoying himself. 'Double *d* is always a "th" sound, but a soft sound, like in "leather", not in "smith." Then, *c* is always a hard sound in Welsh, like in "cat". So is *g*, as a matter of fact – it's always *g* as in "go", not *g* as in "gentle". And the Welsh *w* is like the *oo* sound in "pool", nearly always. So that's why Mynydd Ceiswyn is pronounced Munuth Kice-oo-in.'

Will said, 'But it ought to be *un* at the end, not *in*, because you said the Welsh *y* was like *u* in "run". '

Bran chuckled. 'There's a memory. Sorry. That's one of the times when it isn't. You'll just have to get used to them if you're going to say the places right. After all you can't complain about us not being consistent, not when your old English is full of things like dough and through and thorough.'

Will took the pencil and copied from the map 'Cemmaes' and 'Llangelynin.' 'All right then,' he said. 'If the *c* is hard, then it must be *Kem-eyes.*'

'Very good,' Bran said. 'But a hard *s*, not soft. Said fast it comes out *Kemmess*. Like chemist, without the *t*.'

Will sighed, looking hard at his next sample, 'Hard *g*, and the *y* sound. So it's
. . . *Lan-gel-un-in.*'

'You're getting there,' Bran said. 'All you have to learn now is the one sound
most Englishmen can never manage. Open your mouth a little way and put
the tip of your tongue against the back of your front teeth. As if you're just
about to say *lan.*'

Will gave him a doubtful look, but did what he was told. Then he twitched
his lips upwards, and made a face like a rabbit.

'Stop it,' said Bran, spluttering. 'Get educated, man. Now while your tongue
is there, blow round the sides of it. Both sides at once.'

Will blew.

'That's right. Now, say the word *lan* but give a bit of a blow before you bring
it out. Like this: *llan, llan.*'

'Llan, llan,' said Will, feeling like a steam engine, and stopped in
astonishment. 'Hey, that sounds Welsh!'

'Pretty good,' said Bran critically. 'You'll have to practise. Actually when a
Welshman says it, his tongue isn't like that and the whole sound comes out
from the sides of his mouth, but that's no good for a *Sais*. You'll do all right.
And if you get fed up with trying, you can take the other English way out and
say *ll* like *thl.*'

'Enough,' said Will. 'Enough.'

'Just try one more,' Bran said. 'You wouldn't believe the way some people say
this one. Well, yes you would, because you did too.' He wrote: Machynlleth.

Will groaned, and took a deep breath. 'Well – there's the *y* – and the *ll* –'

'And the *ch* is sort of breathy, the way the Scots say *loch*. At the back of your
throat, like.'

'Why do you people make everything so complicated? Mach . . . un . . .
lleth.'

'Machynlleth.'

'Machynlleth.'

'Not bad at all.'

'But mine doesn't really sound like yours. Yours sounds wetter. Like
German. *Achtung! Achtung!*' Will yelled suddenly at the top of his voice, and
Cafall jumped up and barked, tail waving.

'Do you speak German?'

'Good Lord, no! I heard that in some old film. *Achtung!* Machynlleth!'

'*Machynlleth,*' said Bran.

'You see, yours does sound wetter. Sploshier. I expect all Welsh babies
dribble a lot.'

'Get out of here,' said Bran, and grabbed at him as Will dodged away. They ran down the mountain, laughing, in a wild zigzag, with Cafall bounding joyously alongside.

But halfway, Will stumbled and slowed down; without warning, he felt giddy, his legs weak and unreliable. He staggered to a near-by wall and leaned against it, panting. Bran yelled cheerfully over his shoulder as he ran, satchel flying; then slowed, stopped, looked more carefully and came back.

'Are you all right, then?'

'I think so. Head hurts. It's my stupid legs though, they give out too easily. I suppose I'm still getting better, really – I was ill, for a while –'

'I knew, and I ought to have remembered.' Bran stood fidgeting, cross with himself. 'Your friend Mr Merriman said you'd been even more ill than anyone realized.'

'But he wasn't there,' Will said. 'Well. Not that that means a thing, of course.'

'Sit down,' Bran said. 'Put your head down on your knees.'

'I'm okay. Really. Just have to get my breath back.'

'We're very close to home, or we should be. Just a few hundred yards over that way –' Bran scrambled up on the high dry stone wall to give himself a better view.

But while he stood there, suddenly a great angry yell came from the other side of the wall, and the barking of dogs. Will saw Bran draw himself up tall and straight where he stood on the wall, looking down haughtily. He heaved himself upright to peep over the slate-topped edge, past Bran's feet, and saw a man approaching at a half-run, shouting, and waving one arm angrily; in the other arm he carried what looked like a shotgun. When he came closer, he began calling to Bran in Welsh. Will did not recognize him at first, for he wore no hat, and the tousled head of raw red hair was unfamiliar. Then he saw that it was Caradog Prichard.

When the farmer paused for breath, Bran said clearly, pointedly using English, 'My dog does not chase sheep, Mr Prichard. And anyway he is not on your land, he is over this side of the wall.'

'I tell you that he is a rogue dog, and he has been worrying my sheep!' Prichard said furiously; his English was sibilant, heavily accented, thickened by rage. 'Him and that damn black hound of John Rowlands. I will shoot them both if I catch them at it, you be sure I will. And you and your little English friend there had better keep off my land too, if you know what's good for you.' The small eyes in his flushed, pudgy face glared maliciously at Will.

Will said nothing. Bran did not move; he stood there looking down at the angry farmer. He said softly, 'Bad luck you would have, if you shot Cafall, Caradog Prichard.' He ran one hand through his white hair, pushing it back, in a gesture that seemed to Will oddly affected. 'You want to look more closely at those sheep,' Bran said, 'before you go blaming dogs for what is foxes' work.'

'Foxes!' said Prichard contemptuously. 'I know a fox's killing when I see it, and I know a rogue dog too. Keep away from my land, both of you.' But he was not meeting Bran's eye now, nor looking at Will; he swung round without another word and strode off across the pasture, with his dogs trotting at his heels.

Bran climbed down from the wall.

'Bah!' he said. 'Worrying sheep! Cafall is a match for any working dog in this valley; he would never in the world go wild after any sheep, let alone on Caradog Prichard's land.' He looked at the vanishing Prichard, and then at Will, and smiled. It was a strange sly smile; Will was not sure that he liked it.

'You will find out,' Bran said, 'that people like him are a bit afraid of me, deep down. It is because I am albino, you see. The white hair, and funny eyes, and not much pigment in the skin – a bit of a freak, you might say.'

'I shouldn't,' Will said mildly.

'Maybe not,' Bran said without much belief, acid in his tongue. 'But it is said often enough at school . . . and outside too, by nice men like Mr Prichard. You see, all good Welshmen are dark, dark of hair and dark of eyes, and the only fair-skinned creatures in Wales, in the old days, were the *Tylwyth Teg*. The old spirits, the little people. Anyone as fair as me must have something to do with the *Tylwyth Teg* . . . Nobody believes in such things any more, oh no, of course not, but in the middle of the winter night when the wind is blowing dark and the old television is not on, I bet you half the people in this valley would not like to swear that I could not bring the Evil Eye on them.'

Will scratched his head. 'There was certainly something . . . fidgety . . . in the way that man looked at you, when you said –' He shook his shoulders, like a dog coming out of water. He did not look at Bran; he disliked the shadows of crafty arrogance that this talking had put over the other boy's face. It was a pity, it shouldn't be necessary; one day he would take it away . . . He said, 'Caradog Prichard isn't dark. He has red hair. Like carrots.'

'His family is from Dinas Mawddwy way,' Bran said. 'His mother, anyway. There was supposed to be a whole tribe of villains up there once, all red-haired, real terrors. Anyway there are still redheads come from Dinas today.'

'Would he really shoot Cafall?'

'Yes,' Bran said shortly. 'Caradog Prichard is very strange. There is a saying that anyone who spends the night alone up on Cader will come down next morning either a poet, or mad. And my father says that once when he was young, Caradog Prichard did spend the night alone up on Cader, because he wanted to be a great bard.'

'It can't have worked.'

'Well. Perhaps it worked in one way. He is not much of a poet, but he often acts as if he were more than a little bit mad.'

'What is Cader?'

Bran stared at him. 'Don't know much about Wales, do you? Cader Idris, over there.' He pointed to the line of blue grey peaks across the valley. 'One of the highest mountains in Wales. You should know about Cader. After all it comes in your verse.'

Will frowned. 'No, it doesn't.'

'Oh, yes. Not by name, no – but it's important in that second part. That's where he lives you see, up on Cader. The Brenin Llwyd. The Grey King.'

Grey Fox

Nobody else could feel it, Will knew. As far as outward appearances went, there was no reason why anybody should feel the least unease. The skies were a gentle light blue; the sun shone with unseasonable warmth, so that Rhys sat up on the tractor bare-backed as he ploughed the last stubbly fields, singing a clear tenor over the roar of the machine. The earth smelled clean. Yarrow and ragwort starred the hedgerows white and yellow, with the red berries of the hawthorn thick above them; the sweeping slopes where the valley began to rise were golden-brown with bracken, dry as tinder in this strange Indian-summer sun. Hazy on the horizon all around, the mountains lay like sleeping animals, their muted colours changing with every hour of the day from brown to green to purple and softly back again.

Yet behind all this autumnal gentleness, as he roamed the fields and the gorse-starred mountain, Will could feel tension mounting everywhere, advancing like a slow relentless flood from the high peaks brooding over the end of the valley. Enmity was beginning to push at him. Slowly but irresistibly, the pressure of malevolence was building up to the point where it could break and overwhelm him. And nobody else knew. Only the hidden senses of an Old One could feel the working of the Dark.

Aunt Jen was delighted with the change in Will's appearance. 'Look at you –

only a few days, but you have colour in your cheeks now, and if this sun goes on you will be getting brown. I was writing to Alice last night. I said, you wouldn't know him, he looks like a different boy –'

'Very nice sun, indeed,' Will's Uncle David said. 'But a little too much, for this time of year, thank you. The pastures are getting dry, and the bracken on the mountain – we could do with a bit of rain, now.'

'Hark at you,' Aunt Jen said, laughing. 'Rain is one thing we are never short of here.'

But still the sunny skies smiled, and Will went off with John Rowlands and his dogs to fetch a flock of yearling sheep that was to be wintered at Clwyd Farm. The hill farmer who owned them had already driven them down halfway to another farm at the head of the valley. As he looked at the milling off-white chaos of woolly backs, bobbing and shoving, eighty or so lusty young ewes bleating and baahing in ear-splitting chorus, Will could not imagine how they could possibly be brought intact to Clwyd. When just one sheep broke away from the rest and pranced sideways towards him, where he stood in the field, he could not persuade it back to its fellows even by yelling and pushing and whacking its broad woolly sides. 'Baaaa,' said the sheep, in a deep stupid baritone, as if he had not been there, and it wandered off and began chewing at the hedge. Yet the instant that Tip, John Rowlands's sheepdog, trotted purposefully in its direction, the sheep turned dutifully round and bobbed back to the rest.

Will could not see how John Rowlands communicated with his dogs. There were two: the dappled Tip, named for the splashes of white on his muzzle and the very end of his waving tail, and a bigger, more formidable-looking dog called Pen, with a black, long-haired coat and a crooked ear, torn in some fight long ago. Rowlands needed to do no more than look at them, a smile creasing his lean brown face, with a soft word in Welsh, or a quick whistle, and they would be off on some complicated manoeuvre that the average man could have understood only after ten minutes of detailed explanation.

'Walk at the front,' he called to Will through the deep, unnerving chorus of baaas, as he opened the gate and the sheep poured through into the road like milk. 'Well forward, to wave at any cars coming and stop them at the side.'

Will blinked in alarm. 'But how do I keep the sheep back? They'll all run past me!'

John Rowlands's grin flashed white in the dark Welsh face. 'Don't worry. Pen will see to them.'

And so Pen did; it was as if he had a rope tied round the front of the herd of sheep to keep it in a neat tight curve. Trotting, darting, slinking on his belly, moving always forward, sometimes persuading an errant sheep in the right direction with a curt single bark, he kept them all moving obediently along the road. And Will, clutching the stick John Rowlands had given him, strode ahead bursting with confident pride, feeling as if he had been a real shepherd since time began.

They met only two cars, in fact, all the way down the valley road, but directing even those two to pull in beside the hedge was enough pleasure, with the sheep crowding by in a rippling grey flood. Will was enjoying his job so much that perhaps, he thought afterwards, he let his deeper watchfulness falter. For when the attack came, he had no sense of warning at all.

They were on a lonely part of the road, with barren moorland on one side of the road and dark tree-clad mountainside rising at the other. No fields were cultivated here. Bracken and rocks fringed the roadside as if it were a track over the open mountain. Suddenly Will became aware of a change in the sound of the sheep behind him: a higher note of alarm in their bleating, a flurry of scuffling hooves. He thought at first that it must be John Rowlands and Tip, heading off a runaway; but then he heard a sharp, piercing whistle that in a moment had Pen swinging round at the sheep, growling, barking, threatening them to a standstill. And he heard John Rowlands calling: 'Will! Quick! Will!'

He ran back, skirting the frightened bleating sheep; then jerked to a halt. Halfway past the flock, at the edge of the road, there was a great splash of red at the throat of a single tottering animal, smaller than the rest. Will saw a flicker of movement in the bracken as some unseen creature fled. Away it went towards the mountain, and the fronds waved and then were still. Will watched horrified as the wounded sheep staggered sideways and fell. Its fellows pushed away from it, terrified; the dogs growled and threatened, frantically containing the herd, and Will heard John Rowlands yelling, and the thwacking of his stick against the hard road. He too yelled and waved his arms at the heaving flock of sheep, keeping them together as they tried in panic to break away over the moor, and gradually the nervous animals calmed and were still.

John Rowlands was bending over the injured ewe.

Will shouted, across the heaving backs, 'Is it all right?'

'Not much hurt. Missed the vein. We're lucky.' Rowlands bent down, heaved the inert sheep over his shoulders and grasped its fore and hind feet separately, so that it hung across the back of his neck like a huge muffler. Grunting with effort, he slowly stood up; his neck and cheek were smeared red by the sheep's blood-stained fleece.

Will came towards him. 'Was it a dog?'

Rowlands could not move his head, because of the sheep, but his bright eyes swivelled quickly round. 'Did you see a dog?'

'No.'

'Are you sure?'

'I saw something running away through the bracken, but I couldn't tell what it was. I just thought it must be a dog – I mean, what else could it have been?'

Rowlands did not answer, but waved him ahead and whistled to the dogs. The flock began pouring on down the road. He walked at the side of it now, leaving the rear entirely to Tip; neatly and efficiently the dog kept the sheep moving along.

Soon they came to a deserted cottage set back from the road: stone-walled, slate-roofed, sturdy-looking, but with the glass broken in its two small windows. John Rowlands kicked open the heavy wooden door, staggered inside, and came out without the sheep, breathing heavily and wiping his face on his sleeve. He closed the door. 'Be safe there until we can get back to her,' he called to Will. 'Not far now.'

Before long they were at Clwyd. Will opened the gate of the broad pasture where he knew the sheep were to be kept, and the dogs nudged and nagged them inside. For a few moments the sheep eddied about, bleating and muttering; then they settled down to a greedy rasping nibble of the lush grass.

John Rowlands fetched the Land-Rover and took Will with him to collect the injured sheep; at the last moment the black dog Pen leaped up into the car and settled down between Will's feet. Will rubbed his silky ears.

'It must have been a dog attacked that sheep, surely?' he said as they drove.

Rowlands sighed. 'I hope not. But indeed, I cannot think of any wild creature that would attack a flock, with men and dogs alongside. Nothing but a wolf would do that, and there have been no wolves in Wales for two hundred years or more.'

They drew up outside the cottage. Rowlands turned the car so that its back door would be in easy reach, and went into the little stone building.

He was out again almost at once, empty-handed, looking uneasily about him. 'She's gone!'

'Gone!'

'There must be some sign – Pen! *Tyrd yma!*' John Rowlands went casting around outside the cottage, peering intently at grass and bracken and gorse, and the black dog wove its way round and about him, nose down. Will too peered hopefully, looking for flattened plants or signs of wool, or blood. He saw nothing. A jagged rock of white quartz glittered before them in the sunshine. A woodlark sang. Then all at once, Pen gave one short sharp bark and was off on a scent, trotting confidently, head down, through the grass.

They followed. But Will was puzzled, and he could see the same bafflement on John Rowlands's seamed face – for the dog was tracking through untouched grass, not a stem bent by the passing even of a small creature, let alone a sheep.

There was the sound of water running somewhere ahead of them, and soon they came to a small stream flowing down towards the river, the jutting rocks in its course showing how much lower than usual it was running in the dry spell.

Pen paused, cast up and down the stream unsuccessfully, and came to John Rowlands whining.

'He's lost it,' the shepherd said. 'Whatever it was. Could have been no more than a rabbit, of course – though not too many rabbits I have ever heard tell of would have the sense to hide their trail in running water.'

Will said: 'But what happened to the sheep? It was hurt, it couldn't have walked away.'

'Particularly through a closed door,' Rowlands said drily.

'That's right, of course! D'you think whatever animal attacked it would have been clever enough to come back and drag it away?'

'Clever enough, perhaps,' Rowlands said, staring back at the cottage. 'But not strong enough. A yearling will weigh about a hundred pounds, I near broke my back carrying her a little way. You'd need a mighty big dog to drag that weight.'

Will heard himself say, 'Two dogs?'

John Rowlands looked at him with narrowed eyes. 'You have some unexpected ideas, Will, for one not brought up on a farm . . . yes, two dogs together could drag a sheep. But how would they do it without leaving a great flat trail? And anyway, how could two or twenty dogs open that door?'

'Goodness knows,' Will said. 'Well – perhaps it wasn't any animal. Perhaps somebody drove by and heard the sheep bleating and got it out of the cottage and took it away. I mean they couldn't know we were coming back.'

'Aye,' John Rowlands said. He did not sound convinced. 'Well, if any did that, we shall find the sheep at home when we get there, for it has the Pentref mark on its ear and any local man would know that we winter William Pentref's ewes. Come on, now.' He whistled to Pen.

They were silent on the drive home, each lost deep in concern and baffled conjecture. John Rowlands, Will knew, was worrying over the need to find the sheep quickly, to doctor its wounds. He, Will, had his own worries. Although he had not mentioned it to Rowlands, and hardly dared even to think what it might mean, he knew that in the moment when the wounded sheep had staggered and fallen beside the flock, he had seen something more than that formless twitch of motion in the bracken where the attacker fled. He had seen the flash of a silvery body, and the muzzle of what had looked very much like a white dog.

*

Music was flowing out of the farmhouse in a golden stream, as if the sun were inside the window, shining out. Will paused, astonished, and stood listening. Somebody was playing a harp, long rippling arpeggios soaring out like birdsong; then without a break the music changed to something like a Bach sonata, notes and patterns as precise as snowflakes. John Rowlands looked down at him with a smile for a moment, then pushed open the door and went in. A side door was open into a little parlour that Will had never noticed before; it looked like a creaky-neat Best Room, tucked away from the big kitchen-living room where all the real life of the house went on. The music was coming from this parlour; Rowlands stuck his head round the door, and so did Will. Sitting there, running his hands over the strings of a harp twice his own height, was Bran.

He stopped, stilling the strings with his palms. 'Hullo, then.'

'Much better,' said John Rowlands. 'Very much better, that, today.'

'Good,' Bran said.

Will said, 'I didn't know you could play the harp.'

'Ah,' Bran said solemnly. 'Lot of things the English don't know. Mr Rowlands teaches me. He taught your auntie too, this is hers I'm at.' He ran one finger across the lilting strings. 'Freezing in the winter in this room, always, but it keeps better in tune than in the warm . . . Ah, Will Stanton, you don't know what a distinguished place you are in. This is the only farm in Wales where there are two harps. Mr Rowlands has one in his house too, you see.' He nodded through the window, at the trio of farm cottages across the yard. 'I practise there mostly. But Mrs Rowlands is busy cleaning today.'

'Where is David Evans?' asked John Rowlands.

'In the yard with Rhys. Cowshed, I think.'

'*Diolch.*' He went out, preoccupied.

'I thought you'd be at school,' Will said.

'Half-holiday. I forget why.' Bran wore the protective smoky glasses even indoors; they made him look eccentric and unreal, the inscrutable dark circles taking all expression out of his pale face. He was wearing dark trousers too, and a dark sweater, making his white hair still more striking and unnatural. Will thought suddenly: *he must do it on purpose, he likes being different.*

'An awful thing happened,' he said, and told Bran about the sheep. But again he left out the quick glimpse of the attacker that had made him think it was a white dog.

'Are you sure the sheep was alive when John left it?' Bran said.

'Oh, yes, I think so. There's always the chance someone just stopped and took it away. I expect John's checking.'

'What a weird business,' Bran said. He stood up, stretching. 'I've had enough practising. Want to come out?'

'I'll go and tell Aunt Jen.'

On the way out, Bran picked up his flat leather schoolbag from a chair beside the door. 'I must drop this off at home. And put the kettle on for Da. He comes in for a cuppa, round about now, if he's working near by.'

Will said curiously, 'Does your mother work too?'

'Oh, she's dead. Died when I was a baby, I don't remember her at all.' Bran gave him a strange sideways look. 'Nobody told you about me, then? My dad and I, we're a bachelor household. Mrs Evans is very nice, always. We eat supper at the farm, weekends. Of course, you haven't been here at a weekend yet.'

'I feel as if I'd been here for weeks,' Will said, putting his face up to the sun. Something in the way Bran spoke was making him oddly uneasy, and he did not want to think about it too closely. He pushed it to the back of his mind, to join that image of the flicker of a white muzzle through the bracken.

'Where's Cafall?' he said.

'Oh, he will be out with Da. Thinking I am still at school.' Bran laughed. 'The time we had when Cafall was young, trying to persuade him that school is for boys but not puppies. When I went to primary school in the village, he used to sit at the gate all day, just waiting.'

'Where do you go now?'

'Tywyn Grammar. In a bus.'

They scuffed their feet through the dust of the path down to the cottages, a path made by wheels, two ruts with hummocky grass growing between. There were three cottages but only two were occupied; now that he was closer, Will could see that the third had been converted into a garage. He looked beyond, up the valley, where the mountains rose blue-hazed and beautiful into the clear sky, and he shivered. Though the mystery of the wounded sheep had taken up the front of his mind for a while, the deeper uneasiness was swelling back again now. All around, throughout the countryside, he could feel the malevolence of the Dark growing, pushing at him. It could not focus upon him, follow him like the gaze of a great fierce eye; an Old One had the power to conceal himself so that his presence could not at once be sensed so precisely. But clearly the Grey King knew that he was bound to come, soon, from somewhere. They had their prophecies, as did the Light. The barriers had gone up, and were growing stronger every day. Will felt suddenly how strange it was for him to be the invader; for the Light to be advancing against the Dark. Always before, through all the centuries, it had been the other way round, with the powers of the Dark sweeping in fearsome recurrent attack over the land of men protected in gentleness by the Light. Always the Light had been the defenders of men, champions of all that the Dark came to overturn. Now, an Old One must deliberately reverse the long habit of mind; now he must find the thrust of attack, instead of the resolute sturdy defence which for so long had kept the Dark at bay.

But of course, he thought, this attack itself is a small part of a defence, to build resistance for that other last and most dreadful time when the Dark will come rising again. It is a quest, to awaken the last allies of the Light. And there is very little time.

Bran said suddenly, uncannily echoing the last thread of his thought, 'Hallowe'en, tonight.'

'Yes,' Will said.

Before he could say more, they were at the door of the cottage; it was half-open, a low heavy door set in the stone wall. At Bran's footsteps the dog Cafall came bounding out, a small white whirlwind, leaping and whining with pleasure, licking his hand. It was noticeable that he did not bark. From inside, a man's voice called, 'Bran?' and began speaking in Welsh. Then as Will followed Bran through the door, the man speaking, standing shirt-sleeved at a table, turned in mid-sentence and caught sight of him. He broke off at once and said formally, 'I beg your pardon.'

'This is Will,' Bran said, tossing his bag of books on the table. 'Mr Evans's nephew.'

'Yes. I thought perhaps it was. How do you do, young man?' Bran's father came forward, holding out his hand; his gaze was direct and his handshake firm, though Will had an immediate curious feeling that the real man was not there behind the eyes. 'I am Owen Davies. I have been hearing about you.'

'How d'you do, Mr Davies,' said Will. He was trying not to look surprised. Whatever he had expected in Bran's father, it was not this man: a man so completely ordinary and unremarkable, whom you could pass in the street without noticing he had been there. Someone as odd as Bran should have had an odd father. But Owen Davies was all medium and average: average height, medium-brown hair in a medium quantity; a pleasant, ordinary face, with a slightly pointed nose and thin lips; an average voice, neither deep nor high, with the same precise enunciation that Will was beginning to learn belonged to all North Welshmen. His clothes were ordinary, the same shirt and trousers and boots that would be worn by anyone else on a farm. Even the dog that stood at his side, quietly watching them all, was a standard Welsh sheepdog, black-backed, white-chested, black-tailed, unremarkable. Not like Cafall: just as Bran's father was not at all like Bran.

'There is tea in the pot, Bran, if you would both like a cup,' Mr Davies said. 'I have had mine, I am off over to the big pasture. And I shall be going out tonight, there is a chapel meeting. Mrs Evans will give you your supper.'

'That's good,' Will said cheerfully. 'He can help me with my homework.'

'Homework?' said Bran.

'Oh, yes. This isn't just a holiday for me, you know. They gave me all kinds of work from school, so I shouldn't get behind. Algebra, today. And history.'

'That will be very good,' Mr Davies said earnestly, pulling on his waistcoat, 'so long as Bran takes care to do his own work as well. Of course, I know he will do that. Well, it is nice to meet you, Will. See you later, Bran. Cafall can stay.'

And he went out, nodding to them amiably but with complete seriousness, leaving Will to reflect that after all there was one thing about Owen Davies that was not altogether common; he had not a glimmer of laughter in him.

There was no expression in Bran's face. He said flatly, 'My father is a big one for chapel. He is a deacon, and there are two or three meetings for him in the week. And we go twice on Sundays.'

'Oh,' Will said.

'Yes. Oh is right. Want a cup of tea?'

'Not really, thank you.'

'Let's go out, then.' With absentminded conscientiousness Bran rinsed out the teapot and left it neatly inverted on the draining-board. '*Tyrd yma*, Cafall.'

The white dog bounded happily beside them as they crossed the fields, away from cottage and farm, up the valley towards the mountains and the lone near peak. It stood at a right angle to the mountain behind it, jutting into the flat valley floor.

'Funny how that rock sticks out like that,' Will said.

'Craig yr Aderyn? That's special, it's the only place in Britain where cormorants nest inland. Not very far inland, of course. Four miles from the sea, we are here. Haven't you been over there? Come on, we've got time.' Bran changed direction slightly. 'You can see the birds fine from the road.'

'I thought the road was that way,' Will said, pointing.

'It is. We can cut across to it this way.' Bran opened a gate on to a footpath, crossed the path and scrambled over the wall on the other side. 'The only thing is, you must go quietly,' he said with a grin. 'This is Caradog Prichard's land.'

'Hush, Cafall,' Will said in a heavy stage-whisper, turning his head. But the dog was not there. Will paused, puzzled. 'Bran? Where's Cafall?'

Bran whistled. They both stood waiting, looking back at the long sweep of the slate-edged stone wall along the stubbled field. Nothing moved. The sun shone. Far away, sheep called. Bran whistled again, with no result. Then he went back, with Will close behind, and they climbed over the wall again and went down to the footpath they had crossed.

Bran whistled a third time, and called in Welsh. There was concern in his voice.

Will said, 'Wherever could he have gone? He was right behind me when I came over the wall.'

'He never does this. Never. He will never go from me without permission, or not come when he is called.' Bran gazed anxiously up and down the footpath. 'I don't like it. I shouldn't have let him come so near Mr Prichard's land. You and me is one thing, but Cafall –' He whistled again, loud and desperate.

'You don't suppose –' Will said. He stopped.

'That Prichard would shoot him, the way he said?'

'No, I was going to say, you don't suppose Cafall wouldn't come because he knew he shouldn't go on Mr Prichard's land. But that's silly, no dog could work out something like that.'

'Oh,' Bran said unhappily, 'dogs can work out things a lot more complicated than that. I don't know. Let's try this way. It leads to the river.'

They set off along the path, away from the looming mass of the rock Craig yr Aderyn. Somewhere ahead of them, a long way off, a dog barked.

'Is that him?' Will said hopefully.

Bran's white head was cocked on one side. The dog barked again, closer. 'No. That's John Rowlands's big dog, Pen. But Cafall might have gone that way when he heard him –'

They both broke into a run, along the stony, grass-patched path. Will very soon lost his breath and dropped behind. Bran disappeared round a bend in the path ahead of him. When Will turned the corner himself, two things slammed simultaneously into his consciousness: the sight of Bran – without Cafall – talking to his father and John Rowlands, and the sick certainty that something evil had taken control of everything that was happening now on Clwyd Farm. It was a recognition, like the sudden sensing of an overwhelming sound or smell.

He came panting up to them, as Bran said: '. . . heard Pen bark, and thought he might have come this way, so we came running.'

'And you saw nothing at all?' Owen Davies said. His face was tight with some deep concern. Looking at it, Will felt foreboding clutch at the pit of his stomach.

John Rowlands said, his deep voice strained, 'And you, Will? Did you see anyone, anything, on the path just now?'

Will stared. 'No. Only Cafall, before, and now we've lost him.'

'No creature came past you?'

'Nothing at all. Why? What's wrong?'

Owen Davies said, bleakly, 'In the big pasture up the way, there are four dead sheep with their throats torn out, and there is no gate open or any sign of what can have attacked them.'

Will looked in horror at John Rowlands. 'Is it the same –'

'Who can tell?' said the shepherd bitterly. Like Davies, he seemed caught between distress and rage. 'But it is not dogs, I do not see how it could be dogs. It looks more like the work of foxes, though how that can be, I do not know.'

'The *milgwn*, from the hills,' said Bran.

'Nonsense,' his father said.

'The what?' said Will.

'The *milgwn*,' Bran said. His eyes were still darting round in search of Cafall, and he spoke automatically. 'Grey foxes. Some of the farmers say there are big grey foxes that live up in the mountains, bigger and faster than our red foxes down here.'

Owen Davies said, 'That is nonsense. There are no such things. I have told you before, I will not have you listening to those rubbishy old tales.'

His tone was sharp. Bran shrugged.

But across the front of Will's mind there came suddenly a brilliant image, clear as a film thrown on a screen: he saw three great foxes trotting in line, enormous grey-white animals with thick coats growing to the broadness of a ruff round their necks, and full brush-like tails. They moved across a hillside, among rocks, and for an instant one of them turned its head and looked full at him, with bright unwinking eyes. For that instant he could see them as clearly as he could see Bran. Then the image was gone, they were vanished, and he was standing again in the sunshine, mute, dazed, knowing that in one of the brief communications that can come – very rarely, only very rarely – unguarded from one Old One to another, his masters had sent him a warning picture of the creatures of the Grey King, agents of the Dark.

He said abruptly, 'They aren't tales. Bran is right.'

Bran stared at him, shaken by the crisp certainty in his voice. But Owen Davies looked across in chilly reproof, the corners of his thin mouth turned down. 'Don't be foolish, boy,' he said coldly. 'What can you know of our foxes?'

Will never knew what he could have said in answer, for breaking into the tense stillness of the sunlit afternoon came a shout from John Rowlands, urgent, loud.

'*Tân!* Look over there! There is fire on the mountain! Fire!'

Fire on the Mountain

There was not much smoke, for so much fire. In a line along the lower slope of the mountain, which they could only just see above the hedge from where they stood, flames were blazing in the bracken. It was like a long wound, a gash in the peaceful brown slope, quivering with deadly, ominous life. Yet there was little colour in it, and they were too far away to hear any sound. For a moment Will was conscious only of wonder that John Rowlands should have caught sight of it at all.

Then they were deep in instructions, and the urgency of Rowlands's soft voice. 'Off to the farm, both of you, quick. Call the fire from Tywyn and the police, and then come back with anyone who is there. All the hands you can get. And bring more fire brooms, Bran, you know where they are. Come on, Owen.'

Both men ran up the path across the valley, and the boys dived for the gate that led over the fields to Clwyd Farm. Bran swung his head round in a whirl of white hair: 'Take it *gently*, now,' he said earnestly, 'or you'll be worse ill –' and he was off like a sprinter, leaving Will to close the gate and trot resignedly in his wake.

The telephoning was done by the time he caught Bran up at the farm. David Evans took them with him in the Land-Rover, with Rhys and a tall thin farmer called Tom Ellis who had been there when they arrived. The back of the little car had been hastily filled with fire brooms and sacking, and several buckets that Will's uncle seemed to have small hope of using. The dogs, for once, were left behind.

'They will be no good with fire,' Rhys said, seeing Will cock his head to the plaintive barking. 'And the sheep can get out of the way on their own – indeed they will all be well away, by now.'

'I wonder where Cafall is,' Will said, and then caught sight of Bran's face and wished he had not.

Close to, the fire on the mountain was very much more alarming than it had seemed from a distance. They could smell it now, and hear it; smell the smoke more bitter than a farm bonfire; hear the soft, dreadful sound of flames consuming the bracken, like paper crumpled in the hand, and the sudden crackling roar as a bush or a patch of gorse went up. And they could see the flames, leaping high, bright red and yellow at the edges of the fire but ferocious and near-invisible at its heart.

As they tumbled out of the car David Evans was yelling for the fire brooms. Will and Bran pulled them out: besoms made like those for old-fashioned sweeping, but with the twigs longer and wider-spread. John Rowlands and Bran's father, already equipped, were thrashing at the leading edge of the fire, trying to contain it; but the wind was gusting higher, and the flames, now leaping, now creeping, were soon past them and travelling along the lower edge of the mountain. As they swept upwards, roaring up the hillside through the tinder-dry bracken, Owen Davies jumped out of the way only just in time.

The crackling rose; the air was full of fumes and smoke and whirling black specks of charcoal and ash. Great heat shone out at them. They were all in a line beating at the flames, flailing away with all their might, yet only occasionally extinguishing a spark. John Rowlands shouted something desperately in Welsh; then seeing Will's uncomprehending face near him, gasped out: 'We must drive it higher, before it can reach Prichard's! Keep it from the rock!'

Peering ahead at the great outsweeping rocky slope of Craig yr Aderyn, Will glimpsed for the first time the corner of a grey stone building jutting out beyond its far side. The light glinted on a spray of water flung up beside the house; someone was soaking the land all round it, in an effort to deaden the fire if it should reach that far. But Will, beating hopelessly with his long flat-tipped broom, felt that nothing could halt or check the inferno before them, snarling high over their heads now as it reached a tangle of blackberry bushes. It was like a huge beast raging over the mountain, gobbling up everything in its path with irresistible greed. It was so powerful, and they so small, that even the effort to control its path seemed ludicrous. He thought: *It is like the Dark* – and for the first time found himself wondering how the fire could have begun.

Below them, from the road past the foot of the great Craig, came the clanging of a fire engine's bell, and Will glimpsed patches of bright red through the trees, and a hose snaking through the air. Men's voices were calling faintly and there was a sound of engines. But up here on the slope, the fire was gaining a greater hold, as the gusting wind caught it in patches, and gradually they were forced downwards, into the trees edging the road. In triumphant thunder the fire roared after them.

'Down the road!' the thin man Tom Ellis called. 'Those trees will catch in a minute!'

Will panted along at John Rowlands's side. 'What will happen?'

'Burn itself out, eventually.' But the Welshman's creased face was grim.

Bran came trotting up at his other side, his white skin smudged and dirty. 'This wind is the trouble, taking it up the valley – is Prichard's place really in danger, Mr Rowlands?'

John Rowlands checked his stride for a moment, to gaze all round the sky. Clouds were forming in the blue air now, strange ragged dirty-white clouds that seemed to be coming from no one direction. 'I don't know . . . the wind is for a change in the weather, and it is shifting, but hard to tell where . . . we shall have rain sooner or later.'

'Well,' Will said hopefully, 'the rain will put the fire out, won't it?' But as he spoke, he could hear the crackle and roar of the fire like laughter at his back, and he was not surprised when John Rowlands shook his head.

'Only a great deal of rain . . . the ground is so dry, dry as it never is this time of year – nothing but a downpour will have any effect at all.' He looked round again, frowning at the mountains and the sky. 'Something is strange, about this fire and everything . . . something is wrong . . .' He shook his shoulders, giving up the search, and strode on ahead as they rounded a bend and came towards the fire engine and its thunderous thrumming engine.

Will thought: *Ah, John Rowlands, you see more than you think you see, though not quite enough. The Dark Lord has begun his work in these mountains, the Grey King is building up a wall to enclose the golden harp, and the Sleepers who must be wakened, so that I may not come to them and fulfil the quest. For if he can keep them from the reach of the Light, then the Old Ones will not come into their full power, and there will be none to keep the Dark from rising . . .*

He said, without knowing that he spoke aloud: 'But it won't work!'

A voice said softly in his ear, 'What won't work?' Bran's dark smoky spectacles, shrouding the eyes behind, were staring into his face.

Will looked at him and said with sudden naked honesty, 'I don't know what to make of you.'

'I know you don't.' Bran said, a quirk of a smile twitching his strange pale face. 'But you're going to need me all the same.' He spun round, as smoke from the fire up the hillside came billowing down around them. 'Don't worry,' he said, grinning. 'Nobody else has ever known what to make of me either.' And he was off, spinning, running, almost dancing up the road towards the fire engine.

Will ran after him. And then in a moment both of them were brought up short by a sight more astonishing than any yet. Beneath the looming bulk of Craig yr Aderyn the firemen had two hoses playing, drenching both the mountain and the side of the road in an effort to check the fire from leaping over the Craig and down to Prichard's Farm. Others ran here and there with buckets, fire brooms, anything with which stray sparks might be drowned or beaten out before they gained a hold. The road was buzzing with anxious activity. Yet in the midst of it all, standing rigid and oblivious with fury, stood Caradog Prichard, his red hair bristling, blood on his shirt and a shotgun levelled in one hand – and the other hand out rigid, pointing in accusation as he screamed with rage at John Rowlands.

'Bring me the dog! Bring him! I will prove to you that it was him, him and that freakish white hound of the freak boy Davies! I will show you! Six sheep in my field, there are six of them, with their throats ripped out, dammo, their heads half off – all for black joy, and that is what those bloody dogs had of it and that is what I shall shoot them for! Bring me them here! Bring them! And I will prove it to you!'

The boys stood frozen, gazing at him in horror; he was not for that moment a human being, but a frenzied creature possessed by rage, turned into an animal. All that could be seen in him was the urge to hurt, and it was, as it always will be, the most dreadful sight in the world.

Looking at Prichard with the eye of a human and the vision of an Old One, Will was filled with an overpowering compassion: an awareness of what must inevitably overtake Caradog Prichard if he were not checked, now, for always, in this passion before it was too late. Stop, he longed to call to him: stop, before the Grey King sees you and puts out his hand in friendship, and you, unwitting, take it and are destroyed . . .

Before he thought what he was doing he stepped forward, and the movement brought the red-haired man swinging towards him. The finger wheeled viciously round, jabbing at him through the air.

'You there too, *Sais bach*, you are part of it, you and your uncle's farm. They are Clwyd dogs, these murdering brutes, it is on all your heads, and I will have my due from all of you, from all of you –'

Spittle foamed at the corners of his mouth. There was no speaking to him. Will fell back, and with the fury of Prichard's shouting even the firefighters paused in amazement. There was no sound but the thump of the fire engine's pumping and the crackle of the approaching flames, and no movement for an instant anywhere. Then David Evans pushed forward, a small brisk form with a fire broom in his hand and smudges of soot on his face and shirt, and he took Prichard fearlessly by the shoulder and shook him, hard.

'The fire will be on us in minutes, Caradog Prichard – do you want your farm to burn? All of us here working our hands raw to keep the flames from your roof, and your wife inside there doing the same, and you stand here shouting your silly head off and think of nothing but a few dead sheep! A lot more dead sheep you will have, man, and a dead farm too, if you do not pull yourself together now. Now!'

Prichard gazed blankly at him, the small bright eyes squinting suspiciously in the pudgy face, and then he seemed gradually to wake up, and to realize where he was and what was happening. Dazed, he stared at the flames leaping closer beyond the hedge. The pump of the fire engine rose to a higher pitch, as the workers swung their hoses round to meet the advancing fire; sparks flew in all directions as the beaters thwacked frantically at the bracken. Caradog Prichard gave one short squeal of terror, turned, and rushed back towards his farmhouse.

Without a word Will and Bran rejoined the line of beaters, edging diagonally up the hillside in an effort to keep the fire from sweeping over and beyond the Craig. The sky was growing darker as the clouds thickened and the evening drew on, but there was no hint of rain. Again the wind gusted, dropped to nothing, rose in a sudden new gust; there was no telling what it would do next. More and more strongly Will could feel the enmity of the Grey King thrusting at him from the high peaks at the head of the valley; it made a wall as fierce as the wall of flames roaring towards them from the other direction, though the only one who could feel the force of both, the only one caught between the two, was the Old One, Will Stanton, bound by birth to follow this quest wherever it might lead . . . He was swept up suddenly in a wild exhilaration, bringing energy from nowhere to harden his drooping arms and legs. Yelling with sudden glee, grinning madly at Bran, he whacked at the flames licking the bracken at his feet as if he could flatten them in an instant into the ground.

Then a flash of movement higher up the mountain caught his eyes away from the line of flame, and out of the bare rocks above he saw, flinging itself forward at astonishing speed, the form of a grey-white fox. Brush flying out behind, ears back; it leapt up the towering side of Craig yr Aderyn. Smoke billowed, rising on the wind, and the fox was gone. Will had seen it for only a quick moment.

He heard a high wail from Bran. 'Cafall!'

Then the Welsh boy was scrambling up the slope, ignoring cries of concern from below, ignoring the fire and the smoke and all else except the glimpse of the white animal he had thought was his dog.

'Bran, come back! It isn't Cafall!'

Will climbed desperately after him, his heart thumping as if it would leap out of his chest. 'Bran! Come back!'

Steeper and steeper the slope grew, until they were upon the Craig itself, scrambling through bracken, over slippery grass, round jutting shelves of grey rock. Bran paused at last on one of these, panting, staring wildly about him. Will stumbled up beside him, hardly able to speak.

'Cafall!' Bran shouted into nowhere.

'It wasn't Cafall, Bran.'

'Of course it was. I saw him.'

'It was a fox, Bran. One of the *milgwn*. Bran, it's a trick, don't you see?'

Will coughed, choking in a billowy gust of smoke from the black cloud that wreathed round the slope behind and below them. They could see nothing but smoke and the steep rock, with patches of grey sky above their heads. Below, there was no sign of the farm or men or the valley, and in their ears no sound but the sighing of the wind, and somewhere the harsh faint voices of birds.

Bran looked at Will uncertainly.

'Bran, I'm sure of it.'

'All right. I was so certain . . . I'm sorry.'

'Don't be. It wasn't you seeing. It was the Grey King making you see. But the trouble is, we can't go back that way, the fire's coming up after us –'

'There is a way down the other side,' Bran said, brushing sweat from his eyes. 'No bracken for the fire to burn there, just rock. But it's hard going.' He looked doubtfully at Will's pale smudged face.

'I'm all right. Go on, go on.'

They clambered on up the rough stairway of grass and rock, holding on now with both hands and feet.

'There's a bird's nest here!' Will had glimpsed an untidy pile of twigs and bracken a foot from his head.

'There'd be birds too, if it weren't for the fire. It's a nesting place in spring, I told you. Not just the cormorants – ravens too. Lots of birds . . . which is why they call it Bird Rock, of course. Here –' Bran paused upright on a broad shelf of rock, edged with bracken. 'This is the ridge. It goes down the other side towards Prichard's Farm.'

But Will was standing very still, looking at him. 'Bird Rock?'

'That's right,' Bran said, surprised. 'Bird Rock. Craig yr Aderyn, rock of the birds. I thought you knew that.'

Will said softly, reflectively:

> 'On the day of the dead, when the year too dies,
> Must the youngest open the oldest hills
> Through the door of the birds, where the breeze breaks . . .'

Bran stared at him. 'You mean . . . the door of the birds . . . here?'

'Bird Rock. It must be. I know it. And this is the day of the dead –' Will swung his head sharply, gazing up at the sky where clouds flew like grey puffs of smoke. 'And the wind's changing, feel . . . No . . . Yes, there again . . . A bad wind, a wind from the Dark. I don't like it, Bran, it has the Grey King in it.' He spoke now with no thought of Bran as anything but an ally, ever.

The white-haired boy said bleakly, 'It's swinging to the north. That is the worst wind of all, the north wind. *Gwynt Traed yr Meirw*, they call it, the wind that blows round the feet of the dead. It brings storms. And worse, sometimes.'

The distant crackling of the fire seemed louder now. Will glanced over his shoulder, down the hill; the smoke was thicker there, and he felt more heat in the air. The wind whirled in gusts, catching up cinders and soot from below into strange dark eddies round their heads. All at once Will knew with dreadful certainty that the Grey King was aware of him, precisely aware, gathering his power for attack – and that it was at that first moment of awareness that the fire on the mountain had begun. He flinched in a sudden sense of fearful loneliness. An Old One, alone without others of the Light, was vulnerable to the Dark at its strongest. Though he could not be destroyed for all time, yet he could be disarmed; the full power of a Lord of the Dark could, if it struck him defenceless, blast him out of Time for so great a space that he could be of no help to his fellows until too late. So the Grey King struck now at Will with fire, and with all else that might be at his command.

And Bran was more vulnerable yet. Will swung back quickly. 'Bran, come on, along the ridge to the top. Before the fire –'

His voice died in his throat. Silently on to the ridge round them, out of holes and crevices, round corners and crags, came slinking the grey-white ghostly shapes of the *milgwn*, more than a score of them: heads held low, teeth grinning, a white tip glimmering on each stiffly-held grey bushy tail. Their foxy smell was in the air stronger than the smoke. At their head stood the king fox, their leader, red tongue lolling from a mouth set in a wide dreadful grin, its white teeth long as fingers and sharp as nails, icicles of bone. The eyes were bright; the ruff stood out white round the huge shoulders and neck.

Will clenched his fists, shouting angry words of power in the Old Speech, but the great grey fox did not flinch. Instead it made a sudden sharp leap into the air, straight up on the one spot, as Will had once seen a fox do in a Buckinghamshire field, far away from this valley, to discover what danger lurked in a field of wheat higher than its head. As it jumped, the king fox gave one short, sharp bark, deep and clear. The *milgwn* snarled low. And an abrupt *whoof* of flame shot up at Will's side with a sound like tearing cloth, as the fire on the mountain burst at last on the ridge of Craig yr Aderyn and roared crackling round them in the bracken.

Will shrank back. There was no way of escape but past the king fox. And the big fox crouched motionless, low on its belly, tensing itself to spring.

There was a sudden piercing yell at Will's shoulder. Bran leapt forward, waving in his hand a crooked branch of scrub oak blazing like tinder, a sheaf of flame; he thrust it full into the grey fox's face. Screaming, the animal fell back amongst its fellows, and the foxes milled in confusion. Before the branch could burn down to his arm, Bran flung it aside. But unexpectedly, caught by a gust of wind, it fell over the opposite side of the ridge, down towards the unburned slope. Out it went and over the edge, and down to the far side of the Craig where the fire might not otherwise have gone. There was a gasp of flame as the fire took hold on its new prey. Bran wailed in horror.

'Will! I've been and sent the fire down to Prichard's Farm – we're cut off both ways!'

'The top!' Will called urgently. 'We must get to the top!' With all the certainty of ancient instincts he knew the place they must find; it had begun compellingly to call to him, unseen, waking to his quest. He knew what it would look like; he knew what he must do when they reached it. But the reaching was another matter. Flames crackled at either side of them, scorching their dry skin; ahead, the *milgwn* gathered now in a tight semicircle, waiting, waiting –

Desperately Will put protection about himself and Bran, standing foursquare facing the north and calling some words in the Old Speech: it was the Spell of Helledd, to give freedom to a wanderer against any compulsion by those holding the land over which he roamed. But there was not much hope in him; he knew it could not hold for long. Beside him he heard Bran give a great imploring shout, like a small child calling for help without knowing that he calls.

'Cafall! Cafall!'

And out of nowhere along the ridge towards them came a white streak, leaping at the nearest fox, charging it sideways, so that it spun round with a shriek rolling over and over. The tight semicircle wavered, uncertain. Cafall leapt snarling at the next fox, his jaws closing quick and hard on its shoulder, and the animals squealed dreadfully and twisted away. There in the rent he had torn in the rank of the *milgwn* the white dog stood, belligerent as a bull, with his legs planted firm on the rock, and the message glinting in his strange silvery eyes was clear. Will grabbed Bran by the arm and slipped out with him past Cafall, free, while the panting foxes hesitated.

'Up here, Bran, quick! It's the only place!'

Bran's eyes flickered over black earth and white fur, dark hills and grey sky; he saw the great king fox of the *milgwn* watching them, controlled again, poised for pursuit. Then Cafall, curving to face the animal, began a long crescendo snarl more bloodcurdling than any sound Bran had ever heard in his life. In fulfilment of some long destiny, the dog was making it possible for them to escape. There was no excuse not to obey. With a sudden flooding of trust and humility, Bran turned and scrambled upwards after Will.

Clambering on hands and feet over the rocky ridge, Will made for the place to which they must go; it sang to him, beckoning. Below the rocks to which they clung, smoke swirled like a dark sea; high above, unseen birds screamed and cawed in angry fear. When he could climb no further, Will saw a narrow overhung cleft in the rocks before him, a long slit broadened and eroded by frost and wind and rain. Its grey granite sides were green-patched with lichen. Irresistibly, it summoned him.

He called to Bran: 'In here!' Then his voice rose louder, commanding. 'Cafall!'

The granite sides of the cleft towered three times higher than his head. Entering, Will glanced back over his shoulder; he saw Bran following, bemused, and then a quick white shape slipping after him, as Cafall darted forward, nuzzling his nose briefly into Bran's hand as he passed. Outside on the rock, a shrieking tumult of baffled rage rose from the furious *milgwn*, prevented from entry. Their master's power, Will now knew, was a power over the rock and the mountains and all the high places of Gwynedd; but only over those. Inside the rock and the mountain was a different domain.

He went on. At its far end, the rocky cleft widened a little. The light was dim. Things seemed indistinct, as if in a dream. Outside, the foxes barked and screamed. And then there was nothing more ahead of Will but bare grey rock: a formidable blank wall, ending the cleft. Will stared at the rock, and his mind filled with a warmth of discovery and relief as intense as joy. The dog Cafall was at his side, standing straight and proud as a young horse. Will dropped one hand to rest on the white head. The other arm he raised before him, with fingers stiff outstretched in a gesture of command, and he called out three words in the Old Speech.

And before him, the rock parted like a great gate, to a faint, very faint sound of delicate music that was achingly familiar and yet strange, gone as soon as it was heard. Will walked forward through the rocky doors, with Cafall trotting confidently beside him, head high and tail waving. And Bran, a little hesitantly, followed them.

Bird Rock

There was no way of telling whether they were deep inside Craig yr Aderyn, or had walked through the grey rocky doors into another place and time. It did not matter to Will. Exhilaration was pulsing through him, in this the true beginning of his first full quest as an Old One. Turning to look back, he saw without surprise that the doors through which they had come were no longer there. The rocky wall at the end of the chamber where they now stood was smooth and unbroken, and upon it, high up, there hung a round golden shield, glinting dully in a light that came from somewhere deep within the room.

Will looked tentatively at Bran, but the Welsh boy seemed unperturbed. His pale face was oddly vulnerable without its protective glasses, but Will could read no expression in the catlike eyes; he felt once more an intense curiosity about this strange boy with no colour in him, born into the Dark-haunted valley – mortal, and yet also a creature foreknown by the Old Ones centuries before. How was it that he, Will, an Old One himself, could sense so little of Bran's nature?

'You okay?' he said.

'I'm all right,' said Bran. He was looking up at the walls, beyond Will. '*Duw*,' he said softly. 'Beautiful. Look at those.'

It was a long, empty room. On its walls hung four tapestries, two to each side, their rich colours so deeply gleaming that they too seemed to shimmer in the half-light, like the golden shield. Will blinked in recognition at the images embroidered there, rich as stained glass: a silver unicorn, a field of red roses, a glowing golden sun . . .

All the light in this room seemed, he now saw, to come from only one flame. In an iron holder jutting from the stone wall near the end of the room, a single tremendous candle stood. It was several feet high, and it burned with a white unwavering flame of intense brilliance. The long shadow of the candle lay over wall and floor, motionless, undancing. Its stillness, Will realized, was the stillness of the High Magic, a power beyond Light or Dark or any allegiance – the strongest and most remote force in the universe, which soon in this place he and Bran must face.

There was a faint whistling whine at his side, scarcely audible. He looked down, and saw the dog Cafall gazing backwards at Bran.

Will said softly, 'Go on, then.'

The dog's cold nose nudged his hand, and Cafall turned and trotted briskly back to his master, waving his tail. Bran thrust his fingers into the fur of the dog's head in quick fierce affection, and Will knew that for all his calm appearance there was in his mind an uncertainty approaching panic, which Cafall had sensed and sought to reassure. Will felt a quick tug of sympathy for Bran, but there was no time for explanations. He knew he must trust his instinctive feeling that, in the last resort, the strange remoteness always apparent in Bran would prove to be the strangeness of great strength.

He said aloud, without turning, 'This way.' Then he walked firmly down the long lofty chamber. Bran followed with Cafall; Will could hear the footsteps ringing with his own on the stone-paved floor. He reached the tall candle in the wall. Its iron holder was set into the stone at the level of his shoulder; the smooth white sides of the candle reached far higher, high above his head, so that the white flame glowed up there like a bright full moon.

Will paused. 'First the moon,' he said. 'Then stars and, if all is well, a comet, and then the dust of the stars. And at the last, the sun.'

'What?' said Bran.

Will glanced across without really seeing. Behind his eyes he was looking into his own mind and memory, not at Bran. Here in this place he was an Old One, occupied with the affairs of the Light; nothing else had very much relevance. He said, 'It is the order of things, by which the High Magic shall be known. So that none may come within reach of it except by birthright.'

Bran said, 'I still don't know what you're talking about.' Then he shook his head in quick nervous apology. 'I'm sorry, I didn't mean to sound –'

'It doesn't matter,' Will said. 'Just follow. You'll see.'

The footsteps rang out again, and then they were at the end of the long room and there was nothing before them but a blank hole in the floor. Bran peered at it dubiously.

Will said, 'Do what I do.' He sat on the edge of the rough rectangular opening in the floor, and in a few moments he could see a staircase, running downwards at a steep angle. Cautiously lowering himself, he found the stairway was narrow and dark; it was like going down into a well. When he put out a hand to either side, each hand at once touched rock, and the rock of the roof too was very close to his head. He went slowly down. In a moment he could hear Bran's careful steps following, and the soft scratch of Cafall's paws. For a little while the glimmer from the upper chamber reached down after them, casting wavering patterns of shadow on the close walls, but soon even that faded, and there was no light in the stair tunnel at all. In its sides, Will's fingers found two smooth channels carved to form balustrades, a steadying refuge for the hands of anyone descending. He said quietly, his voice eerily echoing, 'Bran, if you put your hands out –'

'I've found them,' Bran said. 'Like banisters, aren't they? Bright idea of somebody's, that.' The words were cool, but there was tension behind them. Their voices boomed gently in the stairway, muffled as if by mist.

Will said, 'Go carefully. I may stop in a hurry.' He was straining to hear the voice of his instincts; random images and impressions flickered in and out of his mind. Something was calling him, something close, close –

He put out a hand in front of him, just in time to save himself from coming hard up against a blank wall of rock. There was no other stair ahead: only a stony dead end.

'What is it?' said Bran, behind.

'Wait a moment.' An instruction was growing inside Will's memory, like an echo from another world. Standing with his feet planted firmly on the last stair, he put the palms of both hands flat against the rough unseen rock-face barring their way, and he pushed. At the same time he said certain words in the Old Speech that came into his mind.

And the rock parted, silently, as it had when the great doors opened silently on Bird Rock, though no music sounded here. With Bran and Cafall at his heels, Will stepped forward into a faint glow of light that caught him into such wonder that he could only stand and gaze.

They were no longer where they had been. They stood somewhere in another time, on the roof of the world. All around them was the open night sky, like a huge black inverted bowl, and in it blazed the stars, thousand upon thousand brilliant prickles of fire. Will heard Bran draw in a quick breath. They stood, looking up. The stars blazed round them. There was no sound anywhere, in all the immensity of space. Will felt a wave of giddiness; it was as though they stood on the last edge of the universe, and if they fell, they would fall out of Time . . . As he gazed about him, gradually he recognized the strange inversion of reality in which they were held. He and Bran were not standing in a timeless dark night observing the stars in the heavens. It was the other way around. They themselves were observed. Every blazing point in that great depthless hemisphere of stars and suns was focused upon them, contemplating, considering, judging. For by following the quest for the golden harp, he and Bran were challenging the boundless might of the High Magic of the universe. They must stand unprotected before it, on their way, and they would be allowed to pass only if they had the right by birth. Under that merciless starlight of infinity, any unrightful challenger would be brushed into nothingness as effortlessly as a man might brush an ant from his sleeve.

Will stood, waiting. There was nothing else that he could do. He looked for friends in the sky. He found the Eagle and the Bull, with Aldebaran glowing red and the Pleiades glimmering; he saw Orion brandish his club high, encouraging, with Betelgeuse and Rigel winking at shoulder and toe. He saw the Swan and the Eagle flying towards one another along the bright path of the Milky Way; he saw the hazy hint of distant Andromeda, and Earth's near neighbours Tau Ceti and Procyon, and Sirius the dog star. In longing hope Will gazed at them; in hope and in salutation, for during his time of learning the ways of an Old One he had flown amongst them all.

Then the sky wheeled, and the stars slanted and changed; now the Centaur galloped overhead, and the blue double star Acrux supporting the Southern Cross. The Hydra stretched lazily over the heavens, with the Lion marching by, and the great Ship sailed its leisurely, eternal way. And at last a brilliant point of light, with a long curving tail, came blazing into view over half the inverted bowl of the sky, moving past in a long stately progress; and Will knew that he and Bran had survived their first ordeal.

He pressed Bran's arm briefly, and saw a flicker of reflected light as the white head turned.

'It is a comet!' Bran whispered.

Will said softly back, 'Wait. There's more, if all is well.'

The long flaring tail of the comet moved gradually out of sight, down over the horizon of their nameless world and time. Still in the black hemisphere the stars blazed and slowly wheeled; beneath them, Will felt so infinitesimally small that it seemed impossible he should even exist. Immensity pressed in on him, terrifying, threatening – and then, in a swift flash of movement like dance, like the glint of a leaping fish, came a flick of brightness in the sky from a shooting star. Then another, and another, here, there, all around. He heard Bran give a small chirrup of delight, a spark struck from the same bright sudden joy that filled his own being. *Wish on a star*, said a tiny voice in his head from some long-departed day of early childhood: *Wish on a star* – the cry of a pleasure and faith as ancient as the eyes of man.

'Wish on a falling star,' said Bran soft in his ear. All around them the meteors briefly dived and vanished, as tiny points of stardust in the long travel of their cloud struck the aery halo of the earth, burned bright and were gone.

I wish, said Will fiercely in his mind: *I wish ... Oh, I wish ...*

And all the bright starlit sky was gone, in a flicker of time that they could not catch, and darkness came around them so fast that they blinked in disbelief at its thick nothingness. They were back on the staircase beneath Bird Rock, with stone steps under their feet and a curved stone balustrade smooth to the sightless touch of their hands. And as Will stretched out one hand groping before him, he found no blank wall of stone there to bar his way, but free open space.

Slowly, faltering, he went on down the dark stairway, and Bran and Cafall followed him.

Then very gradually faint light began to filter up from below. Will saw a glimmer from the walls enclosing them; then the shape of the steps beneath his feet; then, appearing round a curve in the long tunnelling stairway, the bright circle that marked its end. The light grew brighter, the circle larger; Will felt his steps become quicker and more eager, and mocked himself, but could not help it.

Then instinct caught him into caution, and on the last few steps of the staircase, before the light, he stopped. Behind him he heard Bran and the dog stop too, at once. Will stood listening to his senses, trying to catch the source of warning. He saw, without properly seeing, that the steps on which they stood had been carved out of the rock with immense care and symmetry, perfectly angled, smooth as glass, every detail as clear as if the rock had been cut only the day before. Yet there was a noticeable hollow in the centre of each step, which could only have been worn by centuries of passing feet. Then he ceased to notice such things, for awareness caught at him out of the deepest corner of his mind and told him what he must do.

Carefully Will pushed up the left sleeve of his sweater as far as the elbow, leaving the forearm bare. On the underside of his arm shone the livid scar that had once been accidentally burned there like a brand: the sign of the Light, a circle quartered by a cross. In a deliberate slow gesture, half defensive, half defiant, he raised this arm crooked before his face, as if shielding his eyes from bright light, or warding off an unexpected blow. Then he walked down the last few steps of the staircase and out into the light. As he stepped to the floor, he felt a shock of sensation like nothing he had ever known. A flare of white brilliance blinded him, and was gone; a brief tremendous thunder dazed his ears, and was gone; a force like a blast wave from some great explosion briefly tore at his body, and was gone. Will stood still, breathing fast. He knew that beneath his singular protection, he had brought them through the last door of the High Magic: a living barrier that would consume any unsought intruder in a gasp of energy as unthinkable as the holocaust of the sun. Then he looked into the room before him, and for a moment of illusion thought that he saw the sun itself.

It was an immense cavernous room, high-roofed, lit by flaring torches thrust into brackets on the stone walls, and hazy with smoke. The smoke came from the torches. Yet in the centre of the floor burned a great glowing fire, alone, with no chimney or fireplace to contain it. It gave no smoke at all, but burned with a white light of such brilliance that Will could not look straight at it. No intense heat came from this fire, but the air was filled with the aromatic scent of burning wood, and there was the crackling, snapping sound of a log fire.

Will came forward past the fire, beckoning Bran to follow; then stopped abruptly as he saw what lay ahead.

Hazy at the end of the chamber three figures sat, in three great thrones that seemed to be fashioned out of smooth grey-blue Welsh slate. They did not move. They appeared to be men, dressed in long hooded robes of differing shades of blue. One robe was dark, one was light, and the robe between them was the shifting greenish-blue of a summer sea. Between the three thrones stood two intricately carved wooden chests. At first there seemed to be nothing else in the huge room, but after a moment of gazing Will knew that there was movement in the deep shadows beyond the fire, in the darkness all around the three illuminated lords. These were the bright figures on a dark canvas, lit to catch the eye; beyond them in the darkness other things of unknown nature lurked.

He could tell nothing of the nature of the three figures, beyond sensing great power. Nor could his senses as an Old One penetrate the surrounding darkness. It was as if an invisible barrier stood all around them, through which no enchantment might reach.

Will stood a little way before the thrones, looking up. The faces of the three lords were hidden in the shadows of their hooded robes. For a moment there was silence, broken only by the soft crackle of the burning fire; then out of the shadows a deep voice said, 'We greet you, Will Stanton. And we name you by the sign. Will Stanton, Sign-seeker.'

'Greetings,' Will said, in as strong and clear a voice as he could muster, and he pulled down his sleeve over his scarred arm. 'My lords,' he said, 'it is the day of the dead.'

'Yes,' said the figure in the lightest blue robe. His face seemed thin in the shadows of his hood, the eyes gleaming, and his voice was light, sibilant, hissing. 'Yesssssss . . .' Echoes whispered like snakes out of the dark, as if a hundred other little hissing voices came from nameless shapes behind him, and Will felt the small hairs rise on the back of his neck. Behind him he heard Bran give a muffled involuntary moan, and knew that horror must be creeping like a white mist through his mind. Will's strength as an Old One rebelled. He said in quick cold reproach, 'My lord?'

The horror fell away, like a cloud whisked off by the wind, and the lord in the light blue robe softly laughed. Will stood there frowning at him, unmoved: a small stocky boy in jeans and sweater, who nonetheless knew himself to possess power worthy of meeting these three. He said, confident now, 'It is the day of the dead, and the youngest has opened the oldest hills, through the door of the birds. And has been let pass by the eye of the High Magic. I have come for the golden harp, my lords.'

The second figure in the sea-blue robe said, 'And the raven boy with you.'
'Yes.'

Will turned to Bran, standing hesitantly nearer the fire, and beckoned him. Bran came forward very slowly, feet as unwilling as if they swam against treacle, and stood at his side. The light from the torches on the walls shone in his white hair.

The lord in the sea-blue robe leaned forward a little from his throne; they glimpsed a keen, strong face and a pointed grey beard. He said, astonishingly, 'Cafall?'

At Bran's side the white dog stood erect and quivering. He did not move an inch forward, as if obeying some inner instruction that told him his place, but his tail waved furiously from side to side as it never waved for anyone but Bran. He gave a soft, small whine.

White teeth glinted in the hooded face. 'He is well named. Well named.'

Bran said jealously, in sudden fierce anxiety, 'He is my dog!' Then he added, rather muffled, 'My lord.' Will could feel the alarm in him at his own temerity.

But the laughter from the shadows was kindly. 'Never fear, boy. The High Magic would never take your dog from you. Certainly the Old Ones would not either, and the Dark might try but would not succeed.' He leaned forward suddenly, so that for an instant the strong, bearded face was clear; the voice softened, and there was an aching sadness in it. 'Only the creatures of the earth take from one another, boy. All creatures, but men more than any. Life they take, and liberty, and all that another man may have – sometimes through greed, sometimes through stupidity, but never by any volition but their own. Beware your own race, Bran Davies – they are the only ones who will ever harm you, in the end.'

Dread stirred in Will as he felt the deep sadness in the voice, for there was a compassion in it directed solely at Bran, as if the Welsh boy stood at the edge of some long sorrow. He had a quick sense of a mysterious closeness between these two, and knew that the lord in the sea-blue robe was trying to give Bran strength and help, without being able to explain why. Then the hooded figure leaned abruptly back, and the mood was gone.

Will said huskily, 'Nevertheless, my lord, the rights of that race have always been the business of the Light. And in quest of them I claim the golden harp.'

The soft-voiced lord in the lightest robe, who had spoken first, swiftly stood. His cloak swirled round him like a blue mist; bright eyes glinted from the pale face glimmering in the hood.

'Answer the three riddles as the law demands, Old One, you and the White Crow your helper there, and the harp shall be yours. But if you answer wrong, the doors of rock shall close, and you be left defenceless on the cold mountain, and the harp shall be lost to the Light forever.'

'We shall answer,' Will said.

'You, boy, the first.' The blue mist swirled again. A bony finger was thrust pointing at Bran, and the shadowed hood turned. Will turned too, anxiously; he had half expected this.

Bran gasped. 'Me? But – but I –'

Will reached out and touched his arm. He said gently, 'Try. Only try. We are here only to try. If the answer is asleep in you, it will wake. If it is not, no matter. But try.'

Bran stared at him unsmiling, and Will saw his throat move as he swallowed. Then the white head turned back again. 'All right.'

The soft, sibilant voice said, 'Who are the Three Elders of the World?'

Will felt Bran's mind reel in panic, as he tried to find meaning in the words. There was no way to offer help. In this place, the law of the High Magic prevented an Old One from putting the smallest thought or image into another mind: Will was permitted only to overhear. So, tense, he stood overhearing the turmoil of his friend's thoughts, as they tossed about desperately seeking order.

Bran struggled. The Three Elders of the World . . . somewhere he knew . . . it was strange and yet familiar, as if somewhere he had seen, or read . . . the three oldest creatures, the three oldest things . . . he had read it at school, and he had read it in Welsh . . . the oldest things . . .

He took his glasses from his shirt pocket, as if fiddling with them could clear his mind, and he saw staring up out of them the reflection of his own eyes. Strange eyes . . . creepy eyes, they called them at school. At school. At school . . . Strange round tawny eyes, like the eyes of an owl. He put the glasses slowly back in his pocket, his mind groping at an echo. At his side, Cafall shifted very slightly, his head moving so that it touched Bran's hand. The fur brushed his fingers lightly, very lightly, like the flick of feathers. Feathers. Feathers. *Feathers* . . .

He had it.

Will, at his side, felt in his own mind the echoing flood of relief, and struggled to contain his delight.

Bran stood up straight and cleared his throat. 'The Three Elders of the World,' he said, 'are the Owl of Cwm Cawlwyd, the Eagle of Gwernabwy, and the Blackbird of Celli Gadarn.'

Will said softly, 'Oh, well done! Well done!'

'That is right,' said the thin voice above them, unemotionally. Like an early-morning sky the light blue robe swirled before them, and the figure sank back into its throne.

From the central throne rose the lord in the sea-blue robe; stepping forward, he looked down at Will. Behind its grey beard his face seemed oddly young, though its skin was brown and weathered like the skin of a sailor long at sea.

'Will Stanton,' he said, 'who were the three generous men of the Island of Britain?'

Will stared at him. The riddle was not impossible; he knew that the answer lay somewhere in his memory, stored from the great Book of Gramarye, treasure book of the enchantment of the Light that had been destroyed as soon as he, the last of the Old Ones, had been shown what it held. Will set his mind to work, searching. But at the same time a deeper riddle worried at him. Who was this lord in the sea-blue robe, with his close interest in Bran? He knew about Cafall . . . clearly he was a lord of the High Magic, and yet there was a look about him of . . . a look of . . .

Will pushed the wondering aside. The answer to the riddle had surfaced in his memory.

He said clearly, 'The three generous men of the Island of Britain. Nudd the Generous, son of Senllyt. Mordaf the Generous, son of Serwan. Rhydderch the Generous, son of Tydwal Tudglyd. *And Arthur himself was more generous than the three.*'

Deliberately on the last line his voice rang echoing through the hall like a bell.

'That is right,' said the bearded lord. He looked thoughtfully at Will and seemed about to say more, but instead he only nodded slowly. Then sweeping his robe about him in a sea-blue wave, he stepped back to his throne.

The hall seemed darker, filled with dancing shadows from the flickering light of the fire. A sudden flash and crackle came from behind the boys, as a log fell and the flames leapt up; instinctively Will glanced back. When he turned forward again, the third figure, who had not spoken or moved until now, was standing tall and silent before his throne. His robe was a deep, deep blue, darkest of the three, and his hood was pulled so far forward that there was no hint of his face visible, but only shadow.

His voice was deep and resonant, like the voice of a cello, and it brought music into the hall.

'Will Stanton,' it said, 'what is the shore that fears the sea?'

Will started impulsively forward, his hands clenching into fists, for this voice caught into the deepest part of him. Surely, surely . . . but the face in the hood was hidden, and he was denied all ways of recognition. Any part of his senses that tried to reach out to the great thrones met a blank wall of refusal from the High Magic. Once more Will gave up, and put his mind to the last riddle.

He said slowly, 'The shore that fears the sea . . .'

Images wavered in and out of his mind: great crashing waves against a rocky coast . . . the green light in the ocean, the realm of Tethys, where strange creatures may live . . . a gentler sea then, washing in long slow waves an endless golden beach. The shore . . . the beach . . . the beach . . .

The image wavered and changed. It dissolved into a green dappled forest of gnarled ancient trees, their broad trunks smooth with a curious light grey bark. Their leaves danced above, new, soft, bright with a delicate green that had in it all of springtime. The beginnings of triumph whispered in Will's mind.

'The shore,' he said. 'The beach where the sea washes. But also it is a wood, of lovely fine grain, that is in the handle of a chisel and the legs of a chair, the head of a broom and the pad of a workhorse saddle. And I dare swear too that those two chests between your thrones are carved of it. The only places where it may not be used are beneath the open sky and upon the open sea, for this wood loses its virtue if soaked by water. The answer to your riddle, my lord, is the wood of the beech tree.'

The flames leaped up in the fire behind them, and suddenly the hall was brilliant. Joy and relief seemed to surge through the air. The first two blue-robed lords rose from their thrones to stand beside the third; like three towers they loomed hooded over the boys. Then the third lord flung back the hood of his deep blue robe, to reveal a fierce hawk-nosed head with deep-set eyes and a shock of wild white hair. And the High Magic's barrier against recognition fell away.

Will cried joyously, 'Merriman!'

He leapt forward to the tall figure as a small child leaps to its father, and clasped his outstretched hands. Merriman smiled down at him.

Will laughed aloud in delight. 'I knew,' he said. 'I knew. And yet –'

'Greetings, Old One.' Merriman said. 'Now you are grown fully into the Circle, by this. Had you failed in this part of the quest, all else would have been lost.' The bleak, hard lines of his face were softened by affection; his dark eyes blazed like black torches. Then he turned to Bran, taking him by the shoulders. Bran looked up at him, pale and expressionless.

'And the raven boy,' the deep voice said gently. 'We meet again. You have played your part well, as it was known you would. Hold your head in pride, Bran Davies. You carry a great heritage within you. Much has been asked of you, and more will be asked yet. Much more.'

Bran looked at Merriman with his catlike eyes unblinking, and said nothing. Listening to the Welsh boy's mood, Will sensed an uneasy baffled pleasure.

Merriman stepped back. He said, 'Three Lords of the High Magic have for many centuries had guardianship of the golden harp. There are no names here in this place, nor allegiances in that task. Here, as in other places that you do not know yet, all is subject to the law, the High Law. It is of no consequence that I am a Lord of the Light, or that my colleague there is a Lord of the Dark.'

He made a slight ironic bow to the tall figure who wore the robe of lightest blue. Will caught his breath in sudden comprehension, and looked for the thin face hidden in the hood. But it was turned away from him, staring out into the shadows of the hall.

The central figure in the sea-blue robe stepped forward a pace. There was great quiet authority about him, as if he were confident, without pomp, in knowing himself the master in that hall. He put back his hood and they saw the full strength and gentleness of the close-bearded face. Though his beard was grey, his hair was brown, only lightly grey-streaked. He seemed a man in the middle of his years, with all power undiminished, yet wisdom already gained. *But*, Will thought, *he is not a man at all . . .*

Merriman inclined his head respectfully, stepping aside. 'Sire,' he said.

Will stared, at last beginning to understand.

At Bran's side, the dog Cafall made the same small sound of devotion that he had before. Clear blue eyes looked down at Bran, and the bearded lord said softly, 'Fortune guard you in my land, my son.'

Then as Bran looked at him perplexed, the lord drew himself up, and his voice rose. 'Will Stanton,' he said. 'Two chests stand between our thrones. You must open the chest at my right, and take out what you will find there. The other will remain sealed, in case of need, until another time that I hope may never come. Here now.'

He turned, pointing. Will went to the big carved chest, turned its ornate wrought-iron clasp, and pushed at the top. It was so broad, and the carved slab of wood so heavy, that he had to kneel and push upward with all the force of both arms; but he shook his head in warning refusal when Bran started forward to help.

Slowly the huge lid rose, and fell open, and for a moment there was a delicate sound like singing in the air. Then Will reached inside the chest, and when he straightened again he was bearing in both his arms a small, gleaming, golden harp.

The hint of music in the hall died into nothing, giving way to a low growing rumble like distant thunder. Closer and louder it grew. The lord in the lightest, sky-blue robe, his face still hooded and hidden, drew away from them. He seized his cloak and swung it round with a long sweep of the arm.

The fire hissed and went out. Smoke filled the hall, dark and bitter. Thunder crashed and roared all around. And the lord in the sky-blue robe gave a great cry of rage, and disappeared.

Eyes That See the Wind

They stood silent in the dim-lit darkness. Somewhere out beyond the rock, thunder still rumbled and growled. The torches burned, flickering and smoky, on the walls.

Bran said huskily: 'Was he the – the –'

'No,' Merriman said. 'He is not the Grey King. But he is one very close to him, and back to him he has now gone. And their rage will mount the higher because it will be sharpened by fear, fear at what the Light may be able to do with this new Thing of Power.' He looked at Will, his bony face tight with concern. 'The first perilous part of the quest is accomplished, Old One, but there is worse peril yet to come.'

'The Sleepers must be wakened,' Will said.

'That is right. And although we do not yet know where they sleep, nor shall till you have found them, it is almost certain that they are terribly, dangerously close to the Grey King. For long we have known there was a reason for his hard cold grip on this part of the land, though we did not understand it. A happy valley, this has always been, and beautiful; yet he chose to make his kingdom here, instead of in some grim remote place of the kind chosen by most of his line. Now it is clear there can be only one reason for that: to be close to the place where the Sleepers lie, and to keep their resting-place within his power. Just as this great rock, Craig yr Aderyn, is still within his power . . .'

Will said, his round face grave, 'The spell of protection, by which we came here untouched, has run its course now. And it can be made only once.' He looked ruefully at Bran. 'We may have an interesting reception out there, when we leave this place.'

'Have no care, Old One. You will have a new protection with you now.'

The words came deep and gentle from the top of the hall. Turning, Will saw that the bearded lord, his robe blue as the summer sea, was sitting enthroned again in the shadows. As he spoke, it seemed that the light began gradually to grow in the hall; the torches burned higher, and glimmering between them now Will could see long swords hanging on the stone.

'The music of the golden harp,' said the blue-robed lord, 'has a power that may not be broken either by the Dark or by the Light. It has the High Magic in it, and while the harp is being played, those under its protection are safe from any kind of harm or spell. Play the harp of gold, Old One. Its music will wrap you in safety.'

Will said slowly, 'By enchantment I could play it, but I think it should rather be played by the art of skilful fingers. I do not know how to play the harp, my lord.' He paused. 'But Bran does.'

Bran looked down at the instrument as Will held it out to him.

'Never a harp like that, though,' he said.

He took the harp from Will. Its frame was slender but ornate, fashioned so that a golden vine with gold leaves and flowers seemed to twine round it, in and out of the strings. Even the strings themselves looked as if they were made of gold.

'Play, Bran,' said the bearded lord softly.

Holding the harp experimentally in the crook of his left arm, Bran ran his fingers gently over the strings. And the sounds that came from them were of such sweetness that Will, beside him, caught his breath in astonishment; he had never heard notes at once so delicate and so resonant, filling the hall with music like the liquid birdsong of summer. Intent, fascinated, Bran began to pick out the plaintive notes of an old Welsh lullaby, elaborating it gradually, filling it out, as he gained confidence in the feel of the strings under his one hand. Will watched the absorbed musician's devotion on his face. Glancing for an instant at the enthroned lord, and at Merriman, he knew that they too were for this moment rapt, carried away out of time by a music that was not of the earth, pouring out like the High Magic in a singing spell.

Cafall made no sound, but leaned his head against Bran's knee.

Merriman said, his deep voice soft over the music, 'Go now, Old One.' His shadowed, deep-set eyes met Will's briefly, in a fierce communication of trust and hope. Will stared about him for a last moment at the high torchlit hall, with its one dark-robed figure standing tall as a tree, and the unknown bearded lord seated motionless on his throne. Then he turned and led Bran, his fingers still gently plucking a melody from the harp, towards the narrow stone staircase to the chamber from which they had come. When he had set him climbing, he turned to raise one arm in salute, then followed.

Bran stood in the stone room above, playing, while Cafall and Will came up after him. And as he played, there took shape in the blank wall at the end of the chamber, below the single hanging golden shield, the two great doors through which they had come into the heart of Bird Rock.

The music of the harp rippled in a lilting upward scale, and slowly the doors swung inward. Beyond, they saw the grey, cloudy sky between the steep walls of the cleft of rock. Though fire blazed no longer on the mountain, a strong, dead smell of burning hung in the air. As they stepped outside, Cafall bounded out past them, through the cleft, and disappeared.

Struck suddenly by a fear of losing him again, Bran stopped playing. 'Cafall! Cafall!' he called.

'Look!' Will said softly.

He was half-turned, looking back. Behind them, the tall slabs of rock swung silently together and seemed to melt out of existence, leaving only a weathered rock face, looking just as it had looked for thousands of years. And in the air hung a faint vanishing phrase of delicate music. But Bran was thinking only of Cafall. After one brief glance at the rock, he tucked the harp beneath his arm and dived for the opening through which the dog had disappeared.

Before he could reach it, a whirling flurry of white came hurling in upon them through a cloud of fine ash, snarling, kicking, knocking Bran sideways so hard that he almost dropped the harp. It was Cafall; but a mad, furious, transformed Cafall, growling at them, glaring, driving them deeper into the cleft as if they were enemies. In a moment or two he had them pinned astounded against the rocky wall, and was crouching before them with his long side-teeth bared in a cold snarl.

'What is it?' said Bran blankly when he had breath enough to speak. 'Cafall? What on earth –'

And in an instant they knew – or would have known, if they had had time still for wondering. For suddenly the whole world round them was a roaring flurry of noise and destruction. Broken, charred branches came whirling past over the top of the rocky cleft; stones came bounding down loose out of nowhere so that instinctively they ducked, covering their heads. They fell flat on the ground, pressing themselves into the angle between earth and rock, with Cafall close beside. All around, the wind howled and tore at the rock with a sound like a high mad human scream amplified beyond belief. It was as if all the air in Wales had funnelled down into a great tornado of tearing destruction, and was battering in a frenzy of frustrated rage at the narrow opening in whose shelter they desperately crouched.

Will lurched up on to his hands and knees. He groped with one hand until he clutched Bran's arm. 'The harp!' he croaked. 'Play the harp!'

Bran blinked at him, dazed by the noise overhead, and then he understood. Forcing himself up against the fearsome wind pressing in between the rocky walls, he gripped the golden harp against his side and ran his right hand tremulously over the strings.

At once the tumult grew less. Bran began to play, and as the sweet notes poured out like the song of a lark rising, the great wind died away into nothing. Outside, there was only the rattle of loose pebbles tumbling here and there, one by one, down the rock. For a moment a lone sunbeam slanted down and glinted on the gold of the harp. Then it was gone, and the sky seemed duller, the world more grey. Cafall scrambled to his feet, licked Bran's hand, and led them docilely out to the slope outside the narrow cleft that had sheltered them from the fury of the gale. They felt a soft rain beginning to fall.

Bran let his fingers wander idly but persistently over the strings of the harp. He had no intention of stopping again. He looked at Will, and shook his head mutely with wonder and remorse and inquiry all in one.

Will squatted down and took Cafall's muzzle between his hands. He shook the dog's head gently from side to side. 'Cafall! Cafall!' he said wonderingly. Over his shoulder he said to Bran, '*Gwynt Traed y Meirw*, is that how you say it? In all its ancient force the Grey King sent his north wind upon us, the wind that blows round the feet of the dead, and with the dead is where we should have been if it weren't for Cafall – blasted away into a time beyond tomorrow. Before we could have seen a single tree bending, it would have been on us, for it came down from very high up and no human sighted eye could have seen it. But this hound of yours is the dog with the silver eyes, and such dogs can see the wind . . . So he saw it, and knew what it would do, and drove us back into safety.'

Bran said guiltily, 'If I hadn't stopped playing, perhaps the Brenin Llwyd couldn't even have sent the wind. The magic of the harp would have stopped him.'

'Perhaps,' Will said. 'And perhaps not.' He gave Cafall's head one last rub and straightened up. The white sheepdog looked up at Bran, tongue lolling as if in a grin, and Bran said to him lovingly, '*Rwyt ti'n gi doa*. Good boy.' But still his fingers did not stop moving over the harp.

Slowly they scrambled down the rock. Though it was full morning now, the sky was no lighter, but grey and heavy with cloud; the rain was still light, but it was clear that it would grow and settle in for the day, and that the valley was safe now from any more threat of fire. All the near slope of the mountain, Bird Rock and the valley edge were blackened and charred, and here and there wisps of smoke still rose. But all sparks were drowned now, and the ashes cold and wet, and the green farmlands would not again this year be in any state for burning.

Bran said, 'Did the harp bring the rain?'

'I think so,' Will said. 'I am just hoping it will bring nothing else. That's the trouble with the High Magic, like talking in the Old Speech – it's a protection, and yet it marks you, makes you easy to find.'

'We'll be in the valley soon.' But as he spoke, Bran's foot slipped on a wet rock face and he stumbled sideways, grabbing at a bush to save himself from falling – and dropped the harp. In the instant that the music broke off, Cafall's head jerked up and he began barking furiously, in a mixture of rage and challenge. He jumped up on to a projecting rock and stood poised there, staring about him. Then suddenly the barking broke into a furious deep howl, like the baying of a hunting dog, and he leapt.

The great grey fox, king of the *milgwn*, swerved in mid-air and screamed like a vixen. In a headlong rush down Bird Rock he had sprung out at them from above, aiming straight for Bran's head and neck. But the shock of Cafall's fierce leap turned his balance just enough to send him spinning sideways, cartwheeling down the rock. He screamed again, an unnatural sound that made the boys flinch in horror, and did not stop himself to turn at bay, but rushed on in a frenzy down the mountain. In an instant Cafall, barking in joyous triumph, was tearing down after him.

And Will, up on the empty rock under the grey drizzling sky, was instantly filled with a presentiment of disaster so overpowering that without thought he reached out and seized the golden harp, and cried to Bran, 'Stop Cafall! Stop him! Stop him!'

Bran gave him one frightened look. Then he flung himself after Cafall, running, stumbling, desperately calling the dog back. Scrambling down from the rock with the harp under one arm, Will saw his white head moving fast over the nearest field and, beyond it, a blur of speed that he knew was Cafall pursuing the grey fox. His head dizzy with foreboding, he too ran. Still on high land, he could see two fields away the roofs of Caradog Prichard's farm, and near by a grey-white knot of sheep and the figures of men. He skidded to a halt suddenly. The harp! There was no means of explaining the harp, if anyone should see it. He was certain to be among men in a few moments. The harp must be hidden. But where?

He looked wildly about him. The fire had not touched this field. On the far side of the field he saw a small lean-to, no more than three stone walls and a slate roof, that was an open shelter for sheep in winter, or a storeplace for winter feed. It was filled with bales of hay already, newly stacked. Running to it, Will thrust the gleaming little harp between two bales of hay, so that it was completely invisible from the outside. Then standing back, he stretched out one hand, and in the Old Speech put upon the harp the Spell of Caer Garadawg, by the power of which only the song of an Old One would be able to take the harp out of that place, or even make it visible at all.

Then he rushed away over the field towards Prichard's Farm, where distant shouts marked the ending of the chase. He could see, in a meadow beyond the farm buildings, the huge grey fox swerving and leaping in an effort to shake Cafall from its heels, and Cafall running doggedly close. A madness seemed to be on the fox; white foam dripped from its jaws. Will stumbled breathless into the farmyard to find Bran struggling to make his way through a group of men and sheep at the gate. John Rowlands was there, and Owen Davies, with Will's uncle; their clothes and weary faces were still blackened with ash from the fire-fighting, and Caradog Prichard stood scowling with his gun cocked under his arm.

'That damn dog has gone mad!' Prichard growled.

'Cafall! Cafall!' Bran pushed his way wildly through into the field, scattering the sheep, paying no heed to anyone. Prichard snarled at him, and Owen Davies said sharply, 'Bran! Where have you been? What are you up to?'

The grey fox leapt high in the air, as they had seen it do once before on Bird Rock. Cafall leapt after it, snapping at it in mid-air.

'The dog *is* mad,' David Evans said unhappily. 'He will be on the sheep –'

'He's just so determined to get that fox!' Bran's voice was high with anguish. 'Cafall! *Tyrd yma!* Leave it!'

Will's uncle looked at Bran as if he could not believe what he had heard. Then he looked down at Will. He said, puzzled, '*What fox?*'

Horror exploded in Will's brain, as suddenly he understood, and he cried out. But it was too late. The grey fox in the field swung about and came leaping straight at them, with Cafall at his heels. At the last moment it curved sideways and leapt at one of the sheep that now milled terrified round the gate, and sank its teeth into the woolly throat. The sheep screamed. Cafall sprang at the fox. Twenty yards away, Caradog Prichard let out a great furious shout, lifted his gun, and shot Cafall full in the chest.

'Cafall!' Bran's cry of loving horror struck at Will so that for a second he closed his eyes in pain; he knew that the grief in it would ring in his ears for ever.

The grey fox stood waiting for Will to look at it, grinning, red tongue lolling from a mouth dripping brighter with red blood. It stared straight at him with an unmistakable sneering snarl. Then it loped off across the field, straight as an arrow, and disappeared over the far hedge.

Bran was on his knees by the dog, sobbing, cradling the white head on his lap. He called desperately to Cafall, fondling his ears, dropping his cheek just once, in longing, to rest against the smooth neck. But there was nothing to be done. The chest was a shattered ruin. The silver eyes were glazed, unblinking. Cafall was dead.

'Murdering bloody dog!' Prichard was babbling with fury still, in a kind of savage contentment. 'He'll kill no more of my sheep! A damn good riddance!'

'He was just after the fox. He was trying to save your old sheep!' Bran choked on his words, and wept.

'What are you talking about? A fox? *Dammo*, boy, you are as mad as the dog.' Prichard broke the shell out of his gun, his pudgy face contemptuous.

Owen Davies was down on his knees beside Bran. 'Come, *bachgen*,' he said, his voice gentle. 'There was no fox anywhere. Cafall was going for the sheep, there is no question. We all saw. He was a lovely dog, a beauty' – his voice shook, and he cleared his throat – 'but he must have gone bad in the head. I cannot say that I would not have shot him myself, in Caradog's place. That is the right of it. Once a dog turns killer, it is the only thing to do.'

His arm was tight round Bran's shoulders. Bran looked up at the rest of them, blindly tugging off his glasses and rubbing a hand over his eyes. He said, high, incredulous, 'But did none of you see the fox? The big grey fox that Cafall jumped as it went to kill the sheep?'

John Rowlands said, his voice deep and compassionate, 'No, Bran.'

'There was no fox, Bran,' David Evans said. 'I'm sorry, boy *bach*. Come on, now. Let your father take you to Clwyd. We will bring Cafall after you.'

'Ah,' said Prichard with a sniff. 'You can get that carrion out of my yard as soon as you like, yes. And pay the vet's bill when I have had that sheep seen to, as well.'

'*Cae dy geg*, Caradog Prichard,' said Will's uncle sharply. 'There will be talk of all this sheep attacking business later. You can have a little feeling for the boy, surely.'

Caradog Prichard looked at him, his small eyes bright and expressionless. He motioned to one of his men to take the wounded sheep away. Then he spat, casually, on the ground, and walked off to his farmhouse. A woman was standing there in the doorway. She had not moved through everything that had happened.

Bran's father helped him to his feet, and led him away. Bran seemed dazed. He looked at Will blankly, as if he had not been there.

David Evans said glumly, 'Wait a minute. There is some sacking in the car. I will come and find it.'

John Rowlands stood beside Will in the fine rain, sucking at an empty pipe, looking reflectively down at the still white body with the dreadful red gash in its chest. He said, 'And did you see this fox, Will Stanton?'

'Yes,' Will said. 'Of course. It was in front of us as clear as you are now. It had tried to attack us on Bird Rock, and Cafall chased it down here. But none of you could see it. So nobody will ever believe us, will they?'

John Rowlands was silent for a moment, his creased brown face unreadable. Then he said, 'Sometimes in these mountains there are things it is very hard to believe, even when you have seen them with your own eyes. For instance, there is Cafall, and with our eyes we saw him alone jump at that sheep. And indeed something did sink its teeth into the sheep's throat and must have got a bloody mouth doing it, for there was blood all over the sheep's fleece and it is lucky to be alive. And yet it is a strange thing, which will not go out of my mind – that although poor Cafall lies there with his own blood all over his broken chest, *there is no blood on his mouth at all.*'

PART TWO
The Sleepers

The Girl from the Mountains

Will said, 'Excuse me, Mr Davies, is Bran home from school yet?'

Owen Davies jerked upright. He had been bent over the engine of a tractor in one of the farm outhouses; his thin hair was ruffled and his face smeared with oil.

'I'm sorry,' Will said. 'I made you jump.'

'No, no, boy, that is all right. I was just a bit further away than this engine, I think . . .' He made the quick apologetic grimace that seemed to be as near as he ever came to a smile. All the lines on his thin face seemed to lead nowhere, Will thought: no expression, ever. 'Bran is home, yes. I think you will find him in the house. Or up by . . .' His light, worried voice trailed away.

Will said softly, 'By Cafall.' They had buried the dog the evening before, up on the lower slope of the mountain, with a heavy stone over the grave to keep predators away.

'Yes, I think so. Up there,' Owen Davies said.

Will wanted suddenly to say something, but the words were slippery. 'Mr Davies, I'm sorry about that. All of it. Yesterday. It was awful.'

'Well, yes now, thank you.' Owen Davies was embarrassed, flinching from the contact of emotion. He said, looking down into the tractor's engine, 'It couldn't be helped. You can never tell when a dog may take it into his head to go for the sheep. It is one in a million, but it can happen. Even the best dog in the world . . .' He looked up suddenly, and for once his eyes met Will's, though they seemed to be looking not at him but beyond, into the future or the past. His voice came firmer, like that of a younger man. 'I do think, mind you, that Caradog Prichard was very ready to shoot the dog. That is something very drastic, and not done normally to another man's creature, at any rate not before his face. We were all there, it would have been nothing to catch Cafall. And a sheep-chaser can sometimes be given a home, somewhere away from sheep, without having to be killed . . . But I cannot say this to Bran, and nor must you either. It would not help him.'

His eyes flicked away again, and Will watched, fascinated and disturbed, as the bright echo of another time dropped away like a coat and left the familiar drab Owen Davies with his humourless, slightly guilty air.

'Well,' Will said. 'I think you are right, but no, I wouldn't mention that to· Bran. I'll go and look for him now.'

'Yes,' Owen Davies said eagerly, turning his anxious, helpless face to the hills. 'Yes, you could help him, I believe.'

But Will knew, as he trudged along the muddy lane, that there was small chance he, or anyone of the Light, could comfort Bran.

When he reached the edge of the valley, where the land began to climb, he saw very small and distant above him, halfway up the mountain, the figure of John Rowlands like a toy man. His two dogs, black-and-white specks, moved to and fro. Will looked, irresolute, at the place further down the valley where Bran would be gone to earth: alone with his misery. Then on an instinct he began to climb straight up, through the bracken and gorse. John Rowlands might be a good person to talk to, first.

Nevertheless it was Bran he first saw.

He came upon him suddenly, without expecting it. He was partway up the slope, panting hard as he still did on rising ground, and as he paused for breath, raising his head, he saw there before him sitting on a rock the familiar figure: dark jeans and sweater, white hair like a beacon, smoky glasses over the pale eyes. But the glasses were not visible now, nor the eyes, for Bran sat with his head bent down, immobile, even though Will knew he must have heard the noisy puffing of his approach.

He said, 'Hallo, Bran.'

Bran raised his head slowly, but said nothing.

Will said, 'There was no dog like him, ever, anywhere.'

'No, there was not,' Bran said. His voice was small and husky; he sounded tired.

Will cast about to find words of comfort, but his mind could not help but use the wisdom of an Old One, and that was not the way to reach Bran. He said, 'It was a man that killed him, Bran, but that is the price we have to pay for the freedom of men on the earth. That they can do the bad things as well as the good. There are shadows in the pattern, as well as sunlight. Just as you once told me, Cafall was no ordinary dog. He was a part of the long pattern, like the stars and the sea. And nobody could have played his part better, nobody in the whole world.'

The valley was quiet under its brooding grey sky; Will heard only a song thrush trifling from a tree, the scattered voices of sheep on the slopes; the faint humming, from the distant road, of a passing car.

Bran raised his head and took off his glasses; the tawny eyes were swollen and red-rimmed in his white face. He sat there hunched, knees bent up, arms dangling limp over them.

'Go away,' he said. 'Go away. I wish you had never come here. I wish I had never heard of the Light and the Dark, and your damned old Merriman and his rhymes. If I had your golden harp now I would throw it in the sea. I am not a part of your stupid quest any more, I don't care what happens to it. And Cafall was never a part of it either, or a part of your pretty pattern. He was my dog, and I loved him more than anything in the world, and now he is dead. *Go away.*'

The red-rimmed eyes stared cold and unwinking at Will for a long moment, and then Bran put back his smoky glasses and turned his head to look out across the valley. It was a dismissal. Without a word, Will stood straight again and plodded on up the hill.

It seemed a long time before he reached John Rowlands. The lean, leathery sheepman was crouched half-kneeling over a broken fence, mending it from a prickly skein of barbed wire. He sat back on his heels as Will came panting up, and looked at him through narrowed eyes, his seamed brown face crinkled against the brightness of the sky. With no greeting, he said, 'This is the top level of the Clwyd pasture here. The hill farms have the grazing beyond – the fence is to keep our sheep below. But they are crafty beggars at breaking it, especially now the rams are out.'

Will nodded, miserably.

John Rowlands looked at him for a moment, then got up and beckoned him over to a high outcropping of rock a little way up the mountain. They sat down on its lee side; even there the place was like a lookout post, governing the whole valley. Will glanced round him briefly, his senses alert, but the Grey King still lay withdrawn; the valley was as quiescent as it had been since the moment Cafall had died.

John Rowlands said, 'There is the rest of the fence to check, but I am ready for a break. I have a thermos here. Would you like a mouthful of tea, Will?'

He gave him the thermos top brimming with bitter brown tea. Will surprised himself by drinking thirstily. When he had finished, John Rowlands said softly, 'Did you know you were sitting near Cadfan's Way, here?'

Will looked at him sharply, and it was not the look of an eleven-year-old and he did not trouble to disguise the fact. 'Yes,' he said. 'Of course I did. And you knew that I knew, and that's why you mentioned it.'

John Rowlands sighed and poured himself some tea. 'I dare say,' he said in a curious tone that had envy in it, 'that you could now walk blindfold all the way from Tywyn to Machynlleth over the hills on Cadfan's Way, even though you have never been to this country before.'

Will pushed back his straight brown hair, damp on his forehead from the climbing. 'The Old Ways are all over Britain,' he said, 'and we can follow one anywhere, once we have found it. Yes.' He looked out across the valley. 'It was Bran's dog who found it for me up here, in the beginning,' he said sadly.

John Rowlands pushed back his cloth cap, scratched his head and pulled it forward again. 'I have heard of you people,' he said. 'All my life, on and off, though not so much these days. More when I was a boy. I even used to think I'd met one of you, once, when I was very young, though I dare say it was only a dream . . . And now I have been thinking about the way the dog died, and I have talked a bit to young Bran.'

He broke off, and Will looked nervously to see what he might say next, but did not choose to use his art to find out.

'And I think, Will Stanton,' said the sheepman, 'that I ought to be helping you in any way that you might need. But I do not want to know what you are doing, I do not want you to explain it to me at all.'

Will felt suddenly as if the sun had burst out. 'Thank you,' he said. The smaller of John Rowlands's dogs, Tip, came quietly over and sat down at his feet, and he rubbed the silky ears.

John Rowlands looked down over the bracken-brown slope; Will's gaze followed his. Just above the blackened land where the fire had grazed, they could see the tiny figure that was Bran, sitting hunched with his back to them, his white head propped on his knees.

'This is a very bad time for Bran Davies,' the shepherd said.

'I'm glad he talked to you,' Will said bleakly. 'He wouldn't talk to me. Not that I blame him. He'll be so lonely, without Cafall. I mean, Mr Davies is nice, but not exactly . . . and not having any mother, too, that makes it worse.'

'Bran never knew his mother,' John Rowlands said. 'He was too small.'

Will said curiously, 'What was she like?'

Rowlands drank his tea, shook the cup dry and screwed it back on the flask.

'Her name was Gwen,' he said. He held the flask absentmindedly in his hands, looking past it into his memory. 'She was one of the prettiest things you will ever see. Small, with a clear fair skin and black hair, and blue eyes like speedwell, and a smiling light in her face that was like music. But she was a strange wild girl too. Out of the mountains she came, and never would tell where she came from, or how . . .'

He turned abruptly and looked hard at Will, with the dark eyes that seemed always to be narrowed against fierce weather. 'I should have thought,' he said with sudden belligerence, 'that being what you are, you would know all about Bran.'

Will said gently, 'I don't know anything about Bran, except what he has told me. We are not really so very different from you, Mr Rowlands, most of us. Only our masters are different. We do know many things, but they are not things that intrude on the lives of men. In that, we are like anyone else – we know only what we have lived through, or what somebody has told us.'

John Rowlands nodded his head, relenting. He opened his mouth to say something, stopped, pulled his pipe from his pocket and poked at its contents with one finger. 'Well,' he said slowly, 'perhaps I should tell you the story from the start. It will help you to understand Bran. He knows some of it well enough himself – indeed he thinks about it so much, on his own, that I wish he had never been told.'

Will said nothing. He sat closer to Tip, and put one arm round his neck.

John Rowlands lit his pipe. He said, through the first cloud of smoke, 'It was when Owen Davies was a young man, working at Prichard's Farm. Old Mr Prichard was alive in those days. Caradog worked for his father too, waiting to take over and run the place, though he wasn't a patch on Owen for work . . . Owen was sheepman for Prichard. A solitary chap he was, even then. He was living in a cottage on his own. Out on the moor, closer to the sheep than to the farm.' He puffed out some more smoke, and glanced at Will. 'You have been at that cottage. It is deserted now. Nobody has lived there for years.'

'That place? Where you left the sheep, after –' Startled, Will saw again in his mind the figure of John Rowlands staggering into the little empty stone house in the bracken, with the wounded sheep draped over his shoulders and blood from its fleece on his neck. The little house from which, when they had come back half an hour later, the hurt sheep had vanished without any trace.

'That place. Yes. And one wild night in the winter, with rain and a north wind blowing, there was a knocking at Owen's door. It was a girl, out of nowhere, half-frozen with walking through the storm. And worn out from carrying her baby.'

'Her baby?'

John Rowlands looked down the mountain at Bran's hunched figure, sitting lonely on his rock. 'A sturdy little chap the baby was, just a few months old. She had him in a kind of sling on her back. The only strange thing about him, Owen saw, was that he had no colour in him. White face, white hair, white eyebrows, and very odd tawny eyes like the eyes of an owl . . .'

Will said slowly, 'I see.'

'Owen took the girl in,' John Rowlands said. 'He got her back to life, gradually, with much care, that night and the day after – and the baby too, though babies are tough creatures and he was not in such a bad way. And before twenty-four hours were even gone, Owen Davies was more in love with that strange beautiful girl than I have ever seen a man love a woman. He had never loved anyone much before. Very shy, was Owen. It was like a dam bursting . . . With a man like that, it is dangerous – when at last he loves, he gives all his heart without care or thinking, and it may never go back to him for the rest of his life.' He stopped for a moment, compassion softening his weather-lined face, and sat in silence. Then he said, 'Well. There they were, then. The next day Owen went off to the sheep, leaving the girl to rest in the cottage. On the way home he stopped at my house, on Clwyd here, to get some milk for the baby. We had always been friends since he was a boy, even though I am older. I was not there, but my wife was, and he told her about Gwen and the baby. My Blodwen has a warm heart and a good ear. She said he was like a man on fire, glowing, he had to tell somebody . . .'

Far down on the lower slope, Bran got up from his rock and began roaming aimlessly through the bracken, peering about as though he were looking for something.

'When Owen came back to his cottage,' John Rowlands said, 'he heard screaming. He had never heard a woman scream before. There was a strange dog outside the door. Caradog Prichard's dog. Owen went into the house like a wire snapping, and he found the girl struggling with Caradog. He had come looking to see why Owen had not been at work the day before, had Caradog, and found Gwen there instead, and decided in his dirty way that she must be a light woman, and easy for him to take if he fancied her . . .' John Rowlands leaned deliberately to one side and spat into the grass. 'Excuse me, Will,' he said, 'but that is how I feel when my mouth has been talking about Caradog Prichard.'

'What happened? What did he do?' Will was lost in wonder at this mist of romance surrounding dim, ordinary Owen Davies.

'Owen? He went mad. He has never been a fighter, but he threw Caradog out of the door, and went after him, and he broke his nose and knocked out two of his teeth. Then I arrived, and a good thing I did or he would have killed the man. Blodwen had sent me with some things for the baby. I took Caradog home. He wouldn't have the doctor called. Afraid of the scandal, he was. I cannot say I had very much sympathy for him. His nose has not looked quite the same shape since.'

He glanced down the slope again. Bran's white head was still bent over the ground, as he moved slowly, meaninglessly to and fro.

'Bran may be glad of your company soon, Will. There is not much more to tell, really. One more day and one more night the girl Gwen stayed with Owen in the cottage, and he asked her to marry him. He was such a happy man, the light shone out of him. We saw them for part of that day, and she seemed just as joyful too. But then, just about dawn on the next morning, the fourth day, Owen was wakened by the baby's crying, and Gwen was not there. She had vanished. No one knew where she had gone. And she never came back.'

Will said, 'Bran told me she died.'

'Bran knows she disappeared,' John Rowlands said. 'But perhaps it is more comfortable to believe that your mother died than to think of her running away and leaving you without a second thought.'

'That's what she did? Just disappeared and left the baby behind?'

John Rowlands nodded. 'And a note. It said: *His name is Bran. Thank you, Owen Davies.* And that was all. Wherever she went, she has never been seen or heard of since, nor will she ever be. Owen came to us with the baby that morning. He was out of his head, crazy with losing Gwen. He went up into the hills, and did not come down for three days. Looking for her, you see. People heard him calling, *Gwennie, Gwennie* . . . Blodwen and Mrs Evans, your auntie, looked after Bran between them. A good baby, he was . . . Old man Prichard gave Owen the sack, of course. About that time your uncle David lost a man, so he took Owen on, and Owen moved to the cottage on Clwyd where he lives now.'

'And he brought Bran up as his son,' Will said.

'That's right. With everybody's help. There was a bit of a to-do, but he was allowed to adopt the boy in the end. Most people ended up thinking Bran really was Owen's son. And the one thing that Bran has never been told is that he is not – he believes that Owen is his father, and you must take care you never suggest anything different.'

'I shall,' Will said.

'Yes. I have no worries about you . . . Sometimes I think Owen believes Bran is his real son too. He was always strict chapel, you see, and afterwards he turned even more to his religion. Perhaps you cannot understand this quite, Will *bach*, but because Owen knew it was wrong by the rules of his faith to live those few days alone in the same house with Gwen, then he began to feel that it was just as much wrong as if he and Gwennie, not married to each other, had had a baby together. As if the two of them *had* produced Bran. So when he thinks of Bran – still, to this day – it is mostly with love, but a little bit – with guilt. For no good reason, mind, except in his own conscience. He has too much conscience, has Owen. The people do not care, even the people of his chapel – they think Bran is his natural son, but the tut-tutting was over long ago. They have brains enough to judge a man by what he has proved himself to be, not by some mistake he may or may not have made a long time ago.'

John Rowlands sighed, and stretched, knocked out his pipe and ground the ashes into the earth. He stood up; the dogs jumped to his side. He looked down at Will.

'There was all this at the back,' he said, 'when Caradog Prichard shot Bran Davies's dog.'

Will picked a single blossom from a gorse bush beside him; it shone bright yellow on his grubby hand. 'People are very complicated,' he said sadly.

'So they are,' John Rowlands said. His voice deepened a little, louder and clearer than it had been. 'But when the battles between you and your adversaries are done, Will Stanton, in the end the fate of all the world will depend on just those people, and on how many of them are good or bad, stupid or wise. And indeed it is all so complicated that I would not dare foretell what they will do with their world. Our world.' He whistled softly. '*Tyrd yma*, Pen, Tip.'

Carefully he picked up his loop of barbed wire, and with the dogs following, he walked away beside the fence, over the hill.

The Grey King

Will went slowly across the slope towards Bran. It was a grey day now; the rain had fallen all night, and there was more to come. The sky was lowering, ominous, and all the mountains were lost in ragged cloud. Will thought: *the breath of the Brenin Llwyd* . . .

He saw Bran begin climbing away up the hill, diagonally, in an obvious effort to avoid him. Will paused, and decided to give up. A ridiculous game of dodging across the mountain would do no one any good. And besides, the harp had to be taken to a safe place.

He set off through the wet bracken on the long muddy walk to the far side of Caradog Prichard's farm. His trousers were already soaked, in spite of Wellington boots borrowed from Aunt Jen. Partway, he crossed the land that had been swept by the fire, and a thin mud of black ash clung to his boots.

Will strode along moodily. He glanced round now and then in case Caradog Prichard were about, but the fields were deserted, and oddly silent. No birds sang today; even the sheep seemed quiet, and there was seldom the sound of a car drifting from the valley road. It was as if all the grey valley waited for something. Will tried to sense the mood of the place more accurately, but all the time now his mind was gradually filling again with the enmity of the Grey King, growing, growing, a whisper grown to a call, soon to grow to a furious shout. It was difficult to find attention for much else.

He came to the slate-roofed shelter where he had hidden the harp among the stacked bales of hay. The force of his own spell brought him up standing, ten feet away, as though he had walked into a glass wall.

Will smiled. Then to break the enchantment in the way appointed, he began very softly to sing. It was a spell-song of the Old Speech, and its words were not like the words of human speech, but more indefinite, a matter of nuance of sound. He was a good singer, well-taught, and the high clear notes flowed softly through the gloomy air like rays of light. Will felt the force of the resisting spell melt away. He came to the end of the verse.

Caradog Prichard's voice said coldly behind him, 'Proper little nightingale, isn't it?'

Will froze. He turned slowly and stood in silence, looking at Prichard's pasty, full-cheeked face, with its crooked nose, and eyes bright as black currants.

'Well?' Prichard said impatiently. 'What do you think you are doing here, standing in the middle of my field singing to the hedge? Are you mad, boy?'

Will gaped, changing his face subtly to an expression of total foolishness. 'It was the song. I just thought of it, I wanted to try it out. They say you're a poet, you ought to understand.' He let his voice drop, conspiratorially. 'I write songs, sometimes, you see. But please don't tell anyone. They always laugh. They think it's stupid.'

Prichard said: 'Your uncle?'

'Everyone at home.'

Prichard squinted at him suspiciously. The proud word 'poet' had made its effect, but he was not the kind of man to relax unwarily, or for long. He said contemptuously, 'Oh, the English – they know nothing of music, I am not surprised. Clods, they are. You have a very good voice, for an English boy.' Then his voice sharpened suddenly. 'But you weren't singing English, were you?'

'No,' Will said.

'What, then?'

Will beamed at him confidentially. 'Nothing, really. They were just nonsense words that seemed to go with the tune. *You* know.'

But the fish did not bite. Prichard's eyes narrowed. He looked in a quick nervous movement up the valley towards the mountains, and then back at Will. He said abruptly, 'I don't like you, English boy. Something funny about you, there is. All this about songs and singing does not explain why you are standing here on my land.'

'Taking a short cut, that's all,' Will said. 'I wasn't hurting anything, honestly.'

'Short cut, is it? From where to where? Your uncle's land is all over there, where you came from, and nothing is on the other side of us except moor and mountain. Nothing for you. Go back to Clwyd, nightingale, back to your snivelling little friend who lost his dog. Off. Off out of here!' All at once he was shouting, the pudgy face dusky red. 'Get out! Get out!'

Will sighed. There was only one thing to be done. He had not wanted to risk attracting the closer attention of the Grey King, but it was impossible to leave the harp vulnerable to Caradog Prichard's eye. The man was glaring at him now, clenching his fists in a fit of the same unaccountable vicious rage that Will had seen overtake him before. 'Get out, I tell you!'

There in the open field under the still, grey sky, Will stretched out one arm, with all five fingers stiff and pointing, and said a single quiet word. And Caradog Prichard was caught out of time, immobile, with his mouth half-open and his hand raised pointing, his face frozen in exactly the same ugly anger that had twisted it when he shot the dog Cafall. It was a pity. Will thought bitterly, that he could not be left that way forever.

But no spell lasts forever, and most for only a short breath of time. Quickly Will went forward to the stone shelter, reached in between the bales of hay, and pulled out the gleaming little golden harp. One corner of its frame was caught on an old tattered sack left among the bales; impatiently he tugged both harp and sacking free, bundled them together under his arm. Then he moved round to stand behind Caradog Prichard. Once more he pointed a stiff-fingered hand at him, and spoke a single word. And Caradog Prichard, as if he had never intended to do anything else, plodded off across the field towards his farmhouse without once turning round. When he arrived there, Will knew, he would be convinced that he had gone straight home from the day's work, and he would not have an ounce of memory of Will Stanton standing in a field singing to the sky.

The plodding, paunchy form disappeared over the stile at the end of the field. Will untangled the old sack from the harp's intricate golden frame, and was about to toss it aside when he realized how useful it would be as a covering; a nameless bundle under his arm could be explained away, if he should meet someone, rather more easily than a gleaming and obviously priceless golden harp. As he slid the harp carefully inside the sack, wrinkling his nose at the hay dust puffing out, a movement across the field caught his eye. He glanced up, and for a moment even the harp left his mind.

It was the great grey fox, king of the *milgwn*, creature of the Brenin Llwyd, loping fast along the hedge. In sudden furious hatred Will flung out one pointing arm and shouted a word to stop it, and the big grey animal, no longer on its master's land, tumbled backwards in mid-stride as if it had been snatched up by a sudden tremendous high wind. Picking itself up, it stood staring at Will, red tongue lolling. Then it lifted its long muzzle and gave one low howl, like a dog in trouble.

'It's no good calling,' said Will under his breath. 'You can just stand there till I decide what to do with you.'

But then, involuntarily, he shivered. The air seemed suddenly colder, and across the fields, all around him, he could see creeping in a low ground-mist that he had not noticed before. Slowly it came pouring over the fences, relentless, like some huge crawling creature. From every direction it came, from the mountain, the valley, the lower slopes, and when Will looked back at the grey fox standing stiff-legged in the field, he saw something else that gave a chill of new terror to the mist. The fox was changing colour. With every moment, as he watched, its sleek body and bushy tail grew darker and darker, until it became almost black.

Will stared, frowning. He thought irrelevantly, '*It looks just like Pen.*' And instantly he caught his breath, realizing something that was not irrelevant at all – that it was John Rowlands's dog Pen who, with Cafall, had been accused by Caradog Prichard of the sheep attacks made in reality by the foxes of the Grey King.

Something immeasurably strong was pushing against him, breaking his own enchantment. Whilst Will stood for a moment confused and powerless, the big fox, now black as coal, gave its strange small exultant leap into the air, grinned deliberately at him, and was off, running swiftly across the field. It vanished through the far hedge, in the direction that Caradog Prichard had taken, towards his farm. Will knew exactly what was likely to happen when it got there, and there was nothing he could do. He was held back by the power of the Grey King, and reluctantly now he was facing an idea to which he had not given a thought before: the possibility that this power, much greater than his own, was in fact so great that he might never be able to accomplish his allotted quest.

Setting his teeth, he gripped the shrouded harp beneath his arm and set off across the field towards Clwyd Farm. Carefully he slipped under the barbed wire edging the field, crossed the corner of the next, clambered over the stile leading into the lane. But all the time his steps grew slower and slower, his breathing more laboured. Somehow, there beneath his arm, the harp was growing heavier and heavier, until he could scarcely move for the weight of it. He knew that it was not a matter of his own weakness. Against his resistance, some great enchantment was giving to the precious Thing of Power in his arm a heaviness impossible for any human strength to support. Clutching at the harp, he gasped with pain at its impossible weight, and sank down with it to the ground.

As he crouched there he raised his head and saw that the mist swirled everywhere round him now; all the world was grey-white, featureless. He stared into the mist. And gradually, the mist took shape.

The figure was so huge that at first he could not realize it was there. It stretched wider than the field, and high into the sky. It had shape, but not recognizable earthly shape; Will could see its outline from the corner of his eye, but when he looked directly at any part of it, there was nothing there. Yet there the figure loomed before him, immense and terrible, and he knew that this was a being of greater power than anything he had ever encountered in his life before. Of all the Great Lords of the Dark, none was singly more powerful and dangerous than the Grey King. But because he had remained always from the beginnings of time in his fastnesses among the Cader Idris peaks, never descending to the valleys or lower slopes, none of the Old Ones had ever encountered him, to learn what force he had at his command. So now Will, alone, last and least of the Old Ones, faced him with no defence but the inborn magic of the Light and his own wits.

A voice came from the misty shape, both sweet and terrible. It filled the air like the mist itself, and Will could not tell what language it spoke, nor whether it spoke to the hearing of the ears; he knew only that the things it said were instantly in his own mind.

'You may not wake the Sleepers, Old One,' said the voice. 'I will prevent you. This is my land, and in it they shall sleep forever, as they have slept these many centuries. Your harp shall not wake them. I will prevent you.'

Will sat in a small crumpled heap, his arms across the harp he could no longer hold. 'It is my quest,' he said. 'You know that I must follow it.'

'Go back,' said the voice, blowing through his mind like the wind. 'Go back. Take the harp safely with you, a Thing of Power for the Light and your masters. I shall let you go, if you go back now and leave my land. You have won that much.' The voice grew harder, more chill than the mist. 'But if you seek the Sleepers, I shall destroy you, and the golden harp as well.'

'No,' Will said. 'I am of the Light. You cannot destroy me.'

'It will not differ greatly from destruction,' the voice said. 'Come now. You know that, Old One.' It grew softer, more sibilant and nasty, as if caressing an evil thought; Will suddenly remembered the lord in the sky-blue robe.

'The powers of the Dark and the Light are equal in force, but we differ a little in our . . . treatment . . . of those we may bring under our will.' The voice crawled like a slug over Will's skin. 'Go back, Old One. I shall not warn the Light again.'

Summoning all his confidence, Will scrambled up, leaving the harp on the ground at his feet. He made a mocking little bow to the grey mistiness that he knew, now, he must not look at directly. 'You have given your warning, Majesty,' he said, 'and I have heard it. But it will make no difference. The Dark can never turn the mind of the Light. Nor may it hinder the taking of a Thing of Power once it has been rightly claimed. Take your spell off the golden harp. You have no right to touch it with enchantment.'

The mist swirled darker; the voice grew colder, more remote. 'The harp is not spellbound, Old One. Take it from the sack.'

Will bent down. He tried once more to pick up the sacking-wrapped harp, but it would not move; it might have been a rock rooted deep in the land. Then he pulled the sacking aside to uncover the harp, and took it up, and the shining gold thing came into his hand as lightly as ever it had.

He looked down at the sack. 'There is something else there.'

'Of course,' said the Grey King.

Will ripped the half-rotted sacking so that it lay open; it still seemed quite empty, as it had from the first. Then he noticed in one fold a small highly-polished white stone, no bigger than a pebble. He bent to pick it up. It would not move.

He said slowly, 'It is a warestone.'

'Yes,' the voice said.

'Your warestone. A channel for the Dark. So that when it is left in a certain place, you may know all that is happening in that place, and may put into it your will to make other things happen. It was hidden in that old sack all the time.' A sudden memory flickered in his mind. 'No wonder I lost my hold on the fox of the *milgwn*.'

Out of the mist, laughter came. It was a terrifying sound, like the first rattle of an avalanche. Then instead, and worse, the voice came whispering. 'A warestone of the Dark has no value for the Light. Give it me.'

'You had put it on Caradog Prichard's farm,' Will said. 'Why? He is your creature anyway, you have no need of a warestone for him.'

'That fool is none of mine,' the Grey King said contemptuously. 'If the Dark showed itself to him he would melt with fear like butter in the sun. No, he is not of the Dark. But he is very useful. A man so wrapped in his own ill-will is a gift to the Dark from the earth. It is so easy to give him suitable ideas . . . Very useful, indeed.'

Will said quietly. 'There are such men, of an opposite kind, who unwittingly serve the Light too.'

'Ah,' said the voice slyly, 'but not so many, Old One. Not so many, I think.' It sharpened again, and the mist swirled colder. 'Give me the warestone. It will not work against you, but neither will it work for you. It will always cleave to the earth at the touch of the Light – as would a warestone of yours, if you had one, at my touch.'

'I have no need of one,' Will said. 'Certainly no need of yours. Take it.'

'Stand away. I shall take it and be gone. And if in one night and one day you are not also gone, from this my land, you will cease to exist by the standards of men, Old One. You shall not hinder us, not with your six Signs nor your harp of gold.' The voice rose and swelled suddenly like a high wind. 'For our time is almost come, in spite of you, and the Dark is rising, *the Dark is rising!*'

The words roared through Will's mind as the mist swirled dark and chill round his face, obscuring everything, even the ground beneath his feet. He could no longer see the harp, but only feel it clutched close in both his arms. He staggered giddily, and a terrible chill struck into all the length of his body.

Then it was gone. And he stood in the lane between the hedges, with the harp clasped to his chest, and the valley was clear all about him under the grey sky, and at his feet an empty piece of old sacking lay.

Shakily Will bent and wrapped the harp again, and set off for Clwyd Farm.

He slipped upstairs to his room to hide the harp, calling a greeting to Aunt Jen. She called back over her shoulder without turning, stirring a pot carefully at the stove. But when Will came downstairs again, the big kitchen seemed full of people. His uncle and Rhys were roving restlessly about, faces taut with concern. John Rowlands had just come through the door.

'Did you see him?' Rhys burst out anxiously to Rowlands.

John Rowlands's weather-lined brown face gained a few extra lines as his eyebrows rose. 'Who should I have seen?'

David Evans pulled out a chair and dropped wearily into it. He sighed. 'Caradog Prichard was outside just now. There is no end to this madness. He claims that another of his sheep was worried by a dog this afternoon – killed, this one. He says that it happened right there in his yard, again, and that he and his wife saw everything. And he swears up and down that the dog was Pen.'

'Waving his gun about, he was, the damn lunatic,' Rhys said angrily. 'He would have shot the dog for sure, if you and Pen had been here. Thank God you were not.'

John Rowlands said mildly, 'I am surprised he was not waiting for us at the gate.'

'I told him you were out late on the mountain, after some ewes,' said Will's uncle, his neat head bent, despondent. 'No doubt the fool will be out there looking for you.'

'Shoot a sheep he will, I shouldn't be surprised,' John Rowlands said. 'If he can find the black ewe, that is.'

But David Evans was too shaken to smile. 'Let him do that, and I will have him off to Tywyn police station, dogs or no dogs. I don't like it, John Rowlands. The man is acting as if . . . I don't know, I really think that his wits have begun to turn. Raving, he was. Dogs killing sheep is a bad thing, heaven knows, but he was acting as wild as if it was children had been killed. If he had had children. I think it is as well he has not.'

'Pen has been with me all day, without a break,' John Rowlands said, his deep voice tranquil.

'Of course he has,' said Rhys. 'But Caradog Prichard would not believe that even if he had watched you every minute of the day with his own eyes. He is that bad. And he will be back tomorrow, there is no doubt at all.'

'Perhaps Betty Prichard will be able to make him see reason before then,' Aunt Jen said. 'Though she has never had much luck before, goodness knows. He must be a hard man to be married to, that one.'

John Rowlands looked at Will's uncle. 'What shall we do?'

'I don't know,' David Evans said, shaking his head morosely. 'What do you think?'

'Well,' John Rowlands said, 'I was thinking that if you are not using the Land-Rover in the morning, I might go very early up the valley and leave Pen for a few days with Idris Jones Ty-Bont.'

Will's uncle lifted his head, his face brightening for the first time. 'Good. Very good.'

'Jones Ty-Bont owes you a favour, for borrowing the tractor this summer. He is a good fellow anyway. And one of his dogs is from the same litter as Pen.'

'That is a very good idea,' Rhys said simply. 'And we are out of plugs for the chain saw. You can pick one up in Abergynolwyn coming back.'

Rowlands laughed. 'All settled, then.'

'Mr Rowlands,' Will said. 'Could I come too?'

They had not noticed he was there; heads turned in surprise to where he stood on the stairs.

'Come and welcome,' John Rowlands said.

'That would be nice,' Aunt Jen said. 'I was just thinking yesterday that we hadn't taken you to Tal y Llyn yet. That's the lake, up there. Idris Jones's farm is right next to it.'

'Caradog Prichard will not dream that the dog might be there,' said David Evans. 'It will give him time to cool off.'

'And if the sheep-killing goes on –' Rhys said. Deliberately he left the sentence hanging.

'There's a thought now,' Will's aunt said. 'We must make sure Caradog thinks Pen is still here. Then if he sees Pen with his own eyes savage a sheep again tomorrow, there will be a quick answer for him.'

'Good, then,' John Rowlands said. 'Pen is at home having his supper, I think I will go and join him. We will leave at five-thirty, Will. Caradog Prichard is not the earliest riser in the world.'

'Perhaps young Bran would like to go with you, being a Saturday,' said David Evans, leaning back relaxed now in his chair.

'I don't think so,' Will said.

The Pleasant Lake

Will expected to be the only one stirring in the house, at five in the morning, but his Aunt Jen was up before him. She gave him a cup of tea, and a big slab of homemade bread and butter.

'Cold out there, early,' she said. 'You'll do better with something inside you.'

'Bread and butter tastes five times as good here as anywhere else,' said Will. Glancing up as he chewed, he saw her watching him with a funny, wry half-smile.

'The picture of health you are,' she said. 'Just like your big brother Stephen, at your age. Nobody would guess how ill you were, not so long ago. But my goodness me, it's not exactly a rest cure we've been giving you. The fire, and all this business with the sheep-killing –'

'Exciting,' said Will, muffled, through a mouthful.

'Well, yes,' said Aunt Jen. 'Indeed, in a place where nothing out of the ordinary ever happens, usually, from one year's end to the next. I think I have had enough excitement to be getting along with, for now.'

Will said lightly, deliberately, 'I suppose the last real stir was when Bran's mother came.'

'Ah,' his aunt said. Her pleasant, cosy face was unreadable. 'You've heard about that, have you? I suppose John Rowlands told you. He is a kind soul,

Shoni mawr, no doubt he had his reasons. Tell me, Will, have you had some sort of a quarrel with Bran?'

Will thought: *and that's what you wanted to ask me, with the cup of tea, because you are a kind soul too, and can feel Bran's distress . . . And I wish I could be properly honest with you.*

'No,' he said. 'But losing Cafall has been so bad for him that I think he just wants to be alone. For a while.'

'Poor lad.' She shook her head. 'Be patient with him. He's a lonely boy, and had a strange life, in some ways. It's been wonderful for him having you here, until this spoiled everything.'

A small pain shot through Will's forearm; he clutched it, and found it came from the scar of the Light, his burned-in brand.

He said suddenly, 'Did she never come back at all, ever, Auntie Jen? Bran's mother? How could she just go off and leave him, like that?'

'I don't know,' his aunt said. 'But no, there was no sign of her ever again.'

'In one minute, to go away for ever . . . I think that must bother Bran a lot.'

She looked at him sharply. 'Has he ever said anything about it?'

'Oh, no, of course not. We've never talked about that. I just felt – I'm just sure it must bother him, underneath.'

'You're a funny boy yourself,' said his aunt curiously. 'Sometimes you sound like an old man. Comes from having so many brothers and sisters older than you, I suppose . . . Perhaps you understand Bran better than most boys could.'

She hesitated for a moment, then drew her chair closer. 'I will tell you something,' she said, 'in case it might help Bran. I know you have sense enough not to tell him about it. I think Gwen, his mother, had some great trouble in her past life that she could do nothing about, and that because of that she felt she had to give Bran a life that would be free of it. She knew Owen Davies was a good man and would look after the boy, but she also knew that she simply did not love Owen as deeply as he loved her, not enough to marry him. When things turn out like that, there is nothing a woman can do. It is kindest to go away.' She paused. 'Not kind to leave Bran, you might say.'

'That was just exactly what I was going to say,' said Will.

'Well,' said his aunt. 'Gwen said something to me, in those few days she was here, when we were alone once. I have never talked about it, but I have never forgotten. She said: *If you have once betrayed a great trust, you dare not let yourself be trusted again, because a second betrayal would be the end of the world.* I don't know if you can understand that.'

'You mean she was frightened of what she might do?'

'And more frightened of what she had done. Whatever it was.'

'So she ran away. Poor Bran,' said Will.

'Poor Owen Davies,' said his aunt.

There was a gentle knock at the door, and John Rowlands put his head inside. '*Bore da*,' he said. 'Ready, Will?'

'*Bore da*, John,' said Aunt Jen, smiling at him.

Pulling on his jacket, Will turned suddenly and gave her a clumsy hug. 'Thank you, Aunt Jen.'

The smile brightened with pleasure and surprise. 'We'll see you when we see you,' she said.

John Rowlands said, as he started the car outside the farm gate, 'Fond of you, your auntie.'

Will held open the door for Pen to scramble up; the dog jumped over the seat into the back, and lay docile on the floor.

'I'm fond of her too, very. So's my mum.'

'Be careful then, won't you?' Rowlands said. His seamed brown face was innocent of all expression, but the words had force. Will looked at him rather coldly.

'What do you mean?'

'Well,' Rowlands said carefully, turning the Land-Rover into the road. 'I am not at all sure what it is that is going on all around us, Will *bach*, or where it is leading. But those men who know anything at all about the Light also know that there is a fierceness to its power, like the bare sword of the law, or the white burning of the sun.' Suddenly his voice sounded to Will very strong, and very Welsh. 'At the very heart, that is. Other things, like humanity, and mercy, and charity, that most good men hold more precious than all else, they do not come first for the Light. Oh, sometimes they are there; often, indeed. But in the very long run the concern of you people is with the absolute good, ahead of all else. You are like fanatics. Your masters, at any rate. Like the old Crusaders – oh, like certain groups in every belief, though this is not a matter of religion, of course. At the centre of the Light there is a cold white flame, just as at the centre of the Dark there is a great black pit bottomless as the Universe.'

His warm, deep voice ended, and there was only the roar of the engine. Will looked out over the grey-misted fields, silent.

'There was a great long speech, now,' John Rowlands said awkwardly. 'But I was only saying, be careful not to forget that there are people in this valley who can be hurt, even in the pursuit of good ends.'

Will heard again in his mind Bran's anguished cry as the dog Cafall was shot dead, and heard his cold dismissal: *go away, go away* . . . And for a second another image, unexpected, flashed into his mind out of the past: the strong, bony face of Merriman his master, first of the Old Ones, cold in judgement of a much-loved figure who, through the frailty of being no more than a man, had once betrayed the cause of the Light.

He sighed. 'I understand what you are saying,' he said sadly. 'But you misjudge us, because you are a man yourself. For us, there is only the destiny. Like a job to be done. We are here simply to save the world from the Dark. Make no mistake, John, the Dark *is* rising, and will take the world to itself very soon if nothing stands in its way. And if that should happen, then there would be no question ever, for anyone, either of warm charity or of cold absolute good, because nothing would exist in the world or in the hearts of men except that bottomless black pit. The charity and the mercy and the humanitarianism are for you, they are the only things by which men are able to exist together in peace. But in this hard case that we the Light are in, confronting the Dark, we can make no use of them. We are fighting a war. We are fighting for life or death – not for our life, remember, since we cannot die. For yours.'

He reached his hand behind him, over the back of the seat, and Pen licked it with his floppy wet tongue.

'Sometimes,' Will said slowly, 'in this sort of a war, it is not possible to pause, to smoothe the way for one human being, because even that one small thing could mean an end of the world for all the rest.'

A fine rain began to mist the windscreen. John Rowlands turned on the wipers, peering forward at the grey world as he drove. He said, 'It is a cold world you live in, *bachgen*. I do not think so far ahead, myself. I would take the one human being over all the principle, all the time.'

Will slumped down low in his seat, curling into a ball, pulling up his knees. 'Oh, so would I,' he said sadly. 'So would I, if I could. It would feel a lot better inside me. But it wouldn't work.'

Behind them, Pen leapt unexpectedly to his feet, barking. Will uncoiled like a startled snake; John Rowlands braked sharply, half-turning, and spoke swift and low to the dog in Welsh. But still Pen stood in the back of the Land-Rover stiff as a stuffed dog, barking furiously, and in the next moment, as if he were observing something outside himself, Will felt his own body jerk stiff as he felt the same force. His finger-nails drove into the palms of his hands.

John Rowlands did not stop the car, though he had slowed to a crawl. He gave one sharp look out of his near window at the moorland, through the mist, and accelerated again. In a moment or two Will felt the tension go out of his limbs, and sat back, gasping. The dog too stopped barking, and in the sudden loud silence lay down meekly on the floor as if he had never moved at all.

Rowlands said, with a tightness in his deep voice, 'We have just come past the cottage. The empty cottage, where we lost the sheep.'

Will said nothing. His breath was coming fast and shallow, as it had when he first came out of the worst of his illness, and he hunched his shoulders and bent his head beneath the fierce weight of the power of the Grey King.

John Rowlands drove faster, pulling the tough little car round blind slate-walled turns. The road curved across the valley; great new slopes rose on its eastern side, swooping up into the sky bare and grey, treacherous with scree. Everywhere they loomed over the gentle green fields, dominant, menacing. And then at last there were signs of side roads, and scattered grey slate-roofed houses, and before them, as Rowlands slowed for a crossroad, Will saw the lake Tal y Llyn.

His aunt had called it the loveliest lake in Wales, but lying dark there in the grey morning, it was more sinister than lovely. On its black still surface not a ripple stirred. It filled the valley floor. Above it reared the first slopes of Cader Idris, the mountain of the Grey King, and beyond, at the far end of the valley, a pass led through the hills – away, Will felt, towards the end of the world. He had himself under control now, but he could feel the tension quivering in his mind. The Grey King had felt his coming, and the awareness of his angry hostility was as clear as if it were shouted aloud. Will knew that it could not be long before one of the watchers, a peregrine curving high over the slopes, would catch clear sight of him. He did not know what would happen then.

John Rowlands turned the Land-Rover down a rough track, away from the lake, and before long they came to a farm tucked beneath the lowest slopes of Cader Idris. Will jumped out to open and close the gate, and as he trudged up into the farmyard he saw a small man in a flat cap come out of the house to greet the car. Dogs were barking. He could see one of them waiting a little way off where the farmer had left it: a sheepdog a little smaller than Pen, but with exactly the same black coat, and the splash of white under the chin.

Rowlands broke off an animated Welsh conversation as Will came up to them. 'Idris, this is a new helper I have – David Evans's nephew Will, from England.'

'How do you do, Mr Jones,' Will said.

Idris Jones Ty-Bont twinkled at him as they shook hands; he had enormous and rather prominent dark eyes that made him look disconcertingly like a bush baby. 'How are you, Will? I hear you have been having fun with our friend Caradog Prichard.'

'We all have,' John Rowlands said grimly. He gave a whistle over his shoulder, and Pen leapt out of the car, glanced up as if seeking permission to leave, and trotted off to greet the other black dog. They circled one another amiably, without barking.

'Lala there is his sister, believe it or not,' Idris Jones said to Will. 'Came from the same litter, they did, over Dinas way. That's a while ago, eh, John? Come along inside now, Megan has just made the tea.'

In the warm kitchen, with stout, smiling Mrs Jones who was almost twice the size of her neat husband, the smell of frying bacon made Will ravenous all over again. He filled himself happily with two fried eggs, thick slices of home-cured bacon, and hot flat Welshcakes, like miniature pancakes flecked with currants. Mrs Jones began instantly chattering away to John Rowlands in a contented flow of Welsh, scarcely ever seeming to draw breath, or to give way to a phrase or two in her husband's light voice, or Rowlands's deep rumble. Clearly she was enjoying relaying all the local gossip, and collecting any that might emanate from Clwyd. Will, full of bacon and well-being, had almost stopped paying attention when he saw John Rowlands, listening, give a sudden start and sit forward, taking his pipe out of his mouth.

Rowlands said, in English, 'Up over the lake, did you say, Idris?'

'That's right,' Farmer Jones said, dutifully switching languages with a quick smile at Will. 'Up on a ledge. I didn't have a chance to get too close, being in a hurry after my own sheep, but I am almost sure it was a Pentref ewe. Not dead very long, I think, the birds had not been at it enough – maybe a day or two. What interested me was the blood on the neck. Quite old, it was, very dark, must have been on the fleece a lot longer than the sheep had been dead. And for a sheep that must have been already wounded, that slope was a hell of a funny place to go. Well, I'll show you later.'

Will and John Rowlands looked at one another.

'You think it's *that* sheep?' Will said. 'The one that vanished?'

'I think it may be,' John Rowlands said.

But later, when Idris Jones took them to see the ewe, he would not let Will come close enough to see.

'Not a nice sight, *bachgen*,' he said, looking doubtfully at Will and resettling the cap on his head. 'A sheep when the ravens have been at her for a day or two is a bit of a mess, if you're not accustomed to it . . . wait you here a minute or two, we will be straight back.'

'All right,' Will said, resigned. But as the two men went on up the steep, slippery mountainside, he sat hastily down in a sudden fit of giddiness, and knew that it certainly would not have been a good idea for him to have gone further on. They were on a slope rising above the lake, a broad unprotected sweep of scree and poor grass broken by ledges and outcrops of granite. Further down the valley the mountain was clothed in dark forests of spruce trees, but here the land was bare, inhospitable. The dead sheep lay on a ledge that seemed to Will totally inaccessible; high above his head it jutted out of the mountain, and the pathetic white heap lying on it was not visible from where he sat now. Nor could he see John Rowlands and Idris Jones, climbing higher with the two black dogs.

Two hundred feet below lay the lake, its stillness broken only by one small dinghy moving lazily out from the small anglers' hotel that nestled beneath the mountains at the opposite side. Will could see no other sign of life anywhere on the rest of the lake, or on either side of the valley. The land seemed gentler now, with subtle colour everywhere, for the sun was breaking out fitfully between scudding clouds.

Then there was a scuffling and stumbling above him, and John Rowlands came down the steep slope, planting his heels firmly into the shale lying loose in the thin grass. Idris Jones and the dogs followed. Rowlands's lined face was bleak.

He said, 'That is the same ewe all right, Will. But how she could have got out of that cottage and up here is just beyond me. It makes no sense at all.' He glanced over his shoulder at Idris Jones, who was shaking his birdlike head in distress. 'Nor to Idris either. I have been telling him the story.'

'Oh,' Will said sadly, without bothering now to dissemble, 'it was not very complicated really. The *milgwn* took her.'

He saw from the corner of his eye that Idris Jones Ty-Bont stood suddenly very still, up on the slope, staring at him. Avoiding the farmer's eye, he sat there hugging his knees against his chest, and looked up at John Rowlands unguardedly for the first time, with the eyes not of a boy but of an Old One. Time was growing short, and he was tired of pretence.

'The king of the *milgwn*,' he said. 'The chief of the foxes of the Brenin Llwyd. He is the biggest of all of them, and the most powerful, and his master has given him the way of doing many things. He is no more than a creature, still, but he is not at all . . . ordinary. For instance, he is now at this moment just exactly the colour of Pen, so that it would be hard for any man who, with his own eyes, saw him attacking a sheep, not to think for certain that it was Pen he was seeing attack the sheep.'

John Rowlands was gazing at him, his dark eyes bright as polished stone. He said slowly, 'And maybe before that he might have been just exactly the colour of Cafall, so that also anyone else might have thought –'

'Yes,' Will said. 'They might.'

Rowlands shook his head abruptly as if to cast a weight from it. 'I think it is time we went down off this mountain, Idris boy,' he said firmly, heaving Will to his feet.

'Yes,' said Idris Jones hastily. 'Yes, yes.' He followed them, looking totally bemused, as if he had just heard a sheep bark like a dog and were trying to find a way of believing what he had heard.

The dogs trotted ahead of them, turning protectively now and then to make sure they followed. John Rowlands very soon released Will to walk alone, for single file was the only possible way down the winding, steep path, made by sheep and seldom used by men. Will was halfway down to the lake before he fell.

He could never explain, afterwards, how he came to stumble. He could only have said, very simply, that the mountain shrugged – and even John Rowlands in the height of trustfulness could not have been expected to believe that. Nevertheless, the mountain did shrug, through the malice of its master the Brenin Llwyd, so that a piece of the path beneath Will's feet jumped perceptibly to one side and back again, like a cat humping its back, and Will saw it with sick horror only in the moment that he lost his balance and went rolling down. He heard the men shout and was aware of a flurry of movement as Rowlands dived to grab him. But he was already rolling, tumbling, and it was only a ledge of granite, jutting as the ledge on which they had found the dead sheep, that caught him from rolling the full hundred-foot drop down to the edge of the lake. He came a great thud against the jagged shelf of rock, and cried out in pain as a shaft of fire seemed to shoot blazing up his left arm. But the rock had saved him. He lay still.

Gentle as a mother, John Rowlands felt along the bone of his arm. His face was a strange colour, where the blood had drained away beneath the tan. '*Duw*,' he said huskily, 'you are a lucky one, Will Stanton. That is going to hurt a good deal for the next few days, but it is not broken anywhere so far as I can tell. And it might well have been in smithereens.'

'And the boy at the bottom of Llyn Mwyngil!' Idris Jones said shakily, straightening up and trying to recover his lost breath. 'How the devil did you manage to fall like that, *bachgen*? We were not going so very fast at all, but such a speed you went down –' He whistled softly, and took off his cap to wipe his brow.

'Gently does it,' said John Rowlands, putting Will carefully back on his feet. 'Are you all right to walk, now? Not hurt anywhere else?'

'I shall be okay. Honestly. Thank you.' Will was trying to look around at Idris Jones. 'Mr Jones? What was that you called the lake?'

Jones looked at him blankly. 'What?'

'You said, the boy might have been at the bottom of the lake. Didn't you? But you didn't say Tal y Llyn, you called it by some other name. Llyn something else.'

'Llyn Mwyngil. That is its proper name, the old Welsh name.' Jones was looking at him in a kind of dazed wonder, clearly suspecting the fall had knocked Will on the head. He added absently, 'It is a nice name but not much used these days, even on the Ordnance Survey . . . like Bala too. Now that should be Llyn Tegid as it always was, but they do no more now anywhere than call it Bala Lake . . .'

Will said, 'Llyn Mwyngil, what does it mean in English?'

'Well . . . the lake in the pleasant place. Pleasant retreat. Whatever.'

'The pleasant lake,' Will said. 'No wonder I fell. The pleasant lake.'

'Yes, you could put it that way, loosely, I suppose.' Idris Jones collected his wits suddenly and turned in baffled anguish. 'John Rowlands, what is the matter with this mad boy you have found, standing up here talking semantics on a mountain, when he has just come close to breaking his neck? Get him down to the farm before he falls down in a fit and starts speaking with tongues.'

John Rowlands's deep chuckle had relief in it. 'Come on, Will.'

Plump Mrs Jones clucked over Will in concern and put a cold compress on his forearm. Nobody would hear of his doing anything, or going anywhere. The patchy sunshine was warmer now, and Will found it not unpleasant at all to lie on his back in the grass near the farmhouse, with Pen's cold nose pushing at his ear, and watch the clouds scud across the pale blue sky. John Rowlands decided that he would go to Abergynolwyn, near by, to fetch the spark plug Rhys wanted from the garage there. Idris Jones discovered errands that meant he should go too. They both announced firmly that Will should stay with Mrs Jones and the dogs, and rest. He felt that they were still recovering from his fall themselves, treating him as a fragile piece of china which, since it had magically survived without breakage, should be set very carefully on a shelf and not moved for a special conciliatory length of time.

The Land-Rover chugged away with the two men. Mrs Jones fussed amiably to and fro until she had satisfied herself that Will was not in pain, or any distress, and then went off and settled to pastry-making in her kitchen.

For a while Will sat playing idly with the dogs, thinking of the Grey King in a mixture of brief triumph, resentment, belligerence, and nervousness of what might be going to happen next. For there was no escape now. He had known it, somehow, even when they had left that morning. His way lay firmly on into the middle of the heartland of the Brenin Llwyd. *By the pleasant lake the Sleepers lie . . . On Cadfan's Way where the kestrels call . . .* It had never occurred to him to follow the simplest route out of the conundrum, and go out and walk along Cadfan's Way until it led him to a lake. But there would have been no difference in the end. Sooner or later he would have come here, to Tal y Llyn,

Llyn Mwyngil, the lake in the pleasant place under the shadow of the Grey King.

Taking Pen with him, and leaving a patient resigned Lala behind, he strolled beyond the farm gate and out down the slate-fenced lane. A few late blackberries hung down over the grassy bank, and a woodlark sang behind the fence; it might almost have been summer. But though the sun shone, in the distance over the brambles Will could see mist round Cader Idris's peaks.

He was in a dreamy, suspended state of mind, due partly to the aspirin Mrs Jones had made him take for the pain in his arm, when all at once he saw a boy come hurtling down the lane towards him on a bicycle. Will jumped to one side. There was a squealing of brakes, a flurry of kicked-up slate dust, and the boy collapsed in a pile of legs and spinning wheels on the other side of the lane. His cap tumbled off and Will saw the white hair. It was Bran.

His face was damp with sweat; his shirt clung stickily to his chest, and his breath came in great gulps. He had no time for greeting, or explanation.

'Will – Pen – get him away from here, hide him! Caradog Prichard found out. He's coming. He is as mad as a hatter, he swears he's going to kill Pen whatever, and he's on his way here now, with his gun . . .'

The Warestone

Bran got to his feet, brushing off dust and grass.

Will gaped at him. 'You've just cycled all the way from Clwyd?'

Bran nodded. 'Caradog Prichard came roaring up in his van this morning, looking for Pen. He is dead set on shooting him. I was frightened, Will. The way he looks, he is not like a man at all. And I think he had been hunting all night for John Rowlands and Pen, he was all creased looking, and not shaved.' His breath was coming more normally now. He picked up his bicycle. 'Come on. Quick!'

'Where shall we go?'

'I don't know. Anywhere. Just away from here.' He tugged his bicycle up over the bank edging the lane at the left, and led them off through bushes and trees towards the open moorland that stretched back down the valley, away from the lake.

Will scrambled after him, with Pen at his side. 'But does he really know we're here? He couldn't.'

'That's the only part I don't understand,' Bran said. 'He was having a big argument with your cousin Rhys, about where Pen was, and then suddenly he stopped in the middle of it and went very quiet. It was almost as if he were listening. Then he said, *I know where they are gone. They are gone to the lake.* Just like that. Rhys tried to talk him out of it, but I don't think that worked. Somehow Prichard just knew. I'm positive he's on his way to Ty-Bont. Pen! Hey!' He whistled, and the dog paused ahead, waiting for them. They were walking on rising ground now, through waist-high bracken, on a meandering sheep path.

'How did you get here before him, then?' Will said.

Bran looked over his shoulder with a quick grin; he had moved ahead on the path, pushing his bike. Something seemed to have transformed him out of the figure of despair Will had seen the day before.

'Caradog Prichard will not be too pleased about that,' Bran said solemnly. 'I had my clasp knife in my pocket, you see, and I happened to be passing his van when he was not looking, and I stuck it in his back tyre, and gave it a good jerk. And while I was at it I stuck it in his spare tyre too. You know the way he has the spare bolted onto the side of the van? A mistake, that is, he should keep it inside.'

The tension inside Will snapped like a breaking spring, and he began to laugh. Once he had started, it was hard to stop. Bran paused, grinning, and then the grin became a chuckle and before long they were reeling with laughter, roaring, tottering, clutching at one another, in a wild fit of chortling mirth with the dog Pen leaping about them happily.

'Imagine his face,' Will gasped, 'when he goes tearing off in the van and poof! the tyre goes flat, and he gets out furious and changes it, and goes tearing off again, and poof –'

They collapsed again, gurgling.

Bran took off his dark glasses and wiped them. 'Mind you,' he said, 'it is going to make everything worse in the long run, because he will know very well somebody cut the tyres on purpose, and that will just make him wilder than ever.'

'Worth it,' Will said. Controlled again, but cheerful, he gave Bran a sideways, rather shy glance. 'Hey,' he said. 'It was nice of you to come, considering.'

'Oh, well,' Bran said. He put the glasses back on, retreating once more into inscrutability; his white hair lay in damp-darkened lines across his forehead.

He seemed about to say something else, but changed his mind. 'Come on!' he said; jumped on his bicycle and began pedalling erratically off along the weaving path through the bracken.

Will began to run. 'Where are we going?'

'Goodness knows!'

They careered along in a happy, lunatic chase through the valley: over open slopes, down into hollows; up over ridges, in and out of rounded, lichened rocks; through grass and bracken and heather and gorse, and quite often, on damper ground near one of the little streams that fed the river, through reeds and iris leaves. They had come a long way from the lake; this was the main valley land now, open grazing land, merging into the arable fields of Clwyd and Prichard's Farm further down, past the jutting hills.

Suddenly Bran skidded, tumbling sideways. Thinking he had fallen, Will went to help, but Bran grabbed his arm and pointed urgently across the moorland. 'Over there! On the road! There's a curve a long way down where you can see cars coming, before they get here – I'm almost sure I just saw Prichard's van!'

Will grabbed Pen by the collar and looked wildly about. 'We must get under cover – behind those rocks over there?'

'Wait! I see where we are! There's a better place, just up here – come on!' Bran bumped off again. The big sheepdog slipped from Will's hand and bounded after him. Will ran. They rounded a group of near-by trees, and there beyond it was the glimmer of grey stone and slate, behind a low ruined wall. The cottage looked quite different from behind. Will did not recognize it until too late. Bran had shot inside, thumping open the broken back door, before he could call to prevent him, and then there was no alternative but to follow.

Naked to the eye of the Grey King, feeling the force of the Dark pressing sudden and strong on him like a huge hand, he stumbled after the dog and the white-haired boy into the cottage from which the *milgwn* had stolen the wounded sheep, the cottage where Owen Davies had fought Caradog Prichard for the woman who had borne and deserted Bran; the cottage haunted, now more than ever, by the malice of the rising Dark.

But Bran, propping his bicycle against a wall, was bright and unaffected. 'Isn't this perfect? It's an old shepherd's hut, no one's used it for years... quick, over here – keep your head down –'

They crouched beside the window, Pen lying quiet beside them, and saw through the jagged-edged hole the small grey van passing perhaps fifty yards away on the road. Prichard was driving slowly. They could see him peering from side to side, scouring the land. He glanced incuriously at the cottage, and drove on.

The van disappeared along the road to Tal y Llyn. Bran leaned back against the wall. 'Whew! Lucky!'

But Will was paying no attention. He was too much occupied with shielding his mind from the raging malevolence of the Grey King. He said through his teeth, the words coming slow and dragging, 'Let's . . . get . . . away . . . from . . . here . . .'

Bran stared at him, but asked no questions. 'All right, then. *Tyrd yma*, Pen.' He turned to the dog, and suddenly his voice came high as the wind in the telegraph wires. 'Pen! What is it? Look at him, Will!'

The dog lay flat on his stomach, his four legs splayed outwards, his head down sideways against the floor. It was horrible, unnatural; a position impossible for any normal living creature. A faint whistling whine came from his throat, but he did not move. It was as if invisible pins held him forced flat against the ground.

'Pen!' Will said in horror. 'Pen!' But he could not lift the dog's head. The animal was not paralysed by any natural circumstance. Only enchantment could force him so hard into the earth that no living hand could move him.

'What is it?' There was fear in Bran's face.

'It is the Brenin Llwyd,' Will said. His tone seemed to Bran deeper than before, more resonant. 'It is the Brenin Llwyd, and he has forgotten the bargain that he made when we spoke yesterday. He has forgotten that he gave me one night and one day.'

'*You spoke to him?*' Bran heard his voice come out in a broken whisper, and he crouched there motionless beside the window. But again Will was paying no attention. He spoke half to himself, in this same strange adult voice. 'It is sent not at me but at the dog. It is indirect, then, a device. I wonder . . .'

He broke off and glanced at Bran, waving a finger at him in warning. 'You may watch me if you will, though it would be better not, but you must say nothing, and make no move. Not one.'

'All right,' Bran said.

He watched, crouching on the dirty, broken slate floor in one corner, and he saw Will move to the middle of the room, to stand beside the hideously prostrate dog.

Will bent and picked up a broken piece of wood, from the litter of the empty years that lay scattered everywhere. He touched it to the ground before his feet and, turning, drew a circle about Pen and himself on the floor with the tip of the stick. Where the circle was drawn, a ring of blue flame sprang up, and when it was complete, Will relaxed and stood full upright, like someone freed of a great burden that had been weighing him down. He raised the stick vertically in the air over his head, so that it touched the low ceiling, and he said some words in a language that Bran did not understand.

The cottage seemed to grow very dark, so that Bran's weak eyes, blinking, could see nothing but the blue ring of cold fire and Will's form shadowy in the middle of it. But then he saw that another light was beginning to glow in the room: a small blue spark, somewhere in the far corner, steadily growing brighter until it blazed with such intensity that he was forced to look away.

Will said something, sharp and angry, in the language that Bran could not understand. The circle of blue flames flared high and then low, high and low, high and low, three times, and then suddenly went out. Instantly the cottage was full of daylight again, and the brilliant star of light nowhere to be seen. Bran let out a long slow breath, staring about the room to try and see where the light had been. But the room seemed now so different and ordinary that he could not tell. Nor could he imagine where the circle had been drawn, though he knew it had been round Will.

Will, standing there unmoving, was the only thing in the room that seemed not to have changed utterly, in that one second – and even he seemed now once more different, a boy as he had been, but glaring round the floor irritably as if peering for an errant marble that had rolled away.

He glanced at Bran and said crossly, 'Come and look at this.' Then without waiting, while Bran scrambled nervously up, he crossed to the far corner of the room, crouched, and began riffling through a small pile of bits of stone that lay there, random-scattered and dusty, among the debris. Pushing them aside, he cleared a space in which one small white pebble lay alone. He said to Bran, 'Pick it up.'

Puzzled, Bran reached out and took the pebble. But he found that he could not pick it up. He worked at it with his fingers. He stood up, straddled it, and tried with thumbs and forefingers to pull it up from the floor. He stared at the pebble, and then at Will.

'It's part of the floor. It must be.'

'The floor's made of slate,' Will said. He still sounded cross, almost petulant.

'Well . . . yes. No stones in slate, true. But all the same it's fixed, somehow. Bit of quartz. It won't budge.'

'It is a warestone,' Will said, his voice flat now, and weary. 'The awareness of the Grey King. I might have guessed. It is, in this place, his eyes and his ears and his mouth. Through it – just through the fact of its lying there – he not only knows everything that happens in this place, but can send out his power to do certain things. Only certain things. Not any very great magic. But, for instance, he is able so to paralyse Pen there that we can no more move him than we can move the warestone itself.'

Bran knelt in distress beside the dog, and stroked the head flattened so unnaturally against the floor. 'But if Caradog Prichard tracks us here – he might, his dogs might – then he will just shoot Pen where he lies. And there will be nothing we can do to help.'

Will said bitterly, 'That's the idea.'

'But Will, that can't happen. You've got to do something!'

'There is just one thing that I can do,' Will said. 'Though obviously I can't tell you what it is, with that thing there. It means I shall have to borrow your bicycle. But I'm not too sure whether you should stay here alone.'

'Somebody's got to. We can't leave Pen like that. Not on his own.'

'I know. But the warestone . . .' Will glared at the pebble as if it were some infuriating small child sitting there clutching an object too precious for it to hold. 'It's not a particularly powerful weapon,' he said, 'but it's one of the oldest. We all use them, both the Light and the Dark. There are rules, sort of. None of us can actually be affected by a warestone – only observed. That wretched pebble can give the Grey King an idea of what I do and say here. A general idea, like an image – it's not as specific as a television set, mercifully. It can't do anything to harm me, or stop me doing what I want to do – except through the control it has over objects. I mean, it can't actually affect me, because I am an Old One, but it *can* transmit the power of the Dark – or of the Light, if it happened to belong to an Old One – to affect men, and animals, and things of the earth. It can stop Pen from moving, and therefore stop me from moving him. You see? So that if you stay here, there's no knowing what exactly it's able to do to you.'

Bran said obstinately: 'I don't care.' He sat cross-legged by the dog. 'It can't kill me, can it?'

'Oh, no.'

'Well, then. I'm staying. Go on, off with the bike.'

Will nodded, as if that was what he had been expecting. 'I'll be as quick as I can. But take care. Stay very wide awake. If anything does happen, it will come in the way you least expect.'

Then he was gone out of the door, and Bran was left in the cottage with a dog pressed impossibly flat against the slate floor by an invisible high wind, staring at a small white stone.

'Good day, Mrs Jones. How are you?'

'Well, thank you, Mr Prichard. And you?'

Caradog Prichard's plump pale face was glistening with sweat. Impatience swept away his Welsh politeness. He said abruptly, 'Where is John Rowlands?'

'John?' said cosy Megan Jones, wiping floury hands on her apron. 'There now, what a shame, you have missed him. Idris and he went off to Abergynolwyn half an hour ago. They will not be back until dinner, and that will be late today ... You want to see him urgently, is it, Mr Prichard?'

Caradog Prichard stared at her vacantly and did not answer. He said, in a high tight voice, 'Is Rowlands's dog here?'

'Pen? Goodness no,' Mrs Jones said truthfully. 'Not with John gone.' She smiled amiably at him. 'Is it the man you want to see, or the dog, then? Well, indeed, you are welcome to wait for them here, though as I say, it may be quite a time. Let me get you a cup of tea, Mr Prichard, and a nice fresh Welshcake.'

'No,' said Prichard, running his hand distractedly through his raw red hair. 'No . . . no, thank you.' He was so lost in his own mind that he scarcely seemed to be aware of her at all. 'I will be off to town and see if I find them there. At the Crown, perhaps . . . John Rowlands has some business with Idris Ty-Bont, does he?'

'Oh,' said Mrs Jones comfortably, 'he is just visiting. Since he had something to do in Abergynolwyn anyway. Just a call, you know, Mr Prichard. Like your own.' She beamed innocently at him.

'Well,' said Caradog Prichard. 'Thank you very much. Good-bye.'

Megan Jones looked after him as he swung the grey van hastily round and drove away down the lane. Her smile faded. 'Not a nice man,' she said to the farmyard at large. 'And something is going on behind those little eyes of his that is not nice *at all*. A very lucky thing it was that young Will happened to take that dog for a walk just now.'

Will pedalled hard, blessing the valley road for its winding flatness, and freewheeling only when his pounding heart seemed about to leap right out of his chest. He rode one handed. He had said nothing about his hurt arm, and Bran had not noticed, but it hurt abominably if he so much as touched the handlebars with his left hand. He tried not to think about the way it would feel when carrying the golden harp.

That was the only thing to be done, now. The music of the harp was the only magic within his reach that would release Pen from the power of the warestone. In any case, it was time now to bring the harp to the pleasant lake, to accomplish its deeper purpose. Everything was coming together, as if two roads led to the same mountain pass; he could only hope that the pass would not be blocked by some obstacle able to hinder both at once. This time more than ever, the matter of holding the Dark at bay depended as much on the decisions and emotions of men as on the strength of the Light. Perhaps even more.

Broken sunlight flickered in and out of his eyes, as clouds scudded briskly over the sky. At least, he thought wryly, we've got a good day for it all. His wheels sang on the road; he was nearly at Clwyd Farm now. He wondered how he was to explain his sudden arrival, and equally sudden departure afterwards, to Aunt Jen. She would probably be the only one there. She must have been there for Caradog Prichard's appearance earlier that morning, and the changing of his two mutilated tyres. Perhaps he could say that he had come to get something to help put Prichard off the scent, to keep him from finding Pen ... something John Rowlands had suggested ... but still he would have to leave the house with the golden harp. Aunt Jen would not be likely to let that sacking-swathed object past her sharp eye without at least inquiring what was wrapped up in there. And what possible reason could anyone have, least of all her nephew, for not letting her see?

Will wished, not for the first time, that Merriman were with him, to ease such difficulties. For a Master of the Light, it was no great matter to transport beings and objects not only through space but through time, in the twinkling of an eye. But for the youngest of the Old Ones, however acute his need, that was a talent too large.

He came to the farm; rode in; pushed through the back door. But when he called, no one came. He realized suddenly with a great lightening of the spirits that he had seen no cars in the yard outside. Both his aunt and uncle must have gone out; that was one piece of luck, at any rate. He ran upstairs to his bedroom, said the necessary words to release the golden harp from protection, and ran down again with it under his arm, a rough sacking-wrapped bundle of odd triangular shape. He was halfway across the yard to the bicycle when a Land-Rover chugged in through the gate.

For a second Will froze in panic; then he walked slowly, carefully, to the bicycle, and turned it ready to leave.

Owen Davies climbed out of the car and stood looking at him. He said, 'Was it you left the gate open?'

'Oh, gosh.' Will was genuinely shocked: he had committed the classical farm sin, without even noticing. 'Yes, I did, Mr Davies. That's awful. I'm most terribly sorry.'

Owen Davies, thin and earnest, shook his flat-capped head in reproof. 'One of the most important things to remember, it is, to shut any gate you have opened on a farm. You do not know what livestock of your uncle's might have slipped out, that should have been kept in. I know you are English, and no doubt a city boy, but that is no excuse.'

'I know,' Will said. 'And I'm not even a city boy. I really am sorry. I'll tell Uncle David so.'

Taken aback by this implication of honest confidence, Owen Davies surfaced abruptly from the pool of righteousness that had threatened to swallow him. 'Well,' he said. 'Let us forget it this time, both of us. I dare say you will not do it again.'

His gaze drifted sideways a little. 'Is that Bran's bike you have there? Did he come with you?'

Will pressed the shrouded harp tight between his elbow and his side. 'I borrowed it. He was out riding, and I was . . . up the valley, walking, and I saw him, and we thought we'd have a go at flying a big model plane I've been making.' He patted the bundle under his arm, swinging his leg over the bicycle saddle at the same time. 'So I'm going back now. Is that all right? You don't need him for anything?'

'Oh, no,' Owen Davies said. 'Nothing at all.'

'John Rowlands took Pen to Mr Jones at Ty-Bont all safe and sound,' Will said brightly. 'I'm supposed to be having dinner there, late-ish Mrs Jones said – would it be all right if I took Bran back with me too, Mr Davies? Please?'

The usual expression of alarmed propriety came over Owen Davies's thin face. 'Oh, no, now, Mrs Jones is not expecting him, there is no need to bother her with another –'

Unexpectedly, he broke off. It was as if he heard something, without understanding it. Puzzled, Will saw his face become oddly bemused, with the look of a man dreaming a dream that he has dreamed often but never been able to translate. It was a look he would never have expected to find on the face of a man so predictable and uncomplicated as Bran's father.

Owen Davies stared him full in the face, which was even more unusual. He said, 'Where did you say you and Bran were playing?'

Will's dignity ignored the last word. He kicked at the bicycle pedal. 'Out on the moor. Quite a long way up the valley, near the road. I don't know how to describe it exactly – but more than halfway to Mr Jones's farm.'

'Ah,' Owen Davies said vaguely. He blinked at Will, apparently back in his usual nervous person. 'Well, I daresay it would be all right if Bran goes to dinner as well. John Rowlands being there – goodness knows Megan Jones is used to feeding a lot of mouths. But you must be sure to tell him he must be home before dark.'

'Thank you!' said Will, and made off before he could change his mind, carefully closing the gate after he had ridden through. He shouted a farewell, with just time to notice Bran's father's hand slowly raised as he rode away.

But he was not many yards along the road, riding awkwardly one-handed and slowly with the harp clutched in his aching left arm, before all thought of Owen Davies was driven from his head by the Grey King. Now the valley was throbbing with power and malevolence. The sun was at its highest point, though no more than halfway up the sky in that November day. The last part of the time for the fulfilling of Will's only separate quest had begun. His mind was so much occupied with the unspoken beginnings of battle that it was all his body could do to push the bicycle, and himself, slowly along the road.

He paid little attention when a Land-Rover swished past him, going fast in the same direction. Several cars had passed him already, on both journeys, and in this part of the country Land-Rovers were common. There was no reason at all why this one should have differed from the rest.

The Cottage on the Moor

Alone with the motionless sheepdog, Bran went again to the pile of rubble in the corner of the room and stared at the warestone. So small, so ordinary : it was just like any other of the white quartz pebbles scattered over the land. He bent again and tried to pick it up, and felt the same throb of disbelief when it would not move. It was like the dreadful splayed attitude in which Pen lay. He was looking at the impossible.

It occurred to him to wonder why he was not afraid. Perhaps it was because part of his mind did still believe these things impossible, even while he saw them clearly. What could a pebble do to him ? He went to the door of the cottage and stood staring across the valley, towards Bird Rock. The Craig was hard to see from here : an insignificant dark hump, dwarfed by the mountain ridge behind. Yet that too had held the impossible ; he had gone down into the depths of that rock, and in an enchanted cavern encountered three Lords of the High Magic there . . . Bran had a sudden image of the bearded figure in the sea-blue cloak, of the eyes from the hooded face holding his own, and felt a strange urgent warmth in the remembering. He would never forget that figure, clearly the greatest of the three. There was something particular and close about him. He had even known Cafall.

Cafall.

'*Never fear, boy. The High Magic would never take your dog from you . . . Only the creatures of the earth take away from one another, boy. All creatures, but man more than any. Life they take . . . Beware your own race, Bran Davies – they are the only ones who will ever hurt you. . . .'*

The pain of loss that Bran had begun to learn to conceal struck into him like an arrow. In a great rush his mind filled with pictures of Cafall as a wobble-legged puppy, Cafall following him to school, Cafall learning the signals and commands of the working sheepdog, Cafall wet with rain, the long hair pressed flat in a straight parting along his spine, Cafall running, Cafall drinking from a stream, Cafall asleep with his chin warm on Bran's foot.

Cafall dead.

He thought of Will then. It was Will's fault. If Will had never brought him to –

'No,' Bran said aloud suddenly. He turned and glared at the warestone. Was it trying to turn his mind to thinking ill of Will, and so to divide them? Will had said, after all, that the Dark might try to reach at him in some way he would least expect. That was it, for sure. He was being influenced subtly to turn against Will. Bran felt pleased with himself for noticing so soon.

'You can save the effort,' he said jeeringly to the warestone. 'It won't work, see?'

He went back to the doorway and looked out at the hills. His mind drifted back to thought of Cafall. It was hard to keep away from the last image: the worst, yet precious because it was the closest. He heard again the shot, and the way it had echoed round the yard. He heard his father saying, as Cafall lay bleeding his life out and Caradog Prichard sneered with success: *Cafall was going for the sheep, there is no question . . . I cannot say that I would not have shot him myself, in Caradog's place. That is the right of it . . .*

The right, the right. So very sure his father was always, of the right and the wrong. His father and all his father's friends in chapel, and most of all the minister with his certain-sure preaching of good and bad, and the right way to live. For Bran it was a pattern of discipline: chapel twice on Sundays, listen and sit still without fidgeting, and do not commit the sins the Good Book forbids. For his father it was more: prayer meetings, sometimes twice a week, and always the necessity of behaving the way people expected a deacon to behave. There was nothing wrong with chapel and all of that, but Bran knew his father gave it more of himself than any other chapel member he had ever met. He was like a driven man, with his anxious face and hunched shoulders, weighed down by a sense of guilt that Bran had never been able to fathom for himself. There was no lightness in their lives; his father's endless meaningless penance would not allow it. Bran had never been allowed to go to the cinema in Tywyn, and on Sundays he could do nothing at all except go to chapel and walk the hills. His father was reluctant to let him go to school concerts and plays. It had even taken John Rowlands a long time to persuade him to let Bran play the harp in contests at *eisteddfodau*. It was as if Owen Davies kept both of them, himself and Bran, locked up in a little box in the valley, bleak and lonely, out of contact with all the bright things of life; as if they were condemned to a life in jail.

Bran thought: *It's not fair. All I had was Cafall, and now even Cafall is gone . . .* He could feel grief swelling in his throat, but he swallowed hard and gritted his teeth, determined not to cry. Instead rage and resentment grew in his mind. What right had his father to make everything so grim? They were no different from other people . . .

But that's wrong, said a voice in his mind. You are different. You are the freak with the white hair, and the pale skin that will not brown in the sun, and the eyes that cannot stand bright light. Whitey, they call you at school, and Paleface, and there is one boy from up the valley who makes the old sign against the Evil Eye in your direction if he thinks you are not looking. They don't like you. Oh, you're different, all right. Your father and your face have made you feel different all your life, you would be a freak inside even if you tried to dye your hair, or paint your skin.

Bran strode up and down the cottage room, furious and yet puzzled. He banged one hand against the door. He felt as though his head were about to burst. He had forgotten the warestone. It did not occur to him that this haunting too might be brought by the subtle workings of the Dark. Everything seemed to have vanished from the world except the resentful fury against his father that flooded his mind.

And then outside the cottage's broken front door there was the crunch and squeal of a car drawing up, and Bran looked out just in time to see his father jump out of the Land-Rover and stride towards the cottage.

He stood still, his head singing with rage and surprise. Owen Davies pushed open the door and stood looking at him.

'I thought you would be here,' he said.

Bran said curtly. 'Why?'

His father made the strange ducking movement of his head that was one of his familiar nervous gestures. 'Will was up at the farm, fetching something, and he said you were both up here, somewhere . . . he should be along soon.'

Bran was standing stiffly. 'Why are you here? Did Will make you think something was wrong?'

'Oh, no, no,' Owen Davies said hastily.

'Well then, what –'

But his father had seen Pen. He stood very still for a moment. Then he said gently, 'But something is wrong, isn't it?'

Bran opened his mouth, and shut it again.

Owen Davies came further into the room and bent over the helpless sheepdog. 'How is he hurt, then? Was it a fall? I never saw an animal lie so . . .' He stroked the dog's head, and felt along his legs, then moved his hand to pick up one paw. Pen gave an almost inaudible whine, and rolled his eyes. The paw would not move. It was not rigid, or stiff; it was simply bound fast to the earth, like the warestone. Bran's father tried each of the four paws in turn, and each time could not move any a fraction of an inch. He stood up and backed slowly away, staring at Pen. Then he raised his head to look at Bran, and in his eyes a terrible fear was mingled with accusation.

'*What have you been doing, boy?*'

Bran said, 'It is the power of the Brenin Llwyd.'

'Nonsense!' Owen Davies said sharply. 'Superstitious nonsense! I will *not* have you talk of those old pagan stories as if they were true.'

'All right, Da,' Bran said. 'Then it is superstitious nonsense that you cannot move the dog.'

'It is some kind of rigor of the joints,' his father said, looking at Pen. 'It seems to me he has broken his back, and the nerves and the muscles are all stiffened up.' But there was no conviction in his voice.

'There is nothing wrong with him. He is not hurt. He is like that because —' Bran felt suddenly that it would be going much too far to tell his father about the warestone. He said instead, 'It is the malice of the Brenin Llwyd. Through his trickery Cafall was shot when he should not have been, and now he is trying to make it easy for that crazy Caradog Prichard to get Pen as well!'

'Bran, Bran!' His father's voice was high with agitation. 'You must not let yourself be carried away so by Cafall dying. There was no help for it, *bachgen*, he turned into a sheep-chaser and there was no help for it. A killer dog has to be killed.'

Bran said, trying to keep his voice from trembling, 'He was not a killer dog, Da, and you do not know what you are talking about. Because if you do, why can you not get Pen to move one centimetre from where he is lying? It is the Brenin Llwyd, I tell you, and there is nothing you can do.'

And he could tell from the apprehension in Owen Davies's eyes that deep down, he believed it was the truth.

'I should have known,' his father said miserably. 'When I found you here in this place, I should have known such things were happening.'

Bran stared at him. 'What do you mean?'

His father did not seem to hear him. 'Here of all places. Blood will tell, they say. Blood will tell. She came here out of the mountains, out of darkness to this place, and so this is where you came too. Even without knowing, you came here. And evil comes of it again.' His eyes were wide and he was blinking very fast, looking at nothing.

Suspicion of his meaning began to creep into Bran's mind like an evening mist over the valley. '*Here.* You keep saying, *here* . . .'

'This was my house,' Owen Davies said.

'No,' Bran said. 'Oh, no.'

'Eleven years ago,' Davies said, 'I lived here.'

'I didn't know. I never thought. It's been empty ever since I remember; I never thought of it being a proper house. I come here quite often when I'm out on my own. If it rains. Or just to sit. Sometimes' – he swallowed – 'sometimes I pretend it's my house.'

'It belongs to Caradog Prichard,' his father said emptily. 'His father kept it as the shepherd's house. But Prichard's men live by the farm now.'

'I didn't realize,' Bran said again.

Owen Davies stood over Pen, looking down, his thin shoulders bowed. He said bitterly, 'The power of the Brenin Llwyd, aye. And that was what brought her out of the mountains to me, and then took her away again. Nothing else could have done it. I have tried to bring you up right, away from it all, in prayer and in goodness, and all the time the Brenin Llwyd has been reaching out to have you back where your mother went. You should not have come here.'

'But I didn't know,' Bran said. Anger flared in him suddenly like a blown spark. 'How was I to know? You never told me. There's never anywhere else to go anyway. You don't let me go to Tywyn ever, not even to the pool or the beach after school with the others. Where else do you let me go except out on the moors? And how was I to know I shouldn't have come here?'

Davies said wretchedly, 'I wanted to keep you free of it. It was over, it was gone, I wanted to keep you away from the past. Ah, we should never have stayed here. I should have moved away from the valley at the beginning.'

Bran shook his head from side to side as if trying to cast something away from it; the air in the cottage seemed to be growing oppressive, heavy, filled with prickling tension like the forewarning of a thunderstorm. He said coldly, 'You've never told me anything, ever. I just have to do what I am told all the time. *This is right, Bran, do it, this is for the best, this is the way you must behave.* You won't ever talk about my mam, you never have. I haven't got a mother – well, that's not so unusual, there's two boys at school haven't either. But I don't even know anything about mine. Only that her name was Gwen. And I know she had black hair and blue eyes, but that's only because Mrs Rowlands told me so, not you. You wouldn't ever tell me anything, except that she ran away when I was a baby. I don't even know whether she's alive or dead.'

Owen Davies said quietly, 'Neither do I, boy.'

'But I want to know what she was like!' The tension sang in Bran's head like an angry sea; he was shouting now. 'I want to know! And you're scared to tell me, because it must have been your fault she ran away! It was your fault, I've always known it was. You kept her shut off from everybody the way you've always kept me, and that's why she ran away!'

'No,' his father said. He began walking unhappily to and fro in the little room; he looked at Bran anxiously, warily as if he were a wild animal that might spring. Bran thought the wariness was that of fear; there was nothing else in his experience that he could imagine it to be.

Owen Davies said, stumbling over the words, 'You are young, Bran. You have to understand, I have always tried to do what is right, to tell you as much as is right. Not to tell you anything that might be dangerous for you –'

'Dangerous!' Bran said contemptuously. 'How could it be dangerous to know about my mother?'

For a moment Davies's control cracked. 'Look over there!' he snapped, pointing at Pen. The dog still lay motionless, dreadfully flattened down, like a skin pegged out to dry. 'Look at that! You say that is the work of the Brenin Llwyd – and then you ask how there could be danger?'

'My mother has nothing to do with the Brenin Llwyd!' But as he heard his own words Bran stopped, staring.

His father said bleakly into the silence, 'That is something we shall never know.'

'What do you mean?'

'Listen. I do not know where she went. Out of the mountains she came, and back into the mountains she went, in the end, and none of us saw her again, ever.' Owen Davies was forcing the words out one by one, with difficulty, as if each one gave him pain. 'She went of her own choice, she ran away, and none knew why. I did not drive her away.' His voice cracked suddenly. 'Drive her away! *Iesu Crist*, boy. I was out of my head up in those hills looking for her, looking for her and never finding, calling, and never a word in return. And no sound anywhere but the birds crying, and the sheep, and the wind an empty whine in my ears. And the Brenin Llwyd behind his mist over Cader and Llyn Mwyngil, listening to the echo of my voice calling, smiling to himself that I never should know where she had gone . . .'

The anguish in his voice was so clear and unashamed that Bran fell silent, unable to break in.

Owen Davies looked at him. He said quietly, 'I suppose it is time to tell you, since we have started this. I have had to wait, you see, until you were old enough to begin to understand. I am your legal father, Bran, because I adopted you right at the beginning. I have had you from when you were a baby, and God knows I am your father in my heart and soul. But you were not born to me and your mother. I cannot tell you who your real father was, she never said a word about him. When she came out of the mountains, out of nowhere, she brought you with her. She stayed with me for three days, and then she went away forever. And took a part of me with her.' His voice shook, then steadied. 'She left me a note.'

He took his battered leather wallet out of his pocket and drew from an inner flap a small piece of paper. Unfolding it with great gentleness, he handed it to Bran. The paper was creased and fragile, almost parting at the folds; it bore only a few pencilled words, in a strangely rounded hand. *His name is Bran. Thank you, Owen Davies.*

Bran folded the note again, very slowly and carefully, and handed it back. 'It was all she left me of herself, Bran,' said his father. 'That note – and you.'

Bran could think of no words to say. His head was crowded with jarring images and questions: a crossroads with a dozen turnings and no sign of which to follow. He thought, as he had thought a thousand times since he was old enough, of the enigma that was his mother, faceless, voiceless, her place in his life nothing but an aching absence. Now, across the years, she had brought him another absence, another emptiness: it was as if she were trying to take away his father as well – at any rate the father who, whatever their differences, he had always thought of as his own. Resentment and confusion rose and fell in Bran's mind like the wind. He thought wildly: *Who am I?* He looked at Pen, and the cottage, and the warestone of the Brenin Llwyd. He heard again his father's bitter remembering: *the Brenin Llwyd behind his mist over Cader and Llyn Mwyngil* . . . The names re-echoed round his head, and he could not understand why they should. Llyn Mwyngil, Tal y Llyn . . . the roaring in his head grew; it seemed to come from the warestone. He looked towards the stone. And again, as when Will had been there, the cottage seemed to grow dark, and the point of blue light began to shine out of the dim corner, and suddenly Bran had a strange jolting awareness of a part of his mind he had never been conscious of before. It was as if a door were opening somewhere within him, and he did not know what he would find on the other side. Flashing through his consciousness came a quick array of images, making no sense, like a dream dreamed while waking.

He thought he saw mist swirling on the mountain, and in it the tall blue-cloaked figure of the lord Will called Merriman, hooded, his head bent and his arm outstretched pointing down into a valley at a cottage – the cottage in which Bran now stood. For a flash Bran saw a woman, with black hair blowing, and he felt washed by love and tenderness, so that in longing he almost cried out to keep the feeling from flickering away. But then it was gone, and the mist swirled, and then again the hooded figure was there, and the woman too, looking back at the cottage, stretching out her arms in yearning. Then the figure of the lord called Merriman swept his robed arm around the woman and they were both gone, vanished into the mist, out of sight and, he knew, out of the world. He saw only one other image: far below, through a break in the mist, the water of a distant lake glimmering like a lost jewel.

Bran did not understand. He knew that somehow he was seeing something out of the past concerning his mother, but there was not enough. What had Merriman to do with her coming, with its beginning and its end? He blinked, and found he was staring at his father again. Davies's eyes were wide in concern; he was clutching Bran's arm, and calling his name.

And in the new part of his mind that he had not seen before, Bran knew suddenly that he had now the power to do more things than he could ordinarily have done. He forgot all else that had happened that day, thinking only of the glimpse of his mother on a mountain over a glinting lake; all at once he wanted only to get to Tal y Llyn and the slopes of Cader Idris, to find out if this new part of his mind could sense there some further memory of the way he had begun. And he knew he could do something else, too. Leaping up, he called to the dog in a strong voice that seemed hardly his own, 'Tyrd yma, Pen!'

And out of his flat-pressed paralysis the black sheepdog instantly rose, and leapt, and the boy and the dog ran out and away across the moor.

Owen Davies, his face lined old in fear and concern, stood silently watching for a moment. Then he moved heavily out to the car, and drove out away from the cottage along the road to Idris Jones's farm.

Will rode more slowly than he had expected. The awkward shape of the harp, pressed against his chest, cut into his bruised arm and hurt so much that soon he could scarcely keep from dropping it. He stopped often to change its position. There were other reasons for pausing too, for the ferocity of malevolence building up in the valley now thrust at him like a great hand, pushing him away, threatening to clutch him in the giant fingers and crush him into nothingness. Doggedly Will rode on. First the cottage, then the lake. In the discordant chaos trying to force him back, only the simplest thoughts and images could survive, keep their shape. *First the cottage, then the lake.* He found himself saying it under his breath. Those were the two tasks for the harp that, above all else, he must make sure were carried out in these next two or three hours. The enchanted music must release Pen from the grip of the warestone, in the cottage, so that he would escape Caradog Prichard's gun. That was a simple matter. But then, more important than anything in the world, the music must wake the Sleepers of the pleasant lake, the creatures who slept their timeless sleep beside Tal y Llyn – whoever, and whatever, those creatures might be. For if a Lord of the Dark such as the Grey King could gain so astonishing a power as that now filling this valley, after centuries of murmuring sleep beneath his mountain, then indeed the Dark was rising, and its whole power increasing like a vast cloud threatening to engulf the whole world.

At last he came to the cottage. And found it empty.

Will stood in the bare stone-walled room, baffled and anxious. How could Pen have escaped the power of the warestone? Where was Bran? Had Caradog Prichard come hunting, with aid from the Grey King, and carried them both off? Impossible. Caradog Prichard was an unwitting servant, knowing nothing of his own links with the Grey King; he was a man only, with the instincts of a man – the worst instincts, with the best sadly submerged. *Where was Bran?*

He crossed to the corner of the room. The small white pebble that was the warestone lay just as it had lain before, innocuous and deadly. All around him the force of the Grey King's will beat implacably. *Go away, give up, you will not win, give up, go away.* Will cast desperately about through the powers of his own mind to find out what might have happened to Bran and the dog, but found nothing. He thought miserably: you should never have left them here alone. In a kind of angry self-abasement he leaned down once more and put his hand to the small round stone that he knew would be bound fast to the earth, beyond any ability of his to move it a fraction of an inch.

And the warestone came away as easily as any other stone, and lay loose in his palm, as if asking to be used.

Will stared at it. He could not believe what he saw. What had loosed the grip of the warestone? No magic he knew could do such a thing. It was a part of the Law, that the Light could not budge a warestone of the Dark, nor the Dark influence a warestone of the Light. That monstrous rigidity, once in force, could not be shattered by any but the stone's owner. Who then could have broken the power of the warestone of the Brenin Llwyd, other than the Brenin Llwyd himself, the Grey King?

Will shook his head impatiently. He was wasting time. One thing was certain, at any rate: left now without ownership, its control broken, the warestone was outside the Law and could itself be employed to tell him what had happened to bring it to its strange present state.

Will kept close hold of the harp; he felt he would never put it down again, least of all in this place. But he stood in the centre of the room with the warestone lying in his open palm, and he said certain words in the Old Speech, and emptied his mind and waited to receive whatever kind of awareness the stone could put into it. The knowledge would not be simple and open, he knew. It never was.

It came, as he stood there with his eyes closed and his mind thrumming, in a series of images so rapid that they were like a narrative, a piece of a story. Will saw a man's face, strong and handsome, but worn, with clear blue eyes and a grey beard. Though the clothes were strange and rich, he knew who it was in an instant: the face was that of the second lord in the cavern of Bird Rock, the Lord in the sea-blue robe, who had spoken with such particular – and then unaccountable – closeness to Bran.

There was a deep sadness in the man's eyes. Will saw then the face of a woman, black-haired and blue-eyed, twisted in a dreadful mingling of grief and guilt. And somewhere with them he saw Merriman. Then he was seeing a different place, a low building with heavy stone walls and a cross above its roof – a church, or an abbey – and from it Merriman was leading the same woman, with a baby in her arms. They stood in a high place, on one of the Old Ways; there was a great whirling of mist; a rushing, and a flurry of images so fast that Will could not follow, nor make out more than a flash of the cottage, and an upright smiling Owen Davies with a younger, unlined face; and dogs and sheep and the mountain slopes green with bracken, and a voice calling, 'Gwennie, Gwennie . . .'

Then, clearer than any, he saw Merriman, hooded in the dark blue robe, standing with the black-haired woman up on the slope above the Dysynni Valley, on Cadfan's Way. She was weeping quietly, tears running slow and glinting down her cheeks. She held nothing in her arms now. Merriman stretched out his hand, fingers stiff-straight, and Will heard through the whistle of the wind a thread of bell-like music that, as an Old One following the ways of the Old Ones, he had heard before in other places and times. Then the whirling came again, and all was confusion, though now he knew from the music that what he was witnessing was a travelling back to another age, long ago: the movement through Time that held no difficulty for an Old One, or a Lord of the Dark, though impossible for men except in dreams. In a last flashing image he saw the woman who had been with Merriman turn and go sadly back into the stone-built abbey, and disappear behind its heavy walls. And away alone elsewhere, yet superimposed on the abbey like the reflection in the glass that covers a picture, he saw the bearded face of the lord who had worn the sea-blue robe, with the gold circlet of a king crowning his head.

And suddenly Will understood the true nature of Bran Davies, the child brought out of the past to grow up in the future, and he felt a terrible compassion for his friend, born to a fearsome destiny of which, as yet, he could have no clear idea at all. It was hard even to think about so astounding a depth of power and responsibility. He saw now that he, Will Stanton, last of the Old Ones, had been fated all along to aid and support Bran in time to come, just as Merriman had always been at the side of Bran's great father. The father who had not known of his son's existence, back when he had been born, and who only now, over the centuries, had as a Lord of the High Magic seen him for the first time . . . It was clear enough now how the ownership of the warestone had been broken. Beside a figure of this rank, the power of the Grey King dwindled to insignificance. But – that was true only if Bran truly knew what he was doing. How much of his buried and infinitely powerful nature had really been released? How much had he seen, in the cottage; what images had spun into his own unsuspecting mind?

Clutching the harp, forgetting his hurt arm in his haste, Will ran out of the cottage, clambered on the bicycle and made off along the road to Tal y Llyn. Bran could have gone nowhere else. All roads now must lead to the lake, and to the Sleepers. For at stake was not only the quest of the golden harp, the Sleepers' waking, but a power of the High Magic that could, if still unrecognized and uncontrolled, destroy not only that quest but the Light as well.

The Waking

When Will came to Tal y Llyn, he knew he must try to keep out of sight. There was no way of telling where Caradog Prichard might be; whether he had gone to Idris Jones's farm, where he would have turned from there . . . Will thought of going to the farm to check, keeping hidden round the bend in the lane in case the battered grey van might be there. Then he changed his mind. There was too little time. Clutching his bundle, he rode on past the top of the Ty-Bont lane, and came to the corner where the road curved round the lake.

Tal y Llyn lay before him, rippled by the wind that all day had sent chunky cumulus clouds scudding across the sky. Green with grass and brown with bracken, the mountains swept out and up from its shores at both sides; the dark lake filled the valley all the way to the far end, where mountains met in a great V to make the pass of Tal y Llyn. Will stared at the rippled water.

Fire on the mountain shall find the harp of gold
Played to wake the Sleepers, oldest of the old...

Where should it be played, and when? Not here, out on the unprotected valley road ... He turned left and rode towards the side of the valley where, above the low gentle green fields, the first dark slopes of Cader Idris climbed like a wall roofed by the sky. It was the slope on which they had found the dead sheep; the slope that its master the Grey King had shaken to throw Will down into the lake. Yet the instinct of the Old Ones drove Will to struggle towards it; to make for the stronghold of the enemy, in a deliberate challenge to the furious force driving him back. The greater the odds, he thought, the greater the victory.

There was a muted roaring in his ears, as he rode on with the bundled harp beneath his arm. Nearer and nearer the mountainside loomed above him. Soon the road would curve away. To stay by the lake, he must dismount and climb over the fields and up the slope of treacherous loose scree, to stand isolated overlooking the water. But he felt that was where he must go.

Then swiftly, suddenly, Caradog Prichard stepped into the road in front of him and grabbed the handlebars of the bike, so that Will tumbled sideways into a painful heap on the ground.

As he scrambled up, clutching the harp with an arm now hurting still more, Will felt not anger or fear but acute irritation. Prichard: always Prichard! While the Grey King loomed in dire threat over the Light, Prichard like a squealing mouse must endlessly intrude to tug Will down to the petty rivalries and rages of ordinary men. He glared at Caradog Prichard with a mute disdain that the man had not the wit to recognize as being dangerous.

'Where you going, English?' said Prichard, holding the bicycle firmly. His thinning red hair was dishevelled; his small eyes glittered oddly.

Will said, cold as winter fish, 'That has nothing whatsoever to do with you.'

'Manners, manners,' said Caradog Prichard. 'I know very well where you are going, my sweet young man – you and Bran Davies are trying to hide that other damn sheep-killing dog. But there is not a single way in the world that you are going to keep me from him. What you got there, then, eh?'

In mindless suspicion he reached for the sacking-swathed bundle beneath Will's arm.

Will's reaction was quicker even than his own eye could follow. The harp was far, far too important to be placed in such foolish jeopardy. Instantly, he was an Old One in the full blaze of power, rearing up terrible as a pillar of light. Towering in fury, he stretched an arm pointing at Caradog Prichard – but met, in answering rage, a barrier of furious resistance from the Grey King.

At first Prichard cringed before him, his eyes wide and his mouth slack with terror, expecting annihilation. But as he found himself protected, slowly craftiness woke in his eyes. Will watched warily, knowing that the Brenin Llwyd was taking the greatest of all risks that any lord of the Light or the Dark could take, by channelling his own immense power through an ordinary mortal who had not the slightest awareness of the appalling forces at his command. The Lord of the Dark must be in a desperate state, to trust his cause to so perilous a servant.

'Leave me alone, Mr Prichard,' Will said. 'I have not got John Rowlands's dog with me. I don't even know where he is.'

'Oh, yes, you do know, boy, and so do I.' The words tumbled out of Prichard, nearer the surface of his mind than the wonder at his new gift. 'He has been taken to Jones Ty-Bont's farm, to be kept from me so that he can get back to his murderous business again. But it will not work, indeed no, no hope of it, I am not such a fool.' He glared at Will. 'And you had better tell me where he is, boy, tell me what you are all up to, or it will go very badly with you.'

Will could sense the man's anger and malice whirling round his mind like a maddened bird caught in a room without exit. *Ah, Brenin Llwyd*, he thought with a kind of sadness, *your powers deserve better than to be put into one without discipline or training, without the wit to use them properly* . . .

He said, 'Mr Prichard, please leave me alone. You don't know what you are doing. Really. I don't want to have to hurt you.'

Caradog Prichard stared at him for a moment of genuine blank wonder, like a man in the instant before he understands the point of a joke, and then he broke into gulping laughter. 'You don't want to hurt me? Well, that's very nice, now, I am delighted to hear it, very thoughtful. Very kind . . .'

The sunshine that had intermittently lit the morning was gone now; grey cloud was thickening over the sky, sweeping down the valley on the wind that rippled the lake. Some instinct at the back of Will's mind made him suddenly aware of the greyness growing like a weight all around, and woke the decision that took hold of him as Caradog Prichard's jeering laughter spluttered down into control. He took a step or two backwards, holding the harp close at his side. Then half closing his eyes, he called silently to the gifts that had made him an Old One in full strength, to the spells that made him able to ride the wind, to fly beyond the sky and beneath the sea; to the circle of the Light that had set him on this quest for the last link in their defence against the Dark's rising.

There was a sound like the murmuring sea out of the still lake Tal y Llyn, Llyn Mwyngil, and from the far edge of the dark water a huge wave came travelling. It curled up high and white-topped, fringed with foam as if about to break. Yet it did not break, but swept on across the water towards them, and on its curving peak rode six white swans, moving smooth as glass, their great wings outstretched and touching wing-tip to wing-tip. They were enormous, powerful birds, their white feathers shining like polished silver even in the grey light of the cloud-hung sky. As they drew nearer and nearer, one of the swans raised its head on the curving, graceful neck and gave a long mournful cry, like a warning, or a lament.

On and on they came, towards the shore, towards Will and Caradog Prichard. The wave loomed higher and higher: a green wave, glowing with a strange translucent light that seemed to come out of the bottom of the lake. It was clear that the birds would dive upon them, and the wave break over them and rush forward down the valley, with all the water of the lake in one long rush, sweeping farms and houses and people before it in total devastation, down to the sea.

Will knew this not to be true, but it was the image that he was forcing into Caradog Prichard's mind.

The white swan gave one more whooping, mourning cry, the shriek of a soul in utter emptiness, and Caradog Prichard stumbled backwards, his small eyes bulging in his head from horror and disbelief, one hand clutched in his red hair. He opened his mouth, and strange wordless sounds came out of it. Then something seemed to seize him, and he jerked into a frozen immobility, arms and legs caught at unnatural angles; and the air was filled with a rushing, hissing sound that came so quickly its direction could not be told.

But Will, appalled, knew what it must be. By accepting help from the Dark, the Welshman had doomed his own mind.

He saw in Caradog Prichard's eyes the quick flash of madness as human reason was swept aside by the dreadful power of the Grey King. He saw the mind sway as the body was, still unwittingly, possessed. Prichard's back straightened; his pudgy form seemed to rise taller than before, and the shoulders hunched themselves in a hint of immense strength. The force of the Brenin Llwyd's magic was in him and pulsing out of him, and he stared at the advancing wave and shrieked in a cracked voice some words of Welsh.

And the swans rose crying into the air and curved away on long slow-beating wings, for all at once the rearing wave collapsed, dragged down into heaviness by a tremendous churning and heaving of thousand upon thousand fish. Silver and grey and dark glinting green they boiled on the surface, perch and trout and wriggling eels, and slant-mouthed pike with needle teeth and small evil eyes. It was as if all the fish in all the lakes of Wales seethed there in a huge mass on the water of Llyn Mwyngil, smoothing its surface into a quivering stillness. Yet it was with the use of a voice and a mind no more than human that so great a spell had been cast. A chill struck into Will as he understood this new deviousness of the Brenin Llwyd. There would be no open confrontation. He himself would never see the Grey King again, for in such a facing of two poles of enchantment there was danger of annihilation for one. Instead Will would face, as he was facing now, the power of the Grey King channelled through the mind of an evil-wishing but innocent man: a man made into a dreadfully vulnerable vessel for the Dark. If the Light were to give any final annihilating stroke in this encounter, the Dark would still be protected, but the mind of the man would inevitably be destroyed. Caradog Prichard, if he were still sane now, would be driven then forever into hopeless madness. Unless Will could somehow avoid such an encounter, there was no help for it. The Grey King was using Prichard as a shield, knowing that he himself could remain protected if the shield were destroyed.

Will called out in anguish, hardly knowing he did so, 'Caradog Prichard! Stop! Leave us alone! For your own sake, leave me alone!'

But there was nothing he could do. The momentum of their conflict was already too great, like a wheel spinning faster and faster downhill. Caradog Prichard was gazing in childish delight at the lake of seething fish, rubbing his hands together, talking steadily to himself in Welsh. He looked at Will and giggled. He did not stop talking, but switched to English, the words coming out in a half-crazed conversational stream, very fast.

'You see the pretty creatures now, so many thousands of them, and all ours and doing what we ask, more of a match for six swans than you were expecting, eh, *dewinn bach*? Ah, you do not know what you are up against, enough nonsense we have had now, my friends and me, it is time that you are going to show me the dog, the dog, because anything you do to try and turn us aside will be no use at all. No use at all. So I want the dog now, English, you are to tell me where I can find the dog, and my good gun is there in the car waiting for him and there will be no more sheep-killing in this valley. I shall see to that.'

He was watching Will, the little eyes darting up and down like small fish themselves, and suddenly once more his gaze fastened on the sacking-bundled harp.

'But first I would like to know what that really is under your arm there, boy, so I think you will show me that if you would like us to leave you alone.' He giggled again on the last word, and Will knew that there was no hope now of reaching the side of the mountain, the place from which it would have been safest and most fitting to play the golden harp. He stepped slowly backwards, in a smooth movement designed to keep Caradog Prichard from alarm, and as caution woke too late in the farmer's bright eyes, he slipped the harp out from its covering, laid it crooked in one arm as he had seen Bran do, and swept the fingers of the other hand over its strings.

And so the world changed.

Already now the sky was a heavier grey than it had been, as the afternoon darkened towards evening and the clouds thickened for rain. But as the lilting flow of notes from the little harp poured out into the air, in an aching sweetness, a strange glow seemed very subtly to begin shining out of lake and cloud and sky, mountain and valley, bracken and grass. Colours grew brighter, dark places more intense and secret; every sight and feeling was more vivid and pronounced. The fish covering the whole swaying surface of the lake began to change; flickering silver, fish after fish leapt into the air and curved down again, until the lake seemed no longer burdened with a great weight of sluggish creatures, but alive and dancing with bright streaks of silver light.

And out of the sky at the seaward end of the valley, down towards the lake, another sound rose over the sweet arpeggios lilting to and fro as Will ran his fingers gently up and down the strings of his harp. There was a harsh crying, like the calling of seagulls. And flying in groups and pairs, without formation, came swooping the strange ellipsoid black forms of cormorants, twenty or thirty of them, more than Will had ever seen flying together. The kings of the bird-fishermen of the sea, never normally seen away from the sea and its cliffs and crags, they came skimming down to the surface of Llyn Mwyngil and began snatching up the leaping fish, and Will remembered suddenly Bran's stories of how the Bird Rock, Craig yr Aderyn, is the only place in the world where cormorants are known to gather and build their nests inland, because in the land of the Grey King the coast has no rocky cliffs for such building, but only sand and beaches and dunes.

Down they swept. The fish jumped, sparkling; the cormorants gulped them; swerved away; dived and gulped again. Caradog Prichard gave a cross wail like a disappointed child. The curious light glimmered through the valley. Still Will's fingers flickered over the harp, and the music rippled out deliberate and clear as spring water. He was caught up in a tension that prickled through him like electricity, a fierce anticipation of unknown wonders; he felt as taut as though every hair stood on end. And then, all at once, the fish vanished, the surface of the lake was suddenly smooth as dark glass, and all the cormorants swept upwards in a cloud and curved away, shrieking, disappearing back up the long broad valley to Bird Rock. And through the luminescence that held the valley suspended in daylit, moonlit half-light, Will saw six figures take shape.

They were horsemen, riding. They came out of the mountain, out of the lowest slopes of Cader Idris that reached up from the lake into the fortresses of the Grey King. They were silvery-grey, glinting figures riding horses of the same strange half-colour, and they rode over the lake without touching the water, without making any sound. The music of the harp lapped them round, and as they drew near, Will saw that they were smiling. They wore tunics and cloaks. Each one had a sword hanging at his side. Two were hooded. One wore a circlet about his head, a gleaming circlet of nobility, though not the crown of a king. He turned to Will, as the ghostly group rode by, and bent his smiling bearded head in greeting. The music rippled bell-like round the valley from the harp in Will's hands, and Will bent his own head in sober greeting but did not break his playing.

The riders rode past Caradog Prichard, who stood gaping vacantly at the lake, looking for the vanished wondrous fish, and clearly did not see anything else. *He has the power of the Grey King*, Will thought, *but not the eyes* . . . Then the riders wheeled back suddenly towards the slope of the mountain, and before Will could wonder at it, he saw that Bran stood there on the slope, halfway up the loose scree, near the ledge that had broken his own fall earlier that day. The black sheepdog Pen was beside him, and toiling up the slope after them was Owen Davies, bent and weary, with the same blankness in his face that Caradog Prichard wore. It was not for ordinary men to see that the Sleepers, woken out of their long centuries of rest, were riding now to the rescue of the world from the rising Dark.

But Bran could see.

He stood watching the Sleepers with a blaze of delight in his pale face. He raised one hand to Will, and opened both arms in a gesture of admiration at the playing of the harp. For a moment he seemed no more than an uncomplicated small boy, caught up in bubbling wonder by a marvellous sight. But only for a moment. The six riders, glinting silver-grey on their silver-grey mounts, curved round after their leader and paused for a moment in line before the place on the hillside where Bran stood. Each drew his sword and held it upright before his face in a salute, and kissed the flat of its blade in homage as to a king. And Bran stood there slim and erect as a young tree, his white hair gleaming in a silver crest, and bent his head gravely to them with the quiet arrogance of a king granting a boon.

Then they sheathed their swords again and wheeled about, and the silver-grey horses sprang up into the sky. And the Sleepers, wakened and riding, rose high over the lake and away, disappearing further and further into the gathering gloom of the Tal y Llyn pass and beyond, until they were gone from the valley, and beyond, and could be seen no more.

Will stilled his fingers on the golden harp, and its delicate melody died, leaving only the whisper of the wind. He felt drained, as though all strength had gone out of him. For the first time he remembered that he was not only an

Old One, but also a convalescent, still weak from the long illness that in the beginning had sent him to Wales.

For a flicker of an instant too, then, he remembered what John Rowlands had said about the coldness at the heart of the Light, as he realized by what agency he must have become so suddenly and severely ill. But it was only for an instant. To an Old One such things were not of importance.

All at once he was brushed aside, and a hasty rough hand snatched the golden harp from his grasp. The power of the Grey King seemed gone from Caradog Prichard, but he was not what he had been before it had come.

'So that is what it's all about, then,' Prichard said thickly. 'A bloody harp, a little gold thing just like she was playing.'

'Give it back,' Will said. Then he paused. '*She?*'

'It is a Welsh harp, English, an old one.' Prichard peered owlishly at it. 'What might it be doing in your hands? You have no right to be holding a Welsh harp.' Suddenly he was glaring viciously at Will. 'Go home. Go back where you belong. Mind your business.'

Will said, 'The harp has fulfilled its purpose. What did you mean, *like she was playing?*'

'Mind your business,' Prichard said again, savagely. 'A long time ago, and nothing to do with you.'

From the corner of his eye Will could see that Owen Davies had joined Bran up on the hillside, with Pen darting restlessly between them. Desperately he tried to will Bran to move away, out of sight; he could not understand why he stayed there in the open, where a casual glance would show them to Caradog Prichard. *Move!* he shouted silently. *Go away!* But it was too late. Something, perhaps the sheepdog's anxious wheeling, had caught Prichard's eye; he glanced half-consciously up at the mountain, and he froze.

Every part of the moment seared itself into Will's brain, so that ever afterwards he could feel the quick roaring of impending disaster and see like a bright picture the heavy grey sky, the rearing mountain, the rippling dark lake, the startling patches of colour made by a white-haired boy and a man with flaring red hair: and over it all the strange glow of a light like the warning luminousness hanging over a countryside before a dreadful storm. Caradog Prichard turned towards him a face marked with a terrible mingling of anger, reproach, and pain, and at the heart of them all a thin core of hatred and the urge to hurt back. Looking deliberately into Will's face, he heaved back his arm and flung the golden harp far out into the lake. Ripples circled outward on the dark water, and then were still.

Then Prichard ran, light as a boy, throwing himself forward to the mountain, and to Bran standing there like a figurehead with the dog Pen. At the last moment before the slope he turned aside, along the curving road that led back down the valley; and Will saw that he had left the small grey van there in the road and was running towards it now with desperate speed.

In the same moment he realized why, and flung a great spell of prevention at Prichard – only to have it cast aside by the protection of the Grey King that the farmer, unknowing, still carried with him. Caradog Prichard reached the van, snatched open its back doors and brought out his long-muzzled shotgun, the same gun with which he had shot Bran's dog Cafall. Swiftly he cocked the gun, swung round and began walking, deliberately and steadily, towards the boy and the dog on the hill. He had no need for haste now. There was no cover to which they could run. Will dug his fingernails into his palms, his mind thrashing for an effective defence. Then he heard the sound of a noisy car.

The Land-Rover swung at astonishing speed out of the lane from Ty-Bont Farm, and round the corner to the lake. John Rowlands must have seen Prichard and his van and his gun all in one appalled moment, for the chunky little car rushed forward to a jerking halt almost at the farmer's feet. The door seemed hardly open before John Rowlands's lanky form was out. He stood still, facing Caradog Prichard and the boy and the dog on the hillside beyond. 'Caradog,' he said. 'There is no sheep here with its throat cut. You have no right, and no need.'

Prichard's voice was high and dangerous. 'There is a sheep dead up there now!' And Will saw that the body of the ewe attacked by the *milgwn*, still up there on its ledge, was visible as a white heap from where they stood. He knew then for the first time why the Grey King had made sure that his *milgwn* should bring it to that spot.

'That is a Pentref sheep, from those wintering at Clwyd,' John Rowlands said.

'Oh, very likely,' said Prichard, sneering.

'I will show you. Come up and see.'

'Even if it were, what of that? It is still that murdering dog of yours that does these things – to sheep in your own care too, is it? What is the matter with you, Rowlands, that you keep him?' His face glistening with the sweat of rage, Prichard brought up his gun level with his waist, facing the hill.

'*No,*' John Rowlands said behind him, his voice very deep.

Something in Caradog Prichard cracked, and he swung round to face Rowlands, the gun still pointing. His voice pitched itself higher still, he was like a wire about to break.

'Always pushing your nose in, you are, John Rowlands. Trying to stop me now, the way you stopped me before. You should not have stopped me then, I would have fought him harder and won, and then she would have come with me. She would have come with me, if it had not been for you pushing in.'

His hands were white where they clenched the gun; his words came out so fast they fell over themselves. John Rowlands stood speechless, staring at him, and Will saw understanding gradually follow astonishment on the tough kind face as he realized what Prichard was talking about.

But before he could speak, Owen Davies's voice came unexpectedly strong and clear from the hillside above them, like a bell ringing out. 'Oh, no, indeed, she would not have come with you, Caradog. Never. And you were not winning that fight and you would never have won in a hundred years, and it was lucky for you that John Rowlands did break into it. I did not know what I was doing, but I would have killed you if I could, for hurting my Gwen.'

'Your Gwen?' Prichard spat the words at him. 'Any man's Gwen! That was as clear as the light in the sky. Why else would she choose a man like you, Owen Davies? A lovely wild thing out of the mountains she was, with a face like a flower, and fingers that made music out of that little harp that she carried like no music you ever heard before . . .' For an instant there was a terrible yearning in his voice. But almost as soon again, the tortured, half-crazed face twisted back into malevolence. He looked at Bran's white head.

'And the bastard son there, that you kept all these years to torment me, to remind me – you had no right to him either, I could have looked after her and her child better than you –'

Bran said in a high remote voice, that seemed to come so far out of the past that it put a chill into Will's spine: 'And would you then have shot my dog Cafall, Mr Prichard?'

'Not even your own dog, that animal was not,' Prichard said roughly. 'That was a working dog of your father's.'

'Oh, yes,' said Bran in the same clear distant voice. 'Yes, indeed. My father had a dog named Cafall.'

Will's blood tingled in his veins, for he knew that the Cafall of whom Bran spoke was not the dog Cafall who had been shot, and the father not Owen Davies. So now Bran, the Pendragon, must know of his true, magnificent, dreadful heritage. Then a last sudden astonishment woke in Will's mind. It must have been Owen Davies who gave the dead dog his name, for Bran had said that Cafall had come to them when he himself was only a very small boy. *Why had Owen Davies named his son's dog by the name of the great king's hound?*

His eyes flickered to Owen Davies's thin unprepossessing form, and he saw that the man was watching him.

'Oh, yes,' Davies said. 'I knew. I tried not to believe it, but I've always known. She came from Cader Idris, you see, and that is the Seat of Arthur, in English. With Arthur's son she came out of the past, because she had betrayed the king her lord and was afraid that he would cast out his own son as a result. By enchantment of the *dewin* she brought the boy into the future, away from their troubles – the future that is the present time now for us. And she left him here. And perhaps, perhaps, she would not herself have had to go back into the past, if the fat fool there had not interfered, and heard the harp, and wanted my Guinevere, and tried to take her away.'

He looked coldly down at Caradog Prichard. With a snarl of fury Prichard jerked his gun up to his shoulder, but John Rowlands swiftly reached out a long arm and wrenched it from him before his finger could reach the trigger. Prichard shouted angrily, gave him a great push and leapt away, scrambling up in venomous fury towards the ledge where Bran and Owen Davies stood.

Bran went to Davies and put his arm round his waist, and stood close. It was the first gesture of affection between the two that Will had ever seen. And wondering, loving surprise woke in Owen Davies's worn face as he looked down at the boy's white head, and the two stood there, waiting.

Prichard scrambled towards them, murder in his eyes. But John Rowlands was close behind him. He swung the gun at Prichard like a stick, knocking him sideways, and then seized and held him with the force of a much younger man. Wildly struggling, but grasped into helplessness, Caradog Prichard put back his head and gave a terrible shriek of madness, as all control from the Dark left him, and his mind collapsed into the wreck it must now remain. And with the Sleepers ridden, and the last hope of harming Bran gone, the Grey King gave up his battle.

The echoes of Prichard's shriek became a long howling cry through the mountains, rising, falling, rising, echoing from peak to peak, as all powers of the Dark vanished forever from Cader Idris, from the valley of the Dysynni, from Tal y Llyn. Cold as death, anguished as all the loss in the world, it died away and yet still seemed to hang in the air.

They stood motionless, caught in horror.

And the mist that men called the breath of the Grey King came creeping down out of the pass and down the side of the mountains, rolling and curling and wisping, concealing all it reached, until at the last it cut off every one of them from the rest. A rustling, flurrying sound came out of the mist, but only Will saw the great grey forms of the ghost foxes, the *milgwn* of the Brenin Llwyd, come rushing headlong down the mountain, and plunge into the dark lake, and disappear.

Then the mist closed over Llyn Mwyngil, the lake in the pleasant retreat, and there was a cold silence through all the valley save for the distant bleat, sometimes, of a mountain sheep, like the echo of a man's voice calling a girl's name, far away.

Silver on the Tree

For Margaret

Contents

AUTHOR'S NOTE: in Chapter Three, I have taken the liberty of transplanting Sir Mortimer Wheeler's excavation of the Roman amphitheatre at Caerleon from 1928 to the present day. In Part Four, the five lines attached to the sword Eirias are those once proposed by Robert Graves as an envoie to the ancient Irish 'Song of Amergin'

PART ONE

When the Dark Comes Rising

Midsummer's Eve

Will said, turning a page, 'He liked woad. He says – listen – *the decoction of Woad drunken is good for wounds in bodies of a strong constitution, as of country people, and such as are accustomed to great labour and hard coarse fare.*'

'Such as me, and all other members of Her Majesty's Navy,' Stephen said. With great precision he pulled a tall, heavy-headed stem of grass out of its sheath, and lay back in the field nibbling it.

'Woad,' said James, wiping a mist of sweat from his plump pink face. 'That's the blue stuff the Ancient Britons used to paint themselves with.'

Will said, 'Gerard says here that woad flowers are yellow.'

James said rather pompously, 'Well, I've done a year's more history than you have and I know they used it for blue.' There was a pause. He added, 'Green walnuts turn your fingers black.'

'Oh, well,' said Will. A very large velvety bee, overloaded with pollen, landed on his book and waddled dispiritedly across the page. Will blew it gently on to a leaf, pushing back the straight brown forelock that flopped over his eyes. His glance was caught by a movement on the river beyond the field where they lay.

'Look! Swans!'

Lazy as the hot summer day, a pair of swans sailed slowly by without a sound; their small wake lapped at the riverbank.

'Where?' said James, clearly with no intention of looking.

'They like this bit of the river, it's always quiet. The big boats stay over in the main reach, even on a Saturday.'

'Who's coming fishing?' said Stephen. But he still lay unmoving on his back, one leg folded over the other, the slender stem of grass swaying between his teeth.

'In a minute.' James stretched, yawning. 'I ate too much cake.'

'Mum's picnics are as huge as ever.' Stephen rolled over and gazed at the grey-green river. 'When I was your age, you couldn't fish at all in this part of the Thames. Pollution, then. Some things do improve.'

'A paltry few,' Will said sepulchrally, out of the grass.

Stephen grinned. He reached out and picked a slender green stalk with a tiny red flower; solemnly he held it up. 'Scarlet pimpernel. *Open for sun, closed for rain, that's the poor man's weathervane.* Granddad taught me that. Pity you never knew him. What does your friend Mr Gerard say about this one, Will?'

'Mmm?' Will was lying on his side, watching the weary bumblebee flex its wings.

'Book,' James said. 'Scarlet pimpernel.'

'Oh.' Will turned the crackling pages. 'Here it is. Oh lovely. *The juyce purgeth the head by gargarising or washing the throat therewith ; it cures the tooth-ach being snift up into the nosethrils, especially into the contrary nosethril.*'

'The contrary nosethril, of course,' Stephen said gravely.

'He also says it's good against the stinging of vipers and other venomous beasts.'

'Daft,' said James.

'No it's not,' Will said mildly. 'Just three hundred years old. There's one super bit at the end where he tells you very seriously how barnacle geese are hatched out of barnacles.'

'The Caribbean might have foxed him,' Stephen said. 'Millions of barnacles, but not one barnacle goose.'

James said, 'Will you go back there, after your leave?'

'Wherever their Lordships send us, mate.' Stephen threaded the scarlet pimpernel into the top buttonhole of his shirt, and unfolded his lanky body. 'Come on. Fish.'

'I'll come in a minute. You two go.' Will lay idly watching as they fitted rods together, tied hooks and floats. Grasshoppers skirled unseen from the grass, chirruping their solos over the deep summer insect hum: it was a sleepy, lulling sound. He sighed with happiness. Sunshine and high summer and, rarer than either, his eldest brother home from sea. The world smiled on him; nothing could possibly be improved. He felt his eyelids droop; he jerked them apart again. Again they closed in sleepy content; again he forced them open. For a flicker of a moment he wondered why he would not let himself fall harmlessly asleep.

And then he knew.

The swans were there on the river again, slow-moving white shapes, drifting back upstream. Over Will's head the trees sighed in the breeze, like waves on distant oceans. In tiny yellow-green bunches the flowers of the sycamore scattered the long grass around him. Running one of them between his fingers, he watched Stephen standing tall a few yards off threading his fishing-line through his rod. Beyond, on the river, he could see one of the swans moving slowly ahead of its mate. The bird passed Stephen.

But as it passed, it did not disappear behind Stephen. Will could see the white form clearly through the outline of Stephen's body.

And through the outline of the swan, in turn, he could see a steep slope of land, grassy, without trees, that had not been there before.

Will swallowed.

'Steve?' he said.

His eldest brother was close before him, knotting a leader on his line, and Will had spoken loudly. But Stephen did not hear. James came past, holding his rod erect but low as he fastened the hook safely into its cork handle. Will could still see, through him, the forms of the swans as if in a faint mist. He sat up and stretched out his hand to the rod as James went by, and his fingers moved through the substance of the wood as if there had been nothing there.

And Will knew, with dread and delight, that a part of his life which had been sleeping was broad awake once more.

His brothers walked off to the river, moving diagonally across the field. Through their phantom forms Will could see the only earth that in this elusive patch of time was for him solid and real: the grassy slope, its edges merging into mistiness. And on it he saw figures, running, bustling, driven by some urgent haste. If he stared at them too hard, they were not there. But if he gazed with sleepy eyes, not quite focused, he could see them all, sun-dappled, hurrying.

They were small, dark-haired. They belonged to a very distant time. They wore tunics of blue, green or black; he saw one woman in white, with a string of bright blue beads about her neck. They were gathering bundles of spears, arrows, tools, sticks; packing pots into wrappings of animal skin; putting together packages of what he supposed was meat, in dry rippled strips. There were dogs with them: full-haired dogs with short pointed muzzles. Children ran and called, and a dog lifted his head to bay, but no sound came. For Will's ears, only the grasshoppers chirruped, over the deep insect hum.

He saw no animals but the dogs. These people were travellers; not belonging here, but passing through. He was not even sure whether the land on which they stood, in their own time, lay in his own part of the Thames Valley or in some totally different place. But he knew one thing very clearly, suddenly: they were all very much afraid.

Often they raised their heads, fearfully, and gazed away to the east. They spoke seldom to one another, but worked on, hastily. Something, someone, was coming, threatening them, driving them on. They were running away. Will found himself catching the sense of urgency, willing them to hurry, to escape whatever disaster was on its way. Whatever disaster . . . he too stared eastward. But it was hard to tell what he saw. A strange double landscape lay before him, a firm curving slope visible through the phantom misty lines of the flat fields and hedges of his own day and the glimmering half-seen Thames. The swans were still there, and yet not there; one of them dipped its elegant neck to the surface of the water, ghostly as an image reflected in a window-pane . . .

. . . and all at once, the swan was real, solid, opaque, and Will was no longer looking out of his own time into another. The travellers were gone, out of sight in that other summer day thousands of years before. Will shut his eyes, desperately trying to hold some image of them before it faded from his memory. He remembered a pot glinting with the dull sheen of bronze; a cluster of arrows tipped with sharp black flakes of flint; he remembered the dark skin and eyes of the woman in white, and the bright luminous blue of the string of beads about her neck. Most of all he remembered the sense of fear.

He stood up in the long grass, holding his book; he could feel his legs trembling. Unseen in a tree over his head, a song-thrush poured out its trilling twice-over song. Will walked shakily towards the river; James's voice hailed him.

'Will! Over here! Come and see!'

He veered blindly towards the sound. Stephen the purist fisherman stood casting delicately out into the river, his line whispering through the air. James was threading a worm on his hook. He put it down, and triumphantly held up a cluster of three small perch tied through the gills.

'Goodness,' Will said. 'That's quick!'

Before he could regret the word, James was raising an eyebrow. 'Not specially. You been asleep? Come on, get your rod.'

'No,' said Will, to both question and command. Stephen, glancing round at him, suddenly let his line go slack. He looked hard at Will, frowning.

'Will? Are you all right? You look –'

'I do feel a bit funny,' Will said.

'Sun, I bet. Beating down on the back of your neck, while you were sitting there reading that book.'

'Probably.'

'Even in England it can get pretty fierce, matey. Flaming June. And Midsummer's Eve, at that . . . go and lie down in the shade for a while. And drink the rest of that lemonade.'

'All of it?' said James indignantly. 'What about us?'

Stephen aimed a kick at him. 'You catch ten more perch and I'll buy you a drink on the way home. Go on, Will. Under the trees.'

'All right,' said Will.

'I told you that book was daft,' James said.

Will crossed the field again and sat down on the cool grass beneath the sycamore trees, beside the remains of their picnic tea. Sipping lemonade slowly from a plastic cup, he looked uneasily out at the river – but all was normal. The swans had gone. Midges danced in the air; the world was hazy with heat. His head ached; he put aside the cup and lay on his back in the grass, looking up. Leaves danced above him; the branches breathed and swayed, to and fro, to and fro, shifting green patterns against the blue sky. Will pressed his palms to his eyes, remembering the faint hurrying forms that had flickered up to him out of the past; remembering the fear . . .

Even afterwards, he could never tell whether he fell asleep. The sighing of the breeze seemed to grow louder, more fierce; all at once he could see different trees above him, beech trees, their heart-shaped leaves dancing agitated in a wilder swirl than sycamore or oak. And this now was not a hedge-line of trees stretching unbroken to the river, but a copse; the river was gone, the sound and smell of it, and on either side of him Will could see the open sky. He sat up.

He was high over the wooded valley of the Thames on a curving grassy slope; the cluster of beech trees around him marked the top of the hill like a cap. Golden vetch grew in the short springy grass at his side; from one of the curled flowers a small blue butterfly fluttered to his hand and away again. There was no more heavy hum of insects in valley fields; instead, high over his head through the stirring of the wind, a skylark's song poured bubbling into the air.

And then, somewhere, Will heard voices. He turned his head. A string of people came hurrying up the hill, each darting from one tree or bush to the next, avoiding the open slope. The first two or three had just reached a curious deep hole sunk into the hill, so closely overgrown by brush that he would not have noticed it if they had not been there, tugging branches aside. They were laden with bundles wrapped in rough dark cloth – but so hastily wrapped that Will could see the contents jutting through. He blinked: there were gold cups, plates, chalices, a great gold cross crusted with jewels, tall candlesticks of gold and silver, robes and cloths of glimmering silk woven with gold and gems; the array of treasure seemed endless. The figures bound each bundle with rope, and lowered one after another into the hole. Will saw a man in the robes of a monk, who seemed to be supervising them: directing, explaining, always keeping a nervous watch out over the surrounding land.

A trio of small boys came hurrying up to the top of the hill, despatched by the pointing arm of the priest. Will stood up slowly. But the boys trotted past him without even a glance, ignoring him so completely that he knew he was in this past time only an observer, invisible, not able even to be sensed.

The boys paused on the edge of the copse, and stood looking out keenly across the valley; they had clearly been sent to keep watch from there. Looking at them huddled nervously together, Will let his mind dwell on hearing them, and in a moment the voices were echoing in his head.

'No one coming this way.'

'Not yet.'

'Two hours maybe, the runner said. I heard him talking to my father, he said there's hundreds of them, terrible, rampaging along the Old Way. They've burned London, he said, you could see the black smoke rising in great clouds—'

'They cut off your ears if they catch you. The boys. The men they slit right open, and they do even worse things to the women and girls—'

'My father knew they'd come. He said. There was blood instead of rain fell in the east last month, he said, and men saw dragons flying in the sky.'

'There's always signs like that, before the heathen devils come.'

'What's the use of burying the treasures? Nobody'll ever come back to get them. Nobody ever comes back when the devils drive them out.'

'Maybe this time.'

'Where are we going?'

'Who knows? To the west—'

Urgent voices called the boys back; they ran. The hiding of bundles in the hole was finished, and some of the figures already scurrying down the hill. Will watched fascinated while the last men heaved over the top of the hole a great flat flint boulder, the largest he had ever seen. They fitted it neatly inside the opening like a kind of lid, then unrolled over the top a section of grassy sod. Branches growing from surrounding bushes were tugged across the top. In a moment there was no sign of any hiding place, no scar on the hillside to show that the hasty work had even taken place. Crying out in alarm, one of the men pointed across the valley; beyond the next hill a thick column of smoke was rising. At once, in panic, all the group fled down the grass-skinned chalk slope, slipping and leaping, the monkish figure as hasty and helter-skelter as the rest.

And Will was swept by a wave of fear so intense that it turned his stomach.

For a moment he knew, as vividly as these fugitives, the animal terror of cruel violent death: of pain, of hurting, of hate. Or of something worse than hate: a dreadful remote blankness, that took joy only from destruction and tormenting and others' fear. Some terrible threat was advancing, on these people just as on those others, shadowy forms he had seen in a different, distant past a little while before. Over there in the east, the threat was once more rising, roaring down.

'It's coming,' Will said aloud, staring at the column of smoke, trying not to envision what might happen when its makers came over the brow of the hill. '*It's coming –*'

James' voice said, full of a curious excitement, 'No it isn't, it's not moving at all. Are you awake? *Look!*'

Stephen said, 'What an extraordinary thing!'

Their voices were above Will's head; he was lying on his back in cool grass. It was a moment before he could recollect himself, and stop shaking. He heaved himself up on to his elbows, and saw Stephen and James standing a few paces away, their hands full of rods and fish and bait pails. They were staring at something in a kind of wary fascination. Will craned his head round to the hot humming meadow, to see what held them. And he gasped, as his mind was half torn apart by a great wave of that same blind terror that had swamped him a moment before, a world and ten centuries and yet no more than a breath away.

Ten yards off in the grass, a small black animal was standing motionless, facing him: a lithe, lean animal perhaps a foot and a half long with a long tail and sinuous, curving back. It was like a stoat or a weasel and yet it was neither. Its sleek fur was pitch black from nose to tail; its unwinking black eyes were fixed unmistakably on Will. And from it he felt a pulsing ferocity of viciousness and evil so strong that his mind rebelled against believing it could exist.

James made a sudden quick hissing sound.

The black creature did not move. Still it stared at Will. Will sat staring back, caught up in the unreasoning shout of terror that twanged on through his brain. Out of the corner of his eye he was aware of Stephen's tall form standing at his side, very still.

James said softly, 'I know what it is. It's a mink. They've just started turning up round here – I saw it in the paper. Like weasels, only nastier, it said. Look at those eyes–'

Impulsively breaking the tension, he yelled wordlessly at the creature and slashed at the grass with his fishing rod. Swiftly, but without panic, the black mink turned and slid away through the field towards the river, its long back undulating with a strange unpleasant gliding movement like a large snake. James bounded after it, still clasping his rod.

'Be careful!' Stephen called sharply.

James shouted, 'I won't touch it. Got my rod . . .'. He disappeared along the riverbank, past a clump of stubby willow.

'I don't like this,' Stephen said.

'No,' Will said. He shivered, looking at the place in the field where the animal had stood, staring at him with its intent black eyes. 'Creepy.'

'I don't mean just the mink, if that's what it was.' There was an unfamiliar note in Stephen's voice that made Will abruptly turn his head. He moved to get to his feet, but his tall brother squatted down beside him, arms resting on knees, hands fiddling with the wire leader on a piece of fishing-line.

Stephen wound the line round his finger and back again, round and back again.

'Will,' he said in this strange taut voice. 'I've got to talk to you. Now, while James is off chasing that thing. I've been trying to get you alone ever since I came home – I hoped today, only Jamie wanted to fish –'

He floundered, stumbling over his words in a way that filled Will with astonishment and alarm, coming from the cool adult brother who had always been so much his symbol of everything fulfilled, complete, grown-up. Then Stephen brought his head up and stared at Will almost belligerently, and Will stared nervously back.

Stephen said, 'When the ship was in Jamaica last year, I sent you a big West Indian carnival head, for a Christmas and birthday present put together.'

'Well of course,' Will said. 'It's super. We were all looking at it only yesterday.'

Stephen went on, ignoring him. 'I'd got it from an old Jamaican who grabbed me one day in the street, out of nowhere, in the middle of Carnival. He told me my name, and he said I was to give the head to you. And when I asked how on earth he knew me, he said, *There is a look that we Old Ones have. Our families have something of it too.*'

'I know about all that,' Will said brightly, swallowing the foreboding that hollowed his throat. 'You sent a letter, with the head. Don't you remember?'

'I remember it was a damn funny thing for a stranger to say,' Stephen said. 'Old Ones, we Old Ones. With capital letters – you could *hear* them.'

'Oh not really. Surely – I mean, you said he was an old man–'

'Will,' Stephen said, looking at him with cold blue eyes, 'the day we sailed from Kingston, that old man turned up at the ship. I don't know how he talked them into it, but someone was sent to fetch me to him. He stood there on the dock, with his black, black face and his white, white hair, and he looked quietly at the rating who'd fetched me, until the boy left, and then he said just one thing. *Tell your brother*, he said, *that the Old Ones of the ocean islands are ready.* Then he went away.'

Will said nothing. He knew there would be more. He looked at Stephen's hands; they were clenched, and one thumb was flicking automatically to and fro over its fist.

'And then,' Stephen said, his voice shaking a little, 'we put in at Gibraltar on the way home, and I had half a day ashore, and a stranger said something to me in the street. He was standing beside me, we were waiting for a traffic light – he was very tall and slim, Arab I think. Do you know what he said? *Tell Will Stanton that the Old Ones of the south are ready.* Then he just disappeared into the crowd.'

'Oh,' Will said.

The thumb abruptly stopped moving on Stephen's hand. He stood up, in one swift movement like a released spring. Will too scrambled to his feet, blinking up, unable to read the suntanned face against the bright sky.

'Either I'm going out of my head,' Stephen said, 'or you're mixed up in something very strange, Will. In either case you might have a little more to say to me than *oh*. I told you, I don't like it, not one bit.'

'The trouble is, you see,' Will said slowly, 'that if I tried to explain, you wouldn't believe me.'

'Try me,' his brother said.

Will sighed. Of all the nine Stanton children, he was the youngest and Stephen the oldest; there were fifteen long years between them, and until Stephen had left home to join the Navy, a smaller Will had shadowed him everywhere in silent devotion. He knew now that he was at the ending of something he had hoped would never end.

He said, 'Are you sure? You won't laugh at me, you won't . . . judge?'

'Of course not,' Stephen said.

Will took a deep breath. 'Well then. It's like this . . . This where we live is a world of men, ordinary men, and although in it there is the Old Magic of the earth, and the Wild Magic of living things, it is men who control what the world shall be like.' He was not looking at Stephen, for fear of seeing the changing expression that he knew he would certainly see. 'But beyond the world is the universe, bound by the law of the High Magic, as every universe must be. And beneath the High Magic are two . . . poles . . . that we call the Dark and the Light. No other power orders them. They merely exist. The Dark seeks by its dark nature to influence men so that in the end, through them, it may control the earth. The Light has the task of stopping that from happening.

From time to time the Dark has come rising and has been driven back, but now very soon it will rise for the last and most perilous time. It has been gathering strength for that rising, and it is almost ready. And therefore, for the last time, until the end of Time, we must drive it back so that the world of men may be free.'

'We?' Stephen said, expressionless.

'We are the Old Ones,' Will said, strong and self-confident now. 'There is a great circle of us, all over the world and beyond the world, from all places and all corners of time. I was the last one to be born, and when I was brought into my power as an Old One, on my eleventh birthday, the circle became complete. I knew nothing about all this, till then. But the time is coming closer now, and that is why you were given the reassurances – warnings, in a way – to bring to me, I think from two of the three oldest of the circle.'

Stephen said, in the same flat voice, 'The second one didn't look very old.'

Will looked up at him and said simply, 'Nor do I.'

'For God's sake,' Stephen said irritably, 'you're my little brother and you're twelve years old and I can remember you being born.'

'In one sense only,' Will said.

Stephen stared in exasperation at the figure before him: the stocky small boy in blue jeans and battered shirt, with straight brown hair falling untidily over one eye. 'Will, you're too old for these silly games. You sound almost as if you believed all this stuff.'

Will said calmly, 'What do you think those two messengers were, then, Steve? You think I'm smuggling diamonds, maybe, or part of a drug ring?'

Stephen groaned. 'I don't know. Perhaps I dreamt them . . . perhaps I really am going out of my head.' The tone tried to be light, but there was unmistakable strain in his voice.

'Oh no,' Will said. 'You didn't dream them. Other . . . warnings . . . have begun coming too.' He fell silent for a moment, thinking of the anxious hurrying figures looming misty out of a time three thousand years past, and the Saxon boys, after that, watching terrified for the marauding Danes. Then he looked sadly at Stephen.

'It's too much for you,' he said. 'They should have known that. I suppose they did. The messages had to come by word of mouth, that's the only way secure from the Dark. And after that it's up to me . . .' Quickly he seized his brother's arm, pointing, as the incomprehension on Stephen's face began changing unbearably to alarm. 'Look – there's James.'

Automatically Stephen half-turned to look. The movement made his leg brush against a low bramble clump growing out into the field from the trees and hedge behind. And out of the sprawling green bush rose a flickering, sudden cloud of delicate white moths. They were an astonishing sight, feathery, exquisite. Endlessly flowing upward, hundred upon hundred, they fluttered like a gentle snow-flurry round Stephen's head and shoulders. Startled, he flapped his arms to brush them away.

'Stay still,' Will said softly. 'Don't hurt them. Stay still.'

Stephen paused, one arm raised apprehensively before his face. Over and around him the tiny moths flurried, round and around, wheeling, floating, never settling, drifting down. They were like infinitely small birds fashioned of snowflakes; silent, ghostly, each tiny wing a filigree of five delicate feathers, all white.

Stephen stood still, dazed, shielding his face with one hand. 'They're beautiful! But so many ... what are they?'

'Plume moths,' Will said, looking at him with a strange loving regret, like a farewell. 'White plume moths. There's an old saying, that they carry memories away.'

In one last whirl the white cloud of moths flowed and fluttered round Stephen's uncertain head; then the cloud parted, dispersing like smoke, as in the same curious communion the moths disappeared into the hedge. The leaves enfolded them; they were gone.

James came thudding up behind them. 'Gosh, what a chase! It *was* a mink – must have been.'

'Mink?' Stephen said. He shook his head suddenly, like a dog newly come out of water.

James stared at him. 'The mink. The little black animal.'

'Yes, of course,' Stephen said hastily, still looking dazed. 'Yes. It was a mink, then?'

James was bubbling with triumph. 'I'm sure it was. What a piece of luck! I've been watching out for one ever since that article in the *Observer*. It told you to, because they're a pest. They eat chickens, and all kinds of birds. Someone brought them over from America, years ago, to breed them for the fur, and a few escaped and went wild.'

'Where did he go?' said Will.

'Jumped into the river. I didn't know they could swim.'

Stephen picked up the picnic basket. 'Time we took the fish home. Hand me that lemonade bottle, Will.'

James said promptly, 'You said you'd get me a drink on the way back.'

'I said, if you caught ten more fish.'

'Seven's pretty close.'

'Not close enough.'

'Stingy lot, sailors,' said James.

'Here,' said Will, poking him with the bottle. 'I didn't drink all the lemonade anyway.'

'Go on, Sponge,' said Stephen. 'Finish it.' One corner of the basket was fraying; he tried to weave the loose ends of wicker together, while James gulped his lemonade.

Will said, 'Falling to bits, that basket. Looks as though it belonged to the Old Ones.'

'Who?' said Stephen.

'The Old Ones. In the letter you sent me from Jamaica, with that big carnival head, last year. Something the old man said, the one who gave you it. Don't you remember?'

'Good Lord no,' said Stephen amiably. 'Much too long ago.' He chuckled. 'That was a crazy present all right, wasn't it? Like the stuff Max makes at art school.'

'Yes,' Will said.

They strolled home, through the long feathery grass, through the lengthening shadows of the trees, through the yellow-green flowers of the sycamore.

Black Mink

The way home was a winding way: first through fields and along towpaths, to the place where they had left their bicycles, then along curving small green-shaded roads. Oak and sycamore and Lombardy poplar reached high on either side; houses slept behind hedges fragrant with honeysuckle and starred with invading bindweed. In the distance they could hear the hum of a hurrying, more preoccupied world, and see the cars flicking by on the motorway that straddled the valley of the Thames. It was late afternoon now; the horizons were lost in haze, and clouds of gnats danced in the warm air.

They were cycling along Huntercombe Lane, half a mile from home, past Will's favourite flint-walled, brick-trimmed cottages, when James braked suddenly.

'What's up?'

'Back tyre. I thought it would last, but it keeps getting softer. I can pump it up enough to get home.'

Will and Stephen waited, while he unhitched his pump. Faint voices drifted towards them from further up the road; the road crossed a small bridge, up there, over a stream that meandered through the farm fields on its way to join the Thames. Generally the stream moved so sluggishly that it hardly deserved the name, though on just one wild day of his life Will had seen it in spate. He scooted his bicycle idly up towards it. No sound of running water today; the stream glimmered shallow and still, scummed with green weed like a pond.

Voices came nearer; Will leaned over the side of the little bridge. Below on the bank a small boy came running, panting, with a shiny leather music-case that looked half as big as himself banging against his legs. Three others were in pursuit of him, yelling and laughing. Will was about to turn away, thinking it a game, when the first boy, finding his way blocked by the side of the bridge, twisted, skidded and then turned at bay in a movement that somehow spoke not play but desperation. He was dark-skinned, neatly dressed; the boys following were white, and scruffier. Will could hear them now. One was yelping like a hound.

'Pakkie – Pakkie – Pakkie! Here boy, here boy! Here Pakkie–'

They slid to a halt in front of the small tense figure. Will recognized two of them as boys who went to his own school, a tough troublesome pair much given to gang-rumpus on the playground. One of them smiled a thin nasty smile at the boy they had been chasing.

'Don't want to say hallo, Pakkie-boy? What you scared of, eh? Where you been?'

The boy jerked to one side and lunged, trying to slip past and away, but one of the others stepped swiftly sideways and blocked him. The music-case fell to the ground, and as the small boy leaned to pick it up a large dirty foot came down on its handle.

'Been to piano lesson, has he? Didn't know Pakkies played the piano, did you, Frankie? Only those funny little plinky-plink instruments, *wheee-eeeee-eeeeee*–' He capered about making sounds like a bad violinist; the others gurgled with unpleasant laughter, one of them picking up the music-case and whacking it for applause.

'Please give me back my case,' said the small boy, in a precise, unhappy little voice.

The bigger boy held it high over the water of the stream. 'Come and get it, Pakkie, come and get it!'

Will shouted indignantly, 'Give it back!'

Their heads turned sharply; then the bully's face relaxed into a sneer as he recognized Will. 'Mind your own mucking business, Stanton!'

The other boys hooted derisively.

'You brainless oiks!' Will yelled. 'Always picking on little kids – give it back to him, or –'

'Or what?' said the boy, and he looked at the small smaller boy and smiled. He opened his hand, and let the music-case fall into the stream.

His friends guffawed and cheered. The small boy burst into tears. Will, spluttering, thrust his bicycle aside; but before he could move further a whirl of limbs shot past him and Stephen's tall rangy form was bounding down the slope.

The boys scattered, too late. In only a few paces Stephen had grabbed the ringleader. Holding him by the shoulders, he said softly, 'Get that case out of the water.'

Will watched, motionless, caught by the controlled fury in the quiet voice, but the other boy was riding too high on his own confidence. He twisted in Stephen's grasp, snarling at him. 'You crazy? Get meself all wet for some bleedin' nignog? That little cat-food eater? You think I'm –'

The last word had no chance. With a quick shift of grip Stephen suddenly heaved the boy off his feet and into the air, and dropped him into the scummy green water of the stream.

The splash left silence. A bird chirruped gaily overhead. The two boys on the bank stood motionless, staring at their leader as he slowly hoisted himself up, dripping weed and muddy water, to stand knee-deep in the nearly stagnant stream. He looked at Stephen, his face empty of expression; then bent, picked up the flat leather music-case and held it out, dripping, at arm's length. Stephen handed it to the little boy, and he took it, dark eyes saucer-wide; then turned and fled without a word.

Stephen swung round and climbed back up to the road. As he stepped long-legged over the wire fence, the boy standing in the water came suddenly to life as if released from a spell. He splashed back to the bank, muttering. They heard a few scattered obscenities, then a furious shout: 'You think you're so great, just because you're bigger'n me!'

'The pot is speaking to the kettle,' said Stephen peacefully, swinging his leg over his bicycle.

The boy yelled: 'If my Dad ever catches you, you just wait–'

Stephen paused, propelled himself to the edge of the bridge and leaned over. 'Stephen Stanton, at the Old Vicarage,' he said. 'You tell your Dad he can come and discuss you with me any time he likes.'

There was no answer. James came up at Will's side as they rode away; he was beaming. 'Lovely,' he said. 'Beautiful.'

'Yes,' Will said, pedalling. 'But –'

'What?'

'Oh, nothing.'

'That must have been little Manny Singh,' Mrs Stanton said, digging a large knife into the treacle tart. 'They live at the other end of the village, in one of the houses on that new estate.'

'I know them,' Mary said. 'Mr Singh wears a turban.'

'That's right. They aren't Pakistani, as it happens, they're Indian – Sikhs. Not that it's relevant. What horrible boys those three are.'

'They're horrible to everybody, that lot,' James said, hopefully watching the size of the piece of tart about to be cut for him. 'No relation to race, colour or creed – they'll bash anyone. So long as he's smaller than them.'

'They seemed a little more . . . selective today,' Stephen said quietly.

'I'm not sure you should have dropped him in the water, though,' his mother said placidly. 'Pass the custard round, Will.'

'Richie Moore called the little boy a cat-food eater,' Will said.

Stephen said, 'Pity that stream wasn't ten feet deep.'

James said, 'There's an extra piece of tart there, Mum.'

'For your father,' Mrs Stanton said. 'Eyes off. He doesn't work late for you to pinch his dinner. Don't *stuff*, James. Even Mary's eating more slowly than you.' Then she raised her head suddenly, listening. 'What's that?'

They had all heard the faint noise outside; it came again, louder. Distant squawking sounds rose from the chickens in their yard behind the house; not ordinary squawks of protest or demand, but high cackles of alarm.

Instantly the children stampeded, James even forgetting his treacle tart. Will was first out of the back door – and then instantly, abruptly, he stopped, so that Stephen and James blundered round him and almost fell. They ran on. But Will could feel the sense of malevolence, of immanent undiluted ill-wishing, so strong all around him that he could scarcely move. He stood, shaking. Thrusting against the sensation as against a high wind, he stumbled on after the others. His mind felt thick and slow. He thought, *I have felt this before* . . . But there was no time to remember.

He heard shouting from the yard, and scuffling feet, through the cackling of the frightened birds. In the half-light of the hazy evening he saw Stephen and James dodging to and fro as if chasing something; closer, he thought he saw a small twisting dark body, lithe and swift, darting between them. Stephen grabbed for a stick; whacked at the shape; missed. The stick hit the ground, splintering. A garden fork stood against the fence of the hen run; Will seized it, moving closer. The animal ran past his feet. It made no sound.

'Get it, Will!'

'Hit it!'

Feet flurried, birds squawked, the yard was full of colliding bodies, grey shapes in the dim light. For an instant Will saw the full moon, an enormous yellow arc beginning to rise over the trees. Then James was bumping into him again.

'Over here! Catch him!'

Will had one quick clear glimpse. 'It's another mink!'

'Of course! Over *here*!'

Twisting in its urgent search for flight, the mink was suddenly between Will and the fence, cornered. White teeth flashed. It stood taut, staring, and screamed suddenly, a high angry screech that pierced Will's mind and brought flooding into it the overwhelming awareness of evil he had felt when stepping outside the door. He flinched.

'Now, Will, now! Hard!'

They were both yelling at him. Will swung the garden fork high. The mink stared at him, and screamed again. Will looked at it. *The Dark is rising; killing one of its creatures will not stop the Dark from rising.* He let the fork drop.

James groaned loudly. Stephen leapt to Will's side. The mink, teeth bared, ran straight at Stephen as if to attack him; Will gasped in horror, but at the last minute the creature veered aside and darted between Stephen's legs. Even then it did not run at once for freedom; it dived at a frightened huddle of chickens, seized one by the neck and bit hard at the back of its head, so that the bird went instantly limp. The mink let it drop, and fled into the night.

James was stamping in angry frustration. 'The dogs! Where are the dogs?'

A beam of light wavered outside the kitchen door. 'Barbara took them to Eton to be clipped,' his mother's voice said. 'She's late because of picking up your father.'

'Oh *damn*!'

'I agree,' said his mother mildly, 'but there it is.' She came forward with the light. 'Let's look at the damage.'

The damage was considerable. When the boys had sorted noisy hysterical pullets from their dead companions, they had six fat corpses lying in a row. Each bird had been killed by a vicious bite at the back of its head.

Mary said, bewildered, 'But so many? Why so many? It didn't even try to take a single one away.'

Mrs Stanton shook her head in bafflement. 'A fox will kill one bird and run

off with it, quickly. Which makes more sense, I must say. You say this thing
was a *mink?*'

'I'm sure,' James said. 'There was a piece in the paper. Besides, we saw one
this afternoon by the river.'

Stephen said dryly, 'Looks as though it just enjoyed killing our chickens.'

Will was standing a little way off, leaning against the wall of the barn.
'Killing for the love of it,' he said.

James snapped his fingers. 'That's what the paper said. Why they were pests.
It said the mink was the only animal beside the polecat that killed for the sake
of killing. Not just when it was hungry.'

Mrs Stanton picked up a pair of dangling dead chickens. 'Well,' she said with
brisk resignation, 'bring them in. We'll just have to make the best of it and
hope the wretched animal didn't choose the best layers. And just let him try to
come back . . . Steve, will you tuck up the rest of them?'

'Sure,' Stephen said.

'I'll help,' said James. 'Wow – you were lucky, Steve. I thought it was going
to bite you. Wonder what stopped it?'

'I taste bad.' Stephen looked up at the sky. 'Look at that moon – we hardly
need a torch at all . . . Come on. Wood, nails, hammer. We'll make that hen-run
eternally minkproof.'

Will said, 'It won't come back.' He was looking at the pimpernel flower
drooping wilted and forgotten from Stephen's buttonhole. '*Good against
venomous beasts.* It won't come back.'

James peered at him. 'You look funny. You okay?'

'Of course I am,' Will said, fighting the turmoil in his mind. 'Course I am.
Course . . .'

His head was whirling; it was like giddiness, except that it seemed also to be
destroying his sense of time, of what was now and what before or after. Had the
mink gone, or were they still chasing it? Had it yet come at all; were they
shortly to be attacked, the hens to begin a dreadful frightened clamour? Or was
he . . . somewhere else . . . entirely . . . ?

He shook his head abruptly. *Not yet. Not yet.* 'Dad's tool chest is in the barn
now. He moved it,' he said.

'Come on, then.' Stephen led the way into the wooden outbuilding that was
known, more romantically than it deserved, as the barn. Their house had once
been a vicarage, never a farm, but the chickens and rabbits that their farmbred
mother kept were enough to change its mood.

James snapped on the electric light, and they paused, blinking; then
collected hammer, pliers, stout nails, some chickenwire and several pieces of
left-over half-inch board.

'Just right,' Stephen said.

'Dad made a new rabbit-hutch last week. Those are the bits.'

'Leave the light on. It'll shine out.'

A shaft of light from the dusty window beamed out into the night. They began cutting chicken-wire and fitting together boards, on the far side of the hen-run where the mink had wriggled its way in.

'Will – see if there's another piece of board in there, about a foot longer than this one.'

'Righto.'

Will crossed the moonlit yard towards the stream of yellow light reaching out from the barn. Behind him the sound of Stephen's hammer rang rhythmically over the still-restless murmur of the hens.

And then the whirling took hold of his mind again, and caught his senses into confusion, and the wind seemed to blow in his face. Tap-tap-tap . . . tap-tap-tap . . . the hammering seemed to change, to a hollow metallic sound as of iron striking iron. Staggering, Will leaned against the wall of the barn. The shaft of light was gone, and the moon. The alteration came with no more warning than that: a time-slip so complete that in an instant he could see no trace of Stephen or James, nor any familiar thing or animal or tree.

The night was darker than it had been. There was a creaking sound that he could not identify. He found he was standing against a wall still, but a wall of different texture; his fingers, which had been touching wood, discovered now large blocks of stone, mortared together. The air was still warm as in his own time. From the other side of the wall, he could hear voices. Two men. And both voices were so familiar to Will, out of the other side of his life that his family had never touched or seen, that the small hairs rose on the back of his neck and joy swelled in his chest like pain.

'Badon, then.' A deep voice, expressionless.

'It will have to be.'

'Do you think you can drive them back?'

'I don't know. Do you?' The second voice was almost as deep, but lightened by a warmth of feeling, like a profound amusement.

'Yes. You will drive them back, my lord. But it will not be forever. These men may be driven back, but the force of nature that they represent has never yet been driven back for long.'

The warm voice sighed. 'You are right. This island is doomed, unless . . . I know you are right, my lion. I have known it since I was a boy. Since a day–'

He stopped. There was a long pause.

The first man said gently, 'Do not think about it.'

'Do you know, then? I have never spoken of it to anyone. Well, of course you must know.' He laughed softly; the sound held affection rather than amusement. 'Were *you* there, Old One? You? I suppose you must have been.'

'I was there.'

'All the best men of Britain slaughtered. Every one. Three hundred leaders at the one gathering, *three hundred*! Stabbed, strangled, clubbed, at one sign – I even saw him give the sign, do you know that? I, a boy of seven . . . All dead. My father amongst them. The blood flowed and the grass was red, and the Dark began its rising over Britain –' He choked on the words.

The deep voice said, grim and cold, 'It shall not rise for ever.'

'No, by heaven it shall not!' He had collected himself again. 'And a few days from now Badon shall show that. *Mons Badonicus, mons felix.* So let us hope.'

'The gathering is begun, and men come from every corner of your loyal Britain,' said the first. 'And this night the Circle shall be summoned, the Circle of the Old Ones, to meet this great need.'

Will stood straight, as if someone had called his name. He was so deep in this time now that he had no need of calling. There was no thought, even; only awareness. He turned, and saw light glimmering round the doorway in the stone wall; walked forward to the doorway, jumped suddenly at the sight of two figures armed with sword and spear in front of him, at either side of the door. But neither moved; they stood stiff, at attention, staring ahead.

Will reached out to the heavy, thick-woven curtain that hung over the entrance, and pulled it aside. Bright light blazed into his eyes; he brought up his arm to cover them, blinking.

'Ah, Will,' said the deeper voice. 'Come in, come in.'

Will stepped forward, opening his eyes. He stood there, smiling at the tall robed figure with its fierce proud nose and springing shock of white hair. It was a long time since they had met.

'*Merriman!*' he said. They moved to one another, and embraced.

'How do you, Old One?' the tall man said.

'Well, I thank you.'

'Old One to Old One,' said the other man softly. 'The first and oldest of them, and the last and youngest. And I too greet you, Will Stanton.'

Will looked at the clear blue eyes in the weather-brown face; the short grey beard; the hair still brown but streaked with grey. He went down on one knee, and bent his head. 'My lord.'

The other bent forward in his creaking leather chair and touched Will's shoulder briefly in greeting. 'I am glad to see you. Rise now, and join your master. This part of time is for you two alone, and there is much to do.'

He stood, pushing a short cloak back over one shoulder, and strode to the door, soft-shod feet noiseless on the patterned mosaic floor. Though he was a head short of Merriman's great height, there was an authority in him that towered over any man. 'I will go and hear the new count of men,' he said, turning at the door, over the clatter and scrape of spears as the guards presented arms. 'A night and a day. Be swift, my lion.'

Then he was gone, as if the swirl of the cloak had carried him away.

Will said, 'Those guards didn't challenge me.'

'They had been told to expect your coming,' Merriman said. There was a wry smile on his bleak bony face as he looked down at Will. Then suddenly he put his head back with a quick intake of breath and a sigh. 'Eh Will – how is it with you, in the second great rising? For this now, here, is the first, and I tell you it does not go well.'

'I don't understand, you know,' Will said.

'Do you not, Old One? After all my teaching, and the learning of the Book of Grammarye awhile ago, do you still not understand how time must elude the consciousness of men? Perhaps you are still too close to men yourself . . . Well.' He sat down abruptly on a long couch with curved arms. There was little furniture in the high square room; on its painted plaster walls bright pictures of country summer glowed, sunshine and fields and harvest gold. 'Within the time of men, Will,' he said, 'there are two great risings of the Dark. One is in the time into which you were humanborn. One is here and now, fifteen centuries before that, when my lord Arthur must win a victory that can last long enough to detach these invading ravagers from the Dark that drives them on. You and I have a part to play in the defence against each of these two risings. In fact, the same part.'

'But –' Will said.

Merriman raised one bristling white eyebrow, looking at him sideways. 'If you dare to ask me, *you*, how it is that someone from the future can take part in something that has in that foolish phrase, already happened . . .'

'Oh no,' Will said. 'I shan't. I remember something you said to me once, a long while ago –' He screwed up his face, groping in his memory for the right words. '*For all times coexist*, you said, *and the future can sometimes affect the past, even though the past is a road that leads to the future.*'

A small smile of approval flickered in Merriman's grave face. 'And therefore, now, the Circle of the Light must be called, by Will Stanton the Sign-seeker, who once on a time achieved the joining of the Six Signs of the Light into a circle. It must be called, so that from the one and the same calling it may help the men of this world, both in the time of Arthur and in the time from which you come.'

'So,' Will said, 'I must take the Signs from their refuge, through that most complicated spell we laid on them after they had been joined. I only hope I can find the way.'

'So do I,' said Merriman a trifle grimly. 'For if you do not, the High Magic which guards them will take them outside Time, and the only advantage the Light holds in this great matter will be lost forever.'

Will swallowed. He said, 'I must do it from my own century, though. That was when they were joined and hidden.'

'Of course,' Merriman said. 'And that is why my lord Arthur asked us to be swift. Go, Will, and do what you have to do. A night and a day: that is all the time we have, by the measure of the earth.'

He stood and crossed the floor in one swift movement and grasped Will's arm in the old Roman salute. Dark eyes blazed down from the strange craggy face, with its deep lines. 'I shall be with you, but powerless. Take care,' Merriman said.

Will turned away, to the door, and pulled aside the curtain. Outside in the night there still faintly rang out the metallic hammering, the striking of iron upon iron.

'Wayland Smith works long, this day,' said Merriman behind him, softly. 'And not on shoes for horses, in this time, for horses are not yet shod. On swords, and axes, and knives.'

Will shivered, and without a word went out into the black night. His head whirled, a wind blew into his face – and once more the moon was floating like a great pale orange before him in the sky, and in his arms was a wooden board, and the sound of hammering before him was that of a hammer driving nails into wood.

'Ah,' Stephen said, looking up. 'That looks perfect. Thanks.'

Will came forward and gave him the board.

The Calling

Up in Will's attic bedroom the air was warm and still, furry with summer heat. He lay on his back, listening to the late-night murmur and chink below as the last waking Stantons – his father and Stephen, he thought, from the rumbling voices – made ready for bed. This had been Stephen's bedroom once, and Will had carefully packed up his belongings to let the rightful owner take residence again for the length of his leave. But Stephen had shaken his head. 'Max is away – I'll use his room. I'm a nomad now, Will. It's all yours.'

The last door closed, the last glimmer of reflected light went out. Will looked at his watch. Midnight had passed; Midsummer Day was here now, a few minutes old. Half an hour's wait should be enough. He could see no star through the skylight in his slanting roof, but only a moon-washed sky; its muted brightness filtered down into the room.

The house was muffled in sleep when finally he crept down the stairs in his pyjamas, gingerly treading the furthest corners of those steps that he knew would creak. Outside the door of his parents' room he froze suddenly; his father, snoring in a gentle crescendo, half-woke himself, grunted, turned rustling over and was lost again in soft-breathing sleep.

Will smiled into the darkness. It would have been no great matter, for an Old One, to put the household away into a pause of Time, caught out of reality in a sleep that could not be broken. But he did not want that. There were likely to be enough ways, tonight, in which he would have to play with Time.

Softly down the lower staircase into the front hall he went. The picture he had come to find hung on the wall just inside the big front door, beside the hat-rack and umbrella-stand. Will had brought a small torch with him, but he found he did not need it; the moonlight silvering the air through the hall windows showed him all the familiar figures the picture held.

He had been fascinated by it since he was very small, so small that he had to clamber up on the umbrella-stand to peer inside the dark carved wood of the picture-frame. It was a Victorian print, done all in murky shades of brown; its great attraction was the enormous complicated clarity of its detail. In flowing script it was entitled *The Romans at Caerleon*, and it showed the construction of some complex building. Everywhere crowds of figures tugged ropes, led oxen straining on sturdy wooden yokes, guided slabs of rock into place. A paved central floor was finished, smooth and elliptical, flanked by columned arches; a wall or staircase seemed to be rising beyond. Roman soldiers, splendidly uniformed, stood overseeing the bands of men unloading and tugging the neatly cut stones into place.

Will looked for one soldier in particular, a centurion in the far right-hand corner of the foreground, leaning against a pillar. He was the only still figure in the whole panorama of busy construction; his face, drawn in clear detail, was grave and rather sad, and he was gazing out of the picture, into the distance. That sad remoteness was the reason why Will, when small, had always found himself more intrigued by this one odd figure than by all the rest of the scurrying workers put together. It was also the reason why Merriman had chosen the man for the concealing of the Signs.

Merriman. Will sat down on the stairs, chin on hands. He must think hard and deep. It was simple enough to remember the way in which he and Merriman had managed the hiding of the linked circle of six Signs, the most powerful – and vulnerable – weapons of the Light. Back into the time of this Roman they had gone, and there among the stones whose picture hung before him now, he, Will, had slipped the Signs into a place where they could lie safe and unseen, buried by Time. But to remember that was one thing, to reverse it quite another . . .

He thought: The only way is to live through that all over again. I have to go again, to go once more through everything we did in hiding the Signs – and then, instead of stopping, I shall have to find a way to take them out again.

He was beginning to be excited now. He thought: Merriman can be there but I shall have to do it. *I shall be with you, but powerless,* he said. So he won't be able to show me the moment when I have to say something, or do something, whatever it is; he may not even know when it comes. Only I can choose it, for the Light. And if I fail, we can go no further forward from here . . .

Excitement dwindled beneath the appalling merciless weight of responsibility. There was one key only to the spell that would release the Signs, and only he could find it. But where, when, how?

Where, when, how?

Will stood up. The way out of the spell could be found only by going back into it. So, first he must re-enact the casting of it; turn Time so that once more he could live through the hours, more than a year earlier, when with Will at his side Merriman had –

What had Merriman done? It must be an exact echo.

Putting down his torch, Will stood before the picture on the wall, remembering. He reached out and put one hand on its frame. Then he stood very still, gazing in total concentration at a group of men in the picture's middle distance: men straining at a rope that was pulling a slab of rock towards some point that could not be seen. He emptied his mind of all thought, his senses of all other sight or sound; he gazed and he gazed.

And very gradually, the sound of creaking rope and rhythmic shouts and the grinding of rock against rock began to grow in his ears, and he smelled dust and sweat and dung – and the figures in the picture began to move. And Will's hand was no longer on the wooden picture-frame, but on the wooden side-support of an ox-cart laden with stone, and he stepped forward into the world of the Romans at Caerleon, a boy of that time, cool in a white linen tunic on a warm summer's day, with square stone cobbles uneven beneath his sandalled feet.

'*Heave*-two-three . . . *heave*-two-three . . .' The stone inched forward on its rollers. In other rhythms, the same shouts rang through the air from other groups, soldiers and labourers working together, skins olive or dusty pink, hair curly black or lank blonde. Stone crashed and squealed against stone; men and animal grunted with effort. And Merriman said into Will's ear, from behind him, 'You must be ready to slip the link, when the moment comes.'

Looking down, Will saw the six Signs of the Light, joined by links of gold, clasped about the waist of his tunic like a belt. Bright and dark they lay between the gleaming links, each of the six the same shape, a circle quartered by a cross: dull bronze, dark iron, blackened wood; bright gold, glittering flint, and the last that he would never forget, seeing it sometimes even in dreams – the Sign of water, clear crystal, engraved with delicate symbols and patterns like a circle of snowflakes caught in ice.

'Come,' Merriman said.

He swept past Will, tall in a dark blue cloak that fell almost to his feet, and drew level with the pillar beyond the steaming oxen, where a centurion stood watching a team of workmen lace straps and ropes round the topmost slab of granite on the wagon. Will followed, trying to be inconspicuous.

'The work goes well,' Merriman said.

The Roman turned his head, and Will saw that it was the same sombre figure whose image he had passed almost every day of his life. Bright dark eyes regarded Merriman from a lean, long-nosed face.

'Ah,' the man said. 'It is the Druid.'

Merriman inclined his head in a kind of mock-formal greeting. 'Many things to many men,' he said, smiling slightly.

The soldier looked at him reflectively. 'A strange land,' he said. 'Barbarians and magicians, dirt and poetry. A strange land, yours.' Then he snapped suddenly taut; part of his attention had been all the while on the ox-cart. 'Careful, there! You, Sextus, the rope at that end–'

Men scrambled to balance the descending slab, which had tipped perilously to one side; it came down in safety and the man in command of the team saluted, calling his thanks. The centurion nodded and relaxed, though still watching them. Another wagon rumbled past, laden with long beams of wood.

Merriman looked out at the rising structure before them; their wider view now showed that it was a half-built amphitheatre, stone-walled, with tiers of wood-topped seats rising in a great curving sweep from the central arena. 'Rome has many talents,' he said. 'We have some skill with stone, here, and none can match our great stone circles, with their homage to the Light. But the skill of Roman builders for the daily life of men as well as for worship – your villas and viaducts, your pipes and streets and baths . . . You are transforming our cities, friend, as you have begun transforming the pattern of our lives.'

The soldier shrugged. 'The Empire grows, always.' He glanced at Will, who hovered at Merriman's side watching the team of men swinging the long stone slowly to one side, down from the wagon.

'Your boy?'

'He learns a little of what I know,' Merriman said coolly. 'I have had him a year now. We shall see. He has the old blood in him, from the years before your fathers came.'

'No fathers of mine,' the centurion said. 'I am not Empire-born. I came from Rome seven years back, commissioned into the Second. A long time gone. Rome is the Empire, the Empire is Rome, and yet, and yet . . .' He smiled suddenly at Will: a kind smile, lightening the severe face. 'You work hard for your master, boy?'

'I try, sir,' Will said. He enjoyed following the formal patterning of the Latin; it came without effort to an Old One, as did any language of the world, but brought somehow a particular pleasure because of the echoes of it in his own native tongue.

'The building interests you.'

'Marvellous, it is. The way each piece of stone is cut to fit exactly to the next, or to hold a beam of wood. And the putting them together, so carefully, precisely – they know just what they are doing–'

'It is all planned. Just as anywhere in the Empire. This same amphitheatre has been built in a score of legionary fort towns like this one, from Sparta to Brindisium. Come, I will show you.'

He took Will by the shoulder, with a beckoning glance at Merriman, and led him across the sandy central floor of the arena to a half-finished vaulted arch, one of eight entrances through the rising tiers of seats. 'When my third team brings up that next slab, it will fit here, so – and lock in place, there–'

A column of stone slabs was beginning to rise at the side of the arch. Will peered at the next as it drew close on its rollers, tugged by four sweating soldiers. A grunting, straining team hoisted it into place in the rising arch. It was much larger than the rest: irregular with a large hollow depression in the top, but with one broad, unusually flat surface for the front side. Will saw the incised letters: COH. X. C. FLAV. JULIAN.

'Built by the tenth cohort, the century of Flavius Julianus,' Merriman said. 'Excellent.' And silently, in the Old Ones' manner of speaking into the mind, he said to Will, '*In there. Now.*' At the same moment, he stumbled, knocking clumsily against the centurion's elbow; the Roman turned courteously to catch him.

'Is anything wrong?'

Swiftly Will slipped the belt of linked Signs from his waist and dropped it into the hollow irregularity in the slab's top side over which the next slab of stone would be placed; he pushed earth and stones hastily over it to keep the gleaming metals from view.

'I beg your pardon,' Merriman was saying. 'Foolish – my sandal–'

The soldier turned back; the team came straining up; Will moved quickly aside and the stone slab groaned and squeaked into place. And the circle of Signs was shut into a coffin of stone, to lie hidden for as long as this work of the Roman Empire should survive.

The detached part of Will's mind, aware of everything as a spell-brought echo of things he and Merriman had done before, came jolting now into his consciousness. *Now!* it said. *What next?* For this was as far as those first actions had gone. After this point, on the day of the hiding of the Signs, he had very soon found himself back in his own century, flicked forward in Time with the precious circle hidden safe behind him. So the secret that he must now urgently find, the precious key to their recovery, must lie somewhere in these next moments of Roman time. What could it be?

He looked desperately at Merriman. But the dark eyes over the high curved nose held no expression. This was not Merriman's task, but his own; he must do it alone.

All the same there might be a reason why Merriman was there, for this half of the spell as for the other; even unwittingly, he might have some part to play. It was for Will to discover that part, if it were so, and take hold of whatever might be there for him to take.

Where, when, how?

The centurion shouted commands, and his nearest team of workers swung round and marched back for the next stone. Watching them, the Roman shivered suddenly, and drew his cloak tighter round his shoulders.

'Britain-born, all of them,' he said wrily to Merriman. 'Like you, they find no horror in this climate.'

Merriman made a formless, murmuring sound of sympathy, and for no reason that he could imagine Will found the small hairs rising on the back of his neck, as if in a warning from senses that had no other speech. He stood tense, waiting.

'These islands,' the Roman said. 'Green, I grant you. Well might they be green. Always the clouds, the mist and damp and rain.' He sighed. 'Ah, my bones ache . . .'

Merriman said softly, 'And not the bones only . . . it must be hard, for one born in the sun.'

The centurion stared out over the wooden seats and stone columns, looking at nothing, and shook his head helplessly.

Will said, in a small clear voice that seemed to him to belong to somebody else, 'What is it like, your home?'

'Rome? A great city. But my home is outside the city, in the country – a quiet life, but good –' He glanced at Will. 'I have a son who must now be as tall as you. When last I saw him I could throw him in the air and catch him in my hands. Now my wife tells me he has learned to ride like a centaur, and swim like a fish. Swimming now, perhaps, in the river near my land. I wanted him to grow up there, as I did. With the sun hot on the skin, and the air shrill with cicadas, and a line of cypress trees dark against the sky . . . the hills silver with olive trees and terraced for the vines, with the grapes filling out, now . . .'

The homesickness was a throbbing ache like physical pain, and suddenly Will knew that the answer was here in the air, in this moment of simple unprotected longing with a man's deepest, simplest emotions open and unguarded for strangers to hear and see. This was the road that would carry him.

Here, now, this way!

He let his mind fall into the longing, into the other's pain, as if he were diving into a sea; and like water closing over his head the emotion took him in. The world spun about him, stone and grey sky and green fields, whirling and changing and falling down into place not quite the same as before, and the yearning homesick voice was soft in his ears again; but the voice was a different voice.

The voice was a different voice and the language was changed, to a soft accented English with long slanting vowels. And it was evening now, with a moon-washed silver-dark sky above and shadows all around, shapes and shadows indistinguishable one from the next.

But in the new voice, the ache of longing was exactly the same.

'. . . it's all sun and sand and sea, that part of Florida. My part. Flowers everywhere. Oleander and hibiscus, and poinsettia in big wild red bushes, not shut up in skinny little Christmas pots. And down on the beach the wind blows in the coconut palms and the leaves make a little rattling noise, like a shower of rain. I used to swing on those leaves when I was your age, like swinging on a rope. If I were down there now I'd be out fishing with my dad – he's got a forty foot Bertram, a beauty. Called *Betsy Girl* after Mom. Out through the channel in the mangroves, you go – dark green, like forests in the water. The water's green too till you get way out in the Gulf, and then it's a deep, deep blue.

Beautiful. And you swing the outriggers up with the lines over, and ballyho on, and you'll catch bonita or dolphin, or if you're lucky, pompano. The tourists all want sailfish or kingfish. Day before I left home I got a sixty pound king. Ginny, that's my girl, she took a picture of it.'

Will could see him outlined against the sky, bright and dark by turns now as gathering clouds crossed the moon: a lean young man with long hair caught back in a stubby pony-tail. The soft, remembering voice went on.

'Haven't seen Ginny for eight months. Man, that's a long time. I've got our first day all planned out for when I get home. Keep thinking about it. Long lazy day in the sun, swimming, lying on the beach, surfing maybe. And beer and hamburgers at Pete's. His burgers are just out of this world, big and juicy. Ginny loves them . . . She's so pretty. Long blonde hair. Great figure. She writes me every week. Didn't come over here because her old man's got a weak heart and she felt – ah, she's just a great girl.' He paused, and slowly shook his head. 'Hey, I'm sorry. You really got me going. I guess I didn't know how much I'd been missing . . . people. It's been fun here on the dig, but I'll sure be glad to get home.'

Behind him, a rounded grassy slope rose as skyline; yet although this seemed totally strange, Will had the conviction that somehow he was in the same place as before. Perhaps it was only that linking emotion, the ache in the American's voice, and yet . . .

Merriman's voice said in the dim night, cheerful, breaking the mood, 'He seems to have pressed a button, asking you about home. Have you been here a long time?'

'It'll be a year, by the time I'm through. Not so long really, I guess.' The young man became self-consciously brisk. 'Well, hey, let's show you. I wish this wasn't such a quick visit, professor – there's so much you could see better in the morning.'

'Ah well,' Merriman said vaguely. 'I have appointments . . . Over here, you said?'

'Just a minute, I'll get a lamp. Better than a torch –' The American vanished into a boxlike structure that seemed to be a small wooden shed; a light flared in a window, and then he was back again with a hissing hurricane lamp unexpectedly held aloft, casting a bright pool around them in which Will could see grass at their feet, and Wellington boots on Merriman's trousered legs. Beyond, poles and ropes and small drooping marker-flags jutted from an excavation made into the grassy mound that he had thought a natural slope, as if a giant slice had been cut from an earthen cake. At the inside of the excavation, where it cut furthest into the mound, he could see stones. He could see a stone-paved floor like a stretch of square cobbles; the scattered stones of a fallen arch; rising tiers of stones where once wooden benches had stood . . .

The whirl of others' emotions cleared from Will's mind, and instead wonder and relief and delight flooded into him like a spring tide, and he knew, looking at the stone, that the secret releasing the Signs from their enchantment had been caught at the proper moment indeed.

'You know the background, of course, Professor Lyon,' the young American said. 'Always the mound was known as King Arthur's Round Table, with absolutely no justification of course. And no one could get permission to dig. Or funds for that matter, until this Ford Foundation deal. And now that we finally get inside it, what do we find inside King Arthur's so-called Round Table but a Roman amphitheatre.'

'You'll find a Mithraeum, too, before you're done, I shouldn't wonder,' Merriman said, in a strange brisk professional voice Will had not heard before. 'Caerleon was a major fort, after all – built for keeping down the barbaric British in their mists and fog.'

The American laughed. 'I don't really mind the mists and fog. It's the rain – and all that mud afterwards. They sure knew how to work with stone, those old Empire-builders. Look, here's the inscribed slab I was telling you about – Centurion Flavius Julianus and his boys.'

The lamp hissed, the shadows danced; he led them to a shoulder-high column of great slabs of rock. Will saw the highest, the largest, with its inscribed letters battered now by age. It was newly excavated; an inch of earth still lay over it, where the stone above had slipped to one side.

Merriman took a small torch from his pocket and shone it, quite unnecessarily Will thought, on the inscribed block of stone. 'Very neat,' he said fussily, 'very neat. Here, Will, my boy, have a look.' He handed Will the light.

'We think there were eight entrances,' the American said, 'all vaulted, with this kind of stonework. This must have been one of the two main ones – we only started clearing it this afternoon.'

'Excellent,' Merriman said. 'Now just show me that other inscription you mentioned, would you?' They moved away to one side of the cave-like dig, taking the pool of yellow lamp-light with them. Will stood still. He snapped on the light for a second, to be sure of his step, then turned it off. Putting his hand forward in the darkness of what he knew now was his own time, Midsummer Day a matter of seconds after he had first left it, he reached scrabbling into the earth that had lain since the decay of Rome's Empire, some sixteen centuries before, in the hollow of the big rock of the broken arch. And his fingers met a circle of metal quartered by a cross, and putting down the flashlight to scrabble with both hands in the earth, he drew out the linked circle of Signs.

Very carefully he shook off the dirt, with the circles and their gold links spread wide to keep the metal from rattling. He glanced up. Merriman and the young archaeologist were no more than a glimmer of light, yards away across the excavation. Excitement tight in his throat, Will clipped the belt-like chain of Signs round his waist, tugging his sweater down to cover them. He went forward to the lamplight.

'Ah, well,' Merriman said blandly. 'Time we were going, I'm afraid.'

'It's very exciting,' Will said, bright and enthusiastic.

'I'm so glad you stopped by.' The young American led them to a car parked behind a fence. 'It's been a privilege to meet you, Dr Lyon. I only wish the others had been here – Sir Mortimer will be real sorry–'

In a flurry of farewells he handed them into the car, pumping Merriman's arm in a kind of hearty reverence. Will said, 'You made Florida sound lovely. I hope you see it soon.'

But archaeology had driven his earlier emotion quite out of the young American's mind. Nodding, smiling vaguely, he disappeared,

Merriman drove slowly down the road. He said, his voice changed utterly, 'You have them?'

'I have them safe,' Will said, and a strong hand clenched his shoulder briefly, hard, and was gone. They were no longer master and boy, nor ever would be again; they were Old Ones only, caught out of Time in a task both were long-destined to fulfil.

'It must be tonight, and quickly,' Will said. 'Here, do you think? Now?'

'I think so. The times are linked, by our presence and by the place. Above all by your good work. I think so.' Merriman stopped, turned the car, and drove back towards the excavation. They got out and stood in silence for a moment.

Then they went together into the darkness, skirting the cleared arch and walls, climbing to the top of the grassy mound. There they stood, under a sky dark now with scudding clouds that hid the moon; and Will took from his waist the linked belt of crossed circles that was the symbol of the Circle of the Light, and held it up in both hands. And time and space merged as the twentieth and the fourth centuries became for a Midsummer's instant two halves of a single breath, and in a clear soft voice Will said into the night, 'Old Ones! Old Ones! It is time. Now and for always, for the second time and the last, let the Circle be joined. Old Ones, it is time! For the Dark, the Dark is rising!'

His voice ran strong; he held the Signs high, and a glimmer of starlight flashed on the circle of crystal like white fire. And all at once they were no longer alone on the silent grassy mound. From all the world over, from every point of time, the shadowy forms of men and women from every kind and generation crowded there in the night. A great glimmering throng was gathered, the Old Ones of the earth come together for the first time since, six seasons earlier, the Signs had in their presence been ceremonially joined. The darkness rustled; there was a formless murmuring in the place, a communication without speech.

Merriman and Will stood there together on the hill in the night full of beings, and waited for the one last Old One whose presence would weld this great gathering into an ultimate instrument of power, a force to vanquish the Dark.

They waited, and the night grew brighter with starlight; but she did not come.

The glimmering forms murmured and rippled as though the land blurred, and Will's consciousness, at one with the minds of all his fellows there, was filled with unease.

Merriman said, low and husky, 'I was afraid of this.'

'The Lady,' Will said helplessly. 'Where is the Lady?'

'*The Lady!*' Indistinct as the wind, a long whisper ran through the darkness. '*Where is the Lady?*'

Will said softly to Merriman, 'She came at the turn of the year, the year before last, for the Joining. Why does she not come now?'

Merriman said, 'I think she has not the strength. Her power is worn by resisting the Dark – you and I know well how she has spent herself, in the past. And though she managed the effort for the joining of the Signs, you remember that then she had no strength even to take her leave.'

'Yes,' Will said, remembering a small, fragile old figure, delicate as a wren, standing beside him overlooking a great throng of Old Ones as Merriman stood now. 'She simply . . . faded. And then she was gone.'

'And it seems that she is gone still. Out of reach. Gone until a helping magic may come from the sum of the centuries of this spell-ridden island, to bring her to our need. For the first time, for the only time, the help of mere creatures is needed for the Lady.'

Merriman drew himself up, a tall shadowy hooded figure in the night, dark as a pillar against the sky. He spoke without effort or great force, yet his voice filled the night and seemed to echo to and fro over the unseen heads of that enormous throng.

'Who knows?' he said. 'Who can tell? Oh all you Circle of the Old Ones, who can tell?'

And one voice came out of the night, a deep beautiful Welsh voice, rich and smooth as velvet, speaking with a rhythm that gave it the lilt of singing.

'*Y maent yr mynyddoedd yn canu,*' the voice said, '*ac y mae'r arglwyddes yn dod.*

Which means, being translated, The mountains are singing, and the Lady comes.'

There was a great stir among the aery crowd, and before he could help himself Will let out a cry of joyful recognition at the words. 'The verse! Of course! The old verse from the sea.' He sobered suddenly. 'But what does it mean? We all know that line, Merriman – but what does it mean?'

The question echoed in many voices, whispering and susurrating like the sea when a small breeze rises. The deep Welsh voice said, reflectively, 'When the mountains are singing, the Lady will come. And remember one thing. It is not in the Old Speech, which we all use, that those words have come down to us, but in a younger language – that is nevertheless one of the most ancient used by men.'

Merriman said softly, 'Thank you, Dafydd my friend.'

'Welsh,' Will said. 'Wales.' He stared into blank dark space, where clouds once more were drifting over the moon. He said hesitantly, his mind feeling for the right word, the right idea, 'I am to go to Wales. To that part where I have been once before. And there I must find the moment, the right way . . . Somewhere in the mountains. Somehow. And the Lady will come.'

'And we shall be complete and singly-bound,' Merriman said. 'And the end of all this questing will begin.'

'*Pob hwyl*, Will Stanton,' said the rich Welsh voice gently in the darkness. '*Pob hwyl*. Good luck . . .' And it faded and died into the soft whine of the wind, and all the gathering around them faded too, vanishing away to leave them standing, two lone figures, there in the darkening night on the grass-smooth mound, in the Midsummer Day of the time into which Will had been born.

Will said, 'But for that first time, to which I was called, the rising of the Dark in the time of Arthur . . . We are allowed only a night and a day to bring help there. And I cannot keep to that limit now. So what of the great king, and the battle that is to come at Badon? What will –' He stopped himself, cutting off words that belonged not to Old Ones but to men.

Merriman said, completing it, 'What will happen there? What will happen, what has happened, what is happening? A battle, won for a little while. A respite gained, but not for long. You can see, Will. Things are as they are, and will be. In Arthur's time, we have the Circle to help us, for they have been gathered, and much can therefore be accomplished. But without words from the Lady, the last height of power cannot be reached, and so the peace of Arthur that we shall gain for this island at Badon will be lost, before long, and for a time the world will seem to vanish beneath the shadow of the Dark. And emerge, and vanish again, and again emerge, as it has done through all the length of what men call their history.'

Will said, 'Until the Lady comes.'

'Until the Lady comes,' Merriman said. 'And she will help you to the finding of the sword of the Pendragon, the crystal sword by which the final magic of the Light shall be achieved, and the Dark put at last to flight. And there will be five to help you, for from the beginning it was known that six altogether, and six only, must accomplish this long matter. Six creatures more and less of the earth, aided by the six Signs.'

Will said, quoting, '*When the Dark comes rising, six shall turn it back.*'

'Aye,' Merriman said. Suddenly he sounded very weary. 'Six, for a hard turning.'

On impulse Will quoted again, a whole verse this time, from the old prophetic rhyme that had come gradually to light – a world ago, it seemed to him – with the growing of his own power as an Old One.

> 'When the Dark comes rising, six shall turn it back,
> Three from the Circle, three from the track;
> Wood, bronze, iron; water, fire, stone;
> Five shall return, and one go alone.'

He spoke the last line more slowly, as if he were hearing it for the first time. 'Merriman? That last part, what does it mean? It has never put anything into my mind but a question. Five shall return, and one go alone . . . Who?'

Merriman stood there in the quiet night, his face obscured by shadow; his voice was quiet too, and without expression. 'Nothing is certain, Old One, even in the prophecies. They can mean one thing, or they can mean another. For after all, men have minds of their own, and can determine their actions, for good or ill, for going outward, or turning in . . . I cannot tell who the one may be. None shall know, until the last. Until the . . . one . . . goes . . . alone . . .' He gathered himself, and stood straighter, as if pulling them both back out of a dream. 'There is a long road to tread before that will come, and a hard one, if we are to triumph at the end of it. I go back now to my lord Arthur, with the Signs, and the power of the Circle which only they can call.'

He held out his hand, barely visible in the star-washed darkness, and Will gave him the linked belt of crossed circles, gold and crystal and stone glittering between dark wood, bronze, iron.

'Go well, Merriman,' he said quietly.

'Go well, Will Stanton,' Merriman said, his voice tight with strain. 'Into your own place, at this Midsummer hour, where affairs will take you in the direction you must go. And we will strive at our separate tasks across the centuries, through the waves of time, touching and parting, parting and touching in the pool that whirls forever. And I shall be with you before long.'

He raised an arm, and he was gone, and the stars spun and the night whirled about, and Will was standing moonlit in the hall of his home, his hand on the frame of a sepia Victorian print that showed the Romans building an amphitheatre at Caerleon.

Midsummer Day

At a triumphant trot Will mowed the last patch of grass, and collapsed, panting, draped over the lawn-mower handle. Sweat was trickling down the side of his nose, and his bare chest was damp, speckled with tiny cut stems of grass.

'Ouf! It's even hotter than yesterday!'

'Sundays,' James said, 'are always hotter than Saturdays. Especially if you live in a village with a small stuffy church. James Stanton's Law, you can call that.'

'Go on,' said Stephen, passing with his hands full of twine and clippers. 'It wasn't that bad. And for two horrible little boys you still sound pretty angelic in the choir.' He dodged neatly as Will flung a fistful of grass cuttings.

'I shan't be there much longer,' James said, with some pride. 'I'm breaking. Did you hear me croak in the canticle?'

'You'll be back,' Will said. 'Tenor. Bet you.'

'I suppose so. That's what Paul says too.'

'He's practising. Listen!'

Distant as a fading dream, from inside the house the soft clear tone of a flute rippled up and down in scales and arpeggios; it seemed as much a part of the hot still afternoon as the bees humming in the lupins and the sweet smell of the new-cut grass. Then the scales gave way to a long lovely flow of melody, repeated again and again. Halfway across the lawn Stephen stood caught into stillness, listening.

'My God, he's good, isn't he? What is that?'

'Mozart, First Flute Concerto,' Will said. 'He's playing it with the N.Y.O. this autumn.'

'N.Y.O.?'

'National Youth Orchestra. You remember. He was in it for years, even before he went to the Academy.'

'I suppose I do. I've been away so long...'

'It's a big honour, that concert,' James said. 'At the Festival Hall, no less. Didn't Paul tell you?'

'You know Paul. Old Modesty. That's a lovely-sounding flute he's got now, too. Even I can tell.'

'Miss Greythorne gave it to him, two Christmases ago,' said Will. 'From the Manor. There's a collection that her father made, she showed us.'

'Miss Greythorne ... Good Lord, that takes me back. Sharp wits, sharp tongue – I bet she hasn't changed a bit.'

Will smiled. 'She never will.'

'She caught me up her almond tree once when I was a kid,' Stephen said, grinning reminiscently. 'I came climbing down and there she was out of nowhere, in her wheelchair. Even though she hated anyone seeing that wheelchair. "Only monkeys eat my nuts, young man," she said – I can still hear her – "and you'll not even make a powder monkey, at your age."'

'Powder monkey?' James said.

'Boys in the Navy in Nelson's day – they used to fetch the powder for the guns.'

'You mean Miss Greythorne knew you were going into the Navy?'

'Of course not, I didn't know myself then.' Stephen looked a little taken aback. 'Funny coincidence though. Never occurred to me before – I haven't given her a thought for years.'

But James's mind had already taken off on a tangent, as it frequently did. 'Will, whatever became of that little hunting horn she gave you, the year she gave Paul the flute? Did you lose it? You never even gave it one good blow.'

'I still have it,' Will said quietly.

'Well, get it out. We could have fun with it.'

'One day.' Will swung the lawn-mower round, shoving its handle at James's unready hands. 'Here – your turn. I've done the front, now you do the back.'

'That's the rule,' said their father, passing with a weed-loaded wheelbarrow. 'Fair's fair. Share the burden.'

'My burden's bigger than his,' James said dolefully.

'Nonsense!' said Mr Stanton.

'Well it is, actually,' Will said. 'We measured, once. The back lawn's five feet wider than the front, and ten feet longer.'

'Got more trees in it,' said Mr Stanton, unclipping the catch-box of grass cuttings from the front of the mower, and emptying it into his barrow.

'That makes more work, not less.' James drooped, more dolefully still. 'Going round them. Trimming afterwards.'

'Go away,' said his father. 'Before I burst into tears.'

Will took the box and clipped it back on the mower. 'Goodbye, James,' he said cheerfully.

'You haven't finished yet, either, matey,' Mr Stanton said. 'Stephen needs some help tying up the roses.'

A muffled curse came from the front garden wall; Stephen, embraced by the sprawling branches of a climbing rose, was sucking his thumb.

'I believe you may be right,' Will said.

Grinning, his father picked up the wheelbarrow and prodded James and the lawn-mower up the driveway; Will was starting over the lawn when his elder sister Barbara came out of the front door.

'Tea's nearly ready,' she said.

'Good.'

'Outside, we're having it.'

'Good, better, best. Come and help Steve fight a rose bush.'

Rambler roses, spilling great swathes and bunches of red blossom, grew along and over the old stone wall that bordered the road. Gingerly they untangled the most wildly sprawling arms, drove stakes into the gravelly earth, and tied the branches to keep the billowing sprays of roses off the ground.

'Ouch!' said Barbara for the fifth time, as a rebellious rose-branch scored a thin red line across her bare back.

'Your own fault,' said Will unfeelingly. 'You should have more clothes on.'

'It's a sunsuit. For the sunshine, duckie.'

'Nekkidness,' said her younger brother solemnly, 'be a shameful condition for a yooman bein'. Tain't roight. 'Tes a disgrace to the neighbour'ood, so 'tes.'

Barbara looked at him. 'There you stand, wearing even *less –*' she began indignantly; then stopped.

'Slow,' said Stephen. 'Very slow.'

'Oh, you,' Barbara said.

A car passed on the road; slowed suddenly; stopped; then began backing gradually until it was level with them. The driver switched off his engine, hauled himself across the seat and stuck a heavy-jowled red face out of the window.

'Might the biggest of you be Stephen Stanton?' he said with clumsy joviality.

'That's right,' said Stephen from the top of the wall. He gave one last blow to a stake. 'What can I do for you?'

'Name's Moore,' the man said. 'You had a little run-in with one of my boys the other day, I gather.'

'Richie,' said Will.

'Ah,' said Stephen. He jumped down from the wall to stand next to the car. 'How do you do, Mr Moore. I dropped your son into some water, I believe.'

'Green water,' said the man. 'Ruined his shirt.'

'I should be happy to buy him a new one,' Stephen said easily. 'What size is he?'

'Don't talk rubbish,' the man said, expressionless. 'I just wanted to get the rights and wrongs of it, that's all. Wondered why a young man like you should be playing those sort of games with kids.'

Stephen said, 'It wasn't a game, Mr Moore. I simply felt very strongly that your son deserved to be dropped into the water.'

Mr Moore ran one hand over his large glistening forehead. 'Maybe. Maybe. He's a wild kid, that one. They kick him around, he kicks back. What did he do to you?'

'Didn't he tell you?' Will said.

Mr Moore looked across the low wall at Will as though he were something small and irrelevant, like a beetle. 'What Richie told me, it wasn't something that gets people dropped in streams. So like as not it wasn't true. That's what I want to get straight.'

'He was tormenting a young boy,' Stephen said. 'There's not much point in going into detail.'

'Having a bit of fun, he said.'

'Not much fun for the other one.'

'Richie said he didn't lay a finger on him,' Mr Moore said.

'He just threw his music-case full of music into the stream, that's all,' Will said shortly.

'We – ell,' Mr Moore said. He paused, tapping the edge of the car window absently. 'It was that Indian kid from the Common, I gather.'

The three Stantons stood looking at him in silence. He stared back, blankly. At length Barbara said, in a small polite voice, 'Does that make a difference?'

Before the man could answer, Mr Stanton said amiably from behind them, 'Good afternoon.'

'Afternoon,' said Mr Moore, turning his head, with a tinge of relief in his tone. 'I'm Jim Moore. We were just –'

'Yes, I heard some of it,' Mr Stanton said. He propped himself against the edge of the wheelbarrow he had just set down, and took out his pipe and matches. 'I must say I thought Steve might have over-reached himself a bit that day. Still–'

'The thing is, you can't always believe these people, you see,' said the man in the car, smiling, confident of agreement.

There was a silence. Mr Stanton lit his pipe. He said, puffing, blowing out the match, 'I don't quite follow, I'm afraid.'

Stephen said coldly, 'It wasn't a case of believing anyone, just of what I happened to see for myself.'

Mr Moore was looking at Mr Stanton with a kind of anxious adult *bonhomie*. 'Made a lot of fuss about nothing, that kid, I dare say. You know how they are, always on about something.'

'True, true,' said Roger Stanton, his round face placid. 'Mine usually are.'

'Oh no, no,' said Mr Moore heartily, 'I'm sure your bunch are very nice. I meant coloureds, not kids.'

He went on, ploughing unawares through the silence that came again, 'I see a lot of them at work. I'm in personnel, you know – Thames Manufacturing. Not much I don't know about Indians and Pakkies, after all these years. Of course I've got nothing against them personally. Very intelligent, well-educated, some of them. Got myself an op from an Indian doctor at the Memorial Hospital last year – clever little chap, he was.'

Barbara said, in the same small polite voice, 'I expect even some of your best friends are Indians and Pakistanis.'

Her father gave her a sharp warning glance, but the words went flickering quite over Mr Moore's stubbly head. He chuckled at Barbara, very much the jovial appreciative male indulging a pretty seventeen-year-old. 'Well no, I wouldn't go that far! I'll be honest with you, I don't think they should be here, them or the West Indians. Got no right, have they? Taking jobs that should go to Englishmen, with the country in the state it is . . .'

Stephen said quietly, 'We do have unions, Mr Moore, and they aren't exactly helpless. Most of those famous jobs are the ones Englishmen don't want to do – or that the immigrants do better.'

The man looked at Stephen with resentment and dislike, his thick jaw hardening. 'One of those, are you? A bleeding-heart. Don't try and teach me, young man. I've seen too much of the real thing. One Pakkie family rents a two-bedroom house and the next thing you know, they've got sixteen of their friends and relations living there. Like rabbits. And half of them having babies free on the National Health Service, at the British taxpayer's expense.'

'Remember your Indian doctor?' Stephen said, still softly. 'If it weren't for the immigrant doctors and nurses, the National Health Service would fall apart tomorrow.'

Mr Moore made a contemptuous noise. 'Just don't try and tell me about coloured people,' he said. 'I *know*.'

Stephen leaned back against the wall, twisting a piece of raffia between his fingers. 'Do you know Calcutta, Mr Moore?' he said. 'Have you ever had beggars grabbing at your feet, calling out to you, children half the size of Will here with an arm missing, or an eye, and ribs like xylophones and their legs stinking with sores? If I lived in a place with that kind of despair round me, I think I just might decide to bring up my kids in a country where they'd have a better chance. Specially a country that had exploited my own for about two hundred years. Wouldn't you? Or Jamaica, now. Do you know how many children get to a secondary school there? D'you know the unemployment rate? D'you know what the slums are like in Kingston? Do *you* know—'

'Stephen,' said his father gently.

Stephen stopped. The raffia string in his hands snapped.

'So what about it? All that stuff?' The man's face had darkened. He leaned belligerently out of the window; his breath came more quickly. 'Let them solve their own problems, not come whining over here! What's all that have to do with us? They don't belong here, none of 'em; they should all be thrown out. And if you think they're so bloody marvellous you'd better go and live in their lousy countries with them!' He caught Mr Stanton's calm eye suddenly and tried visibly to control himself, jerking his head back from the window and sliding across into the driver's seat.

Mr Stanton came close to the wall, where the car stood, and took his pipe from his mouth. 'If your son shares your views, Mr Moore,' he said clearly, 'as I am glad to find my son shares mine, then the stream episode isn't hard to explain, is it? We only have to decide what reparation you'd like.' The pipe went back between his teeth, abruptly.

'Reparation hell!' The man started his engine with a deliberate roar. He leaned over the seat, shouting above the noise. 'You just see what happens to anyone laying a finger on my boy again, for the sake of some snivelling little wog, that's all. Just see!'

He lurched back at the wheel and drove off, gears snarling. They stood looking at the car.

Stephen opened his mouth.

'Don't say it,' said his father, 'don't say it! You know how many there are. You can't convince them and you can't kill 'em. You can only do your best in the opposite direction – which you did.' He looked around, embracing Will and Barbara in a rueful smile. 'Come on. Let's go and have tea.'

Will came last, trailing despondently. From the moment when he had heard the man in the car begin to shout, and seen the look in his eyes, he had been no Stanton at all but wholly an Old One, dreadfully and suddenly aware of danger. The mindless ferocity of this man, and all those like him, their real loathing born of nothing more solid than insecurity and fear . . . it was a channel. Will knew that he had been gazing into the channel down which the powers of the Dark, if they gained their freedom, could ride in an instant to complete control of the earth. He was filled with a terrible anxiety, a sense of urgency for the

Light, and knew that it would remain with him, silently shouting at him, far more vividly than the fading memory of a single bigot like Mr Moore.

'Come on, Tarzan,' said Paul, thumping his bare shoulder as he came past out of the house. So Will came back, slowly, into the other part of his mind.

They all gathered for tea as though the disturbing Mr Moore had never been. By one of those unspoken censorships that come sometimes in close families, those who had seen him made no mention of him to those who had not. Tea was laid out on the orange wicker table, glass-topped, that stood outdoors with its matching chairs in high summer. Will's spirits began to rise. For an Old One with the tastes and appetite of a small boy, it was hard to despair for long over the eternal fallibility of mankind when confronted with home-made bread, farm butter, sardine-and-tomato paste, raspberry jam, scones, and Mrs Stanton's delicious, delicate, unmatchable sponge-cake.

He sat on the grass. His senses were crammed with summer: the persistent zooming of a wasp lured by the jam; the grass-smell of James's partly cut lawn mingling with the scent of a nearby buddleia bush; the dappled light all around him as sunshine filtered through the apple tree overhead, lush in full green leaf now, with small green apples beginning to swell. Many of the apples were fallen already, victims of over-population, never to grow. Will picked up one of the little thick-stemmed oval objects and gazed at it pensively.

'Put it down,' Barbara said. 'This'll taste better.' She was holding out a plate with two scones spread thickly with butter and jam.

'Hey,' said Will. 'Thanks.' It was a small warm kindliness; in a family as big as the Stantons', self-service was the general rule. Barbara smiled at him briefly, and Will could sense her formless maternal concern that her youngest brother had been upset by the violence of the man in the car. His spirits lifted. The Old One within him thought: *The other side. Don't forget. There's always the other side of people too.*

'Three and a half more weeks of school,' James said, in a tone that was half delight, half grumble. He looked up at the sky. 'I hope the holiday's all like this.'

'The long-range forecast says it will begin pouring with rain the day you break up,' said Paul seriously, folding a piece of bread-and-butter. He went on, through a mouthful, 'It's due to go on for three weeks without stopping. Except once, for August week-end.'

'Oh no!' said James, in unguarded horror.

Paul looked at him owlishly over his horn-rimmed glasses. 'There may very well be hail. And on the last day of July they're expecting a blizzard.'

James's face relaxed into a grin, as relief twined with shame-faced rage. 'Paul, you swine. I'll–'

'Don't kill him,' Stephen said. 'Too fatiguing. Bad for digestions. Tell me what you're going to do for the holidays, instead.'

'Scout camp, some of the time,' James said happily. 'Two weeks in Devon.'

'Very nice too.'

'I'm doing summer courses at the Academy – and playing in a jazz club at night,' Paul said with a crooked grin.

'Good Lord!'

'Ah, the worm turns. Not exactly your kind of jazz, though.'

'Better nor nowt. What are you going to do, Will?'

'Loaf about, like me,' said Barbara comfortably, from an armchair.

'Well as a matter of fact,' Mrs Stanton said, 'Will has an invitation he hasn't heard about yet. Quite a surprise.' She leaned forward with the teapot and began filling cups. 'Your Aunt Jen telephoned this afternoon from London – she and David are up for a day or two, with some group from Wales. And she wanted to know, Will, if you'd like to spend part of the holidays at the farm – as soon as school ends, if you like.'

Will said slowly, 'That's good.'

'Wow!' said James. 'Don't tell Mary, she'll be livid – she thought she was going to get invited back to Wales this year.'

'Jen said something about Will getting along very well last year with a rather lonely boy who lived there,' Mrs Stanton said.

'Yes,' Will said. 'Yes, I did. His name was Bran.'

'You'll have to make sure it's a working holiday, you know,' said his father. 'Make yourself useful to your uncle. I know that part of Wales is almost all sheep, but it's a busy time of the year on any farm.'

'Oh yes,' Will said. He picked up another of the small immature apples and twirled it round and round, fast, by its stem. 'Yes. There'll be a lot of work to do.'

PART TWO

The Singing Mountains

Five

'Have we been here before?' Barney said. 'I keep feeling—'

'No,' Simon said.

'Not even when you were little, and I was a baby? You might have forgott·n.'

'Forgotten this?'

Simon swung one arm rather theatrically to embrace the panorama that lay spread around them, where they sat on the wiry grass halfway up the mountain, among spiny bushes of brilliant yellow gorse. Over all the right-hand half of their view was the blue sea of Cardigan Bay, with its long beaches stretching far into the haze of distance. Directly below them lay the green undulations of Aberdyfi golf course, behind its uneven dunes. To the left, the beaches ran into the broad estuary of the River Dyfi, full and blue now with water at high tide. And beyond, over the flat stretch of marsh on the other side of the river-mouth, the mountain mass of Mid-Wales rolled along the skyline, purple and brown and dull green, its colours shifting and patching constantly as clouds sailed over the summer sky past the sun.

'No,' Jane said. 'We've never been to Wales before, Barney. But Dad's grandmother was born here. Right in Aberdyfi. Perhaps memories can float about in your blood or something.'

'In your blood!' Simon said scornfully. He had recently announced that instead of going to sea, he proposed to become a doctor, like their father, and the side-effects of this weighty decision were beginning to try Jane and Barney's patience.

Jane sighed. 'I didn't mean it like that.' She groped in her shirt pocket. 'Here. Halfway snack time. Have some chocolate before it melts.'

'Good!' said Barney promptly.

'And don't tell me it's bad for our teeth, Simon, because I know it is.'

'Course it is,' said her elder brother with a disarming grin. 'Utter disaster. Where's mine?'

They sat munching fruit-and-nut chocolate for a contented space, gazing out over the estuary.

'I just know I've been here before,' Barney said.

'Don't keep on,' Jane said. 'You've seen pictures.'

'I mean it.'

'If you've been here before,' Simon said, long-suffering, 'you can tell us what we'll see when we get to the top of the ridge.'

Barney turned, flipping his blonde forelock out of his eyes, and stared up the mountain, over the bracken and the green slope. He said nothing.

'Another ridge,' Jane said cheerfully. 'And from that one you'll see another.'

'What'll we see, Barney?' Simon persisted. 'Cader Idris? Snowdon? Ireland?'

Barney looked at him for a long blank moment, his eyes empty. He said at last, 'Someone.'

'Someone? Who?'

'I don't know.' He jumped up suddenly. 'If we sit here all day we'll never find out, will we? Race you!'

He leapt up off the slope, and in an instant Simon was bounding confidently after him. Jane watched them, grinning. In the last year or so, though her younger brother had remained fairly neat and small, Simon seemed to have sprouted legs far too long for his body, like a giraffe. There were very few family races now that he failed to win.

Both boys had disappeared above her. The sun was hot on the back of her neck, as she climbed slowly after them. She stumbled on an outcrop of rock, and paused. Somewhere far away on the mountain a tractor's engine purred; a pipit shrilled overhead. The rocky outcrops led to the top of the ridge here in an erratic progression, through bracken and gorse and billowing piles of heather; hare-bells starred the low sheep-cropped grass, and little creeping white flowers she did not recognize. Far, far below, the road wound like a thread past the dune-fringed golf course, and the first grey roofs of Aberdyfi village. Jane shivered suddenly, with a sense of being very much alone.

'Simon!' she called. 'Barney!'

There was no answer. The birds sang. The sun beat down out of a lightly-hazed blue sky; nothing moved anywhere. Then very faintly Jane heard a strange long musical note. High and clear, it was like the call of a hunting horn, and yet not so harsh or demanding. It came again, closer. Jane found that she smiled as she listened; it was a lovely beckoning sound, and suddenly she was filled with an urgent desire to find out where it came from, what instrument could play so beautiful a note. She went on more swiftly up the hillside, until all at once she was over a last rocky edge and could see before her the first few yards of the ridge of the hill. The long sweet note came again. and on the highest grey granite outcropping that met the sky, she saw a boy, lowering from his lips the small curved horn with which he had just blown a call over the mountains, out into nowhere. His face was turned away from Jane, and she could see little except that he had longish straight hair. Then as he moved one hand in an automatic swift gesture to push back the hair from his forehead, she knew suddenly and positively that she had seen that gesture before, and knew who this boy was.

She went forward up the last slope to the rock, and he saw her and stood waiting.

Jane said, 'Will Stanton!'

'Hello, Jane Drew,' he said.

'*Oh!*' Jane said happily. Then she paused, surveying him. 'I can't think why I'm not more surprised,' she said. 'The last time I saw you was when we left you on Platform Four at Paddington Station. A year ago. More. What are you doing on the top of a mountain in Wales, for goodness' sake?'

'Calling,' Will said.

Jane looked at him for a long moment full of remembering, thinking back to a dark adventure in a beleaguered Cornish village, where her Great-Uncle Merriman had brought her and Simon and Barney together with an unremarkable round-faced, straight-haired Buckinghamshire boy – who had seemed to her in the end as alarming and yet as reassuring as Merriman himself.

'Different, I said you were then,' she said.

Will said gently, 'You three are not altogether ordinary, as you very well know.'

'Sometimes,' said Jane. She grinned at him suddenly, reaching back to hitch up the ribbon on her pony-tail. 'Mostly we are. Well. I said I hoped we should see you again someday. Didn't I?'

Will grinned back, and Jane remembered the way his smile had always transformed his rather solemn face. 'And I said I was pretty sure you would.' He came a few paces down the rock, then paused and raised the horn to his lips again. Tilting it to the sky, he blew a string of short staccato notes and then one long one. The sound curved out into the summer air, then down, like an arrow dropping.

'That'll bring them,' he said. 'They used to call it the *avaunt*.'

The note of the horn was still echoing round Jane's head. 'It's a lovely, lovely sound, not a bit like the ones they use for fox-hunts. Not that I've ever heard those except on television. That one – it's just – it's *music* –' She broke off, flapping one hand wordlessly.

Will held up the small curved horn, looking at it with his head on one side. Though it seemed old and battered, it gleamed like gold in the sunlight. 'Ah,' he said softly. 'Two occasions there will be, for its using. That much I know. The second is hidden to me. But the first time is now, for the gathering of the Six.'

'The Six?' Jane said blankly.

'We are two,' Will said. She stared at him.

'Jane? Jane!' It was Simon's voice, loud and peremptory, from over the ridge. She turned her head.

'Jane – Oh there you are!' Barney clambered over the rock a few yards away, turning over his shoulder to call, 'Over here!'

Will said in the same tranquil voice, 'And then there were four.'

Both boys' heads swung round in the same instant.

'*Will!*' Barney's voice was a yelp.

Jane heard the sharp inward gasp of Simon's breath; then he let it out in a long slow hiss. 'Well ... I'll ... be ...'

'Someone,' Barney said. 'Didn't I tell you? Someone. Was that you blowing the horn, Will? Let's see, do let me see!' He was hopping about, reaching, fascinated.

Will handed it over.

Simon said slowly, 'You can't tell me this is a coincidence.'

'No,' Will said.

Barney was standing still now on the rock, holding the small battered horn, watching the sun glint on its golden rim. He looked over it, at Will. 'Something's happening, isn't it?' he said quietly.

'Yes,' said Will.

'Can you tell us?' Jane said.

'Not yet. In a little while. It's the hardest thing of all, and the last thing. And ... it needs you.'

'I should have known.' Simon looked at Jane with a small wry smile. 'This morning. You weren't there. Dad happened to mention who it was that suggested we stay at this particular golfing hotel.'

'Well?'

'Great-Uncle Merry,' Simon said.

Will said, 'He will be here before long.'

'It really is serious,' Barney said.

'Of course. I told you. The hardest, and the last.'

'It really had better be the last,' Simon said rather pompously. 'I start boarding school after these holidays.'

Will looked at him. The corner of his mouth twitched.

Simon seemed to hear in his mind the echo of his own words; he looked down, scuffing at the grass with one foot. 'Well I mean,' he said. 'I mean my holidays will be even more different from all the others', so we may not be going to . . . to the same places all the time. Right, Jane?' He turned in appeal to his sister; then paused. 'Jane?'

Jane was gazing past him, eyes wide and fixed. She was seeing, now, nothing but a figure on the mountain, a figure standing looking at them, outlined by the blazing light of the high-summer sun. It stood slim and straight. Its hair was like a silver flame. She had a sudden extraordinary sense of great rank, of high natural degree, almost as if she were in the presence of a king. For a moment she resisted a strong irrational impulse to curtsey.

'Will?' she said softly, without turning her head. 'Then there were five, Will?'

Will's voice came strong and casual and eminently normal, snapping the tension. 'Hey Bran! Over here! Bran!' He pronounced the name with a long vowel, Jane noticed, like the sound inside farm, or barn. She had never heard a name like it before. She had never seen anyone like this before.

The boy on the skyline came slowly down towards them. Jane stared at him, hardly breathing. She could see him clearly now. He wore a white sweater and black jeans, with dark glasses over his eyes, and there was no colour in him anywhere. His skin had a strange pale translucence. His hair was quite white; so were his eyebrows. He was not merely blonde, as her brother Barney was blonde, with his mop of yellowish hair falling over a sun-browned face. This boy seemed almost crippled by his lack of colour; its absence hit the eye as hard as if an arm or a leg had been missing. And then he pulled off his glasses as he drew level with them, and she saw that after all the lack was not total; she saw his eyes, and they too were like nothing she had seen before. They were yellow, tawny, flecked with gold, like the eyes of an owl; they blazed at her, bright as new coins. She felt a sense of challenge – and then she was conscious of her staring, and though she would never normally have shaken hands with anyone her own age, in a kind of apology she thrust out her hand towards him.

'Hallo,' she said.

Will said at once, beside her, matter-of-fact, 'That's Bran Davies. Bran, this is Jane Drew. And Simon, he's the big one, and Barney.'

The white-haired boy took Jane's hand briefly, awkwardly, and nodded at Barney and Simon. 'Pleased to meet you.' He sounded very Welsh.

'Bran lives in one of the houses on my uncle's farm,' Will said.

'You have an uncle down here?' Barney's voice was high with astonishment.

'Well, actually he isn't my real uncle,' Will said cheerfully. 'Adopted. He married my mum's best friend. Comes to the same thing. Like you and Merriman. Or is he your real great-uncle?'

'I've never really known,' Simon said.

'He probably isn't,' Jane said. 'Considering.'

Barney said pertly, 'Considering what?'

'You know perfectly well.' She was uneasily conscious of Bran silently listening.

'Yes,' Barney said. He handed the small gleaming horn back to Will. Instantly Bran's cold golden eyes were on it; then up glaring at Barney, fierce, accusing.

'Was that you blowing the horn?'

Will said quickly, 'No, of course not, it was me. Calling, like I said. Calling you, and them.'

Something in Jane's mind flickered at the note in his voice: a small strange difference, so slight that she could not be sure she was not imagining it. It seemed a kind of respect, that Will did not show even when he spoke to Merriman. Or not respect, but an . . . awareness of . . . of *something* . . . She glanced quickly, nervously at the white-haired boy and then away again.

Simon said, 'Have you known Will for long?' His tone was carefully neutral.

Bran said calmly, '*Calan Gaeaf* last year, I got to know Will. Last *Samain*. If you can work that out, you'll know how long. You staying at the Trefeddian then, you three?' He pronounced it *Trevethian*, natural and Welsh; not as they had themselves when they first arrived, Jane painfully remembered.

'Yes,' she said. 'Daddy's playing golf. Mother paints.'

'Is she good?' Bran said.

'Yes,' Barney said. 'Very.' Jane could hear the same wariness in his voice as there had been in Simon's, but without hostility. 'I mean she's a real painter, not just hobby stuff. She has a studio, shows in galleries, all that.'

'You're lucky,' Bran said quietly.

Will was looking at Simon. 'Is it hard to get away?'

'From the A.P.s? Oh no. Mother takes off in the car with her easel, Father's on the golf course all day.' Glancing at Bran, Simon added, 'Sorry – A.P.s – Aged Parents.'

'Believe it or not,' Bran said, 'they teach Dickens in Welsh schools too.'

'Sorry,' Simon said stiffly. 'I didn't mean–'

'That's all right.' Bran smiled suddenly, for the first time. 'We are going to be doing things together, Simon Drew. I think we had better get along. Don't worry. I am not one of those Welshmen with a chip. No fixations about the snotty English, or being a subject race, and all that. No point, is there, when the Welsh are so clearly superior?'

'Bah, humbug,' Will said cheerfully.

Barney said rather hesitantly, looking at Bran, 'You said, *We're going to be doing things together* . . . Are you one of – are you like Great-Uncle Merry and Will?'

'In a way I suppose I am,' Bran said slowly. 'I can't explain. You'll see. But I am not one of the Old Ones, not a part of the Circle of the Light as they are . . .' He grinned at Will. 'Not a *dewin*, a wizard, like that one there, with all his tricks.'

Will shook his round head with only half a smile. 'We need more than tricks, this last time. There is something we have to find, all of us, and I don't even know what it is. All we have is the last line of an old verse, that you three heard, once upon a time, when first we deciphered it. It was in Welsh, which I can't possibly remember, but in English it meant, *The mountains are singing, and the Lady comes.*'

'*Yr mynyddoedd yn canu,*' Bran said, '*ac y mae'r arglwyddes yn dod.*'

'Wow,' Barney said.

'The Lady?' Jane said. 'Who is the Lady?'

'The Lady is . . . the Lady. One of the great figures of the Light.' Unconsciously Will's voice seemed to deepen, taking on an eerie resonance, and Jane felt a prickling along her spine. 'She is the greatest of all, the one essential. But when a little while ago we called the Circle together, all the Old Ones of the earth out of all time, for the beginning of the end of this long battle, the Lady did not come. Something is wrong. Something holds her. And without her we can go no further. So the first thing that I – all of us – must do now is find her. With only four words to help us, that do not mean very much to me. *The mountains are singing.*'

He stopped abruptly, and looked around at them all.

'We need Great-Uncle Merry,' Barney said gloomily.

'Well, we haven't got him. Yet.' Jane sat down on the nearest rock, playing with a stem of the heather that grew round it in springy mounds of purple and green. Beside her, poking through a clump of dead brown gorse, grew a cluster of the little nodding harebells of the Welsh uplands: delicate pale-blue caps quivering in the slightest breeze. Jane touched one of them gently with her little finger. 'Isn't there any Welsh place name that helps?' she said. 'Nothing that means the Singing Mountain, or anything like that?'

Bran was pacing to and fro, hands in pockets, the dark glasses back again over his pale eyes. 'No, no,' he said impatiently. 'I have thought and thought, and there is nothing at all like that. Nothing.'

'Well,' said Simon, 'how about any very old places – I mean old old, like Stonehenge? Ruins, or something?'

'I have thought of that too and still there is nothing,' Bran said. 'Like, there is a stone in St Cadfan's Church in Tywyn that has on it the oldest piece of Welsh ever written down – but all that tells is where St Cadfan is buried. Or there is Castell y Bere, a ruined castle, very romantic, right near Cader. But that wasn't built till the thirteenth century, when Prince Llewellyn wanted to make himself a headquarters to rule all of Wales that the English hadn't grabbed.'

'No chip?' Barney said mischievously.

The dark glasses glared at him; then Bran grinned. 'History I am telling you, boy, not comment. Old Llewellyn had the chip . . . and a fine one too, like Owain Glyndwr later . . .' The grin faded. 'But none of that takes us anywhere either.'

'Isn't there anything to do with King Arthur?' Barney said.

And he and Jane and even Simon could feel the sudden weight of silence around them like a blanket. Neither Will nor Bran moved; they simply stood looking at Barney. And the emptiness of the mountain, up there on top of the world, was all at once so oppressive that every smallest sound seemed to take on immense significance. The rustle of heather as Barney shifted his feet; the deep distant call of a sheep; the persistent tuneless chirruping of some small unseen bird. Jane and Simon and Barney stood very still; surprised, uncertain.

Will said at last, lightly, 'Why?'

'Barney has a fixation about King Arthur, that's all,' Simon said.

For an instant Will paused still; then he smiled, and the strange oppressiveness fell away as if it had never been there. 'Well,' he said, 'there's the biggest mountain of all, next to Snowdon – Cader Idris. Over there. It means in English "the seat of Arthur".'

'Any good?' said Barney hopefully.

'No,' Will said, glancing at Bran. He offered no explanation for the total finality in his voice. Jane found herself resenting the feeling of exclusion that was growing in her.

Bran said slowly, 'Or there's one other. I hadn't thought about it. Carn March Arthur.'

'What's that mean?'

'It means, the hoof of Arthur's horse. It is not much to look at – just a mark on a stone, up behind Aberdyfi, on the mountain above Cwm Maethlon. Arthur is supposed to have pulled an *afanc*, a monster, out of a lake up there, and this is the footprint his horse made. when he was leaping away.' Bran wrinkled his nose. 'Of course it is all rubbish, so I never gave it a thought. But – the name is there.'

They looked at Will. He spread his hands. 'We have to start somewhere. Why not?'

Barney said hopefully, 'Today?'

Will shook his head. 'Tomorrow. It's a long way home from here, for us.'

'Carn March Arthur will be a longish walk,' Bran said. 'The quickest way from this side is up past the vicarage on a path over the mountain. Not so nice in summer, because of visitors' cars. Still. If you can get to the Square in the morning, perhaps we can too. Depends if we get a lift again, eh, Will?'

Will looked at his watch. 'Twenty minutes before we meet him. Let's go and ask.'

Jane never could remember, afterwards, the precise manner of the asking, though over and over again she tried. As they slithered and leapt over the grass and heather of the mountain ridge, there was little time for talking, and she felt obscurely that however much breath Will had he would not have explained much more about John Rowlands.

'He's shepherd on my uncle's farm. Among other things. He's . . . special. And this week he goes to a big annual market in Machynlleth, up the Dyfi valley. You must have come through it, on the way down.'

'Slate roofs and grey rock,' Jane said. 'Grey, everything grey.'

'That's the one. For the three days of the market now John is driving there every day, through Tywyn and Aberdyfi. That's how we got here today. He dropped us off this morning and he's picking us up now. So perhaps we can persuade him to do the same tomorrow.'

Will slowed on a gentler, grassy slope as they came to a stile, and stood diffidently aside to let Jane climb over first.

'D'you think he will?' she said. 'What's he like?'

'You'll see,' said Will.

But all that Jane saw, when they trotted breathless down the last side road and out on to the main road by the village station, was a waiting Land-Rover with a frowning face in the window. It was a brown, lean face, much lined; dark-eyed, given now a mask of severity by the joined brows and straight unsmiling mouth.

Bran said something penitent-sounding, in Welsh.

'It is not good enough,' John Rowlands said. 'Ten minutes we have been sitting here. I told you five o'clock, and Will has a watch.'

'I'm sorry,' Will said. 'It was my fault. We met some old friends of mine on the mountain. Visiting from London. This is Jane Drew, and Simon, and Barnabas.'

'How d'you do?' John Rowlands said gruffly. The dark eyes flickered over them.

Jane said, before her brothers could speak, 'How d'you do, Mr Rowlands, I'm sorry they're late. We slowed them down, you see, not being so good at running down mountains.' She gave him a small hopeful smile.

John Rowlands looked at her more carefully. 'Hmm,' he said.

Bran cleared his throat. 'It is not the best time to ask, but we wondered if you would bring us in with you again tomorrow. If Mr Evans would let us go.'

'I am not at all sure about that,' John Rowlands said.

'Oh come along now, John.' Unexpectedly a soft, musical voice came from inside the car. 'Of course David Evans will let them go. They have worked hard these last few days – and there is nothing much doing on the farm, except waiting for what comes from market.'

'Hmm,' John Rowlands said again. 'Where will you be going?'

'Up over Cwm Maethlon,' Bran said. 'To show these three Panorama Walk, and all that.'

'Go on, John,' said the soft voice coaxingly.

'Pick up afterwards on time, is it?' The lines on the strong dark face were relaxing gradually, as if it had been an effort for them to make a frown in the first pláce.

'Honest,' Will said. 'Truly.'

'I shall go without you if you're not here. Then you would have to make your own way back.'

'All right.'

'Very well then. I will drop you here at nine, and pick you up at four. If your uncle agrees.'

Will stood on tiptoe to see past him into the car. 'Thank you, Mrs Rowlands!'

Amusement creased John Rowlands' eyes, and his wife leaned past him, laughing at them. Jane liked her instantly; it was a face like the voice, gentle and warm and beautiful all at once, with a glow of kindliness.

'Enjoying your stay?' Mrs Rowlands said.

'Very much, thank you.'

'Happy Valley and the Bearded Lake tomorrow, then, is it?'

Jane looked at Will. There was barely a fraction of a second's hesitation, and then he said heartily, 'Yes, that's right.. Real tourist stuff. But I've never seen them either.'

'Lovely up there,' Mrs Rowlands said warmly. 'John had better drop you in the Square, you can all meet by the chapel.' She smiled at Jane. 'It's a long walk, you know. Take your lunch. And good strong shoes, and jackets in case of rain.'

'Oh, it won't rain,' Simon said confidently, looking up at the hazy blue sky.'

'You're in Snowdonia now, boy,' Bran said. 'Mean annual rainfall a hundred and fifty inches, high up. Only place that didn't die of the drought, back in nineteen seventy-six. Bring a raincoat. See you tomorrow.'

He and Will climbed into the back of the car, and the Land-Rover roared away.

'A hundred and fifty inches?' Simon said. 'That's impossible.'

Barney hopped happily round in a circle, kicking a stone. 'Things are happening!' he said. Then he paused. 'I wonder if Will should have said where we were going?'

'That's all right,' Jane said. 'He said John Rowlands was special.'

'Sounds a touristy kind of place anyway,' Simon said. 'I don't suppose it'll be any help at all.'

The Bearded Lake

There was no rain at first, though clouds swirled over the blue sky like billowing smoke. Silent for want of breath, they toiled up the long winding lane that led from the village of Aberdyfi into the hills. The road rose very steeply, climbing out of the broad valley of the Dyfi estuary, so that whenever they paused to look back they could see, spread beneath them, a widening sweep of the coast and hills and the broad sea, with the silver ribbon of the Dyfi River snaking through gleaming acres of brown-gold sand left by the falling tide. Then another bend in the lane cut away all this southern view, and they were left climbing towards the mountains of the north, not yet visible.

High grassy banks enclosed them in the lane, banks as high as their heads, starred with yellow ragwort and hawkweed, white flat heads of yarrow, and a few late foxgloves. Higher yet above the banks, hedges of hazel and bramble and hawthorn reached to the sky, heavy with half-ripe berries and nuts, and fragrant with invading honeysuckle.

'Keep in,' Will called from the rear. 'Car!'

They pressed themselves against the grass wall of the lane, dodging the prickly embrace of bramble shoots, while a bright red mini whipped past in a tenor snarl of low gear.

'*Visitors!*' Bran said.

'That's the sixth.'

'We're visitors too,' Jane said.

'Ah, but such a superior brand,' said Barney solemnly.

'At least you are walking on your legs,' Bran said. He resettled the peaked Swedish-type cap he wore over his white hair, and gave it a resigned tug. 'All these cars, they are like flies on a sunny day, this time of year. And because of them, up in the wild places you find not just the sheep and the wind and the emptiness now, but little wooden chalets for people from Birmingham.'

'No way out of it, is there?' Simon said. 'I mean there don't seem to be many ways left of making a living, round here, except tourism.'

'Farming, too,' said Will.

'Not for many.'

'True enough,' Bran said. 'The ones who go away to college after leaving school, they never come back. Nothing for them here.'

Jane said curiously, 'Will you go away?'

'*Duw,*' Bran said. 'Have a heart. That's years away, anything could happen. Power stations in the estuary. Holiday camps on Snowdon.'

'Watch out!' Simon said suddenly. 'Another one!'

This time the car was pale blue, chugging and coughing past them like a small tank. Two small children could be seen fighting in the back seat. It disappeared round the next bend.

'Cars, cars,' said Will. 'D'you know there's even something on the Machynlleth road called a chaltel? A *chaltel!* Presumably a cross between a motel and –' He broke off, staring at the road ahead.

'Look at that! Golly!' Barney grabbed Jane's arm, pointing. 'Whatever are they?'

Paused halfway across the lane a few yards ahead of them were two strange sinuous animals, as big as cats but slender-bodied. Their fur was reddish-ginger, like the coat of a red fox; they had cat-like tails, held just above the ground. Their heads were turned, bright-eyed. They stared at the children. Then first one and then the other, deliberately, without haste, turned back and made off in a slinking, undulating motion across the road, apparently disappearing into the bank.

'Stoats!' Simon said.

Barney looked doubtful. 'Weren't they too big?'

'Much too big,' said Bran. 'And these had white only on the muzzle. A stoat has a white belly and chest.'

'What were they, then?'

'*Yr ffwlbartau.* Polecats. But I've never seen one bright red before.' Bran went forward and peered cautiously at the bank, raising a warning hand as Simon joined him. 'Careful. They are not nice creatures . . . There's a rabbit hole. They must have taken it over.'

'Funny the cars don't seem to bother them,' Barney said. 'Or people, for that matter.'

'They are not nice,' Bran said again, looking thoughtfully at the hole. 'Vicious. Not afraid. They even kill for fun.'

'Like the mink,' Will said. His voice was husky. Impatiently, he cleared his throat. Jane noticed with surprise that he seemed to have turned very pale; sweat glistened on his forehead, and one of his hands was tight-clenched.

'Mink?' Bran said. 'Don't have those in Wales.'

'They look like those. Only black. Or brown, I think. They . . . enjoy killing, too.' Will's voice still seemed strained. Jane watched him out of the corner of her eye, trying not to appear curious.

'There's a farm just round the corner, that might be why they're about the place in daytime.' Bran seemed to have lost interest in the polecats; he strode off up the lane. 'Come on – it's a long way yet.'

Jane paused to pull up a sock and let the boys pass her; then followed, alone and thoughtful. Above the farm the lane widened a little; the grass banks dropped to a mere foot or so, topped sometimes by wire fencing. The way led more gently upward now, through rock-studded grassland where Welsh Black cattle grazed here and there, or stood contemplatively in the middle of the road. Jane warily skirted a large bullock, and tried to collect the elusive feelings that were running like quicksilver in and out of her mind. What was happening? Why was Will anxious, and why did Bran on the contrary seem to feel nothing, and anyway who *was* this Bran? She felt a vague formless resentment of the way his presence somehow complicated their relationship with Will: *it's not just us any more*, she thought, *the way it was last time* . . . And over everything she was beginning to feel a great unease about whatever lay ahead, as if some sense at the back of her mind were trying to tell her something she did not consciously know.

Then walking blindly on she bumped into Barney, and found all the others standing still in sudden silence, and looked up and saw why.

They were on the rim of a magnificent valley. At their feet the hillside dropped away in a sweep of waving green bracken, where a few sheep precariously grazed on scattered patches of grass. Far, far below, among the green and golden fields of the valley floor, a road ran like a wavering thread, past a toy church and a tiny farm. And across the valley, beyond its further side patched blue with cloud-shadows and dark with close-planted fir, there rolled in line after line the massing ancient hills of Wales.

'Oh!' Jane said softly.

'Cwm Maethlon,' Bran said.

'Happy Valley,' said Will.

'Now you see why they call this path Panorama Walk,' Bran said. 'This is what brings the cars. And walkers too, fair play.'

'Wake up, Jane,' Will said lightly.

Jane was standing quite still, staring out over the valley, her eyes wide. She turned her head slowly and looked at Will, but did not smile. 'It's . . . it's . . . I can't explain. Beautiful. Lovely. But – frightening, somehow.'

'Vertigo,' Simon said confidently. 'You'll feel better in a minute. Don't look over the edge.'

'Come on,' Will said, expressionless, suddenly reminding her of Merriman. He turned and continued up the path along the edge of Happy Valley. Simon followed.

'Vertigo, my foot,' Jane said.

Bran said curtly, 'Frightening, my foot, too. If you start listening to silly feelings, up here, you will never stop. Will has enough to worry about without that.'

Astonished, Jane stared, but he had turned and was plodding up the road again with Simon and Will.

She looked crossly after him. 'Who does he think he is? My feelings are in my head, not his.'

Barney stuck his fingers into the knapsack straps over his shoulders. 'Now perhaps you'll understand what I meant yesterday.'

Jane raised her eyebrows.

'Up on the hill over the sea,' Barney said. 'That was sort of frightening too. When I was sure I'd been there before, and you both said rubbish. Only, I've been thinking – it's really more like living inside something that happened before. Without its really having happened at all.'

They went on in silence after the others.

The rain began soon afterwards: a gentle persistent rain, from the low grey clouds that had been growing steadily larger and had begun to merge now into a covering over all the broad sky. They pulled anoraks and raincoats from the rucksacks and went doggedly on along the high moorland road, between open grassy slopes with no shelter anywhere.

One by one, cars came back down the road past them. Round one last bend, the paved road ended at an iron gate, and a footworn earthen track went on instead, past a lone white farmhouse and away over the mountain. Five cars were parked tipsily on the grass before the gate; back down the mountain came a straggle of damp holiday-makers with drooping headscarves and complaining children.

'There's one thing to be said for rain,' Barney said. 'It does wash the people away.'

Simon glanced back. 'Gloomy-looking lot, aren't they?'

'Those two kids from the blue car are still thumping one another. I suppose anyone'd look gloomy with brats like that.'

'You aren't long out of the brat stage yourself, chummy.'

Barney opened and shut his mouth, hunting the right insult; but then glanced at Jane instead. She stood silent, unsmiling, gazing at nothing.

'You aren't still feeling odd, Jane?' Simon peered at her.

'Look at them,' Jane said in a strange small, tight voice. She pointed ahead to Will and Bran, trudging one after the other up the track through the grass: two matching figures in oilskins rather too big for them, distinguishable only by Bran's cap and the sou'wester pulled low over Will's head. 'Look at them!' Jane said again, miserably. 'It's all mad! Who are they, where are they going, why are we doing what they want to do? How do we know what's going to happen?'

'We don't,' Barney said. 'But then we never have, have we?'

'We ought not to be here,' Jane said. Impatiently she tugged the hood of her anorak closer over her head. 'It's all too . . . vague. And it doesn't feel right. And' – the last words burst out defiantly – 'I'm scared.'

Barney blinked at her, out of the folds of an enveloping plastic mackintosh. 'But Jane, it's all right, it must be. Anything to do with Great-Uncle Merry –'

'But Gumerry isn't *here*.'

'No, he's not,' Simon said. 'But Will's here, and that's just about the same.'

Surprise sang through Jane's head. She stared at him. 'But you never liked Will, not really. I mean I know you never said anything, but there was always . . .' She stopped. Firm ground seemed to have become suddenly shaky; Simon was now so much bigger than she, as well as being almost a year older, that somehow she had imperceptibly begun to take him more seriously than before, paying attention to his opinions and prejudices even when she disagreed with them herself. It was unnerving to find one of those opinions turning itself upside down.

'Look,' Simon said. 'I don't pretend to understand anything that's ever happened to us with Great-Uncle Merry and Will. But there's not much point in trying, is there? I mean basically it's very simple, it's a matter of – well, there's a good side and a bad, and those two are absolutely without question the good side.'

'Well, of course,' Jane said pettishly.

'Well then. Where's the problem?'

'It's not a *problem*. It's that Bran. It's just – oh dear, you wouldn't understand.' Jane poked dolefully at a tuft of grass.

'They're waiting for us,' Barney said.

High up on the path beyond the farmhouse, beside another gate, the two small dark figures stood turned, looking back.

'Come on, Jane,' said Simon. He patted her tentatively on the back.

Barney said, in a sudden rush of discovery, 'You know, if you're really scared – it isn't like you – you ought to think whether you're being' – he flapped one hand vaguely – 'being got at.'

'Got at?' said Jane.

'The Dark,' Barney said. 'You remember – the way it makes something wriggle into your mind and say *I don't want you, go away* . . . Makes you feel something terrible is going to happen.'

'Yes,' Jane said. 'Oh yes. I do remember.'

Barney hopped in front of her like some small fierce animal. 'Well, if you fight it, it can't get hold. Push it off, run away from it –' He grabbed her sleeve. 'Come on. Race you up the hill!'

Jane tried to smile. 'All right!'

They rushed up the path to the waiting figures on the hill, raindrops scattering from their coats as they ran. Simon followed, more slowly. He had been listening with only half his attention. The rest had been caught, while Barney spoke, by two sinuous red animals slinking into the bracken from a thicket of gorse; and then out of the gorse, if he had not been imagining it, two bright pairs of eyes, watching them.

But it seemed a bad moment to mention that to Jane.

Bran said, as they watched Barney and Jane running towards them up the path. 'What was that all about, d'you think?'

'They could just have been discussing whether it was time for lunch,' Will said.

Bran pulled his glasses down his nose, and the tawny eyes regarded Will steadily for a moment, between the dark lenses and cap. 'Old One,' Bran said softly. 'You know better than that.' Then he pushed his glasses back and grinned. 'Anyway, it's too early.'

But Will looked soberly down at the approaching figures. 'The Light needs those three. It always has, in this whole long quest. So the Dark must be watching them very hard, now. We must stay close to them, Bran – especially Barney, perhaps.'

Barney came panting up to them, his hood flapping on his shoulders and his yellow hair damp-dark with rain. 'When's lunch?' he said.

Bran laughed. 'Carn March Arthur is just over the next slope.'

'What does it look like?' Without waiting for an answer Barney was gone, trotting up the path, mackintosh flapping.

Bran turned to go after him. But Jane was in his way. She stood there, breathing unevenly, looking coolly at them both in a way Will did not recognize. 'It won't do, you know,' she said. 'We're all marching along as if everything was ordinary but we just can't go on pretending to one another.'

Will looked at her, patience battling urgency in his mind; his head dropped for a moment on to his chest and he let out a short hiss of breath. 'All right then. What do you want us to say?'

'Just something about what we might find, up there,' Jane said, quavering, exasperated. 'About what we're *doing* here.'

Bran was on the words like a terrier at a bone, before Will could open his mouth. 'Doing? Nothing, girl – you will probably have nothing to do but look at a valley and a lake and say, oh, how pretty. What's the fuss? If you don't like the rain, wrap yourself up and go home. Go on!'

'Bran!' Will said sharply.

Jane stood very still, eyes wide.

Bran said angrily, 'The hell with it! If you have seen the raising of fear, and the killing of love, and the Dark creeping in over all things, you do not ask stupid questions. You do what you are intended to do, and no nonsense. And so that is what we should all be doing now, going on to where we might perhaps find out the next right move.'

'And no nonsense!' said Jane tightly.

Simon came up behind her, silent, listening, but she paid no attention.

'Right!' Bran snapped.

Watching Jane, Will felt suddenly that he was seeing someone he had never met before. Her face was drawn into furious lines of emotion that seemed to belong to someone else.

'You!' Jane said to Bran, pushing her hands fiercely into her pockets. 'You, you think you're so special, don't you, with the white hair and the difference, and the eyes behind those silly glasses. Super-different. You can tell us what we ought to do, you think you're even more special than Will. But who are you, anyway? We never met you at all until yesterday, in the middle of nowhere on a mountain, and why should we get into danger just because you –' Her voice quivered and dwindled, and she swung away from them, up the hill, towards Barney's small eager vanishing form.

Simon began to go after her and then paused, irresolute.

'Special, is it?' Bran said softly as if to himself. 'Special. That's nice. After all the years of people sneering and muttering about the boy with no colour in his creepy skin. That's lovely. Special. And what is this about the eyes?'

'Yes,' Will said shortly. 'Special. You know it.'

Bran hesitated; he pulled off his glasses and stuffed them in his pocket. 'That is separate. She knows nothing of that. And that is not at all what she meant.'

'No,' Will said. 'But you and I may not forget it for a moment. And you may not . . . let go, like that.'

'I know,' Bran said. 'I'm sorry.' He looked deliberately at Simon as he spoke, including him in the apology.

Simon said awkwardly, 'I don't know what all this is about, but you shouldn't be bothered by Jane flying off the handle. It doesn't mean anything.'

'Doesn't seem like her,' Will said.

'Well . . . now and then she does it, these days. A sort of flare-up . . . I think,' Simon said confidingly, 'she's going through a *stage*.'

'Maybe,' Will said. He was looking at Bran. 'Or maybe it is Jane we should be specially watching?'

'Come on,' Bran said. He brushed raindrops from the brim of his cap. 'Carn March Arthur.'

They climbed on, to the line where the green grassy slope met a grey sky. On the downward sweep of the path on the other side, Jane and Barney were crouched beside a small out-cropping of rock, identical with every other rocky scar on the hill but singled out by a neat slate marker like a label. Will came slowly down the path, his senses open and alert as the ears of a hunting dog, but he felt nothing. Glancing across, he saw the same blankness on Bran's face.

'There's a sort of carved-out circle here that's supposed to be where the hoof of Arthur's horse trod – look, it's marked.' Barney measured the hollow in the rock with his hand. 'And another over there.' He sniffed, unimpressed. 'Pretty small horse.'

'They are hoof-shaped, though,' Jane said. Her head was down, her voice slightly husky. 'I wonder what really made them?'

'Erosion,' Simon said. 'Water swirling round.'

'With dirt rubbing,' Bran said.

Jane said hesitantly, 'And frost, cracking the rock.'

'Or the hoof of a magic horse, coming down hard,' Barney said. He looked up at Will. 'Only it wasn't, was it?'

'No,' Will said, smiling. 'Hardly. If Arthur had ridden over every hollow called Arthur's Hoofprint, or sat on every rock called Arthur's Seat, or drunk from every spring called Arthur's Well, he'd have spent his whole life travelling round Britain without a stop.'

'And so would the knights,' Barney said cheerfully, 'to sit round every hill called King Arthur's Round Table.'

'Yes,' Will said. He picked up a small white quartz pebble and rolled it round and round his palm. 'Those too. Some of the names mean . . . other things.'

Barney jumped up. 'Where's the lake, the one he's supposed to have taken the monster from?'

'Llyn Barfog,' Bran said. 'The Bearded Lake. Over here.'

He led them on, down the path into a hollow between hill-tops, curving round a slope; the rain, which had been gentle, began here to whip at their faces in uneven gusts, as the high wind eddied round the gullied land. The cloud was low over their heads.

'Such a funny name, the Bearded Lake,' Jane said. The words were aimed at Bran, though she walked without looking at him; Will felt a pang of compassion for her groping unspoken apology. 'Bearded. Not exactly romantic.'

'I'll show you why in a minute,' Bran said without rancour. 'Watch where you tread, now, there's boggy patches.' He strode ahead of them all, dodging tussocks of reedy grass that marked wet ground. And then Will looked up, and suddenly there ahead of him through the driving rain he could see the far side of the Happy Valley again, misted and grey. But this time, on this side, on their own steep edge over-hanging the valley, there lay a lake.

It was a strange small reed-edged lake, little larger than a pond; its dark surface seemed curiously patched and patterned. Then Will saw that its open surface was rippled by the wind, but that only a small part of it was open, a triangle at the closest end of the lake. All the rest of its surface, from the end at the edge of the valley to a trailing V-shape in the centre, was covered with the leaves and stems and creamy white bloom of waterlilies. And from a singing in his ears like the sudden rise of waves on a loud sea, he knew too that somewhere up here, after all, was the place to which they were intended to come. Something waited for them here, somewhere up on this rolling rock-strewn mountaintop, between the Happy Valley and the estuary of the Dyfi River.

Through a mist that was not the rain in the air but a blurring inside his mind, he saw with a vague distant surprise that this feeling did not seem to have come to Bran. The white-haired boy stood on the path with Simon and Jane, one hand raised over his eyes against the wind and rain, the other pointing.

'The Bearded Lake – see, it's the weed on the water that gives it the name. Some years when there is not much rain it gets much smaller, and the weed is left all around it like a beard. John Rowlands says perhaps the name is not from that, perhaps long ago there was much more water in the lake and *it* would spill out over the edge of the mountain and down into the valley in a waterfall. That could be, too. But a long time ago indeed, the way it looks now.'

The little lake lay dark and silent under the shifting grey sky. They could hear the wind whining over the hills, and rustling through their clothes. Down in the valley, far away, a curlew gave its sad ghostly call. Then closer by, somewhere, they heard a muffled shout.

Barney turned his head. 'What's that?'

Bran looked across the lake at the slope that seemed to be the highest part of the mountain on which they stood. He sighed. 'Visitors. Shouting for the echo. Come and see.'

Will lagged behind as they balanced their way one after the other along the muddy, rock-strewn path edging the lake.

He gazed out once more across the water, and its white-starred green carpet of weed, to the far shore where the land fell abruptly away into the valley. The rain blew back into his eyes, the mist whirled over the hills. But nothing came into his consciousness; nothing spoke to him. There was only the strong sense pulsing through his mind that they were in the presence of the High Magic, in some form he did not understand.

So then Will followed the others, along the path and round the next high slope. He found them standing on a bluff overlooking a flat hollow in the hills perhaps fifty yards square, a space much like the one occupied by the Bearded Lake, but here holding only the bright patches of coarse reedy grass that warned of marsh. A man and woman wearing startling orange anoraks stood lower down the slope, with three children of assorted sizes roaming about them shouting across the flat green hollow. A steep cliff-like rock on the opposite side threw an echo back.

'Hey! . . . *Hey* . . .'

'Ooooo! . . . *Ooooo* . . .'

'Baa baa black sheep . . . *black sheep . . . sheep . . .*'

'Hey fat face! . . . *face . . . face . . .*'

Jane said, 'If you listen carefully it's really a double echo, the second very faint.'

'Fat face!' shouted the most raucous of the children again, delighted with himself.

Barney said in a clear precise voice, 'Funny how people can never think of anything intelligent to shout to make an echo.'

'It's like never knowing what to say to find out if a microphone's working,' Will said. 'Testing testing, one two three.'

'The English master at school has a very rude rhyme he uses for that,' Simon said.

'You can't shout rude rhymes for an echo,' Barney said coldly. 'Echoes are special. People ought to . . . to sing to them.'

'Sing!' said Jane. The small children were still screeching at the mountain; she looked at them with distaste.

'Well, why not? Or do some Shakespeare. Simon was Prospero last term – why not a bit of that?'

'Were you really?' Bran looked at Simon with new interest.

'Only because I was the tallest,' Simon said depreciatingly. 'And had the right kind of voice.'

'Fat face!' shouted all the awful children together.

'Oh really!' said Jane, losing patience. 'What's the matter with their stupid parents?' She swung round irritably, and walked a little way back down the slope. The wind seemed less gusty here, and the rain had calmed to a fine mist. Underbrush scratched at her ankles; the slope was thick with heather and low-growing bilberry bushes, studded here and there with tiny blue-black berries among the leaves.

The others' voices receded as she wandered away. She thrust her hands deep into her pockets and hunched her shoulders as if to shake something from her back. *Black dog on my shoulder*, she thought wrily: it was the family term for a brief bad mood, generally her own these days. Yet somehow this time, Jane felt, there was more than a mood invading her mind; this was a strangeness she could not define, had never known before. A restlessness, a half-fearful anticipation of something part of her seemed to understand and part not . . . Jane sighed. It was like being two people at once: living with someone without having the least idea what the other would do or feel next.

A flash of orange caught her eye through a gap in the hilly skyline; the noisy family was leaving, the mother dragging one rebellious child crossly by the arm. They disappeared behind the slope, heading for the path. But Jane did not go back to the others; she wandered aimlessly still on her own, through the heather and the wet grass, until suddenly the wind was cold on her face again and she found she was back at the Bearded Lake. From behind, she heard a faint laugh and a call from Barney, and then the same call again: a summons for the echo. She stood looking bleakly out over the dark weed-shrouded water, at the distant valley beyond. The wind sang in her ears. The cloud of the heavy grey sky was so low now that it blew ragged over the hilltop in white tails and tatters of mist, whirling down to the lake, curling, blowing away into the valley. The whole world seemed grey, as if all colour had drained from the summer grass.

In an eddy of the wind that brought a sudden stillness after it, Jane heard Simon's voice faintly behind her, a sudden snatch of sound. '. . . *thou earth, thou! Speak!* . . .' And very faintly indeed, perhaps only in imagining, she heard the echo: '. . . *speak* . . . *speak* . . .'

Then some words came in another voice, clear and strange, and she knew that it was Bran calling in Welsh; and again the echo came faintly back, bringing the words to her again, familiar even while meaningless.

The wind flurried, the mist blew in a ragged shroud over the far side of the lake, hiding the Happy Valley. And on the echo of Bran's call, as if following a cue, a third voice came, singing, singing so high and sweet and unearthly that Jane stood without breathing, caught out of movement, feeling every stilled muscle and yet as totally transported as if she had no body at all. She knew it was Will; she could not remember if she had ever heard him sing before; she could not even think, or do anything but hear. The voice soared up on the wind, from behind the hill, distant but clear, in a strange lovely line of melody, and with it and behind it very faint in a following descant came the echo of the song, a ghostly second voice twining with the first.

It was as if the mountains were singing.

And as Jane gazed unseeing at the clouds blowing low over the lake, someone came.

Somewhere in the shifting greyness, a patch of colour began faintly to glow, red and pink and blue merging into one another too fast for the eye to follow. Glimmering soft and warm on the cold mountain, it held Jane's gaze as hypnotically as a flame; then gradually it began to focus itself, and Jane blinked in disbelief as she realized that a form was taking shape around it. Not definite clear shape, but a suggestion, a hint of what might be seen with the right eyes . . .

The brightness grew more intense until suddenly it was all contained in a glowing rose-coloured stone set into a ring, and the ring on the finger of a slender figure standing before her, leaning a little as if resting on a stick. There was at first such brightness around the figure that Jane could not look directly at it; instead her eyes flickered down to the ground on which it stood, only to realize with a shock that no ground was there. The figure was floating before her, an isolated fragment of whatever world lay there behind the greyness. It was the delicate form of an old lady, she saw now, wearing a long light-coloured robe; the face was fine-boned, kindly yet arrogant, with clear blue eyes that shone strangely young in the old, old cobweb-lined face.

Jane had forgotten the others, forgotten the mountain and the rain, forgotten everything but the face that watched her and now, gently, smiled. But still the old lady did not speak.

Jane said huskily, 'You are the Lady. Will's Lady.'

The Lady inclined her head, a slow graceful nod. 'And since you can see that much, I may speak to you, Jane Drew. It was intended, from the beginning, that you should carry the last message.'

'Message?' Jane's voice came out in a whisper.

'Some things there are that may be communicated only between like and like,' the sweet soft voice said from the mist. 'It is the pattern of a child's game of dominoes. For you and I are much the same, Jane, Jana, Juno, Jane, in clear ways that separate us from all others concerned in this quest. And you and Will are alike in your youth and your vigour, neither of which I share.'

The voice grew fainter, as if with a great weariness; then rallied, and the light glowed more brightly from the rose-coloured ring on the Lady's hand. She drew herself upright, and her robe shone clear white now, bright as a moon over the grey lake.

'Jane,' she said.

'Madam?' Jane said at once, and without any self-consciousness she bowed her head and dipped one knee almost to kneeling, oblivious of her jeans and anorak, as if she were dropping a deep curtsey of respect, out of another age.

The Lady said clearly, 'You must tell him that they must go to the Lost Land, in the moment when it shall show itself between the land and the sea. And a white bone will prevent them, and a flying may-tree will save them, and only the horn can stop the wheel. And in the glass tower among the seven trees, they will find the crystal sword of the Light.'

Her voice wavered, ending in a gasp, as if clutching for some last strength.

Jane said, struggling to hold the words, struggling to hold her image of the Lady, 'In the glass tower among the seven trees. And – a white bone will prevent them, and a flying may-tree save them. And only the – the horn will stop the wheel.'

'Remember,' the Lady said. Her white form was beginning to fade, and the glow dying in the rose of the ring. The voice grew softer, softer. 'Remember, my daughter. And be brave, Jane. Be brave . . . brave . . .'

The sound died, the wind whirled; Jane stared desperately out into the grey mist, searching to see the clear blue eyes in the old, lined face as if only they could fix the words in her memory. But she was alone among the dark hills and the lake with the low clouds blowing, and in her ears only the wind and the last imagined thread of a dying voice. And, now, as if it had never left her consciousness from the first instant, there came instead the clear high echo-twined melody of Will's voice, that had seemed to her like the mountains singing.

Suddenly the singing broke off. Will's voice flung through the air in a hoarse, urgent shout. 'Jane! Jane!' The echo followed it '...*Jane!*...*Jane!*...' like a whispered warning. In quick instinct Jane swung round towards the voice, but saw only the green slope of the hill.

Then she looked back at the lake, and found that in the brief moment of her turning, such horror had arisen before her that panic engulfed her like ice-cold water. She tried to scream, and brought out only a strangled croak.

Out of the dark water an immense neck rose, swaying before her, dripping, tipped by a small pointed head, open-mouthed, black-toothed. Two horn-like antennae moved sluggishly to and fro on the head, like the horns of a snail; a fringe like a mane began between them and ran down the whole length of the neck, bent to one side by the water that hung from it, dripping slimily into the lake. The neck rose higher and higher, huge, endless. Gazing in motionless terror Jane saw that it was everywhere a dark green, shot with a strange dull iridescence, except on the underside that faced her, a dead silvery-white like the belly of a fish. High over her head the creature towered and swayed, menacing; the air was filled with a stench of weed and marsh-gas and decaying things.

Jane's arms and legs would not move. She stood, staring. The great serpent lunged to and fro towards her, nearer, nearer, blindly searching. Its mouth hung open. Slime dripped from the black jaws. It swung close to her, reeking, dreadful, and seemed to sense her; the head drew back to strike.

Jane screamed, and closed her eyes.

Afanc

In the hollow beside the echo rock, all other sound had seemed to die away when Will began to sing. The loud wind dropped, and Simon, Bran and Barney stood motionless, astonished, listening. The music fell through the air like sunlight; a strange, haunting melody, like nothing they had ever heard before. Will sang, standing there unselfconscious and relaxed, with his hands in his pockets, his high clear choirboy's voice singing words of a tongue none of them could recognize. They knew that this was the music of the Old Ones, shot through with an enchantment that was more than melody. The clear voice soared through the mountains, entwining with its echoes, and listening they stood rapt, caught up out of time.

But then suddenly the song broke off in the middle of a note, and Will reeled back as if he had been struck in the face. They saw his face twisted by horror, and he threw back his head and yelled, in dreadful unboyish warning, 'Jane! Jane!'

The echo threw the words back at them: *'Jane ... Jane!'*

But before the first echo came, Bran had begun to move. He came rushing past Simon and Barney, as if flung forward by the same urgent impulse that had hold of Will. His cap tumbled off, his white hair blew like a flag as he went leaping over the grass and the rocks, away towards the Bearded Lake, away on a pursuit of something none of them could see.

The monstrous head swung past Jane's face, once, twice, three times; not quite close enough to touch, but each time fanning past her a wave of abominable decay. Jane opened slits of eyes, peering through the shaking hands she held over her face, convinced she was still alive only by feeling a powerful urge to be sick. It was impossible that anything so hideous could exist; yet the creature was there. Her mind clutched for support, wavering beneath an awful awareness of evil. It was *wrong*, this thing from the lake: malevolent, vicious, full of the festering resentment it had nursed through the centuries of some terrible nightmare sleep. She could feel its will groping for hers, just as the blind head groped through the air before her. And then breaking into her head like a howl, yet not with any sound to be heard with the ears, the voice came.

'Tell!'

Jane shut her eyes tight.

'Tell me!' The command beat at her mind. *'I am the afanc! Tell me the instruction that comes only through you! Tell!'*

'No!' Desperately Jane tried to shut off her mind and her memory.

'Tell! Tell!'

She tried to find images to hold as a defence against the hammer-blow demands; she thought of Will's pleasant round face, with the straight brown hair falling sideways; she thought of Merriman's fierce eyes beneath his bristling white brows; of a golden grail and the finding of it. Reaching closer, into the last few days in Wales, she thought of John Rowlands' lean brown face, and the gentle kindly smile of his wife.

But even as she began to find a steadiness, suddenly it shattered, and the high shrieking voice broke again into her mind and beat and beat at her, until she felt she would go mad. She whimpered, staggering, holding both hands to her head.

And all at once, mercifully muffling the high shriek, came another voice, gentle, reassuring: *It's all right, Jenny, it's all right*, and relief flooded warm through her mind, and after it came only darkness . . .

They saw her crumple and fall in a heap on the wet grass, as they came stumbling up from the echo rock. Simon and Barney started forward, but Will seized each of them in an astonishing grip, and even tall Simon was held helpless by the hand clamped like a steel band round his arm. They gasped at the sight of the *afanc*, thrashing furiously now in the lake with its great neck bending to and fro. And then they saw Bran, upright and bare-headed, standing angry in challenge before it on a tall rock, with his white hair blowing in the wind.

The creature screamed in fury, stirring a foam in the lake, throwing it up to join the gusting ragged cloud and the blowing rain so that all the world seemed one whirling grey mist.

'Go back!' Bran shouted across the lake towards it. 'Go back where you should be!'

From the horned head in the mist a high thin voice came, cold as death; they shuddered at the sound.

'I am the *afanc* of Llyn Barfog!' the high voice cried. 'This place is mine!'

Bran stood unmoving. 'My father cast you from it, away into Lyn Cau. What right had you to return?'

Up on the hillside, Will felt Barney's hand clutch convulsively at his sleeve. The younger boy was looking up at him, very pale. '*His father, Will?*'

Will met his gaze, but said nothing.

The water churned, the voice was angry and obstinate. 'The Dark outlived that lord, the Dark brought me home. The Dark is my master. I must have what the girl will tell!'

'You are a stupid creature,' Bran said, clear and contemptuous.

The *afanc* roared and screamed and thrashed; its noise was terrifying. But gradually now, they began to realize that it was no more than noise: that in spite of the creature's horrifying bulk, it seemed to have the power only to utter threats. It was a nightmare – but no more than that.

Bran's white hair gleamed like a beacon through the grey mist; his lilting Welsh voice rang out over the lake. 'And your masters are stupid too, to think that the mere force of terror could overcome one of the Six. This girl, she has seen more dreadful sights than you, and stood the test.' His voice hardened into a command, sounding suddenly deeper and more adult; he stood erect, pointing. 'Go, *afanc*, back to the dark water where you belong! Go back to the Dark, and never come out again! *Ewch nôl! Ewch y llyn!*'

And suddenly there was total silence over the lake, but for the wind whistling and the patter of the rain on their clothes. The huge green neck bowed and coiled in submission, dripping slime and weed; and the horned snail-like head dipped into the water and slowly the creature disappeared. A few large sluggish bubbles broke on the dark surface of the lake, their ripples spreading to be lost in the water-lily leaves. And then there was nothing.

Will let out a yell of exuberant relief, and with Simon and Barney he went slithering and sliding down the grassy slope. Jane was sitting at the bottom of the slope, on the grass edging the reeds that fringed the lake; her face was pale.

Simon crouched beside her. 'Are you all right?'

Jane said, illogically, 'I was watching him.'

'But you didn't hurt yourself? When you fell?'

'Fell?' Jane said.

Will said gently, 'She'll be all right now.'

'Will?' Jane said. She was looking out across the lake, to where Bran still stood motionless on his rock. Her voice shook. 'Will . . . Who – what – is Bran?'

Simon helped her to her feet, and the four of them stood looking at Bran. The white-haired boy turned slowly away from the lake, pulling his coat closer at the collar, shaking his head dog-fashion to get rid of the rain.

'He is the Pendragon,' Will said simply. 'The son of Arthur. Heir to the same responsibility, in a different age . . . When he was born, his mother Guinevere brought him forward in Time, with Merriman's help, because once before she had deceived her lord and she was afraid Arthur would not now believe that Bran was truly his son. And she left him here, so that he grew up in our time in Wales, with a new father who adopted him. So he belongs to this age just as much as we do, yet at the same time he does not . . . And sometimes I think he is exactly aware of all this all the time, and other times I think one side of his life is for him no more than a dream . . .' His voice quickened, became more matter-of-fact. 'I can't tell you any more now. Come on.'

They went, each one hesitant, to meet Bran, through the rain that was growing heavier again now. He grinned cheerfully at them, totally without strain, and wrinkled his nose. '*Daro!*' he said. 'What a nasty!'

'Thank you, Bran,' Jane said.

'*O'r gore,*' said Bran. 'You're welcome.'

'Will it really never come back *ever*?' Barney said, looking fascinated at the lake.

'Never,' Bran said.

Simon took a deep breath and let it out again. 'I shan't laugh at stories of the Loch Ness Monster from now on.'

'But this one was a creature of the Dark,' Will said. 'Made out of the stuff of nightmare, in order to break Jane. Because they wanted something that she had.' He looked at her. 'What happened?'

'It was when you sang,' Jane said. 'And the echo sang with you. It sounded ... it sounded ...'

'*The mountains are singing,*' Bran said slowly. '*And the Lady comes.*'

Jane said, 'And she did come.'

There was silence.

Will said nothing. He stood staring at Jane with a strange medley of emotions crossing his face: blank astonishment, chased by envy, followed by the dawning of an understanding that relaxed into his usual amiable look. He said softly, 'I didn't know.'

'This ... Lady –' Simon said. He stopped.

'Well?' said Jane.

'Well ... where did she come from? Where is she now?'

'I don't know. Either of those things. She just ... appeared. And she said –' Jane paused, a warmth running through her as she remembered those things the Lady had said for her, Jane, alone. Then she put them aside. 'She said, tell him, that they must go to the Lost Land, when it shows itself between the shore and the sea. She said, a white bone will prevent them, and a – a flying may-tree will save them. And –' She shut her eyes, trying desperately to remember the right words. 'And only the horn will stop the wheel, she said. And they will find the crystal sword of the Light in the glass tower among the seven trees.'

She let out a quick breath, and opened her eyes. 'That's not perfect, but it's what she said. And then she ... went away. She seemed awfully tired, she just sort of faded out.'

'She is very tired indeed,' Will said soberly. He touched Jane's shoulder briefly. 'You did marvellously. The moment the Dark sensed she had told you, they must have come rushing, sending the *afanc* to shock you into giving up what she had said. That was their only possible way – they couldn't have heard it for themselves. There is a protection sometimes round the Six, through which the Dark cannot see or hear.'

'But there's only five of us,' Barney said.

Bran chuckled. 'That one is so sharp he will cut himself.'

Barney said hastily, 'I'm sorry – I know. Of course things work just the same whether it's five or six. But where *is* Great-Uncle Merry?' For a moment his voice dropped unwittingly into the unselfconscious plaint of a small child.

'I don't know,' Will said. 'He'll come, Barney. When he can.'

Simon suddenly gave a gigantic sneeze, ducking his head. Rainwater ran off the edge of his hood in a thin stream. No mist blew over the lake now, and the clouds seemed higher, broken, racing across the sky in a wind they hardly felt, there below. But the rain fell steadily.

'Where is the Lost Land?' said Barney.

'We shall find it,' Will said. 'When the time comes. No question. Come on, let's go down before we all get pneumonia.'

They went single file back over the path edging the lake, hopping over puddles, skirting patches of mud; then trooped through the long wet grass towards the little grey outcrop of Carn March Arthur, and the path back over the ridge. Jane turned for one last look at the lake, but it was hidden by the slope.

'Will,' she said. 'Tell me something. Just about a second before I saw that – that thing, I heard you shout *Jane!* Like a warning.'

Barney said promptly, 'Yes, he did. He looked awful – as if he could already see it.' He realized what he had said, and looked thoughtfully at Will.

'Could you?' Jane said.

Will brushed his hand over the top of the slate marking Carn March Arthur, which Bran, ahead of them, had passed without a glance. He walked on in silence. Then he said, 'When the Dark comes, anywhere, we can feel it. It's like, I dunno, like an animal smelling man. So I knew – and I knew you were in danger, so I had to yell.' He glanced back at Jane over his shoulder with a shy half-grin. '*Halloo your name to the reverberate hills,*' he said.

'Huh?' said Simon, beside her.

'You aren't the only one who knows a few bits of Shakespeare,' Will said.

'What's that one?'

'Oh – just some speech we had to learn last term.'

'The reverberate hills,' said Jane. She looked back at the hill that rose behind them now, masking the echo rock. Then she frowned. 'Will – if you could sense the Dark, why couldn't you sense the Light?'

'The Lady?' Will shook his head. 'I don't know. That was her doing. For her own reasons. I think – I think perhaps there will be a test for each of us, before all this is done. Each time different and each time unexpected. And maybe the Bearded Lake was yours, Jane, yours on your own.'

'I hope mine isn't like that,' Barney said cheerfully. He pointed. 'Look – the clouds are breaking up.'

Hints of blue were emerging in the sky to the west, among the racing ragged clouds; the rain had dwindled to a fine sprinkle, and was dying altogether now. They went on down the hill, past the small white farm built sturdy as a fort

against winter gales; through other gates, over the clanking metal pipes of a
cattle grid set to keep the wandering Welsh Black bullocks within bounds. The
Happy Valley unfolded far below them again, the last low shreds of mist
blowing away past the mountains of its further side. Sunshine flickered now
and then through the clouds, and the air grew warmer; jackets were opened,
and raincoats shaken free of water. As if to give final proof that the rain was
over, a small car came humming up the hill past them, bringing the first of the
next flow of visitors to wander the hillside among the sheep-droppings and
rabbit holes; to collect feathers, and the tufts of greyish wool that barbed-wire
fences grab from sheep, and small rough pebbles of white quartz. Will found
himself trying hard to remember that he had no right whatsoever to resent
these people wandering through the bracken and the heather, the gorse and the
harebells, dropping their cigarette ends on the short, springy grass.

Seagulls keened in the distance. As the track swung round a hill, suddenly
there ahead they saw the sea, and the broad estuary of the Dyfi, with the silver
thread of the river wandering through glistening stretches of golden low-tide
sand.

They all stopped to stand and gaze. Sunshine shafting out from between the
clouds sparkled on the river, glimmered on the sandy bar that lay across its
entrance to the sea.

'I'm hungry,' Barney said.

'Now that's a good idea,' said Simon. 'Lunch?'

Bran said, 'Rocks to sit on, though – try up here.'

They clambered up the slope edging the track, to the unfenced land where
the cattle grazed. Several large black bullocks lumbered reproachfully out of
their way. In a few moments they were over the crest of a small ridge, with the
track out of sight behind them and the sea and the estuary lying spread below.
They perched on humps of slatey rock and fell upon their sandwiches. The wet
grass smelt clean, and somewhere a skylark bubbled its long ecstatic song. High
overhead a small hawk hung in the air.

Jane said, looking out over the estuary as she munched, 'What an enormous
lot of flat land there is on the other side of the river. Miles of it, miles and miles,
before the mountains start again.'

'*Cors Fochmno*,' Bran said, his strange white hair drying fluffy in the sun.
'Bog, most of it – see the drainage channels, all so straight? Some very
interesting plants there are, over in that part, if you are a botanist. Which I am
not . . . And old things have been found there, a golden girdle with spikes on it,
once, and a gold necklace, and thirty-two gold coins that are in the National
Museum now. And there are stumps of drowned trees out there on the sands,

near the dunes. Some on this side of the river too, on the sands between
Aberdyfi and Tywyn.'

'Drowned trees?' Simon said.

'Sure,' Bran said. He chuckled. 'From the Drowned Hundred, no doubt.'

Barney said blankly, 'Whatever's that?'

'Haven't you heard that old story yet? About where the Bells of Aberdyfi
ring, all ghostly out at sea on a summer night, over there?' Masked by the dark
glasses that covered his pale eyes once more, Bran got to his feet and pointed
out at the mouth of the estuary, all of it sunlit now beneath wider patches of
blue. 'That was supposed to be *Cantr'er Gwaelod*, the Lowland Hundred, the
lovely fertile land of the King Gwyddno Garanhir, centuries ago. The only
trouble was, it was so flat that the seawater had to be kept out by dykes, and one
night there was a terrible storm and the sea-wall broke, and all the water came
in. And the land was drowned.'

Will stood up and came quietly forward to stand beside him, looking down
at the estuary. He tried to keep the excitement from his voice. 'Drowned,' he
said. 'Lost . . .'

The mountain was very quiet. The skylark had finished its song. Very far
away once more they heard gulls faintly crying, out over the sea.

Bran stood very still, without turning. 'Dear God,' he said.

The others scrambled to their feet. Simon said, *'The Lost Land?'*

'I have known that old story always, as well as I know my own name,' Bran
said slowly, 'and yet I never thought . . .'

'Could that really be it?' Simon said. 'But—'

Barney burst out, 'It has to be! It couldn't be anything else! Isn't that right,
Will?'

'I think so,' Will said. He was trying to stop his face from breaking into a
broad stupid smile. Confidence was running through him like the warmth of
the sun. He could feel again, rapidly growing as strong as before, the sense of
the High Magic all around. It was a kind of intoxication, a wonderful
expectancy of marvellous things: the feeling of Christmas Eve, or the new-
green mist of trees in early spring, or the first summer-holiday sight of the sea.
Impulsively he stretched both arms upward, as if to catch a cloud.

'Something –' he said, talking out of his feelings, without any thought of
what he said. 'There's something –' He whirled about, staring round him on
the mountain; delight was singing all through him, he scarcely knew that the
others were there. Except one of them.

'Bran?' he said. 'Bran? Do you feel it – do you –' He flapped one hand
impatiently as he found he had no words; but then looked and knew that he
needed none, from the rapt astonishment on Bran's pale face. The Welsh boy

too turned, looking out over the mountains, out at the sky, as if hunting for something, trying to hear a voice calling. Will laughed aloud, to see the reflection of the same indefinable joy that flooded his own mind.

Jane, behind them, watching, sensed the intensity of their feeling and was afraid of it. Unconsciously she drew closer to Simon, and reached an arm to keep Barney beside her; and chilled by the same instinct Barney did not resist, but stepped slowly backward, away from Will and Bran. The Drews stood there, three together, watching.

And out over the hill, a mile beyond in the blue and gold patterning of the estuary, a flickering of the air came, like the quiver of heat that is over a paved road in high summer. At the same time a whispering music drifted to their ears, very distant and faint, but so sweet that they strained to hear it better, yet could never catch more than a hint of the delicate elusive melody. The quivering air grew bright, brighter, glowing as if it were lit from within by the sun; their eyes dazzled, but through the brightness they seemed to see a changing out in the estuary, a movement of the water.

Although the tide was already low, there seemed to be more sand shining golden now beyond the furthest low-tide mark. The waves had stilled, the water had begun to go back. Further and further the white rim of the blue sea withdrew, and the shore rose out of it; first sand, then the glimmering green of weed. But it was not weed, Jane saw incredulously, it was grass; for after it, as the sea fell back and back, there rose trees, and flowers, and walls and buildings of grey stone, blue slate and glimmering gold. A whole city lay there, growing gradually out of the retreating sea: a live city, with here and there thin strands of smoke rising from unseen fires through the unmoving summer air. Towers and glittering pinnacles reached up like guardians, over the flat fertile land patched green and gold, stretching beside the mountains. And far away at the distant edge of the new land, where the blue of the vanished sea at last began again, they glimpsed a pencil of light standing, a faraway tower gleaming like white fire.

Up on the highest ridge of the slope, looking out over the Lost Land and the city that seemed to govern it, Will and Bran stood together, outlined against the blue sky. They seemed to Jane to be poised there, expectant, like musicians waiting for the first sweep of the conductor's baton. She saw Will raise his head suddenly and look out to sea. And then the brightness that filled the air began to grow again, dazzling, blinding, so that only the faintest outline of the strange land could be seen through it, and it seemed to Jane as she flinched back, shielding her eyes, that the luminous air drew itself into a shining broad ribbon like a road, stretching from their feet far, far out into the air and over the valley, down beyond the mouth of the Dyfi River.

She heard the sound of the music again, lovely and elusive, and she saw Will and Bran step together on to the bright road of light and move away, over the river, through the air, into the haze and towards the Lost Land.

Her arm tightened across Barney's shoulder, and at her other side she felt Simon's hand touch her own. They stood together in silence.

Then the music dwindled into the sound of gulls crying, far away, and the shining road of light faded, and with it the figures that had been walking upon it. And as brightness fell from the air they saw, looking out over the estuary, no towering city, no new green fields, no thin smoke rising, but only the sea and the river and the low-tide shore just as they had been in the beginning.

Simon and Jane and Barney turned, in silence, and gathered coats and the remnants of picnic lunches into the rucksacks, and walked back to the road.

Three from the Track

They walked in single file, back along the path over the hills. The wet grass glittered in the sunshine now; raindrops hung sparkling on bracken, heather, the patches of yellow-starred gorse.

Barney said, 'What are we going to say?'

'I don't know,' Jane said.

'We'll have to meet John Rowlands in the Square, where they were going to,' Simon said. 'And say – and say–'

'Better if we don't,' Jane said suddenly. 'Then he'll just think they're late, and go without them. He warned them he would, remember?'

'That won't solve anything for long.'

'Maybe they won't need long.'

They went on in silence. At the turn where the path curved back down towards Aberdyfi, Jane paused and stood gazing ahead over the fields, over to the next ridge of high moorland where they had first encountered Will and Bran.

She pointed. 'Can't we go on over the hills, and down to the hotel from the ridge?'

Simon said doubtfully, 'There isn't any footpath.'

'Be a lot quicker than going down to the village,' Barney said. 'And we shouldn't see Mr Rowlands either.'

'There's bound to be a sheep trail at least, after this field,' Jane said.

Simon shrugged. 'I don't care. Go on then.' He seemed detached, indifferent, as though his mind were still half-paralysed. Jane swung open the gate to the first field that would lead them away from the little road, and he followed listlessly.

Barney trotted behind, taking the gate from Jane; but before he could swing it shut again, suddenly ahead of him Jane screamed, a dreadful high muffled sound. She seemed to leap into the air, cannoning sideways into Simon; Simon too yelled, and then he and Jane were flinging themselves at Barney, pushing him back through the gate. And behind them in a horrible hasty flash Barney saw, coming at them from all parts of the field, the red rippling bodies of dozens of polecats like the two they had seen on the road before, on their way up the mountain.

Desperately Simon slammed the gate shut, in a hopeless instinctive clutch at defence. But instantly the animals were after them as before, pouring through the open rails that would have kept out nothing smaller than a sheep. The children kicked out at them; the lithe red creatures slipped aside and were at their heels again in a moment, white teeth glinting, black eyes shining; never biting, always nagging, hovering, chivvying. Driving ... *driving*, Barney thought suddenly; driving us, as if we were sheep and they were sheep-dogs. He glanced up, and saw that the small hard bodies darting sideways against his ankles were pushing towards the open gate of the farm they had passed earlier that day. Deliberately he turned away, and at once the animals were at his heels, hissing, snapping, making dreadful small yipping sounds, turning him; until in spite of himself Barney turned back to Simon and Jane, and all three of them flung themselves for refuge towards the yard of the farm.

'Slowly, now!' The voice was warm, relaxed, amused; as Jane skidded desperately into the farmyard she glimpsed the figure of a woman ahead, holding out an arm to catch her. The smiling face seemed somehow familiar ... Jane thought no further, but collapsed in exhausted relief against the comforting outstretched arm. Behind her, Barney glanced apprehensively over his shoulder – and saw that every single polecat had disappeared.

'Goodness me now!' The woman's voice was gentle. 'Break your necks you will, tearing in here like that as if the devil were at your heels. What is the trouble, what's wrong?' Then she looked more closely at Jane. 'Why, I know you – you're the children who were with Bran and Will Stanton, yesterday.'

Barney said suddenly, 'You're Mrs Rowlands!'

'Yes indeed.' Blodwen Rowlands' voice sharpened. 'What is wrong, has something happened to the boys?'

They stared at her, unable for a moment to gather enough wit for an answer.

'No no,' Jane said then, stumbling. 'No . . . they're all right, they . . . went down. They said they were going to meet you in the Square.'

'That is right.' Mrs Rowlands' round face cleared. 'Came up here just for John to see Llew Owen, we did, we were just on our way down now. We did wonder whether we might meet the boys on the way.' She looked at Jane in concern. 'Your hair is all wet, *cariad*, that rain must have caught you . . . Now why were you three in such a fright?'

'Not a fright really,' Simon said gruffly. Now that every trace of the polecats had gone, he was beginning to feel shame at his panic. 'It was just –'

'There were these animals,' Jane said, too exhausted to pretend. 'Polecats, Bran said they were. We'd seen two this morning, near here. And then just now on the path, lots of them just jumped at us out of nowhere – and – and – they were horrible. Their teeth –' She gulped.

'Oh dear me,' Mrs Rowlands said comfortingly, cossetingly, as if to a small child. 'Never you mind now, there's nothing now, they've gone . . .' She put her arm round Jane's shoulders and led her towards the farm. Simon made a face at Barney that said: *She doesn't believe it.* Barney shrugged, and they followed.

Before they reached the farmhouse John Rowlands came out of its door; they could see his Land-Rover parked close by. He knew them at once; surprise creased his lean brown face.

'Well well,' he said. 'Three out of five – and where are my two?'

'They went on down,' Barney said, all blithe self-possession now, keeping instinctively as close to the literal truth as Jane had done. 'We thought we'd go across the top and then down to the Trefeddian that way. But there didn't seem to be a path.'

'Hard to find it nowadays,' John Rowlands said, 'since all those new houses down the hill have covered up the path. Gone, it is, the old way we went when I was a boy.' He had cast one sharp look at Jane's pale face, but seemed disinclined to question them further; there was a preoccupied look behind his eyes.

'Come with us,' Mrs Rowlands said. 'Give you a lift, now.' She waved farewell to the farmer's wife emerging inquiringly from the farmhouse, and opened the Land-Rover's back door.

'Yes, of course,' John Rowlands said.

'Thank you very much.' They climbed in. Jane peered closely at hedgerow and field as the car turned out into the lane, and saw Barney gazing too, but there was no sign of anything except white fool's parsley, and rose-bay willowherb tall in the grass, and the sweep of the tall green hedges above.

Simon, sitting beside her, saw the strain in her face and brushed a fist gently against her arm. He said, very low, 'But they *were* there.'

The Land-Rover crept down the last elbow turn of the steep little road and into Chapel Square, there to wait in line while a miniature traffic jam of cars fidgeted in the single tiny one-way street leading to the main road.

'Goodness gracious,' Blodwen Rowlands said. 'Look at them all. I want to call in at Royal House, John, but how you will find a parking place I cannot think.'

'We shall just have to be visitors, and go in the car park,' John Rowlands said, swinging to the right and edging through sweaters and parkas, push-chairs and buckets and spades, their owners all vaguely wandering or gazing out at the sea.

The Land-Rover was left in the park, its square roof looming over its smaller neighbours like a landmark. They threaded their way back along the crowded streets; Mrs Rowlands paused beside a shop-window filled with jerseys and swimsuits and shorts.

'*Wyt ti'n dwad i mewn hefyd, cariad?*'

'No, I won't come,' John Rowlands said, pulling his pipe from his pocket and peering into its bowl. 'We will be over on the wharf, I dare say. The best place to look out for Bran and Will. No hurry, Blod, take your time.'

He led the children across the road, between a huge black shed labelled Outward Bound Sea School and a cluster of masts, their rigging gently singing in the breeze, where the boats of the Aberdyfi Yacht Club lay in lines on the beach. Sand spilled out over the pavement.

They walked across the wharf and out on to the short dog-leg jetty. John Rowlands paused, filling his pipe from an old black leather pouch. 'A different jetty we had here when I was a boy,' he said absently. 'All of wood, great beams of black creosoted timber . . . We used to climb all over them at low tide, and fall off where the green weed was slippery, and fish for crabs.'

'Did you live here?' Barney said.

'See over there?' Following John Rowlands' pointing finger, they looked back at the long terrace of stately, narrow, three-storey Victorian houses that stood facing out over the road, over the beach, to the mouth of the Dyfi River and the sea.

'That one in the middle, with the green paint,' John Rowlands said, 'that's where I was born. And my father before me. He was a sailor, and so was *his* father. My grandfather Captain Evan Rowlands of the schooner *Ellen Davies* –

he built that house. All built by the old captains, they were, the houses along that road, in the days when Aberdyfi was still a real shipping port.'

Jane said curiously, 'Didn't you want to be a sailor too?'

John Rowlands smiled at her through puffs of blue smoke as he lighted his pipe, dark eyes narrowed by the lines of his brown face. 'Once I did, I dare say. But my da was drowned when I was six, you see, and my mother took my brothers and me away from Aberdyfi then, back to her parents' farm near Abergynolwyn. Back in the hills near Cader Idris – behind the valley where you were today. So what with one thing and another, it was sheep for me, not the sea.'

'What a shame,' Simon said.

'Oh, not really. The shipping days have been gone a long time now, and even the fishing too. They were dying already in my father's time.'

Barney said, 'Fancy him drowning. A sailor.'

'A lot of sailors can't swim,' Simon said. 'Even Nelson couldn't. He used to get seasick, too.'

John Rowlands puffed reflectively. 'For a lot of them there was never time to learn, I fancy. The men in those sailing ships – no playing in the sea for them. The sea was their mistress, their mother, their living, their life. But everything serious. Nothing for fun.' He turned slowly back towards the street, his eyes carefully searching – just as, Jane suddenly realized, they had been already searching the wharf and the beach. 'I don't see any sign at all of Bran and Will. How long before you left, was it, that they came down?'

Jane hesitated, and saw Simon open his mouth and shut it again, confused. Barney simply shrugged.

She said, 'About – about half an hour, I suppose.'

'Perhaps they caught a bus?' Barney said helpfully.

John Rowlands stood for a moment, pipe between teeth, his face without expression. He said, 'Have you known Will Stanton for long?'

'We were all on holiday together once,' Jane said. 'About two years ago. In Cornwall.'

'Did anything . . . unusual . . . happen on that holiday?' The Welshman's voice was casual still, but suddenly he was looking very closely and specifically at Simon, the dark eyes bright and intent.

Simon blinked, taken by surprise. 'Well – yes, I suppose.'

'What sort of thing?'

'Just . . . well, just things.' Simon's face was flushed; he floundered, caught between honesty and bewilderment.

Jane saw Barney's face crease in a resentful frown. She said, surprised at the cool self-possession in her voice, 'What do you mean exactly, Mr Rowlands?'

'How much do you three know about Will?' John Rowlands said. His face was unreadable, his voice curt.

'Quite a lot,' said Jane, and her mouth shut sharply like a closing door. She stood looking at him. On either side of her she could feel Simon and Barney rigid and challenging as herself; the three of them arrayed against questions that, they instinctively knew, nobody outside the pattern of their dealings with Merriman and Will should be bothering to ask.

Rowlands was looking at her now: a strange searching uncertain look. 'You are not like him,' he said. 'You three, you are no more than I am, you are not . . . of that kind.'

'No,' Jane said.

Something seemed to collapse behind John Rowlands' eyes; his face twisted into a kind of taut despair, and Jane was all at once rocked by distress as she saw him gazing at her in open appeal. '*Diawl*,' he said, tight and unhappy, 'will you stop mistrusting me, for the love of God? You cannot have seen more of the nature of those two than I have seen, this past year. Those two – for Bran is someone you may know nothing about at all. And there is fear shouting all through me now, about what may be happening to them, about who may have taken hold of them, at a time when they may be in worse danger than they have ever been before.'

Behind Jane's shoulder Barney said suddenly, 'He means it, Jane. And Will did trust him.'

'That's true,' Simon said.

'What did you mean, Mr Rowlands,' Jane said slowly, 'about what you had seen, this past year?'

'Not a year all spread out,' John Rowlands said. 'Last summer it was, when Will came visiting his uncle. As soon as he came to the valley, things . . . things began to happen. Forces woke that had been sleeping, and people grew and changed, and the Grey King of Cader Idris rose in his power, and fell again . . . it was all a confronting between the Light and the Dark, and I did not understand what it was all about and I did not want to.' He looked at them, grave and intent, his pipe forgotten in his hand. 'I have told Will that, all along,' he said. 'I know he is part of the power called the Light, and Bran Davies perhaps even deeper into the pattern. But that is enough for me. I will help Will Stanton when he needs me, and Bran, too, because I feel for him as if he were my own – only, I do not want to know what it is that they are doing.'

Barney said curiously, 'Why not?'

'Because I am not of their kind,' John Rowlands said sharply. 'And nor are you either, and it is not proper.' For a moment he sounded stern, censorious – and very sure of himself.

Simon said unexpectedly, 'I know just what you mean. I've always felt the same. And anyway we don't really know either.' He looked at Jane. 'Do we?'

She had opened her mouth to protest, but now she paused instead. 'Well . . . no. Great-Uncle Merry never said anything much. Only that the Dark is rising. or trying to, and must be stopped. Everything we did seemed to be a step on the way to somewhere else. Something else. And we never really have known what.'

'Safer for you that it should be so,' John Rowlands said.

'And for them too, right?' said Simon.

John Rowlands gave his head a small wry shake that was like a shrug; smiled, and began re-lighting his pipe.

Jane said, 'I don't think we shall be seeing Will and Bran here, Mr Rowlands. They went away, somewhere. Safe. But . . . a long way away.' She looked out at the estuary, where a few white sails tacked to and fro over the blue water. 'I don't know for how long. An hour, a day . . . They . . . they just went.'

'Well,' John Rowlands said, 'we shall just have to wait and see. And I must dream up something to tell to Blodwen, because to this day I do not know whether she has any idea at all of what is in those two boys. I think not, really. She has a warm heart and a wise head, bless her, and she is content to be fond of them for what they seem to be.'

A motor-boat whizzed past on the river behind them, almost drowning his voice. Somewhere the beat of rock music thumped insistently through the warm air; it rose and then retreated, as a group of people carrying a portable radio passed on the wharf. Looking over at the road, Jane saw Blodwen Rowlands emerge from the draper's shop and pause on the crowded pavement; then she was cut out of view, as a large motor-coach crept with difficulty down the village street.

John Rowlands sighed. 'Look at it all,' he said. 'How it has changed, *Aberdyfi fach*. Of course that had to come, but I remember . . . I remember . . . in the old days, all the old fishermen used to be in a line over there, leaning on that rail in front of the Dovey Hotel, over the water. And when I was a lad about Barney's age one of my favourite things was to hang around and listen to them, when I was allowed. Lovely it was. They remembered so far back – a hundred years and more, it would be now. Back to the days when nearly all Aberdyfi men were sailors, my *taid*'s time, when the masts bristled thick as a forest along the wharf by here, loading up slate from the quarries. And there were seven yards building ships in the river, seven, building dozens of ships – schooners and brigs, and small boats too . . .'

His deep Welsh voice made a threnody, recalling and mourning the lost days that even he had not seen, except through others' eyes. They listened in silence, fascinated, until the present sounds and sights of the crowded summer resort seemed to retreat, and they could almost imagine that they saw tall ships coming into the river round the bar, and stacks of cut slate piled around them on a different wharf, built of black wood instead of concrete.

A seagull rose slowly into the air from the end of the jetty, crying out, slow and harsh and sorrowful, and Jane turned her head to follow the flap and sweep of its black-tipped wings. The breeze seemed to feel stronger than before against her cheek. The gull swung sideways past them, close, still crying . . .

. . . and when Jane brought her gaze down again from watching it, she saw the wooden beams of the jetty black beneath her feet, stacked with rows of grey-blue slate, and beyond, on the river, a tall ship coming in close towards land, flapping and creaking as men hauled down her sails.

Jane stood motionless, staring. She heard laughter, and shrill voices, and milling round her on the jetty came a gaggle of small boys, pushing and hopping and thrusting one another aside in perilous clamour along the edge. 'Firsties . . . firsties . . . get off my foot, Freddie Evans! . . . look out! . . . don't shove! . . .' They were a mixture, clean and grubby, barefoot and booted, and one of them, yellow-haired, bumping and laughing among the rest, was her brother Barney.

Jane could only think, ridiculously, '*But in those days they'd have been speaking Welsh . . .*'

Further along the jetty she could see Simon talking earnestly in a group of two or three boys his own age. They turned to watch the ship draw gradually closer. With a snapping rush of canvas her mainsail came down in a heap, to be seized and furled; she was a brigantine, square-rigged on the foremast and fore-and-aft rigged on the main, and only two foresails now hung billowing to draw her inshore. Her figure-head glinted beneath the jutting bowsprit: a lifesize girl, with streaming golden hair. On the bow Jane could read the name now: *Frances Amelia*.

'Carrying timber,' John Rowlands' deep voice said beside her. 'See some of it stowed there on the deck? Mostly for John Jones the builder, that will be – he has been expecting it. A cargo of yellow pine, from Labrador.'

Jane glanced at him; his face was tranquil, the pipe still clenched between his teeth. But on the hand that reached up to the pipe now there was tattooed between the knuckles a small blue star that she had not seen before, and at his throat he wore the wing collar and high-necked jacket of the nineteenth century. He had become someone else, belonging to this other time, and yet somehow was still himself as well. Jane shivered and closed her eyes for a moment, and did not look down to see how she herself was dressed.

Then there was a flurry and a sudden shriek from the edge of the jetty, where more and more people had gathered. Peering vainly past the heads, Jane could see only that the brigantine had begun to dock, lines flying down from bow and stern to be caught and made fast by darting figures ashore. From the end of the jetty where the small boys had gone running, there came out of a group of women a noisy scolding eruption, and all at once Barney and another boy, both very white in the face, were being dragged back towards Jane by a bustling distressed woman in bonnet and shawl. It was recognizably Blodwen Rowlands, yet a Blodwen Rowlands who did not seem to know Jane as Jane. She spoke to the world at large, scolding, yet in warm concern, 'Always the same it is, this silly game to be the first to touch the ship that comes in, and all of them in the way there hindering the men . . . One day one of them is going to get killed, and it was as near as a whistle for these two today, did you see them? Right on the edge, losing their balance, the side of the boat like to crush them against the jetty if there had been no one there to grab them out of it . . . aah!' She gave each boy a little exasperated shake. 'Have you forgotten last week, when Ellis Williams fell in?'

'And Freddie Evans the week before,' said the boy with Barney, in a pert, lilting voice. 'And much worse, that, because Evans the Barber was waiting for him with a strap when he got out, and beat him all the way home.'

'Mr Evans to you, young monkey,' said Mrs Rowlands, trying to suppress a smile. She gave Jane a little humorous shrug, released the boys with one finger wagging at them as she turned, and went back to the group of women greeting sailors on the ship.

'I like her,' Barney said cheerfully. 'She probably saved my life, you know that?' And he grinned at Jane and ran off with the other boy, disappearing along the road, behind the great stacks of slate.

Jane turned to call, but no sound came. Beside her, John Rowlands was shouting to one of the men aboard the *Frances Amelia*. 'Iestyn! Iestyn Davies!'

'Evan boy!' the man called back, white teeth flashing. And even while the name pulled her, Jane thought again of the strangeness that there was no Welsh to be heard, and then suddenly knew that of course all the speaking that she could hear was indeed in Welsh, her own included, with no word of English used anywhere at all.

'After all,' she said shakily, knowing with no reason that Simon was now at her side, and turning to him, 'it's no more odd to understand a language that you don't know, than to be switched into a time before you were born.'

'No,' Simon said, in a voice so reassuringly his own that Jane felt dissolved in relief. 'No, not really odd at all.'

John Rowlands called, beside them, 'What news of the *Sarah Ellen*?'

The man stared. 'You haven't heard?'

The man on the *Frances Amelia* paused, put down the line he was coiling, called a few words to someone else on board, and leapt over the gunwale and down to the jetty. He came up to John Rowlands, his face lined with concern. 'Bad news, Evan Rowlands, very bad. I am sorry. The *Sarah Ellen* foundered off Skye two days ago, with all hands. We heard yesterday.'

'Oh my God,' John Rowlands said. He put out a hand, gropingly, and clutched the man's arm for an instant; then turned and moved away, stumbling, as if he were suddenly old. His face was grey and hurt. Jane longed to go after him, but she could not move. How was it possible to comfort grief that was naked on a living face, and yet had been gone and forgotten for a hundred years? Which was more real: her own bewilderment, or Evan Rowlands' pain looking out of his grandson's eyes?

The man called Iestyn said, looking after John Rowlands, 'And his brother aboard.' He looked round, at the two or three other men who had been standing near, and his face was grave. 'Something is not good. That was the fourth boat built by John Jones Aberdyfi to go down in three months, and all of them new boats too. And it was not a great storm that took the *Sarah Ellen*, they say, but only a heavy following sea.'

'They are all the same,' one of the men said. 'They dip the stern under. Every one of his vessels does it now, and then there is strain and the leaks come, and down she goes.'

'Not every one,' another man said.

'No, not every one, that is true. John Jones has built some very good boats indeed. But the bad ones . . .'

'I have heard it suggested,' said the man called Iestyn, 'that it is not in the design but in the building. That it is not John Jones' fault at all, but one of his sawyers. And any work that he handles –'

He broke off, conscious suddenly of Jane's anxious stare, and switched on to his face a broad deliberate smile. 'Waiting as usual, is it, like all the young ones, but too polite to ask?' He reached into one capacious jacket pocket and brought out a square package. 'Here – put some in my pocket for the first of you who would come smiling and begging, I did. And for not asking at all you shall inherit it, little one.'

'Thank you,' said Jane, and for the second time that day startled herself by dropping a little bobbing curtsey. Folded in paper in her hands he had put four enormous wood-hard ship's biscuits.

'Off with you,' said the man amiably. 'Into the oven in a dish, covered with milk, isn't it, and a knob of butter on top, lovely. Lord knows it is good someone enjoys the hard biscuit the way you all do. Not so good half-way across the Atlantic, I can tell you. By then you would swap the lot for a good warm slice of *bara brith*.'

The others laughed, and suddenly it was as if the last two words had turned a key back again to relock a door. For now they were speaking unintelligibly in Welsh together, and Jane knew that the difference was not in the language they used but in her own hearing of it. She had been able to understand it for a short enchanted while; now she could not. She clutched at Simon's unfamiliar stiff sleeve, and drew him away.

'What's happening?'

'I only wish I knew. There's no logic to it. Everything all mixed up.'

'Where are we? And when? And why?'

'The why is the biggest.'

'Let's go and find Barney.'

'I know. All right.' As they walked over the broad-spaced timbers to the street, Jane glanced sideways at her tall brother; somehow in the rough old-fashioned suit he seemed taller than ever, and more controlled. Had he changed too? No, she thought: *it's just that I wouldn't normally bother to think what he's like at all . . .*

They were walking up the road, past little cottages gay with roses and snapdragon and sweet-smelling stock; past terraced houses far grander and newer looking than they had seemed in the days that were yet to come; past a resplendent coaching inn with its board hanging newly painted: *The Penhelig Arms*. Two men walking ahead of them greeted a stumpy sun-tanned figure standing in the doorway of the inn. 'Good day, Captain Edwards.'

Jane thought: *We are back in Welsh again . . .*

'Good day.'

'Did you hear about the *Sarah Ellen*, then?'

'I did,' said Captain Edwards. 'And I remembered what we spoke of, and I was thinking of paying a call upon John Jones.' He paused. 'And on one of his men, maybe.'

'Perhaps we might go with you,' one of the two men said, and as he turned Jane saw with a shock that it was John Rowlands again. She had not recognized him; not only the clothes were different, but the walk as well.

A sound of hammering came from somewhere below the road, down by the sea, and a high rhythmic screeching that Jane could not identify. At a cautious distance she and Simon followed the three men, to the edge of the road where it overlooked a flat yard just above the high-tide mark.

The shipyard was surprisingly simple: a couple of sheds, with next to them a curious box-like structure, leaking threads of steam. It was perhaps two feet high and wide but very very long, dozens of feet long, and attached to it by a pipe was a big metal boiler. Nearby, the rough skeleton of a boat lay in a wooden cradle: a long keel branched by the bare oaken ribs to which only a few planks had as yet been set. Huge baulks of timber, the yellowish-white colour of pine, lay piled on the ground and beside them gaped a long deep pit, deeper than the height of a man, where sawyers cut the wood into planks. Jane stared, fascinated. A piece of timber lay lengthwise over each pit, supported on small logs set across; one man stood below it and another above, and between them they worked up and down a long saw, set in a frame, which produced the rhythmic shrieking she had heard from a distance. Two other sawyers worked in a similar pit close by. Others were shifting the timber, stacking planks, tending the steaming boiler, beneath which a fire burned so hot as to be almost invisible in the warm summer air.

A boy looked up and saw the three sailors, and gave a kind of salute; he ran to the sawyer working on top of one of the pits, shouting to be heard over the rasp of the saw.

'Captain Humphrey Edwards and Captain Ieuan Morgan, it is, and Captain Evan Rowlands, up aloft there.'

The sawyer signalled to his partner, stilling the long blade before it came down again for the next cut. He stared up. Jane, peeping over the side of the rough rock-edged road, saw a pudgy face topped by astonishingly bright red hair; the man was scowling, with no sign of friendship or welcome.

'John Jones has gone to the wharf,' the red-haired man called. 'To see to a shipment of pine just come in.' He bent down again, dismissively.

'Caradog Lewis,' said the stumpy captain from the inn. He did not raise his voice, but even at normal pitch it was the kind of voice accustomed to being heard above a gale at sea.

The red-haired man jerked up petulantly, hands on hips. 'There is work to do here, Humphrey Edwards, if you please.'

'Aye,' John Rowlands said. 'It is your work we should like to talk to you about.' He stepped over the low rocky wall and went down a flight of rough steps to the sawpits; the others followed him. So, a little later when no one was paying attention, did Simon and Jane.

'What boat is this you are working on, Caradog Lewis?' said Captain Edwards, looking thoughtfully at the graceful curving frame, all ribs and keel, standing skeletal on the stocks.

Lewis looked at him sourly, as if about to snarl, but seemed to change his mind. 'She is the schooner *Courage*, for Elias Lewis. I should have thought you would have known that. Seventy-five feet, and a month overdue already. And over there –' he nodded at a half-rigged hull already launched, floating in the dock, 'that is the *Jane Kate* for Captain Farr. They will be floating her spars over from Ynyslas tomorrow, and high time too.'

'And you had a hand in both of them,' John Rowlands said.

'Well of course, man,' said Lewis irritably. 'I am top sawyer for John Jones, isn't it?'

'And no doubt responsible for much,' said Captain Edwards, stroking his side-whiskers. 'John Jones being a busy man, with a great many keels laid down on one another's tails these last few years.'

'Well?'

'The *Integrity* was your work too?' John Rowlands said. 'And the *Mary Rees*? And the *Eliza Davies*?' Each time Lewis nodded his red head impatiently. Rowlands went on, biting off his words like a child biting a biscuit. 'And the *Charity*? And the *Sarah Ellen*?'

Lewis scowled. 'You choose the ships of unfortunate men.'

'Yes I do indeed.'

The sawyer and the other shipyard workers had put down their tools and came drifting close to listen; they stood in a group, restless, eyeing the captains resentfully.

'I have just heard about the *Sarah Ellen*.' Lewis shrugged, with shallow regret. 'It is a pity, about your brother. But no new thing in this village.'

'No new thing among the ships that you work on,' Humphrey Edwards said.

Caradog Lewis's pale face flushed with anger, and Jane saw his hands tighten into fists. 'Now look here –' he began.

'You look here to us, Caradog Lewis,' said the third man, who had not spoken since they entered the yard. He was a small olive-skinned man with a fringe of grey beard. 'Two of those boats I have watched at sea, keeping company on the Labrador run, and both had the same failing, and that none of John Jones' designing if I know him. Careless he is and a little greedy for work, so that he has not the time to supervise as those builders do who will not work on more than one keel at a time. But it is not his doing, for a boat to dig in her stern and founder in a following sea. That is the work of a man every time giving more length at the stern than there should be, and more than a few times letting planks go by that were steamed too quick and had cracks beginning.'

A rumble of anger came from the listening workers.

The red-haired man was wet at the mouth with rage; he could scarcely speak. 'Prove it, Ieuan Morgan!' he hissed. 'Prove one small part of that! You think you can prove I have deliberately sent men to their deaths?'

'There must be some way to prove it,' John Rowlands said, his voice grim and deep, 'for true it is without a doubt. There is more in you than you show.

We have been wondering a long time, we three, and now this loss of the *Sarah Ellen* is too much. And we are sure.'

'Sure of what?'

'That you are . . . different, Caradog Lewis. With loyalties that are not like those of other men. Serving in some dreadful way a cause that is not that of men at all.'

The words had such cold conviction in them that the men near Caradog Lewis shrank unconsciously away from him a little; and Lewis sensed it, and yelled at them in sudden fury so that they dived back at the nearest piece of work. But there was no fury in the way Caradog Lewis looked then at John Rowlands; there was instead an icy arrogant hatred that made Jane shiver, because she had seen it before, once, in a man dedicated to working the will of the Dark. Lewis, with his pasty face and his raw red hair, did not seem to be totally a creature of the Dark, but he was the more frightening as a result; such malice living without apparent reason in an ordinary man was something Jane could hardly bear to contemplate. She could sense anger rising in him like steam in a near-boiling kettle.

Lewis came slowly towards the three men, clear of his sawpit. He said tightly, 'I am a man as you are, Evan Rowlands, and I will show you that I am.' And all at once he seemed to erupt, flinging himself on John Rowlands, his face twisted horribly by snarling rage. Caught off-balance, Rowlands was thrown backwards in a rattling shower of grey slate, and Lewis was after him like a dog, arms flailing, smashing. The two other captains rushed to part them, but now the men from the shipyard had dropped their tools and come deliberately in the way, and there was suddenly a great mêlée on the ground. Stocky Captain Edwards knocked a man down, with a horrible click of teeth as his knuckles met the man's head; then he disappeared beneath a trio of others, and beside him, shouting and fighting, Ieuan Morgan hauled them away. Caradog Lewis, struggling with Rowlands, stumbled to his feet, gasping with malice, and reached for balance to kick with his hard-booted foot. Jane shrieked, and then Simon was past her in a flurry of arms and legs, clutching at Lewis, crying out as the toe of one heavy boot met his own shin.

Simon was never quite sure precisely what happened then. Fighting to drag Caradog Lewis away from John Rowlands' inert form, he found himself suddenly thrust down towards the sea in Lewis's grip, quite unable to resist. They splashed into the water together, still upright, still struggling, and suddenly Simon felt himself jerking outward, falling, falling, and the water closing cold over his head and no bottom to be felt with his feet beneath the sea. One brief touch of the sand he had with one foot, and then the water was swinging him round, a current catching him, pulling him deeper, deeper, alone. He reached up for air, kicking desperately; caught one breath; was swung around again by an eddy, reached out in frantic efforts to swim, his arms and legs heavy with the weight of the old-fashioned suit. There was a roaring in his ears, a blurring in his eyes; the water whirled him round and around.

Simon fought to keep back panic. He had a secret and terrible fear of deep water, even though he could swim well; three years earlier in a dinghy race on the Thames he had fallen from a capsizing boat and come up underneath the floating mainsail, kept down from the air like a cork in a sealed jar. He had panicked then, splashing wildly, only by pure chance reaching the edge of the sail, and then in a desperate gurgling flurry the shore. Now he could feel the same panic rising again in his throat and mind; rising like the waves that whirled him about with only an occasional snatch of breath; rising to blur his brain, to swamp out all thought –

He thrust it away. He fought and fought; fought to keep in his mind the feel of each arm, each leg; to move as he chose to move, to seek the rhythm of swimming instead of the mindless flurrying of horror and despair. So by great effort, he kept from panic.

But still the water was there all around, less violent now, cradling him, and again he was going down. Water pressed in on him, it was in his ears and his eyes and his nose. Now it seemed not frightening but lulling, mothering, as if it were not after all alien, but his own element. It welcomed him, gently, as if he quite naturally breathed water, like a fish. Gentle, gentle, all-enveloping, relaxing, like the feeling of the moment before falling gradually asleep . . .

Something, someone, seized Simon from behind in a fierce grip, two strong hands on his shoulders, pushing him upward, upward and out into bright air. Light cut into his eyes. Water bit the back of his throat. He gasped, retching, choking. The water swished in his lungs with each gurgling snatch at breath. Simon heard terrible frantic bubbling gasps and realized appalled that he was making them himself.

Then there was solid sand beneath his feet. The swimmer released him. Simon stumbled forward on to his hands and knees, and strong hands laid him on the beach, turned his head sideways and pressed down on his back. Water poured from his nose and mouth; he coughed, retching. The hands gently helped him to sit up. Simon sat with his head on his knees, breathing at last without the dreadful gurgling, without gasping, more slowly. He brushed his wet hair from his eyes, sniffing, and looked up.

First he saw Jane, wide-eyed, white-faced, crouching. Beside her a man was bent on one knee, his great height apparent even while stooped. His dark clothes dripped water. The face frowning in concern into Simon's was angular and craggy, dark eyes shadowed in deep sockets, bristling white eyebrows dripping water down the sides of the beak-like nose. The thick white hair, grey with wetness, lay in a tangle of loops and horns all over his head.

Simon said, in a high weak husky voice that was not his own, 'Oh Gumerry.'

He stopped, feeling a prickling in his eyes. He had not used that pet name for a long time.

'That was brave,' Merriman said.

He pressed one hand on Simon's shoulder, and glanced up at Jane, beckoning her closer. Then he stood up. Jane put a diffident arm round Simon's shoulder, to help as he turned to watch.

John Rowlands was standing close by on the beach, dripping from head and clothes. Jane said in Simon's ear, 'He jumped in the sea after you, trying to reach you, when –' her voice seemed to dry into nothing; she swallowed – 'when Great-Uncle Merry just . . . just came *up*, out of nowhere.'

Merriman loomed before them, angular in his wetness, tall as a tree. Before him on the beach, the men of the shipyard stood motionless in a group, with the two grey-whiskered captains angry and silent nearby. Caradog Lewis stood in the midst of the shipwrights, red hair gleaming. He was staring at Merriman transfixed, like some small animal caught in mid-stride by an angry badger or a fox.

And the anger in Merriman's eyes as he looked at the red-haired man was of such depth that both Simon and Jane, watching, shrank from it. Caradog Lewis moved slowly back, cringing, seeking escape. Then Merriman reached out one arm with the first finger stiff, pointing, and the man froze, pinned into stillness once more.

'Go,' Merriman said softly, in his deep voice like black velvet. 'Go, you who have sold yourself to the Dark, back from this bright Aberdyfi of the river to Dinas Mawddwy where you came from. Go back to where the Dark lurks in the hills round Cader Idris in the realm of the Grey King, where others wait in black hope like yourself. But remember that since you have failed in this attempt here, your masters now will have no time for you. So beware after this, in years to come, that you keep your sons and your daughters, and the sons of your daughters, away from any trifling with the Dark. For the Dark in its vengefulness will surely destroy any one of them that it can take into its power.'

Without a word Caradog Lewis turned and walked away over the crackling grey slate, up the rough steps and away along the road, until they could no longer see him. Merriman looked at Simon and Jane; then he turned towards the sea, past the silent men and the shipyard huts and the half-built ship, and in a strange gentle gesture he opened his arms wide, like a man stretched on waking, looking up at the sky.

And out of nowhere a seagull came swooping past, low over the water, harshly crying. Their eyes followed it ... followed ...

... and when it rose again out of sight suddenly they found that they were dressed once more in the jeans and shirts of their own time, standing on a narrow slatey beach a few feet below the level of the iron-railed pavement, alone with John Rowlands and Merriman. In Simon's right hand was a piece of flat slate; his first finger was curled round it as if for throwing. He looked down at it, shrugged, bent, and skimmed it over the surface of the water. It bounced impressively in a long skipping trail.

'Eight!' Simon said.

'You always win,' said Jane.

Their clothes were dry; only Jane's hair was damp still, from the rains of the morning. There was nothing to show that Simon, Merriman and John Rowlands had ever been in the sea. Jane peeped at John Rowlands as he stood there blinking in perplexity, and she knew that he did not remember anything. He looked about, dazed; then he caught sight of Merriman and became very still. He stared at him for a long moment.

'*Daro*,' he said at last, huskily. 'What is this? You. You! I have never forgotten you, from when I was a boy. Do you remember? *Is* it you?'

Jane and Simon stood listening, puzzled.

'You were Will's age then,' said Merriman, looking at him with half a smile. 'Up on your mountain. And you saw me ... riding.'

John Rowlands said slowly, 'Riding on the wind.'

'Riding on the wind. I wondered, after that, if you would remember. There was no harm in it, if you did – who would have believed you? But I put it into your mind that you had dreamed it, to leave you at rest.'

'And indeed I did think that I had dreamed it, until this moment that I see the same face again, unchanged after so long. And wonder why it is here.' John Rowlands turned his head and looked at Simon and Jane. 'This is Will's master, is it not? And known to you as well.'

Simon said automatically, 'Great-Uncle Merry.'

John Rowlands' voice rose, incredulous. '*Your great-uncle?*'

'A name,' Merriman said. His eyes clouded; he looked away over the estuary at the sea. 'I must go. Will needs me. As the Dark knew, Simon, when it caught you in peril in a time from which only I could ransom you, by leaving the place where I was.'

'Are they all right?' Simon said.

'They will be, if all goes well.'

Jane said anxiously, 'What can we do?'

'Be on the beach at sunrise. Your beach,' Merriman said. He looked at her with an odd strained smile, and pointed up the road. 'And take your small brother home to tea.'

Turning, they saw Barney's yellow-haired figure prancing towards them down the road, with Blodwen Rowlands in his wake; and when they turned back again to the beach and the sea, Merriman was not there.

PART THREE
The Lost Land

The City

Down through the bright haze the strange road brought them, arching like a rainbow. Will and Bran found that they made no move of their own. Once they had stepped on to its surface, the road took them up, took them through space and through time with a motion they could not afterwards describe. Then out of that brightness they were down in the Lost Land, and the road was gone, and all else vanished from their minds as they looked up at the place where they were.

They stood high up, on a golden roof, behind a low lattice of wrought gold. Behind them, and at either side, stretched the roofs of a great city, gleaming, spires and towers and turrets crowding the skyline, some golden as the place where they stood, some dark as black flint. The city was very quiet. This seemed to be early morning, cool and silent. Before them, as far as they could see, a luminous white mist lapped round the broad-topped trees of a park. Dew glistened on the trees. Somewhere, beyond the park, the sun was rising into a haze of cloud.

Will gazed out at the trees. They were not packed close together in the random clusters of the wild, but well-spaced, each broad and proud and full; they rose out of the mist like glimmering green islands in a grey-white sea. He saw oak and beech and chestnut and elm; the shapes were as familiar as the buildings around him were strange.

Bran said softly, at his side, 'Look!'

He was pointing past Will's back. Turning, Will saw among the peaks and ridges of the roofs a great golden dome, topped with a gold arrow pointing westward to the blue horizon-line of the sea. The sides of the dome caught the early sun, glittering; he realized that they were banded, up and down, with panels of crystal running between strips of gold.

Bran peered, cupping his hands around his smoky glasses. 'Is it a church?'

'Could be. Looks a bit like St Paul's.'

'Or one of those Arab whatsits. Mosques.'

They spoke in whispers, by instinct. The place was so quiet. Nothing anywhere broke the silence of the city, except once, for a few seconds, somewhere far off among the tops of the trees, a seagull's plaintive cry.

Will looked down at his feet. The roof on which they stood seemed to enclose them, its latticework of wrought gold stretching all round like a fence. He reached out. The top bar would not move. It was perhaps half his height; he thought of climbing over, but changed his mind at the sight of the sheer drop, twenty feet down to the next roof, on the other side.

Bran too reached out and took hold of the lattice in front of him; then suddenly he gasped. Beneath his touch, the whole criss-cross panel moved; swung free, balanced on a lower bar, then dropped down from his hands over the edge of the roof, lengthening in hinged sections as it fell, like a folded ladder opening.

'Clang! . . . clang! . . . clang! . . . clang!' The metallic sounds rang out over the roofs, cracking the silence, ending in a resonant crash as the final section of the ladder-like golden framework hit the roof below. All over the silent city the echoes rose like birds.

Will and Bran stared about them, watching for movement, for the waking of someone, somewhere, that such a clattering must surely bring. But there was nothing.

'Dozy place, isn't it?' said Bran, a small shake in his voice beneath the bravado; and with Will following close after, he swung himself over the edge and clambered down the ladder of gold.

They stood now on a broad lower roof, slanting more gently downward, crossed with raised strips of some darker metal that served as ridges down which they could walk. At the bottom edge of this roof, expecting to find themselves over a perpendicular wall, they found instead a great sweeping stairway of grey stone, with the glitter of granite, stretching down from the very rim of the roof, far down into the mist and the trees.

Together they ran down the steps, keeping close, and as they ran, the mist below them faded into nothing, falling back so that the trees stood clear over a sweep of green grass. And they saw at the bottom of the stone steps, waiting, two horses standing saddled and bridled; untethered, with the reins laid loose over their necks. They were beautiful gleaming animals, lion-coloured, their long manes and tails yellow-white against the golden hide. The bits between their teeth, and their stirrups, were of silver, and the reins were red plaited silk. Will went up to the first and laid a wondering hand on its neck, and the horse blew softly through its nose and ducked its head as if inviting him to mount.

Bran said, gazing bemused at the horses, 'Can you ride, Will?'

'Not really,' Will said. 'But I don't think that will matter.' And he put one foot in the horse's stirrup and without sound or effort he was up on its back, smiling down, gathering up the reins. The second horse pawed the ground, and nudged gently at Bran's shoulder with its nose.

'Come on, Bran,' Will said. 'They've been waiting for us.' He sat there, self-possessed as a huntsman, a small stocky figure in blue jeans and sweater on the tall golden horse, and Bran shook his head in wonder and reached for the saddle-bow. He was up, mounted, before he had a chance to think about it. The horse tossed its head and Bran caught the reins as they fell towards him.

'All right,' said Will gently to his horse, stroking its white mane. 'Take us where we should go. Please?' And the two horses moved off together, unhurried, confident, walking the stone-paved street at the base of the long sweep of rising stone steps.

The trees of the broad green park towered over them at one side, shading the road, lush and dew-flecked and cool. Sunlight lay on the grass between them in bright pools, but there was no sound. No birds sang. Only the clop-clop of the horses' hooves rang through the quiet city, changing to a hollower, deeper sound as the two golden horses turned abruptly away from the park and into a narrow side street. Great grey walls loomed up on either side, huge blank expanses of grey stone, without a window anywhere.

The street grew narrower, darker. Without altering their steady pace the horses went on between the towering walls, while Will and Bran sat loosely holding the reins and glancing nervously about.

They turned a corner. Still the high blank walls enclosed them, in a narrow alley, with the sky no more than a thin blue strip overhead. But this time they could see a small wooden door set into the wall at their right, and when they drew level with this door both animals stopped, and began tossing their heads and pawing at the ground. Will's horse shook its head from side to side, so that the silver harness musically rang and the long mane rippled and flowed like white-gold silk.

'All right,' Will said. He dismounted; so did Bran. As soon as their riders were on the ground, the two horses turned without hurry in a brief confusion of clopping hooves and jingling harness, and together they trotted up the alley, back the way that they had come. Their bright loose tails swung like torches in the shadowy street.

'Beautiful!' Bran said softly, watching the golden shapes disappear.

Will was standing before the door, studying its plain wooden surface. It was dark and pitted as if by age. Absently he thrust his thumbs into his leather belt, and one of them met the curve of the small brass horn that he had blown on the mountain, in another life and another world. Unhooking the horn from his belt, he held it towards Bran.

'We've got to stay close together, whatever happens. You keep hold of one side of this and I'll take the other. That'll help.'

Bran nodded his white head and slipped the fingers of his left hand through the single loop of the horn. Will looked again at the door. It had no handle, no bell, no lock or keyhole; no means at all of opening it that he could see.

He raised one hand and knocked, firmly.

The door swung outward. There was no one on the other side. Peering, they could see nothing within but darkness. Each gripping one side of the little hunting-horn as if it were a lifebelt, they went in, and behind them the door swung shut.

A glimmer of light from somewhere, untraceable, showed them they were in a narrow corridor, low-roofed, ending a few yards ahead where a ladder rose upwards out of sight.

Will said slowly, 'I suppose we go up there.'

'Is that safe?' Bran's voice was husky with uncertainty.

'Well, it's all we can do, isn't it? And somehow nothing seems to be telling me not to. You know?'

'That's true. It doesn't feel . . . bad. Mind you it doesn't feel too good either.'

Will laughed softly. 'That's going to be the same everywhere here. The Dark has no power in this land, I think – but nor does the Light.'

'Then who has?'

'I suppose we shall find that out.' Will took a firm grip on the horn. 'Keep hold. Even if it'll be awkward climbing up there.'

They went up the broad-runged ladder, one close after the other, still linked by their talisman, and emerged into an area so totally unexpected that for a few moments they both stood there motionless, looking.

They had come up through an open trapdoor, close to one end of a long gallery. The floor stretched before them in curious sections, one after the other, on differing levels, so that one might be higher than the one before, and the next lower than either. The place seemed to be a kind of library. Heavy square tables and chairs filled it, separated by low stacks of bookshelves, and the wall on their left was covered entirely with books. The ceiling was wood-panelled. The right-hand wall was not there.

Will stared, but could not understand. At his right, in this long room, a kind of carved wooden balustrade ran all the length of the floor. But no wall was beyond it, nor anything else visible: only blackness. Blank dark. There was no sense of an emptiness, or a perilous void. There was simply nothing.

Then he saw movement in the room. The first people they had seen in this land were appearing, through a door at the far end of the long gallery; drifting, singly, men and women of all ages, dressed in a variety of simple clothes that seemed to belong to no particular age. There were not many of them. One by one, each figure silently settled, collecting a pile of books from the shelves and sitting down with them at a table, or standing browsing over a single book. Not one of them paid the smallest attention to Will or Bran. One man came up close beside them and stood frowning at the shelves lining the wall at their backs.

Will said to him, greatly daring, 'Can't you find it?' But the man made no sign of noticing. His face lightened suddenly; he reached out and took a book, and went back with it to sit down at a table nearby. Will peered at the title of the book as he went past, but it was written on the cover in a language he could not understand. And when the man opened the book, its pages were quite blank.

Bran said slowly, 'They can't see us.'

'No. Nor hear us. Come on.'

They walked carefully together up the long gallery, skirting intent seated figures, cautious not to trip or nudge. Nobody gave any flicker of notice as they passed. And whenever they looked down at a book that a man or woman was reading, they found that its pages seemed to bear no writing at all.

There was no real door at the far end of the gallery, but instead an opening in the panelled wall, from which a strange corridor led. This too was entirely panelled in wood; it was more like a square tunnel than a corridor, slanting down at a steep angle, turning corners in a zig-zag pattern, to and fro. Bran followed Will without question; he said only, once, with sudden helpless force, 'This place doesn't *mean* anything.'

'It will, when we arrive,' Will said.

'Arrive at what?'

'Well – at the meaning! At the crystal sword . . .'

'Look! What's that?'

Bran had stopped, head up, wary. Ahead of them as they turned a corner, the last section of the zig-zag slope was white and glaring, filled with strong light blazing in from whatever lay beyond. For an instant Will had a dreadful sense that they were descending into some great pit of fire. But this was a cold light, fierce without brilliance. He turned the last corner, stepping into the full light, and a strong resonant voice said ahead of him out of the brightness, 'Welcome!'

A great empty expanse of floor stretched before them, its walls lost in shadow, its roof too high to be seen. In the middle of the space stood a single figure, dressed all in black. He was a smallish man, not much taller than themselves, with a strong-featured face creased by humour at the eyes and mouth, though with no sign of a smile now. The hair of his head was grey, tight-curled as a mat, and he had a neat, crisp curling grey beard with a curious dark line down the centre like a stripe. He spread both arms and turned a little, as if offering them the space around him. 'Welcome,' he said again. 'Welcome to the City.'

They stood together before him. Bran took a step forward, letting go the horn. He said, 'Is there only the City, in the Lost Land?'

'No,' the man said. 'There is the City, and the Country, and the Castle. And you shall see all of them, but first you must tell us why you have come.' His voice was warm and ringing, but there was still wariness in it, and still he did not smile. He was looking at Will. 'Why have you come?' he said again. 'Tell us.'

As he spoke he made a small motion with one open hand towards the space before him. Will looked, and gasped. His head sang with shock; all at once he was very cold.

Out there, in a vast space that had been darkness a second before, stretched a huge crowd of blank upturned faces, row upon row, thousands of people. In tiers, in endless galleries they sat, staring at him. Their awareness pressed down on him like an unbearable weight, paralysing his mind; it was like facing the whole world.

Will clenched his fists, and felt the cool metal of the hunting-horn still against his fingers. Taking a deep slow breath, he said in a loud clear voice, 'We have come for the crystal sword.'

And they laughed.

It was not tolerant, friendly laughter; it was horrible. A deep roar rose from the vast audience there, swelling like long thunder, mocking, jeering, breaking over him in a wave of contempt. He could see individuals, pointing, mouths wide with scornful mirth. The ocean of their loud mockery engulfed him so that he trembled, and knew himself to be small, insignificant, dwindling down . . .

Bran's voice, beside him, shouted furiously into the uproar, '*We have come for Eirias!*'

All sound vanished, as totally as if someone had turned a switch. In an instant, all the jeering faces were gone.

Will drooped suddenly, hearing his tight-held breath go out in a small weak gasp.

Bran said again, wonderingly, to himself, 'We have come for . . . Eirias.' He seemed to be tasting the name.

The man with the grey beard said softly, 'You have, indeed.' He stepped forward, hands outspread. Taking each of them by the shoulder he turned them to face the black emptiness where the endless rows of faces had been.

He said, 'There is nobody there. No one, nothing. Nothing but space. They were all . . . an appearance. But look up. Look up, behind you. And there you shall see –'

Automatically they turned; and stood, staring. Over their heads, like a balcony suspended in the air, was the bright-lit gallery through which they had walked among the unheeding reading people. Everything was there, the books, the shelves, the heavy tables. The readers still moved idly to and fro, or stood gazing at the shelves. And the space through which they were looking into the room was the fourth wall which had seemed not to be there.

Will said, 'This place is a theatre come to life.'

The man fingered the point of his beard, pushing it forward with one finger. 'All life is theatre,' he said. 'We are all actors, you and I, in a play which nobody wrote and which nobody will see. We have no audience but ourselves . . .' He laughed gently. 'Some players would say that is the best kind of theatre there can be.'

Bran smiled in response, a small rueful smile. But Will was still listening to a single word echoing inside his head. He said to Bran, 'Eirias?'

'I didn't know,' Bran said. 'It just . . . came. It's a Welsh word. It means a big fire, a blaze.'

'And the crystal sword blazes indeed,' said the bearded man. 'Or so they tell, for few living have ever seen it, within memory here.'

'But we must find it,' Will said.

'Yes,' the man said. 'I know why you are here. When you are asked questions in this land, it is not for our want of the answers. I know who you are, Will Stanton, Bran Davies. Perhaps even better' – he looked hard for an instant at Bran – 'than you know yourselves. And as for me, you will know me soon. You may call me Gwion. And I shall show you the City.'

'The Lost Land,' Bran said, half to himself.

'Yes,' said the man called Gwion. He was a lean, neat figure in his black clothes; his beard glinted in the bright light from overhead. 'The Lost Land. And as I said to you, there lie within it the City, and the Country, and the Castle. And the Castle is where you must go, in the end, but you cannot get there except by way of the rest. So here you will begin, within the City, my City which I greatly love. You must take good note of it, for it is one of the wonders of the world that will not come again.'

He smiled at them, a brilliant sudden smile that lit his face with warmth and affection, and lit their own spirits simply by looking.

'See!' he said, swinging round, opening his arms to the back of the space that was like a stage. And the bright-lit gallery overhead disappeared, and the light grew diffuse, glowing all around, and suddenly they found they were in a great open city square. It was edged by pillared grey-white buildings gleaming in the sunlight, filled with people and music and the calls of traders at bright-coloured stalls, and the sparkle and splash of water flung high by fountains.

The sun was warm on their faces. Will felt delight rushing through him as if the blood in his veins were dancing, and he looked at Bran and saw the same joy shining in his face.

Laughing at them, Gwion drew them across the square, through the crowd, among the people of the Lost Land.

The Rose-Garden

Faces flashed round them like a kaleidoscope's shaken images. A child swung a handful of bright streamers before their eyes, laughing, and was gone; a hopeful flurry of green-necked pigeons swooped by. They passed a group of people dancing, where a tall man decked with red ribbons played the flute, a gay, catchy little tune; they stumbled, almost, at a place on the smooth grey paving, over a fragile crumpled-looking old man who was drawing with chalks on the ground. Will had a sudden startled glimpse of the picture, a great green tree on a rounded hill, with a bright light shining out of its branches, before the flute-player led the dancers past him in a flurry of music, and he was whirled away.

Gwion's bearded face was still there in the crowd, moving beside him. 'Stay close!' he called. But Will noticed now that no other eyes than Gwion's ever met their own in this crowd. The people all around seemed able to see him now, and glanced as they would glance at any other passerby, instead of turning a blind unwitting face to someone who was, for them, not there. Yet nobody properly looked at him, or at Bran; there was no recognition, no glimmer of the interest they showed in one another. He thought: we have come a little way along – we are *here* now, but only just. Perhaps they will really see us, later on, if we do well at whatever it is we are expected to do . . .

Laughter swelled in the crowded square, from a circle of grinning faces watching a juggler. Marvellous smells wafted past from stalls selling food. A fine spray caressed Will's face, and he saw the glittering drops of a fountain, tossed in a diamond stream up to the sun and down again. He saw Bran in front of him, pale face alight behind the dark lenses, laughing as he shouted something to Gwion. Then there was a stir in the crowd, heads turning; bodies pressed back against Will. He heard the hooves of horses, the jingling of harness, a creaking and a rumbling of wheels; through the heads of the crowd he could glimpse riders bobbing by, bareheaded, dressed in blue. The rumbling grew; he could see a coach now, its roof dark blue and splendidly curlicued in gold, and blue plumes tossing before it from the foreheads of tall midnight-black horses.

Hoofbeats slowed, wheels squeaked on the stone street; the coach stopped, rocking gently to and fro. Gwion was close again, drawing Will and Bran forward. The crowd parted easily, respectfully, each one making way instantly at the sight of Gwion's erect grey head. Then the coach was before them, suddenly enormous, like a shining blue ship swaying there on strong leather straps hung from a high-wheeled curved frame. A crest was engraved in gold on the glossy door, higher than Will's head. The black horses stamped and blew. There was no coachman to be seen.

Gwion opened the coach door and, reaching inside, swung down a step for mounting.

'Come, Will,' he said.

Will looked up, uncertain. Shadows hid the inside of the coach.

'No harm,' Gwion said. 'Trust your instinct, Old One.'

Will looked sharply, curiously, at the smile-creased eyes in the strong face. He said, 'Do you come too?'

'Not yet,' Gwion said. 'You and Bran, at first.'

He helped them up, and shut the door. Will sat looking out. Around Gwion the crowd eddied and chattered once more, beginning to resume its own affairs, patchwork-bright in the sunshine. The coach, inside, was cool and dim-lit, with deep padded benches, leather-smelling. A horse whinnied; hooves clattered, and the coach began to move.

Will sat back, looking at Bran. The white-haired boy pulled off his glasses and grinned at him.

'First horses, then a coach-and-four. What'll they offer us next, then? Think they'll have a Rolls-Royce?' But he was not listening to himself; he blinked at the buildings moving past the windows, and propped the dark glasses back on his nose.

'A great bird,' Will said softly. 'Or a griffon, or a basilisk.' He too looked out again at the brightness, moving with the jolting sway of the leather-slung coach. Few people were to be seen here. They were moving along a broad street lined by curving arcades of houses that seemed to him startlingly beautiful, with their clear lines and arched doors and wide-set, even windows, and walls of warm golden stone. It had never really occurred to him to think of buildings as beautiful before.

Bran said haltingly, speaking the same thought, 'It's such a . . . well-made place.'

'Everything the right shape,' Will said.

'That's right. I mean, look at that!' Bran leaned forward, pointing. Set among the houses was the high curving entrance to a magnificent pillared courtyard. But the coach had passed before they could see what lay inside.

The world seemed to dim a little; Will saw that the sunlight was gone. They sat swaying in the coach, hoofbeats loud in their ears. Still the light seemed to die.

Will frowned. 'Is it getting dark?'

'Must be clouds.' Bran stood, braced between seats, and gazed out, clutching the door. 'Yes, there are. Big grey clouds, up there. Looks like a real summer storm cooking up.' Then his voice rose a little. 'Will – there were riders dressed in blue in front of us, weren't there?'

'That's right. Like in a procession.'

'No one there now. Nothing ahead. But something . . . following.'

The tightness in his voice brought Will jerking to his feet, to peer out past the white head. Outside their rocking small space the broad street had grown so murky now that it was hard to see clearly; a dark group of figures seemed to be moving behind them, keeping the same speed, coming a little closer perhaps. He thought he could hear other hoofbeats behind the clatter of their own. Then instinct struck at him and his hand tightened on the window-frame: something was coming, something back there, of which he should be afraid.

'What's the matter?' Bran said; and gasped, as a sudden lurch sent him sprawling back on to the seat of the coach. Will staggered back, dropping beside him. The noise of the coach grew, jingling, thundering; they were flung to and fro, from side to side, as the coach pitched and tossed like a boat on an angry sea.

Bran yelled, 'We're going too fast!'

'The horses are frightened!'

'What of?'

'Of . . . of . . . back there.' Words would not come; Will's throat was dry. Bran's white face danced before him; the Welsh boy had pulled off the sheltering glasses again in the gloom, and there was fear in his strange tawny eyes. Then the eyes widened; Bran clutched Will's arm.

Outside, a flurry of dark figures came whirling past, on either side; horses furiously galloping, manes and tails flying on the wind, and dark cloaks streaming out behind the figures of hooded men riding. Here and there one figure was white-cloaked among the dark mass. They saw no faces inside the hoods. Nothing but shadow. There was no telling whether any faces were there to be seen.

But one figure, taller, came galloping past to the window of the flying coach, swaying out there in the grey half-light. The head turned towards them. Will heard Bran's stifled gasp.

The head tossed, flicking back the side of the flowing hood. And there was a face: a face which Will recognized with dread as it stared at him, filled with hatred and malevolence, bright blue eyes burning into his own.

Will heard a husky croak that was his own voice.

'Rider!'

White teeth flashed in the face, in a dreadful mirthless smile, and then the hood fell back. The cloaked figure leaned forward, urging on its horse, and vanished ahead of them into the dark mass of riding shadows. Hoofbeats thickened the air, beat at their hearing; then began to fade.

The world seemed to grow a little less dark, the frantic tossing of the coach to slow gradually down.

Bran was staring at Will, rigid. '*Who was that?*'

Will said emptily, 'The Rider, the Black Rider, one of the great Lords of the Dark —' Suddenly he sat straight, fierce-eyed. 'We mustn't let him go, now he's seen us, we must follow him!' His voice rose, shrill and demanding, calling as if to the whole coach, as if it were a live thing. 'Follow! Follow him! Follow!'

The coach lurched faster again, the noise grew, the horses flung themselves frantically forward. Bran grabbed for support. 'Will, you're mad! What are you doing? Follow . . . *that?*' His horror brought the word out in a half-shriek.

Will crouched in a swaying corner, his face set. 'We must . . . we have to know . . . Hold on. Hold on. *He* makes the terror, by his riding — if we chase, it grows less. Hold tight, wait and see . . .'

They were moving fast now, but without the wildness of panic. The horses kept up a steady strong gallop, swinging the coach like a child's toy on a string. The light grew and grew as if no cloud were anywhere near, and soon sunlight was shafting in again at them through the open windows. Arched stone buildings still edged one side of the broad street, but on the other side now they saw tall trees and smooth grass, stretching into a green distance; paths and gravelled walks criss-crossed the sweep of the grass, here and there.

'It must be . . . that park.' Bran's voice swung in gulps between one bounce and the next. 'The one we saw . . . at the beginning . . . from the roof.'

'Perhaps it is. Look!'

Will pointed; ahead, two riders had turned from the road and were cantering, without apparent haste now, down one of the small roads across the park. A strange pair they made, two ritualistic figures like images from a chessboard: a rider in black hood and cloak on a coal-black horse, a rider in white hood and cloak on a horse white as snow.

'Follow!' Will called.

Bran peered back up the long empty sweep of the road as they turned from it. 'But there were so many – like a big dark cloud. Where did they go?'

'Where the leaves go in autumn,' Will said.

Bran looked at him and seemed suddenly to relax; he grinned. 'There's poetic, now.'

Will laughed. 'It's true. Of course, the trouble with leaves is, they grow again . . .'

But his attention was on the two tall riding figures starkly outlined ahead against the soft green of the park. In a few moments the White Rider, as he felt he must call him, dropped aside and trotted quietly away. The coach went on, following the black upright form of the other.

Bran said, 'Why should some of the Riders of the Dark be dressed all in white and the rest all in black?'

'Without colour . . .' Will said reflectively. 'I don't know. Maybe because the Dark can only reach people at extremes – blinded by their own shining ideas, or locked up in the darkness of their own heads.'

The wheels made a crunching sound on the path. They began to see formally patterned flower-beds laid out at either side, with white stone seats set between them, and here and there people sitting on the seats, or strolling, or children playing. Not one of these gave more than a brief glance of mild interest at the Black Rider stalking ahead on his tall black horse, or the plumed stallions pulling the swaying blue coach with its gold-crested door.

Bran watched one old man glance up, look at the coach, and turn back at once to his book. 'They can see us, now. But they seem . . . they don't *care*.'

'Maybe they will, later,' Will said. The coach stopped. He opened the door, pushing the step down with his foot. They jumped down to the crunching gravel of the white path; then, as they saw what was all around them, both paused, held for a moment by delight.

The air was heavy with fragrance, and everywhere there were roses. Squares, triangles, circles of bright blossom patched the grass all around, red and yellow and white and all colours between. Before them was the entrance to an enclosed circular garden, a tall arch in a high hedge of tumbling red roses. They walked through, almost giddy with the scent. In the great circle of the garden inside, formal balustrades and seats of white marble were set round a glittering fountain where three white dolphins endlessly leapt, spouting a high triple spray of tasselled drops with a faint arching rainbow caught over all by the sun. And as if to offset the cool lines of the marble, mounds of roses billowed everywhere, enormous bushes growing rampant, tall as trees.

Before one of the largest shrubs, a spreading sweetbriar with small pink flowers and a fragrance wafting from it sweet as apples, there stood like a black brand the figure of the Rider on his tall dark horse.

Will and Bran drew level with the fountain and paused, facing the man and horse a little way off. The black horse side-stepped, stamping, restless; the Rider twitched sharply at his rein. He put back his hood a little way, and Will saw the fierce, handsome face that he had seen earlier in his life, and a glint of the red-brown hair.

'Well, Will Stanton,' said the Rider softly. 'It is a long road from the valley of the Thames to the Lost Land.'

Will said, 'And a long road from the ends of the earth, to which the Wild Hunt harried the Dark.'

A grimace like pain flicked over the Rider's face; he turned his head a little so that it was shadowed by the hood, though not quickly enough to hide a dreadful scar across all his further cheek. But the turning was brief; in another instant he was erect again, his back a straight proud line.

'That was one victory for the Light, but one only,' he said coldly. 'There will be no other. We have reached our last rising, Old One; we are at the flood. You have no way of stopping us now.'

'One way,' Will said. 'Just one.'

The Rider turned his bright blue eyes from Will to Bran. He said formally, almost chanting, 'The sword has not the power of the Pendragon until it is in his hand, nor does the Pendragon exist in his own right until his hand is on the sword.' The blue eyes shifted back to Will, and the Rider smiled, but the eyes stayed cold as ice. 'We are before you, Will Stanton. We have been here since first this land was lost, and you may try as you will to take Eirias the sword from the hand that holds it now, but you will not succeed. For that hand is ours.'

Will could feel Bran turn to him in quick baffled concern, but he did not look at him; he was studying the Rider. The confidence in the man's face and bearing was immense, seeming a total arrogance, and yet something in Will's instincts told him that it was not altogether complete. Somewhere vulnerability lay; somewhere there was a crack, a tiny crack, in the Dark's certainty of triumph. And in that crack was the only hope the Light had left, now, to check the rising of the Dark.

He said nothing, but stared at the Rider for a long time, steadily, holding his gaze, until at last the blue eyes flickered briefly aside like the eyes of an animal. Then he knew that he was right.

The Rider said lightly, to cover the movement, 'You would do well to forget the foolishness of pursuing impossible ends, while you are here, and instead enjoy the wonders of the Lost Land. There is none here to help the Dark, and equally there is none here to help you. But there is much to enjoy.'

The black horse shifted restlessly, and he twitched at the rein, turning the horse a few steps towards a climbing rose brilliant with enormous buds and full, down-curved yellow flowers.

With an assured, almost affected gesture the Rider bent and broke off one yellow rose and sniffed it. 'Such flowers, now. Roses of all the centuries. *Maréchal Niel*, here, never such a scent anywhere . . . or that strange tall rose beside you with the small red flowers, called *moyesii*, that goes its own way, sometimes blooming more heavily than any other rose and then perhaps for years not blooming at all.'

'Roses are hard to predict, my lord,' a voice said easily, conversationally; then a small edge came into it. 'And so are the people of the Lost Land.'

And Gwion was there, suddenly, a neat dark figure standing beside the fountain. They could not see where he came from; it was as if he stepped out of the rainbow floating over the glittering drops.

The Rider's horse stepped uneasily once again; he had difficulty stilling it. He said coldly, 'A hard fate will come to you, minstrel, if you give aid to the Light.'

'My fate is my own,' Gwion said.

The black stallion tossed its head; it seemed now, Will thought, to be straining to get away from the high-hedged garden. He glanced over his shoulder at the rose-bright arch through which they had come in, and saw, standing out there, dazzling in the sunlight, the still form of the white-cloaked rider on the white horse.

Gwion's gaze followed him. He said softly, 'Oho.'

'I am not alone in this land,' the Rider said.

'No,' Gwion said. 'Indeed you are not. The word was about that the greatest Lords of the Dark were gathered in this Kingdom, and I see it is true. Indeed you have all your strength here – and you will have need of it.' He spoke lightly, without stress, but the last few words were dragged deliberately slowly, and the Rider's face darkened. With an abrupt gesture he pulled his hood about his face, and only the voice, hissing, came from the shadow.

'Save yourself, Taliesin. Or be lost with the useless hopes of the Light! Lost!'

He wheeled his horse round, the black cloak swinging; his words flickered out like stones. 'Lost!' He gave rein to the restless horse and it sprang towards the arch, the White Rider wheeling in greeting as it approached; a thunder grew suddenly, rapidly out of the distance, and the horsemen of the Dark who had passed Will and Bran earlier came rushing through the park like a great cloud marring the bright day. They bore down on the waiting horses of the two Riders, the Lords of the Dark, and enveloped them and seemed to carry them off; the dark cloud disappeared along the road and the thundering died. And Will and Bran and Gwion stood alone among the roses, in the City, in the sweet-scented garden of the Lost Land.

The Empty Palace

Will said, 'Taliesin?'

'A name,' Gwion said. 'Just another name.' He put his hand out caressingly to a spray of white roses beside him. 'Do you like what you see of my City, now?'

Will did not quite return his quick smile. Something had been nibbling at his mind. 'Did you know we should see the Rider, when you sent us off in the coach?'

Gwion grew sober, fingering his beard. 'No, Old One, I did not. The coach was simply to bring you here. But perhaps he knew that. There is little the Dark does not know in the Lost Land. Yet also there is little that they can do.' He swung abruptly towards the fountain. 'Come.'

They followed him to a spot before the centre of the fountain, where the water flung up in a glittering spiral from the intertwined white dolphins. Nearby climbed the biggest of all the great sprawling rose-bushes, a tall mound of delicate white dog-roses as broad as a house. A fine spray from the fountain spangled their hair and dampened their faces; Will could see the sparkling drops caught even in Gwion's grey beard.

'Look for the arch of the Light,' Gwion said.

Will gazed at the dancing water, the gleaming dolphins, the four-petalled roses; everything blurred together. 'You mean the rainbow?'

It was there again suddenly, a sun-born curve of hazy colour within the fountain, with the hint of another faint rainbow arching above.

Gwion said softly, behind them, 'Look well. Look long.'

Intent and obedient they stared at the rainbow, gazed and gazed until their eyes dazzled in the sunlight reflecting from the marble and the leaping water. Then suddenly Bran cried, 'Look!' – and in the same instant Will started forward, clenching his fists. They could see, faintly outlined behind the rainbow, the figure of a man seeming to float in the air; a man in a white robe with a green surcoat, head drooping, every line of his body drawn down by melancholy – and in his hand a glowing sword.

Will strained to see more clearly, hardly daring to breathe. The figure half-raised its head, almost as if it sensed their gaze and were seeking to look back; but then lethargy seemed to overtake it again and the head drooped, and the hand . . .

. . . and nothing was there but the rainbow, arching through the fountain's glittering spray.

Bran said, his voice tight, '*Eirias*. That was the sword. Who was the man?'

'So sad,' Will said. 'Such a sad man.'

Gwion let out a long breath, breaking his own tension. 'Did you see? You saw clearly?' There was anxious appeal in his voice.

Will looked at him curiously. 'Didn't you?'

'This is the fountain of the Light,' Gwion said. 'The one small touch of the Light's hand that is allowed in the Lost Land. Only those who are of the Light may see what it has to offer. And I am . . . not quite of the Light.' He was looking keenly at Will and Bran. 'You will know that face again? The sorrowful face, and the sword?'

'Anywhere,' said Will.

'Always,' Bran said. 'It was –' He stopped, perplexed, and looked at Will.

Will said, 'I know. There's no way of describing. But, we shall know him. Who is he?'

Gwion sighed. 'That is the king. Gwyddno, Lost King of the Lost Land.'

'And he has the sword,' Bran said. 'Where is he?' A curious intentness seemed to take possession of him, Will saw, whenever there was any mention of the crystal sword.

'He has the sword, and perhaps he will give it to you if he hears you when you speak to him. He has not heard anybody for a long time – not because he cannot hear with his ears, but because he has shut himself up in his mind.'

Bran said again, 'Where is he?'

'In his tower,' Gwion said. 'His tower in *Caer Wydyr*.' As he spoke the Welsh words, Will realized suddenly that the faint lilt to his speaking of English had all along been the accent of a Welshman; though less pronounced than Bran's.

'*Caer Wydyr*,' Bran said. He looked at Will, his forehead wrinkling. 'That means, the castle of glass.'

'A glass tower,' Will said. 'Which you can see in a rainbow.' He looked back at the spiralling jets of the fountain shooting up, breaking, falling in diamond rain over the shining backs of the dolphins. Then he paused, peering more closely. 'Look down there, Bran. I hadn't noticed. There's something written on the fountain, right down low.'

They both bent to look, hands shielding their faces from the spray. A line of lettering was incised in the marble, half hidden by grass; the letters were patched green with moss.

'*I am the* . . .' Will parted the grass with his hands. '*I am the womb of every holt.*'

Bran frowned. '*The womb of every holt.* The womb is where you come from in the mother, so that must be – the beginning, right? But holt? What's a holt?'

'A refuge,' Gwion said quietly.

Bran pushed his dark glasses down his nose and peered at the carved words. 'The beginning of every refuge? What the heck does that mean?'

'That I cannot tell you,' Gwion said. 'But I think you should perhaps remember it.' He pointed out through the arch, at the blue coach waiting. 'Will you come?'

Will said, as they climbed up the folding step into the coach, 'What is that golden crest on the door, with the leaping fish and the roses?'

'A Dyfi salmon, that fish,' Gwion said. 'The heralds will call it, later, *Azure, a Salmon naiant Or between three Roses Argent seeded and barbed.*' He swung himself up over their heads to sit as coachman, gathering up the reins, and the last words came down faintly. 'That is the crest of Gwyddno the king.'

Then he flicked the reins and the black horses tossed their plumed heads and they were away, swinging and rattling through the gardens of the broad green park and out into the City's stone streets. Here and there groups and pairs of people were walking; they lifted their heads, now, as the coach jingled by, and looked after it with surprise and sometimes curiosity. None offered any greeting, but none ignored their passing as before; this time, every head turned.

The coach slowed; they swayed round a bend. Looking out, Will and Bran saw that they were turning in at the arched entrance to a courtyard. High pillared walls rose on all sides, set with tall nine-paned windows; fantastic pointed towers rose above the balustraded line of the roof. Every window was blank; they saw no face anywhere.

The coach stopped; they climbed out. Before them a narrowing stone staircase rose to a square pillared doorway ornamented with carved stone scrolls and figures – and, dominating the rest, a replica of the crest of the leaping fish from the carriage door. Will and Bran glanced at one another, and then ahead. The door stood open. Nothing but darkness was visible within.

Gwion said, behind them, 'It is the palace of Gwyddno Garanhir. The Empty Palace, it has been called, since the day when the king retreated to his castle by the sea and never afterward came out. Go inside, the two of you together. And I will meet you in there, if you find your way.'

Will looked back. The splendid coach and the midnight-black horses were quite gone. The great courtyard was empty. Gwion stood at the bottom of the steps, a neat dark figure, his bearded face upturned and sudden lines of anxiety written unaccountably clear upon it. He was tense, waiting.

Will nodded. He turned back to the immense open doorway of the palace. Bran stood there gazing in at the murk. He had not moved since before Gwion spoke. Without turning his white head he said, 'Come, on, then.'

They went in, side by side. With a long creak and a deep-echoing crash the huge door slammed shut behind them. Instantly the darkness burst into a blaze of white light. Will had a second in which to see Bran recoil, shielding his eyes, before the impact of what lay before them hit him and he gasped aloud.

All around, in an endless fierce glitter, were countless repeated images of himself and Bran. He spun round, staring; the Will-images spun round too, a long chorus-line retreating into space. He shouted, instinctively expecting an infinitely repeated echo to go bouncing to and fro, just as the reflections before him echoed through his sight. But only the one sound rang dully around them, and then died.

It was the sound that somehow gave Will a sense of the shape of the place where they stood: long, narrow.

'Is it a corridor?' he said, bemused.

'Mirrors!' Bran was looking wildly to and fro, eyes screwed into slits even behind the dark glasses. 'Mirrors everywhere. It's *made* of mirrors.'

Will's head steadied out of its whirling bewilderment; he began to sort out what he could see. 'Mirrors, yes. Except for the floor.' He looked down at glimmering darkness. 'And that's black glass. Look, up and down. It's a corridor, a long curving corridor all made out of mirrors.'

'I can see too many of me,' Bran said with an uneasy laugh. There was a flash of white at each face as all the endless lines of Bran-images instantaneously laughed – and then sobered, staring.

Will took a few uncertain steps, flinching as the rows of reflected figures moved with him. The curve of the corridor opened before him a little, reflecting nothing but its own brilliance, like a gleaming empty page in a huge book. He reached out and tugged at Bran's sleeve.

'Hey. Walk alongside me. If there's someone else to look at, even out of the corner of your eye, all those reflections don't make you so giddy.'

Bran came with him. He said uncertainly, 'You're right.' But when they had gone forward a little way he stopped suddenly; his face looked pinched and ill. 'This is *awful*,' he said, his voice tight. 'The glass, the brightness, all of it pressing in so close. Pressing, pressing, it's like being in some terrible kind of box.'

'Come on,' Will said, trying to sound confident. 'Maybe it opens out round that bend. It can't go on forever.'

But as they rounded the curve, peopling the glass walls with their endlessly reflected figures, they came only to a pair of sharply angled corners, breaking the reflections into even more wildly repeated lines, where another mirrored corridor crossed the first so that they had now a choice of three forward directions to take.

Bran said unhappily, 'Which way?'

'Goodness knows.' Will reached into his pocket and brought out a penny. 'Heads we go right or centre, tails we go left.' He spun the coin, caught it, and held out his arm.

'It's tails,' Bran said. 'Left, then.'

'Whoops!' Will had dropped the penny; they heard it roll and spin. 'Where is it? Ought to be easy enough to find here . . . Funny how there don't seem to be any joints anywhere in the glass – it's like being inside a sort of square tube –' He caught sight of the strain on Bran's face, and was shaken. 'Come on – let's get out of here.'

They went on, up the left-hand turning. But the glass corridor, identical with the first, seemed endless; it stretched on and on, curved sharply to the left, then straightened again. Their footsteps rang out, dropping into immediate silence whenever they paused. At length they came to another crossroads of corridors.

Bran looked round despondently. 'Looks just the same as the other one.'

A glitter that was not glass drew Will's eye to the floor; stooping, he found it was his penny. He straightened, swallowing hard to muffle the sudden hollow feeling in his throat, and held out his hand to Bran.

'It is the same. Look.'

'*Duw*. We've come in a circle.' Bran looked at him, frowning. 'You know what? I think we're in a maze.'

'A maze . . .'

'A maze of mirrors. Now there's something to spend your life in.'

'Gwion knew, didn't he?' Will thought back, to the grey-bearded face looking up at him tense with concern. 'Gwion said, *I shall meet you, if you find your way . . .*'

'You know anything about mazes?'

'I was in one at Hampton Court once. Hedges. You had to keep turning right on the way in, and left on the way out. But that one had a centre. This one –'

'Those curves.' Bran looked less ill now that he had something to puzzle him. 'Think. Think. We went to our right when we started off, and it curved . . .'

'It curved to the left.'

'And then we came to the crossing, and we took the furthest corridor on the left, and *it* curved to the left and brought us back to the crossing in a circle.'

Will closed his eyes and tried to visualize the pattern. 'So turning left must be wrong. Do we turn right then?'

'Yes, look,' Bran said. His pale face was alight with an idea now. Opening his mouth wide, he breathed a long breath over the mirrored wall of the corridor, and drew with his finger in the patch of mist an upward spiral pattern of a series of loops, rising without touching one another. The curving tops of the loops faced the left. It looked like a drawing of a very loose spring standing on end.

'It has to look like this. See that first loop? That's the pattern we've walked so far. And mazes always repeat themselves, right?'

'So if it goes one loop after another, it's a spiral,' Will said, watching the mist-drawing gradually fade. 'And we wouldn't have to go round each whole loop, we could just go up that side on the right where each loop crosses itself.'

'By turning right every time. Come on.' Bran slid triumphantly towards the right-hand corridor.

'Wait a minute.' Will breathed at the wall, and drew the spiral again. 'We're facing the wrong way. See? We've been all the way round the first loop, so now we're facing backwards, back the way we first came. And if we turn right now, we shall really be turning left.'

'And just loop the loop again. Sorry, yes. In too much of a hurry, I am.' Bran swung his arms sideways and did a neat jump to turn himself in the other direction. He looked with dislike at the endless reflections of himself that had echoed the jump. 'Come on, I *hate* these mirrors.'

Will looked at him thoughtfully as they followed the curving right-hand corridor. 'You really mean that, don't you? I mean I don't like them either, they're creepy. But you –'

'It's the brightness.' Bran looked round uneasily, and quickened his step.

'And more than that. All that reflecting, it *does* something, it's like having your mind sucked out of you. Aah!' He shook his head for want of words.

'Here's the next crossroads. That was a lot quicker.'

'So it should be, if we've really got the answer. Turn right again.'

Four times they turned to the right, trooping along with their long, long rows of reflected images keeping endless step.

And then suddenly, curving after the fourth turn, they came face to face with themselves: startled figures staring back out of a blank mirrored wall.

'No!' Will said fiercely, and heard his voice tremble as he saw Bran's head and shoulders droop in despair.

Bran said quietly, 'Dead end.'

'But how could we have gone wrong?'

'Pity knows. But we did. I suppose we have to go back and . . . start again.' Bran let his knees crumple, and sat down in a heap on the black glass floor.

Will looked at him in the mirror. 'I don't believe it.'

'But there it is.'

'I mean, I don't believe we have to start again.'

'Oh yes we do.' Bran looked up bleakly at their reflected images: the blue sweater and jeans of the standing figure, the white head and dark glasses of the figure hunched on the floor. 'Once this happened to us before, once a long time ago – finding a blank wall stopping us. But that was where your magic as an Old One could help. It can't here, can it?'

'No,' Will said. 'No, not in the Lost Land.'

'Well then.'

'No,' Will said obstinately. He bit at a thumbnail, staring round at the blind mirrored walls that could give back nothing but what they were given to reflect, and that yet, somehow, seemed to hold within them a spacious world of their own. 'No. There's something . . . there must be something we ought to be remembering . . .' He looked down at Bran, his eyes not quite seeing him. 'Think: what has Gwion said to us in all the time since we first saw him, that seemed to be anything like a message? What has he *told* us to do?'

'Gwion? He told us to get into the coach . . .' Bran scrambled to his feet, his pale forehead furrowed, as he thought backwards. 'He said he would meet us if we found our way – but that was the very last thing. Before that . . . there was something he said we should remember, you're right. What was it? Remember, he said, remember . . .'

Will stiffened. 'Remember. The face of the man in the rainbow, and after that another thing, the writing on the fountain. *I think you should perhaps remember . . .*'

Remembering, he stood very straight, stretching out both his arms stiff in front of him, and pointing all ten fingers at the mirrored glass wall that barred their way.

'*I am the womb of every holt,*' he said, slowly and clearly, in the words that they had read through the muffling grass on the mossy stone of the fountain in the park.

And above their heads on the glass, faintly and gradually, another single line of words began to glow, growing brighter and brighter until their brilliance flashed out dulling any other light around them. They had just time to look at the words and comprehend them : *I am the blaze on every hill.* And then the light grew for an instant intolerably strong so that they flinched away from it, and with a strange soft sound, like an explosion muffled by many miles' distance, all the glass walls enclosing them shattered and musically fell.

And they stood free, with the bright words hanging in the darkness before them, and the maze of mirrors gone as if it had never been there.

The Journey

The blazing words faded from the air above Will's head, leaving the imprint of their brightness so that for a few moments the letters still hung ghostly across his vision. Beside him he heard Bran let out a long slow breath of relief.

Gwion's voice said warmly, from the shadows, 'And you did find your way.'

Blinking, Will saw him standing before them, in a high vaulted hall whose white walls were hung with rich tapestries and brilliant paintings. He looked back. There, across the hall, was the great carved door which had slammed behind them when they had first found themselves in the maze. Of the maze itself there was no sign at all.

Bran said, with a quiver still in his voice, 'Was it real ?' Then he gave a small shaking laugh. 'There's a silly question, now.'

Gwion came forward to them, smiling. '*Real* is a hard word,' he said. 'Almost as hard as *true*, or *now* . . . Come. Now that you have proved yourselves by breaking the barrier of the City, I may set you on the way to the Castle.'

He pulled back a tapestry curtain on the wall, revealing the entrance to a

narrow circular staircase. He beckoned, and in line they went up the stairs:
Will followed Gwion's feet, quiet in their soft leather shoes; the stairs seemed
to wind endlessly up and up, in curving sections. On and on they went, for so
long a climb that his breath began to rasp and he felt they must be hundreds of
feet into the sky.

Then Gwion said, 'Hold a moment,' and paused. He took something from
his pocket. It was a heavy iron key. In the dim light from one of the narrow
opaque windows set into the staircase wall, Will saw that the top of the key was
wrought into a decorative pattern: a circle, quartered by a cross. Will stared,
motionless. Then he looked up and saw Gwion's dark eyes glittering
enigmatically down at him.

'Ah, Old One,' Gwion said softly. 'The Lost Land is full of signs from long
ago, but few of its people now remember what the signs mean.'

He opened the small door barring their way, and suddenly sunlight was
pouring down on them, washing away the last oppressive memories of the
mirrored maze.

Will and Bran came out with their faces up to the blue sky as if they were
prisoners emerging from jail. They found themselves behind a balustrade of
wrought gold, looking out over the gold and glittering roofs of the City and the
mounded green sweep of the park, just as they had done in the very beginning
– but from a greater height than before. In a moment or two they saw that the
balcony on which they stood was the lower rim of a great curving white and
golden roof – and they realized that it was this, the palace of King Gwyddno,
the Empty Palace of the Lost Land, which was topped by the marvellous dome,
banded in crystal and gold, that they had first seen glittering in the dawn.
Craning his neck, Will thought he could just make out the very top where the
golden arrow pointed to the western sea.

Gwion came and stood at their backs, pointing in the same direction. Will
noticed a ring on his fourth finger, with a dark stone carved into the shape of a
leaping fish.

Out along the line of his arm, they saw the roofs of the City end, giving way
to a green-gold patchwork of fields stretching into a haze of heat. Far, far away
in the distance through the haze Will thought he could see dark trees, with
behind them the purple sweep of mountains and the long glimmer of the sea,
but he could not be sure. Only one thing out there seemed distinct: a glowing
pencil of light rising out of the hazy green blur where the Lost Land seemed to
meet the sea.

'Look at that,' Bran said. For a moment his hand hovered in the air beside
Gwion's, its fingers looking milky-pale and very young beside the lean brown
hand with its dark ring. 'That, there – we saw it from the mountain, Will,

remember? Above Cwm Maethlon.' He glanced ruefully at Will. 'Another world, isn't it? D'you know, I had completely forgotten them? D'you think they are all right?'

'I think so,' Will said slowly. He was staring out still at the hazed horizon, but not seeing it: lost in a concern that had been flickering through his mind since first they came to the Lost Land. 'I wish I knew. And I wish I knew where Merriman is. I can't . . . reach him, Bran. I can't reach him. I can't hear him. Even though I think he meant to be with us, here.'

'So he did, Old One,' Gwion said unexpectedly. 'But the enchantment of the Lost Land keeps him away, if he has missed the only moment for breaking it.'

Will turned sharply to him, a deep instinct stirring. 'You know him, don't you? Some time a long way back, you have been close to Merriman.'

'Very close,' Gwion said, with an ache of affection deep in the words. 'And one thing I am permitted to say to you, now that you have spoken of him to me. He should have been here to join you, in this palace. But I am beginning to fear that in some way the Dark has held him back, in that other world of yours. And if now he has lost the moment for entering the Lost Land, he cannot now come.'

Will said, 'Not at all?'

'No,' Gwion said.

Will suddenly realized how much he had been hoping for Merriman's strong presence to be there, soon, soon, as a support. He swallowed down panic, and looked at Bran.

'Then we have nothing but what the Lady said. That we shall find the crystal sword in the glass tower, among the seven trees, where the – the horn will stop the wheel.'

Bran said, 'And a white bone will prevent us, and a flying may-tree will save us. Whatever that may mean.'

'The glass tower,' Will said again. His eyes went back to the gleaming pencil on the horizon.

Gwion said, 'That is Caer Wydyr, out there where you are looking. The Castle of the Lost Land, with its glass tower. Where my master sits, wrapped in a deathly melancholy that none can take away.' His voice was bleak and sad.

Will said hesitantly, 'May we know more than that?'

'Oh yes,' Gwion said sombrely. 'There are things I must tell you, of the Land and of the sword, for Merlion's sake. As much as I can.' He came to the edge of the golden balustrade and gripped its rim with both hands, looking out over the city. His beard jutted, and the strong nose was outlined against the sky; he looked like a profiled head from a coin.

He said, 'The Land is neither of the Dark nor the Light, nor ever was. Its enchantment was of a separate kind, the magic of the mind and the hand and the eye, that owes no allegiance because it is neither good nor bad. It has no more to do with the behaviour of men, or the great absolutes of the Light and the Dark, than does the blossom of a rose or the curving leap of a fish. Yet our craftsmen, the greatest ever in Time or out of it, did not . . . care to work for the Dark. They did their most marvellous work for the Lords of the Light. They wove tapestries, carved thrones and chests, forged candlesticks of silver and gold. They wrought four of the six great Signs of the Light.'

Will looked up quickly.

Gwion smiled at him. 'Ah, Sign-seeker,' he said gently. 'Long long ago in the Lost Land, forgotten by all its people now, there was the beginning of that gold-linked chain of yours, iron and bronze and water and fire . . . And at the last, a craftsman of this land made the great sword Eirias for the Light.'

Bran said, tense, 'Who made it?'

'It was made by one who was close to the Light,' Gwion said, 'but who was neither a Lord of the Light nor one of the Old Ones – there are none such bred in this land . . . He was the only one who had the skill to make so great a wonder. Even here, where many are skilled. A great craftsman, unparalleled.' He spoke with a slow reverence, shaking his head in wonder, remembering. 'But the Riders of the Dark, they could roam freely through the land, since we had neither desire nor reason to keep any creature out – and when they heard that the Light had asked for the sword, they demanded that it should not be made. They knew, of course, that words already long written foretold the use of Eirias, once it was forged, for the vanquishing of the Dark.'

Will said, 'What did he do, the craftsman?'

'He called together all the makers in the land,' Gwion said. He tilted his head a little higher. 'All those who wrote, or brought life to others' words or music, or who made beautiful things. And he said to them, I have this work in me, I know it, that will be the peak of everything I can ever make or do, and the Dark is trying to forbid me to do it. We may all suffer, if I deny them their will, and I cannot therefore be responsible alone for deciding. Tell me. Tell me what I should do.'

Bran was gazing at him. 'What did they say?'

'They said, *You must make it.*' Gwion smiled, proudly. 'Without any exception. *Make the sword*, they said. So he went away into a place of his own, and made Eirias, and in a land of wonders it was the most wonderful and powerful thing that had ever been made. And the fury of the Dark was very great, but impotent, for the Dark Lords knew that they could neither destroy a work created for the Light, nor steal it, nor bring any . . . harm to its creator.'

He fell silent, gazing out at the misted horizon.

'Go on,' Bran said urgently. 'Go on!'

Gwion sighed. 'So the Dark did a simple thing,' he said. 'They showed the maker of the sword his own uncertainty and fear. Fear of having done the wrong thing – fear that having done this one great thing, he would never again be able to accomplish anything of great worth – fear of age, of insufficiency, of unmet promise. All such endless fears, that are the doom of people given the gift of making, and lie always somewhere in their minds. And gradually, he was put into despair. Fear grew in him, and he escaped from it into lethargy – and so hope died, and a terrible paralysing melancholy took its place. He is held by it now, he is held captive by his own mind. He, and the sword Eirias that he made; with him. Despair holds him prisoner, despair, the most terrible creation of all. For in great men, the mind can produce giant spectres of great power. And King Gwyddno is a great man.'

'The King!' Will said slowly. 'The King of the Lost Land made the sword?'

'Yes,' Gwion said. 'Long, long ago the king went alone into his castle, into the glass tower of Caer Wydyr. And he made the sword Eirias, and there he and the sword have been, alone, ever since. Held in a trap made by the king himself. And only you, perhaps, may spring that trap.' He seemed to be speaking to both of them, but he was looking at Bran.

Bran said, his pale face drawn by horror, 'All alone? All alone since then? Hasn't anyone ever seen him?'

'I have seen him,' Gwion said. But there was suddenly such pain in his voice that no one asked him anything more.

The sun was warm on their faces; heat grew in the gold and crystal banding of the dome, and the roofs of the City shimmered before them. Somewhere in the distance, out over the green fields of the Lost Land, Will heard a seagull cry.

He had a sudden illusion of Merriman's presence, and at once then a sense of great urgency. Merriman was not there, not even to be heard in the mind: he knew it, and yet the urgency lingered, as if it were an echo from something happening somewhere else, a long way away. Will looked at Gwion's face and could see the awareness of it there too. Their eyes met.

'Yes,' Gwion said. 'It is time. You must journey to the Castle, across the Country that lies between, and that I have made possible as far as I can. But I cannot tell you what you may encounter on the way, nor protect you against it. Remember, you are in the Lost Land, and it is the enchantment of the Land which is in command here.' He looked anxiously out at the gleaming distant tower on the horizon. 'Look well, now, at the place where you must go, and set your minds on reaching it. And then, come.'

They looked once at the finger of light, far out in the haze, and then they followed Gwion back down the staircase, into the Empty Palace where no king now lived. But even though the king was gone, they saw now that the palace still held others beside Gwion – and they found that they had been there before.

When they were halfway down the curving staircase, Gwion opened a door in the wall that Will had not noticed before. He led them down a different stair, straight and shallower, in towards the centre of the palace. And all at once they heard a faint murmur of voices ahead, and found themselves in a long wood-panelled room filled with books and bookshelves and heavy tables.

It was the long gallery, the room like a library. Will's eyes went to the side wall and saw that there still was the darkness, empty space with no light or shadow visible: the great theatre in which all life might be played. Other things, though, were not the same as before. People crowded the room now, filling it with a warm buzz of conversation, and any who glanced up at the three of them standing in the doorway smiled, or raised a hand in greeting.

They walked through, up and down over the strangely differing levels of its floor; many people they passed spoke a word or two to Gwion, and the warmth was clear in every face that looked at Will and Bran. One woman touched Will gently on the shoulder as they went by, and said, 'Safe journey to you.' As he looked up, startled, he heard a man beside them say softly to Bran, '*Pob hwyl!*'

Bran said in his ear, '*Good luck*, he said. How do they all know?'

Will shook his head, wondering. They followed Gwion's neat dark-clad figure down the room, walking quickly, and then at the far end a man who had been standing bent over a large book on a table straightened and turned as they approached, putting out a hand to halt them. Will thought he remembered the face as that of the man to whom he had spoken when they had first been in the room: a man who had not then seemed to see or hear him, and who had been reading a book whose pages were blank.

'See, before you go,' the man said, with the lilt of North Wales stronger in his voice than Will heard it from Gwion or even Bran. 'There is a part of this book that you must see, and remember.'

'Remember . . .' said Gwion softly, looking at them, and the echo woke in both their minds. The book lay open before them on the heavy oak table; on one curving vellum page was a painting, and on the other a single line of words.

Will was staring at the picture. In a stylized green world of trees and lawns, among beds of roses bright as those where they had encountered the Rider, it showed the figure of a young woman, fair-haired, robed in blue, standing looking out at them. Her face was heart-shaped, fine-boned, delicately beautiful; she was serious, neither smiling nor sad.

'It is the Lady!' Will said.

Bran said in surprise, 'But you said she was very old.' He reflected for a moment. 'Of course, that just depends, doesn't it?'

'It is the Lady,' Will said again, slowly. 'There's that big rose-coloured ring on her finger, too, I've never seen her without it. And look there – in the picture behind her, isn't that –'

'The fountain!' Bran peered closer, looking over his glasses. 'It's the same fountain, the one we were at in the park – and so that must be the same rose garden. But how –'

Will had his finger on the line of thick black manuscript on the facing page. He read aloud, '*I am the queen of every hive.*'

'Remember,' the man said. He closed the book.

'Remember,' Gwion said. 'And then go.' Facing them, he put one hand briefly on a shoulder of each and looked carefully into their eyes. 'Do you know this place, the gallery we are in? Of course. So you will remember the way by which you came into it, that you must follow now. I stay here, for a while. There are men and women of some art in this place, and they will tell me what they can of Merriman. I will be with you again, but you must go on, now, at once.'

Will looked down, and found the square open trapdoor in the floor, and the ladder leading down beneath. 'That way?'

'That way,' Gwion said. 'And then, take what you will find, and the finding will start you on your way.' The strong grey-bearded face broke into its warm, illumining smile. 'Go well, my friends.'

Down into the shadows Bran and Will clambered, more confident than when they had scrambled up the ladder in the early morning, linked by the little horn that hung forgotten again now from Will's belt. On level ground once more, they groped their way forward in the murk, and came to the small wooden door. Will felt its pitted surface with the flat of his hands.

'No handle or anything on this side, either.'

'It opened outwards, didn't it? Perhaps you just push.'

And at the first gentle pressure the door did swing outward, so that they stood blinking for a moment at the light of the street outside. Then they went out, the door swinging shut behind them with a crash that showed it would not open so easily again. And there in the narrow shady street, waiting for them, were the two white-maned golden horses they had ridden there so long and so short a time ago.

The horses tossed their heads as if in greeting; the silver harness rang like sleighbells. Without a word Will and Bran swung themselves up into the saddles, with the same unaccountable ease as before, and the horses trotted away up the narrow street, between the high grey walls with the thin bright strip of blue sky far above.

They came out into a broader place, filled with people who seemed at once to recognize them; who stood waving, calling out in greeting. The horses walked carefully through the crowd; the calling grew into a spasmodic cheering; children ran alongside them, laughing and halloo-ing. Bran and Will grinned at one another in pleased embarrassment. On they went, down the broad paved street, until they reached a towering wall, with a great gateway in it through which the road ran. Through the arch they could see a glimpse of green fields and distant trees.

The crowds stood thick before the arch, but the golden horses went stepping on, never pausing, nudging their way gently through.

'Good fortune to you!'

'Safe travelling!'

'A good journey!'

All around, the people of the City called and waved; children ran and danced and shouted; a group of girls beside the gate stood laughing and throwing flowers. Will put up his hand half in self-defence and caught a wide red rose; looking down, he saw the dark-haired girl who had thrown it blushing and smiling. He grinned at her, and stuck the flower into his top pocket.

Then all at once they were outside the great gate of the City, and all the crowd was gone. Before them lay broad green fields, and a rough sandy road stretching brown-gold into the distance with a wood beyond. The voices from the city died away. Somewhere a lark sang in the summer sky; a blue sky, patched here and there with puffy fair-weather clouds, the sun high amongst them now. The horses turned up the sandy road and went on without breaking step, at a steady walk.

Bran eyed the flower in Will's pocket. 'Oooh!' he said in a mocking falsetto. 'A red rose, is it?'

Will said amiably, 'Get lost.'

'Not so pretty as Jane, that one who threw it.'

'As who?' Will said.

'Jane Drew. Don't you think she's pretty, then?'

'I suppose so, yes,' Will said, surprised. 'I never thought about it.'

Bran said, 'One good thing about you, you're uncomplicated.'

But Will's mind had jumped backward. He wound the loose rein thoughtfully round one finger as he swayed steadily to and fro on the tall horse. 'I hope they're all right, back there.'

Bran said, roughly, abruptly, 'Better forget them, for now.'

Will looked up sharply. 'What d'you mean?'

Without speaking, Bran pointed out to one side, past him. In the distance across the flat green fields Will saw a patch of black and white, moving fast, in a direction parallel to the road along which they were travelling. He knew it could only be the Riders of the Dark, heading, like themselves, for the Castle of the Lost Land.

The Mari Llwyd

They watched the troop of Riders, miniature in the distance, moving fast across the fields. Will's horse tossed its head suddenly, snuffing the air, and began to quicken its pace.

Bran came up level with him. 'They're going a good lick. Trying to get to the Castle before we do?'

'I suppose so.'

'Shall we race?'

'I don't know.' Will looked down at his restless mount. 'The horses want to.'

Bran was sitting poised in the saddle, his pale face alert; he smiled. 'Think you can stay on?'

Will laughed, a sudden wild exhilaration seizing him. 'Just watch!' He gave no more than a flick to the reins before the horse was off, leaping out, galloping eagerly along the hard sandy track. Bran was beside him, leaning forward, white hair flying, yelling with delight. On and on they went, past stretches of ripening oats and wheat, past fields where placid cattle grazed – some the familiar black, but many pure white. The horses ran smoothly, confidently. In the distance, the Riders of the Dark raced parallel: then, after a while, disappeared behind the far edge of the wood which lay in the centre of the Country, between the City and the Castle of the Lost Land.

Will had assumed that their own road too would skirt this wood, on the nearer side. But when he raised his head out of the whirl of riding, he found that they had not turned; instead the trees seemed to be reaching out around them, cutting off their view of the shining glass tower. He and Bran were galloping straight towards the wood, and the wood was growing, rising before them, far darker and more dense than it had seemed before.

The horses began to slow their pace.

'Come on!' Bran twitched his reins impatiently.

'They know best,' Will said. 'I don't like the looks of that wood.'

Bran glanced up, flinching at the size of the dark mass looming ahead. 'They aren't stopping, though. Why didn't they go around it?'

'I suppose they have to go where the track goes. And I didn't notice where it *was* going. Should have done.'

'We both should have done. Oh well.' The horses were walking again now. Bran pushed one arm across his forehead. 'Lord, it's hot. The sun's still high.'

The woodland was sparse and open at first, leafy with bracken and undergrowth, still bright through the dappling shade. The road, though narrowed to a track, wound through the trees clear and sandy, but gradually it became less distinct, with patches of grass growing in the sand and the arms of creeping plants reaching across, and now the air was cool as the wood grew deeper. The horses stepped warily, in single file. Few birds sang here. Will and Bran began to be conscious of the silence. The trees were larger and thicker; the wood went on and on.

Will tried for as long as he could to ignore the feeling drifting insidiously into his mind as the light grew dim and the trees more dominant, but he knew he was afraid.

There was nothing to be heard now but the soft rise and fall of the horses' feet. The path they trod was completely overgrown yet still visible; covered, as if to mark it from its surroundings, by a mat of some small creeping weed with dark green leaves. Somewhere among the trees edging the path ahead, a bird whirred abruptly away; the horses checked nervously.

'They're as scared as I am,' Will said, trying to brighten his voice. A branch rustled nearby in the wood, and he jumped.

Bran looked round in the gloom. He said uneasily, 'Should we go back?' But as if in answer the horses began walking steadily forward again. Will stroked the light mane on the neck before him; the horse's ears were laid back flat, but still he went doggedly on.

'Perhaps it's just a . . . barrier,' he said suddenly. 'Like the maze. Perhaps they know there's not really anything to be scared of.'

Some unseen creatures rose in the underbrush beside the path and went crashing off through the still trees and the green seas of fern all around; Will and Bran gasped, but this time the horses walked on unheeding. The trees interlaced overhead. Will rode with his teeth clenched, fighting off panic, comforted only by the steady swaying of his tall horse. The air was cool and damp; they crossed a small sluggish stream half-buried in fern. Then almost imperceptibly, the horses' pace began to quicken. Light began to filter through the branches overhead once more; sand appeared between the tight-woven green leaves of the matted path.

'We're coming out!' Bran said in a half-whisper high with relief. 'You were right, the horses knew it was just spookiness. We're coming out!'

The horses began to trot, an easy swinging motion; they tossed their heads as if from a sense of release. Will felt the pounding of his heart slide back to normal; he sat up straighter, ashamed of his fear, and looked up at the thinning trees.

'Blue sky again, look. Ouf, what a difference!'

And so they were both relaxed in the saddle, holding loose reins, looking up unprepared, when suddenly one of the horses gave a high terrified whinny, and both shied, rearing, as something large and loud rushed at them out of the trees. And before they knew it Will and Bran were jerking backward, clutching wildly for rein or saddlebow, tumbling helpless to the ground. The two golden horses bolted in panic across the rough sedgy pasture that stretched away from the wood.

Will had a quick glimpse of the thing that was chasing them. He cried out, in horror and disbelief, 'No!'

Bran gave a croaking shout without words, and they stumbled up and fled unthinking over the fields. In the heat of the summer sunshine Will felt cold. His head sang. He wanted to be sick. He was too frightened even to think of fear.

It was the skeleton of a giant horse, staring with the blind eye-sockets of a skull, running and leaping and prancing on legs of bone driven by ghostly muscles long rotted away. It caught them almost at once. Faster than any living horse it galloped and without any sound. Silently it overtook them, head turned, grinning, an impossible horror. The white bones of its great rib-cage glittered in the sun. It tossed its dreadful silent head, and red ribbons dangled and fluttered like long banners from the grinning lower jaw.

The creature was playing with them, driving them this way and that, as a kitten plays with a beetle. It leapt to and fro before them, then stopped in its tracks, hooves skidding in the sandy soil. Then with the leering skull thrust out, jaws open wide, it charged at them in terrible silence – and was suddenly past them, behind them, waiting again. Swinging round wildly, Bran stumbled and fell.

The skull tossed on the spine that was a neck; the teeth glittered, the red ribbons danced round a strange broken stump in the centre of the bony forehead. In the same soundless menace it stood watching them out of the blind skull, hoof and bone pawing at the ground. Will swallowed.

'You all right? Get up!'

Bran was sitting up, blinking wide tawny eyes; his glasses were gone. 'The *Mari Llwyd!*' he whispered. 'The *Mari Llwyd!*' He was staring at the thing as if bewitched.

'Get up, quick!' Will had glimpsed a refuge nearby. In panic he dragged Bran to his feet. The spectre began to circle them, slowly, silently.

'Over here! Come *on!*'

It was a building, he saw. The strangest of buildings: a small low house made of blocks of grey stone, with a once-thatched roof covered in turf and straggling grass and a great swathe of branches blossoming white. A hawthorn tree was growing there from the ancient roof, a low tree not much bigger than a bush.

Bran stood transfixed, his eyes on the skeleton. 'The *Mari Llwyd!*' he whispered again.

'Close your eyes!' Will said fiercely. He thrust his hand in front of Bran's face to cut off the sight of the monstrous horse, and in the same moment the right words came to him. 'Quick, think, what did the Lady say?'

'The Lady?' Bran said dully. But his head turned.

'What did the Lady say to Jane? Think!'

'To Jane.' Bran's face began to clear. 'To tell us . . . a white bone will prevent you . . . and a flying may-tree –'

'Will save you. Look at it. Look at it!' Will turned him to the stone house with the blossoming white tree growing from its roof. The thing stalking them wheeled closer, closer. With a sound like a sob Bran stumbled forward; Will pushed him in through the door and slammed it shut behind them. He stood leaning against it, gasping for breath. There was a prickling silence outside.

Bran looked down at his hands. He was still clutching the saddlebag from his vanished horse, as if it were a lifebelt. Dropping it on the floor he rubbed his stiff fingers and looked at Will. 'Sorry.'

But Will was not listening; he had crossed to the one small window that let in a dim shadowy light through the chunky stone wall. A broken shutter hung from the window-frame; there was no glass. Will's face was pale; Bran saw fear in it.

Will said huskily, 'Can you look?'

'I'm all right now.' Bran came to stand beside him. And when he looked through the window he clutched Will's arm without knowing it, so hard that the fingertips dug in deep and afterwards left a mark behind.

The great white skeleton of the horned horse, dead and yet alive, was wheeling to and fro in front of the cottage, to and fro, to and fro. Its four bony legs danced beneath the curving empty white strips of the rib-cage and the flattened arcs of the hip-blades. The long beribboned skull was jerking up and down in a dreadful dead frenzy, faster and faster; each time it faced the cottage it dropped its forehead like a charging bull and paused for an instant before turning restlessly away and wheeling to and fro once more.

Will whispered, 'It's going to run at us. Charge at the door. What can we do?'

'Block the door? Would that stop it?'

'Not a hope.'

'Isn't there *anything* you can do, make happen –'

'We're in the Lost Land . . .'

And the monstrous thing out there in the sunshine made one last great curving turn before it would charge at the door to burst in to their destruction. Wheeling deliberately close to the window of the house, out of its hollow-eyed skull the creature laughed dreadfully, soundlessly in at them for a second. It was the last second. As the thing passed so close, a long flurry like snow came down past the window from above, a fluttering flickering cloud of white flakes falling on the apparition, all the petals of the hawthorn tree falling, dropped in a long soft shower. And the horse that was the skeleton of a horse collapsed, as if the strings had been cut from a marionette, and fell apart. Every bone fell from every other bone, clattering down to the ground, rattling as clear now as all had been silent before. And nothing was left but a heap of white bones gleaming in the sun, bleached, long dead, with faded red ribbons drooping from the long grinning skull that lay askew on top of the pile.

Bran let out a long soft breath, his hands going up to cover his eyes; he swung aside and slumped gently down to the floor. So it was only Will, standing wide-eyed in wonder beside the window, who saw the flurry of white petals rise again, fluttering, alive, like a great crowd of feathery white plume moths he had seen before, somewhere, somewhere – and rise flickering into the sky and out of sight, far away.

Will turned unsteadily, uncertain whether to trust his knees. He stood gazing at the dim-lit room. It was a little while before he properly saw anything. But as his churning senses began to calm again, he found he was looking at the door: an ancient door of rotting, battered wood, which would have withstood no impact of any kind at all. He could see some words written over it, with the faint glimmer of gold in them. There was not enough light to read what they said. Will went shakily across and pushed open the door; brightness came in.

Bran said slowly, behind him, reading: '*I am the shield for every head.*'

'And it's written inside, where we couldn't see it,' Will said, stepping back to peer up at the words. 'So we might never have dared to come in, if it hadn't been for what the Lady said.'

Bran was sitting up, arms over his knees, white head drooping. '*Duw*. That . . . thing . . .'

'Don't talk about it,' Will said: a shiver went over him like a cold breeze. Then he remembered something. 'But Bran, what was the name you called it? When it had you . . . hypnotized . . . you called it something in Welsh.'

'Ah,' Bran said. 'The original Nightmare, that thing. There is an old Christmas custom, in South Wales, of something called the *Mari Llwyd*, the Grey Mare – a procession goes through the streets, and a man dressed up in a white sheet carries the skull of a horse stuck upon a pole. He can make its jaws open and shut and pretend to bite people. And one Christmas when I was very small the Rowlands took us down there visiting, my Da and me, and I saw the *Mari Llwyd* and it frightened the lights out of me. Terrible. Screaming nightmares for weeks.' He looked up at Will with a weak smile. 'If anyone had really wanted to put me out of my head, they couldn't have chosen a better way.'

Will came back into the room, leaving the door open and sunlight shafting in. 'Was it the Dark? Hard to tell. One way or another it must have been. Some ancient haunting of the Lost Land, woken by –'

'By the Riders, maybe,' Bran said thoughtfully. 'The Riders, passing.' He reached for the saddlebag he had dropped on the rough slate floor, and looked inside. 'Hey – food! You hungry?'

'A bit,' Will said. Prowling round the cottage, he peered into the only other room, at the back, but decided from the smell and tatters of ancient hay that it had only ever been used for animals. In the main room, the walls were drystone, heavy chunks of rock and slate fitted together without mortar; there was no furniture of any kind, though a few rough shelves were attached to one wall. It was a far cry from the sophisticated elegance of the City. But as he ran his finger idly along a shelf Will came upon one unexpected object: a small mirror, set in a heavy oak frame carved with a pattern of leaping fish. He rubbed the dirt from the glass with his sleeve, and propped the mirror up on its shelf.

Bran came up behind him. 'Here, cup your hands, boy. Gwion's Health Food we have here – two apples and a big bag of hazelnuts. Shelled, mind you. Have some, they taste wonderful.' Cheerfully chewing, he looked up and saw Will staring at the mirror. He grimaced. '*Ach y fi!* Haven't you had enough mirrors for a while?'

Will scarcely heard. Looking at Bran's reflection in the mirror, he could see another familiar face behind him.

'Merriman!' he cried joyously, whirling round.

But behind him he found only Bran, mouth half-open as the cheerful enjoyment on his face changed to alarm. The room was empty, save for the two of them.

Will looked back at the mirror, and Merriman was still there. The shadowed eyes in the angular face stared at him, from behind Bran's puzzled reflected head.

'I am here,' said Merriman to him out of the mirror. His face was drawn and anxious. 'With you and yet not with you, and I must tell you that Bran can neither see nor hear me, since he is not yet grown to power . . . I am not allowed to come to you, Will, or even speak in the ways of the Old Ones. As Gwion told you, I had only one moment in which to pass through the Law of the Lost Land, and just as that moment came, the craft of the Dark caught me back to another time. But we have this crack of an instant. You do well. Be confident. There is nothing you cannot do now, if you try.'

'Oh dear,' Will said. His voice sounded to him small and lost, and suddenly he felt small and lost indeed.

'What's the matter?' Bran said, perplexed.

Will did not hear him. 'Merriman, are the others all right?'

'Yes,' Merriman said sombrely. 'In danger – but all right for now.'

A panic of loneliness fluttered at the back of Will's mind, yet somehow the memory of the destruction of the nightmare horse helped to keep it at bay. 'What must we do?' he said.

Bran was standing very still, staring at him in the mirror without a word.

'Remember the Lady's words, as you have done.' There was trust in Merriman's reflected face. 'Go on now, and take care to remember other things you have been told, there in the Lost Land. You can do no more than your best. And remember one thing from me, Will – you may trust Gwion with your lives. As once long ago I trusted him with mine.' An affectionate warmth deepened his voice. He gave Will one last hard look. 'The Light will carry you, once you return with the sword. Go well, Old One,' he said.

Then he was gone.

Will turned aside from the mirror, letting out a long breath.

Bran said in a whisper, 'Was he here? Has he gone?'

'Yes.'

'Why couldn't I see him? Where was he?'

'In the mirror.'

'In the *mirror*!' Bran looked at it fearfully. Glancing down, he found the bag of nuts forgotten in his hands, and thrust it at Will. 'Here. Eat. What did Merriman say?'

Suddenly hungry, Will stuffed his mouth with hazelnuts. 'That it's certain he can't come to the Lost Land,' he said, muffled. 'That we have to go on alone. To remember things we've been told – like that, he must mean.' He pointed to the writing over the cottage door. 'And – that we can trust Gwion.'

'We knew that already,' Bran said.

'Yes.' Will thought of the lean figure with the strong grey-bearded face and the brilliant smile. 'I wonder who Gwion is? And what he is . . .'

'He is a maker,' Bran said unexpectedly.

Will paused in his chewing. 'A what?'

'He is a bard, I would bet. He has the callouses from the harp on his fingertips. But mostly it was the way he spoke of the makers, of all kinds, when he was telling us the king's story. With love . . .'

'And he and Merriman must have gone through great danger together, once . . . Well, I suppose we shall find out sometime. Here –' Will handed over the bag of nuts. 'You have the rest. They *are* good. Did you say there were apples?'

'One each.' Bran passed one over, and began rolling up the saddlebag.

Will went to the doorway, biting into his apple; it was small, hard and yellow, but astonishingly sweet and juicy. The heap of white bones lay dead and bleached in the sunlight; he tried not to look at it, but raised his gaze out to the Country.

'Bran! See how close we are!'

The sun was high in a blue sky flecked with puffy white clouds. Out over the rough pastureland, perhaps a mile away, a glittering tower rose from a clump of tall trees; the sunlight struck from it so brightly that its brilliance dazzled them.

Bran came out. They stood looking at the Castle for a long moment. Beyond it, the Lost Land ended in the flat shimmering horizon of the blue sea. Will turned from it for a last look at the low, spreading hawthorn tree that grew from the roof of the little house. He stared. The tree that had been covered in milky white blossom, the enchanted snowstorm to destroy the *Mari Llwyd*, was thick now with bright red berries, clustering along the branches, brilliant as flame.

Bran shook his head in wonder. Both he and Will wordlessly touched the sturdy stone wall of the cottage, in an instinctive grateful farewell. Then they set out on foot across the tussocky grass of the pasture, towards the glittering pointing tower.

And when they looked back once more at the little shielding house with the tree growing from its roof, they saw no house there at all, but only a thicket of clustering hawthorn bushes, red-berried, growing in the open field.

Caer Wydyr

Though they tried, they never found the road again. There was no sign anywhere of the golden horses; panic had taken them far away. So Will and Bran turned their faces towards the shining tower and tramped over the rough reedy grass of the pastureland, through clumps of gorse on the firm ground and soggy patches of marsh on lower land where the water still lay. All the Lost Land was low: a coastal plain, with the sweep of Cardigan Bay at their left hand and the mountains rising hazily purple-brown far inland, to the right. Somewhere ahead, Will realized, the River Dyfi must run, towards a mouth considerably further out to sea than the one he had known before. It was as though all the coast of their own time had been given an extra half-mile stretch on its seaward side.

'Or rather,' he said aloud, 'given back the land it lost.'

Bran looked at him with a half-smile of understanding. 'Except that it hasn't been lost yet, has it?' he said. 'Because we've gone back in time.'

Will said pensively, 'Have we?'

'Well of course we have!' Bran stared at him.

'I suppose so. Back, forward, forward, back.' Will's mind was drifting. He looked out to a sweep of yellow irises among the reeds of a boggy area they had been carefully skirting. 'Pretty, aren't they? Just like on the farm, near the river.'

'We must be getting near a river ourselves,' Bran said, eying him a little uncertainly. 'Very wet, it is. I'm parched.'

'Listen!' Will said. 'Can you hear running water?'

'Won't be any good to us even if it is – probably brackish,' Bran said, but he cocked his head to listen. Then he nodded. 'Yes. Up ahead. Past those trees.'

They went on. The bright tower loomed higher now, though almost obscured by trees. They could see that it was topped by a banded dome of crystal and gold, exactly like the dome of the king's palace in the city. There was even an identical golden arrow at the very top, pointing out at the sea.

Then they were among a group of scrubby willow trees, with the sound of water growing, growing, and suddenly they came upon a reed-fringed stream, moving curiously fast for water on such flat land. Curving round to meet them, it seemed to flow from the direction of the City out to join the River Dyfi on its way to the sea. The water looked clear and cool.

'I'm *thirsty*!' Bran said. 'Cross your fingers.' He dipped one hand in the water and tasted; then made a horrible face.

Will groaned in disappointment. 'Salt?'

'No,' Bran said, expressionless. 'It's perfectly good.' He dodged Will's grinning lunge and they both stretched out on the grassy riverbank and drank thirstily, splashing their hot faces until their hair was wet and dripping. In a gentle patch of water on the lee side of a rock Will caught sight of Bran's reflection, and was held by it. Only the glint of the tawny eyes was properly like Bran, for the reflected face was darkened by shade and the wet hair seemed streaked dark and light. Yet somehow Will felt a strange flash of recognition of the whole changed image. He said sharply, 'I've seen you look like that before, somewhere.'

'Of course you've seen me before,' Bran said lazily. He put down his head and blew bubbles into the water, breaking the reflection. The water rippled into a hundred different surfaces, glinting, whirling; there seemed all at once a great deal of white in the pattern. Some small warning note rang in Will's mind. He rolled over, and saw against the sky, standing over them, the hooded White Rider on his white horse.

Bran brought his head out of the water, spluttering, pulling a green strand of weed from his mouth. He rubbed the water from his eyes, looked up – and was suddenly very still.

The White Rider looked down at Will with bright eyes set in a dim white face shadowed by the hood. 'Where is your master, Old One?' The voice was soft and sibilant and puzzlingly familiar, though they knew they had not heard it before.

Will said shortly, 'He is not here. As you know.'

The White Rider's smile glinted. 'And he told you no doubt that something had prevented him from coming, and you were simple enough to believe him. The Lord Merriman is more shrewd than you, Old One. He knows the danger that is here, and takes care not to be exposed to it.'

Will lay back deliberately on his elbows. 'And you are more than simple, if you think to afflict me with such talk. The Dark must be in a sad way, to use the tricks of idiots.'

The White Rider's back straightened; he seemed indefinably more dangerous than before. 'Go back,' said the soft hissing voice coldly. 'Go back, while you still can.'

'You cannot make us go,' Will said.

'No,' said the White Rider. 'But we can make you wish you had never come. Especially . . .' his gleaming eyes flickered towards Bran . . . 'especially the white-haired boy.'

Will said softly, 'You know who he is, Rider. He has a right to a name.'

'He is not yet in his power,' the White Rider said, 'and until then he is nothing. And therefore he will be nothing forever, no more than a child of your century, for without your master you have no hope of gaining the sword. Go back, Old One, go back!' The soft voice rose to a nasal, ringing demand, and the white horse shifted uneasily. 'Go back,' the Rider said, 'and we will give you safe passage out of the Lost Land to your own time.'

The horse shifted again. Exclaiming in irritation, the White Rider gave rein and wheeled it round in a wide circle to calm its restlessness.

'Look!' Bran whispered. He was staring at the ground.

Will looked down. Under the high fierce sun, his shadow and Bran's lay short and stumpy together on the uneven grass; but as the White Rider and his horse curved back towards them, the grass beneath the four hooves lay bright and unshaded.

'Ah yes,' Will said softly. 'The Dark casts no shadow.'

The White Rider said, clear and confident, 'You will go back.'

Will stood up. 'We will not go back, Rider. We have come for the sword.'

'The sword is neither for us nor for you. We shall let you go, in safety, and the sword will stay with its maker.'

'Its maker made it for the Light,' Will said, 'and when we come for it, he will give it to us. And we shall then indeed go away in safety, my lord, whether the Dark allows it or not.'

The lord in the white cloak looked down at him, his womanish mouth relaxed into a strange, unnerving sneer of relief. 'If that is what you expect from the Land,' he said, 'then you are such fools that we have nothing to fear from you.'

And without another word, he turned his horse's head and trotted away beside the curving river, out of sight behind the trees.

There was a silence. The water murmured.

Bran scrambled to his feet, looking uneasily after the Rider. 'What did he mean?'

'I don't know. But I didn't like it.' Will shivered suddenly. 'The Dark is all around us. Can you feel it?'

'A little,' Bran said. 'Not really, not the way you do. I feel just . . . this is a *sad* place.'

'Home of a sad king.' Will looked around. 'Should we follow the river?'

'Looks like it.' They could see the dome and the golden pointing arrow of the Castle reaching up out of the trees, past the curve round which the river disappeared.

The riverbank was grassy; there was no path, but no trees or bushes grew out to impede their way. The river itself remained narrow, perhaps twenty feet across, but its bed between the coarse grass of the banks grew broader and broader, a shining expanse of sand. It was clear golden sand now, without the murkiness of mud.

'Tide's low,' Bran said, seeing Will look at it. 'Like the Dyfi. That sand'll be covered when the tide starts coming in, and the river will grow twice its size. It's beginning to, already. Look.'

He pointed; Will saw the water eddying in the river, as the direction of its flow began to change. The main stream in the centre still flowed out to the sea, but at either side the tidal flow from the sea came creeping in.

'Couldn't drink from it now,' Bran said. 'Too salt.'

The river broadened as they walked farther, and the incoming tide grew more powerful; on the farther bank the trees were smaller and more sparse. They had an occasional glimpse of the broad estuary beyond the scrub and pasture, and the mountains rising far back. Then all at once they saw a square brown sail, and foaming towards them on the tidal current came a boat. Its sail bellied out at right angles to the mast between two sturdy wooden yards; almost at once these clattered to the deck, and the sail came down.

The boat swung towards the bank beside them. Will peered in astonishment at the figure furling the sail.

'It's Gwion!'

Gwion, lean and black-clad, leapt up nimbly into the bow with a line, and jumped ashore as the boat nudged the bank. He glanced at Will and Bran, his familiar smile breaking above the neat grey beard; then called something in Welsh over his shoulder to the boat. A chunky man with black hair and a red-brown face stood there at the long tiller behind the single stubby mast; it was a broad-beamed boat, not unlike a ship's lifeboat. The man called back to Gwion. Will looked enquiringly at Bran.

'About mooring the boat,' Bran said. 'And catching the tide, though I – *tafla 'r rhaff yna i mi*,' he said suddenly to Gwion, reaching for a second line thrown from the boat, and together they moored her fore and aft to a pair of trees, swaying in the river as the tide washed by.

'Well done to be here safe,' Gwion said, a hand pressing each on the shoulder. 'Now then, come on.' He set off at once along the riverbank, at a smart pace.

Will followed; he felt as though a great knot of tension had been loosed between his shoulder blades.

'Explain, explain,' said Bran, lengthening his stride to keep up. 'How did you get here? Why the boat? How did you know where to find us, and when?'

Gwion smiled at him. 'When you are in your full power, Bran Davies of Clwyd, you will be confident as Will here and not bother to ask such questions. I am simply here, because you will need me. And thus I break the law of the

Lost Land, which is to have no dealing with either Light or Dark when they are in conflict. As I shall go on breaking that law, I have no doubt, until the tail-end of Time. Gently, now . . .' His voice dropped and he slowed his pace, stretching both arms sideways to hold them back.

They had come to an end of the scattering of wind-curved oak and pine that fringed this edge of the river. Before them now was the Castle of the Lost Land, a shining tower rising over a circle of tall trees.

Gwion was suddenly sober; he dropped his arms, and stood for a moment as if he had forgotten Will, Bran, himself and everything except the sight of the lonely glittering tower there before him.

'*Caer Wydyr*,' he said softly, almost whispering. 'As beautiful as it has always been. And my great grieving king shut away inside never seeing its beauty. With indeed no one at all, in all the Lost Land, able to see its beauty except the Lords of the Dark.'

Will looked all around, restlessly. 'And they are everywhere, and yet not to be seen.'

'Everywhere,' Gwion said. 'Among the guardian trees. But they cannot harm the trees, just as they cannot touch the king or his castle.'

The great trees grew round the tower in an irregular circle, lapping it with their leaves and branches; it rose from them like an island from a green sea.

'Seven trees, the Lady said.' Bran turned to Will. 'Seven trees. Just as the seven Sleepers woke over Llyn Mwyngil, once before our eyes, to ride away into tomorrow.' The tawny eyes were glittering in his pale face; he stared all around, unafraid, as if in challenge, caught up for a moment in a feverish confidence Will had not seen before.

Will said slowly, 'But there were six Sleepers.'

'Seven there will be,' Bran said, 'seven at the end. And not then Sleepers by name, but Riders, like the Lords of the Dark.'

'Here is the first tree,' Gwion said. His voice was without expression, but Will felt he was deliberately turning the talk aside. Facing them, close to the river, was a crowded clump of slender trunks, green-barked, with broad round dancing leaves.

'*Y gwernen*,' Bran said. 'Alder. Growing with its feet wet, the way it does in our valley too, with John Rowlands cursing it up and down for a weed.'

Gwion broke three small twigs from an alder branch, taking each at the joint where it would not bend or fray. 'A weed-wood sometimes perhaps, but a wood that will neither split nor decay. The tree of fire, is alder. There is in it the power of fire to free the earth from water. And that we may need. Here.' He gave each of them a twig and went on, towards the broad sweeping canopy,

slender-branched, long-leafed, of a willow tree. Again he broke off three sprays
and held out two.

'Willow, the enchanter's tree,' Will said, his mind flickering a long way back
to a certain ancient book shown him by Merriman when he was learning how
to use the gifts of an Old One. *'Strong as a young lion, pliant as a loving woman,
and bitter to the taste, as all enchantment in the end must be.'* He smiled wrily at
Gwion. 'They taught me my trees once, a while ago.'

Gwion said quietly, 'So they did indeed. Tell me the next.'

'Birch,' said Will. A great knotted white tree rose before them, hard catkins
dancing from its long thin brown twigs. Beneath the fluttering green leaves it
was an old, old tree, with white-spotted scarlet toadstools growing between its
roots and the long self-healed split of an ancient wound bringing the first signs
of decay to its trunk.

Bran said in unthinking surprise, 'I never saw a birch tree out here before.'
Then he looked at Will and grinned, mocking himself. 'No – nor a great glass
tower either, nor a may-tree growing from a roof.'

'You say nothing foolish,' said Gwion mildly, giving them twigs from the
birch tree. 'In this my time it is warmer and drier here in Wales than in yours,
and we have forests of alder and birch and pine trees, where you have only oaks
and the foreign trees that will be brought in by new men. And those' – he
paused for an instant – 'not in quite the same place as these trees of my day.'

A kind of terror caught at Will's mind for a moment as he realized what
Gwion must mean; but the Welshman drew them swiftly on, past the big
birch tree, and suddenly the glass tower, Caer Wydyr, was facing them, visible
for the first time from bottom to top, and they saw that it rose not from the
ground, from the golden sand and green bank of the estuary, but from a great
jagged rock. The stone was unfamiliar; it was neither the spangled grey of
granite nor the grey-blue of slate, but a deep blue-black, studded here and there
with bright slabs of white quartz. And they saw now that the sides of the tower
itself were built too of a glassy rocklike quartz, white, translucent, with a
strange milky glow. Slits of windows were set into the circling walls, here and
there, and the surface was totally smooth.

'Is there no door?' Bran said.

Gwion gave no answer, but led them over the long coarse grass towards two
other full, massive trees. The first was not tall, but broad and spreading, with
the blunt rounded leaves and budding feathery nuts of half the hedges of
England and Wales.

'Hazel for healing,' Gwion said, taking three twigs.

'And for feeding starving travellers,' said Bran.

Gwion laughed. 'Were they good, then?'

'Marvellous. And the apples too.'

Will said remembering, 'Apple is another of the trees.'

'But first, holly.' Gwion turned to a forbidding dark mound of a tree with a smooth grey trunk, its glossy dark green leaves sharp-spined on the lower branches and mild ovals above. He picked only the twigs with prickled leaves, and again handed them one each.

'And from the apple,' he said, smiling, 'you may take fruit as well. But I must be the one to pluck the twigs, from every tree.'

'Why?' Bran said, as they went on through the grass.

'Because otherwise,' Gwion said simply, 'the tree would cry out, and the law would come into force, by which neither Light nor Dark may make any move for their own ends within the Lost Land.' He paused for a moment, looking at them intently, fingering the neat dappled grey beard. His voice was grave. 'Make no mistake now, the Lost Land is not a gentle place. There is a hardness here, and an indifference to all emotions other than those belonging to the Land, that is another face of the beauty of the rose garden, and the skill of the craftsmen, the makers. Do not underestimate that.'

Bran said, 'But only the Dark really stands in our way.'

Gwion tilted his chin in a curious arrogant motion, yet with lines of pain clear about the mouth. He said quietly, 'Where do you think the *Mari Llwyd* was called from, to drive you out of your wits almost, Bran Davies? Who do you think devised the mirrored maze? What is it that faces you now in the untasted despair of the task that is almost impossible, the task of reaching the Lost King and his crystal sword? Do you think the Dark has much to do with all this? Oh no. Here the Dark is next to helpless, compared to the powers that belong to this place. It is the Lost Land that you pit yourself against here, with all to win or all to lose.'

'And that is the Wild Magic,' Will said slowly. 'Or something very close.'

'A form of it,' Gwion said. 'And more besides.'

Bran was standing uncertain, blinking at him. 'And you are part of it?'

'Ah,' Gwion said reflectively. 'I am a renegade part, going my own way. And although I love my own land most deeply, no good will come to me here.' He turned his broad smile on Bran suddenly like a beam of warmth, nodding ahead. 'Look there – go on, help yourself.'

An ancient, sprawling apple tree curved to the ground before them like a bent-backed ancient man; it was the only tree that grew low and spreading, and did not tower above their heads. Small yellow apples, and others smaller yet but bright green, studded its dark branches among the sparse leaves. Bran stared. 'Last year's apples as well as this year's?' He pulled off a yellow apple and bit into its juicy hardness.

Gwion chuckled. 'Two years they hang there sometimes. This is a pippin from a long time before your own, remember. There are many things in your own day that were not dreamed of, except by Old Ones, in this age when the Land was lost. But equally there were once other remarkable things that have vanished forever, lost with the Land.'

Will said gently, 'Forever?' He picked a yellow apple and held it up, his eyes smiling at Gwion.

Gwion looked back at him with a strange faraway look on his strong bearded face. 'For ever and ever, we say when we are young, or in our prayers. Twice, we say it, Old One, do we not? For ever and ever . . . so that a thing may be for ever, a life or a love or a quest, and yet begin again, and be for ever just as before. And any ending that may seem to come is not truly an ending, but an illusion. For Time does not die, Time has neither beginning nor end, and so nothing can end or die that has once had a place in Time.'

Bran stood turning his pale face from one to the other of them, chewing his apple, saying nothing.

Will said, 'And here we stand in a time long gone, that has not yet come. *Here.*'

Bran said suddenly, unexpectedly, 'I have been here before.'

'Yes,' Gwion said. 'You were born here. Among many trees like this one.'

Will glanced up quickly, but the white-haired boy said nothing more. Nor did Gwion, but moved forward and broke three blackish gnarled twigs from the old apple tree.

A voice came from behind their backs instead: a soft voice, with an unidentifiable accent to it. 'And the boy who was born here may well find himself staying here – for ever and ever.' A malicious mockery sharpened the tone, flicking like a whip. 'And that is a very long time, my friends, however metaphysical we may become about its meaning.'

Will turned slowly, deliberately, to face the tall dark-cloaked figure seated on the great black stallion. The Black Rider had put back his hood; the sunlight glinted on his thick chestnut hair, with its reddish glitter like the fur of a fox, and his bright eyes blazed like blue coals. Behind him, further away, other mounted figures stood silently waiting, riders all in black or all in white, one beside every tree and others scattered further back than Will could plainly see.

'There are no more warnings now, Old One,' the Black Rider said. 'Now it will be a matter of simple challenge, and threat. And of promise.'

Gwion said, his voice strong and deep, 'Dark promises have no force in this land, my lord.'

The Black Rider glanced down at him as he might have glanced at a dog, or a toddling child. He said contemptuously, 'It is wiser to fear the word of a Lord of the Dark than to heed that of a minstrel to a lost king.'

Premonition prickled like some fast-crawling creature all across Will's body; it sang in his mind: *Oh, oh, you will be sorry for that word* . . . But Gwion showed no hint of reaction; he simply moved forward, as if the Black Rider had not been there, and strode past him to the enormous sturdy oak tree in whose shade the dark figure stood.

'No leaf-collecting here, little player,' the Rider said mockingly. 'The king of trees is out of your reach, I think.'

The warning shudder ran through Will even more strongly. Gwion's face was impassive. Carefully and with dignity he reached up one lean brown arm to its full length; caught a jagged-leaved branch, snapped it, and broke it into three.

The Rider said sharply, 'I promise you, minstrel, that if you get into that tower, you will never come out again.' They saw the dreadful scar on the side of his face as he turned his head.

'You can do nothing to prevent us, my lord,' Will said. Drawing Bran with him, he went towards Gwion and the great oak.

The Black Rider relaxed suddenly, smiling. 'Oh, I have no need,' he said, and slowly he eased his marvellous night-black stallion to sidestep away so that there was a clear view of the rearing glass tower before Will and Bran.

Will stopped, with a groan of dismay that he could not hide. The Black Rider gave a high snickering laugh. It was all too plain now what he had meant.

The great door of Caer Wydyr was visible at last, high on the rocky base at the top of a steep rough-hewn flight of steps. But it was a door barred against entry by an enchantment Will could never have imagined. Before it, spinning so fast that it was like a bright disc, hung a gigantic wheel. There was no axle, nor any kind of support. The wheel hung there in the air, deadly, forbidding approach, flashing round and round with a speed that gave out a menacing hum.

Bran said in a whisper, '*No!*'

From the Lords of the Dark on their black and white horses, stirring among the trees, there came a rustling of mockery, of malice satisfied. The Black Rider laughed again, an unpleasant menacing sound.

Swinging round in hopeless confusion, Will caught Gwion's bright eyes gazing at him, holding him, gleaming over the strong face and the strange dark stripe of its grey beard. Saying: I must tell you but I cannot tell you – *think* –

And Will thought and suddenly knew

'Come on!'

Seizing Bran by the arm, he broke into a run and rushed up the steps of the great rock on which the tower stood, away from the mocking Dark, until he was on the top step, so close to the whirling wheel that it seemed likely to cut him in half. The humming shriek of its spinning filled their minds. Gwion was behind them, white teeth flashing in eager delight. Will bent to Bran's baffled, anxious face and said in his ear: 'And what last thing did the Lady say?'

He saw relief break like a wave, and heard the words choke out: '*Only the horn can stop the wheel –*'

And Will reached to his belt and took the little gleaming hunting-horn that hung there. He paused, drew in a deep breath, put back his head and blew a single long clear note, high and lovely, singing out like a harmonic over the terrible hum of the spinning sharp wheel. And the wheel spun down at once to a half, as if an immense force were stopping it, while a long howling shriek of rage rose from the Riders of the Dark below. Will and Bran had an instant to see that the wheel had four spokes, quartering the circle, before Gwion was urging the two of them in turn through the nearest quarter, and slipping through after them.

Gwion pressed the bunch of seven twigs that he held into Will's hand, and without looking at him Will knew now what to do. Seizing the twigs from Bran's hand too, so that he held all three bunches together, he reached out urgently through the spokes of the wheel, where a surge of darkness and fury and menace was streaming towards them up the steps to the tower. With all the force he could manage, he flung the twigs out into the Dark. An immense force like a soundless explosion swept outwards from the tower, and the great wheel began to spin again.

Faster and faster it whirled. The hum rose, the entrance was barred by spinning enchantment with the frustrated Dark screaming in shock and rage below, and Will and Bran and Gwion stood in a soft translucent brightness inside the glass tower of the Lost King.

The King of the Lost Land

They stood staring at one another. Outside the tower the fury of the Dark rose as if the whole world were roaring; Will hunched his shoulders instinctively, feeling the force of it like a blow.

And then suddenly, it was gone. The tumult dropped, vanished altogether; they could hear nothing at all but the faint hum of the wheel whirling outside. The abrupt change was more unnerving even than the noise had been.

'What are they doing?' Bran said. He was taut as a tight-wound spring; Will could see a muscle twitching at the side of his jaw.

'Nothing,' Will said, with a confidence that was not real. 'They can do nothing here. Forget them.' He stared round the square room, filling the length and breadth of the tower, into which they had just come. 'Look!'

Brightness was everywhere: a soft greenish light filtered through the quartz-like walls of the room. It could be a cave of ice, Will thought. But this was a cluttered, busy place, as if someone had left it in a hurry while preoccupied with some great complex matter. Piles of curling manuscript lay on the tables and shelves, and on the thick rush mat that covered the floor; against one wall an enormous heavy table was littered with strips of shining metal and chunks of glass and rock, red and white and greenish-blue, all among an array of delicate gleaming tools which reminded Will of the workshop behind his father's jewellery shop at home. Then his eye was caught by something high on the wall: a plain round shield, made of gleaming gold.

Gwion leapt light-footed up on to a table and took the shield down from the wall. He held it out.

'Take this, Will. Three shields, once in the days of his greatness, King Gwyddno made for the Light. Two of them were taken by the Light to places where danger might come, and the third they left here. I have never known why – but perhaps this moment now is why, and has been all along. Here.'

Will took the round gleaming thing and slid his arm through the holding-straps on the inner side. 'It's beautiful,' he said. 'And – so are the other two that he made. I have seen them, I think. In . . . other places. They have never been used.'

'Let us hope this one need not be used either,' Gwion said.

Bran said impatiently, 'Where is the king?' He was looking up at a curving wrought-iron staircase, wonderfully curlicued, which spiralled its way up to disappear through an opening in the high glassy ceiling of the room.

'Yes,' Gwion said. 'Up there. We shall go up, but you must let me lead. We shall come to certain rooms in which you will see no one, and at the last we shall come to the king.'

He set one hand on the curving rail of the staircase, and looked hard at Will. 'Where is the belt of Signs?'

'It is at the Battle of Mount Badon,' Will said wistfully. 'Where Merriman took it to the great king, for as much of the winning as can be achieved there. And it will be at the last encounter too, when the Lady comes and all the power of the Light is joined. But not until then. And then only if –' He stopped.

'Eirias,' Bran said, his voice tight. 'Eirias.'

Gwion said swiftly, 'Do not say the name yet! That must wait. Only in the sword's own presence may it be named by its name, inside this tower. Come.'

They climbed the spiralling staircase, up and up through rooms that were scattered with the impedimenta of living, of eating and sleeping, and yet had, too, the strange deserted look of places left abandoned for a long time. And then Will, last in line, came up to find Bran and Gwion standing silent in a great room unlike any that had gone before. The light filtering through these walls was not cool and icy-green, but dimmer, more subdued, for they stood now inside a great hemisphere, banded in gold and translucent glass so that Will knew it must be the domed top of the tower, from whose peak a golden arrow pointed out at the sea.

The dome was warm, its floor striped with the sunlight that slanted in through the banded roof; and yet it was a strangely gloomy place, bringing a heaviness to the senses. The room held only one square table, set to one side, a carved wooden screen, and a scattering of big high-backed chairs, as sturdy as if they were carved from solid blocks of wood.

'Gwion?' a voice said.

Soft echoes whispered round the dome. It was a husk of a voice, low and without strength. It came from a tall chair facing away from them on the far side of the dome; they could see nothing but the chair's back.

'I am here, my lord,' Gwion said. His eyes were warm, and there was love and patience in his voice, as if he spoke to a troubled child. 'And . . . and two from the Light are with me.'

There was a long pause, with no sound in it except the faint crying of a distant seagull outside the dome.

The voice said at last, cold and abrupt, 'You betray me. Send them away.'

Gwion crossed the room swiftly and dropped on one knee before the tall carved chair; in the bands of dim light through the roof they saw his lean brindle-bearded face upturned to the unseen king. He said, loving loyalty bright as a flame in his face, '*I betray you, my lord?*'

'No, no,' the voice said wearily. 'I know better. But you must send them away, minstrel. In that, *you* should know better.'

Will said impulsively, coming forward, 'But Majesty, the danger is too great.' He paused just behind the chair; he could see one thin hand lying limp on the chair-arm, wearing on one finger a great dark-stoned ring like Gwion's ring. He said, in as level a voice as he could manage, 'My lord, the Dark is rising, in its last great attempt to take control of the earth from men. And we of the Light cannot prevent that attempt unless we are armed with all the Things of Power made for our purpose. We have all of them but the last, the crystal sword, which long ago you made for us, my lord the king – and which now you guard.'

'I guard nothing,' the voice said listlessly. 'I exist merely.'

Will said, 'But the sword is here, as it has been always since its making.' He eyes were roving round the room in search as he spoke. 'We may not take it unless you give it to us. Give it to us now, Majesty, I beg you.'

'Leave me alone,' the voice said. 'Leave me alone.' It was full of an aching sadness that made Will long to give some comfort; but the urgency of his quest was louder yet in his mind.

'The sword is for the Light,' he said persistently, 'and to the Light it must go.' He was looking at a wonderfully carved wooden screen that stood against the slanting wall of the dome, near where the king sat. Was it there simply as a lovely object to be looked at, or to hide something else from view?

The voice said with dull petulance, 'You do not say "must" to me, Old One. If Old One is what you are. I have forgotten all such names.'

Behind Will, Bran said sharply, 'But we must have Eirias!'

The thin hand on the chair tightened briefly into life; the fingers curled, then fell back again. 'Gwion,' said the empty voice, 'I can do nothing for them. Send them away.'

Gwion still knelt, looking up, his face lined with concern. 'You are weary,' he said unhappily, dropping all ceremony. 'I wish you were not always alone.'

'Weary of life, minstrel. Weary of the world.' The voice was a winter leaf blown by the wind: withered, dry. 'No purpose, no savour. Time tosses my mind where it will. And my useless life is the empty cawing of a crow, and any talent I once may have had is dead. Let the toys that it made die with it.'

The slow words came from so deep a despair, like a black pit giving back no sound when a stone is dropped in, that the small hairs crawled on the back of Will's neck. It was like listening to a dead man speak.

Bran said clearly, coldly, 'You speak like the *Mari Llwyd*, not like a king.'

The fingers of the hand curled in again briefly, and then again lay limp. Into the voice crept the weary contempt of long, long experience faced with the blind ignorant vigour of hope. 'Boy, callow boy, do not speak to me of life that you have not lived. What do you know of the weight that drags down a king who has failed his people, an artist who has failed his gift? This life is a long cheat, full of promises that can never be kept, errors that can never be righted, omissions that can never be filled. I have forgotten as much of my life as I can manage to forget. Go away, so that I may be free to forget the rest.'

As Will stood, speechless, held by the dreadful deep self-loathing in the husky voice, Bran came up level with him. And all Will's senses shouted at him suddenly that a change had begun; that from this moment Bran would no longer be merely the strange albino boy with the tawny eyes, obscure in a North Wales valley where the villagers looked at him sideways and the children mocked his pale face and white hair.

'Gwyddno Garanhir,' Bran said in a quiet command as cold and hard as ice, with the Welshness very strong in his voice, 'I am the Pendragon, and the destiny of the Light is in my hands to be held or lost. I will not countenance despair. Eirias is my birthright, made by you at my father's bidding. Where is the crystal sword?'

Will stood trembling, his fingernails digging into his palms.

Very slowly, the figure in the chair leaned forward a little and turned towards them, and they saw the face of the king just as they had seen it in the rainbow over the fountain in the rose garden, a little and a long while before. It was unmistakable: a thin face with cheekbones high as wings and lines carved deep in the flesh by sadness. Great channels of despair slanted down from nose to jaw, and shadows lay round the eyes like dark mountain pools. The king glanced first at Will, and then he saw Bran. His face changed.

He sat there motionless, dark eyes staring. There was a long moment of silence, and then the king said, whispering, '*But it was a dream.*'

Gwion said softly, 'What was a dream, Majesty?'

The king turned his head to Gwion; there was a heart-breaking simplicity in him suddenly, like a small child telling a secret to a friend.

'I dream, endlessly, my minstrel,' he said. 'I live in my dreams – they are the only thing this emptiness has not touched. Oh sometimes they are black and dreadful, nightmares from the pit . . . But most of them are wonderful, full of happiness and lost joy, and delight in making and being. Without my dreams, I should have gone mad long ago.'

'Ah,' Gwion said wrily, 'that is true of many men in this world.'

'And I dreamed,' the king said, looking wonderingly again at Bran, 'of a white-headed boy who would come and bring both an end and a beginning. The son of a great father, with all his father's strength in him and more besides. And it seemed to me that I had known the father once, long ago – though I cannot tell where or when, through the mist the emptiness has put in my mind. The white-haired boy . . . there was no colour in him anywhere, in my dream. He had a white head, and white brows, and white lashes to his eyes, and he wore dark circles of glass to protect those eyes from the sun, but when the circles were taken away you could see that the eyes were enchanted, the golden eyes of an owl.'

He stood up, shakily supporting his thin frame on one hand against the chair. Gwion lunged forward to help, but the king raised his other hand.

'He came running,' he said, 'he came running to me across the room there, and the sunlight was in his white hair and he laughed at me, and it was the first music of that kind that this castle has heard for so long, so very long.' There was a softening in the grim-set features like a faint glimmer of sunshine in a cloud-grey sky. 'He brought an end, but a beginning. He took away the haunting of this place. He kneeled down before me, in my dream, and he said –'

Bran laughed softly; Will could feel all the angry tension fall away out of him. The white-haired boy took a few quick steps forward and knelt before the king, and said, smiling up at him, 'And he said, *There are five barriers to be broken to reach the crystal sword, and they are told in five lines that are written in letters of golden fire over the sword itself. Shall I tell you what they are?*'

The king stood looking down at him with a life waking in his eyes that had not been there before. 'And I said, *Yes, tell me.*'

'And when I have told you,' Bran was looking up into his eyes in a closeness like an embrace, no longer quoting now, 'then that will be a falling away of the fifth barrier, Majesty, is not that so? For we have come through four of them already – the words are witness. And if I can break open your despair, which is the tomb of all your hope, then will you let me take the sword?'

The king said, his eyes fast on Bran, 'Then it will be yours.'

Bran slowly stood up before him, and took a breath, and in the Welsh music of his voice the words came out as a lilting chant.

> 'I am the womb of every holt,
> I am the blaze on every hill,
> I am the queen of every hive,
> I am the shield for every head,
> I am the tomb of every hope –
> I *am Eirias!*'

And King Gwyddno let out a long, long sigh like the sound of a wave of the sea washing over sand, and with a sudden crash the carved wooden screen that stood against the wall of the dome fell apart in two pieces, and lay on the ground. And glowing in golden letters on the banded wall they saw the lines that Bran had just spoken aloud, clearly written, and below them on a slab of slate lay like a bright icicle a crystal sword.

The king moved slowly, stiffly, across the smooth rush-matted floor; on the back of the dark green surcoat he wore over his white robe they saw embroidered in gold the royal crest with its roses and leaping fish. King Gwyddno took the sword in his hand, and turned his melancholy drooping body towards them again. He ran one finger along the chased flat side of the sword blade, wonderingly, as if in disbelief that he could ever have made so lovely a thing. Then taking the sword by the cross-piece of its hilt, so that it hung pointing downwards, he held it out to Bran.

'Let the light go to the Light,' he said, 'and Eirias to its inheritor.'

Bran took the sword by the hilt, turning it carefully so that it pointed now straight upward. Instantly he seemed to Will to grow somehow a little more erect, more commanding; the sunlight blazed in his white hair.

Somewhere outside the tower, from far away, there came a long low rumbling like thunder.

The king said expressionlessly, 'Now let come what may.'

He put his hand up to his head suddenly and rubbed his brow. 'There was ... there was a scabbard. Gwion? I made a scabbard for the sword?'

Gwion's smile lit his face. 'You did, Majesty, of leather and of gold. And there must be a breaking of the emptiness, as you call it, in your mind – or you would not remember that.'

'It was . . .' The king's forehead creased, he closed his eyes as if in pain. Then abruptly he opened them again, pointing across the domed room to a plain chest of light-coloured wood, with the figure of a man riding a fish painted in blue on its side.

Gwion went to the chest, and put back the lid. He said after a moment, 'There are three things.' A strange note was in his voice, of some emotion Will could not comprehend.

The king said vaguely, 'Three?'

Gwion drew from the chest a scabbard and swordbelt of white leather set with strips of gold. 'To mask the blaze a little,' he said with a smile, holding it out to Bran.

'Bran,' Will said slowly, listening to deep faint stirrings within his mind. 'I think ... you should not put the sword into the scabbard yet, not for a moment.'

Bran, sword and scabbard in either hand, looked at him with raised eyebrows, and an arrogant tilt to his white head that had not been there before. Then he gave a quick shiver and was Bran again, and said merely, 'All right.'

Gwion said, still at the chest, 'And there is – this.' His voice shook, and his hand too, as he took out a small bright harp. He looked across the room at his king. 'Not a few moments ago, my lord, I was longing to have my harp that I left in the City, so that I could play for you as I did in the old days.'

The king smiled, lovingly. 'That too is your harp, minstrel. Long ago I made it for you, in the first days in the tower when I was struggling against despair, struggling still to work . . .' He shook his head, wondering. 'I had forgotten, it is so long . . . I had chosen to be alone, so that all others were barred from this place by the wheel, yet I missed you and your music so greatly that I made the harp. For my Gwion, for my Taliesin, for my player.'

'And I shall play it for you in a little,' Gwion said.

'You will find it in tune,' the king said, and his smile held an echo of the maker's pride in the thing made.

Gwion put down the harp and reached again into the chest; he brought out a small leather bag gathered at the neck by a cord. 'This is the third thing,' he said, 'but I do not know what it is.'

He pulled open the neck of the bag, and a stream of small blue-green stones tumbled out into his other hand, smooth, shiny, rounded as though by the sea. One of them fell to the floor; Will picked it up and rolled it round his palm, watching the pattern of colour in its sleek irregular shape.

The king glanced at the stones briefly. 'Pretty, but worthless,' he said. 'I do not remember them.'

'You meant to work with them once, perhaps.' Gwion poured the stones back into the bag; Will held out the one that had fallen.

Gwion smiled at him suddenly. 'Keep it,' he said lightly. He picked out another stone and held it to Bran. 'And one for you, Bran. Each of you should have a talisman. A piece of a dream to take away with you, from the Lost Land.'

The king said softly, vacantly, 'Lost . . . lost . . .'

The distant deep rumbling came again outside, louder than before. All at once the sunlight shafting in through the banded roof faded, and the dome seemed much darker.

Bran looked around. 'What is it?'

'It is the beginning,' the king said. His thin voice was stronger now, more alive as his face was more alive, and though the resigned acceptance in it was very plain, there was no hint now of the dreadful black emptiness of despair.

Will said, on instinct, 'We must not stay under this roof.'

Gwion sighed. He looked at Will with wry affection, and Will never afterwards forgot the look: the humorous wide mouth drawn almost into sadness by the lines of experience running down from nose to jaw; the bright eyes, smiling; the crisp curly grey hair, the odd dark stripe in the grey beard. He said to Gwion in his mind: *I like you.*

'Come,' Gwion said. With the harp in one crooked arm he went to a part of the curved wall that seemed no different from any other part, reached up, and with one strong pull slid a whole wedge-shaped section of it to one side. The opening gaped like a triangular door. Outside they saw the sky a dark, dark grey.

Gwion stepped out, down to a balcony. Following him, Will saw a golden balustrade, and realized that this too was identical with the balcony that ran round the dome of the Empty Palace, in the City. But as he looked out from the tower all thought dwindled away.

Westward over the sea, a gigantic bank of dark cloud was massing: heavy, mounded, yellowish-grey. It seemed to writhe, growing and swelling as if it were a live thing. Will's fingers curled tightly round the strap of the golden shield that he still held on one arm. Bran came out on to the balcony behind him, and last of all came the king: frail now, supporting himself on the side of the opening in the roof, breathing suddenly faster as though the keener outside air were something his lungs had not felt for a long, long time.

The low, distant rumbling still filled the air, coming in like a mist from the westward horizon, where the great clouds rolled. Yet it was not the rumbling of thunder; it was a deeper, more insistent sound, like nothing Will had heard before.

'Be ready,' Gwion said softly, behind him.

Will turned and found himself looking straight into the smile-creased dark eyes. He saw calm determination there, and self-possession, but beneath all else a flicker of dreadful blank fear.

'What is it?' he whispered.

Gwion took his harp and drew a series of soft beautiful arpeggios from the strings. He said, as lightly as if it were a casual joke, his eyes imploring Will to ignore the terror behind them, 'It is the death of the Lost Land, Old One. It must come, when the time comes.' His fingers began patterning the notes into a gentle melody, and the king, leaning against the shining wall of the dome, murmured with pleasure.

The rumbling from the western horizon rose. A wind blew against their cheeks, and stirred their hair: a strange warm wind. Will raised his head, sniffing; all at once the summer air seemed full of a smell of the sea, of salt and wet sand and green weed. The light was dying, the cloud spreading grey over the sky. He heard a faint sound like creaking over his head, and looked up sharply. On top of the dome the pointing golden arrow, still gleaming even in the murky light, was swinging gently round: turning, turning quite around, until it pointed inland, away from the sea. A brightness in the sky beyond it caught Will's eye, and he gasped, and saw that Bran was staring at it too.

Far away out there, on the far side of the Lost Land, over the roofs of the City still dimly visible in the dwindling light, sudden sprays of light were springing up like fountains, to blaze for a second and vanish again. Like bursting stars, fireworks leapt, splashing the dark sky with brilliant red, green, yellow, blue: erupting over the City in joyous arches of light. There was a wonderful unafraid gaiety in all the sudden brilliance, as if children were flinging blazing branches out from a fire into a looming wild night. Will found himself smiling and yet close to tears; and in the same moment he heard, very faintly over the low roar filling the world now from the west, the high joyous sound of many bells ringing, somewhere out there, somewhere in the City. Gwion softly shifted the tune and the time of his melody so that his harp chimed in with the bells, and Will breathed fast as he stood on the balcony looking all round at the livid menacing sky and the dark sea and the brilliant gay fireworks challenging both. He was filled with a wild exhilaration that was terror and delight in the contemptuous defiance they flung out to their doom.

Sea grew dark as sky; there was a new rumbling now as the waves grew, their angry tops visible far out, gleaming, throwing spray. The wind blew more strongly, whipping the king's thin hair across his face. Will put up his shield as a shelter. Gwion, still playing, moved back slowly towards the opening in the dome of the tower, moving so that the king moved before him, supported by the wall. And then with a great splitting flare of lightning the sky roared, and the sea seemed to cry out, and a huge wall of water came thundering towards them from the sea, over the sand and reedy marsh, swallowing trees and land and the lines of the river, spreading, swirling, wild. Bran gripped Will's arm with one hand, and Will saw, turning, that the sword Eirias was gleaming bluish-white as if from the inner heat of a fire.

In the dark sky over the City the fireworks suddenly ceased, and the sound of the bells became a long jangling confusion, wild over the lilt of Gwion's harp. Then they too abruptly stopped. But Gwion's music went on. The sea struck at the tower somewhere below; they felt it shake beneath their feet. Wave after wave came roaring, the sea rose higher, the king's light voice called out on the warm fierce wind, 'Lost! Lost!' And out of the raging sea came sailing impossibly towards them, slantwise down the great waves, the chunky boat with its black-haired captain and single tight-filled brown sail, and from his place at the tiller the sailor reached out an arm to Will and Bran, beckoning, the deck of his vessel almost level for a moment with the balcony of the tower.

'Go!' Gwion shouted to them; he stood leaning sideways, his shoulder supporting the failing king.

'Not without you!'

'I belong here!' They saw only the last flash of a smile over the shadowy bearded face. 'Go! Bran! Save Eirias!'

And the words hit Bran like a spur, and he seized Will and leapt with him into the boat tossing an arm's length away. The boat plunged down the side of a wave; for an instant they heard Gwion's harp sweet and faint through the thundering sea, until one single shattering blinding streak of brilliance came out of the sky and struck the tower, splitting the dome in two, and the golden arrow was driven from the roof as if it were suddenly a live malevolent thing and came hurtling over the waves down towards them. Out of an instinct not his own Will flung up the golden shield with both his arms, and the flashing arrow struck the shield and in a great flare of yellow light both vanished, flinging Will down on his back in the leaping boat.

His head rang, his eyes blurred. He saw Bran standing over him with the sword flaming blue in his hand, he heard the waves roar, he saw the lean dark face of the ferryman twisted with effort, as the man struggled to keep the boat heading away from harm. The world tossed and roared in a dark endless turmoil, with no count of time passing.

And then there was a lurch so violent that Will lost all consciousness, and when he opened his eyes he was in a world of grey light and soft sound, the gentle murmuring of small waves on a beach, and he and Bran were lying on a long stretch of sand, in a clear morning, with a whitish-blue sky overhead. The crystal sword gleamed white in Bran's hand, the scabbard lay at his side. The great beach reached far before them into the estuary of the River Dyfi; green sandhills glimmered at its far edge, and beyond over the mountains and the grey roofs of Aberdyfi came the first golden edge of the rising sun.

PART FOUR
The Midsummer Tree

Sunrise

Jane had gone out before five, from the sleeping hotel. She did not wake her brothers. Irrationally but strongly she felt that when Merriman had said, 'Be on the beach at sunrise,' he had meant the words particularly for her. The boys, she thought, could follow in their own time.

So she slipped out alone into the grey morning, and crossed the silent road and railway track, hearing only the surf a distant thunder on the beach beyond. A dozen startled rabbits bounded away from her as she crossed the railway, their white scuts bobbing. Now and then a sheep's deep call floated down from the mountain. The morning was colourless and cold; Jane shivered, in spite of her sweater, and ran over the rolling golf course towards the high dunes. Then she was climbing through long wiry marram grass, with the dew-darkened sand sifting cold through her sandals, until the last step brought her breathless to the top of the tallest dune and the world opened before her in a great sweep of brown sand and grey sea, its flat horizon dissolving into mist where the arms of Cardigan Bay embraced the sea and the sky.

Something lay at her feet on the crest of the dune; looking down, Jane found a small brown rabbit. Its eyes were open and unblinking; it was dead. When she stepped over it she saw with a shock that its stomach had been torn open and the guts ripped out, before the rest of the untouched furry body had been tossed casually aside.

Jane went on down the dune in long sliding steps, more slowly, wondering for the first time what she should expect to see when the sun rose.

She crossed the dry sand above highwater mark, scarred with the footprints of yesterday's holiday-makers and their dogs. Then feeling suddenly vulnerable she went on, out to the vast exposed sweep of sand that fills the Dyfi estuary at low water, and stretches for ten miles and more up the coast on either side. Nothing was before her but the grey sea and sky and the long soft-roaring line of the surf. Through the sandals her feet could feel the hard rippled pattern left on the sand by the waves.

Flocks of roosting gulls rose lazily as she reached the smooth wet sand nearer the sea. Dunlins swooped, piping. Round any tide-left heap of seaweed thousands of sand-hoppers busily leapt, a strange flurrying mist of movement in all the stillness. The record of other flurrying was written already on the hard sand: gouges and claw-marks and empty broken shells, where hungry herring gulls at dawn had seized any mollusc a fraction too slow at burrowing out of reach. Here and there an enormous jellyfish lay stranded, with great slashes torn out of the translucent flesh by the seagulls' greedy beaks. Out over the sea the birds coasted, peaceful, quiet. Jane shivered again.

She veered to the left and walked towards the great jutting corner of sand where the River Dyfi met the sea. A thin sheet of water spread rapidly towards her feet; the tide was coming in, advancing more than a foot every minute over these long flat sands. On the corner of the estuary Jane paused, isolated far out on the enormous beach, feeling small as a shellfish under the empty sky. She looked inland, to the village of Aberdyfi lying on the river, with the mountains rising on either side, and she saw that the sky over the huddle of grey slate roofs was pink and blue, mounded with reddish clouds. And then, behind Aberdyfi, the sun came up.

In a brilliant yellow-white glare the fierce globe rose out of the land, and Jane swung round again, back towards the sea. All the greyness had gone. Suddenly now the sea was blue, the curving wavetops shone a brilliant white; seagulls gleamed white in the air and in a long roosting line on the golden sandbar in the mouth of the river, where they had not even been visible before. Her shadow lay long and thin before her on the sand, reaching out to sea. Each shell had its own dark clear shadow now, each strand of weed, even the ripples of the sand. Only the mountains across the estuary were dark and obscure, vanishing into cloud; at their feet a long white arm of mist shrouded the river. Overhead in the blue sky high bars of cloud were moving fast inland, row after row, but the wind that she could feel rising down here, cold on her face, was blowing from the land out to the sea.

Now in the sunlight Jane saw clearly the small hieroglyphs written by the feet of birds all round her on the sand: the arrowhead footmarks of gulls, the scutter of sandpipers and turnstones. A black-backed gull swooped overhead, and its yelping, yodelling cry faded into the wind, a long laugh ending in a husky croak. A high piping came from the sea's edge. The water ran in faster,

faster, over the flat sand. All at once Jane too began to run, away from the sea, towards the sun. The clouds flew over her head faster than she, rushing eastward; yet into her face the rising wind blew, stronger and stronger, picking up the sand as it rose, in long streamers and trails. It blew into her eyes in a fine stinging mist; she ran more slowly, staggering against it, leaning into it, seeing only the flying streams of bright sand.

Voices called her name; she saw Simon and Barney rushing towards her from the dunes. She thought: *they came sooner than I expected* . . . But something drove her to ignore them, to run on; even as they came up level with her she flung herself forward, eastward into the wind, with the boys at her side.

And then they stumbled as ahead of them two figures took shape in the flying sand, against the brilliant sun, like apparitions in a golden mist. The bars of cloud overtook the sun and the blazing light died, all colour dropping away, and before them stood Will and Bran. And bright against his white sweater and jeans Bran carried a gleaming sword.

Barney's yell was pure triumphant delight. 'You've got it!'

'Hey!' said Simon, beaming.

Jane said weakly, 'Oh goodness. Are you all right?' Then she saw the sword. 'Oh Bran!'

The wind whistled softly past them on the beach, chill but more docile now, blowing gritty streamers of sand against their legs. Bran held out the sword toward them, slantwise, turning the two-edged blade so that even beneath the clouding sky its engraved surface glittered and danced. They saw that a thin core of gold ran down the centre of the crystal blade from the handle, a golden handle behind an ornate crosspiece hilt, inlaid with mother-of-pearl.

'Eirias,' Bran said. 'Yes, very beautiful.' He was staring at the sword through narrowed eyes; his dark glasses were gone, and without them his face looked oddly naked and very pale. He turned inland slowly, the sword in his hand turning as if it were leading him. 'Eirias, blazing. Sword of the sunrise.'

'Reaching to the sunrise,' Will said.

'That's right!' Bran looked at him quickly, in a kind of grateful relief. 'It does, it turns to the east, Will. It – pulls, like.' He pointed the sword high towards the glow in the cloud cover behind which the newly risen sun shone.

'The sword knows why it was made,' Will said. He looked deeply tired, Jane thought: drained, as though strength had run out of him – whereas Bran seemed full of new life, vibrant as a taut wire.

The world brightened and filled with sudden colour as the sun shone out for a moment through a gap in the cloud. The sword gleamed.

'Sheathe it, Bran!' Will said suddenly.

Bran nodded, as if the same quick wariness had struck his own mind, and they watched in astonishment as he seemed to mime the raising and thrusting of the sword into an imaginary scabbard on an imaginary sword belt at his side. But as he thrust the sword down, it disappeared.

Jane, staring with her mouth open, found Bran looking at her. 'Ah, Jenny,' he said softly. 'You can't see it now?'

She shook her head.

'So no other . . . ordinary person will either, I suppose,' Simon said.

Barney said, 'What about the Dark?'

Jane saw both Bran and Will glance up instinctively, warily, out at the sea. She turned, but saw only the golden bar and the white waves, and the blue sea creeping closer in over the long sands. She thought, *what's been happening to them?*

As if in answer Will said, 'There's too much to tell. But it's like a race, now.'

'To the east?' Bran said.

'To the east, where the sword leads us. A race against the rising.'

Simon said simply, 'What d'you want us to do?'

Will's straight brown hair was falling over his eyes; his round face was intent, concentrated, as if he were listening and speaking at the same time, repeating some inner voice. 'Go back,' he said, 'and you will find things . . . arranged so that other people will not get in the way. And you must do what is arranged.'

'By Great-Uncle Merry?' Barney said hopefully.

'Yes,' Will said.

The sunlight died again, the wind whispered. Far out at sea the clouds were thicker, darker now, massing.

'There's a storm-front building,' Simon said.

'Not building,' Bran said. 'Built, and on its way.'

'One thing,' Will said. 'This now is the hardest time of all, because anything may happen. You have seen the Dark at work, you three. You know that although it may not destroy you, it can put you in the way of destroying yourself. So – your own judgement is all that can keep you on the track.' He was looking at all three of them anxiously.

Simon said, 'We know.'

The wind was growing stronger; it began to tug at them again, lashing their legs and faces with sand. The clouds were solid over the place where the sun had disappeared, the light as cold and grey now as when Jane had first come down to the beach.

Sand whirled up in strange clouds from the dunes, flurrying, swirling, and suddenly there was a sound out of the gold-brown mist, a muffled thudding like the sound of a heart beating, but diffused all round them so they could not tell where it began. Jane saw Will's head go up stiff and alert, and Bran too turn in search like a questing dog; suddenly the two of them were standing back to back, covering each direction, watchful and protective. The thudding grew louder, closer, and Bran suddenly swept his arm up holding the sword Eirias, bright with a light of its own. But in the same moment the muffled sound was a thunder all around them, close, close, and out of the whirling sand came a white-robed figure galloping on a tall white horse. The White Rider sent his horse on one thundering pass beside them, the white hood hiding his face, white robe swirling, and at the last instant as they flinched away he leaned swiftly sideways from the saddle, sent Simon sprawling on the sand with one swinging blow, snatched Barney up into his grip, and disappeared.

The wind blew, the sand scurried and leapt, and there was no longer anyone there.

'Barney!' Jane's voice cracked. 'Barney! Will – where is he?'

Will's face was twisted with concern and an intent listening; he looked at her once, blindly, as if not sure who she was. Waving back over the dunes he said hoarsely, 'Go back – we will find him.' Then he was standing with Bran, each of them with one hand on the hilt of the crystal sword, Bran glancing sideways at him as if waiting for instruction; and Will said, '*Turn,*' and without letting go of the sword they disappeared in the blink of an eye as if they had never been there. All that Jane and Simon had was the dark ghost that is left inside the eye by a vanished bright light, for in the last moment they had seen blue-white flame blaze up and down the length of the sword.

'They'll bring him back,' Simon said huskily.

'Oh Simon! What can we do?'

'Nothing. Hope. Do what Will told us. Aaah!' Simon ducked his head, blinking. 'This damn sand!' And as if in retort the wind dropped suddenly down to nothing, and the whirling sand fell to the beach, to lie in utter stillness, with no sign at all of its manic blowing except the telltale little escarpment of sand sloping back from every exposed shell or pebble on the beach.

In silence they tramped back together towards the dunes.

Nothing took shape in Barney's mind but the whirling sense of speed, and then a dim growing awareness of restraint, of his hands tied before him, and a bandage over his eyes. Then rough hands were moving him, prodding him forward to stumble over stony ground. Once he fell, and cried out as his knee hit a rock; voices spoke impatiently in a strange guttural tongue, but after that a guiding hand was slipped beneath his arm.

He heard military-sounding commands, and the walking grew smoother; doors opened and closed, and then he was stopped and the covering pulled from his eyes. And Barney, blinking, found himself being studied by a weather-beaten dark-bearded face with bright dark eyes: wise eyes, deepset, that reminded him of Merriman. The man was leaning against a heavy wooden table; he wore trousers and jerkin of leather over a thick woollen shirt. Still gazing at Barney, eyes flicking from his face to his clothes and back again, he said something curtly in the guttural speech.

'I don't understand,' Barney said.

The man's face hardened a little. 'English indeed,' he said. 'The voice to match the hair. Have they reached such a pass that they must use children now as spies?'

Barney said nothing, since he felt he was spying indeed, peeping out of the corners of his eyes to discover where he might be. It was a low, dark room with wooden walls and floor and beamed roof; through a window he glimpsed outer walls of grey stone. Men who seemed to be soldiers stood grouped around; they wore only a kind of leathern armour over rough clothes, but each had a knife at his belt, and some carried bows as tall as themselves. They were looking at him with hostility, some with open hatred. Barney shivered suddenly, in fear, at the sight of one man's hand playing restlessly with his knife. He looked up desperately at the dark-eyed man.

'I'm not a spy, truly. I don't even know where I am. I was kidnapped.'

'Kidnapped?' The man frowned, uncomprehending.

'Stolen. Carried off.'

The dark eyes grew colder. 'Stolen, to be brought to my stronghold, in the one part of Wales where no Englishman even of my allies dares set foot? The Marcher Lords are foolish, and do many stupid things in their rivalries, but none is quite as stupid as that. Try again, boy, if you wish to save your life. I can see no reason yet why I should not listen to my men, who are anxious to hang you by the neck in the next five minutes, outside that door.'

Barney's throat was dry; he could scarcely swallow. He said again, whispering, 'I am not a spy.'

From the shadows behind the leader the man with the knife said something roughly, contemptuously, but another laid a hand on his arm and stepped forward, speaking a few soft words: an old man, with a heavily wrinkled brown face and wisping white hair and beard. He was looking closely at Barney.

Suddenly another soldier came hurrying into the room and spoke rapidly in the guttural tongue; the bearded leader let out an angry exclamation. He said a few brief words to the old man, nodding in Barney's direction, then swung preoccupied out of the room with men close around him. Only two soldiers remained, guarding the door.

'And where were you stolen from, boy?' The old man's voice was soft and lisping, with a heavy accent.

Barney said miserably, 'From – from a long way away.'

Bright eyes watched him sceptically through the wrinkles. 'I am Iolo Goch, bard to the Prince, and I know him well, boy. He has had bad news, and it will not help his mood. When he comes back I advise you to tell him the truth.'

'The Prince?' Barney said.

The old man looked at him coldly, as if Barney were questioning the title. 'Owain Glyndwr,' he said with chilly pride. 'Prince, indeed. Owain ap Gruffydd, Lord of Glyndyvrdwy and Sycharth, Yscoed and Gwynyoneth, and now in this great rebellion proclaimed Prince of Wales. And all Wales is with him against the English, and Henry Plantagenet cannot catch him, nor hold even his English castles here or the towns they are pleased to call English burghs. All Wales is rising.' A lilt came into his voice, as if he were singing. 'And the farmers have sold their cattle to buy arms, and the mothers have sent their sons to the mountains, to join Owain. The Welshmen who work in England have come home, bringing English weapons with them, and the Welsh scholars at Oxford and Cambridge have left their books, to join Owain. And we are winning. Wales has a leader again. And Englishmen will no longer own Welsh lands and despise and rule us from Westminster, for Owain ap Gruffydd will lead us to set ourselves free!'

Barney listened helplessly to the passion in the frail voice, his uneasiness growing. He felt very lonely and small.

The door crashed open, and Glyndwr was there again among his men, scowling, silent. He glanced from Barney to Iolo Goch; the old man shrugged.

'Listen to me now, boy,' said Glyndwr, his dark-bearded face grim. 'There is a comet in the sky these nights, to show my coming triumph, and on that sign I shall ride. Nothing shall stop me. Nothing – least of all the thought of tearing apart a spy from King Henry who refuses to tell his sending.' His voice rose a little, quivering with control. 'I have just heard that a new English army is camped the other side of Welshpool. You have one minute remaining to tell me who sent you into Wales, and whether that army knows I am here.'

Only one thought sang through the fear loud in Barney's head now: *He may belong to the Dark, don't talk, don't tell him who you are* . . .

He said, choking, 'No.'

The man shrugged. 'Very well. I have sent to speak once more with the one who brought you to me. The light-voiced one from Tywyn, with the white horse. And after that –'

He broke off, staring at the door, and as Barney turned his head the whirling seemed to be back, the speed and the turning, turning . . .

. . . and turning, turning, Will and Bran, each holding the gleaming crystal sword, found themselves suddenly still now. A heavy wooden door before them burst open, and inside in a low-roofed dark room they saw a group of armed men. One stood separate, a dark bearded man with an air of authority, and before him was Barney standing very small and tight-faced. Several of the men lunged forward in shouting confusion, and the bearded one snapped one sharp word and they fell back instantly like startled dogs, swift but reluctant, looking at their leader with an astonishment that was almost suspicion.

Will's senses as an Old One were vibrating like a harp-string. He stared at the man with the beard, and the man stared back for a moment and then gradually the grim lines of his face were relaxing, changing, becoming a smile. An unspoken greeting in the Old Speech came into Will's mind, and aloud the man said, in halting English, 'You are come to a wild time, Sign-seeker. But welcome, if my men do not take you for another English informer such as we have here.'

'Will,' Barney said huskily, 'he keeps telling me I'm a spy and they want to kill me. Do you know him?'

Will said slowly, 'Greetings, Owain Glyndwr.'

'The greatest Welshman of all.' Bran was gazing in awe at the bearded man. 'The only one ever to unite Wales against the English, through all the quarrelling and feuding.'

Glyndwr was looking at him with narrowed eyes. 'But you . . . you . . .' He glanced uncertainly at Will's blank expressionless face, and shook his head crossly. 'Ah no, nonsense. No place for dreams in my head, with the last and hardest battle waiting us. And the bloody English coming up like ants in spring.' He turned to Will, waving a hand at Barney. 'Is the boy with you, Old One?'

'Yes,' Will said.

'That explains much,' Glyndwr said. 'But not his stupidity in failing to tell me so.'

Barney said defensively, 'How was I to know you weren't part of the Dark?'

The Welshman put back his head with a curt incredulous laugh, but then straightened, looking with something like respect. 'Well. True. Not badly done. *Sais bach*. Take him now, Sign-seeker.' He reached out one strong arm and propelled Barney backwards as if he had been a toy. 'And go about your purposes in my land in peace, and I will give you any support you need.'

'There will be great need,' Will said grimly, 'if it is not already too late.' He pointed to the sword that Bran was already holding out before him, in wonder and alarm; the blade was flickering again with blue light, as it had done at the destruction of the Lost Land, as it had done at the rushing descent of the Dark that had carried Barney away.

Glyndwr said abruptly, 'The Dark. But this is my stronghold – there can be none of the Dark here.'

'There are many,' said a soft voice at the door. 'And by right, since you let the first of them in.'

'*Diawl!*' Glyndwr sprang upright, instinct pulling a dagger from his belt; for in the doorway, between two armed men frozen helplessly out of movement, stood the White Rider, a robed figure with eyes and teeth gleaming out of the shadows of the white hood.

'You sent for me, Owain of Gwynedd,' the Rider said.

'Sent for you?'

'*The light-voiced one from Tywyn, with the white horse*,' said the White Rider mockingly. 'Whom your men welcomed so warmly for the gift of a spying English boy.' The voice hardened. 'And who claims in return now another boy, of more significance, and with him the sword he carries.'

'You have no claim over me,' Bran said with contempt. 'The sword brings me into my power and out of your reach, in this time or any other.'

Owain Glyndwr looked at Bran, at Will, and back at Bran: at the white hair and the pale face with its tawny eyes, and the sword-blade flickering with blue flame.

'The sword is two-edged,' the White Rider said.

Bran said, 'The sword belongs to the Light.'

'The sword belongs to no one. It is in the possession of the Light only. Its power is the power of the Old Magic that made it.'

'Made it at the command of the Light,' Will said.

'And yet also the tomb of every hope,' said the Rider softly, masked still by the white hood. 'Do you not remember, Old One? It was written. And there was no word as to whose hopes should be entombed.'

'But they shall be your own!' Owain Glyndwr said suddenly, and he snapped some words in Welsh to his men and sprang towards the back wall of the room, reaching for something. Soldiers flung themselves at the white-robed form of the Rider. None managed to touch him; they fell sideways, backwards, colliding with some hard invisible wall, and the Rider lunged forward at Bran. But Bran swept the sword Eirias to and fro before him as if writing in the air, and the sword left a sheet of blue flame hanging and the Rider fell back with a shriek. Even as he moved he seemed to change, to multiply as if suddenly there were a crowd with him; but Owain was calling, urgently and Will dared not wait to see, but followed the rest through a doorway they had not seen before.

Then leather-clad Welsh soldiers were pushing them on to the backs of a string of sturdy grey mountain ponies, and past slate cliffs and stone walls and through green lanes they trotted swiftly and silently where Owain led. The roar and confusion of the Dark rose behind them, and with it the clash of swords and the song of arrows from long bows, and voices shouting in English as well as Welsh. Will said nothing, but he knew that another battle as well as their own was beginning there, the reason for the Dark's choice of this time for their new hostaging, and that Owain was not in the place where he must have ached to be.

Only when they reached a mountain path where the land rose very steeply, and Owain motioned them to dismount and to follow him on foot, did Will look openly back – and saw smoke rising from the grey roofs they had left, and flame leaping.

Owain said, bitterly, 'The Norman rides always on the back of the Dark, as the Saxon did, and the Dane.'

Barney said unhappily, 'And I'm all those things mixed up, I suppose. Norman and Anglo-Saxon *and* Dane.'

'In what century?' Glyndwr said, pausing to stare ahead up the mountain.

'The twentieth,' Barney said.

The Welshman stopped very still for a moment. He looked at Will. Will nodded.

'*Iesu mawr,*' Glyndwr said; then he smiled. 'If the Circle spreads that far forward, it is not so bad to find failure here, for a time. Until the last summoning of the Circle, outside all Time.' He looked down at Barney. 'No worry about your race, boy. Time changes the nature of them all, in the end.'

Bran said from above them, urgently, 'The Dark is coming!' In his hand Eirias was burning a brighter blue.

Owain looked down the mountain the way they had come, and his mouth tightened. Will turned too, and gasped; a sheet of white flame was moving steadily towards them up through the bracken, without sound or heat, remorseless in its pursuit of those it sought to destroy. A troop of Glyndwr's soldiers stood directly in its path.

'It is not so bad as it seems,' the Welsh leader said, watching Will's face. 'Glyndwr has the tricks of an Old One, be assured.' The white teeth flashed in his dark face, and he clapped Will on the shoulder, pushing him. 'Go,' he said, 'go up that path, and you shall shortly be where you are meant to be. Leave me to take the Dark on a dance into these hills. And if my men and I shall seem to be kept in these hills forever, that will not be such a bad thing, for it will prove to my people that the Lord of the Dark was wrong, and that hope does not lie dead in a tomb but is always alive for the hearts of men.'

He glanced at Bran and raised his dagger in a formal salute. '*Pob hwyl*, my brother,' he said gravely. Then he and his men were gone, darting back down the mountain, and Will led the way up the path on which he had been set. It wound between bleak points of grey rock, narrower and narrower, until they came to a sudden turn where the rock overhung the path and each of them had to bend his head to pass beneath a low natural arch. And at the moment when all three of them were in line, on that piece of the path which lay under the rock, there was a whirling and a turning of the air about them, and a long, strange, husky shrieking in their ears, and when the giddiness went out of their minds they were in a different place and a different time.

The Train

Simon and Jane had left the dunes and crossed the golf course, coming to the wire fence edging the railway track, when they heard the strange noise. It rang out over their heads on the wind: a clear startling metallic clang, like the single blow of a hammer on an anvil.

'What was that?' Jane was very jumpy still.

'Railway signal. Look,' Simon pointed to the lonely pole standing beside the track ahead. 'I never noticed it was there before.'

'Must be a train coming.'

Simon said slowly, 'But the signal's gone to "Stop".'

'Well, the train's already been by, then,' Jane said without interest. 'Oh Simon, I wish we knew what's happening to Barney!' Then she broke off, listening, as a long, shrieking, husky whistle came on the wind, from a long way off towards Tywyn. They were standing close to the railway fence now. The whistle came again, louder. There was a humming in the rails.

'There's the train coming now.'

'But such a funny noise –'

And they saw in the distance, against the growing grey clouds, a long plume of white smoke, and heard the rising roar, closer and closer, of a fast-moving train. Then it came into sight, round the distant bend, and grew clearer, rushing at them, and it was like no train they had ever seen there before.

Simon gave a great whoop of astonished joy. 'Steam!'

Almost at once there was a sudden hissing and groaning and scraping as the train came closer to the signal and the driver flung on his brakes; black smoke belched from the funnel of the enormous green locomotive harnessed to the long train – longer than any normally on that line, a dozen carriages or more, all gleaming as if new in two colours, chocolate brown below and a creamy almost-white above. The train slowed, slowed, its wheels screeching and whimpering on the track; the vast engine came slowly past Simon and Jane standing wide-eyed at the fence, and the driver and fireman, blue-overalled, dusty-faced, grinned and raised hands in greeting. With a last long whish of steam the train stopped, and stood still, hissing gently.

And in the first carriage, a door swung open and a tall figure stood in the doorway, with one hand outstretched, beckoning.

'Come on now! Over the fence, quickly!'

'Great-Uncle Merry!'

They clambered over the wire fence and Merriman hauled them one by one up into the train; from the level of the ground the door was almost as high as their heads. Merriman swung the door shut with a solid crash; they heard the clang of the signal again as its arm went down, and then the locomotive began to stir, a slow heavy chuffing rising in speed and sound, with the dunes slipping past outside, faster and faster, swaying, rocking, clickety-clacking, the wheels beginning to sing.

Jane choked suddenly and clutched at Merriman.

'Barney – they've taken Barney, Gumerry –'

He held her close for a moment. 'Quietly, gently now, Barney is where we are going.'

'Truly?'

'Truly.'

Merriman led them to the first compartment in the swaying train, its long plush seats quite empty. He closed the sliding glass door behind them, and they collapsed on to the padded cushions.

'That engine, Gumerry!' Simon, an expert railway-fancier, was lost in admiring wonder. 'King class, from the old Great Western, ages ago – and this old-fashioned carriage – I didn't think they even existed any more, outside a museum.'

'No,' Merriman said vaguely. Sitting there he looked the same rumpled figure who had wandered occasionally into their lives for as long as they could remember; his long bony frame wore a nondescript dark sweater and trousers, and his thick white hair was tousled. He was staring out of the window; the little compartment was suddenly dark, lit only by a dim yellow bulb in the ceiling, as the train dived into a succession of short tunnels and came out beyond Aberdyfi, running again along the river. A small station whisked by.

'Is it some special train?' Simon said. 'Not stopping at stations?'

'Where are we going?' said Jane.

'Not too far,' Merriman said. 'Not very far.'

Simon said abruptly, 'Will and Bran have the sword.'

'I know,' Merriman said. He smiled proudly. 'I know. Rest now a little, and wait. And – do not show surprise at meeting anyone on this train. No matter who it may be.'

Before they could wonder what he might mean, a figure stopped in the corridor outside their compartment. The windowed door slid open, and John Rowlands stood there, swaying with the motion of the train. He looked spruce and unfamiliar in a dark and rather baggy suit; he was staring at them in amazement.

'Good day, John Rowlands,' Merriman said.

'Well fancy that now,' John Rowlands said blankly. He smiled slowly at Jane and Simon, and nodded; then he looked at Merriman, a strange look, wary and puzzled. 'Funny places we do meet in,' he said.

Merriman gave an amiable shrug.

'Where are you going, Mr Rowlands?' Jane said.

John Rowlands grimaced. 'Shrewsbury, to the dentist. And for Blod to do a bit of shopping.'

The train's whistle shrieked, and another small station flashed by. They were deep in the hills now, travelling through cuttings, with little to be seen outside the windows but high grassy banks blurred by speed. In the train corridor someone approached John Rowlands; he straightened, standing back.

Simon said politely, 'Hallo, Mrs Rowlands.'

Jane heard the warm Welsh voice.

'Well here is a nice surprise then! I wondered who John was talking to. Not having seen anyone we knew get on the train at Tywyn.'

There was a faint question in the words, but Simon rode over it.

'Isn't it a marvellous train? Steam!'

'Just like in the old days,' John Rowlands said. 'Must be some sort of anniversary, revival, whatever. I thought I was back thirty years when she came into the station.'

'Won't you come and sit in here with us, Mrs Rowlands?' Jane said.

'That would be very nice.' Smiling, Blodwen Rowlands moved into the doorway, so that she could see Jane; her eyes flickered past to Merriman.

'Oh,' said Jane. 'Mrs Rowlands – this is our great-uncle, Professor Lyon.'

'*Sut 'dach chi?*' said Merriman's deep voice, expressionless.

'How do you do?' said Blodwen Rowlands, nodding, still smiling. She added, to Jane, 'I will just get my bag,' and disappeared along the corridor.

'I didn't know you spoke Welsh,' Simon said.

'On occasion,' Merriman said.

'Like a native,' said John Rowlands. He came into the compartment and sat down next to Simon. Two figures passed in the corridor, then another, without looking in.

'Is the train full?' Jane said, looking after the last retreating back.

'Filling up,' Merriman said.

Mrs Rowlands came back with her handbag and hesitated in the doorway.

'Would you like the corner?' said Jane automatically, moving up the seat towards Merriman.

'Thank you, my dear.' Blodwen Rowlands gave her the astonishing smile that made her face glow with warmth, and sat down next to her. 'And where are you all going?' she said.

Jane looked into her eyes, so friendly and close, and paused. A great sense of strangeness swept over her; there seemed to be no light in Blodwen Rowlands' eyes, as if they were not rounded but flat. She thought: *Don't be silly*; blinked, looked away and said, 'Great-Uncle Merry's taking us out for the day.'

'To the Marches,' Merriman said in the deep unemotional voice he used for strangers. 'The Border country. Where all the battles so often began.'

Blodwen Rowlands took some knitting from her bag, a bright red bundle, and said, 'Very nice.'

The train swayed and sang. A large man passed slowly in the corridor, paused, looked in, and gave a courteous half-bow towards Merriman. They all stared at him. He had indeed a striking appearance; his skin was very black and his thick hair snow-white. Merriman inclined his head gravely in return, and the man moved away. Jane became conscious of a rapid clicking sound; Mrs Rowlands had started knitting very fast.

Simon said in a fascinated hiss, 'Who was that?'

'An acquaintance of mine,' Merriman said.

Down the corridor in the same direction, limping, leaning on a stick, came an elderly lady in an elegant but old-fashioned coat, with a toque-like hat set at a dashing angle on her head and a certain wild wispiness about her pinned up grey hair. She nodded in at Merriman. 'Good day, Lyon,' she said in a resonant, imperious voice.

Merriman said gravely, 'Good day, madam,' and the lady's sharp eyes flickered over them all and then she was gone.

Four small boys ran past, laughing, clattering, boisterous.

'What weird clothes!' said Jane with interest, leaning to peer after them. 'Sort of tunics.'

The train swayed and lurched, roaring round a bend, and she sat back again rather suddenly.

Simon said thoughtfully, 'Some kind of uniform, maybe.'

Mrs Rowlands took out a second ball of wool from her bag, yellow, and began knitting it together with the red.

'A busy train,' John Rowlands said. 'If there were more like this they might not be talking about closing the line.'

Simon stood up, steadying himself against the door jamb. 'Excuse me a moment.'

'Certainly,' Merriman said. He began an amiable conversation with John Rowlands about the necessity for railway services, while Mrs Rowlands listened, rapidly knitting, and Jane watched the purple-brown sweep of the mountains and the close grassy banks alternately flashing by. Simon disappeared for a long time, then stuck his head in the door.

'Show you something,' he said casually to Jane.

She went out with him; he closed the door and drew her to the end of the corridor, where a locked door ended the coach.

'This is the front end of the train,' Simon said in a peculiar voice. 'There's nothing this side of our compartment.'

'So?' said Jane.

'So if you think about all those people who've been coming past –'

Jane gasped; it came out as a sort of hiccup. 'They came from this end! All of them! But they couldn't have!'

'But they did,' Simon said. 'And I bet you there'll be more after we go back. The train's pretty full already, as far as I went. With the most peculiar mixture of people, in all different clothes. All kinds and colours and shapes. It's like the United Nations.'

They looked at one another.

Jane said slowly, 'Better go back, I suppose.'

'Look normal,' Simon said. 'Concentrate.'

Jane was trying so hard to concentrate that she went past the door of their compartment to the next. A man sitting in the corner there facing her looked up as she approached, and smiled through the window a sudden warm broad smile of recognition. He was an oldish man with a round, weather-beaten face and wiry grey eyebrows; his hair fluffed out in a grey tonsure round a bald head.

'Captain Toms!' Jane said joyfully, and then she blinked, or the air seemed to blink, and there was no one there.

'What?' Simon said.

'I thought –' Jane said. 'I thought I saw someone we used to know.' She looked hard at the empty seat; there was nobody in the compartment at all. 'But – I didn't.'

'Normal, now,' Simon said. He opened the sliding door of their own compartment and they went back in.

They sat in silence, while voices eddied round them and Mrs Rowlands' needles furiously clicked. Jane leaned her head back, looking out of the window, letting the rhythm of the wheels carry her mind. They clattered and clacked, merging with the needles' sound; with a twitch of nightmare she felt they were chattering: *into the dark, into the dark, into the dark.*

Then all at once Jane's mouth was dry, and her fingers clutched at the seat. Like a mist she could see in the fields outside a group of horsemen riding, galloping, leaping hedges, and though the train was rushing at full speed yet they were riding as fast as the train . . .

In troops and streams they rode, some all in black and some in white. And as the massing grey clouds came rolling in from the west the horsemen were galloping now through the clouds, through the sky, as if the clouds were great grey mountains and hills.

Wide-eyed, Jane hardly dared move. She edged one hand along the seat towards Merriman, and before it reached him his own strong hand was holding hers for a moment.

'Don't be afraid, Jane,' he said in her ear. 'This is the Rising, yes, the last pursuit. And the danger will grow now. But they will not touch this time-train of ours, for we carry on it something of their own.'

The train, thundering, rocked furiously along the track. The compartment grew dim as the sky outside darkened with cloud and rushing figures; the rhythm of Mrs Rowlands' busy needles faltered, and Jane saw the bright colours waver as her fingers slowed. The sound of the train began to change; the beat of its wheels fell off, the pitch of its fast song dropped; there was a sharp muffled report under the wheels somewhere a little way ahead, and then another, and the train began gradually to slow down.

'Maroons!' John Rowlands said in astonishment. 'The old maroons going off, that they used to put on the track for fog warnings.' He looked out of the window. 'And indeed that sky is so grey it might well be fog, now.'

The brakes skirled at the train's wheels; the flying landscape slowed, and suddenly the whirling riders were lost in the cloud; grey cloud was everywhere, and swirling mist. Hissing, rattling, the train slowed to a crawl, and all at once a little station was slipping up to them outside the windows. Simon jumped up, pulling Jane out into the corridor; they peered out. The station seemed to be a single platform in the middle of nowhere, without a name, and only a single arch-like structure indefinite in the mist. Beyond, dimly visible through a gap in the cloud, a long hill rose on the horizon ahead. Then slowly, gradually, three vague forms emerged from the arch.

Simon stared at them. 'Quick! Jane, open the door!' He lunged past her and turned the long handle, thrusting the door outward, reaching down. And Bran and Will and Barney climbed into the train.

'*Oh!*' Jane said, quite unable to say anything else, and she gave Barney a quick hard hug, and to her surprise Barney hugged her back. The train began to move. In clouds and swirls the mist came swooping round the platform and the dim arch, as if all were dissolving into emptiness, and from the compartment behind them Blodwen Rowlands' musical voice said in pleasure, 'Well Bran, *cariad*, how lovely! Are the trials in Shrewsbury, then? John never said –'

'I was telling Blodwen yesterday,' John Rowlands' deep careful voice broke in, before Bran could speak, 'about you boys going to help Idris Jones ty-Bont with getting the sheep to the sheepdog trials. His turn to supply them for the heats, it is, having no dogs of his own entered this year. I think he is chairman, isn't it, Bran?'

'Yes,' Bran said smoothly, as they crowded into the compartment. 'And we had to pick up a few more sheep out here, so no more room for us on the lorry, and Mr Jones put us on the train. A surprise to see you, now.'

'And the little one going too, now there's fun for him,' said Mrs Rowlands, smiling at Barney as if it were the most natural thing in the world for him to be helping herd sheep.

Barney smiled dutifully back, said nothing, but slid into the space beside Simon. The train swayed and sang, rushing at full speed again; the mass of the long low hill was rising ahead now like a wall. The grey clouds swept overhead. Hollow-throated, Jane saw the riders again, crowds and streams of them, flying through the sky. Panic gripped her; where were they riding to, where was the train rushing, where –?

'Sit by me, lovely,' said Mrs Rowlands to Bran, an affectionate tug at his arm bringing him down abruptly to the seat between her and Jane. Hastily making room, Jane wondered if the sword were still in the scabbard unseen at Bran's side.

Will stood swaying in the doorway, one hand at either side of the doorframe. He said, looking at Merriman as if at a stranger, 'Many people on the train?'

'It is really quite full,' said Merriman with the same stiff politeness.

And suddenly the engine gave a great shriek, and the train dived under the hill. In one gulp a tunnel swallowed it, and darkness was all around, a low roaring close in their ears, the sulphurous train-smell filling the air they breathed. Jane had a quick glimpse of apprehension on Mrs Rowlands' pleasant face. Then she forgot it in the overwhelmingly vivid sense of the way they were driving into the earth, through the mountain, under tons and fathoms of rock, as the train's track carried them inexorably on.

Gradually she began to feel that they were no longer in a train at all, that the bounds of the small boxlike room in which they sat were beginning to fade. Everyone was there still; the figures sitting, and Will surveying them from what had been the doorway; but now a strange glow had begun all around them, as if it were their speed made visible, as if the glow itself were whirling them along. She felt that they were rushing through the earth, riding on some power of their own, and a great company of people with them, all flying helter-skelter eastward. The glow of light around them grew and grew, became bright; they were contained in brightness, as if they rode on a river of light.

Jane saw wonder and incomprehension on John Rowlands' strong weather-lined face. Blodwen Rowlands gave a sudden whimper of fear; she scrambled to her feet, dropping her knitting on the floor, and lurched over to sit by his side. Rowlands put a comforting arm around her, the support of long affection. 'There now, *cariad*,' he said. 'There now, don't be afraid. Just rest easy, and trust them. Will's Mr Merriman will keep us out of harm.'

But both Will and Merriman now, Jane saw in astonishment, were on their feet and standing before Blodwen Rowlands; both motionless, yet giving an impression of immense silent menace, the menace of accusation. Behind them, Bran stood up slowly, and with the same curious play-acting gesture that Jane remembered from the beach, he drew the invisible sword from the invisible scabbard at his side. And suddenly the sword was there, terrible, naked, gleaming, and the length of its crystal blade was flickering with blue fire.

Blodwen Rowlands shrank back, pressing against her husband's side.

'What is it?' said John Rowlands in angry distress, staring up at Merriman's silent towering form.

'Keep them away from me!' Mrs Rowlands cried. 'John!'

John Rowlands could not stand up, with the weight of her pressing him back, but he seemed to grow more upright as he stared up at them, accusing, reproachful.

'Leave her alone now, you people, whatever you are doing. What has she to do with your concerns? She is my wife and I will not have her frightened. Leave her alone!'

Bran stretched out the tip of the sword Eirias, with the blue flames dancing up and down all its length, and held it so that the tip was between Will and Merriman, pointing at Blodwen Rowlands' contorted face.

'Cowardly it is,' he said in a cold adult voice, 'to shelter behind those who love you, without giving love in return. Very clever, of course. Almost as clever as being in the right place to help the growing up of a strange pale boy out of the past – and making sure he never does or says or thinks anything without your knowing all about it.'

'What is the matter with you, Bran?' said John Rowlands in anguished appeal.

The brightness carried them on, singing like the train, hollow in the hill.

Merriman said in his deep voice, expressionless, 'She belongs to the Dark.'

'You're mad!' John Rowlands' hand tightened on his wife's arm.

'Our hostage,' Will said. 'As the White Rider of the Dark took Barney hostage thinking to get Bran and the sword in exchange. A hostage for our safe running, now.'

'Safe running!' Blodwen Rowlands said in a new soft voice, and laughed.

John Rowlands sat very still, and Jane winced at the horrified disbelief beginning to dawn in his eyes.

Mrs Rowlands' laughter was cold, and her voice was all at once oddly different, soft and sibilant but with a new force behind it. Jane could not believe that it was coming from the familiar warm friendly face she could still see.

'Safe running!' said the voice, laughing. 'You run to your destruction, all of you, and the sword will be no saviour. The Dark is massed and waiting, with your hostage here to guide it. Risen and waiting, Lyon, Stanton, Pendragon, risen and waiting. And not all your Things of Power will help you to the tree, when you rush out of the earth in a moment now and the Dark force falls upon you.'

She stood up, John Rowlands' hand dropping limp away from her, to lie on the seat like a discarded glove while he sat there appalled and staring. She seemed to Jane taller, gleaming in the misty brightness with a light of her own. Deliberately Blodwen Rowlands moved towards the point of the sword Eirias, and Bran slowly put up the sword, letting the point rise so that it would not touch her, and Will and Merriman moved aside.

'Eirias may not destroy the Lords of the Dark,' Blodwen Rowlands said triumphantly.

'None but the Dark may destroy the Dark,' Will said. 'That is a part of the law that we have not forgotten.'

Merriman took one step forward. Suddenly he was the focus of everything around them; of all the Six, of all the power and intention of the Light driving, driving through the stone and the land towards its mysterious goal. He stood tall in the brightness, his white hair gleaming above the long cloak of dark blue that he wore now, and he raised one arm and pointed at Blodwen Rowlands.

'The Light throws you from this stream of Time,' he said, his voice ringing as the song of the train had rung through the hollow land. 'We drive you before us. Out! Out! And save yourself as best you can, when you fly forth ahead of this great progress, and the terrible force of your Dark falls upon you thinking to ambush the Light.'

Blodwen Rowlands gave a thin cry of rage, the sound of it clutching Jane by the throat with horror; and she seemed to spin round, and change, and whirl away into the dark space around them as a white-robed form on a galloping white horse. Leaping high, caught up in fury and fear, the White Rider rose out of the brightness in which they travelled and was gone, ahead of them, into a misty darkness where nothing could be seen.

The River

The great formless vehicle of the Light rushed on through the mountain as if it were a vessel carried along by an underground river. John Rowlands sat still and silent with a face like stone, and they did not look at him for more than an instant; it was not bearable.

At last Jane said, '*The tree*, Gumerry? What did she mean? She said, *Not all your Things of Power will help you to the tree.*'

Merriman stood tall and imposing in his dark cloak, its hood falling like a cowl over his neck. His white hair gleamed in the brightness all around, and so did Bran's beside him; they looked like two figures from some unknown race.

'The midsummer tree, in the Chiltern Hills of England,' Merriman said. 'The tree of life, the pillar of the world . . . Once every seven hundred years it may be seen in this land, and on it the mistletoe that will bear its silver blossom on that one day. And whoever shall cut the blossom, at the moment when it opens fully from the bud, shall turn events and have the right to command the

Old Magic and the Wild Magic, to drive all rival powers out of the world and out of Time.'

Barney said, almost whispering, 'And we're going to the tree?'

'That is where we are going,' Merriman said. 'And so is the Dark, following the path it has been planning all along, to make the final moment of its last and greatest rising the moment when the silver is on the tree.'

'But how can you be sure we shall cut the blossom, and not the Dark?' Jane could see nothing but the rushing brightness all around them, but for an instant she had a fierce image of the grey sky filled with riding Lords of the Dark, with Blodwen Rowlands, the White Rider, laughing long cold laughter at their head.

'We have the sword Eirias,' Merriman said, 'and they do not. And although it is two-edged and may be possessed by either Light or Dark, yet it was indeed made at the command of the Light. If Bran can keep the sword safe, and if the Six and the Circle can keep Bran safe, then all will be well. *And where the midsummer tree grows tall*,' his voice deepened with the lilt of the verse, '*by Pendragon's sword the Dark shall fall.*'

Will glanced automatically at the crystal sword, glinting in Bran's hand. The blade was clear now, the blue flickering fire gone. But as he looked, it seemed to him that on the very point of the blade the dancing blue fire again began to grow – very faint and dim at first, but growing, creeping inch by inch up the blade towards the golden hilt. And the movement of the rushing river of light about them began to change; it became more pronounced, as though they were indeed tossing upon a river. They seemed to be in a boat, the six of them and John Rowlands; Will knew it even though he could see nothing tangible around them at all.

His eye came to Barney, and stopped, and he smiled to himself. The younger boy was sitting oblivious to anyone around him, grinning a private grin of pure pleasure in the sensations swirling through his mind. The fear put into him by Glyndwr's men had evaporated, and there was no ounce of nervousness in him now, but only wonder and astonishment and delight.

Barney looked up suddenly as if he knew Will was looking at him; the grin widened and he said, 'It's like the best kind of dream.'

'Yes it is,' said Will. 'But don't . . . relax into it. You can't trust what will happen.'

'I know,' Barney said equably. 'Honest. I know. But all the same . . . *woo!*' It was a head-back, beaming, yelping shout of joyful excitement, spontaneous and startling, and every face turned; their apprehensiveness faded for a moment, and even Merriman, stern for the first instant, laughed aloud. '*Yes!*' he said. 'We need that as much as the sword, Barney.'

And then suddenly they were out into the day, into grey skies with a watery sun trying in vain to break through thickening cloud, and they could see that their boat was a long high-prowed deckless vessel set with thwarts, and that there were other boats before and behind them of the same shape, filled with figures who could not properly be seen. The mist hovered about them again, and with it a wavering of the air like the tremor of heat, though there was no heat. Will heard a faint familiar music in the air, delicate and fleeting. He looked out at the water and saw glimmering wavelets and an indistinct shore, with green fields beyond, and the shadowy figures of men and horses. For an instant the mist parted, in drifting tatters, and he saw hills rising behind, and the smoke of fires, and an army gathered there waiting, rank after rank of men, many of them on horseback, on small sturdy muscular animals that looked as tough and dark and determined as the riders they bore. It was a cavalry armed with glinting swords, waiting, tense. Then the mist closed again and there was only grey-white space.

'Who are they?' Simon said hoarsely.

'You saw them, then?' Will glanced round; the three of them were grouped beside him, with Bran and Merriman standing remote in the bow of the boat, and John Rowlands a grim hunched figure in the stern.

'Who are they?' Jane said. All three Drews seemed deeply intent, staring vainly into the mist. Will could see Barney's hands convulsively opening and closing, as if longing to be put to use.

Sounds came out of the greyness suddenly, vague, confused, from every direction at once: the clash of weapons, the neighing of horses, the shouts and screams and triumphant yells of men fighting. Simon spun about, his face twisted with frustration. 'Oh where are they, what is it? *Will!*' It was a cry for help, pleading.

Merriman's deep voice said from the bow, with an ache of the same desperation, 'You may well yearn towards it. It is the first making and breaking of your land, this long-worked land so many centuries on the anvil. It is *Mons Badonicus*, the Battle of Badon, where the Dark comes rising and . . . *How goes the day?*' The voice rose into a searching shout, a question asked of no one visible, thrown at random into the grey mist.

And out of the mist as if in answer a long shape loomed: a boat longer and larger than their own, taking shape nearer the bank as they drifted towards it on the stream. It was decked with weapons, filled with armed men, with plain green flags flying at stem and stern; it seemed the boat of a general, rather than a king. But there was the bearing of a king in the figure at its prow: a square-shouldered man with sunburned face and clear blue eyes; brown hair streaked with grey, and a short grey beard. He wore a short blue-green cloak the colour of the sea, and beneath it armour like that of a Roman. And round his neck, half-hidden but glittering with a light like fire, he wore Will's linked circle of Signs.

He looked at Merriman, and raised a hand in triumphant salute. 'We go well, my lion. We have them, now, at last; they will go back to their own lairs and settle, and leave us to live in peace. For a while . . .'

He sighed. His bright eyes moved to Bran, and softened. 'Show me the sword, my son,' he said.

Bran had been gazing at him, unwavering, since the boat had first appeared. Now without a flicker of change in his intent gaze he drew himself upright, a slim pale figure with his colourless face and white hair, and raised the blue-flaming blade of Eirias in a formal salute.

'And still it flames for the Dark. Still the warning.' The words were another sigh.

Bran said fiercely, 'But in this time too we shall drive out the Dark, my lord. We shall come before them to the tree, and then drive them out and away, out of Time.'

'Of course. And I must return something that was brought to my aid, and that has served its purpose and must now serve yours.' He put back his cloak and lifted the linked Signs from around his neck: 'Take them, Sign-seeker. With my blessing.'

Will came to the edge of the boat and took the gleaming chain from the strong brown hands; he put it about his own neck, feeling the weight pull at his shoulders. 'Thank you, my lord.'

Mist whirled round the two boats on the grey river; lifted for a moment to give a glimpse of the crowded armada of shades behind and before; then fell again, leaving all indefinite and vague.

'The Circle is complete, but for the one,' Merriman said. 'And the Six are strong together.'

'Indeed they are, and all is well done.' The keen blue eyes flickered over Jane and Simon and Barney, standing silent and awed, and Arthur gave them a nod of greeting. But his head turned again to Bran, as if by compulsion, back to the pale vulnerable figure standing there holding the sword Eirias, his white hair sleek in the mist and the tawny eyes creased a little against the light.

'And when all is done, my son.' The voice was soft now. 'When all is done, will you sail with me in *Pridwen*, my ship? Will you come with me to the silver-circled castle at the back of the North Wind, where there is peace beneath the stars, and the apple orchards grow?'

'Yes,' said Bran. 'Oh yes!' His pale face was alight with joy and a kind of worship; Will thought, looking at him, that he had never seen him fully alive before.

'And it will be an easier rest than the last, and without end. Unlike the other.' Arthur looked away into the mist, his bearded face sorrowful, looking at the time past from which he spoke to them. 'For our great victory against the Dark at Badon does not last so very long. We British stay untroubled in our own parts of these islands, and the English peaceably in theirs, and the Pax Arturus thrives for a score of years. But then the Saxons come again, those bloody pirates, a trickle and then a flood, battering westward through our land, from Kent to Oxford, from Oxford to the Severn. And the last of the old world is destroyed, our cities and our bridges and our language. All vanishes, all dies.'

There was anguish in the voice now; it was a long aching lament. 'Lost, all lost . . . The savages bring in the Dark, and the servants of the Dark thrive. Our craftsmen and our builders leave, or die, and none replace them except to deck out barbaric kings. And on our roads, on the old ways, the green grass grows.'

'And men flee westward,' Merriman said gently, out of the bow of their vessel, 'to the last corners of the land where the old tongue lives, for a while. To those places where the Light waits always for the force of the Dark to ebb, so that the grandsons of the invaders may be gentled and tamed by the land their forefathers despoiled. And one of those fleeing men carries a golden chalice called a grail, that bears on its side the message by which a later time will be able better to withstand the last and most menacing rising of the Dark – when it will rise not through the spilling of blood but through the coldness in the hearts of men.'

Arthur bent his head in a kind of apology. The mist blew round him; he seemed fainter now, the sea-blue cloak less bright. 'True, true. And the grail is found, and all the other Things of Power, by the six of you, and the Light thus fortified so that all of us in the Circle may come to its aid at the end. I know, my lion. I do not forget the hope promised by the future, even though I weep for the pain suffered by my land here in the past.'

The river began to swing the boats apart; the sound of battle and of triumphant shouting rose again from the mists around them. Arthur's voice grew distant, rising in a last call.

'Sail the river. Sail on. I shall be with you in a little while.'

And the ship and its flags and armed men were gone into the bright mist, and instead a darkness came whirling around them, on both sides of the gleaming stream, a darkness as deep and vast as the sea, battering at their minds, rising, enveloping.

John Rowlands rose slowly to his feet in the stern of the boat where he had been silently sitting. Will could see him only as a vague shape; he could not tell how much Rowlands saw of what was happening.

Rowlands reached out an arm into the darkness, standing pressed against the gunwale of the boat, and with fear and longing in his voice he called out something in Welsh. And then he called, 'Blodwen! *Blodwen!*'

Will closed his eyes at the pain in the voice, and tried not to hear or think. But John Rowlands came stumbling up the boat towards them, his head turned for guide towards the blue-flaming blade of the sword in Bran's hand, and when he reached them he put out one hand and grasped Merriman by the shoulder.

Light glimmered round them as if they carried the moon in their vessel, sailing through clouds, yet the light came only from the sword, burning like a cold torch. John Rowlands said, taut with anguish, 'Was she always so? Always . . . from outside the earth, like yourself?' He was gazing at Merriman like a man begging for his life, pleading. 'Was not one part of it ever real?'

Merriman said unhappily, 'Real?' For the first time since Will had come to know him, his voice was without authority, seeking, lost. 'Real? When we live in your world as you do, John, those of the Light or those of the Dark, we feel and see and hear as you do. If you prick us, we bleed, if you tickle us, we laugh – only, if you poison us we do not die, and there are certain feelings and perceptions in us that are not in you. And these in the last resort have dominion over the others. Your life with your Blodwen was real, it existed, she felt it just like you. But . . . there was another more powerful side to her nature as well, of which you never had sight.'

John Rowlands flung out one arm and struck the side of the boat a fierce blow that his hand did not seem to feel. 'Lies!' The word was a shout. 'That is all it was, a deceiving, a pretending! Can you deny that? I have been living my life on a lie!'

'All right.' Merriman's broad shoulders drooped for a moment, then slowly straightened. His voice seemed to Will to hold a great weariness. 'I am sorry, John. Do you blame the Light? Would it have been less of a lie if you had never discovered the Dark?'

'The hell with both of them,' John Rowlands said bitterly. He stared coldly at Merriman, at Bran, at Will, and his voice rose in anger and misery. 'The hell with all of you. We were happy, before any of this. Why couldn't you leave us alone?'

And while the words rang in the air, to all of them on the boat a figure appeared immediately out of the whirling misty darkness as if riding on the echoes of the angry voice: a dark shape, riding. Each of them saw it in a different way, this towering figure, cloaked, the hood put back from the arrogant head.

Bran saw the Lord of the Dark who had hounded Will and himself through the Lost Land, in wild pursuit through the City, in wait beside the Castle, in roaring fury at their achieving of the sword.

Jane and Simon and Barney saw a figure they had hoped to forget, from days earlier in their lives when they had been caught up in a search for the grail of the Light: a black-haired, black-eyed man named Hastings, fierce and powerful, and in the end raging with the urge for revenge.

Will saw the Black Rider, riding his black stallion in a whirling cloudy turret of the Dark, with one side of his face turned away out of sight. He caught the glare of a blue eye beneath glinting chestnut hair, and the sweep of a robed arm as the Rider turned in his saddle, pointing at Bran. The tall horse reared up over them, hooves glinting, eyes white and wide. Beside him, Will saw Jane instinctively duck.

'A challenge, Merlion!' the Black Rider called. His voice was clear but faint, as if muffled by the surrounding dark. 'We claim there is no place for the Pendragon, the boy, in this flight and this quest. A challenge! He must go!'

Merriman swung round, turning his back in contemptuous dismissal. But the Rider did not move, but stayed by them, his spinning dark tower of cloud rushing with them down the misty river – yet moving gradually more slowly, slowly, just as the boat on which they themselves travelled, Will realized, was slowing now. Soon it was motionless, resting on the still water. For a moment there came a break in the misty darkness ahead, as if a watery sunlight were breaking through; they saw hints of green fields, of swelling green hillsides and the darker green of trees, all hung still with ragged mist so that nothing was properly distinct.

And then through the mist came flying a pair of swans, their great white wings beating the air so that the wind sang through the feathers. They flapped slowly overhead, now visible, now gone, now bright again, through the patches of mist, and then both dived and came awkwardly down, on either side of the boat, skidding into the river, settling, long necks taking back their peaceful graceful curve. And in the moment of raising his eyes from the two handsome birds, Will saw as if standing high on the prow of their boat the figure of the Lady.

She was neither old nor young, now, her beauty ageless: she stood a straight upright figure with the wind blowing round her the folds of a robe blue as an early morning sky. Will leapt forward, overjoyed, reaching out a hand in welcome. But the Lady's fine-boned face was grave; she looked at Will as if she did not properly see him, and then at Merriman, and then at Bran. Her gaze flickered over the others, with a hint of a pause for Jane, and then came back to Merriman.

'The challenge holds,' she said.

Will could not believe what he heard. There was no emotion in the musical voice; it stated merely, without expression but with utter finality. Merriman took one quick unthinking step forward and then stopped; Will, not daring to look up, could see the long fingers of one gnarled bony hand curve tight into a fist, the nails cutting into the palm.

'The challenge holds,' the Lady said again, a faint quiver in her voice. 'For the Dark has invoked the High Law against the Light, claiming that Bran ap Arthur has no rightful place in this part of Time, and may therefore not take the journey to the tree. That challenge is their right, and must be heard. For without the hearing, the High Magic will let nothing go further forward in this matter.'

The beauty of her face was a grave sadness, and she reached out one arm, graceful as a bird's wing in the falling folds of the blue robe, and pointed the five fingers of her hand towards Bran. For an instant a breeze blew on the still river, and there was a hint of a delicate music in the air; and then the blue light died out of the blade of Eirias, and in a strange slow movement without a sound the sword fell to the deck of the ship. And Bran stiffened and then stood motionless, upright, his arms at his sides, a slim dark-clad figure with the face almost as white now as the hair, caught out of movement as if out of all life. A misty brightness took shape and hovered all about him, like a cage of light, so that he was still in their company and yet kept separate.

The Lady looked out into space at the hovering figure of the Black Rider in the cloudy dark.

'Speak your challenge,' she said.

The Rising

The Black Rider said, 'We challenge the boy Bran, of Clwyd in the Dysynni valley in the kingdom of Gwynedd, called Bran Davies for his father in the world of his growing, called the Pendragon for his father the Pendragon in the world from which he came. We challenge his place in this business. He has not the right.'

'He has the right of birth,' Will said sharply.

'There lies the challenge, Old One. You shall hear.' The Black Rider could not now be seen; his voice came hollowly out of the dark turmoil beyond the mist. Will had the sudden sense of an endless army of unseen forms behind him, out there in the dark; he looked quickly away.

The Lady's clear voice said, overhead, 'Whom do you seek to judge the challenge, Lord of the Dark? For you have the right to choose, as the Light has the right to approve or deny your choice.'

There was a deliberate pause. All at once the Rider was visible again, a distinct figure; his hooded head turned toward Merriman.

'We choose the man, John Rowlands,' he said.

Merriman glanced down at Will; he said nothing, either aloud or in the silent speech of the Old Ones, but Will could feel his indecision. He was filled with the same vague suspicion himself – *what are they up to?* – but it fell back, like a wave that breaks over a rock, when he thought of John Rowlands and their long reasons for trusting his judgement.

Merriman nodded. He lifted his wild-haired white head. 'That is agreed.'

John Rowlands was paying them no attention. He stood in the middle of the boat, with Jane, Barney and Simon grouped beside him on a thwart as if they had drawn close for comfort, though for whose comfort Will would not have cared to tell. Rowlands was gazing at Bran, his lean, lined brown face tight with anxiety. His dark eyes flickered to the tranquil, gleaming form of the Lady and then back to the bright mist enclosing Bran. 'Bran *bach*,' he said unhappily, 'are you all right?'

But there was no answer, and instead the Lady turned her grave face to Rowlands and he was suddenly very still, looking up at her, a silent awkward figure with the dark formal suit sitting on his lithe frame as if it belonged to someone else.

'John Rowlands,' the cool, musical voice said, 'there will be things said to you now, by the Lords of the Dark and of the Light, and you must listen to each with good attention, and weigh in your own mind the merit of what is said by each. And then you must say which you think is in the right, without fear or favour. And the power of the High Magic, which is present in this place as it is everywhere in the universe, will put its seal on your decision.'

John Rowlands stood there, still looking at her. He seemed caught in awe, but there were spots of colour on his high cheek-bones, and the finely modelled mouth was set in a straight line. Very quietly, he said, '*Must?*'

Will flinched, and carefully did not look at the Lady; he heard Merriman hiss softly between his teeth.

But the Lady's voice grew quieter, more gentle.

'No, my friend. This matter holds no compulsion. We ask a favour of you, to make such a judgement. For in this world of men it is the fate of men which is at stake, in the long run, and no one but a man should have the judging of it. Have you not said as much yourself, to the Old Ones, here and elsewhere?'

John Rowlands turned and looked at Will, without expression. Then he said slowly, 'Very well.'

Suddenly Will was conscious of a crowding of the Old Ones, an immense array of shadowy presences, all around him and behind him on the still, misted river; hovering in the unseen vessels like their own that he had glimpsed, just as they had travelled across the miles and years of the island of Britain in the vehicle that had taken the appearance of a train. It was as if he heard the murmuring of a great crowd, as he had heard the whole Circle of the Old Ones gathered twice before in the course of his life; yet there was no sound, he knew, but the whispering of the wind in the trees that edged the river. Holding in his mind the sense of their attendance, and his awareness of Merriman's tall blue-robed form at his side, he looked hard and openly at the whirling black mist of the Dark as he had not dared look before. The voice of the Rider came strong and confident out of it.

'Judge then. You know that the boy Bran was born in a time long past, and brought into the future to grow there. His mother brought him, because she had once in her own time greatly deceived her lord and husband Arthur, and although the boy was his true son she feared that he would not believe that was so.'

John Rowlands said emptily, 'Men may be deceived indeed.'

'But men forgive,' the Rider said swiftly, smoothly. 'And the boy's father would have forgiven, and believed Guinevere, if he had had the chance. But a Lord of the Light took Guinevere through Time, at her asking, and so there was no chance and the boy was taken away.'

Merriman said, soft and deep, '*At her asking.*'

'But,' the Rider said, 'and mark this, John Rowlands – but, not to a *time* of her asking.'

Will felt a coldness creeping into his mind: a dreadful misgiving, like a tiny crack that grows in a great secure dike holding back the sea. Merriman's robe rustled, beside him.

The Rider's voice was quiet and confident. 'She came to the mountains of Gwynedd, with her child, without thought of the time to which she came. And a man of the twentieth century, called Owen Davies, fell in love with her, and took her and reared her child as his own when she vanished away again. But that century was not of her choosing. She went where the Lord of the Light took her, she did not care. But the Light had great care.'

Suddenly his voice rose, and became harsh and accusing. 'The Light chose, and made sure that Bran ap Arthur, Bran pen Dragon, came to this time to grow into the right place at the right moment for the working of the quest of the Light. Thus all the old prophecies have been fulfilled only by their manipulation of Time. And that is a twisting of the terms of the High Magic, and so we claim that the boy Bran, who is here only through the craft of the Light, should go back to the time in which he belongs.'

John Rowlands said thoughtfully, 'Send him back more than a thousand years? And what language were men speaking here then?'

'Latin,' Will said.

'He has very little Latin,' John Rowlands said, looking out at the dark mist beyond the river.

'You are frivolous,' the voice out of the darkness said, curtly. 'He may be taken out of time merely, as he is now, so long as he plays no part in this present matter.'

'Not frivolous,' John Rowlands said, softly still. 'I am simply wondering how a boy can be said to belong to a time whose language he does not even speak. Just wondering, sir, in order to judge.'

Merriman said, without moving from his place at the stern of the boat, 'Belonging. That is the answer to this challenge. Whether it was the boy's mother or the Light who chose the time into which he came to grow up, or whether the choice was random, nevertheless he has attached himself to that time. He has bound himself by love to those with whom he has lived there, most particularly Owen Davies his adopted father, and Davies' friend – John Rowlands.'

'Yes,' Rowlands said, looking up in the same swift anxiety as before to the strange cage of misty light in which, dimly, they could see Bran held motionless.

'Such loving bonds,' Merriman said, 'are outside the control even of the High Magic, for they are the strongest thing on all this earth.'

But then out of the darkness beside them, over the still water, from no direction that they could tell, a frightened voice cried urgently, 'John! John!'

John Rowlands' head jerked upright, wary and yet longing.

'That's Mrs Rowlands!' Jane whispered.

'Where is she?' Barney swung all round, for the voice had seemed to come out of the air.

'There!' Simon was pointing. His voice trailed away. 'There . . .'

They could see only her face, dimly lighted in the churning darkness beside the boat, and her hands, out-stretched. She was gazing imploringly at John Rowlands, and her voice was the soft warm voice they had known in the beginning, and it was full of fear.

'John, help me, help – I have no hand in all these things, I am possessed. There is a mind of the Dark that comes into my own, and then . . . I say things, and I do things, and I do not know what they are . . . John, we too have loving bonds of our own. *Shoni bach*, you must help, they say they will let me go free if you will help them!'

'Help . . . them?' John Rowlands seemed to speak with difficulty; his voice sounded slow and rusty.

'Set right the balance,' the Black Rider said curtly. 'Give us the proper decision, that the Light is not entitled to the help of the boy Bran. And we will leave the mind of your wife Blodwen Rowlands, and give her back to you.'

'Oh please, John?' Mrs Rowlands reached out her arms to him, and the appeal in her voice was so poignant that Jane, listening, could hardly bear to keep still. The things she had learned about Blodwen Rowlands vanished totally from her mind; she could hear only the unhappiness and yearning of one human being cut off from another.

'Possession.' There was the same odd creaking quality in John Rowlands' voice, as if he were forcing the words out. 'It is like the possession by demons, you mean, that they used to speak of in the old days?'

The Black Rider gave a low bubbling laugh, a cold sound.

Blodwen Rowlands said eagerly, 'Yes, yes, it is the same. It is the Dark taking over my mind and making me into something else while it is there. Oh John *cariad*, say what they want, so that we can go home to the cottage and be as happy again as we have been all these years. This is all a terrible dream – I want to go home.'

John Rowlands' fists clenched tight as the plaintive musical voice rose in appeal; he gazed at his wife's face long and closely. Turning, uncertain, he looked up at Merriman and Will, and last of all at the high remote form of the Lady, but each one of them looked back at him expressionless, without any sign of threat or appeal or advice. John Rowlands looked again at Blodwen – and suddenly Jane felt a hollow feeling of shock at the pit of her stomach, for the look that she saw on his face now was like a sad farewell for something that is forever gone.

His voice was low and gentle, and they could barely hear it over the soft whimpering of the breeze on the riverbank.

'I do not believe any power can possess the mind of a man or woman, Blod – or whatever your name should really be. I believe in God-given free will, you see. I think nothing is forced on us, except by other people like ourselves. I think our choices are our own. And you are not possessed therefore, you must be allied to the Dark because you have chosen to be – terrible though that is for me to believe after all these long years. Either that, or you are not human, wholly a creature of the Dark, a different creature whom I have never really known.'

The soft deep voice hung over the misty river, and for a moment there was no sound or movement anywhere, from the indistinct flotilla of the Light or the teeming black emptiness of the dark. Blodwen Rowlands' glimmering face was there still, and the towering figure of the Rider.

John Rowlands' deep whisper went on, as if he were speaking his thoughts to himself. 'And as to Bran, that is a matter of a boy whose choice at first was not his own, but who has lived his own life since then. Which is all that you can say of most of us, in the end. He has indeed made loving bonds for himself with his father – adopted father, if you like. And with me, and with the others who have watched him grow up on Clwyd Farm. Though not with my wife, as I had thought.' His voice husked to nothing, and he swallowed and was silent for a moment.

Jane was watching Blodwen Rowlands' face; she saw it begin gradually to harden. The longing dropped away like a mask, leaving indifference and a cold rage.

'If I am to judge,' John Rowlands said, 'then I judge that Bran Davies belongs to the time in which both he and I live our lives. And that since he is not separate, as I am, but has thrown in his lot with the Light and risked much for them – then there is no reason why he should not be free to help their cause. As . . . others . . . are free to help the Dark if they choose.'

He looked up at the Lady. 'There's my judgement, then.' His voice seemed deliberately rough and rural, as if he were trying to isolate himself.

The Lady said clearly, 'The High Magic confirms it, and thanks you, John Rowlands. And the Light accepts that this is the law.'

She turned a little towards the bank of the river, to the churning darkness behind the mist; the brightness seemed to grow around her, and her voice rose. 'And the Dark, Rider?'

The wind was rising, tugging at her long blue robe; somewhere far off, faint thunder rolled.

The Black Rider said in quiet fury, 'It is the law.' He came a little way out of his dark refuge, and put back his hood, and his blue eyes glinted in the scarred face. 'You are a fool, John Rowlands! To choose to destroy your home, for the sake of a nameless cause –'

'For the sake of a boy's life,' John Rowlands said.

'He was always a fool, always!' Blodwen Rowlands' voice came out of the darkness, strident, stronger than before; it was again the voice of the White Rider, and suddenly, listening, Will knew that he had always heard the likeness of the two but never thought to add them together, and he saw from Jane's face that she had in her mind the same fearful parallel.

The thunder rumbled again, closer.

'A soft one, *yn ffwl mawr* !' Blodwen Rowlands cried. 'A shepherd and a harp-player! Fool! Fool!' And her voice rose high into the whine of the rising wind and was carried away into the darkening sky. All around them the mist was darkening now, and the sky above was solid with clouds so dark a grey as to be nearly black.

But the Lady raised her arm and pointed the five fingers of her hand at Bran, where he stood motionless in his cage of bright mist. There was a hint of music in Will's ears, though he did not know if anyone else heard, and then Bran was standing there clear, with the sword Eirias in his hand, and the blade of the sword was flaming with cold blue light.

Bran raised Eirias in the air like a brand. Swelling behind him and all around, Will felt the company of the Light advancing, driving on, and he saw that their boat was moving again, the water lapping past the bow, choppier now, with small waves raised by the rising wind. He knew that the other vessels of their shadowy fleet were moving too. But at the same time the sky was growing darker, darker yet, filled with great billowing clouds.

The wind gusted suddenly higher; he saw the Lady's robe swirl round her slender form and Merriman's dark cloak billow out like a spinnaker over the bow. And then for an instant all light was blotted out around them, as with a roar the whirling tornado of the Dark rose into the sky, travelling over and before them, circling the horizon to collect its final strength.

Only one streak of light still glowed. Standing in the bow of their boat, Bran swept the crystal sword before him in a blue line cutting the air, and the dark mist parted in a ragged, widening gap. They saw green fields rising before them, and suddenly they were all standing on a smooth green slope, on grass, with the river no more than a distant murmur in their ears.

'Stay close, all Six,' Merriman said. He led them up the grassy slope. The chain of Signs rang musically round Will's neck. He could feel the myriad shadowy forms of the Circle all about them, shielding them, pressing them on. John Rowlands moved beside the Lady, blank-faced, as if in a trance. Thunder growled overhead.

Then the last of the mist blew away, and in the dim light beneath the lowering sky they saw a line of trees before them, a wood of beech trees capping a round chalk hill – and, gradually appearing on the slope in front of the wood, a single huge tree. It took shape under their eyes, a shadowy outline becoming steadily more solid and real; it rose and filled out and its broad leaves rustled and tossed in the wind. Its trunk was as thick as ten men, its branches spread wide as a house. It was an oak tree, more vast and ancient than any tree they had ever seen.

Overhead, lightning ripped one of the dark clouds, and the thunder came thumping at them like a huge fist.

Barney said, whispering, 'Silver on the tree . . . ?'

Bran pointed Eirias up into the tree, in a sweeping triumphant gesture. 'See, where the first branch divides – there!'

And through the swaying branches they could see the mistletoe, the strange invading clump of a different green than the green of the oak: the twining stems and the small leaves, growing upon the tree, glimmering a little with a light of their own. Will gazed at the plant and seemed to see it changing, flickering; he blinked in vain to make out something in the middle of the clump.

Merriman's dark cloak blew round him in the rising wind. 'There will be one spray of blossoms only,' he said, his deep voice rough with strain. 'And we shall see each bud break, and when every small bright flower on that spray is in bloom, only then do we cut the spray. Then, and not before and not afterwards, but only in that one moment, does the great spell have force. And in that moment too, he who cuts the mistletoe must be kept from attack by the Six, each with one of the Signs.'

He turned his deep-shadowed eyes on Will, and Will reached to his neck to take off the gold-linked circle of the Signs.

But before he could touch them, white lightning suddenly flashed far closer than before from the dark cloud-base overhead. Will saw Merriman's tall form stiffen, facing the great tree. He too turned, seeking the mistletoe, and saw all at once that a glint of light fierce as fire came from the middle of the strange green clump. The moment was coming; the first bud on the spray of the mistletoe flowers had broken into bloom.

And with it, the Dark came rising.

Will had never, by any enchantment, known what it would be like. Long afterwards, he thought that it must have been like what happens to a mind that goes instantly and totally mad. And worse, for here the world went mad. Like a soundless explosion the immense force of the Dark's power rocked everything round him, rocked his senses; he staggered, reaching blindly for support that was not there. The appearances of things ran wild; black seemed white, green seemed red; all flickering and throbbing as if the sun had swallowed the earth.

A great scarlet tree loomed over him against a sky of livid white; the others of the Six, flashing in and out of sight, were like negative images, blurred forms with black teeth and empty white eyes. The endless dull roar of thunder filled his ears and his mind; he felt sick and ill, cold and hot at once, his eyes closing to slits, a constriction growing in his throat.

Unable to move any limb, he saw through leaden eyelids that Simon and Jane and Barney had collapsed to the ground; moving with tremendous effort, as if held down by weights, they struggled in vain to get up. Darkness loomed over them; slowly turning his heavy head, Will saw in sick horror that half the sky, half the world, behind him was filled with the whirling black tornado of the Dark, spinning between cloud and earth, more vast than his senses could comprehend. He saw Bran, staggering, holding up a blue streak of flame as if for support. Bright blue, he thought, I've never seen a brighter blue, except the Lady's eyes. *The Lady, where is the Lady?* And he could not move to look for her, but crumpled to his knees while the world wove to and fro in his spinning gaze. It was only by simple accident that his feeble hand hit the circle of Signs hanging from his neck.

Then all at once he could see clearly, and wonder caught him as he saw. Down across the storming sky, cleaving the monstrous grey-black clouds, came six horsemen, riding. Three on either side they came, silvery-grey glinting figures on horses of the same strange half-colour: galloping, cloaks flying, with drawn swords in their hands. One of them wore a glinting circlet about his head, but Will could not clearly see his face.

'The Sleepers ride!' Bran called to him. Will saw him leaning back in an intent curve, staring upward, clear against the green grass with his white hair and blue-flaming outflung sword. 'The seven Sleepers, changed now to Riders, just as I said they would be!'

'But still I remember there were six Sleepers,' Will said softly to Merriman, so softly that he knew Bran could not hear. 'Six Sleepers, oldest of the old, that once we woke out of their long sleep beside the lake, with the golden harp.'

Merriman neither moved nor spoke, but stood looking at the terrible sky. And as Will gazed up at the wheeling Riders of the Light, a long brightness began to glow in the east. And like a white sun rising, another figure came leaping across the sky: a different rider of a different shape, like no shape ever born on the earth.

He was a tall man riding a brilliant white-gold horse, but his head was horned like the head of a stag, with shining antlers curving out in seven tines. As Will gazed, he raised his great head, yellow light flashing from tawny round eyes like the eyes of an owl, and he gave a call that was like the halloo a huntsman blows on the horn to call up hounds. And through the sky after him, belling and baying, came flowing an endless pack of huge ghostly white hounds, red-eared, red-eyed, fearsome creatures running inexorable on a trail no living power could turn. They milled round the feet of the Huntsman's horse, high up there in the sky, as he laughed dreadfully over them in delight of the chase; they thronged round the silver-grey horses of the Sleepers waiting restlessly to join their hunt.

And then the Huntsman in a wild shout gave the call to let loose the chase, and he and the ghost-grey swordsmen, seven riders, were leaping through the clouds with the Hounds of Doom flooding after them, red eyes burning, a thousand throats giving tongue like the whickering of migrant geese: the Wild Hunt, in full cry against the Dark for the last time.

The vast storm-cone of the Dark lashed and thrashed about the sky as if in agony, and its tip seemed to split away. A horrible flailing filled the sky, until with one last convulsive lunge that seemed to bring half the clouds in the heavens down to the earth, the huge tornado-like black pillar rushed away and upward, out into nowhere, with the Sleepers and the Wild Hunt in howling merciless pursuit.

But great Herne the Hunter reined in his white-gold mare, leaping high in the heavens with the force of her arrested speed, and he turned seeking through the torn and rushing clouds with his tawny wild eyes. And in sudden new terror Will saw what he sought, the peak of Dark power that would never flee: the two huge figures, indestructible now in their full power, of the Black Rider and the White Rider of the Dark, curving out of the sky on a long rushing lunge down to the grassy Chiltern hill and the enchanted tree.

Will heard Simon shout from beside the tree, the first sound any one of the Six had made in all their breathless watching, and he turned back to see flashing on the tree new small brilliant points of light as more buds on the green patch of mistletoe burst into their magical bloom. His hands went to his neck, in the same instant that he heard Merriman's silent cry of command in his mind, and he tore off the circle of Signs. High in the sky the Riders, grown now to huge size, came rushing closer towards the earth. Will shouted to Simon and Barney and Jane, '*Six Signs shall burn!* Take one for each, and circle the tree!'

They were at his side, eager, reaching, and in the gold-linked chain each Sign in turn came easily away from the rest as the gold seemed to melt and vanish like wax. Simon took the smooth black Sign of Iron and rushed with it to the tree, to stand against the gnarled enormous trunk holding it high in challenge; Jane followed with the gleaming Sign of Bronze, Barney with the rowan-born Sign of Wood. There they stood, brave and quivering, staring terrified at the monstrous Riders galloping headlong down from the high clouds, down to consume them. Swiftly Merriman joined them with the brilliant gold Sign of Fire, Bran holding the crystal Sign of Light with the Sword, to leave Will swinging round last of all with his back to the tree, holding up in defiance the glittering black flint Sign of Stone. And the Riders were upon them, with bright lightning and deep thunder that came from no cloud but out of the dark air; their huge horses reared up, screaming, lashing out with wild deadly hooves. Herne's great horned figure rode at the Dark Lords in attack from above, and the force of all the unseen shades of the Circle was holding, barring, wrestling them below, with the Lady as its shining focus, but the strain was near to breaking-point. And in a burst of brilliance, the last flower on the mistletoe burst into bloom.

Bran reached up, his white hair flying, swinging Eirias over his head to cut the spray; but with the Sign of Light in his left hand he had only one arm for the long crystal blade, and his balance would not hold. He cried out in desperation. The Black Rider's eyes blazed blue as sapphires and he lunged forward in triumph, straining to break through the strength of the Circle and reach the shining bloom with his own sword. But suddenly John Rowlands was at Bran's side, pale and grim; he seized the Sign of Light and thrust it out against the rearing attack, the shimmering crystal circle frail in his big brown hand.

And Bran, free now to use both arms, swung the glittering blade of the sword Eirias at the green mistletoe within the oak, and cut the stars of bright blossom from the tree. As the spray parted Merriman turned, tall and triumphant, and caught the blossom before it fell; he swept round, blue cloak billowing, and in a swift breathtaking movement flung it up into the sky. And the mistletoe blossom changed in that instant into a white bird, and the bird flew up into the sky and away, away through the broken white clouds scudding now across the blue, away into the world.

Each of the Signs held there in each of six hands blazed suddenly with a cold light like fire, too bright for eyes to watch, and with two mingling voices crying out in fear and despair the great rearing figures of the Black Rider and the White Rider of the Dark fell backwards out of Time and disappeared. And each of the six hands suddenly was empty, as each Sign burned with its cold fire into nothing and was gone.

One Goes Alone

They stood in silence about the tree, unable to speak.

High up where a last few tatters of storm cloud blew dark across the sun, Herne the antlered Hunter put back his fierce head and gave a long triumphant cry, the gathering call that is lifted up by the horn when the quarry is slain. His white mare leapt across the sky, whinnying high and clear like the singing of the wind on the hill, curving down to a place where a stream of high wind-blown cloud lay like a river across the sky.

Out and down the Hunter leapt, and in the very instant that he seemed to plunge into the river of the sky and disappear, instead they saw sailing out from that same point the great ship *Pridwen*, graceful and high-prowed, with the green standard of the Lord Arthur rippling out at bow and stern. Closer and closer she came, sailing on the wind, and among the Six beside the tree Will saw Bran slowly raise the sword Eirias and thrust it down into the scabbard visible now at his side. It was a strange reluctant gesture that Will could not interpret. He stared at his friend, at the pale face and the tawny eyes beneath the white hair, but he could see no expression there as Bran watched the long ship sail towards them, down the sky. He found himself reflecting instead, not for the first time, that Bran's golden eyes were curiously like those of the Wild Huntsman, Herne.

And then the ship *Pridwen* was upon them, and he was looking instead at the blue-grey eyes and weathered, brindle-bearded face of the leader-king, Arthur.

Arthur was looking past him, at the fragile slim blue-robed figure of the Lady, standing a little apart from them all. He stepped from the prow of the boat where he stood, and down to the land, and he knelt on one knee before the Lady and bent his head. 'Madam,' he said, his voice as warm with the pleasure of living as when Will had first heard it, 'your boatman awaits.'

Will stood with his head singing in bewilderment, feeling the baffled awe of the three Drews beside him.

The Lady came forward to the boat, with a beckoning touch on Arthur's arm in the casual closeness of those who belong to the same family. 'It is done,' she said. Suddenly there was a deep weariness in the music of her voice, that spoke of great age in spite of the calm ageless beauty of her fine-boned face. 'Our task is accomplished, and we may leave the last and longest task to those who inherit this world and all its perilous beauty.'

She looked back at them all, and as if in farewell she smiled at Barney, at Simon and more lingeringly at Jane. Then she looked at John Rowlands, standing empty-eyed and stiff beside the broad oak tree, and she moved swiftly to him and took both his hands.

Rowlands looked at her, his dark Welsh face drawn down by lines at nose and mouth that had never seemed so marked before.

'John,' the Lady said softly. 'In all this great matter you have done more for your world than any of us, even before your courage at the end – for you could have retreated into an unseeing happiness of your own and yet gave it up. You are a good and honest man, and for a time now you must be an unhappy man. But – it is only for a time.' She released his hands, but still gazed commandingly into his eyes, and John Rowlands looked back at her without awe or subservience, and shrugged. He said nothing.

'You have made a hard choice,' the Lady said, 'and lost the pattern of your life thereby. I cannot give you back your Blodwen, that ambitious fallen figure. But I can give you another chance gentler than the first. In a moment you will be back in your own world and time, and there you will find that the . . . appearance of your wife has had some tragic accident, and died. It is for you to decide whether or not, in that moment, you want still to remember all that has happened to you. You may indeed remember the hard truth about the Light and the Dark, and the true nature of your wife, if you wish.'

John Rowlands said, expressionless, half to himself, 'It is very strange, there was one thing she would never tell me. It was a joke with her – she never would tell me where or when she was born.'

The Lady reached out a hand in pity, then let it fall. 'Or,' she said gently, 'instead you may forget. You may, if you wish, forget all that you have seen ever of the Lords of the Dark and the Light, and although you will then have perhaps a deeper grief at the loss of your wife, you will mourn her and remember her as the woman you knew and loved.'

'That would be living a lie,' John Rowlands said.

'No,' Merriman said from behind him, very strong and deep. 'No, John, for you did love her, and all love has great value. Every human being who loves another loves imperfection, for there is no perfect being on this earth – nothing is so simple as that.'

'It is for you to choose,' the Lady said. She moved to the boat and paused beside it, looking back.

John Rowlands stood facing them all, still without visible emotion; then he turned his dark eyes to the Lady and a warmth came into them. 'I cannot choose, this time,' he said with a wry smile. 'Not such a choice as that. Will you by your grace do it for me?'

'Very well,' the Lady said. She raised her arm, pointing. 'Walk away from me, John Rowlands, and when you turn you will find a path at your feet.

Follow it. In the moment that you pass the one tree, you will be gone from here and instead be on another path in your own valley, that you know far better than this. And whatever is in your mind then will be whatever choice I have made for you. And – we wish you well.'

John Rowlands bent his head for an instant; then looked from one to another of them with a half-smile that held no happiness, but great affection. He looked last at Bran. '*Mi wela'i ti'n hwyrach, bachgen,*' he said. Then he turned and walked away towards the immense spreading oak, on a path that no one else could see, and as he drew level with the tree he was no longer there.

The Lady sighed. 'He shall forget,' she said. 'It is better so.'

Arthur put out a hand to her, and she stepped down into the boat. A rising wind blew, rocking *Pridwen* on the river of the sky, and suddenly Will had the sense once more of a huge throng, and knew that all the Old Ones of the Circle were making their way aboard, to sail with the Lady and the king. At the ship's mainmast now the vast sail rose, square, billowing, marked with the cross within a circle, the Sign of the Light. He heard the cries of sailors; timbers creaked, halyards clattered against spars.

Will glanced at the three Drews beside him, and saw on their faces the beginning anguish of loss, and a long emptiness. But he could not keep his eyes for more than a moment from the great ship. He looked back, and in the ghostly throng of beings on her decks he saw in one quick flash after another the faces of those he had known, on this journey and on other journeys, in this time and other times. A tall burly figure in a smith's apron raised a long hammer in salute; he saw a bright-eyed small man in a green coat wave to him, and an imperious grey-haired lady, leaning on a stick, make him a formal little bow. He had the flash of a smile from a stout brown-faced man with a tonsure of white hair; he saw Glyndwr, and the frail form of the King of the Lost Land; and then with a jerk of his heart he saw Gwion, looking at him, smiling his brilliant smile. Then the wind began to grow stronger out of the clouds, and the sail billowed and flapped as if impatient, and the faces merged into the misty crowd.

Arthur stood in the prow, his bearded head outlined against the sky, and held out his hand to Bran. His warm voice rang out, triumphant and welcoming. 'Come, my son!'

Bran came quickly towards him; then paused. He was close to Merriman, his white hair and pale face almost luminous against Merriman's deep-blue cloak. Will looked on sadly, knowing it would be for the last time, seeing in Bran's face a mixture of longing, and determination, and regret.

'Come, my son,' said the warm deep voice again. 'The long task of the Light is over, and the world is freed of the peril of dominion by the Dark. Now it is all a matter for men. The Six have performed their great mission, and we have fulfilled our heritage, you and I. And now we may have rest, in the quiet silver-circled castle at the back of the North Wind, among the apple trees. And those we leave behind may think of us in greeting each night, when the crown of the North Wind, the Corona Borealis, rises above the horizon in its circlet of stars.'

He reached out an arm again. 'Come. There is a tide in this matter which is almost at the full, and I do not sail on the ebb.'

Bran looked at him in yearning, but he said clearly, 'I cannot come, my lord.'

There was a silence, into which only the wind softly sang. Arthur let his arm come slowly down to his side.

Bran said, stumbling, 'It is what Gwion said, when the Lost Land was to be drowned and he would not leave it. *I belong here.* If it is a matter for men now, as you say, then the men are going to have a hard time of it and perhaps there are things, later, that I might be able to do to help. Even if there are not, still I . . . belong. *Loving bonds,* Merriman said. That is what I have, here. And he said' – he was looking up at Merriman, beside him – 'that those bonds are outside the High Magic, even, because they are the strongest thing on the earth.'

Merriman stirred; from his mind Will could feel something like awe.

'That is true,' Merriman said. 'But consider well, Bran. If you give up your place in the High Magic, your identity in the time that is outside Time, then you will be no more than mortal, like Jane and Simon and Barney here. You will be the Pendragon no longer, ever. You will remember nothing that has happened, you will live and die as all men do. You must give up all chance of going out of Time with those of the Light – as I shall go before long, and as one day long hence Will will go too. And . . . you will never see your high father again.'

Bran turned sharply towards Arthur, and as he watched the two stare at one another, Will saw again the tawny eyes of Herne the Hunter in Bran's face, and yet a look of Arthur too, as if all three were one and the same. He blinked, wondering.

All at once Arthur smiled, proud and loving, and he said softly, 'Go where you feel you should go, my son Bran Davies of Clwyd, and my blessing go with you.' He stepped down over the side of the boat again to the grassy bank, and held his arms open, and Bran ran to him and for a moment they stood close.

Then Arthur stepped back, smiling, and Bran, looking up at him all the while, drew Eirias white and gleaming from the scabbard at his side, slipped the swordbelt over his head, and held out both sword and scabbard to his father. Will heard Merriman sigh gently, as if in release, and found his own fists unwittingly clenched. And Arthur took Eirias in one hand and the scabbard in the other, and sheathed the sword. He looked for a moment past

Bran to Merriman, and his eyes smiled, though his mouth was serious now. 'I will see you in a little while, my lion,' he said, and Merriman nodded his head.

Then the king stepped back into his ship *Pridwen*, and the broad sail filled and bellied out, and with all the host of shades of Light looking back, without sign of farewell or any ending, the ship sailed across the sky. Small sunlit clouds lay scattered there, so that the blue sky was like a sea scattered with small islands, and there was no telling whether the ship was in sea or sky when it disappeared.

Bran stood watching until there was no ship to watch, but Will could see no regret on his face.

'That must have been what John Rowlands meant,' Bran said quietly.

'John Rowlands?' said Will.

'In Welsh. When he left. He said to me, *See you later, boyo.*'

Jane said slowly, 'But – he didn't know you would come back.'

'No,' Bran said.

Merriman said, 'But he knows Bran.'

Bran looked up at him, very young and vulnerable suddenly, with his pale eyes unprotected, and the astonishing burden of the sword Eirias taken from his side. 'Was it the right thing to do?'

Merriman threw back his awesome white-maned head as impulsively as a schoolboy, and let out a hoot of breath that was the most unguarded sound they had ever heard him utter. 'Yes,' he said, sobering suddenly. 'Yes, Bran. It was the right thing, for you and for the world.'

Barney moved at last, from the place on the grassy slope where he and Simon and Jane had been standing close for a long time, watching in a wondering silence. He said anxiously, 'Gumerry? Are you really going away, or will you stay too?'

'Oh Barnabas,' Merriman said, and Jane found herself turning to him in swift motherly concern, there was such weariness in his tone. 'Barnabas, Barnabas, time passes, for the Old Ones even as for you, and though the seasons turn in every year much as in the one before, yet the pattern of the world is different in every year that goes by. My time is done, here, my time and the time of the Light, and there will be other work for us to do elsewhere.'

He paused, and smiled at them, the weariness fading a little from his bony deep-lined face, with the fierce hawk-like nose and the shadowed eyes. 'Here now are the Six,' he said, 'together for the first and last time in the place that was destined for us, on a chalk hill in the Chiltern Hundred of Buckinghamshire, where centuries ago men fleeing from the Dark tried vainly to hide their treasures, and gave prayers to the sky for safety. Look at it now. Look well. Keep a little of it alive.'

So, wondering what he might mean, they looked hard and long, at the slope of smooth green grass with tiny orange-yellow toadflax growing here and there, and small blue butterflies fluttering. They looked at the copse of beech trees capping the hill, and the broad mysterious oak tree standing just below the wood; at the clear blue sky scattered with puffy white clouds.

And then, although Merriman made no move, each of them blinked suddenly as their vision seemed to blur; and they staggered a little, with a singing in their ears and a giddiness taking away their balance. They saw everything about them shiver strangely, as if the air were dancing in the heat of a fire. The outlines of the giant oak wavered, grew dim, and disappeared: the green of the hill darkened, and the shape of its slope was no longer a smooth arc. Though the sun still shone, there were darker patches on the hill now, of yellow-flecked green and brown and purple, where gorse and bracken and heather grew. Other shapes rose in the distance, faraway mountains misted grey and blue on a hazy horizon; and when they turned to look over their shoulders they saw spread below them a broad valley golden with sand, and the winding silver thread of a river making its way out to the immense blue sea. They could hear the erratic aimless calling of sheep, now and then in the silence, basso profundo answered by tenor; somewhere far below them a dog barked. And over their heads, gliding down from the Welsh hillside to the river and the sea, came a single seagull, keening its one repeated melancholy cry.

Merriman took a long gentle breath, and let it out again. He said once more, softly, 'Look well.'

Jane said in a very small voice, looking out at the bar of golden sand that the river had set as guard against the sea, 'Shall we never see you again?'

'No,' Merriman said. 'None of you, except my Will the watchman there. That is the only right way.'

There was a command and a clear strength in his voice that caught each of them into stillness, gazing at him, held by the bright dark eyes and the bleak face.

'For remember,' he said, 'that it is altogether your world now. You and all the rest. We have delivered you from evil, but the evil that is inside men is at the last a matter for men to control. The responsibility and the hope and the promise are in your hands – your hands and the hands of the children of all men on this earth. The future cannot blame the present, just as the present cannot blame the past. The hope is always here, always alive, but only your fierce caring can fan it into a fire to warm the world.'

His voice rang out over the mountain, more impassioned than any of them had ever heard a voice before, and they stood quiet as standing stones, listening.

'For Drake is no longer in his hammock, children, nor is Arthur somewhere sleeping, and you may not lie idly expecting the second coming of anybody now, because the world is yours and it is up to you. Now especially since man has the strength to destroy this world, it is the responsibility of man to keep it alive, in all its beauty and marvellous joy.'

His voice grew softer, and he looked at them with the faraway dark eyes that seemed to be looking out into Time. 'And the world will still be imperfect, because men are imperfect. Good men will still be killed by bad, or sometimes by other good men, and there will still be pain and disease and famine, anger and hate. But if you work and care and are watchful, as we have tried to be for you, then in the long run the worse will never, ever, triumph over the better. And the gifts put into some men, that shine as bright as Eirias the sword, shall light the dark corners of life for all the rest, in so brave a world.'

There was a silence, and the small sounds of the mountain drifted back into it: the faint calls of sheep, the humming of a distant car, and far above, the cheerful trilling of a lark.

'We'll try,' Simon said. 'We'll try our best.'

Merriman gave him a quick startling grin. 'Nobody can promise more than that,' he said.

They looked at him mournfully, unable to grin in return, weighed by the melancholy of parting. Merriman sighed, and swept his midnight-blue cloak around him and back across a shoulder.

'Come now,' he said. 'The oldest words have it the best – *be of good cheer*. I go to join our friends, because I am very tired. And none of you will remember more than the things that I have been saying now, because you are mortal and must live in present time, and it is not possible to think in the old ways there. So the last magic will be this – that when you see me for the last time in this place, all that you know of the Old Ones, and of this great task that has been accomplished, will retreat into the hidden places of your minds, and you will never again know any hint of it except in dreams. Only Will, because he is of my calling, must remember – but the rest of you will forget even that. Goodbye now, my five companions. Be proud of yourselves, as I am proud of you.'

He embraced each one of them in turn, a brief hug of farewell. They were grim-faced, and their eyes were wet. Then Merriman went up the mountain, over the springy grass and the outcrops of slate, through the browning bracken and the yellow-starred gorse, and paused only when he was at the very top, outlined against the blue sky. They saw the familiar tall figure, standing very erect, with the fierce-nosed profile and the springing shock of white hair, blowing a little now in the wind that had risen out of nowhere. It was an image that would flicker in and out of their dreams for the rest of their lives, even when they had forgotten all else. Merriman raised his arm, in a salute which none of them could bear to answer, and then in a subtle inflection of movement the arm stiffened, the five fingers spread wide and pointed at them –

And a wind whirled on the hill, and the slope against the sky was empty, and five children stood on the roof of Wales looking out over a golden valley and the blue sea.

'It's a terrific view,' Jane said. 'Worth the climb. But the wind's made my eyes water.'

'It must blow like anything up here,' said Simon. 'Look at the way those trees are all bent inland.'

Bran was gazing at a small blue-green stone in the palm of his hand. 'Found this in my pocket,' he said to Jane. 'You want it, Jenny-oh?'

Barney said, gazing up over the hill, 'I heard music! Listen – no, it's gone. Must have been the wind in the trees.'

'I think it's time we were starting out,' Will said. 'We've got a long way to go.'

When the Dark comes rising, six shall turn it back;
Three from the circle, three from the track;
Wood, bronze, iron; water, fire, stone;
Five will return, and one go alone.

Iron for the birthday, bronze carried long;
Wood from the burning, stone out of song;
Fire in the candle-ring, water from the thaw;
Six Signs the circle, and the grail gone before.

Fire on the mountain shall find the harp of gold
Played to wake the Sleepers, oldest of the old;
Power from the green witch, lost beneath the sea;
All shall find the light at last, silver on the tree.

And here ends the sequence named

The Dark is Rising

Choosing a brilliant book
can be a tricky business...
but not any more

www.puffin.co.uk

The best selection of books at your fingertips

So get clicking!

Searching the site is easy – you'll find what you're looking for at the click of a mouse, from great authors to brilliant books and more!

Everyone's got different taste . . .

I like stories that make me laugh

Animal stories are definitely my favourite

I'd say fantasy is the best

I like a bit of romance

It's got to be adventure for me

I really love poetry

I like a good mystery

Whatever you're into, we've got it covered . . .

www.puffin.co.uk

Psst!
What's happening?

sneakpreviews@puffin

For all the inside information on the hottest new books,

click on the Puffin

www.puffin.co.uk

hotnews@puffin

Hot off the press!

You'll find all the latest exclusive Puffin news here

Where's it happening?

Check out our author tours and events programme

Best-sellers

What's hot and what's not? Find out in our charts

E-mail updates

Sign up to receive all the latest news
straight to your e-mail box

Links to the coolest sites

Get connected to all the best author web sites

Book of the Month

Check out our recommended reads

www.puffin.co.uk

Choosing a brilliant book
can be a tricky business...
but not any more

www.puffin.co.uk

The best selection of books at your fingertips

So get clicking!

Searching the site is easy – you'll find what you're looking for at the click of a mouse, from great authors to brilliant books and more!

Everyone's got different taste . . .

I like stories that make me laugh

Animal stories are definitely my favourite

I'd say fantasy is the best

I like a bit of romance

It's got to be adventure for me

I really love poetry

I like a good mystery

Whatever you're into, we've got it covered . . .

www.puffin.co.uk

Psst!
What's happening?

sneakpreviews@puffin

For all the inside information on the hottest new books,

click on the Puffin

www.puffin.co.uk

hotnews@puffin

Hot off the press!
You'll find all the latest exclusive Puffin news here

Where's it happening?
Check out our author tours and events programme

Best-sellers
What's hot and what's not? Find out in our charts

E-mail updates
Sign up to receive all the latest news
straight to your e-mail box

Links to the coolest sites
Get connected to all the best author web sites

Book of the Month
Check out our recommended reads

www.puffin.co.uk

Choosing a brilliant book
can be a tricky business...
but not any more

www.puffin.co.uk

The best selection of books at your fingertips

So get clicking!

Searching the site is easy – you'll find
what you're looking for at the click of a mouse,
from great authors to brilliant books and more!

Everyone's got different taste . . .

> I like stories that make me laugh

> Animal stories are definitely my favourite

> I'd say fantasy is the best

> I like a bit of romance

> It's got to be adventure for me

> I really love poetry

> I like a good mystery

Whatever you're into, we've got it covered . . .

www.puffin.co.uk

Read more in Puffin

For complete information about books available from Puffin – and Penguin – and how to order them, contact us at the appropriate address below. Please note that for copyright reasons the selection of books varies from country to country.

www.puffin.co.uk

In the United Kingdom: Please write to Dept EP, Penguin Books Ltd,
Bath Road, Harmondsworth, West Drayton, Middlesex UB7 ODA

In the United States: Please write to Penguin Putnam Inc., P.O. Box 12289,
Dept B, Newark, New Jersey 07101–5289 or call 1–800–788–6262

In Canada: Please write to Penguin Books Canada Ltd,
10 Alcorn Avenue, Suite 300, Toronto, Ontario M4V 3B2

In Australia: Please write to Penguin Books Australia Ltd,
P.O. Box 257, Ringwood, Victoria 3134

In New Zealand: Please write to Penguin Books (NZ) Ltd,
Private Bag 102902, North Shore Mail Centre, Auckland 10

In India: Please write to Penguin Books India Pvt Ltd,
11 Panscheel Shopping Centre, Panscheel Park, New Delhi 110 017

In the Netherlands: Please write to Penguin Books Netherlands bv,
Postbus 3507, NL–1001 AH Amsterdam

In Germany: Please write to Penguin Books Deutschland GmbH,
Metzlerstrasse 26, 60594 Frankfurt am Main

In Spain: Please write to Penguin Books S. A., Bravo Murillo 19,
1° B, 28015 Madrid

In Italy: Please write to Penguin Italia s.r.l.,
Via Felice Casati 20, I–20124 Milano

In France: Please write to Penguin France S. A.,
17 rue Lejeune, F–31000 Toulouse

In Japan: Please write to Penguin Books Japan, Ishikiribashi Building,
2–5–4, Suido, Bunkyo-ku, Tokyo 112

In South Africa: Please write to Longman Penguin Southern Africa (Pty) Ltd,
Private Bag X08, Bertsham 2013